It's not easy to find
THE NEW BODY.

You'll Need:
  Manny
  Natalie
  Justin
  Barry
  Lena
  D. Wayne
  Leonard

But mostly, you'll need yourself and the power
to say No to your obsession and Yes to life!

Just ask Cynthia

THE
NEW
BODY

JAMES FRITZHAND

AVON
PUBLISHERS OF BARD, CAMELOT, DISCUS, EQUINOX AND FLARE BOOKS

THE NEW BODY is a work of fiction. The details, the names, and the characters are not intended to, and do not, relate to any real persons living or dead.

AVON BOOKS
A division of
The Hearst Corporation
959 Eighth Avenue
New York, New York 10019

ISBN: 0-380-00547-6

First Avon Printing, April, 1976

AVON TRADEMARK REG. U.S. PAT. OFF. AND
FOREIGN COUNTRIES, REGISTERED TRADEMARK—
MARCA REGISTRADA, HECHO EN CHICAGO, U.S.A.

Printed in Canada

For Florence
much loved and much remembered

and for Duff
who never stopped answering my questions

Droll thing life is—that mysterious arrangement of merciless logic for a futile purpose. The most you can hope from it is some knowledge of yourself—
Joseph Conrad

Money, position, health, handsomeness, and talent aren't everything.
Kurt Vonnegut, Jr.

From the mouth of a peasant to the ears of God.
Russian proverb

CONTENTS

THE NEW BODY

PROLOGUE:

Anybody

"FAT'S A STATE OF MIND," Cynthia said, assuming the authoritative tone she used on lecture tours. "That's what it all boils down to. You find yourself living in someone else's body. It's plump and padded and it doesn't break easily. But it really isn't your body, that's the point. It's a prison, a shell, a part of you that has to be shattered before you ever find out who you really are. But the thing is, once you start to realize this, to see what you're doing to yourself, everything begins to slide into place. You've made the connection, the realization. Now, you have to begin the process of bursting out of the old body and into the new one. Get me?"

The young man didn't answer.

She saw the top of his head, his hair cut fashionably short. She heard him mutter something, not a word or a comment so much as a low and guttural sound. Incommunicative. Then he looked up from behind the mask of his camera and said, "Perfect. Now just turn your head a little more . . . no, not so much. A little more to the right. That's it. Just pretend you're gazing out the window."

The window was framed with mirrored panels. There were no draperies, no distractions. Beyond the double thickness of glass the city seemed to lurch drunkenly in the heat. "Why would I be gazing out a window?" she said. "I have work to do, right? So isn't that the picture we want to present? I mean, you don't want the readers of *Newsweek* to think I just sit at my desk and waste time all day. Or do you?" She enjoyed teasing him, goading him on. He was so earnest and serious that she couldn't help herself. And when he raised his head once again, she was certain he'd caught her wink. It wasn't seductive as much as conspiratorial, as if to say we're in this together, so let's make the best of it.

"Miss . . . Ms. Morgan. Please," Peter McGuire said. "Just a little more patience. Okay? We're almost done. Promise."

"I could tell you things about promises, too," she said. "Things that'd make your hair stand on end. But I'll spare you, Peter . . . just this once. Anyway, it's Mrs., just for the record." Then she threw her head back. There was a rush of reddish hair and she turned her lips up in a grin. Coolly self-confident, she held the pose. The shutter sounded abnormally loud, a click that jarred her like chalk against a blackboard.

Fourth grade, clear as daylight. Miss Abbott always in a black dress. *Now children, let's not make fun. Fat's not at all a kind thing to say.* She was heavy too, come to think of it. P.S. 189 and guess who's stuffing her face with too much cake and pie, charlotte russes for days. "Chubby" Margold, the darling of Crown Heights. Lena's adorably "big" little girl. A laugh a minute. But it was fun, she told herself. Sure. Lots of giggles . . . all at my expense, of course.

"Finished?" she asked.

"Just a few more shots. You don't have an appointment or anything, do you? I mean, I'm not keeping you, am I?"

"No. I cleared my calendar, just for you." Well, I shouldn't complain. How often does this body get on the cover of *Newsweek.*

It was less a question than a statement of fact. She looked around the office, her eyes darting, shifting, scanning and appraising. All the material objects, the possessions she had acquired, were rendered cool and sharp before her. It was more of a living room than an office. Its simplicity, the crispness of white walls, white surfaces, all pleased her critical eye. There were keepsakes and souvenirs, keys to cities and a wall of glossy black and white photographs, the plaque they'd presented when she was named Brooklyn's Woman of the Year.

I've had good times, she thought. Again she heard the click of the shutter. But she wasn't counting or looking at Peter now. Instead, she glanced around the room. Lush was her word for it. Spacious. Nothing tacky about

4

the office Billy Baldwin had personally designed for her. It had all the right touches, from the grass matting he had used to repave the parquet floor—"Textures, love, that's what we're looking for. Bare office floors are déclassé. Remember that"—to the white muslin and beige-white ticking on the square and angular sofas and chairs. Tropical plants—orchids, numerous exotic species of jungle palm—arched upwards toward the recessed lighting. The room was thin, modular, nothing to conjure up images of weight. Or fat. It's all clean and chic and in perfect taste, she thought, recalling how Leonard Frankel nearly had a heart attack when she presented him with the bill.

"It's p.r.," she had told him. "You have to show the public that you don't cut corners. That when you do something, you do it right. Big."

"But seventeen thousand dollars? It's obscene," and he'd thrown up his hands in a gesture she decided was unworthy of either him or the Yiddish Theater, where it had no doubt originated. "You know, you get more impossible with each passing day, Cynthia. From better to worse."

"You're making it hand over fist, Mr. Frankel," she replied. "So if I were you, I wouldn't complain."

He hadn't, after that. The corporation paid the decorator for his services, down to the last penny. Baldwin called, though, to tell her Leonard had quibbled over the price of an antique Japanese screen, the one hint of serene color he'd insisted on employing. But other than that, the money kept coming, and checks from NuBodies Inc. didn't bounce.

"How about some informal shots, now that the big one's out of the way?" she asked. She eased her desk chair back and got to her feet. Like the room, her dress was muted, bone-colored. Neutral and flattering, all at the same time. It was a thin, skinny synthetic that clung in all the right places. That was the image she wanted to present.

"Sure. Why not. I still have plenty of film." He turned his head around, taking in everything she had just been examining. "Why don't you stand over there?" He pointed to the one cluttered area in the office, a wall of identically framed photographs ("Cynthia, how can you. It's . . . it's not even outré, raffiné," Baldwin had moaned) which faced the white marble Parsons table that was her desk.

5

"Isn't it too busy?"

"Not really," as if he didn't like to be told his business. "I'll bleed out the background if it gets to be too much."

She moved into place, looking for something, perhaps something to pull it all together. It was a need she felt, a desire to give the last ten years solidity and form. Behind her was the snapshot she'd taken at the Tony Awards, just a few months before. Patrick Casey, the television personality; his manager Gene Burr; three others—all youngish men of somewhat indeterminate age, all impeccably dressed as if they were gracing the table with their presence. She'd always wanted to be surounded by handsome men. It had long been a recurring fantasy and at the Tonys they had come to her, attracted by the glamor of a name, a body the public thought it owned.

But we've had laughs, good times, she thought. That's what it's all about. I don't need hassles. No way. No how.

"Fantastic. Hold it hold it." The shutter clicked louder than ever. "Great. You're gonna love that one."

"What kind of camera are you using? I just bought my son a Leica."

"A Leica?" his voice registering a nice piece of change. "That's an expensive proposition."

"You're telling me. But, you know," though she was sure he didn't, "it was a birthday present. I decided to splurge."

"This is a Nikon," and again he fixed her permanently against a backdrop of the past. The photographs were all links, separate tentacles to events spanning the last ten years of her life.

"How much they paying you, Pete? Or do you mind my asking? I'm just curious that's all." Peter was a freelance photographer. Although he didn't look hungry, there was a thin attenuated air about him, especially around the mouth. It made her think of a racehorse and then, amidst the running, the sleekness and precision and muscular control, she saw her son. Barry's face passed out of her mind just as quickly, and Cynthia turned away, wondering if she was blushing.

"Five hundred," he told her.

"You're selling yourself cheap. That's one thing I've learned over the years. Never sell yourself short. You should have demanded another two-fifty, at the very least."

"I would have lost the job. Magazines are the cheapest

6

outfits to deal with. They count every penny." He let the camera dangle around his neck. "And lucky for me, they made the rare exception and didn't send down someone on their masthead, somebody on staff."

"That's it?" she said when he made no move to resume shooting.

"That's it. All through. You were beautiful. Thank you."

"My pleasure," she said, mouthing the words like a line she'd rehearsed way in advance, months if not years before. She moved back to her desk. "You know, I should have you speak to my editor over at our magazine."

"What magazine is that?"

For a moment she was surprised. The monthly had a circulation of well over a million. But McGuire wasn't overweight. He had no need for dieting hints, weight-reduction recipes and down-to-earth feature stories and articles all patterned after the pep talks which had made her famous. *"NuBodies* Magazine," she said. "But as I was saying, my editor's always moaning about how hard it is to find good people. Talented people." She paused and ran the tip of her tongue across her lips. "Who knows, he might be able to give you a few assignments."

"Sounds terrific," Peter said, taking the bait. "I'm always in the market for more work."

Aren't we all, she thought, saying, "Well I'll call him then. It couldn't hurt. Needless to say, I carry a certain amount of weight around here." She laughed at the pun. But there was also a hint of nervousness, self-consciousness too. The false frivolity in her voice disturbed her. She tapped her glossy fingernails against the top of the desk, eyeing the young man as he began to put away his equipment. His jeans were stretched tight across his lean, muscular buttocks. His body was lanky, swift. Tight, she decided, without a trace of flab.

"Tell me, Pete." She stopped abruptly, not sure if she was about to do the right thing. "Why don't we talk about this . . . the photographic assignments I mean, over drinks. Say . . . seven-thirty, or is that too late for you?"

He looked up and grinned. Again she thought of her son, wondering what he was doing this afternoon, if he was just lying around the pool. Like a bum. Or maybe . . . no, she thought. I don't want to deal with it. Not now. Not today. I have enough on my mind as it is.

"This evening?" he said.

Christ, he won't commit himself to anything, will he. "Yes, this evening. I hope I wasn't too difficult a subject."

"Not at all," he said. "If you think you're a perfectionist, you should have seen Barbara Walters—"

"You did that cover shot, too?" She was impressed and let him know it. A little flattery, ego-boosting, always went a long way. That was something else she'd learned firsthand, from personal experience. "Well that's not my scene, thank God. I hate to give anyone a hard time. It's just not the way I'm built, if you know what I mean."

"You were really good, no kidding," he said. "And I appreciate it, Mrs. Morgan, I really do."

"Good. I'm glad." She didn't know what else to say. I'd just like to get the hell out of New York already, that's what. If it wasn't for this goddamn gala, I'd be back in L.A. Where I belong. Pat and I would be having drinks, then dinner at Le Restaurant. Someplace smart. But easy, too. No fuss, no hassles. She sighed and flashed him a grin she hoped he'd find endearing. "The truth of it is, the older I get, the less sure I become. The less certain. About everything. Understand?"

"You're not so old."

"Forty-five," and then silence. Sometimes I'm just plain idiotic. She rushed forward, trying to recover her poise, saying. "But you're very kind. Very sweet, too. And you're right, because I really do feel younger than I did, say ten years ago when I was Cynthia Morgan the blimp."

"You have a terrific body. What I mean is," and she was delighted to see the color rise adolescently in his cheeks, "to look at you now, you'd never know you once had a weight problem—"

"You put it so discreetly," she said with a laugh.

"No, I mean it. I've seen the old photos—"

Again, she interrupted. "The jolly blimp of Crown Heights rides again."

"But I couldn't even believe it was you, that's what I'm trying to say."

"Well, that's what NuBodies is all about. So what do you say? Just drinks and some nice conversation and we'll talk about your work." She didn't want to beg. Yet that's precisely what I'm doing. It doesn't end, Cynthia, does it.

"Sure," he said at last. "Seven-thirty?"

"Seven-thirty," she repeated. She scribbled her address

8

on a slip of paper, the top of which bore the headline, NUBODIES INC., CYNTHIA MORGAN, PRESIDENT. "I'm at the Sherry-Netherland." When he reached across her desk for the paper she was again reminded of her son. But the differences were obvious. McGuire was doing something with his life. Barry wasn't. Their fingers touched and then she eased herself back in her chair. Fixing him with her stare, her eyes narrowed, she whispered, "This place is filled with a lot of phonies and old farts. Plain talk."

He was laughing when, as if on cue, the doorknob turned and the paneled door swung open. There was only one person she knew of who didn't need to knock, didn't need to be cleared with her secretary. I'll have to get around to dealing with that, too, she thought.

"Pardon me, young lady," said the man in the wide-lapeled poison-green Meledandri suit, "but could you tell me the way to the Obesity Clinic? I seem to have lost my bearings."

"Your marbles, you mean," she said and stayed put, not bothering to get up from her swingback chair. "D. W., this is Peter McGuire, the talented . . . no, the extremely talented photographer *Newsweek* sent over to do the cover shot. Peter, this is D. Wayne Eliot, my creative director."

"Nice to meet you," Peter said. He swung his leather carrying case over one shoulder and hitched his fingers into the back pockets of his faded blue jeans.

"Did she give you a hard time?" D. W. asked, keeping his eyes on the young man.

"Not in the least," Peter said with a boyish grin. "She was an angel. Couldn't have been more cooperative . . . or photogenic." He looked back at Cynthia and winked.

"Really?" and D. W. raised his eyebrows. "That doesn't sound like the Cynthia Morgan I know. I was positive I'd hear whips cracking."

"He's jealous of my beauty," Cynthia said, one eye on D. W.—the embodiment of sartorial splendor—, the other on McGuire—sloppy and loose and as eclectically attired as her office was decorated.

"Not your beauty, my dear. It's your body I'm after." He growled and made a move to paw her, the buckles of his Gucci loafers clicking like the shutter of a camera. Then he moved closer and Cynthia caught the signal, the way he glanced almost imperceptively at Peter McGuire and then back at her, questioning without saying a single word.

She chose to ignore his curiosity. "You had your chance, Eliot, and you muffed it," she said. "So don't blame me." Peter was now at the door. Again, she didn't bother to get to her feet, but rocked back and forth in the chair. "Thank you again, Peter. We'll be speaking, I'm sure."

"I'm sure," D. W. parroted.

"Nice meeting you, Mr. Eliot," the photographer said. Then he looked back at Cynthia, even as he started to open the door. "And good luck with your gala. I'll be there in September to take some more shots for the magazine. But I hope it's a big success, I really do."

"It's going to be the smash hit of the century," D. W. called out. The door closed and he leaned over the desk, palms flat against the slab of highly polished marble. "Just your type, wasn't he. Humpy, too."

"Humpy, yes. My type . . . that's something I didn't even think about," she said, still appreciating the way Pete had handled his exit. "Besides, I'm old enough to be his mother."

"That's never stopped you before," he said, sneering. "Do I hear strains of sour grapes?"

"You do not."

"Good, I was hoping you'd say that. But in any event, my dear, don't ever say D. W. doesn't have your best interests at heart, because I do. He showed up, didn't he? They're putting you on the cover, aren't they?"

"And why not?" She wanted to say there was only one Cynthia Morgan, but she was certain he'd never understand. So she kept her mouth shut and raised the lid of a gold box engraved with her initials. She found a cigarette and didn't wait for D. W. to dig up his lighter. "He's just a nice sweet boy. Very sensitive. Not like you, you lech."

"Ah, so that's what they're calling me these days. Well, it's better than being known as schmuck." He pulled up a beige-and-white chair and again she heard the buckles of his loafers playing "Jingle Bells." Then, sprawling insolently, his body sinking into the down cushions, he said, "Anyway, it's just another reason why you adore me, Margold."

"Morgan," she said sharply. "You made me change it, so let's keep it that way."

10

D. W. clucked his tongue. He ran his fingers through his Brillo black hair. "Why so touchy, kiddo? Did he put you off? Or shall I say, turn you down?"

"God, is that all you think about? Sex."

"Sex and NuBodies, though not necessarily in that order, of course," he said with a smirk.

She ignored the latter, an expression of supreme and overbearing self-confidence. "I don't know, I'd just like to get back to the Coast, that's all. This place," and she waved her hand about the office, "is starting to give me the creeps. I feel claustrophobic. At least in California I get to see grass on occasion."

"Well, the gala was your idea, not mine," he reminded her. "NuBodies' coming of age . . . isn't that the way you wanted it billed? The tenth anniversary of America's largest and most successful weight-reduction business."

"It's not a business. It's . . . it's a way of life."

D. W. made a face. The tops of his ears, pointed as a satyr's, stuck out through his clipped and layered hair. "A way of life? Shit, do you really believe all that crap?"

"What are you talking about?" she said, raising her voice. "Of course I believe it. If I didn't, I wouldn't be here."

"Cynthia, this is D. W. you're talking to, not a reporter from *Newsweek*."

"I don't know what you're talking about, you know that. And do me a favor and stop jiggling your leg. Those are the noisiest shoes ever invented. I don't understand why they're such a status symbol. Everyone and his mother is wearing them."

He uncrossed his legs and smiled. "But as I was saying before I was so rudely interrupted, see what a little pressure in the right places can do. A guarantee of advertising, a certain number of pages spread out over the next twelve months and presto change-o, you've got your picture smeared over the cover of one of the biggest weeklies in the country. It's as simple as that."

"You make it sound so cheap. And shady, unethical," she replied. "It's not as if I bought the cover, for God sakes."

"No dear, *you* didn't buy it. NuBodies did. There's a difference."

"So I'm learning." She inhaled deeply, flicked the ash off the end of her cigarette. It landed in the middle of a small Steuben bowl. "How much is it costing us, by the way?"

"To feed your ego?"

"I'm not going to answer you."

"Okay, don't. But what's the difference, anyway. We're making it faster than we can spend it, so what's another hundred thou, specially for advertising."

"Do you like the dress I picked out?" she asked, purposely changing the subject. "I wanted to keep it simple. Classic."

"Halston?"

She nodded her head.

"I didn't know he made half-sizes."

"You know," Cynthia said, trying not to smile since that was precisely what he was expecting, "you are the most obnoxious person I have ever met. Bar none. Don't you ever take anything seriously, anything at all?"

D. W. cracked his knuckles, yawned, rolled his dark brown eyes left and right and gave her a Howdy Doody grin. "If I decided to be serious, my dear, they'd have shipped me off long ago . . . like your son, I might add."

She winced and bit down on her lower lip. "You're a flashy sonuvabitch, Eisenstern."

"If it's all the same to you, I prefer Eliot, my darling," he said, still managing to keep a straight face.

"You'll always be Eisenstern to me," she replied, taking on his mannerisms, the same rude and blasé tone she realized made him feel self-important. It's my fault too, she thought. I indulged him, constantly. Let him ride roughshod over me, that's the expression. I let him get away with blue murder, just like my kids. "Do me a favor and just leave my children out of this, if you don't mind. The less said about Barry, the better. For all of us."

"I was just trying to get you to smile."

"Yeah, some smile. I should live so long." Barry looked up at her from a silver-framed photograph. She reached out and traced the outline of his face with the tip of a manicured finger. "I get more aggravation from that one than I know what to do with. Everyone has normal children, except me."

"Poor thing," D. W. said with a snicker. His lips were pulled back for a moment, exposing two rows of evenly spaced, expensively capped teeth. "How you've suffered for their sins. Cynthia Morgan, the unhappy million-airess."

"You're damn right I've suffered. You know, money isn't everything—"

"But it helps."

"It helps but it's not the be-all and end-all of my existence, that's the point. But you know what? I'm not going to suffer any longer. No more. I'm not going to be a patsy for anyone. From now on in it's Cynthia—first, last, and always."

"From now on in?" he said with another sly grin that made her want to scream. "You mean for the last ten years, don't you?"

"We are really being adorable today, D. W. Absolutely amusing beyond belief. And kind. Yes, let's not forget what a kind sweet person you are. Now what can I do for you because if I don't get out of my office I'm going to start climbing the walls." She ground out her cigarette against the side of the ashtray and reached for another, waiting for him to answer. "Come on, let's get it over with, whatever it is. I have no more patience, if you want to know the truth."

"Nothing really," he said, immediately putting on his best business voice. "Just wanted you to know how the gala's shaping up."

"Well?"

"For starters, we finally got a commitment from Hope."

"From Hope, or Hope's manager?"

"From Hope, personally," he said. "I was on the phone with him this afternoon."

"How much is he asking?"

"Too much, but it's all tax deductible so what's the difference."

"And Pat Casey?"

D. W. nodded his head. "No sweat. He loves your ass, you know that. Besides, after all those parties you've been giving for him in L.A., he wouldn't dare say no. Oh, before I forget, the contract's signed for Shea Stadium. We sent out the last batch of tickets to all the franchises, so we're right on schedule. Everything's going like clock-work."

That's refreshing, and she said, "And we're going to fill the place, I hope?"

"I hope," he repeated. "It's a tough nut to crack.

13

You've got to remember that we're not dealing with Carnegie Hall or the Felt Forum. Shea has a seating capacity of over 55,000."

"And right now, today, if I remember my figures correctly, we have something like 400,000 active members enrolled in NuBodies classes. And three times that many, if not more, have been through the course. They've reached goal weight, I mean. So how can you say you're worried about getting . . . what was that figure you just quoted?"

"Fifty-five thousand."

"You mean to say you don't think we'll get that many members, ex-members too, don't forget, to come to the gala?"

"I'm not saying that. I'm just saying that we're dealing with a lot of people, that's all."

"I've been dealing with a lot of people all my life. They believe in me and I believe in them. So if I were you, I wouldn't worry about filling Shea Stadium. The problem we're gonna have to face is how to turn away the overflow without hurting anyone's feelings."

"That should be our biggest problem."

"It will be," she said. "Wait and see."

"Well, that's about it, I guess. I think I've covered everything." He got to his feet and smoothed out the wrinkles in his trousers. He was thirty-four, she recalled. But he still looked as impossibly boyish as he had nearly ten years before, when they'd first met. Ever since then, ever since D. W. had come to work for NuBodies, there had never been a question of things "going like clockwork," of getting everything done. If something needed taking care of, D. W. was always around to tie up all the loose ends, to soothe ruffled feathers, to assuage egos and pat backs and charm the pants off anyone who might be giving the corporation a hard time.

It was a quality Cynthia appreciated. So it was no wonder that she had learned to put up with his flashy remarks, his needle-sharp barbs. There had never been anyone to replace D. W., even when she'd made a point of scouring the market for a new brain to pick, a new idea man, a new source of creative inspiration and untiring imagination.

Untiring. Yes, that was the word for him. D. W. always looked as if he'd just awakened from the soundest of

14

sleeps. She'd never figured out the way his head worked, the fact that he might be saying one thing yet thinking something else entirely. The longer they had worked together, the more she had put her trust in him. Business-wise, that is. Now, things had happened, events had conspired—especially in recent months—to make her wonder if he just didn't have her over a barrel, if he still had the interests of the corporation at heart.

"What are your plans?" he asked as he stood by the door.

"Long-range or immediate?"

"Immediate," he said. "How about dinner tonight? I could get us a table at Lutèce, and you know how much you like their food. All I have to do is call."

"I'd love to, but I can't." He was being too friendly, too considerate. She didn't want to get trapped into something she couldn't get out of, not when it had happened so many times in the past. "I really want to go to bed early tonight, thanks all the same. I feel exhausted, run-down."

"How about drinks then, my apartment or the hotel. It doesn't matter, one way or the other. Whichever's more convenient for you is fine with me."

She wondered why he was pursuing the issue, solicitous to the point of fawning, if only to get his way. What's he feeling guilty about? she asked herself. But instead of turning the question back at him, she said, "No, I think I'll take a raincheck. I'm just not up to it."

"Leonard wanted to see you about something, before I forget." The door opened a crack and she heard her secretary clicking away at the typewriter. The phone rang once, twice, and the pecking stopped abruptly.

"NuBodies, good afternoon," the voice came back to her.

"If Leonard wants to see me, he knows exactly where to find me," she said.

"Do you want me to tell him in those exact words?" D. W. asked. He shifted his weight from one foot to the other, his hands balled into fists, their outline visible behind the pockets of his pleated trousers.

"Tell him whatever you like. But I'm not his flunky and I don't intend to turn into one. He's still my partner. And I'm still . . . Christ, he's such a pain in the ass. I'll call him," and she lifted the receiver.

15

D. W. closed the door softly behind him. The moment it clicked shut she put down the phone and buzzed her secretary. "Judy, do me a favor and cancel my appointments for the rest of the afternoon, will you."

"Anything the matter, Mrs. Morgan?"

"No, it must be the heat, that's all." The office was air-conditioned. Her secretary—a former NuBodies member, as were most of the clerical staff—obviously knew enough to remain silent, not to question her. "I think I'll go back to the hotel and take a nap. I feel drained."

"Do you want me to forward your calls?"

"Absolutely not." She paused and glanced toward the windows, catching her reflection in one of the mirrored panels. "Maybe I'll have my hair done, I don't know. Is Phil downstairs?"

"Since three."

"Fine." She released the button and got to her feet. Something has to be done, she thought. The problem is, I just don't know what it is.

Ten minutes later she was sliding into the back seat of her limousine. Her driver closed the door behind her, and she took a deep breath, feeling like a little kid playing hooky. The car was air-conditioned. But when Phil opened the door by the driver's seat, the heat and humidity of New York in July barreled into her. Outside, the street seemed to glisten and drip with sweat. People walked bowed over, weighed down by the oppressive humidity.

"You can't go out," Phil said. He glanced back at her and smiled. "Impossible. Muggy's not even the word for it. Believe me, worse. People are dropping like flies all over town; I heard it on the radio. And what's worse than that, there's gonna be no letup in sight. So where to, Cynthia? You want me to drop you back at the hotel?"

"I guess so." She settled back as he pulled away from the curb. From where she sat she could read the lines of Phil's neck. It was a map she had known, memorized, for nearly seven years. At least *he* never gives me hassles. Dependable, always there when I need him.

There were few people she could say that about, few people with whom she had that kind of unique and special rapport. It had never been anything but Cynthia and Phil, never Mrs. Morgan unless there was someone else sitting alongside of her in the back seat. And even

16

then he was never the obsequious shuffling chauffeur. He had his dignity and she appreciated the way he projected a sense of self, self-worth as well. He was her driver, but he was also her friend, confidant when she chose to place him in that role, or just good company when she needed someone to talk to.

"Did you have lunch?" she asked. "We could stop at the Stage."

"Thanks, but I had a bite while you were upstairs. How'd the photography thing work out? Did the guy know what he was doing?"

"He wasn't bad," she said, thinking, I opened my big mouth and now I don't even know how to get in touch with him, cancel it. In fact, I don't even know if I want to cancel drinks. I don't even know what I want. Period. "I bet you'd be happier if we were back on the Coast. The truth?"

She saw his eyes reflected in the rearview mirror. Hooded, framed by bushy unkempt brows and tired purplish pouches, they held her for a silent moment. "It sure beats this nonsense," he said, gesturing with one hand to the traffic backed up along Madison Avenue. "Not even four, not even rush hour mind you, and look at it. At least when you want to get somewhere in L.A., you just hop on the freeway and bim-bam-biff, you're there in no time at all. Here, people have heart attacks behind the wheel, conditions are so screwed up."

"Well, we could go back for a couple of weeks, but what's the point? Soon as the gala's over with in September, I'm going to grab the first plane out. What gets me is I don't even know how I lived here all my life. I must've been out of my mind."

They stopped at the corner of Madison and Fifty-seventh and waited for the light to turn green. The IBM clock read 3:47. She glanced down at her watch again, but there was no need to correct it. "You know, I'm bored, believe it or not," she said. "I don't know, Phil, I'm just not myself these last few weeks."

"Anything I can do?"

"I'll let you know if I think of something." She tried to smile, but her lips felt parched, the skin pulled taut, about to crack. What is it? she asked herself. Isn't 'malaise' the word for it? But what am I so malaised about? I have a gorgeous home. I'm making it hand over fist, no financial

17

worries or aggravations whatsoever. People recognize me on the street; some even ask for my autograph. I'm going to be on the cover of *Newsweek*. So what am I complaining about. "I'm not complaining, I'm just . . . Phil, do me a favor and take the next right."

"Go east?" and three lines appeared, one after another and all screwed up tight across his forehead. "Don't you want me to take you back to the hotel?"

"No," she said. "I changed my mind. Take the FDR Drive down to the bridge. I want to go to Brooklyn. I haven't been since—"

"You were just—"

"I know, but still."

"Brooklyn?" he said, shaking his head. The lines deepened, eroding his brow. "Homesick?"

"No, just . . . just curious, that's all."

He turned right at the corner.

At Third Avenue she could see a long drooping line of New Yorkers bending around the corner like a length of melted taffy. They were backed up the way the traffic had been, halfway down the block. "They gotta be crazy," Phil said. "Standing on line for a movie in this kind of heat, you gotta be nuts."

"It's cool inside."

They sped past the theater as the moviegoers fanned themselves with copies of *Cue* magazine and *The New York Times*.

The traffic thinned out considerably at the drive. A breeze, stale with the smell of combustion and industrial pollution, seeped through the crack she had made in the window. The East River was dark with oil slicks, smooth as freshly laid tar, black as licorice. A garbage scow moved lethargically up the river in the direction of the Bronx.

If I was going to the Bronx, I'd take my time, too, she thought. This time she smiled genuinely and without effort. An adventure, that's what it is. "I'm going back to my roots, Philly, that's what I'm doing. Isn't it true . . . I mean, don't they all say you can't go home again."

"What's the point?" he said, while on their right Peter Cooper Village slipped by like a mirage. Stuyvesant Town loomed up behind the buildings and housing projects. She decided the air smelled different uptown. Sweeter, with the scent of money, the slick aroma of spare

18

change and houses in the suburbs, away from the heat and the bad element, as her mother always called it. "Where in Brooklyn, by the way?"

"The old neighborhood. I never took you there before. You're gonna get an education, Philly, a college degree, let me tell you," she said with a grin. The thought of going back, returning to Crown Heights and the street where she had lived so many years, where she and Manny had raised a family, somehow made her feel alive, refreshed. Recharged with energy, she breathed deeply once again, satisfied that everything would work out for the best. Out of the old body and into the new, she thought. Out of the lousy mood and into the good one. You've got to fight your problems, not give in to them. You can't let them get the best of you, no matter what. That's the secret, the key to it all. You can't wallow around in self-pity, letting the talkers, the phonies, run you ragged. If I gave in years back I'd still be a size forty-six. Can you imagine, tipping the scale at over two-hundred-fifty pounds, no wrist bones in sight for over twenty years and a triple chin, to boot. I was as big as a horse. No, a truck. Better yet, I was a mess, plain talk.

Crossing the Brooklyn Bridge, Phil asked for instructions. She told him the simplest way to get to Eastern Parkway and sat up straight, eyes turning left and right. The hum of the air-conditioning unit muted the sounds of the city. But everything was still crystal clear, laid out before her like a panorama of the past. They drove past the Squibb factory and she remembered how she'd always had an aversion to the taste of their toothpaste. Then the Watchtower building was behind her and the staggered lights were green all the way up Flatbush Avenue. Beyond the empty Fox Theatre they sped, deep into the welfare zone.

"What kind of neighborhood we going to?" Phil asked.

"Crown Heights, where I grew up. Where I lived out the dull drama of my days. Now doesn't that sound melodramatic, eh Philly." She laughed and suddenly clapped her hands. They won't believe it, seeing Chubby Margold after all these years. Thank God Manny doesn't live on the block anymore. That's all I'd need, to see him again— the other one too. "See, Phil, no one can ever say Cynthia's lost touch. And no one can call me a snob, either."

"You're no snob," he said, "never were. But I still can't

19

figure it out. What's the great draw? Flatbush itself, that I'd understand. But Crown Heights is filled with blacks and Hasidim. Who needs it?"

"We'll see, we'll see," her voice promised, confident that the changes she would notice would all be small, minor compared to the changes she had made in her own life. "But this is where it all happened, don't you see? I was a fatty here, Phil. I used to waddle down these streets, trudging from Jack's Appetizing Store to the Normandie Bake Shop, stuffing my face with chopped herring on onion rye and prune danish. My kids went to school here. Manny had his shop on Winthrop Street, maybe five blocks from the house. I lived here, don't you see?"

"So?"

"So haven't you ever been curious to go back home?"

"To Ralph Avenue? No way. It's a regular jungle these days. Besides, home's California. You got me out of the city—"

"By pulling teeth."

"Well, you got me out, so what's the difference. Who needs to . . . how should I put it? Yeah, who needs to dredge up old memories? Makes no sense, if you ask me."

"Since when have you become such a cynic? I thought you were the biggest softie in the business."

"Who? Me? And what business ya talkin' about?" and he tapped himself on the chest and lifted his head so she could see the way he was grinning. "Naw, not this Phil. You must mean someone else. This Phil's hard as nails, always was."

"Talker," and she leaned back in her seat. Things still crowded in on her, the session with Pete McGuire, the date she had made with him, D. W.'s wisecracks and the fact that she hadn't bothered speaking to Leonard Frankel, vice president of the corporation. In recent weeks all of her energies had been devoted to the gala, the huge promotional event which would herald NuBodies' tenth anniversary, its "coming of age."

D. W. had seemed a little bit worried about it and she wondered why. The company had never been in better shape. Only last month shares of common stock had risen sharply, while the rest of the market continued to react sluggishly, fighting what the Administration still insisted was *stagflation,* a sideways waffling of the economy.

20

"Did you see the ad we put in the *Times?*"

"Which one?" Phil asked. "Today's paper?"

"Yesterday's," she replied. "A two-page spread, all about the gala. Oh, by the way, I didn't tell you Bob Hope's going to be there."

"He's gonna cost you."

"Sure he's costing us, but I'm going to give my members the best show they've ever had. When people pay five and ten bucks a ticket, they want to get their money's worth. And that's exactly what I'm going to give them, a show that's going to be unbelievable. We're going all out, lining up the biggest names in the business."

"Barry and your mother gonna fly in for it?"

"It's up to them," she said and lapsed into silence.

They turned onto Eastern Parkway. The memorial arch at Grand Army Plaza, the Brooklyn Public Library's main branch right behind it, began to bring back one flicker of memory after another. One day maybe fifteen years before, she'd taken Barry and Natalie to the library. Barry was ten at the time, her daughter almost three years younger. Afterwards they'd gone to the zoo in Prospect Park. It was safe in those days and she could still taste the cotton candy, the Sabrett frankfurter, so good she used to say "it melts in your mouth," eaten under the shade of the hot dog cart's orange umbrella.

That's three you had already mommy, Barry had complained. So? Natalie had two and look how much older I am, she said. I'm hungry. Your mommy's a big woman. If I don't have something to put inside my stomach I'm gonna faint on the street. How'd you like that to happen, Barry sweetface? You don't want your mother to fall down on the street just because she's hungry, do you? That's all you do, he said. Wherever we go that's all you do is eat. You and the elephants.

I should have slapped him in the teeth. Manny would have, for being so fresh. But I couldn't, even then. *I could eat you up, you're so adorable.* He believed me, too. He thought I'd really gobble him up like a sandwich. Must've been . . . what, sure maybe six years old, so gorgeous people would stop me on the street, ask if he was in the movies that's how beautiful a child he was. And when I said I'd eat him up he started to cry. *You're too sensitive for your own good, Barry Margold. I don't know who in the family you take after. Not me. Not Daddy or Nat,*

21

either, he said. Gramma Lena, that's who. She can wear anything, tight stuff, high-heel shoes, anything she wants. Crazy Moshe from the candy store said she's a firebrand. Is that good? It means your grandma's a bundle of energy. Not like you, he said.

Sure I was tired; my mouth was always going, that's why. But I was happy. Once . . . once, wasn't I? "Turn down Utica Avenue, Philly, right at the next light." At the corner she saw the Famous Restaurant on one side of the parkway and Dubrow's Cafeteria on the other. The first was known for its vegetarian cutlets, the second for potato pirogen. Both looked shabbier than she remembered. And she remembered too that it had been close to ten years since she'd tasted pirogen, a doughy pouch filled with a hot spicy mixture of potatoes and onions. I used to eat a dozen at a time, with a full pint of sour cream on the side. Afterwards, *What'll it be for dessert, Manny? You know how much you favor their rice pudding. They make it just the way you like it. Me, I'm gonna have myself a strawberry shortcake. I've been thinking about it all day, tell you the truth. And to the waiter, an old friend by then, Hermie don't you dare skimp on the whip cream or I'll take it out of your tip . . . you know I'm only kidding, pulling your leg. You know I love you; who else gives me such good attention every time I walk in here. But I'm off my diet till Monday, so what the hell. Another few calories ain't gonna kill me. Right? And Manny said, Sure. And Hermie said, Absolutely. Eat, enjoy. You only live once.*

What the hell, what was the difference between weighing two forty-seven and two fifty-two. It didn't show. I was a forty-six. I had the large sizes market sewn up tight. Fifty-six-inch hips. *I'm giving you double the value for your money, Manny, two for one. Think of it that way.* He did, that was just the problem. It didn't bother him.

"Well?" Phil said.

She felt herself jerking her head up, as if she'd been dozing. "Boy, I'll say the neighborhood's changed," she said. She recognized no old and familiar faces. Most of the shops she had patronized now looked back at her through the blinded eyes of boarded-up storefronts. Or else they had passed into different hands. Leon's Haute Coiffure, where her friend Henny used to give her manicures—"Not so red, doll, please. I'm a big woman, not a

22

vampire"—and where she'd sell out her stock of costume jewelry on a Saturday afternoon to help make ends meet, was now the Ashanti Salon de Beauté. Black Afro-styled wigs graced the window. The "natural look" was in evidence everywhere she turned her eyes.

"Pull up at the corner," she said. "I'll just stop in at the luncheonette and see if Claire and Bernie are still in business." The taste of English muffins drenched in salt butter, egg creams with a sweet residue of chocolate syrup coating the bottom of the soda fountain glass, hot fudge sundaes and double-dip cones, was right on the tip of her tongue. I haven't allowed myself to indulge that way in years, she thought. That's all I think about, maintaining the image . . . here she is folks, Streamlined Cynthia, at your service.

"I don't like the idea you walking around this kind of neighborhood," Phil told her.

"Don't be silly, this is where I grew up, for God sakes." She pointed to the street sign. "Montgomery Street and Utica Avenue. I lived right down the block. Believe me, it's as safe as Madison Avenue. Besides, I'll only be a minute. I'm just going to stop in and say hello, that's all. They'd never forgive me otherwise. Afterwards we can drive around and I'll show you everything, promise."

His look was dubious, doubtful. Watchdog, forever protective of what she knew he thought of as "her best interests," Phil made a petulant, worried face. But he double-parked at the corner, just the same.

"Sit, sit," she said, one hand already on the door. "I'm perfectly capable." What she was afraid to say, to admit, was that she didn't want to make "a stink," a scene. She didn't want to be seen waiting for her chauffeur to open the door for her so she could step out of her limousine, looking for all the world like a movie star, a rich bitch, a snob. "Relax," she told him. "It'll take all of two minutes." And then, when he didn't answer, "You want to come in with me, have a cold drink?"

"No thanks. I don't trust 'em. I'll sit and watch the car."

Cynthia felt his eyes on her back as she slid her legs over the side, held onto the edge of the door and stepped outside. The heat was worse than ever. It knocked against her like fists, wave after wave of open oven doors as she

23

hurried into the luncheonette. Bernie had had the store air-conditioned early in the Sixties, a closet-sized unit that made many of his old customers complain about drafts. But now, as she pushed the swinging door forward and found her fingers surprised at the presence of a protective metal grate, a formidable iron screen, the cool blasts of air were a welcome relief against the unbearable humidity.

Here, at least, nothing had changed.

She saw it all at once, a totality, complete and whole. The same row of red leatherette stools. Bernie stood behind the counter, a small dapper moustached man, his apron as white and snowy and virginal as it had been the last time she had seen him. Wielding a knife to halve a sandwich was Claire, his wife. Same bad teeth, Cynthia thought as the brown-haired woman, the roots untouched, turned her eyes in her direction. The knife didn't slip from her fingers. But her mouth dropped open. Blindly she scooped the crisp toasty sandwich onto a green Melmac plate, tossed a slice of sour pickle onto the side and shoved it across the counter.

"I don't believe it, I just don't believe it," she said, wiping her hands dry on her apron.

Cynthia couldn't stop smiling. She squeezed in behind the counter, something she had never been able to do when she was hitting two fifty-two pounds. Now her body fit, not even snugly. There was room to spare, to spread out, to move between the boxes of El Productos and the canisters of pretzel sticks and licorice.

"Who's that?" Bernie said, transferring the stub of a cigar from one side of his mouth to the other.

"Who do you think?" she said with a laugh.

"Chubby Margold?" he said, as unbelieving as his wife. "Naw, you're puttin' me on."

"It's Cynthia," Claire said, giving him an elbow in the ribs. "What are you talking, this is Cynthia, our Cynthia." She pushed her way forward and wrapped her arms around Cynthia's waist. Again, it was something few people could accomplish in years past. "I can't believe it. What the hell are you doing here, a person like you?"

"A person like me is just like a person like you. You look fabulous, Claire, just fabulous. But then again, you were always as skinny as my mother, knock wood."

24

"How is she, by the way?" a look rushing into her eyes that seemed to hope for the best.

"As gorgeous as ever," and Claire was immediately relieved. "She lives out in California with me. She hasn't aged a day."

"Good for her," Claire said. "Who needs Brooklyn, anyway."

"We do," Bernie said. "It's our bread and butter. But California . . . so what brings you all the way back here?"

"Business."

"Sure, of course," he said. "I should've known. But you picked the wrong time of year with heat like this. Anyway, what are you drinking, Cynthie? It's on me."

"The usual," she said and began to laugh when he remembered.

"I can't get over it, you look so fabulous," Claire kept repeating, her eyes roaming up and down Cynthia's body. She took in everything: the Halston dress, the Cartier watch and Hermès bag, the gold jewelry and look of complete and total prosperity. "You haven't gained a pound, either. Remarkable, just remarkable."

"How could I?" Cynthia said. "NuBodies works, or haven't I already told you that."

"I saw you on the TV, not two months ago. That panel show—"

"David Susskind."

"That's the one. You were fantastic, Cynthia. What answers. Ask Bernie, he'll tell you. You put Atkins and Stillman in their place, no foolin'. So what do you think of our little store?" She waved her hand around, taking in the row of stools, the banquettes in the rear.

"The same. Hasn't changed. It looks like home. So how's business?"

"Good, bad. Nothing fabulous. It's a slow day. The heat." She leaned closer. "I can't talk now," her eyes motioning back to the two customers at the counter. Their doleful curious black faces gazed at Cynthia as they munched their sandwiches.

"One chocolate egg cream coming up," Bernie said. He slid the foaming drink in her direction.

"It's been a long time," she said.

"You mean to say they don't know how to make egg creams in L.A.?" Bernie asked, amazed.

25

"What L.A.? She's living in Hollywood with the movie stars, aren't you, Cynthia?"

"Beverly Hills," she said. "But they know how to make them. Thing is, I never allow myself. You know," and she patted her flat stomach, hoping the waistband of her girdle didn't show. After all, there was such a thing as going overboard, ruining a good impression.

"Beverly Hills, that's some fancy neighborhood," Bernie muttered. He looked up and his face suddenly brightened. "Well drink up, Cynthie. It isn't every day—"

The foam coated her upper lip. The mixture of chocolate syrup, milk, and club soda was cool and tingly. It slid down her throat and brought back a thousand little bubbles of time, trickles of memory.

"Boy, where's it all gone. I'm gettin' gray and look at you. You look younger than you did ten years ago, the truth." Bernie told her.

"He still has eyes for a pretty face," Claire said with another nudge in his ribs.

"So tell us, what brings you back to Brooklyn?" he asked.

She put down the glass and wiped her lips with a paper napkin. "Lonesome I guess. Boy, hasn't the neighborhood changed though. I wouldn't have recognized it."

"You Cynthia Morgan, the NuBodies lady?" one of the customers asked. He slipped off his stool and sidled up to her.

"That's me," she said.

"You know, my wife went to that NuBodies school, over on Empire Boulevard. I want to thank you. Ask Bernie here. How does Dee look, tell the lady."

"His wife dropped fifty pounds," Claire said, nodding her head vigorously up and down. "The before and after . . . like day and night. You wouldn't know it's the same woman, honest to God. Am I exaggerating, Bernie?"

"Not in the least," he said.

"Fifty-*two* pounds, please," the heavyset man said. "Lady, I want to shake your hand. You know, ever since Dee dropped that weight she's been like a new woman. Keeps me on my toes." He flashed a grinning mouthful of teeth and extended his hand. His palm was warm, his grip firm and friendly. Thankful.

"So what's holding you back?" she said with a good-natured grin.

26

"Ah, well, I like to eat, what can I say," he laughed. "So what do I owe you, Bernie?"

"Dollar fifty-seven."

"A good customer, has breakfast here every morning," Claire said as soon as the man was out of earshot. "And he wasn't kidding about his wife, either."

Cynthia finished the egg cream and slid the empty glass back onto the counter. "How are your children?" she asked.

"Eddie just bought a house out on the Island. He's doing very well." She rapped her knuckles on the formica counter. "And Joanie just had a little girl. She lives down in Atlanta—"

"Atlanta? No kidding."

"Her husband's a teacher. Has a very good job there, and it's such gorgeous country she doesn't want to move back," Claire went on. "And what's with your two? Any grandchildren yet?"

"No," she said, trying to smile. "But you know what they say. I live in hope."

"Barry . . . what's he doing?" Bernie asked.

"Keeping himself busy," she said quickly.

"Well, that's good. Long as he keeps out of trouble," Claire replied, just as hurriedly.

"And Natalie, she still—"

"She's taking her Masters, University of California," Cynthia said, knowing they'd never catch her in a lie.

"Good school, good school," Bernie said.

"She always had her nose in a book, you remember."

"Sure," Claire said, nodding her head. "Smart as a whip, that one was."

"Tell me, you ever see . . . you know, Manny?" Bernie asked.

"What kind of questions you asking, imbecile," Claire said angrily. She pushed Bernie back and stepped in front of him. "He's a real snoop, my husband. Don't listen to him."

"Well, my . . . uh's . . . waiting outside. I've got to run. Have to get back into the city." She checked her watch. "You two look fabulous. It was good seeing you."

"Say hello to your mother," Claire said.

"I will, I promise. I'm sure she'll be tickled pink to hear I saw you. Stay well." She leaned over the counter and pecked Bernie on the cheek.

27

"What? No kiss for me, too?" Claire said with a laugh.

"What did I say that was so terrible you have to go and embarrass me like that?" she heard Bernie say as she pushed the door open and stepped out onto the street.

Then Phil was jumping out of the front seat to hold the door open for her.

"I should have brought a photographer along," she said. "We could've taken some pictures for the magazine." Sure, local girl makes good. What a laugh.

"Where to?"

"Back into town."

"I thought you wanted to drive around the old neighborhood, see the sights."

What sights? she thought. "No, I don't think so, Phil." She heard herself sighing. "What they say is right. You can't go home again. It just doesn't work." It just doesn't pay, either.

She was on her third consecutive cigarette and her second Scotch and soda when she heard him at the door. The knock was low-pitched, soft and gentle. Hesitant, too. "One minute," she called out. She got to her feet and turned to face a gilt-framed mirror above the couch. Her fingers moved birdlike at her hair, brushing it back from her eyes. I look tired, she thought, tired and unsure of myself. Well, it's too late now.

She unlocked the door, stepped back and waved him inside. He'd changed out of his jeans and into a pair of European-cut high-waisted trousers. She decided they made him look even younger than he really was. "Good evening, Mrs. Morgan," Peter said, bending forward so that it looked like he was bowing from the waist.

"Cynthia. The one thing I'm not is a formal person. You know," she said as she walked to the bar, "I just hate to stand on ceremony. It's so . . . so phony. What are you drinking, Peter?"

"Do you have any wine open?"

"No, I'm sorry. But let me call down and order a bottle. White or red?"

"No, please," he protested. "It's not necessary. Scotch?"

"Dewars or Cutty?"

"Dewars is fine. Just a splash of water and ice."

He was exactly on time, as if he were punching in at a time clock for a job. Cynthia poured a liberal amount of Scotch into a rocks glass, added two ice cubes and a finger of water. She mixed it with the tip of her pinkie, licked her finger dry and brought, the drink over to where he was sitting on the couch.

Then, pulling up a velvet lady-chair, she sat down and raised her glass. "Cheers," she said, clicking glasses.

"Salud."

She took a swallow and felt the liquor settling in her stomach. She already had a glow on and because of the two drinks she'd had earlier, she realized she'd have to have next to nothing for dinner. "I see you brought along your camera. Mixing business with pleasure, eh?"

"Just a habit," he said. "It's sort of become an extension of my body, if you know what I mean."

Everyone is a born qualifier, including me, she thought. She nodded her head. Unable to come up with a clever rejoinder, a suitable analogy, she leaned back in the chair and ran the tip of one finger around the rim of her glass. "So tell me about yourself, Pete," she said at last. She crossed her legs and pulled the hem of her dress down over her knee. The sole of one alligator shoe tapped against the thick pile carpet.

"What's to tell," and he took another swallow. He set his drink down on the coffee table in front of him and folded his hands in his lap.

"Come on," she said, smiling. "You can do better than that. Besides, you didn't strike me as the shy silent type, not by a long shot."

"Oh, I'm not shy," he said. He looked up at her and grinned. "Silent . . . on occasion."

"Are you a New Yorker? Originally, I mean?"

"No way," he laughed. "Would you believe Carbondale, Illinois?"

"No I wouldn't," she said. "But it couldn't have been that bad. You certainly look like you survived the ordeal."

"An ordeal's putting it mildly. But New York's my home, has been for about five years now. I live down in SoHo."

"Like it?"

"Very much. I share a loft with two other guys."

"It's cheaper that way."

"Considerably." He raised his glass again and she held her smile.

"Speaking of Carbondale, we just opened a franchise there, a couple of months ago."

"People need help just about everywhere, I guess."

"You can say that again."

There was something strained about small talk, meaningless chatter. All at once she felt foolish and ancient, having put herself in what she now decided was a ridiculous situation. Again, almost against her will, it came back to her that she was old enough to be his mother. What was I expecting? she wondered. What, he's just going to sweep me off my feet and carry me into the bedroom like the other one did, is that it?

The thought had crossed her mind. But now, watching Peter while she toyed idly with her drink, she became less certain of her motives, her real desires. There was something vaguely discomforting and incestuous about contemplating going to bed with Peter McGuire. Thoughts of her son rushed in and out of her head, looking for a permanent place to settle. She felt as if they wanted to hole in and claim her complete and undivided attention, just as Barry himself had often tried to do when he was a child.

You want to get burned twice, is that it? she asked herself, saying aloud, "How did you get into photography, Peter?"

"Just bought myself a camera, I guess," he replied. "I was thirteen or fourteen at the time. It was a Brownie Hawkeye . . . remember them? Anyway, I guess I got the bug. I'm like a junkie, cause I haven't been able to keep my finger off the shutter ever since."

"You must meet a lot of interesting people in your work." Before he could answer she tapped her fingers nervously against the arm of the chair. There was no other movement in the room. She felt penned in, trapped. "Christ, what a thing to say. Aren't we two being witty, scintillating as all get-out."

As if he were responding to her words, Peter unsnapped the leather case protecting the camera. He checked the light meter and got to his feet. Cynthia sat and watched him, staring at the round glass eye of the Nikon. Cameras, snapshots, family albums, say cheese and smile, had always fascinated her. But though she had loved looking at photos, she had always shunned having her picture taken. "People'll look at me and laugh," she used to say. "They'll remember how ugly I was, what a fat little girl I used to be." And in reply, her mother would always be there to kiss her on top of the head and murmur, soft and sibilant, "Fat? What fat? What kind of nonsense is that? You've got big bones, that's all. By me you'll never be fat. By your mother you're a beauty, my most beautiful little girl in the world."

As she had lost weight, as the pounds had melted like a dish of ice cream left out in the sun, her feelings had changed. She wanted to see herself, her "new" self as it were. She wanted to hold that vision, fixed and permanent, in both of her hands and say, "This is what I was. But I'm not going to be like that, not ever again." Small wonder she had always insisted that all NuBodies members take a photograph on their first day at class. "The *before*," she would tell them, "is going to be the best reminder of the *after*. When you see the change, the difference losing weight makes in your personal appearance, your whole outlook, you'll know exactly what I'm talking about." Perhaps too it was the confrontation, forever different, of viewing herself captured on a piece of coated stock. She might change, but the photo would always remain, immutable as the calories she had collected the way some people collect stamps and coins.

As Peter stepped back and got ready to once again claim the Cynthia of the moment, the instant, her mood brightened and she lifted her eyes. He was staring at her, just as fixedly as she had been staring at the lens of his camera. "Don't think I've forgotten," she said, "because I haven't."

The shutter clicked and he moved to the side.

"What?"

"I'm not a woman who shoots her mouth off, just remember that."

The shutter clicked and he moved in for a close-up.

"I never thought you were."

"Well, I'm not. When I say I'll do something, I do it. Tomorrow morning I'm going to speak to my editor. You have anything against . . . how shall I put it? Work on a more commercial level? I mean, less than art studies, portraits."

31

"Not at all," he said. "When I first started out I ran an ad in the *Voice.* 'Photographer available for weddings, confirmations, and bar mitzvahs.' It paid the bills."

"Let me touch up my makeup, run a comb through my hair."

"You look perfect, Cynthia. Artfully casual."

"Aren't you a charmer," and she laughed as the shutter clicked. How our founder entertains at home, as seen in her lavish suite at New York's incomparable Sherry-Netherland Hotel. She could even see the layout, the written copy: 'On an unbearably hot and muggy New York evening, we had the rare pleasure of speaking to Cynthia Morgan, president of NuBodies. Looking cool and serene in her tastefully decorated . . .'

"Say cheese and smile," he said with a laugh, a giggle that seemed to get stuck in his throat.

He's forcing it, she thought. The sound of the clicking shutter exploded in her ears. All she saw was the camera, Peter's pale and watery blue eyes poised above the black box. Then he was putting the Nikon down on the coffee table and moving back to her. His hands reached for her shoulders and she involuntarily leaned back in the chair. The wooden frame dug against her neck and spine.

"Say cheese and smile," he said again and he found her lips and jabbed his tongue deep inside her mouth.

Cynthia murmured a protest, relaxed and held onto his arms. Peter's eyes were still open, wide and staring. She returned his look which told her nothing except perhaps that he wanted to see her as she really was. She could see her face reflected in his pupils, glassy and minute. His fingers stroked back and forth. His tongue was a zoom lens, probing still deeper. His face was a Polaroid, taking quick ten-second shots of her.

I must be out of my mind, she thought and eased him back, even as he grabbed for her breasts.

Peter was not about to give up so easily.

He was down on his knees before the chair. She blushed, embarrassed by this show of affection, passion. He tickled her stockinged legs with the tip of his tongue, sliding his hands up along the insides of her thighs.

"Peter, I don't think—"

"Shh," he whispered. "Trust me."

What a line if ever there was one, she thought as he

tried to ease her off the chair and down onto the carpet. There was no reason to stop, to deny herself the pleasure of the moment. He was young and attractive, sexy in a lanky hillbilly kind of way. What harm would it do? An orgasm was an orgasm was an orgasm. Besides, it'll make me forget my troubles, she told herself. But at the same time she thought, I'm acting like an ass. He's still a baby, a kid.

"Peter, really, I don't think so," she said, more forceful than before.

"Come on."

"No really."

"But I thought—"

"No doll, honest. I just asked you up for drinks, that's all. Don't spoil it, okay?"

"Sure, whatever you say." He picked himself up off the floor and returned to the couch. When he raised his glass to his lips she didn't miss seeing the tremor in his hands. He was red-faced, embarrassed. She knew what he was thinking and she wanted to ease him out of the suite and be alone.

"A favor's a favor," she said. "I didn't mean for you to think there were any strings attached."

"I didn't," he insisted. "You're . . . you're just a very attractive woman, Mrs. Morgan."

"Cynthia," she said like a mechanical toy, thinking, That's it. The Cynthia Morgan doll. Wind her up and she loses weight. "And I thank you, I really do. And you're a very handsome man, Peter McGuire. But it's just . . . I don't know, it's just not the right . . . time maybe. Whatever. Maybe some other time, okay?"

"Sure, whatever you say," he said again.

She straightened up and stood by the side of the chair, looking down at him. Then she moved to the bar, resolutely and confidently, she hoped, to mix herself another drink. When she didn't ask him if he needed a refill, Peter got the message exactly the way she had intended. He fitted his camera back into its case, patted his pockets as if to make certain he hadn't left anything behind and then moved up to her.

His lips nibbled the back of her neck. But the gesture was perfunctory, meaningless. She knew he was trying to exit as gracefully as possible. "I'll send you the proof sheet," he promised.

33

"Please do. I can always use good photographs. And thank you for coming."

"Thanks for having me."

He was at the door, a slice of hall carpet at his feet, the sound of the elevator a dull rumble behind him, when she turned around and said, "Sticky of me, but you remind me of my son. Too much, I guess."

Without answering, he closed the door behind him.

She turned away and swallowed her drink, neat.

Less than an hour later she was reclining in the tub. The color TV had been wheeled to the bathroom door and from where she lay in the cool sudsy water, Cynthia had a perfect and unimpeded view of the twenty-four-inch screen. No steak tartare for me tonight, she thought. What was it, four drinks? Three? Five? I lost track. "You've been a bad girl, Cynthia. Alcoholic beverages are a no-no. They're not allowed. You weren't playing fair, according to the rules . . . the ones *you* made up, remember?" Then, "The hell with the rules. I feel like I'm in a strait jacket, that's what."

"And now from Hollywood," announced the newscaster, "our very own and very lovely Rhonda Grahame."

Talk about plastic people, she thought, spreading the bubbles over her legs.

"Good evening, this is Rhonda Grahame, reporting from Hollywood. Rumor has it that superbitchy superstar Suzann Jaffe—"

They pay her a fortune, too, she thought. She remembered meeting the gossip columnist at a party at Patrick Casey's house, over a year before. *A lackluster lacquered loser, he called her. Her name used to be Ginsberg. She wrote a tattletale column for her grade school paper. Once a bigmouth, always a bigmouth. It's in the blood, my dear. And it's far from blue, I assure you.*

"—Tudor & Sons, whose last best seller, *Naked in Kingdom Come*, outsold *The Godfather* by over a million copies, announced today the publication of what they describe as the most daring and raunchy exposé ever allowed in print. Don't worry, Jackie O., this one isn't about you. It's called *The Fat Lady* and its author, one-time scriptwriter turned scandalmonger, Justin Rodell, suggests his book may just be about 'the life and hard times' of Cynthia Morgan, founder of that nationwide chain of weight-reduction schools, NuBodies—"

"What the—" she sat up in the tub and reached for a towel.

"—and according to Rodell, there's more juicy unexpurgated gossip per printed page than anything the public has read in years. We even understand the treasury department has gotten into the act. Well, good luck, Mr. Rodell. Let's hope you don't get hauled into court. And if you're listening out there, have a good read, Mrs. Morgan. This is Rhonda Grahame, reporting from Hollywood, wishing you all good-night." The teased hair, white-blonde on the color screen, disappeared and a commercial for dog food came on in its place.

Cynthia sat in the tub, not believing what she had just heard. "Treasury department? Justin Rodell?" she said aloud. "Justin Rodell, my friend Justie, Burr's client . . . he's done what? *The Fat* what? I don't believe it—that little—" and she grabbed hold of the towel rack and got to her feet.

She stepped out of the tub, threw on her terrycloth robe, and hurried into the bedroom.

Cynthia knew who to call. She didn't need to consult her address book. She had memorized D. W.'s two phone numbers long before. The one he gave out to everyone but his closest friends linked up with a recorded message which began with a selection from Shchedrin's ballet, *Anna Karenina*. Recherché, he had termed it. The second number had no taped introduction. It was the latter that she now dialed, one hand searching for a cigarette and a light. Trickles of water dripped down her legs. She pulled the robe tightly around her and tried to remain calm, but it was as difficult as losing weight.

"Good evening, Eliot residence."

It was D.W.'s Filipino houseboy.

"Andres, this is Mrs. Morgan. Is Mr. Eliot in?"

"Oh, good evening, Mrs. Morgan. How are you?"

"Furious. So angry I want to scream. Can you put him on. It's important."

"Mr. Eliot, I'm afraid, is indisposed at the moment. I can have him call you back—"

"I don't care who he's in bed with, Andres. I want to speak to him."

35

"Well . . . yes, well let me see if I can get him, Mrs. Morgan," he said. "One moment, please."

She cradled the receiver against her ear and flicked her cigarette at the ashtray. She missed, brushed the gray-white ash off the top of the mahogany night table and tried to be patient. But it was no use. The more she thought about what she had just heard, the more infuriated she became. Justin Rodell, she thought, what I didn't do for him, the money I didn't spend. How dare he, *The Fat . . .* what was it? *The Fat Woman, The Fat Loser*. Something like that. And what about the treasury department? Don't tell me he's gotten the IRS on my back. Stupid accountant—

She heard a sound like the rustle of sheets. "Hello, my sweetest, dearest Chuck," D.W. said. "You can hang up now, Andres. I've picked up." There was a click as the houseboy hung up the extension phone. "Sorry I kept you, darling. One of those things, you understand."

"Did you just hear what I did?"

"What?"

"That loudmouth from Hollywood, Rhonda whatever her name is, was just on the news. The one who has nothing better to do with her life than talk about people."

"Rhonda Grahame, you mean? Scandal Unlimited."

"You're damn right, scandal unlimited. He's written a book, an exposé. All about me. *The Fat* something or other. What gall, what audacity, and after all the money I invested in him this is how he treats me."

"Who, my dear? Who the hell are you talking about?"

"Justin Rodell. You remember him, Gene Burr's client, the writer."

"Oh yes, Justin. What about him?"

"That's what I've been trying to tell you, if you'd only listen—"

"Well Cynthia, you sound so overwrought and you're speaking a mile a minute that I can't understand a word you're saying. Start from the beginning, sweetheart."

Sweetest, dearest, darling, sweetheart. What's worse, I never can tell if he's serious or putting me on. "I repeat, Rhonda Grahame was just on television. She announced to her coast-to-coast audience that Justin Rodell has written a big fat filthy exposé, *The Fat* something or other."

"*The Fat Lady.*"

"That's it," she said and stopped short. "How do you know about it?"

"Finish first."

"What's to finish? It's all about me, NuBodies, the works. And the treasury department is in on it, or something."

"So?"

"So you don't think I'm just going to sit back and let him get away with it, do you?"

"Get away with what, Cynthia? What?"

"You know damn well what. Lies, that's what."

"But you haven't even read the book yet."

"Why, have you?"

"As a matter of fact," he said, drawing out the words at an impossibly slow and collected rate, "I have."

"What do you mean, you have? And you didn't tell me about this? You just let it sit there, like it happens every day!"

"Cynthia, calm yourself, for God sakes. If you don't you'll start eating again, remember that."

"Listen, I don't know what's going on here, Eliot. But I don't like it, not one iota. What about the book? When did you read it?"

"The publisher sent me galleys, a month or two ago. Just to make sure we wouldn't hit them with a libel suit."

"And you never told me about it?"

"Well, why aggravate you unnecessarily? You were up to your ass in work. I didn't want to put any undue pressure on you, that's all."

"What pressure? What in God's name gives you the right to decide what I can and cannot see, or read for that matter? Ford's President now, not Nixon."

"That's very funny," he said. "But to be quite honest, I just exercised what I felt was a modicum of common sense. So calm down and stop sounding so hysterical. It's very grating, if you want to know the truth."

"I want to know the truth about the book," she said and blew furiously at her cigarette.

"It's . . . it's heavy stuff, revealing, what else can I say."

"Heavy stuff?" she said incredulously. "Just heavy? What kind of stuff, may I ask? And where does the government fit in, while we're at it?"

"I don't remember," he said. "Look, you'll read it, you'll see for yourself. He's gone and interviewed a lot of people, taken down their recollections—"

"About who?"

"Who do you think. It's about you, Cynthia. It's all about you."

"It's all about me. How charming, how absolutely delightful," she said. "You know what, Eisenstern. You're . . . you're treacherous, that's what. And deceitful, on top of everything else. How could you do this to me? You get galleys and you don't say a word? It's just plain inconceivable. A book's about to come out that could do NuBodies irreparable damage and you just sit around on your backside and say it's heavy stuff. I don't believe you, you know that."

"Believe whatever you want to believe, Cynthia, but I really must get off. You called at an inopportune time. We'll discuss this tomorrow, when you're in a better frame of mind."

"What? Now you're dismissing me? Listen, D. W. You work for me, remember that."

"Don't threaten me, Cynthia. You know I don't like to be pushed. It goes against my grain."

"I'll go against your grain, all right, you phony you. I want him stopped, do you hear me. I want to sue. We'll slap a libel suit on them, that's what. An invasion of privacy, or something. You're the one who's responsible for this and you're gonna pay the piper, too. If you'd shown me the galleys we could have hauled them into court months ago. Now it may be too late. That's all we need, after all the time and energy—not to mention money, we've poured into the gala."

"I'm responsible?" he exclaimed. She could see him thumping his fist against his chest, his naked chest at that, laughing at her. "I'm responsible? You know, you're crazy. You're the one who's responsible for it, not me. You ran your life according to your own rules, not anyone else's, Cynthia. In case no one's told you by now, you stepped on a lot of toes along the way."

"What way?"

"Baby, you're not worth close to ten million just because you lost over a hundred pounds in the last ten years," he said.

His voice, shrill and accusing, rose up in the air like the smoke from her cigarette.

"And if it wasn't for me, David Wayne Eisenstern, you'd still be living in a railroad flat with a Pullman kitchen, not some Park Avenue duplex with servants and unlimited expense accounts, and stock options, and profit-sharing and anything else you wanna name. And your house on the Island, too. Let's not forget that, either. And after all I've done for you, you tell me to forget about it? I want you to get on the phone right this minute and call Louis Nizer, or Belli or someone big, it doesn't matter."

"What for? What good will it do? Besides, anybody could've written the book. If not Rodell, then someone else."

"But I am not *anybody*. I am somebody, not just a nothing, a nobody off the street." She felt she was knocking her head against a wall, for all the good it was doing. "I can't figure you out, never could. Never could say no to you either, that was my problem, from the start. And I thought Barry was a difficult case. You put him in the little leagues." She stopped and caught her breath. "I repeat, D. W., we're going to sue the pants off them, Rodell *and* his publisher, the two of them. You read the book; you know what's in it."

"I'll talk to you tomorrow, Cynthia. Just stop over-reacting. Good-night."

"Overreacting! Don't you hang up on me. I'll . . . I'll fire you first!" she yelled.

"You forget, you can't."

The connection was severed.

"What is going on here?" she said. "What's happening that they all think nothing of ruining my reputation, my business?" She felt as though she were on a carousel, a merry-go-round, rushing headlong in unending tightening circles. No one was there to catch her if she lost her balance and started to fall. She felt hunger too, the old hunger she had dreamt of for years upon years, reveries of roasts, dreams of deli sandwiches, triple-thick and overstuffed. Cream pies, chocolate cookies, turnovers filled with poppyseed paste. The inside of her mouth

39

was dry. She flicked the ash off the end of her cigarette and tamped it out with a swift jabbing motion of her hand. Then she got to her feet and moved across the bedroom. She found her battered, dog-eared address book in the inner zippered pocket of her leather bag.

Thumbing through the pages, Cynthia was confronted with an abbreviated diary of her past failings and accomplishments. A for Antonio, P.; B for Burr; E for Evans, Gerald; F for Fisher, D. and Frankel, Leonard and Jeanette. J as in Jameson, Richard. Names of franchise owners and NuBodies members, names and addresses of doctors, dentists, stockbrokers, Halston's home number, Billy Baldwin's *pied-à-terre*, her salesman at Tiffany, the soft-spoken one who took such good care of her at Cartier. Names and private numbers of Hollywood supernumeraries, directors, press agents. R for Rodell, Justin.

She reached for the phone and dialed, breaking a fingernail with a soft splintering crack. "Shit," she whispered and sucked on the wounded finger as she waited for the phone to ring at the other end. Just a cookie, maybe a saltine. Something. She heard the dull rumbling in her stomach. The "lion of hunger" she used to call it. She'd been listening to that trapped beast for years. Now its roar was petulant and insistent, louder than she had ever recalled. A little black coffee, a slice of cake. Just to fill the gap, she thought.

"What number are you calling, please?"

"Hello? Who is this?" This is the party to whom you are speaking. But no, that's in my head. Why am I laughing?

"This is the operator, miss. What number are you calling, please?"

She glanced down at the open page of the address book. "One second," barely able to read her own handwriting. "Here it is. Operator, I'm trying to reach 861–1358."

"861–1358 is no longer in service."

"What's the new number then?"

"I'm sorry, but the new number has been withheld at the customer's request."

"So there's no way I can get in touch with my party, is there?"

"No, I'm afraid not. It's the company's policy not to give—"

She hung up and dialed again.

A morbid wail of androgynous music greeted her ears. David Bowie or Lou Reed, Alice Cooper maybe. Someone like that. She knew the names all right, but not their music. "Hello? Hello? I can't hear you. Who is this? This is Mrs. Morgan."

"Good evening, Mother. And how are you this evening?" the voice replied. It was attenuated, epicene. It sounded as if it were dripping with syrup, sluggish as hot fudge poured languidly over a sundae. "How is every little thing in Fun City, mother?"

"Barry, what's going on there? I can't hear you."

"I'm listening to music, mother. A few friends, what they call out here an intimate informal gathering. Is there anything I can do for you?"

"Did you listen to the news yet?"

"Television? Ugh, I have better things to do with my time."

"I can just imagine. Remember Justin Rodell, that writer?"

"Who?"

They don't want to listen. All of them. "How many people are over there, Barry?"

"A small gathering of arcane types, mother. I'm sorry I can't hear you better. It must be a bad connection. Are you in good health?"

"I'm in perfect health—"

"I can't hear. The connection's dreary. You sound a little drunk, too. I'll call tomorrow."

"I'm not drunk; who gave you that idea?"

"Goodnight, mother."

Dead as the last time, she heard the empty buzz of an open connection. She dialed again, hanging up before the phone began to ring at the other end. Lena's not home, she realized. She's in Palm Springs, soaking up the sun. Good for her arthritis. What could she say that she hasn't already? *I spoiled you rotten and look where it got me, nowhere.*

Scribner's was closed, as was Brentano's and Rizzoli. She called information, got the number for the Doubleday branch on Fifth Avenue. "Doubleday. We're just about to close. May I help you?"

"Yes you can. I'm looking for a copy of a new book. It's . . . it's called *The Fat Lady*."

"Clever title," the voice said. "Who's the author?"

"Justin Rodell."

"How do you spell that?"

"Rodell, Rodell," she said impatiently.

"Well, I know *you* know it, but I don't."

Don't answer. "Rodell," she repeated. "R-O-D-E-double L as in libel."

"R-O-D-E-L-L. One moment, let me check."

That wait seemed interminable. She nursed her splintered fingernail, unable to reach the emery board she kept in her bag, when the salesman returned to the phone. "It's on order, but it hasn't arrived yet, I'm afraid."

"Well, when are you expecting it in?"

"I couldn't say. Next week or three. One never knows with New York publishers. It's a big order but we could reserve a copy for you."

"No, I don't think so. It's not necessary. Thank you." She hung up.

The phone was a direct link to her lack of will power. I'll show them, all of them, that's what I'll do. I'll make him pay through the nose, that phony. The money I poured into that one and he goes and writes . . . "Hello, operator, get me room service, please." She looked at her torn fingernail. Let them all break, let them all go to hell so that bitch can get on the air and say eat your heart out, Mrs. NuBodies. "Hello? Room service? Yes, good evening. Actually it's not . . . no, the room is fine, really it is. But thank you anyway. This is Mrs. Morgan in 917. Yes. Yes, are you still serving? Marvelous. I'd like to order dinner. No, I don't need a menu. Send up a sirloin, medium-rare. That's right, not too well done. I hate it when it gets like leather. Yes, absolutely sour cream on the baked potato. What do you have for dessert? Mousse? Sure, why not. Chocolate mousse'll be delicious. A little pound cake, too, if you have it. And do me a favor, doll, and toast it. That's right, just lightly so it gets a little brown. Right, it's much tastier that way. Black coffee . . . on second thought, cream and sugar, actually. How long will that take? Only twenty minutes. Marvelous. I'll be waiting."

But in the meantime, there was always the bowl of

fruit sitting on the coffee table. She wheeled the TV back into the living room, switched channels until she got the late movie, and settled back on the couch. Fruit's allowed, she thought, reaching for a nectarine. What's another few calories, when you get right down to it . . .

BOOK ONE:

The Nobody

November 1962

"WHAT'S ANOTHER FEW CALORIES, when you get right down to it. That's what I always say. I mean," and she held the Fig Newton between two fingers, waving it before her mother's face, "a cookie's just a cookie. No big deal." Before Lena could say a word, agree or disagree as the mood might take her, Cynthia raised her hand abruptly. The cookie disappeared between her lips. Her eyes closed for a moment as she bit down. The outer layer was sweet and hard, protecting the fig filling and keeping it from drying out. The inside of the cookie was moist and almost gooey. The filling got stuck between her teeth and along her palate. She chewed vigorously, gulped loudly, swallowed just as energetically.

"True," Lena said. "Besides, figs are good for regularity."

"What's taking so long, honey?" Manny called from the living room. "A man comes home from work he likes to see his supper on the table."

"Another five minutes," she yelled back. "Tops." Then she looked at her mother and smiled. "Knock wood, he has a good appetite. That's one thing I've never had to worry about."

"I wish your father ate half as good," Lena Winick replied. "A nibble here, a nibble there. How he manages to keep up his strength is a miracle."

"What do you mean? He's not eating?"

Lena pursed her lips. Her thin and angular body was held rigidly at attention, pulled taut as the pained expression on her face. She nodded her head. "Not like he used to. Says he's not hungry, hasn't got an appetite. What, I'm gonna force him, at his age? You at least, I never had problems with. I put something down in front of you and you ate, like a person."

Two persons, she thought. "I don't like the way that sounds."

"Well it's the truth. What can I do about it, spoonfeed him?"

"That's no answer." She turned back to the counter near the sink. Then, with deft precise motions, she finished slicing the tomatoes for the salad.

"Well?" her mother persisted. "What can I do? You tell me."

"I don't know, mom," she said. "But just do me a favor and sit down and relax. Everything's under control. The chicken's almost done, the grapefruit's already cut. Everything's taken care of." She popped another cookie into her mouth and arranged the tomato slices around the rim of a gold glass plate. The seeds dripped down and made a wet sloppy puddle in the middle of the plate. They had no taste and she didn't bother to wipe them off or remove them with the edge of a spoon. Instead, she covered the drippings with wedges of lettuce, cut in thick chunks the way Barry liked. Next came spears of cucumber, pale green and chewy, then narrow lengths of fresh green pepper. "Manny loves his vegetables," she said, almost as if she were talking to herself. "Me, I could live without them." She reached for the box of Fig Newtons.

"What are you eating so many cookies for?" Lena said as she pulled a chair out and sat down at the table. "You'll ruin your appetite."

"It won't happen."

In the living room the TV was on. Chet Huntley's voice came back to her, sharp and articulate. "The President met today with astronaut Wally Schirra, whose historic flight in Mercury VIII last month—" Manny loves his news, too, she thought. So what's the big rush about sitting down to eat. Besides, I made him a bite when he came in from work, so what's he so hungry about.

"What's for supper, ma?"

"Roast chicken," she said, bending over the sink so he wouldn't see the box of cookies.

"I brought cream soda and sour pickles, Barry," Lena said. "Your favorite."

"I hate chicken."

"Then don't eat it," Cynthia told him. "No one's forcing you."

"It doesn't have any taste," he said.

"I made it spicy this time. It has plenty of taste, believe me." She wiped her hands on a dish towel and took the plate of raw vegetables to the table. If he saw the box, she couldn't do anything about it. Barry was leaning against the side of the fridge, his legs crossed, his lips curled down in annoyance.

"What do you want your mother to do, darling? Make ten different dishes?" Lena asked. "This isn't a restaurant, you know. She has her hands full as it is."

"She's done it before," he said.

"Sure, give him lobster tails, fried shrimp, you're his best friend. Give him roast chicken and you're an enemy of the people," Cynthia replied, trying to get Barry to smile. When she didn't succeed, when he remained unmoved, unimpressed by her efforts, she went back to the fridge and opened the door. She beckoned him forward with a single cocked finger. "Come here, smart guy. Let me show you what I got for you." Barry leaned forward and looked inside the refrigerator. "Ebinger's cake," she said, pointing to the neatly tied box.

"What kind?"

"What kind do you think? Your favorite."

"Mocha cake?" and his eyes opened wide.

"What else," Lena said from the table. "You think your grandmother forgets. Not for her Barry, she doesn't."

"You haven't eaten any yet, ma, have you?"

She knew she shouldn't have expected anything less than this, but she still had hoped. Now, it didn't matter anymore. "Eaten it?" she said, trying to sound self-righteous, indignant. She tapped her fingers against her chest. Instead of striking bone, they disappeared as if into the depths of a feather pillow. "Don't be silly. Why would I want to eat cake when I made so much food for dinner?"

"Last time there was just one measly little piece left." He stepped back and slipped out of the room as silently as he had entered.

"Did you hear that?" Cynthia said, still following him with her eyes as he walked through the foyer and then turned right to enter the living room. "A mouth that doesn't stop, from one minute to the next. As handsome as he is, that's how fresh he is."

"You spoiled him, that's why."

"*I* spoiled him?" raising her voice, only to be cut off as Manny called out from the living room.

"Honey, your husband's starving! I have pains already."

He's the pain, she thought. Then she raised her voice again. "Another minute! What's the big rush? The chicken'll be gamey."

"The man's hungry," Lena said.

"The man's always hungry." She stopped, gripped the edge of the counter and breathed deeply.

"What's the matter?"

"Nothing, just a little short of breath, that's all. I'm not as young as I used to be."

"Thirty-three and she's complaining about being old," Lena said to the cardinals which flew across the kitchen wallpaper. "I should be thirty-three and you should be my age, then you'll first know what old is all about. Cynthia, it's not a question of age and do me a favor and put away that box of cookies before you finish all of them. It's a question of weight. You're just not as thin as you used to be, that's all."

"Mother, I was never thin," she said. "If there's one person in the world who knows that, it's you."

"And for your information, you were in such a hurry you were one month premature."

Sure. I was hungry, even then, she thought.

"Cynthia," her mother continued, "you didn't even weigh six pounds when you were born, that's how skinny you were."

"Well, then just be thankful I'm still around."

"What kind of talk is that?" her mother asked, taking her seriously, literally. "Believe me, a little constructive criticism, a word to the wise, never hurt anybody."

"I know all about it. Last time I tried to diet they nearly put me in the hospital, I got so weak."

"God forbid you should ever be in a hospital," Lena said. "Sure, black coffee and cottage cheese. Some terrific diet that was. A diet for lunatics, if you ask me."

It was better than sunflower seeds and milk. "Well, I'm off it, so what's the difference." Her flat backless slippers slapped alternately against her feet and the linoleum which covered the kitchen floor. The beat was slow, the tempo plodding. She knew herself well enough to realize she would have to take her time in the future. Rushing around, trying to do ten different things at once, only made her hungry. And short of breath. Even now, even after she had stopped for a moment, she could still feel her heart beating rapidly, her pulse fast and agitated.

She bent down, held onto the top of the range for additional support and opened the oven door. The two roast chickens were like twin works of art. "Gorgeous," she said. She found a potholder and removed the roasting pan from inside the hot oven.

"They look beautiful," her mother said from her vantage at the table.

"They should. They cost an arm and a leg."

"Prices . . . isn't it a disgrace? What they're asking for fresh poultry they used to get for steak."

"And what they're asking for steak the middle-class can't even afford," Cynthia replied. "Last week I made a chuck steak for Manny and the kids. Now you know how fabulous a good piece of chuck can taste—"

"If you cook it long enough."

"I cooked it plenty," Cynthia said. "And it was still tough. And mind you, it was top quality meat."

Lena clucked her tongue, totally sympathetic. She got to her feet and moved to the door. "Children, you can come in now. Everything's on the table. It'll get cold."

Cynthia was mashing the potatoes when Manny came into the kitchen. "It's about time," he said.

"You were watching the news."

"I was starving, that's what I was doing."

"Jack, sit over here," Lena said. "Next to me."

Cynthia watched her father moving to the table. He didn't exactly drag and shuffle his feet. But the old bounce—what she'd always called the old bounce, at least—was missing. His color's bad, she thought. Not about to let it pass, she spoke up, even before Barry and Natalie had taken their seats. "Dad, when was the last time you went for a checkup?" And to her daughter, "Natalie, sweetheart, sit next to your brother so there'll be room for me at the table."

"She takes up two places," Barry said.

"Who's asking you, bigmouth," Manny told him. "Natalie, don't mind him. He's only teasing."

51

"He always teases," Natalie said, squeezing behind the table to get to her seat.

"Jack, come, sit by me," Lena said.

"Pop, you didn't answer me."

"What?" He looked up at her and again she thought how bad his color was, a waxen pallor that made his cheeks look as if they were coated with paraffin.

"I tried to get him to go, not two weeks ago," Lena said. She spread a napkin over her lap and lifted her spoon. "Like pulling teeth. Hates doctors like poison."

Jack waved his hand. "I'm tired. A man lives as long as I have, he gets a little tired. Cynthia, I'm entitled, wouldn't you think. It's not as if I've loafed all my life."

"No one's accusing you of being lazy, dad."

"He's the one person who isn't," Lena said. She spread a second paper napkin over her husband's lap and dug the spoon into her grapefruit.

"I don't like the way you look, pop, that's all."

"He didn't sleep well last night," Lena said.

"That's right," Jack agreed. "All I need is a good night's rest and I'll be fine."

"Eat, go ahead. Start. I'll be right there." She tasted the potatoes and corrected the seasoning, adding more salt, a touch of pepper, another tablespoon of butter.

"Natalie, move over. There's no room," Barry said. He looked over at his mother. "How am I supposed to eat when she takes up half the table?"

"He's kicking me, that's why," Natalie said.

"I will not have fights at the dinner table," Manny told them. He swallowed another grapefruit section and for a moment all Cynthia heard was the sound of their appetites at work. "Sweet as sugar," Manny said under his breath.

"He's still kicking me under the table, daddy."

"Do you want me to separate you, the both of you," Cynthia said sharply. She took her place at the table, looked down at her plate and smiled to herself. Then she slid the spoon down into the grapefruit half, snared a precut section, thought of the chicken, and brought the loaded spoon back up to her mouth.

She was halfway through the appetizer when Natalie pushed her chair back and made a move to get to her feet. "Leave me alone," Natalie said, the corners of her eyes moist, her cheeks red as the radishes Cynthia had forgotten to add to the plate of raw vegetables.

Maybe I should cut them up now, she thought. Instead, she said, "You heard your father. And sit down Natalie and finish your food. Do you want us to lose our appetites the way the two of you keep carrying on."

"It'll never happen."

"What did you say, Barry?" she asked.

"Nothing."

"You did too," Natalie said. She pushed her chair forward and once again lifted her spoon. "And stop squirting me."

"You see this, Barry?" Manny raised his hand, the fingers held tightly together, the palm flat and menacing as a fly swatter. "You know where it'll go, don't you, if you carry on anymore?"

"He didn't mean it," Cynthia said. "Did you, sweetheart?"

"I'm not hungry," he said. He leaned back in his chair and crossed his arms.

I could kill him, she thought. Spoiled isn't even the word for him. Mom's right, that's what gets me. I'm a sucker, a real patsy. "Everyone eat. There's plenty." She attacked the grapefruit with gusto. "It needs a little sugar."

"Mine's sweet," Lena said.

"So how's my boy coming along?" Jack asked his grandson.

"He studies with a record now, pop. Every word . . . like an actor," Cynthia said. The last section removed, she lifted the grapefruit shell and squeezed the juice out onto her spoon. She could smell the chicken as it cooled on top of the range. She sensed the way the warm juices would run in her mouth, the way the mashed potatoes—swimming in butter—would cling to her palate. Abruptly she pushed her chair back and got to her feet. As soon as I eat I'll think more clearly, she told herself. Lena made a move to rise. "Sit, ma, I can do it," she said, stacking the plates.

"Manny, do me a favor and open a window."

"Jack, you're hot?" Lena asked.

"The oven was on, that's why," Cynthia said. She carried the two chickens back to the table. "Manny honey,

53

do the honors." And to her mother, "He carves like a dream."

"There's good money in the butcher business," Jack said.

For a moment Cynthia was afraid Manny would say something, something that would take away from the pleasure of a Friday night dinner with all of her family assembled together, seated around the oval-shaped formica table. But rather than criticize his father-in-law for implying he was an inadequate breadwinner, Manny ignored the remark, rubbed his hands together, and lifted the carving utensils.

"There's plenty," Cynthia said quickly. "Take all you want. And fresh bread. I bought an onion rye. It's still warm."

"You can do without the bread," Lena said.

"She sure could," Barry seconded.

"What is this *she* business, young man? *She* is your mother, just remember that."

"He remembers, Manny. He loves me very much. Barry, take a drumstick, honey. You like the dark meat, so take it." Before I do, she thought.

Again, there was silence as Manny carved the chickens and plates were passed around the table. From where she sat, nearest to the fridge and across from her husband, Cynthia had a view of the courtyard beyond the window. The clothesline whistled softly, sliding back and forth along the rusted metal pulleys. The white cotton curtains fluttered like wings, now that the window was open. She felt herself shivering. It was drafty, but her father had complained of being hot, so she made no move to close the window. Cynthia looked over at him. He ate slowly, tentatively, she decided. Again she wondered why her mother hadn't been more forceful with him.

"You really should go for a checkup," she said.

"What's this checkup business all of a sudden? Believe me, I'm fine. What are you getting so excited about, anyway?"

"I'm not getting excited, dad. I'm just worried about you, that's all," she said with a mouthful of food. "You don't look . . . I don't like your color. It's . . . it's pasty looking."

"Sure, I told him he should take a week off and go

54

down to Florida, rest up. But no, not Jack Winick. You'd think he was a partner in the firm the way he's so afraid to take time off . . . and it's coming to him, mind you. It's his vacation from last year and he still refuses to budge."

"It's the busy season," Jack said. "I can't just walk out on the man."

"And why not? He's giving you such benefits?" She looked up at Cynthia. "No health plan, no pension, no insurance even. Twenty-some-odd years with the company and you know what you'll get when you retire, Jack . . . a gold watch which you need like a hole in the head, and a boot in the pants."

"What's a pension?" Natalie asked.

"You'll never need one," Barry said. "You can always live off your fat."

"That's enough, bigmouth!" Cynthia yelled. "Apologize to your sister, this instant, do you hear me?" When he kept silent, she leaned forward in her chair. "I am talking to you, Barry."

"I didn't say anything." He looked down at his plate.

"You did too, you liar," Natalie said. "He calls me that all the time, daddy. Not just now."

"Well, that's what everyone else calls her, so what's the matter if I do," Barry said. "Fat Nat, that's what they say at school."

"Fat what?" Lena asked.

"Nothing. He didn't say anything, Lena. Did you, Barry?" Jack asked.

Cynthia, her mouth still filled with chicken, sighed deeply and contentedly, even if she did feel like a spectator at an all too familiar melodrama. She swallowed, took a sip of cream soda, and said, "Why two children, a brother and a sister, can't get along in this day and age is beyond me. And if I hear you refer to Natalie as fat, I will wash your mouth out with soap, Barry. Personally. Just remember that."

"He says it all the time," Natalie repeated. She raised her small round face and demanded to be heard. Cynthia held her tongue, but Natalie didn't wait any longer. "And you know what else? He says it about you too, mommy."

"Tattletale," Barry hissed.

"Natalie, that's enough. Finish your dinner," she said. The food should have tasted bitter in her mouth. But it didn't. Rarely had there been a time when she had lost her appetite. Crises only served to make her hungrier. Now she ate more than she had planned, picking the bones as clean as a scavenger searching for every last fiber of meat, flesh.

"Here, I can't finish, Natalie. Have mine." Lena stood up, leaned over the table and scraped half a chicken breast onto the girl's plate.

"What do you say, Natalie?" Cynthia asked.

"Thank you, grandma."

"That's better." Satisfied, she helped herself to another serving of mashed potatoes. "How's everything? No one's touching the salad." She lifted the plate and speared a slice of tomato and a length of cucumber.

"Dee-lish," was Lena's comment.

"Terrific, honey. The chicken's perfect," Manny said. "Not too dry."

Jack and Barry kept silent, not doing the meal the justice Cynthia felt it deserved. "Barry, you're not getting up from this table until you eat some more." She looked at her mother. "He weighs less than his sister, and he's two years older. Skin and bones. But cake he'll eat."

"Go figure children," Lena said with a shrug.

I can't, she thought, that's just it. Barry resembled Manny's side of the family. But Manny was heavy, and even that, she realized, was just a nice way of putting it. Natalie, on the other hand, looked like her, the same natural reddish-brown hair, the same rounded features and dark piercing eyes. Angry eyes, someone had once called them. "Look how nicely your sister eats," she said.

"I'm not hungry. I told you that," Barry replied.

"Don't force him, Cyn," Manny said. "If the boy says he's not hungry, he's not hungry. Here kiddo, give your pop your plate. Nothing gets wasted in this house." He looked around the table and grinned. "That's me, Manny Margold, garbage collector."

"Manny, there's more," she said.

"I have plenty, plenty."

I have plenty, too, she thought. More than I can handle.

At least she'd temporarily tamed the lion of hunger; there were no dissatisfied roars from her stomach, no sense of dizziness, shortness of breath, fatigue. She was still hungry, but she decided to save some room for the mocha cake. And when that went there was the bag of danish she'd bought that afternoon. And there'll be leftovers for tonight and tomorrow, she thought. And I really should try to watch my weight. Tomorrow. But it's Saturday. Who ever heard of starting a diet on a Saturday? You gotta be out of your mind.

"I apologize," Barry said.

No one had prompted him and she was pleased. "I told you he's good," she spoke up, beaming with approval. "Didn't I say he's a good child?"

"Of course he is," Lena said. "Jack, you're not eating."

"You'll excuse me," he said. "I'm going to take a nap."

Cynthia managed to ease her chair back. She held onto the edge of the table and slowly maneuvered herself onto her feet, nearly upsetting her plate in the process. You can't move that quickly, she told herself. "Use the kids' room, Pop. The beds are all made."

"Nothing with nothing."

"He works too hard," Lena said.

"I'll make a pot of coffee." She moved between the stove and the refrigerator, even as she heard her father walking slowly down the hall to the bedroom, even as she thought of the cake that was yet to be devoured. He's not young anymore. And I'm three years past thirty and I feel like I'm ready to retire. I shouldn't be this tired. What's happened to all my old energy? Sure, I don't eat enough. Everyone's on my back. *How could she let herself go like that?* Diet, reduce, diet, reduce. Lose weight, slim down. *You have such a pretty face it's a shame, a pity.* Everyone begrudges me that little bit extra. Everyone, including myself.

"The cake is fabulous," Lena said as she poured the coffee. "Isn't it good, Barry?"

"It's the only kind of cake I like," he said. This time he didn't hesitate to scrape his plate clean.

She cut him another piece and then sat down at the table. "Did you ever hear of a kid not liking sweets?" she said. "That's my Barry. Give him a raw carrot and he's happy. Cookies, chocolate pudding . . . forget it." The mocha icing had turned hard. She took her time, savoring each mouthful. But when she made a move to cut herself another slice, her mother reached out and covered the top of the cake with the flat of her hand.

"It's enough. Let the kids have it."

"Mother," she said, making no effort to mask the angry tone of her voice. "Another piece won't kill me."

"You don't know when to stop, dear," still holding her hand over the cake so that Cynthia would have to draw blood if she wanted to cut herself another piece.

Barry looked at her and held up his plate. "I'll have your piece, mom."

"What is this, a conspiracy?" certain that the two of them had winked.

"We worry about your health," Lena said. "Cynthia . . . you weigh two hundred and forty pounds, for God sakes. Exercise a little self-control."

"How can I? Did you see what my living room furniture looks like? I've had it since the day I got married, since day one." She tried to laugh, but no one was buying it. "And it's two hundred and *thirty-seven* pounds, thank you. And tell Manny that too, while you're at it. He's thirty pounds heavier."

But he'd already excused himself, taking his coffee and cake into the living room. The television was on. She heard him working, fastening key cases to a cardboard display card as he watched the tail end of Don Ameche's "International Showtime." He works like a dog, seven days a week. And we still worry about money. Too bad I wasn't born rich. Someday . . . right?

"Someday it would be nice if we didn't have to worry about money, if we didn't have to live in a four-room apartment," she repeated to Manny later that evening. They were alone in their bedroom, Barry and Natalie fast asleep across the hall. "And did you see how white my father was when he left. No color and he was sweating, in November no less. I don't like it, Manny. He looks terrible."

"He's getting old, honey."

"What do you mean, *old*. He's not even sixty-five yet."

"Well, that's not young. He's not a kid anymore."

"Neither am I."

"Come on, you're a baby. You're still my baby." He leaned over and kissed her lightly on the lips. Then, reaching around, he managed to drape his arm over her shoulders.

58

She snuggled closer and the bedsprings creaked. Even though the frame was reinforced, several boards concealed beneath the box spring, the mattress still sagged under their combined weight. "Nothing comes easy in this family," she said. Then, unable to help herself, she sighed deeply. "What's worse. I sound like I'm giving up. And at thirty-three that's . . . that's disgusting, if you want to know the truth."

"Who said anything about giving up?" He released her, turned slowly onto his side and stared into her eyes. "What's the matter, hon? I always know when something's bugging you. So tell me, get it out."

"I'm hungry." She made a move to pull back the covers, even though getting out of bed was a considerable effort, a feat of balance and weight distribution.

"Come on. The truth. What's the matter?"

"My father, for starters. My fresh-mouthed son, for another. Natalie for a third. Tell me this . . . when was the last time either of them had a friend in? You know, just someone from school. A classmate. Or even one of the kids on the block."

"I don't know," he admitted. "I come home from work at six o'clock. Most people eat around then."

"Well I'm here most of the day and I can't remember the last time. How do you like that?"

"So?"

"So why do you think it's like that? I mean, Manny, is he ashamed of me, is that it?"

"Of course not, Cyn. Whatever gave you that idea?"

"He did." She pulled the covers up over her shoulders and heard her stomach growling. "And they do call her that. I heard them myself."

"Call who what? What are you talking about?"

"Nothing. I forgot to brush my teeth." Fat Nat, I heard it with my own two ears. Ten years old and she weighs more than her brother.

"Cynthia . . . please. You had a big dinner. It's not necessary. I mean, I'm trying to cut back, so why can't you?"

"Who said anything about eating?" she snapped. "Did I mention food? Did I?"

"Well . . . not exactly."

"Then don't say it. I'm full; how do you like that? I'm not the least bit hungry." She struggled to get her legs over the side of the bed, fell back, and tried again. A whale, that's what I feel like, a landed whale, beached or whatever happens to them when they're out of water. I feel out of water even though I don't belong in water, which is worse. Once on her feet, it was easy. As she passed the dressing table mirror the sight of her night-gowned figure made her start with surprise. Foreshortening, that's all it is, she said to herself. A walking tent, foreshortened or not. A size forty-six—barely, barely—circus tent. All I have to do is pass out tickets.

She locked the door behind her and turned on the cold water tap. The faucet leaked, but the sound promised toothpaste, soap, the ritual of bedtime ablutions and personal hygiene. Satisfied, she raised one hand and reached for the shower rod. Steadying herself, she leaned forward and eased the bathroom window up. Outside on the sill, cool and comforting to the touch, she found a box of cookies. Fig Newtons. Her favorite. She left the window open, stepped back, and leaned against the sink. It wobbled.

He won't hear me, she thought as she opened the box. I'm lucky it didn't rain. I should buy myself a tin, like they have for those luscious fancy English biscuits. She glanced at her fingers, instantly recalling in a surge of pain the embarrassment of her wedding. The Case of the Ring that Didn't Fit, she thought ruefully. The Adventure of the Whispering Pews. It was all there, right in front of her, the humiliation she tried to hide when Manny attempted to push the gold marriage band onto her finger. *It won't go on, he whispered. And she, hissing between clenched teeth, I don't care if you have to break my finger, but make it fit.* Despite the fumbling, it hadn't. Later, a jeweler had made it several sizes larger, commenting that her ring size was "most unusual," meaning it was a man's size, not a woman's.

Now, she bit down, cracked the smooth outer layer and tasted the delicious fig filling on her lips and tongue. Better, much better, she decided. If he's ashamed of his own mother then he's no son of mine. And if he says one more thing to Natalie I will give him such a slap in the teeth he's not going to forget it so quickly.

Problem was, she'd never hit him in the past, never able to bring herself to touch him with anything less than a caress.

She chewed slowly, contemplatively, enjoying the sweet fig preserves sandwiched in the cookie. Then she reached for another. She turned up the water and bent down to flush the toilet. What he doesn't know won't kill him, she thought. A third cookie followed the second. Then she had a fourth, stifled an impulse to make it an even half-dozen, and returned the all but empty box to the sill. She lowered the window, once again hiding the cookies from view. It was better than concealing them in the dirty clothes hamper. Besides, several months before, Manny had discovered in that hiding place, a cache of sour balls and a sticky brown paper bag filled with peanut brittle. She didn't want to take any more chances, any unnecessary risks.

The less he knows, the better. Besides, I have a large frame, that's why. It's not as if I can't lose weight if I wanted to. It's just that I have big bones. That's all it is, just a case of big bones and a glandular condition . . . or maybe even bad heredity. Anyone can see that at a glance. All they have to do is ask.

Forman—Manny to everyone but the IRS—always claimed that selling was an art, that the presentation was worth twice as much as the actual product. "It's like a three-act play," he explained. "Act One is when you walk in. The curtain goes up and you make your entrance, all smiles and charm. The hook is baited, get the picture? Act Two is the pitch, the spiel. You keep their interest going, see. Get them personally involved, not only with the merchandise, but with yourself as well. That's what I mean when I keep saying my customers are my greatest friends. And why not? They're responsible for helping me put food in my family's mouth. Without them I'd be out in the cold. Now Act Three's the windup, the climax. And the curtain comes down when you ring up the sale, when the money changes hands. I hate taking checks, but that's part of business, so it's hard to get around it. Just make sure you know who you're dealing with and it shouldn't be a problem. But remember, Cynthia. Always smile and never stop talking. You catch them off their guard that way. Before they realize it, they're going along with you. Buying it. And usually more than they bargained on, on top of everything else."

"You make it sound like a shyster operation."

"What shyster? I'm a shyster, a con man? I'm a hard worker. I bust my chops, day in day out. The merchandise sells, so what's the difference. In the end, the long run, no one loses out, including the final customer."

He examined her case the first day she went out. "Well?" she asked. "What do you think?"

"A little velvet, honey, that's what it needs. Mind you, I'm strictly the middleman, the jobber. Leather goods, key chains, they're another story altogether. But with jewelry, good stuff like this," and he fingered a medallion that hung from a thick plated metal chain, "you need a little more polish. Razzmatazz. That's what women like. You've gotta make it showy, presentable. I don't want you to be a flash in the pan, Cyn, the first day out. I mean, this isn't junk . . ."

"It's just costume jewelry, Manny."

"Well, what's the matter with that. *You* wear it, don't you?"

"Sure, but—"

"Sure but nothing. Line the case with some nice velvet, a maroon or a dark red would look perfect. This stuff'll sell itself, Cyn. All you have to do is pour on the charm and smile."

Pour on the charm and smile, she repeated to herself. Easy as pie, Cynthia. It'll sell like hotcakes . . . and how do hotcakes sell? You'll be filling orders left and right.

She lined the case with a piece of wine red velour she found at a remnant sale. Manny provided the hooks to secure the sample pieces—the bangle bracelets, the chains, pendants and earrings—to the thick supple cloth. But the moment she chalked up her first sale, she immediately forgot the three-act play on the art of salesmanship. It wasn't in her nature to give people a line, to tell them one thing when she might be thinking something else entirely. If a pair of hoop earrings looked ridiculous on a blue-haired grandmother, she subtly suggested something else, steering the woman's taste to something more conservative, fitting, and appropriate. "Trust me. These other ones are you to a tee. Try them on. I dare you to tell me I'm wrong. Believe me, when it comes to good taste, I know what I'm talking about . . . better than Maxwell House."

They laughed. And they bought.

It was a small operation, certainly not like Manny's far more extensive—though not particularly profitable or lucrative—business. But the small operation nevertheless provided her with an additional twenty or thirty dollars a week. She was putting the money aside to pay for Barry's bar mitzvah. Not that she was religious. She always insisted she kept God in her heart. Not that her parents, or Manny's for that matter, were strictly Orthodox, either. But she wanted to give the boy a party for his friends, just like all the other youngsters in the neighborhood.

Fortunately, luckily, she'd been having her hair done at Leon's for nearly as long as he owned the beauty parlor. So when she asked him if he'd mind letting her sell to his customers, a kind of informal concession, he made no objections whatsoever. "You want to peddle, Cynthia, go peddle. It'll keep them occupied when they're under the dryers. Just don't get under my operators' feet, that's all. Anything else and you're in business."

Peddle she did, even though the very sound of the word left a bad taste in her mouth. Saturday mornings she arrived with her leatherette case. "Your jewelry lady is right on time. Have a piece of candy, gorgeous. Have I got a pair of earrings for you." Her purse was stuffed with caramels, Life Savers, peppermints, coffee-flavored Hopjes. The patter came naturally, effortlessly. She wooed them with a smile she didn't have to question or put on with spirit gum. It was real, all right. It came from inside, "from the heart." She liked people and she liked getting attention. She was their roly-poly, gold-plated fashion coordinator. She made them laugh—at her and at themselves. She catered to their vanity. And in the end she felt she made them all look pretty, special.

"You know what the zodiac is? You don't!" forming an exclamation mark with her wide-open and patently astonished lips. "I'm telling you, it's going to be the hottest fashion look in the next five years, maybe longer. Ask anyone in the know. Ask Jackie Kennedy, and she has more taste in her little finger than I have in my whole body . . . and it's a pretty hefty-sized body, doll. But seriously, what sign are you? You don't know that, either?" and now her hands would fly up in dismay, stabbing incredulously at the air. "When were you born? No, not the year, don't worry, doll. No one's asking your age.

63

Besides, you're younger than I am. Just the month." Then, "Aha, a Scorpio, just as I thought. I could tell from your eyes. Very tricky, secretive people, Scorpios." She'd lean over, force a hairnet to be lifted, claim the attention of an interested ear. "The sexiest sign in the zodiac, that's Scorpio." The laughter was reciprocal. She would launch into, "Is this not stunning? Have you ever seen a pendant like this? Come on, the truth. Of course you haven't. That's because Cynthia gets exclusives. You couldn't buy this in Abraham & Straus or Macy's for love or money."

She had zodiac pendants and earrings with cultured pearls you couldn't tell from the original, "even if you were in the business, which I know for a fact you're not." She had bracelets of sterling silver, "what they cost me I can't even afford to sell, that's how low my mark-up is." But even more than her work with the case crammed with trinkets culled from discontinued items and manufacturers' end-of-season sales, she had a good time. So did her customers, the clientele who frequented Leon's Haute Coiffure.

She arrived the following morning, but even she was the first to realize that her good cheer was laid on a bit too thick, her smile pasted across her lips. "Something's on your mind, isn't there?" her friend Henrietta asked.

"I don't know," she said. "My folks came over for dinner last night and my father . . . he just wasn't his old self."

The manicurist asked, "Has he seen a doctor?"

"That's just it. He's afraid of doctors, hates them like poison. I called this morning, but no one was in." Then she stepped back, an artist surveying a work-in-progress. "I don't believe it," she said. "You look absolutely fabulous, Henny. I mean, you always look beautiful, but—"

"Ten pounds . . . poof," Henrietta said, blowing a kiss into the hairspray-scented air.

"Ten pounds? What do you mean?"

"Just what I said. I lost ten pounds. In *one* week, Cynthia, can you imagine. Next week I'm going to lose another ten, mark my words."

"Sure, you must've starved yourself," Cynthia replied. She put her case down on one of the empty chairs in the front of the beauty parlor, the "shop" as Henrietta called it.

"I did not," her friend insisted. "In fact, I ate better than I have in years. Three square meals a day. It's all part of the diet."

"That's a diet?" and she made a face. "I go on that kind of diet every day of my life. Come on, there's no such thing. How can you eat and lose weight? It doesn't make sense. Believe me, I've tried them all."

"But this one's different."

"That's what they all say. Remember my bout with safflower capsules? I was so oily I sort of slipped around the neighborhood. Talk about greasy. Or how about Margold's famous itsy-bitsy diet, the one where I let myself have anything I wanted, so long as it was in teeny-weeny amounts."

"Cynthia, I'm serious. I'm telling you, this diet works."

"Yeah, sure. They all work . . . for the first seven days. After that, forget it." She waved at a neighbor who had just walked in. "Hello, beautiful. How's your gorgeous hubby?"

"Cynthia, I mean it," Henrietta said again.

"I have big bones," she said, unwrapping a caramel. "Diets don't work for me. I've tried them all, every last one, and it's always the same. You lose ten pounds and the next week you put them right back on again." She popped the candy into her mouth. "But I have a new item. You're going to love it." She bent down, opened the case and displayed her velvet-lined trays. "A chain belt. The newest thing. Bergdorf's in Manhattan is going to go in for it big this coming spring. I have the manufacturer's word."

"Henrietta," came Leon's voice from the rear of the shop. "Mrs. Bolen is waiting to have her hair washed."

"Let her wait," Henrietta said under breath. She edged closer. "A twenty-five cent tip, I get from that one. Can you imagine the nerve it takes? I'd be ashamed if it was me."

"Some people are givers and some are takers," Cynthia said. As Henrietta moved to the back of the shop, she kept her eyes on her friend. Ten pounds, and it shows. On me you wouldn't notice a thing. Amazing, she thought. Henny wasn't hitting close to two forty. But she was still a long way from a size sixteen. Where do they all get the will power, that's what I want to know.

"I'm in a buying mood, Cynthia dear. What kind of goodies did you bring this morning?"

She turned around. Up went the smile. She put on the charm and started going through her paces. "It's the only one I have. Don't tell Mrs. Bolen or she'll have a fit because I swore on a stack of bibles I'd save it for her and her alone."

"Mrs. Bolen? The dentist's wife?"

She whispered, "The *orthodontist's* wife, get my drift?"

By the time twelve o'clock rolled around, she had gathered over twenty-five dollars in sales and orders. She packed up her case, waved good-bye, and headed directly to Claire and Bernie's luncheonette on the next corner. She was famished. Her throat was dry from talking, and she had the beginnings of a headache from having inhaled hairspray and "God knows what."

Outside on the street she breathed deeply, fumbling with the oversized buttons on her coat. Take your time, no rush, she thought as she walked slowly down the street, trying to steer clear of Fox's Nut Shop. Something twisted up inside of her. She needed a sandwich, a cup of hot coffee, more than a pound of cashews or a bag filled with chocolate bark. *It's a crying shame.* That's what one of the women had said. Not directly, of course. Not to her face. But she had heard the comment, all the same. The customer had been referring to her and no one else. Why can't I do it? she asked herself, feeling the chill November air buffeting her cheeks. If Henny can do it, why can't I?

But Henny didn't have big bones and a large frame. She was shorter by a good two or three inches and she didn't even weigh two hundred pounds, nor did she have problems with fat genes and a sluggish glandular system. Her body didn't suffer from torpid endocrines or whatever. Nor had the manicurist ever been a fat baby, a fat child, a fat teenager, and a fat wife.

Sure, she realized, she's not married, that's why she can diet. She can hardly boil water. If she had to contend with a husband and two growing kids day and night, she wouldn't be able to maintain her strength. She'd have to eat more. It just makes sense.

"There she is, just like clockwork," Claire called out the moment she stepped inside the luncheonette. "We were just talking about you."

Cynthia smiled. "No wonder my ears were ringing."

66

"I was just telling Bernie here that it just doesn't seem like a Saturday until you come in for lunch. What'll you have today, Chubby?"

No, she didn't wince. It bounced off her, rolled off like water on a duck's back. That was the old adage, wasn't it? Nothing fazed her, least of all her nickname. "What's your special today?" she asked. She set down her case and slowly maneuvered herself up onto a stool. The edge of the counter dug into her stomach, but she hated eating alone at a table in the back.

"I have a brisket of beef that's outstanding," Bernie said, his cigar stuck like a wedge between his lips. "I made it myself. Fresh, not two hours ago."

"No, I don't think so," she said. "I'm sure it's beautiful, but I'm not in the mood for something so heavy."

"A little fresh egg salad on an onion roll?" Claire suggested. "Or maybe you'd prefer whole-wheat toast. It'll take no time at all."

"No, I just had eggs this morning for breakfast." She leaned over, her eyes moving rapidly and excitedly from the steam trays to the stainless steel tubs of refrigerated salad. "How about shrimp salad for a change? That sounds perfect. Nice and refreshing."

Claire hung over the counter. "Not fresh," she mouthed without speaking the words aloud.

Disappointed, Cynthia nodded her head. "Salmon salad?" she whispered.

In response, Claire made a circle with her thumb and forefinger. She shook her head approvingly. "I can swear by it, believe me. What kind of bread you want it on?"

"Rye toast," she said promptly. "And a cup of coffee." That's not a big lunch. I worked hard all morning, anyway. I have to keep up my strength, take care of myself.

"How ya doin', Chubby?"

"Hello, beautiful."

"How's the jewelry business?"

People came and went, nearly all of them familiar, friendly faces. She was a fixture in the neighborhood. Born on the block, she'd returned after her marriage. Every day she saw people she had known since she was a little girl. It was safe, easy. But there would always be that half-heard whispered comment, that infamous "it's a pity, such a shame." The words went with her like a badge, went with her "sweet face" and "darling per-

67

sonality." But no one called her fat, or even pleasantly plump. Either she was Chubby or Manny's wife, Barry and Natalie's mother, Lena Winick's only child from down the block.

"Mommy, mommy!"

She put down the cup of coffee and tried to swivel around on the stool. But she was wedged, stuck as tightly as an anchovy in a vacuum-packed metal tin. She jerked her head over her shoulder as Natalie grabbed hold of the long voluminous hem of her old winter coat. "What's the matter, sweetheart? You want some lunch, something to eat? Sure you do, come," and she patted the vacant stool right alongside of her. "Sit by me and we'll have a nice lunch together, just the two of us."

"She's getting so big," Claire said, adding quickly, "I mean tall. I wouldn't have recognized her."

"Mommy, where have you been, they've been trying to get you all morning," Natalie said in a rush. She tripped on the words and held fast, refusing to let go of Cynthia's coat.

"I was at the beauty parlor. Who's been trying to get me?" she asked. Natalie was the emotional one in the family. Barry may have been sensitive, and in all the wrong and petulant ways, but his sister had a loose edge of compassion that went far beyond her meager years. It was this crumbling façade she now stared at, visible in her daughter's reddened face and wildly imploring hands.

"Daddy was and grandma," Natalie said.

She understood immediately and reached for her bag. "How much do I owe you, Bernie?" And to Natalie, "Who? Grandma's been trying to get me on the phone, is that it?"

Natalie seemed to shudder and sink back. Her head jerked up and down with emphatic insistence. "Grandpa Jack is sick," she said, whispering as though she feared the very sound of the word, as though she were reluctant to let the others know what was wrong.

Bernie said, "Dollar ten."

She put down a dollar bill, a nickel, and a quarter, waved a mechanical good-bye and followed her daughter out of the luncheonette. "Button up, Natalie. It's very chilly out. Where's your father?"

They turned the corner and she squinted, narrowing her eyes.

"Waiting in front of the house."

"What happened?"

"I don't know 'cept grandma's been calling all morning," she said again.

"I called the beauty parlor but they said you'd already left," Manny told her when she reached the house. He was standing in front of the entrance to the six-story apartment building, his arms crossed over his prominent and bulging stomach.

"And? And?" she asked.

"Your father," he said, holding the car door open for her.

She'd barely noticed the pale blue Ford station wagon he'd been leaning against. "What about my father? What happened, Manny?"

"It's all right, Cynthia. Just a . . . just a small stroke—"

"A small what?" she exploded, trying to slide down onto the front seat. She hit her elbow against the edge of the dashboard. Wincing with pain, she nevertheless managed to haul herself onto the seat. "Natalie, watch your fingers," she said. She slammed the car door shut as Natalie crawled into the back seat. "Lock your door, honey." Manny was already behind the wheel. She turned her head to the side as he started the car. "What? A what?" she asked, refusing to believe what she had heard the first time.

"He had a heart attack, Cyn. I'm sorry. This morning."

"Where? What happened he's still a young man I don't understand." Her head was shaking and she couldn't stop her lips from trembling. "I left my sample case in the luncheonette; they'll hold it for me. Where Manny? When did this happen?"

"At the doctor's office. He was waiting to have a checkup."

Jack lay on his back, his head flat against the pillows, held rigidly at what she shuddered to think was a strange and unnatural angle. She moved to the front of the bed, close to the I.V. unit, closer still to his crescent of face. Then, reaching out a hand, Cynthia touched his fingers. They lay against the smooth white sheets, prominently veined, liver-spotted, unmoving. Jack's eyes were blank and dim. She'd never seen them that way before, so devoid of life, so lacking in animation. She ran her fingers along his arm and his cheek, brushing his forehead with quick butterfly movements, fluttering and unsettling. "Papa? Pop, it's Cynthia. Can you hear me?"

The eyes, the empty unclear brown eyes, blinked, blinked again. "Lena said you'd come," Jack whispered. He seemed to be urging his lips to move, urging his throat to make sounds, to articulate thoughts. He tried to raise his head but he was too weak. His neck was gaunt. The muscles stood out like strips of catgut. His skin was tinged with a pale yellow.

"Dad, everything's going to be okay. I spoke to the doctors. You'll just have to rest up, that's all." She tried to sound gay, watching him as a smile slowly took form across his lips. "You'll be up and out of here in no time, no time at all," she continued. Behind her Lena was crying, whimpering into a crumpled tissue.

"I went," he whispered. "Didn't I go? I was right there, in his office. Life's . . . funny. How's my baby, my sweetest beautiful girl?"

"She's fine, dad. I'm fine. You'll just have to rest, take it easy, stay off your feet for a couple of weeks," she said. She wasn't certain if she believed the words. Jack was in the intensive care unit. The cardiologist assigned to the case had told her it was impossible to make any predictions or venture a prognosis. They'd have to wait, sit tight, see what developed. *But in a man of his age, there's no way to tell what the outcome will be.*

"I warned him. I begged him to go," Lena said.

"Ma, please. Stop it now. Come on. He's getting the best of care," she said.

"You . . . you wouldn't think your ole man'd be so weak," Jack said, once again trying to smile.

"I begged him. I should've gotten down on my hands and knees to make him listen."

"Lena come, we'll go outside. Take a breather," Manny said.

"Go, have a cigarette, a cup of coffee," Cynthia urged. Then they were alone together, the father and his only child. She pulled up a chair and sat down alongside the bed. She reached for his hand and held onto his fingers, squeezing them gently. His chest rose and fell beneath the spotless hospital-white sheets.

"Where's my little Natalie? And the bar mitzvah boy?"

"Downstairs, in the waiting room, dad. They won't let her . . . them, I mean, come up. They're too young. They're not old enough, the both of them."

"Who's watching?"

"Barry's watching her," she lied. She'll be all right, she told herself. She's a very responsible little girl. The receptionist had promised to keep an eye on her, so she wasn't worried. And Manny'll go down soon and buy her a soda, or something. Something. Barry was probably in the park, playing with his friends. He didn't even know what had happened. It's for the best, she decided. He's too young. He doesn't have to know about sickness so early in his life.

She opened her bag and reached for a candy. She removed the cellophane wrapper and bit down on the toffee. Sweetness flooded her mouth. She felt she could now think more clearly, as if there were a direct link between sugar content and mental acumen, emotional control. Strength, she thought. You have it or you don't and that's the whole point. That's what it all comes down to.

"Promise me," he said. His eyes closed and the muscles smoothed out across his face. His color was even more pallid than it had been the night before. His flesh looked waxen, without tone or texture.

Tears dripped down her cheeks and she brushed them aside with a quick wiping motion of her hand. She fumbled in her bag for a tissue. He'll be all right. Just has to rest. He's still young, a young man. He's been working too hard, that's why.

"Promise," her father whispered.

She leaned forward in her chair, feeling her bulk, her weight, settling and readjusting itself. The chair creaked dangerously. Her father's voice was faint and weak, but she had no difficulty understanding what he was trying to say to her. "What, pop? Promise you what? What do you want me to promise?"

"The eating," he said. His eyelids floated up like those of a doll turned on its back. Once again she stared at his distant, remote eyes. They held no clue, no expression. She had to go by the tone of his voice and nothing else. "You were, were so beautiful, such a beautiful child.

71

It's . . . it's too much already, sweetface. It's no good. It'll, it'll make you sick, like me. You and Manny both." He stopped, closed his eyes. The sheets barely stirred. "Tell him," he whispered.

"Pop, rest, you're talking too much. It's no good."

"It'll make you sick," he said. "Like me."

"You're not sick," she hurried to say. "Nothing's damaged. As God is my witness that's what the doctor said. No . . . no pathological damage, pop."

"No good, it's no good." He sank back against the pillows. His head slipped to the side, revealing the hollow concavity of an ashen gray-stubbled cheek. His lips parted, and she heard a deep rattling sound. She sat by the edge of the bed, her hands folded in her lap. She swallowed what was left of the toffee and reached blindly, automatically it seemed, for another. Her stomach muscles churned spasmodically in pain. *No good, it's no good.* And when was it ever? Tell me that. When was it ever good? When did I ever live without worrying? When did anything ever come easy for this family?

After dropping Lena off in front of her apartment on Lefferts Avenue, they drove home in silence. Her mother had refused to spend the night, insisting she would be fine, that she had her own home, that she liked her privacy. "I'll only be in the way, sweetheart. But thank you. I know you love me and I'll be okay. I want to go back to the hospital this evening, after he has his supper. Do me a favor and eat something. You'll feel better."

"Is grandpa gonna be okay?" Natalie asked.

"He's going to be fine, darling. He just has to rest and take it easy. But he's going to be fine in no time at all." She listened to the sound of her voice, the repetition of familiar words, a recording she'd already committed to memory. Why don't I believe it myself? she wondered. I'm so afraid and all he could think of was me. *Promise me . . .*

When the phone rang at three o'clock that morning, she knew what to expect before she picked up the receiver.

For a woman who had never moved quickly—or so she had long since come to believe—who had made up for the slowness of physical motion with the swiftness of speech, Cynthia found herself rushing at a breathless and

72

agonizingly hurried pace. She took cabs and subways and buses, squeezed through turnstiles, and lost the buttons off her winter coat. She took the Long Island Railroad to Farmingdale and then a taxi to the cemetery to purchase a plot. She took the IRT to Livonia Avenue and then a bus down Rockaway Parkway to make the necessary arrangements at the funeral home. Manny was working. He couldn't afford to lose a day's pay. Barry, now that she needed him, responded in a way she still found difficult to believe. He was the very picture of compassion and understanding, waiting in front of school at three o'clock to take his sister home, to seat her at the kitchen table and make sure she had her requisite milk and cookies. He'd always hated playing babysitter in the past. Now he never said no, nor refused to accept the responsibilities she thrust into his hands. Lena sat alone in her three-room apartment. Immobilized by the speed of events, the permanence of death, she was unable to grasp what had happened. The solitude of being a widow stunned her. She said little. Her eyes were always wet, hollow, devoid of anything but the most despondent and lachrymose of expressions. Cynthia grieved for her helplessness, the loneliness which quickly overtook her before she herself could do anything to stop it.

"I'll take care of it, ma. I'll attend to everything. Just sit. I don't want you rushing around. Please, leave everything to me."

She ate constantly now, eating on the run. Cold drinks and moldy Swiss cheese sandwiches on the train, slices of pizza in Brownsville, franks and knishes on Rockaway Parkway, chocolate bars from subway vending machines. Calories were her metaphor of grief, a way of overcompensating for her loss. She refused to wallow in self-pity. Her father deserved more than that, had always respected her strengths, her sense of self-sufficiency. So no one had to call upon her to perform her filial duties. No one had to ask her to arrange for the funeral and burial, to make the seemingly endless phone calls to friends and neighbors and relatives.

Perhaps hardest of all was her visit to the savings bank on Eastern Parkway. She'd had an account there for years, a passbook that had grown only fitfully. The charm, the easy banter, the playful persuasiveness which had served her so well in the past, was now lost. It evaded her grasp. It went out the window, she thought, the minute the phone rang.

"I need a loan," she said, overflowing the narrow chair. "I've had an account here since I got married, but my husband doesn't make enough and social security won't pay for the funeral."

"What funeral, Mrs. . . . ?"

"Mrs. Margold, Mrs. Forman Margold. Here's my bankbook. It's all here." She tried to laugh. "The story of my life. My father died and he had no insurance, no pension. Nothing. Worked like a dog and . . . you see, if my mother lays out the six hundred for the funeral . . . I went all over, that was the cheapest I could find. I mean, I can't bury him in a cardboard box for God sakes, can I." Deaf to his expressions of sympathy and condolence, she said, "I'm sorry," and reached for a tissue to wipe her eyes. "If my mother pays she'll have nothing left. It'll wipe her out. I'm working part-time. I'll pay it back."

"And your husband? Is Mr. Margold working?"

"He's never stopped working, seven days a week, but it's just enough to make ends meet. All I have is this four hundred and seventy-five dollars." All I have to show for thirteen years of marriage. "I was saving it from my job. I sell jewelry, costume jewelry part-time, to pay for my son's bar mitzvah. You know what a bar mitzvah is, don't you, Mr. Flynn?"

"Certainly I do, Mrs. Margold. I understand your . . . your predicament."

"I'm not religious," she felt compelled to add. "But it's for him, my father I mean. For his memory. He never lived to see his grandson be bar mitzvahed and I don't care if I have to scrub floors, the boy's going to get a party like everyone else."

"How much were you thinking of asking for, Mrs. Margold?" Mr. Flynn spread forms out across the top of his desk. He held a slim gold fountain pen in one hand and Cynthia was unable to keep her eyes off it. The pen reminded her of a magic wand. A flourish, a wave, and all her wishes would come true. But she knew that Cinderella lived in a mythical storybook kingdom. She knew that the fairy godmother wasn't named Flynn, nor was she an officer of a savings bank.

"Six hundred. That's all. Just to pay for the funeral

expenses." She dug into her handbag. "I have it all here, the itemized bill. See," and she thrust it into his hands. "No flowers, nothing fancy. No extras. The bare minimum, bare essentials I mean. I left a deposit, fifty dollars with the funeral people."

"Do you have any charge accounts, Mrs. Margold?" he asked, examining the wilted, many-times folded and unfolded sheet of paper.

"No. I've always paid for everything with cash. My husband doesn't believe in charging."

"That makes things more difficult, I'm afraid."

"Because I paid cash?" she asked in disbelief.

"We have no way of establishing your credit rating, if you'd be a good risk or not."

"But I have this bankbook. Take a look at it. I've been depositing for over ten years." And again she thought, All I have to my name, less than five hundred dollars.

"I know it's an unfortunate situation," he said. "But wait a moment. Do you own an automobile?"

"Yes, a station wagon, a Ford," she said quickly. "And it's all paid for, complete."

"That improves things considerably."

The car served as collateral. When she left the bank two hours later she was soaking wet. Her dress clung to her overheated body in damp and sticky pleats. Never, she vowed, will I go through that again, as long as I live. I'll get a job, something. But who'd want to hire a two-hundred-fifty-pound workhorse, a fat dynamo. I couldn't even fit behind a desk. *Promise me, sweetface.* Dad, you just don't understand. If it was anything else . . . I've tried, believe me. I can't help myself. I'm like a magnet. Wherever there's food, I start eating. I gained ten pounds this week alone, pop. I want to be thin, slim like everyone else. But I just can't help myself. I just can't do it.

She avoided the revolving door, knowing from past experience that she'd never fit. Instead, she took the side entrance and stepped into Dubrow's Cafeteria. A nice meat loaf sandwich, she thought. Besides, I need the protein.

December 1962

MANNY INSISTED Cynthia needed a night out.

She bundled up against the cold. She was ashamed of her coat, even though she'd managed to find a new set of buttons to replace the ones she had lost the week of her father's death. Now that it was all behind her, now that she had stood at the graveside and listened to the rabbi recite kaddish, she realized what they meant when they all said, "Life must go on." She had never questioned that, nor the wisdom of such a course of action. But now that it was over and the last of the sympathy calls had been made, there was a feeling that something was undone, incomplete, not yet finished.

She was ashamed of her overcoat, a vast woolen tent which reached down to the middle of her calves. A horse blanket, that's what it is, she thought. But she couldn't afford to buy a new coat and she buttoned up in silence, refusing to stare at her reflection in any number of mirrors hanging in the apartment. She gave Barry "strict instructions," kissed her children goodbye—"And there's plenty to eat in the icebox if you get hungry and don't get into fights. I'm warning you"—and followed Manny out of the apartment.

The evening promised a movie, relaxation. "It'll get your mind off the war," Manny said.

The war against what? she asked herself. The war against sorrow or the war against calories? Or the war against both. Her father's voice still made itself known in a hundred little ways. Her thoughts were forever returning to the last time she saw him, lying sticklike and weak in the hospital bed. What kind of thing was that to say,

76

'Stop eating'? The man was dying and he worried about my weight.

She wanted to discount it, declare his sentiments absurd, ridiculous. Ludicrous to the extreme, the nth degree. But no matter how hard she tried to forget, the words stuck like a gear jammed inside her head. It's silly, to go on a diet in his memory, she decided. Yet there had been other voices too, all saying the same kind of thing. Friends and relatives had come to the apartment to pay their respects. She and her mother had sat on hard wooden stools, following religious traditions, customs they neither questioned nor fully understood. It was simply a matter of how it was done and Cynthia had obeyed, even as she'd listened to the telling creak of the mourning stool, knowing a soft cushion was not a way of offering sorrow, the pain of loss. The stool seemed to measure her weight, protesting her lack of self-control, not her lack of feeling. For nearly a week she sat on the straining wooden stool. The visitors came with baskets of fruit, boxes of Barton's continental miniatures, pounds of roasted cashews and bags of bridge mix. They brought platters of cold cuts and sour cherry tomatoes, barbecued chickens so she and Lena wouldn't have to cook, containers of potato salad and cole slaw, hard candies that were "good for the throat." Food was love, had always been an expression of concern. Now it was no different and the coffee table in the living room creaked under another kind of weight, another measure of devotion.

It seemed her mouth never stopped moving. She didn't talk so much as eat, unable to resist the delicacies her guests brought to the apartment. "Eat, you'll feel better," Lena kept saying. "Me . . . I just don't have a stomach for food." I eat for the two of us, Cynthia thought. That's why she's always been so thin. I inherited papa's fat genes, that's the reason, the whole cause of it all. Jack had never had much of a weight problem, but she refused to take this into account. An aunt on her father's side had been laid to rest in a specially built casket, designed to accommodate her unusually large frame. *Unusually large,* that's it, she decided. Aunt Bess had big bones too, just like me. She weighed nearly three hundred pounds when she passed away. But ask anyone who remembers, and I remember even though it was nearly twenty years ago. She didn't drop dead because she was fat. It had nothing to do with it. Even the doctors said so.

But now there was something else on her mind. It had nothing to do with her inability to control, or even curb, her appetite, her compulsive eating habits. It was a question of money, hard cash, not calories. Cynthia had already come to a decision, even before she left the apartment. She said nothing about it as they drove to Flatbush Avenue. She buttoned her lips as they searched for a parking spot, rather than spend the two or three dollars it would cost to leave the car in a lot. She held her tongue all during the double feature as she and Manny ate hot buttered popcorn in the balcony of the RKO Kenmore on Church Avenue. Stewart Granger was starring in the *Swordsman of Siena*. Don Murray was forever rescuing Christine Kaufmann in *Escape from East Berlin*. Then the lights came up and still she kept silent as they bundled up

Christmas decorations were strung across Flatbush Avenue, garlands of tinsel and winking popsicle-colored neon lights. People walked hurriedly, heads hunched down once again and stepped outside.

into their shoulders, coat collars riding high along their invisible necks. The air was sharp and tingly and her breath formed a cloud before her face. After sitting in a smoke-filled balcony, she inhaled deeply, drawing down the crisp air as if it were a kind of vaporous food.

"Both of them were stinkeroos," Manny announced, "a waste of money. A lot of propaganda, fascist stuff, if you ask me. We should have gone to see *Gypsy*, or Peter Sellers at the Astor. Well, it's too late now, so what's the difference. Better than staying home, right?" He shoved his ungloved hands down into the pockets of his coat. "Where to, honey? Jahn's or Garfield's? It's up to you."

The first was an ice-cream parlor, the second a cafeteria. Jahn's catered to the high-school crowd. Hot fudge sundaes, banana splits, pie à la mode, pancakes prepared any number of ways were the mainstay of its menu. It was noisy and brightly lit, its genuine plastic turn-of-the-century decor considered charming and atmospheric. Cynthia considered it dangerous territory and tried to exercise discretion and self-control.

"I could do without the ice-cream, if you want to know the truth," she said.

"I guess you've got a point. There are too many kids at Jahn's, anyway. Garfield's is more our kind of crowd."

Although she didn't agree, there was no sense arguing, especially since she had a considerable amount of persuading still ahead of her. So they crossed Flatbush Avenue, arm in arm, and ducked out of the cold. Cynthia claimed a table for two in the rear while Manny grabbed a tray and took his place in line. She'd already told him what she wanted and now she sat in front of a neatly folded machine-dispensed paper napkin, her coat draped over the back of her chair. All around her middle-aged couples were eating, bent over in heated conversation. Garfield's was known as a meeting place. Many of the over-thirty crowd who frequented the cafeteria had either never said "I do," or else had lost mates through natural or unnatural causes. Bouffant hairdos and false eyelashes were as much in abundance as sapphire pinkie rings and purple Italian knit shirts.

I want something more from my life, she told herself. I don't want to grow old sitting here on a Saturday night, thinking up ways to cheat on my husband or spend his money, looking for some big spender from the garment center.

She craned her head around and smiled to herself. The sight of several other overweight women made her feel more confident and assured. I'm not the only one, she thought. I'm not the only one with a freak hormone system, a glandular imbalance. All the same, she wished there was a pill, some kind of simple medication she could pop into her mouth as easily as a candy, to shut off her appetite like a valve. She'd taken diet pills but they'd made her nervous and high-strung, short-tempered. Her mother had told her they'd make her sick. Manny had agreed. She stopped taking them and the fifteen pounds she had lost seemed to bounce back into place.

"They were all out of smoked whitefish, so I bought you lox instead. Nova Scotia. It's not as salty as the other kind," Manny said when he returned to the table. He set down the overloaded tray and she reached out to remove her plate and cup of coffee.

"I didn't want any cream cheese," she said. "I'm trying to cut down."

"On what? Air?"

She ignored his heavy-handed sarcasm. "You know

what. My weight, Manny. I'm trying to watch myself . . . for a change."

"Well, scrape it off then. Use your knife." He bit into his bagel and Cynthia saw his eyes close in contentment.

She didn't bother to remove the cream cheese. She raised the bagel and lox with two fingers and took her first bite. Keep your eyes open, she thought. Jesus Christ, Cynthia, there's more to life than food. Grab hold of yourself, for God sakes. You're looking at this bagel like it's an emerald or something.

"What's the matter?" he said.

She finished chewing what was in her mouth, swallowed, and returned the bagel to the plate. "You know me like a book, don't you."

"After thirteen years of marriage, I should hope so," Manny said with a laugh. "Do you want me to call the kids and see if everything's okay? Is that it?"

"No," she said. "I'm not worried. Barry's been behaving himself lately. Besides, he knows to call Lena if something's the matter."

"So relax and take it easy, enjoy yourself," he said. "You're sitting there like you're seeing your whole life go by. I don't understand."

"I don't either." She listened to the sigh escaping from between her lips, hating the sound as much as everything it stood for. Stop it, this instant, she told herself. The very mood of self-pity angered her. She refused to fall victim, to fall into its nice easy trap, wading right out into the middle of self-inflicted pain. "I have something to discuss with you," she said. She fortified herself with another bite, then cleared her throat with a sip of hot coffee.

"About what?"

"My mother," she replied.

"Go on. What about Lena?"

"She has no money—"

"So what else is new?" He made a sound halfway between a laugh and a jeer. "Neither do we, for all intents and purposes. But we manage. We survive."

"Barely."

"Come on, Cynthia. I'm doing the best I can, the best I know how. You know that as well as I do. I'm trying to build up the business. It just takes time, that's all. You've got to be patient with me."

"I realize that." Once again she lifted the coffee cup to her lips, her eyes looking beyond Manny to the table right behind him. That could be me, she thought, watching a stout—which is just a nice way of putting it, too—well-dressed woman consuming a piece of Boston cream pie. Do I look like that? She has so many chins I can't even begin to count them. Are my arms that flabby—loose pieces of meat, like the wattle of a turkey? Is my neck that invisible? Does she have to add extra elastic to her bras, or does she have them all custom-made, the way I can't afford?

The woman wore an elaborate hat, a trick Cynthia had often used to draw attention away from her weight problem. Sure, that's just it, she thought, my weight problem. Not my fat problem or my obsessive-compulsive eating habits. But my weight problem . . . sure, that's a nice clinical way of putting it. Yes, I have a weight problem. I've gone to all the top men in the field, weight problem specialists. They all agree it's a sluggish thyroid, coupled with a lazy metabolism. Some people have all the luck . . .

"Well?" Manny said. "What is it then?" She watched him as he turned his head over his shoulder and then looked back at her. "Some people just don't know how to control themselves," referring to the woman with the Boston cream pie.

"So what's that chocolate eclair doing on your plate?" she asked. She pointed to the dessert he was just about to tackle. "You could do without it, too, for your information."

"You serious? I thought you'd finally given up all that diet nonsense. You told me yourself it doesn't work for you."

"Well, how am I supposed to even try to watch my weight and cut back when you sit there eating like a horse."

"Hey, just a minute, Cynthia. I don't eat like a horse and I don't need my wife to insult me, either. If you want to try to cut down, that's your business. But leave me out of it. I don't want to be involved. I carry my weight very well. Everyone says so."

Everyone but your wife, that is, she thought.

"And furthermore," he went on, "I remember the last

81

time, when you were on those lousy diet pills. You were impossible to live with, in case you've forgotten."

"I haven't forgotten," she said. She finished the bagel, wiped her mouth and added another spoonful of sugar to her coffee. Manny was halfway through the eclair when she decided to broach the subject once again. "Manny, I have to discuss something with you. It's about Lena."

"I know," he said and she could see the custard filling sticking to his lips. "You told me already. We're all in the same boat. No money. So what do you want me to do about it, honey? I can't very well subsidize her, can I?"

"Subsidize?" she repeated. "Who said anything about subsidize?"

"Well, you're saying she has no money."

"Manny," and she leaned over the table and pulled his attention away from the half-eaten eclair. "I'm talking about the facts of life, and not the birds and the bees, either. You know as well as I do that my father left nothing behind. After she got through paying the hospital bills, she didn't even have enough for the funeral. That's why I had to take out that loan."

"So? What does that have to do with us? You were a good daughter. How many other daughters would have done half as much as you did? Answer me that."

"But that's not the point. I did what I had to do, don't you see that?"

"I don't think I'm following you, Cynthia."

No, because you don't want to, she thought. But belligerence would get her nowhere, so she said, "Manny, the woman doesn't have a penny. She doesn't have a pot to pee in, okay. There, plain talk and pardon me for putting it so crudely. But that's the God's honest truth, whether you want to hear it or not."

"So, I'm listening," he said. "So what else is new."

She recognized the cynical expression on his face, the way the corners of his mouth turned down for a brief but indelible instant. He reached into his coat pocket and pulled out a pack of cigarettes. She waited until he found a match. He inhaled and blew the smoke out of the side of his mouth so that it drifted away, temporarily silencing her. She watched the trail of smoke break up, caught by invisible currents of air. A second unwitting semaphore followed the first and she took a deep breath, steeling herself for what she had consciously held back from saying.

82

"Manny, I'm talking about economics. Just her social security won't pay the rent."

"Well I certainly can't afford to help her out, honey, much as I'd like to. Believe me, if I was a rich man do you think I'd say no to her for one minute? You know how fond I am of your mother. We've always been on the best of terms."

"I realize that," she replied, "and that's why I think it won't be such an . . . an untenable situation."

"An untenable what?"

"Manny," and again she breathed deeply, trying to be as terse and succinct as possible, if only to get it over with as quickly as she could. "She's going to have to move in with us. We can't get around it."

He gagged and sprayed coffee clear across the table. Then he started to cough. "Sorry about that. It went down the wrong pipe. I'll wipe it up."

Wrong pipe my eye, she thought. She watched him dabbing at the table with his napkin.

"Well, go on," he said with another sputter in his voice. "I'm listening."

"I fail to see the humor," she said. "All I said was that Lena's going to have to move in with us. There's nothing we can do about it."

"There's nothing we can do about it?" he said with a rising inflection. It was a tone of voice she recognized, one he had used whenever he wanted to express disbelief and disagreement. "And where do you propose she sleep? On the ceiling?"

"We'll buy a convertible, a Castro or something. She can sleep in the living room. There's plenty of closet space—"

"Cynthia, we live in a four-room apartment. Am I making myself perfectly clear? Four rooms, period. We get under each other's feet as it is. How do you think it'll be with another adult there? Impossible, that's what. It's absolutely an impossibility. If we had our own home, it would be another story altogether. But not in a four-room apartment. No way, honey. It's absolutely out of the question."

"Do you want her to end up on the street, is that it?" she said. Just take it easy, control yourself. One thing at a time. It's not as if he's such an unreasonable man. He

83

just has to be sweet-talked, that's all. So calm down, take it slow, step by step.

"End up on the street?" he repeated. He slouched back in his chair and looked at her smugly. "Believe me, it won't happen."

"I'm telling you, Manny, she doesn't have a dime to her name. When my father was working it was one thing. He brought home a paycheck every week. And even then they just about managed to make ends meet, living hand-to-mouth. Day-to-day."

"They never lived day-to-day and let her get a job if she has no money."

"At her age? Who're you kidding. And don't ever imply that my mother's lazy, either. She worked like a dog for years, just remember that."

"Okay, okay," he said. "Don't get so upset. And stop raising your voice at me. People can hear."

Like I give a good goddamn. "Do you want me to get down on my hands and knees and beg you, is that it?" I sound like Lena, she realized. But there has to be some way to get through to him.

"No one's asking you to beg, honey. But I don't even think you've thought this thing through. We'll have no privacy. We'll get on each other's nerves. You know what happens when a mother-in-law moves in."

"I don't know," she said, "because Lena never lived with us. Besides, it'll only be a temporary situation."

"Why temporary? She's going to inherit a fortune? Some rich uncle is going to drop dead and leave her a million bucks, is that it?"

"I'm not even going to answer you, you know that," she said. "Manny, this is no laughing matter."

He picked at his teeth with the corner of a matchbook. "All right, I'm sorry. I apologize. I didn't mean to sound sarcastic. Listen, why can't she apply for welfare if she can't afford to pay her rent?"

"Because I will not allow my mother to be degraded that way, that's why."

"There's nothing degrading about it, Cynthia. It's home relief. My folks were taking supplementation when I was a kid. It wasn't a sin, a crime or something."

"They pay next to nothing," she told him. "And I'll say it once again. It's only going to be a temporary situation. I'm going to go out and look for a job. How do you like that? And as soon as I get situated and save up a little money, she'll be able to get her own apartment again. But right now she has no one to turn to but us."

"You, get a job?" he asked, amazed.

"That's right. I'm going to get a job. Natalie's old enough to take care of herself. She's not a baby anymore."

"She's only ten years old."

"One of the other mothers can pick her up after school and bring her home. What am I saying?" She shook her head in confusion. "*Lena* can take her to school in the morning and pick her up in the afternoon. Believe me, it would give her the greatest of pleasure to be useful. She doesn't like to sit around all day, in case you're interested."

"So it's settled then. You've made up your mind. Once again Cynthia gets her way, is that it?"

"Manny, I'm an only child. Have pity on the woman. I'm all she's got. So don't deny me this. Please."

He dug the side of his fork into the eclair, cut off a piece and brought it up to his mouth. "If I said I didn't have the strength to argue with you, I'd be lying. You want Lena so bad, you can have her. But I want to tell you one thing, Cynthia, so you won't ever say that I didn't warn you. It's not going to work."

"It's only temporary," she said again, suppressing a smile of relief. "Just until I find a job and save some money. You'll see, honey. Everything's going to work out for the best."

"As your mother always says, 'From your mouth to God's ears.'" He finished the chocolate eclair and scraped his plate clean.

"No, I'm not actually looking for Christmas work, Miss Harvey," Cynthia said. "I realize it's probably a bit too late for that—"

"Oh it is, I can assure you. It most certainly is."

"Yes, well, actually I was in the market for something not so . . . temporary, if you know what I mean."

She was seated alongside a scarred oak desk, one that brought to mind a childhood of public schools, Miss Abbott and other old-maid teachers. The desk was located in a glassed-in cubicle, the cubicle part of a series of identical narrow partitioned rooms which comprised the offices of French & Friedlich, Employment Counselors. In one damp and anxious hand Cynthia still clutched the advertisement torn from the morning's paper.

COST OF LIVING GOT YOU DOWN?
DON'T WORRY, YOU'VE GOT A FRIEND
AT FRENCH & FRIEDLICH.
WE HAVE JOBS ALL OVER TOWN!

SECRETARIES
TYPISTS
BOOKKEEPERS
RECEPTIONISTS

OUR LISTINGS ARE ALL FEE PAID
Come in today and see Loretta Harvey

FRENCH & FRIEDLICH
EMPLOYMENT
COUNSELORS
1631 BROADWAY at 51 St.

"I see, I see," Loretta Harvey replied. Her eyes were turned down to the application Cynthia had filled out a few minutes before. "You have no prior experience, no clerical skills, Mrs. Margold?"

"No, not really," she admitted. "I took an academic diploma. But I thought all a receptionist needed was personality." She smiled brightly and refolded her hands across her lap. The air was close, tight. She wished someone would open a window. She wished Loretta Harvey, career consultant—according to the neatly lettered nameplate sitting on her desk—would look up at her, confront her eye to eye, if only for a moment. But she kept her eyes glued to the application form, avoiding Cynthia's questioning glances.

"No experience," she said again. Finally she looked up, raising her untweezed brows. Her lips were drawn thin and tight across her mouth. "Don't you think it's . . . it's inadvisable to seek employment at this time, Mrs. Margold?" she asked. She tapped the eraser end of a pencil against the application.

"Why at this time?" Cynthia asked, trying not to stare at the woman's dirt-encrusted fingernails. "I mean, your ad said . . ." and she waved the crumpled clipping as if she were trying to fan herself.

"Oh, I'm well aware of what the ad says, dear. I wrote it myself. But really, the thing is . . . most employers would be reluctant to take a chance training a new girl, especially if you're going to be expecting in just another few months. It's not for me to say one way or the other, or pass value judgments, dear. But what purpose would it serve finding yourself a situation at this late date? Wouldn't it make more sense to wait until the baby is born before looking for work?"

"The baby?" Cynthia whispered. The color rose in her cheeks, a hot blush she was unable to control. She felt her eyes growing moist. "The baby is born?"

"That's right, Mrs. Margold. It's just a matter of common sense, wouldn't you agree. But what I *can* do for you in the meantime is hold onto this," and she indicated the application form, "until you're ready to . . . uh . . . look for employment once again. I'm sure that by then we'll have something right up your alley." She beamed at Cynthia, holding the smile as if it were fastened with two thumbtacks at each corner of her mouth.

"Yes, you're absolutely right," Cynthia managed to say. She got slowly to her feet and held onto the back of the chair for additional physical support. Her thighs rubbed against each other, bruised and prickly-heated. "I shouldn't, shouldn't push myself, I guess."

"If I were in your shoes, dear—and between you and me I wish I were, to tell you the truth—I'd sit home like a lady and take it easy. I bet you didn't even tell your husband you were looking for a job."

"No," she whispered. "I didn't, didn't mention it. Well, thank you, Miss Harvey." She forced her lips up, smiled bravely and turned towards the door.

"The best of luck, Mrs. Margold, the very best of luck."

"Thank you," Cynthia replied. "Thank you for everything." Thank you for every . . . little . . . thing.

"Well?" Manny asked. "How'd it go?"

Lena seconded with, "So, are you going to be a career girl?"

87

They stood in the foyer as if reviewing troops, calculating military strength. Cynthia wanted to say the usual thing, a flashy, flip remark about how she had no strength left. But it wasn't so much that she was physically tired as mentally exhausted, emotionally drained.

"Not yet," she said, putting up what she had begun to think of as her brave little smile of determination. "But it's only the first day out, so what do you expect."

"Take your time, honey," Manny said. "No one's rushing you. Lena made supper. Everything's on the table; it's all ready. We expected you back an hour ago."

It was nearly six-thirty. The midtown offices had been closed since five, but Cynthia had not taken the subway immediately after her last interview. She told herself she didn't want to do battle with the rush hour. But it was more than that. She needed time and she found herself walking, heading in a vague southerly direction. She had left the offices of French & Friedlich, holding the smile balanced precariously upon her lips. She didn't want it to slip off until she was safely outside and her privacy was assured. Only then did she allow herself a moment of despair. She brushed two stray maudlin tears into oblivion, dried her eyes and crossed Broadway. Standing under the marquee of the Winter Garden Theatre, where *Carnival* was being heralded as "America's Magical Musical," she closed her eyes for a moment and let the sounds of the city take hold. When she blinked and looked up, nothing had changed, neither her mood nor the snarled line of traffic extending as far as she could see.

French and company had been her fourth stop. Earlier in the day she had gone to another agency and the personnel offices at Macy's and Bloomingdale's.

Standing under the marquee, she turned her lips up, raising them in yet another brave little grin. Then she headed downtown, stopping at the next corner to slip silently and unhappily into Chock Full O' Nuts. "A nutted cheese sandwich," she told the woman at the counter.

"Anything to drink?"

"Choc . . . no, just black coffee, please." Too bad they only hire colored women here. And even if they didn't, they probably would give me a song and dance about eating up the profits. The man sitting on her left was making quick work of a slice of peach pie. She watched his fork rise and fall, empathizing with his taste buds, the rhythmic tempo of his appetite. The syrupy fruit was golden, the flaky crust capped by a dab of whipped cream. She bit into her nutted cheese and tried to tear her eyes away from the pie. This is better for you. It's loaded with protein, vitamins, she thought. It's good for the . . . baby.

"Tomorrow's another day," Manny said as she hung up her coat. "Don't let it get you down, honey. I mean, how many people hook up with a job the first day out?"

"I'm going to hold off until after Christmas," she told him. "They're just not hiring now. I should've spoken to someone in the know. It's the wrong time of year. Come January, maybe things'll open up more."

"Sure," he said. "Don't worry about it. It's only another week or so, so don't aggravate yourself."

"I assure you," she said, slamming the closet shut, "I'm not about to let that happen."

"Dinner's on the table!" Lena called out.

"It'll get cold," Manny said. He put his hands on her shoulders and peered into her eyes. "Hey, what's this funny mood you're in."

"No mood."

"Come on, I know you better than you think I do. Listen, Cynthia, it's not worth getting upset about. Am I breathing down your neck? Am I?"

"No."

"So don't worry about it. Your mother is a pleasure to have around, honest to God. And she can stay here for as long as she pleases, even if you do get a job. Okay? Feel any better?"

"It's just too much, Manny," she said. "It's just gotten to be too much."

"What?" He looked at her curiously, his hands still resting on her shoulders. "What has?"

"Everything," she said. She slipped free and moved to the door. "Come, you must be starved."

"I had a big lunch." He followed her out of the bedroom.

So did I, she thought. Enough for two.

January 1963

SITTING IN THE STATION WAGON Manny used for business, Cynthia hugged her side of the seat and kept her eyes glued straight ahead. Don't look at him, she thought. Don't say a word. Of all the nerve . . . how dare he?

"It was your fault, too," he said. "You don't know when to stop eating, that's your problem."

"And you don't know when to stop drinking, moron," she snapped. "So do me a big favor and keep your mouth shut. And watch your driving unless you want to get us killed."

"It would solve a lot of problems."

"I'm sure it would, Forman, I'm sure it would."

They rode in silence, from Sheepshead Bay all the way up Ocean Parkway. Some New Year's Eve this was, she thought. I've never been so embarrassed in all my life, the way he couldn't keep his hands to himself.

"In case you're interested," she said, "your friend Harold is never going to invite you to his home again, pig."

"What did you call me?"

She ignored the growl in his voice, low-pitched and guttural. "You heard me, Forman. I said pig. P-I-G as in someone who paws someone else's wife. And she's not even pretty, that's what gets me. A mousy little phony with an annoying laugh and you have to go and pick on her. You don't even have good taste, Margold."

"You can say that again. I picked you. That was mistake number one."

"You're damn tootin' it was. I was a big fool, to fall in love with someone who can't hold his liquor, starts to

90

feel up someone else's wife like he's in high school again, a real big man. That's some mature kind of behavior, Forman. I'm surprised Harold didn't take a swing at you. And in front of everyone, every person there knew what was going on in the den. But you could've given a damn, you were so high."

"Cynthia, I'm not going to answer you. Harold's wife puts out a plate of shrimp and five minutes later it disappears."

"I wasn't the only one who ate it."

"Like fish you weren't the only one. Is that all you can do, just eat? Sure, no wonder you didn't find yourself a job when you went looking. Who the hell would want to hire a fat slob like you?"

She wanted to throw herself on him. "I want you to drop dead, Forman. That's all, just drop dead and leave me alone with your vicious . . . that's right, your vicious and disgusting mouth. Fat? I'm fat? And what are you, Mr. Skin and Bones? Two hundred and eighty pounds—"

"Seventy."

"Big deal. You can't even see your thing, moron, that's how disgusting you are."

"Me?" he said, thumping himself on the chest. "I'm the disgusting one? Ask your son who's disgusting, Cynthia. He's embarrassed to be seen with you because you're so . . . obese. You have no self-control. You don't know when to stop, when to quit when you're ahead."

"Who can be ahead married to you," she replied. "Sure, no wonder I have problems. A man can't even make a decent living so no wonder I eat. It's out of frustration, that's why, because when it comes to being a breadwinner you stink, period."

"I'll remember that," he said.

"Do that." Terrific year this is going to be, she thought. It got off to a wonderful start, absolutely fabulous. He'll sleep on the couch, that's where. Lena can share the bed with me. I don't want him near me and he smells of booze, all that liquor he drank it'll be a miracle if we both get home alive. "That was a red light you just went through. Do you want to get arrested or is that part of being a big man?"

He didn't answer.

After Manny had left the apartment the following morning, she sat at the kitchen table nursing her second cup of coffee and her third slice of pound cake. "I'm not taking sides so don't ask me to," Lena said. "I'd be a lousy mother and a lousier mother-in-law if I got involved in your squabbles, Cynthia."

"I assure you, it was more than a squabble."

"You want to know something, sweetheart? Maybe you forget, but your father and I had plenty of fights in our lifetime. Plenty, up to here," and she drew a line over the top of her head. "But it's normal. Two people can't agree on everything. So he got a little high. So big deal, it was New Year's Eve, Cynthia. People always drink a little more than they should at a party. It's only natural."

"You weren't there, mother. You didn't hear what he said to me, the names he called me. The . . . language, the foul abusive language he used."

"And you didn't say the same kind of things back?" Lena asked. "Come on, admit it."

"It's my turn!" Natalie called out from the living room.

"It's not, it's mine."

"Leave it alone, Barry. Ma! Ma, he's hitting me!"

"Stop fighting!" she yelled. She got to her feet.

"Children are children, what do you expect," Lena said.

"He won't let me watch my program," Natalie complained as Cynthia stepped into the living room.

"It's my turn now," Barry said. "She's been watching all morning."

Natalie shouted, "Liar!"

"I'm in no mood this morning," she told them. "Do you want me to pull the plug out, or can the two of you try to get along for a change."

Barry said, "It wasn't my fault. You always blame me."

"I don't always blame you and no one said it was anybody's fault," she replied, trying to remain calm, patient. "We'll flip a coin."

"It's not fair," Barry insisted. "She watched her programs all morning. Now I want to get a chance to see my stuff."

"How old are you, Barry?"

"What does that have to do with it?" he said. "Fair's fair."

"She's a little girl, Barry. Act your age!"

Barry sat cross-legged on the floor. But now he scrambled to his feet and rushed past her. "Two fatsos!" he yelled. "Two big fatsos!"

She caught up to him in the foyer, even as he struggled to pull on his coat. Cynthia lunged forward and grabbed him by the hand. "What did you call me, you spoiled brat?" Her voice cracked and she began to shake him, enraged by what he had said.

"Nothing. Let go of me. I didn't say anything." He tried to wiggle out of her grasp. But the more he worked to pull himself free, the tighter she maintained her grip on his wrist.

"I'll teach you to open a mouth to me, you fresh kid," and swinging her hand out, she slapped him across the face. Her hand stung from the blow and she closed her eyes in momentary disbelief, as if she doubted what had come to pass. The imprint of her palm and five fingers left a fiery red tattoo along one downy cheek.

Barry jerked back and pulled himself free. He lifted his face and stared at her with narrowed, cornered eyes. There were no tears, no liquid overflowing lids. His expression was at once hostile and defiant.

"I'm sorry," she whispered. It was the first time she had ever hit him and now she was angry with herself for having lost control. "But you don't know when to stop, Barry. You don't know when to leave well enough alone. You provoked me."

Lena appeared in the doorway.

"At least grandma doesn't look like . . . she looks normal," Barry blurted out. He ran toward the door.

"Put on your rubbers!" Cynthia yelled. "It's snowy out. You'll catch cold." But he was already gone. The front door slammed behind him and from the living room she could hear the cackling laughter of Woody Woodpecker. I can't take it anymore, she thought. I've had it. I've reached the end of my rope. It has to get better because it can't get any worse. It just can't.

"I'll put up a pot of coffee, Cynthia."

"No, Henny, please. Don't bother. I had so much coffee this morning it's coming out of my ears."

"Well, I'll make some instant for myself then. You sure?"

"Positive."

"I had too much to drink last night, tell you the truth. I still feel a little dizzy." Henrietta pulled her housecoat tightly about her and moved to the Pullman kitchen at the opposite end of the room.

Cynthia listened to the slap of her slippers. The sounds of children playing in the street below filtered through the windows. She raised her eyes and looked at her friend. "You lost more weight," she said.

"Does it show?"

"Absolutely. It definitely does. That's some fantastic diet, isn't it?"

"The best," Henrietta said. She turned her head over her shoulder. "And what's so good about it, Cynthia, is that it's easy as pie, no kidding. You eat three full meals a day. You can even have snacks, certain kinds of courses. But it's unbelievable how simple the whole thing is. A size sixteen is big on me already—that's how much weight I've lost."

"It shows," she said again. It does, too. It really does. She looks ten years younger. Cynthia cleared her throat then and edged forward in the chair. "Henny, I've made up my mind. And this time I'm serious, I mean it. I don't care if I have a nervous breakdown in the process, but there has to be an answer."

"To what?"

"To this . . . this fat," she said, her voice loud and sharp, as piercing as her son's insults. She kneaded the loose tier of fat girdling her waist. "I'd like to rip it off," she said, pinching herself. "It's abnormal. The way I've let myself go. I'm ashamed, Henny. I just don't know how to cope anymore."

A blue flame shimmered and danced beneath the aluminum pot. Henrietta turned around and leaned against the edge of the sink. Her movements were tight and cramped in the Pullman kitchen, the row of appliances seemingly installed more for show than utility. "That bad?"

"That bad. Worse than bad," Cynthia replied. She wanted to cry, to let loose, to give vent to her emotions. But something held them in check, not so much the fear of being embarrassed, as an unwillingness to sink any lower, to hate herself more than she did. "Everything's getting screwed up royally. Manny, the kids . . . everything, Hen. It has to stop somewhere. It just has to."

"Cynthia, honey, if I can do it, so can you," Henrietta told her. Her slippered feet padded across the wall-to-wall carpeting. She sank down on the sofa and reached for Cynthia's hands. "Listen to me, just listen for a minute. This diet works. I'm telling you that it's not even hard. Instead of junk food like sweets, sodas, and candy bars, and crap like that, I've been snacking on cold vegetables—"

"I hate cold vegetables. I hate hot vegetables, too." Except potatoes.

"You can't hate them as much as you hate that," Henny replied. She let go of Cynthia's hands and pointed at her bulging stomach.

"I went looking for a job two weeks ago and they thought I was pregnant," Cynthia whispered. "Pregnant, like I was ready to have a baby. I look at myself in the mirror but I'm the worst judge of my appearance, always have been. If I start telling myself I look too heavy, I put a scarf around my neck or buy a new pair of earrings. I dress up my face, while the rest of me goes to pot. See this blouse?"

"What about it?"

"It was always big on me, Henny. It could fit on an elephant, damn it, and now it's getting snug. I already reinforced one of the seams, but it doesn't help. And it's a good blouse. It's not a piece of junk. It cost plenty. It's good material and it's shredding. Look." She turned to the side and pointed at the worn fibers. "It was always big on me, that's what I'm trying to point out. Now it's too tight."

Henrietta nodded her head and got slowly to her feet. "I have a number I want you to call. You'll make an appointment, same as I did. You'll go down and see them and they'll help you out. If you want it bad enough, that is."

"I do," Cynthia replied. "I'm ashamed and I'm disgusted. I hit my kid this morning because he called me fatso. I mean, I'm like a child, hiding boxes of cookies on the window sill so Manny doesn't see them. You know, he's at least twenty pounds heavier than me and not much taller and he looks thinner than I do, Henny. I don't even carry my weight well anymore. It just hangs out, all over the place."

"Wait a sec." She disappeared into the bedroom.

Cynthia heard her rummaging through her drawers. She leaned back in the club chair and tried to ignore the creak of the overtaxed wooden frame. I'll break her furniture yet, she thought.

A child's voice called out from the street, "Anyone around my base is it!" They were playing hide-and-seek. She heard another child yell, "I see Diane behind the black car. Come out, come out, wherever you are."

That's me, too, she thought. Like the real me's in hiding, covered up by all this flab.

"Here it is," Henrietta said. She came back into the living room and handed her a thin, stapled booklet.

"My passport to fame and fortune, eh?"

"No, just your ticket to a more normal life."

"And a more normal waistline," Cynthia said, trying to smile. She stared at the pamphlet which announced, YOU TOO CAN BE THIN. "And happy," she said aloud. "So what do I do?" She was afraid to open to the first page, afraid to see the lists of Dos and Don'ts.

"You call them up and make an appointment. Once you get down there, they take over."

"Who are these people, anyway?" Cynthia asked. "Don't they have something better to do with their time than worry about the fatties of the world?"

"Go ahead, be a cynic. Go ahead and laugh. You can laugh all the way to three hundred pounds, if that's what you want, Cynthia."

"No," she said, serious once again. "I . . . I won't let myself. I'd kill myself first." She looked down at the pamphlet. It was put out by Kings County Hospital, the massive city-run institution on Clarkson Avenue, just a short bus ride from where she lived. "Aren't they all booked up? Maybe they won't be able to take me for a couple of months," she said, almost hopeful that would be the case.

"It won't happen," Henny said, shaking her head. "See what it says next to the phone number. The Hotline. That's what they call it. Someone's stationed at their phones twenty-four hours a day, seven days a week. All you have to do is pick up the receiver and dial. Come on, we can do it right now and get it over with. It won't take but a minute."

"On New Year's Day?" She tried to mask the alarm rising up in her voice. "Let me wait, just until tomorrow. I'll call tomorrow morning, honest."

"Cynthia, should I tell you how many times I've heard

96

you say that. Tomorrow is another day. It worked for what's her name—"

"Vivien Leigh."

"Very good," Henny said with a grin. "But you're not Scarlett O'Hara, Cynthia. You have a weight problem, same as I did—and still do."

"Still do?" She wrinkled up her eyes. "What kind of problem do you have? You're almost a fourteen."

"And for my height I should be between a ten and a twelve. And I will be. Every week I lose a little more."

"I'd be happy to get down to a size twenty, between you and me. As far as I'm concerned, that would be perfect."

"Don't set limits for yourself, Cynthia. Remember that. When you get to the hospital, they weigh you and then they tell you what your goal weight should be."

"Goal weight?"

"What you want to get down to. If you follow their diet, you won't have any problems, I promise you."

"You and umpteen doctors from here to Connecticut. Believe me, I've tried them all. I've tried everything— pills, shots. I even had myself hypnotized once. I only put my foot down when some doctor wanted to give me electroshock therapy."

"The only shocking thing about this diet is that it works."

"My friend the convert," she said. "Next thing you know, you'll go around preaching, like the diet's gospel or something." And to herself, I'll believe it when I see it, not before. With difficulty she got to her feet.

"It's all up to you now, Cynthia. Like I said, if you want it bad enough, you can do it."

"Okay already," she snapped. "I told you I'm going to call. I have the number memorized, that's how serious I am about it."

"See? You're even getting angry at me, and for no reason at all. Cynthia, if you want to be roly-poly for the rest of your life, I'm going to love you just as much, believe me. You called *me,* just remember that."

"I know and I'm sorry if I was short with you. You know you're my dearest friend. I mean, if I can't talk to you, who can I talk to, other than Manny of course. And at the moment we're having a little bit of trouble communicating." She didn't want to go into it, rehashing the events of the previous evening. Henny didn't press her for details. She walked her to the door and turned on the hall light.

Then she gave Cynthia a hug, kissed her on the cheek and said, "It works. Believe me, it works."

"It better," Cynthia said, "because I don't have any other choice."

"The choice is yours, Miss . . . ?"

"Mrs. Margold."

"As I was saying, Mrs. Margold, if you don't try to deal with your problems there's no getting around them. I can set up an appointment for you to visit our Corpulence Unit—"

"Corpulence what?"

"Our Corpulence Unit," the woman on the other end of the line repeated. "Staff psychiatrists have discovered that people suffering from weight problems respond much better to oblique, rather than direct, references to their condition. Studies have shown that such words as overweight, obesity, and the like, generally have a negative connotation. Therefore we refer to our clinic as the Corpulence Unit."

"I see. Well I'm corpulent, no two ways about it. And I need help. You can't be more direct than that, can you?"

"No, you can't," the woman said, chuckling softly. "I have an opening for this coming Friday."

"Friday?" Cynthia said. It was all happening too quickly. She hadn't counted on getting an appointment so easily. "Can't we make it for Monday?"

"Monday it is," the woman said promptly. "Ten-thirty, Mrs. Margold. Use the Kingston Avenue entrance, right near the doctors' residence. You can't miss it. There's a big sign. And thank you for calling. I'm sure you won't regret your decision."

"I hope so." She hung up and took a deep breath. "It's now or never, Margold," she said aloud. "There's no turning back."

She spent the remainder of the week trying to prepare herself for the appointment. First on the list was an attempt to patch things up with Manny. She failed on New Year's Day, but the following evening decided to try once again. Pressing a ten dollar bill into Lena's hand, she got her mother to take the children out for Chinese food. Alone in the apartment when Manny returned from work, she made no bones about the fact that she was unhappy they had quarreled.

"It's stupid to walk around not saying a word to each other," she announced. "I mean, we're not children anymore, Manny. We both got angry and hot around the collar and we shot our mouths off. Foolishly. I apologize for insulting you. I just wasn't thinking straight, you got me so annoyed."

"*I* got *you* annoyed?" he said. "That's a joke. Who the hell am I around here, anyway. Just a poor slob who breaks his back trying to make a living so my wife shits on my head and insults me."

"I'm sorry. I apologize. What more do you want me to do, Manny? You said some pretty ugly things yourself."

"That's because you goaded me on."

She decided not to answer. "And I have something else to tell you."

"What? You're running off to join the Peace Corps."

"Manny, be serious. I have an appointment Monday. I'm going down to Kings County to speak to some people about my weight problem. I'm going to try to lose—"

"You're gonna go on another diet, and make us all crazy in the process? That's a laugh." He headed toward the bedroom to hang up his clothes.

Cynthia wasn't about to give up so easily. She hadn't expected his stubborn streak. His pride's shot to hell, she thought. And it's my fault, the things I said to him. "Manny, I want to be pretty again," she said. She stood by the bedroom door, watching him as he unbuttoned his shirt.

"Pretty? For who?"

"For you," she said.

"Well that's a load of bullshit," he said gruffly. "You're Cynthia, you're my wife. My wife's the most beautiful woman in the world, don't you forget that."

All she could do was smile, smile and move across the room to press herself against him. "I'm sorry," she whispered.

"It's okay. I've forgotten it already. It's over and done with and there's no sense battling. It's kid stuff." His hands, the calloused tips of his fingers, slid up and down her back. He pressed himself closer against her and she knew what he wanted even before he began to pull her blouse out from around the waistband of her skirt.

She wanted to please him, to smooth things over, to satisfy his physical appetites, but it wasn't because she herself felt a reawakening of desire. It had been so long since she needed him for that that now she was momentarily confused, never having expected Manny to respond so ardently. He held her face in both of his hands, cupped her cheeks with his rough weathered palms and slid his lips and tongue back and forth across her mouth.

She eased herself back long enough to say, "They went out for dinner. Lena took them for Chinese."

"You're a smart cookie," he said, laughing. Gently he urged her down onto the bed.

Relax, just relax, she kept repeating to herself. Who else wants you as much as he does? Who else could put up with you? Or be able to get their hands around your waist. The rough mat of hair covering his chest brushed against her skin. "Manny honey, don't forget to use something." She closed her eyes, trying to make herself feel the same way she had when they'd first gotten married.

"I will," he muttered, quickly unzipping his pants. "Don't worry about a thing."

It was easier said than done.

The girdle dug into her flesh, biting ridges of elastic teeth. I dreamed I was a size twelve in my Maidenform . . . but they don't even make them for the big-girl market. Stop looking at yourself. You should drape a sheet over the mirror, mourn for the loss of your svelte lines, your youthful figure. Problem was, it was never youthful and the lines were never svelte, far from it. When I was sixteen I wore a size sixteen dress. No, it was an eighteen. Memory doesn't serve me. Nothing does. This darned zipper is stuck.

It wasn't stuck. She had gained more weight than she had imagined, than she had dared to realize or accept. The zipper wasn't broken. Now, standing in the middle of the bedroom, Cynthia cursed her appetite, her lack of will power, her nonexistent self-control. She turned her back to the mirror and struggled to pull the zipper up.

It didn't budge.

The skirt was the same chocolate brown worsted she'd worn on her interviews. It wasn't this tight three weeks ago, she thought. She sucked in her breath, strained to hold what was left of her stomach muscles and finally managed to pull the metal zipper all the way up to the waistband of her skirt. Don't breathe. Don't move or the whole thing'll rip in two.

Woodenly she stepped to the closet and took what seemed a forever amount of time bending down to retrieve a pair of shoes. They were flats. Heels never stood up for more than a week of normal use. Inevitably, invariably—even when she'd spent close to twenty dollars outfitting herself at Coward's, known for the fine quality of their sturdy footwear (so said the ads)—she would crush the heels like papier-mâché beneath her heavy step.

What's the rush? You've got plenty of time.

She sat down on the edge of the bed and felt the wave of dizziness come and go. I bent down too quickly, she thought, that's why. Then she squeezed first one foot and then the other into the brown calfskin shoes. She glanced at her watch, checked the time, and decided she was still in good shape. It's still early, not even ten. And the bus takes ten minutes, the most. Less than a dozen stops.

Now that she'd managed to zip up the skirt, she dared not attempt to tuck a blouse inside the straining woolen garment. Instead, she found an old favorite. An old warhorse is what it is, she thought as she pulled on an off-white overblouse that buttoned down the back. A little lipstick, a nice pin, and we're all set, Margold. And with time to spare. You can even stop for a cup of coffee since you were such a good girl this morning to go without breakfast.

The last button straining to rip through its hole, she straightened up and moved back to the vanity table. She selected a pair of clip-on earrings, two round gold buttons Manny had bought her for her last birthday. Then she applied a soft red shade of lipstick to her upper lip, pursed her lips together and then blotted away the excess with a tissue.

A little powder and you're in business. Now is that a pretty face? It has lots to commend it, lots, Cynthia. She gave her hair a quick swipe with a comb. Perfect. You'll walk in and they'll know they're looking at a person who takes pride in her appearance. If I had a decent coat to put on my back it would be another story, but I can always take it off the minute I walk inside.

"Can I come in? Are you decent?" Lena asked from the other side of the bedroom door.

As decent as I'll ever be, under the circumstances, she thought, saying, "All set, mom. How do I look? Presentable?"

The hinges creaked. She tried to ignore the falling chip of paint that settled like a snowflake on the carpeting.

Lena said, "You look like a dream. Stunning. They'll know who they're dealing with."

Yeah, a fat woman. "Let's hope so, mom. Can you help me on with my coat?"

"With pleasure."

If it's tight I'll shoot myself, she thought. Ever so carefully she eased her arms into the sleeves of her winter coat.

"Perfect," Lena said. "Gorgeous."

Cynthia made a face.

"What's the matter, your mother can't give you a compliment for a change. With a face like yours—"

"Yes, I know, mother. If I ever write an autobiography," though God knows who'd want to read about fat Cynthia Winick Margold, "that's what I'm going to call it. *With a Face Like Yours,* the true story of a fat mama."

"I don't know why you say such things. A few pounds and you'd be just right. If you get too thin you know what happens to your face."

"Yes, people would finally be able to see what it really looks like," for a change.

"Cynthia."

"I was only kidding, mother. Well, kiss me goodbye and wish me luck."

"I wish you luck every minute of the day. Believe me, before I close my eyes at night I lie in bed and I think, 'Let my daughter be happy. Let her life be a little bit easier.' You're always on my mind, Cynthia. Constantly."

"Thank you, mother. You know I feel the same way about you. But if I gave you a hug I'd only crush you."

"Cynthia!"

"I was just teasing you, mom." She bent down and Lena pecked her on the cheek.

"Just bundle up. It's very treacherous outside. I don't want you to catch a draft."

"Mothers are the same all over, aren't they?"

"A mother lives for her children, just remember that. And don't worry. I'll pick Natalie up at three, so take your time. There's no rush to get home."

At the end of her street, she stood patiently in front of the painted yellow line of the bus stop. There was no promise of snow in the air, just one of those endlessly blue skies and clear blue days that New York—Brooklyn as well—can often boast about. The sidewalks had been cleared and gray patches of slush littered the gutters. A freshet of water gurgled down the nearest storm sewer. She breathed deeply, savoring the luminous clarity of the air, trying to ignore the dull warning rumble that was not overhead thunder but gastric unrest.

I'll stop and have myself a nice cup of coffee. Black, she told herself. She stepped toward the edge of the sidewalk and turned her head to the left. The square green front of a bus was just about visible. Slipping wetly, it splashed through the puddles of half-melted snow and gave its passengers a fine view of the fence bordering Lincoln Terrace Park.

You have plenty of time. She checked her watch again. It was exactly ten o'clock. You'll be early. And what are you so anxious and worried about? They're not gonna cut you up for experiments, stupid. What did Henny say? First they weigh you and then they tell you how much you have to lose. Easy as pie . . . and that's a definite Don't, anyway you slice it. Sure, go ahead and make jokes. When it gets down to the nitty-gritty, Mrs. M., this is no laughing matter.

When the bus pulled up in front of the stop, she stepped back to avoid being splashed. The driver came to a full stop and the doors opened wide. She gripped the metal handrail and lifted herself up, straining and puffing and breathing hard. She gave a little gasp when she cleared the three steps with their rubber runners. The doors closed behind her. The bus swayed and she deposited her fare and moved to the back.

So you take up close to two seats. So what? It's almost empty.

She balanced her handbag on her lap and stared at the opposite window, watching a procession of semi-attached

103

houses and then the Safeway supermarket pass in and out of her view. Across the aisle a little boy was fidgeting in his seat, bundled up in a navy blue snowsuit. He caught her glance and raised one small pudgy hand. His index finger shot out. He pointed at her and nudged his mother with his elbow.

"Malcolm, I told you never to point, it's impolite," the mother hissed. She pushed the child's hand down and flashed a smile in Cynthia's direction.

"But look how fat she is," the youngster whispered.

Cynthia would have liked to slip under her seat. Only thing is, I'd never fit. She looked down at her lap. I could balance three babies on my knees with no trouble at all. She opened her bag and reached inside. Cellophane crackled like static electricity. She found a neatly wrapped cherry sour ball. "C'mere," she said, smiling and wiggling a finger at the boy's staring red-cheeked face. And to the mother, now gripping the child with a protective, fearful set of fingers, "Just a sucking candy."

"Go ahead," Cynthia heard her say.

The boy slipped off the seat and grabbed for a post as the bus lurched around a corner. Cynthia caught him before he fell. She deposited the hard candy in the palm of his hand.

"What do you say to the nice lady?" the woman spoke up.

"Thank you," Malcolm replied.

Satisfied, she turned her head to the side and kept her eyes glued to the window. Even if he points at me again, I won't be able to see. And what I don't see, doesn't hurt me.

One block from the doctors' residence on Kingston Avenue, she got off the bus and headed straight for a luncheonette on the corner. It was Claire and Bernie's in miniature, with only two narrow tables near the phone booths in the rear, a row of not more than six stools facing the counter. Her place was wiped clean with a damp cloth and a paper napkin laid down in front of her.

"What'll it be?" the owner asked.

"Just a cup of coffee." She pulled the sleeve of her coat back just far enough and just long enough to see the face of her watch. Ten-fifteen. I can relax, take my time.

The coffee was served immediately. She blotted the wet saucer with another napkin and raised the cup to her lips.

It was too strong and bitter for her. "You have a little cream?" she asked.

"For you, anything," the counterman said with a laugh. He plunked down a metal creamer.

Maybe just one teaspoon of sugar otherwise I'll get a sour stomach. She added it carefully, purposely trying to be stingy.

"That's it, just the coffee?" the man asked, writing it up on his pad. "We have some beautiful danish. They just brought it in this morning. Take a peek." He motioned to the covered cake plate not far from where she balanced on the rickety stool. Heaped beneath the clear plastic were an array of sweet rolls, cinnamon buns, prune and apricot danish, plump flaky turnovers. "Trust me," the man said. He removed the plastic lid and extended his hand, palm up. "If you don't like it I won't charge you, but you've never tasted danish the way we have here."

"No, I don't—" she started to say.

"So fresh it melts in your mouth." He removed a cinnamon bun with two fingers, laid it out like a work of art on a plate and set it down alongside her coffee. "Danish like this you can't even find anymore, for love or money."

"I really—"

"Try it. Would I steer you wrong, a nice-looking woman like you." He turned away, as if to give her the privacy of testing it out on her own.

Don't, she told herself. Ten minutes from now they're going to weigh you, for God sakes. She wondered if they'd ask her to open her mouth the way you did when you bought a horse. Her teeth were good, but she didn't have a toothbrush to remove the telltale particles of pastry, the sticky residue of cinnamon, the soggy flakes of dough. They'll find out I had forbidden food and they'll tell me I'm a foregone conclusion. 'Hey you, foregone conclusion. Out. Out.' A broom, they'll use a broom yet, sweep me out with all the other miserable fatties of the world, the landed whale of Crown Heights, the only woman in the neighborhood who can claim the title Miss Zeppelin of 1963.

"The longer you wait, the less fresh it gets," the man behind the counter said with another toothy laugh. "Go ahead, it doesn't bite."

She picked up the cinnamon roll, closed her eyes as if to make it disappear, and opened her mouth.

"Good? Is that not danish like they used to make when you and I were kids?"

"Delicious," she said, wiping her lips with yet another paper napkin. The man was at least fifteen years older than she. We weren't kids together, she thought. How old does he think I am, anyway? Then she took another bite. The cinnamon coating, laced with crystals of hard rock sugar, literally melted in her mouth. She took another sip of coffee and sighed softly and gently and happily to herself.

By the time she had finished eating, the thunder in her stomach had subsided. She washed her mouth with the last of the coffee, dried her lips, carefully eased herself off the stool, and headed toward the door.

"Was I right?" he called out after her.

"I knew you had an honest face, minute I walked in," she said. Then, still grinning, still tasting the cinnamon on her lips and tongue, she opened the door and stepped outside. That's the problem, she thought. No one knows how to live, how to have a good time, enjoy themselves. They all push me. They all want me to be just like them.

She started down the block. Halfway there, the doctors' residence and its neighboring Corpulence Unit visible through the bare denuded branches of city sycamores, she stopped and tried to catch her breath.

What am I doing? she thought. Where am I running? I'm gonna put myself through hell, for what? So I can lose twenty pounds and gain it back all over again? If there was a diet that worked I would have found it already. Besides, Henny never had as healthy an appetite as I do. For her it was just a matter of being lazy, letting herself go, eating all the wrong things. Sure, she never cooks for herself. Restaurant food day and night could kill anyone. But the minute she took herself in hand, presto the weight fell off like nobody's business.

She pulled up her sleeve and looked at her watch. It was ten thirty-two.

That's right, if I walk in late and whatever they do has already started, what's the point. They'll tell me to go home and come back tomorrow, or next week if they don't have room for me. Look at all the time I wasted. I ate up a whole morning and for what, to be told to get on a scale and be insulted. They'll probably have a load of doctors standing by, taking down my measurements. Sure, here's another tub of lard, fellers. Watch she doesn't break the scale. Who cares . . . I'm living proof why one of out five people in the country don't walk around looking like death, because at least they're like me. At least they have a little meat on their bones. All those women in their size sevens can go to hell. I'm gonna kill myself, have a nervous breakdown, for what? To be told if my kid leaves something over on his plate, I can't do his dinner justice? For what, so they can say starve yourself and faint on the street when you get weak, no one's gonna be there to pick me up anyway.

"I won't," she whispered. I won't subject myself. I won't allow them.

She took a cab home and thought, I don't have the strength to wait for buses. I didn't even have a proper breakfast; no wonder I have a migraine headache coming on.

"What are you doing home so early?" Lena asked. "I told you not to worry. I was just straightening up." Her hair was wrapped in an old cotton scarf and she was armed with a feather duster. Bottles of furniture polish, cans of floor wax, ammonia, and a tin pail, were set out on top of the sink. The house had a lemony odor. The living room windows were opened wide and fresh air circulated from one room to the next.

"I have a splitting headache," Cynthia said. She left her coat draped over the back of a kitchen chair and headed for the bathroom. Three aspirins and five minutes later she was back in the kitchen.

"Sure, you didn't eat a proper breakfast, that's why your head hurts. You didn't put something in your stomach. Let me make you a bite. How about a nice grilled cheese sandwich and a sliced tomato? It'll take no time."

"No," she said.

"What d'you mean? You're not hungry?" Lena asked, frowning in disbelief.

"Of course I'm hungry. I'm always hungry, that's just the problem. But this time I'm not going to give in. Mother, I was halfway down the block. I mean, I could see the clinic from where I was standing."

"So? What did they say to you?"

"They didn't say anything, that's the point. I never
107

walked inside. I started convincing myself what a big mistake it would be."

"Well, if you're going to go into a major depression because of a diet, it's not worth it. That's my opinion. You've always done what you wanted, anyway, so what's the good of talking. A grilled cheese sandwich? Yes or no?"

"No."

Instead, she changed out of her skirt and blouse and good shoes, replacing them with an old faded housedress and backless slippers. The headache was a dull insistent throbbing, a pounding far off in the back of her skull. She tried her best not to think about it. Rather than dwell on her unhappiness or than sit around and first feel sorry for herself and then start to eat—indiscriminately and ravenously—she found a roll of Scotch tape and pasted the printed diet to the door of the refrigerator. Then, starting with the Hollywood cabinets above the sink and moving on to the fridge, she began to remove all and everything she would henceforth be forbidden to eat.

On the formica kitchen table she set out the following: a can of dried coconut, Planter's peanuts, three boxes of Fig Newtons, Saltines and Ritz crackers, a can of French's gravy, a jar of honey, a quart of butter pecan ice-cream, six tins of sardines and another of anchovies, imitation maple syrup, rice, mayonnaise, strawberry jam, grape jelly, peanut butter. Behind the pots and pans she kept under the sink cabinet she found a half-eaten bag of potato chips and nearly a pound of peanut brittle she had completely forgotten about, not even remembering when she'd first hidden it away. In the freezer compartment, invisible behind a frozen ball of chopped meat, she removed two doughnuts wrapped in aluminum foil.

Then she went into the bedroom and shut the door. Beneath her neatly folded undergarments she retrieved three chocolate bars, candy corn, Reese's peanut butter cups, red hots, and Milk Duds. At the bottom of her closet, down on her hands and knees, she lifted three shoe boxes and pulled out the fourth. Inside was a veritable treasure-trove, a portable and miniature candy store: three boxes of jelly beans in assorted flavors, sticks of licorice, a bag of M & M's. Not to mention honey crisps, chocolate-covered cherries leaking red sticky syrup, peppermints, Chuckles, Raisinettes, Clark bars, Life Savers,

Charms, Hershey bars of several varieties, pistachio nuts —both red and natural—Indian nuts still in their shells, pumpkin seeds coated with hard white salt, candies shaped like peanuts, chocolates shaped like coffee beans, cocoa almonds, jellied fruit slices.

When she got to her feet she was dizzier than she had been earlier in the morning. The blood had rushed to her head and she had to sit on the bed until the feeling of nausea passed. Then she brought all the things she had found into the kitchen and piled them onto the table. Lena was standing by the doorway, watching her with strangely frightened eyes.

"Don't worry, mother. I'm not having a nervous collapse," she said. She hunted up a shopping bag and began to toss the foodstuffs out of sight, off the table and into the brown paper bag. "This is just the start of something new. And do me a favor and go into the bathroom. There's a box of cookies outside on the window sill. Could you bring them in for me."

"I'm going to call a doctor."

"You're not going to call anyone, mother. I'm fine. Believe me, I'm better than I've ever been. I've just reached the end of my rope, that's all. If my friend Henny can lose weight, so can I. I'm going to stop acting like a child and start taking care of myself, for a change."

"You're . . . you're crazy," Lena whispered. "You call this normal behavior?" Nevertheless, she stepped out of the kitchen and headed down the hall to the bathroom.

Anything else? she thought. She shut her eyes and tried to think. Then, smiling to herself, she set down the overloaded bag on the floor and walked into the living room. Down on all fours again, she reached under the couch and snagged something wrapped in wax paper. She didn't bother opening it. I don't even remember when I put it here, she thought. She'd wrapped up a supply of lemon drops, laying them in for the winter. Now, she didn't even want to look at the sugar-coated sucking candies. She didn't want to let her eyes linger on anything she was no longer allowed to eat.

Lena came back with the box of Fig Newtons. "It's soaking wet," she said in disgust.

"Good. Just throw it into the bag, Mother."

"Cynthia, you're not going to waste all that good food, are you? I mean, candy's one thing, dear. But good mayonnaise? Sardines? And the kids like peanut butter . . ."

"They'll learn to live without it," she replied. "Barry had too many cavities this year, anyway. He ran up a fortune at the dentist. Natalie's old enough to start watching her weight, same as me. It's time."

"What about Manny?"

"What about him?" She lifted the heavy shopping bag in both of her arms, cradling it like an infant. "Do me a favor and hold the door open. I want to throw this down the incinerator."

"You'd think money grows on trees around here the way you're throwing out good—"

"Mother, I don't want to discuss it, okay? Just hold the door for me. Please."

The bag didn't fit in the incinerator chute. She had to remove one item after another, tempting herself all over again. She tried her best to keep her eyes averted, as if there were something obscene about what she was about to do. Like old friends, throwing out my bosom buddies, she thought to herself. She listened to the cans and jars and bottles and boxes thumping their way down the shaft to the basement incinerator. Finally there was nothing left but the bag itself. She wadded it into a ball, pushed it into the gaping mouth of the chute, and slammed it shut.

The start of something new, she thought again. The start of a new me.

This time she wasn't about to go back on her words, or the promises she had made to herself. "This time I'm going to ride out the storm," she said aloud, "come hell or high water."

February 1963

"You KNOW, I think you've lost a little weight, Cynthia."

"Really? Does it show?"

"Yes, honest to God it does. You're on a new diet or something?"

Cynthia nodded her head. "Nine pounds in three weeks. Not a record, but you know what they say . . . slow and steady wins the race. And I brought you that pin you wanted me to order. It just arrived the other day."

"Aren't you sweet. I thought you'd forgotten."

"Now would I forget something for you, one of my best customers? When I make a promise, I keep it," she said. She raised her eyes and caught sight of Henny in the back room. She had on a new white uniform, a size fourteen. The change in her friend, a change which seemed to go above and beyond losing weight, only served as an added inducement for Cynthia. She might have given up on the idea of going to the Corpulence Unit, but there was no reason why she couldn't follow the prescripts and requirements of the diet by herself in the privacy of her own home.

That clear and luminous January morning three weeks ago was the perfect day to start a diet, she decided. The new regime, as she liked to call it, already had had its share of rocky and uncertain moments. For one, Manny refused to join her or be a partner to her goals. He re-refused to cut down or change his eating habits, "one iota." Natalie ignored her warnings about sweets, junk food, eating on the sly. Every morning Lena looked at her as she gobbled down all that she was allowed for breakfast:

111

one slice of bread, a glass of juice or half a grapefruit, an egg or a small amount of cottage cheese, and black coffee. And every morning she would say from across the table, "I don't like the way you look. You're going to kill yourself, starving like this."

"I'm not starving. I'm eating the right kind of foods."

"You call that a breakfast?" Lena said. "That's not enough to sustain a midget."

"If I get hungry I can always have a piece of celery or a carrot stick or some cucumber."

"What are you, Bugs Bunny all of a sudden? You never ate raw vegetables when you were a baby."

"Well, I'm not a baby anymore, mother. And if I feel hungry and that's all I'm permitted to eat, then that's all I'm going to eat. You know, it doesn't make things any easier for me when you're not on my side, rooting for me."

"How can I be on your side when your face is all pinched up and shriveled like a peanut."

All she could do was sigh and clean her plate. All she could do was try to forget the constant craving for sweets, the way she bypassed her favorite food stores. She was afraid that any moment she would lose control, rush inside and devour endless quantities of danish pastry, cookies, fruit pies, candies, ice-cream sodas.

Only Barry encouraged her, delighted that she had finally decided to take herself in hand. And when, just a few days before, he had asked her if he could invite a friend over for dinner, Cynthia felt so good that she wanted to cry. That's right, she thought. I'm doing it for my kid as much as I am for myself. What kind of mother would I be if he spent his whole life being ashamed of me. Will power's a sign of maturity; self-control is just another way of saying I'm finally becoming emotionally stable. If my kid is proud of me then dammit I'm going to stick through this to the bitter end.

For three weeks, twenty-one difficult and sometimes impossible days, she had not faltered in her resolve. Oh, there had been nights—too many, as far as she was concerned—when she awakened to listen to the lion of hunger demanding its share. She would rise from her bed and pad silently as a jungle cat into the kitchen. There, holding the refrigerator door ajar and bathed in its icy glow, she would stand for minutes on end and stare at the shelves. Manny might have brought home a strawberry shortcake for dessert. Even Barry might have unknowingly contributed to her weaknesses and fears with a pint of coffee ice-cream. Her hands would shake, her fingers tremble. It was like having a fit, but for three weeks she reached for the celery, the carrots, the cucumbers and green pepper, the sour pickles and radishes. Don't look at anything else, she would say to herself, repeating the words over and over again. Remember, what you don't see won't hurt you.

Determined to go down to two hundred pounds by the time Barry was bar mitzvahed, she fought her cravings twenty-four hours a day. But for every compliment and encouraging remark, there were equal numbers of outbursts from Manny or cynical comments from her mother.

Lying in bed at night she listened to the unhappy creak of the springs as Manny tossed restlessly—hungrily, she thought—from one side to the other. She listened when he woke in the middle of the night, letting his appetite get the best of him. She heard him eating cookies in the kitchen and tried to blot out the sounds. All I have to do is get up and join him, simple as that.

She never realized how heavy he was until her own weight had become an embarrassment. Now, his body seemed to crush against her. "Manny, you're hurting me," she had said. He rolled off her and turned away. "But you hurt me. I can't help it."

"When we were married you couldn't wait for me to get home at night. Now, once a month and you put up a fight. Am I supposed to be pleased, or should I just shut my mouth and grin and bear it?"

"I didn't put up a fight. You know I love you."

"Stop bullshitting around, Cynthia."

"Well," and she stammered out with, "there are other ways of doing it, you know. Other positions."

"Forget it," he said. "Just forget it ever happened."

If he was thinner, solid and muscular, built like a brick wall . . . but he isn't.

That night she had two stalks of celery and an entire can of cooked mushrooms. And still she was hungry.

Those were some of the horrors, the "crazies" she'd been going through. But then there was the pleasure of hearing someone like Mrs. Bolen, the orthodontist's wife, saying, "Let me look at you. I heard you're on a diet."

Cynthia obliged her, turned full-face, and waited for yet another verdict.

"I can see the change," Mrs. Bolen said. "No question about it." She nodded her head, flashed a set of perfectly capped white teeth and sat down under the nearest dryer.

"That's all I hear around here, don't eat this and don't eat that," Manny yelled. "Well let me tell you something, misues. Don't tell me how to run my life. Do you got that, you got it straight? I'll eat whatever I goddamn please and not you or anyone else for that matter is gonna interfere."

"You'll eat yourself right into a grave," she said, the words a slow burn.

"That's my business," he said, "not yours."

"You're getting to be as big as a house," she said, staring at his eyes. They were critical, suspicious.

"Cynthia, I'm warning you. I'm fed up with all your carryings-on. Just mind your own goddamn business and butt out of it. If I want to eat coconut custard pie, I'm gonna eat it, no matter what you say."

"Some example you set for your kids," she said. She looked away, totally disgusted with what she thought of as his lack of self-control. "Did you see how much weight Natalie's put on this month? Like she's taking on all the pounds I've lost. And for what? What does it prove, except to make her more unhappy. Or maybe she just wants to be like her big fat daddy, that's what!"

He didn't hit her, though she fully expected him to explode and lose his temper. Instead, Manny turned away and stormed into the living room, catching the heel of his shoe as he rounded the bend in the hallway. A black scuff mark showed his angry passage.

"I'm not saying anything, not a word," Lena spoke up from her place at the kitchen table. She looked down at her coffee cup and Cynthia moved back to the sink.

"I need this, right. I need it like a hole in the head," she muttered. "No cooperation, no encouragement, nothing. He'd rather I was a fat pig, that's what, instead of someone who's not ashamed to walk out on the street." She held a saucer under the hot water and wiped it clean

114

with a sponge. Then it suddenly slipped from her fingers, hit the metal drain, cracked, and broke apart.

"Did you hurt yourself?" Lena asked with a start. She was halfway to her feet.

"Sit, nothing happened. Just broke a little plate, that's all." She removed the broken pieces with thumb and forefinger before finishing what was left of the dirty dishes.

"I told you I'd wash up."

"It's okay, mom. I'm almost done." The last dish and final utensil clean and sparkling, she dried her hands with a length of paper toweling before returning to the table. Her black coffee was now tepid and lukewarm. She freshened it and sat down across from her mother. "Am I wrong?" she asked. "Am I so wrong that all I want is for him to try it out with me?"

"He doesn't want to, Cynthia. You can't force the man."

"The man," she said, biting at the words like a seamstress snapping thread between her teeth, "is getting out of hand, that's what *the man* is doing. Do you know what it's like getting into—forget it. I'm sorry I even brought it up. I shouldn't subject you, mother."

"That's what a mother's for," she replied.

It was the remark Cynthia had expected to hear. But now that Lena had spoken, she realized that nothing had changed. No opinions had really been voiced, no decisions discussed or bandied about. "You're still on his side, aren't you?"

"It's not a matter of taking sides, I told you that. I just don't think it's worth all the aggravation, that's all. Cynthia, this is the third time this week the two of you have had words. The way you're at each other's throats—instead of getting better, it gets worse."

"Well I need some encouragement, moral support, for God sakes. I'm breaking my back trying to be thin and attractive. For him, as much for Manny as for myself. You'd think he'd realize that, say a kind word, lift my spirits up a little or be constructive. Forget it." She waved her hand, erasing the words. "He'd rather I was a fat slob for the rest of my life. Well I'm not going to be. I'm not a hippo. I'm not going to let myself be put on display like someone in a freak show. I'd die first."

"Don't talk about dying. We had enough deaths this year."

"I'm sorry. I didn't mean it that way."

"All I can say is, it's your life—"

"It most certainly is. You just said it all, a mouthful." She lifted her spoon and began to finish off what was left of the baked apple.

"Well, worrying about everything you eat could make anybody a little antsy. I mean, there's such a thing as carrying something to an extreme."

"You *have* to select the right foods, mother. You think it's fun; you think I get a kick out of being so fussy? Believe me, it's a pain. But I do it. I'm following the diet, remember that. People who know everything there is to know about nutrition wrote it, not some quack who'd prescribe pills and all sorts of nonsense. This is all commonsense dieting. You're never supposed to go hungry."

"But you do. You told me so yourself."

"Sure I get hungry," she said. She scraped the inside of the apple, getting at every last bit of warm fruit. "But that's because I got into the habit of eating out of frustration. If I didn't like the way I looked, I ate a pound of peanut brittle. If I didn't like the idea of constantly worrying about money, making ends meet, I'd finish off a box of cookies. Simple neurotic solutions to complicated problems. But that's not a way to spend your life, mother. It just isn't. And if Manny would start realizing that, things would be entirely different."

She raised her head and listened. From the bedroom came the strains of a boy's high-pitched voice, melodic, rising and falling. It was Barry, chanting the passage from the Torah he would read at his bar mitzvah.

"It's for him, as much as it is for me." And for my father, may he rest in peace. All that was left of the apple was its shell. She put down her spoon, glad she hadn't cheated, hadn't added a little bit of brown sugar to sweeten up the soft, pulpy fruit. "Next month my kid's going to be just as proud of me as I'm going to be proud of him, mark my words."

"We should all live so long," Lena said with a sigh that was loud, skeptical, and unsympathetic.

Cynthia decided not to answer. She didn't want any discussions, any more arguments. The less said, she told herself, the better.

116

March 1963

AGAIN THERE WAS RUNNING, errands to be attended to, business to deal with. First the invitations had to go out the day after they arrived a week late from the printer. MR. & MRS. FORMAN MARGOLD CORDIALLY INVITE YOU . . . nearly fifty envelopes had to be stamped and addressed. Final arrangements had to be made with the caterer on Eastern Parkway. The bar mitzvah was scheduled for the end of the month, even though Barry had "officially" turned thirteen late in February.

"Availability, Mrs. Margold, that's the problem," the caterer had told her. "Believe me, if I could squeeze you in any earlier, I'd bend over backwards doing it. But I can't. It's the season, what can I say."

She had no idea there was such a thing as a bar mitzvah season. Weddings were for June, for bar mitzvahs . . . the man could not be swayed. And besides, she'd waited too long, afraid she might not have enough money saved, what with making the loan payments and hustling her jewelry case from one beauty parlor to another. She'd ceased giving Leon's an "exclusive," realizing that there was money to be made up and down the length of Utica Avenue. There were at least half a dozen other beauty parlors and each Saturday she made her rounds, wheedling, cajoling, spinning amusing stories and receiving a fair share of compliments as a result of her slow—but steady—weight loss.

After the invitations were mailed, she spent three afternoons going downtown with Barry. As soon as he came home from school the two of them made their way up the sloping hill that was Utica Avenue, boarding the subway at Eastern Parkway. First stop was Abraham & Straus in downtown Brooklyn. "I want an Ivy League suit," Barry said. "With cuffs on the pants and a vest and three buttons on the jacket. Black."

"You're not going to wear a black suit, so just get it out of your head," she said. "Just forget it. I don't like seeing children in black."

"I'm not a child."

"You'll always be my child," she said. "But black is for old men. You're thirteen. You need something more youthful. Black is morbid." She opened her purse, removed a clear plastic bag and untied the knot she had made at the top. "Want one?" she asked. She pulled out a carrot stick.

"No thank you, and what's so unyouthful about black? I don't think it's morbid. I like black."

"A nice brown, a tweed. Or maybe a glen plaid. Very handsome. Listen to your mother for a change instead of being so stubborn." She took a bite, chewed thoughtfully and decided she felt very proud of herself, having successfully avoided the hot pretzel stand she'd seen on the subway platform.

The boys' shop at A&S had racks of suits—worsteds and flannels, summer-weight gabardines and poplins, blends, corduroys, shetlands, and cotton twills. "I don't like it," Barry said, posing for her in front of a three-paneled dressing mirror. "It doesn't fit right."

"It fits beautifully."

"Listen to your mother, sonny. It's what everyone's wearing."

"I don't like it. It makes me look stupid."

"Go fight with children," Cynthia sighed. And to the salesman, sharkskin-suited and eager to make his commission, "He has a mind of his own. Always has."

They made stops at Crawford's, Ripley's, Robert Hall, Browning King and several others. Finally on their third day out, they ventured into Manhattan to try their luck at Macy's.

"It looks fabulous on you. Ask the man. Doesn't the suit look stunning? Tell my son, before I have heart failure," she said, trying to laugh. "In all of New York, there isn't a suit for him."

"Your mother's right, sonny. The fit is perfect. It doesn't need any work at all. You could walk right out of the store wearing it, it looks that good. You have enough room in the crotch?"

"Check it, will you?" she said.

Barry stepped out of reach. "I don't like it," he said. And to Cynthia, "I want a suit from Brooks Brothers." He edged closer and lowered his voice. "It's cheap looking, mother."

"Cheap looking?" She refused to believe what she had heard.

"Brooks Brothers," he said again, already slipping his arms out of the sleeves of the suit jacket.

The salesman said, "You won't find prices like this at Brooks Brothers, that I can promise you, lady."

"Let me talk to him."

"Sure, take your time." The man walked off, disappearing between the garment racks. "Listen, Barry. I don't know where you get your ideas from. We can't afford Brooks Brothers prices. You're going to outgrow the suit anyway. When will you wear it again?"

"I have other bar mitzvahs to go to," he insisted. "And parties. Let's just look, see what they have. All this stuff is garbagy, mom. Please. Please."

"How about Wallach's? They have some very nice merchandise. I'll even take you to Rogers Peet."

He shook his head.

I can't fight with him, she thought. If he doesn't find a suit today they'll never have it ready in time for the party. Then I'll really be in trouble and that's all there is to it.

"Let's just see what they have," he said again. "You don't want me to look lousy, do you?"

"Go, change your clothes. I want to get out of here already; I'm sweating bullets it's so hot." And to the salesman at Brooks Brothers, farther uptown, she said, "My son is looking for a nice simple, dignified suit. As year-round as possible. And not too tight because he's still growing."

"I want it in black," said Barry.

"You're not getting black," she hissed, "so just drop the subject."

"Why don't you take a seat while I try a coat on to determine your son's proper size," the salesman suggested.

Now they're talking, she thought. Everywhere else they

119

hustle you in and out like they're doing you a favor or something. "Remember, black is out of the question. Anything else, as long as it's appropriate for a young man. I don't want him looking like an undertaker—"

"Mother," he said, frowning in annoyance.

Where does he get these airs, all of a sudden? she wondered. She sat herself down in a red leather chair, pleased that nothing creaked or strained or moved precariously beneath her weight. And I still have to find a dress for myself. At least Lane Bryant's open late tonight. I'm glad he's with me. He has such good taste, an eye for color, he'll know what's right more than I will.

She let her eyes move slowly over the floor. There was an air of respectability that delighted her. Everyone spoke in hushed subdued voices. The other mothers she saw shopping with their children all seemed to have stepped off the pages of *Vogue* or *Women's Wear Daily*. Not one was heavier than a size fourteen. They wore smart little dresses, form-fitting coats, high-heeled shoes with matching leather bags. Am I ever going to look like that? she asked herself. She hadn't weighed herself in several days, afraid to confront the irrevocable decision of the bathroom scale. But she'd kept to the diet, never cheating, not even once. Maybe I'm retaining water or something. I just can't see any great change. My clothes are a little looser on me, but then again they were always huge so what's the difference.

"This is exactly what I want," Barry said a few minutes later. He stepped in front of her and held himself stiffly at attention.

"I've given him plenty of room in the jacket. You wouldn't want it any larger or it would hang on the boy. The trousers need shortening but the waist is fine," the salesman commented.

"What do you think?" Barry asked. He smiled hopefully.

"Turn around," she said, knowing even then that she was trying to find fault with the brown herringbone suit he now wore. It had a vest, a three-button jacket, all the Ivy League details he had said he wanted. And what was more, one look and she knew she'd never have the heart to say no.

"Well?" he asked, more expectant and anxious than ever.

"Step a little closer to me, Barry." She remained in the chair, trying to stay calm and detached. He looks like he belongs on Park Avenue, she thought. She reached out and examined the price tag clipped to the sleeve of the jacket.

"That reflects our spring clearance price," the salesman said promptly.

The suit had been reduced from eighty-five dollars to sixty-four ninety-nine, at least twenty dollars more than she had been prepared to spend. She remembered too that he needed a new dress shirt, a tie, and a pair of shoes. Where's all the money going to come from? she thought. If Manny finds out he'll cry bloody murder. He doesn't spend this kind of money on himself, so how can I start explaining a sixty-five dollar suit. He'll blow his stack.

"What's the wool content?" she asked, hoping she sounded casual and vaguely disinterested, a woman who never bothered to look at prices.

"It's a hundred percent wool, madam. Are you familiar with the quality of our garments?"

"I am," Barry said quickly. "What do you think, sir?"

"I think it looks fine on you, son. We've sold quite a number of these suits to other young men. It's a popular choice."

"Did you hear that, ma?"

"How soon can you have it ready?" she asked.

Barry's face lit up.

His smile's worth a million dollars, she thought. The hell with anything else. If it's going to make my kid happy, it's worth every penny. She got to her feet and motioned to the salesman. He stepped toward her, his polished cordovan wingtips squeaking softly with each step he took. "Can I speak to you a moment?" she said, indicating with her eyes that she didn't want her son to overhear their conversation.

"Certainly. As I said, I can rush it through in less than a week, if that's convenient."

"A week would be perfect. But I'd like to open a charge, if it won't be too difficult."

"I'm sure it won't be a problem, madam. If you'll follow me upstairs to the credit department, we can fill out an application."

"And I'll leave a deposit on the suit, in any event," she

said. She didn't want the salesman to think she was trying to put anything over on him. "And we'll need a nice white button-down shirt and a tie, when you get the chance."

"I know one that'll go perfectly. Your son has excellent taste, I might add."

"That's for sure." She looked at Barry. He stared at the buttoned front of his new vest, a sly delighted smile visible on his lips. "Wait here, sweetheart. I'll be down in five minutes."

An hour later, Barry sat smiling in an overstuffed wing chair, clutching a blue Brooks Brothers box with a gold elastic band. Inside, nestled between layers of tissue paper, was an oxford cloth shirt and a striped silk rep tie. Cynthia looked at him as she stepped out from behind the dressing room curtains. "I should have worn low heels," she told the woman who was taking care of her. "It's hard to tell in flats."

"I don't like the color, mother," Barry said from where he was sitting. "It's not becoming. It's . . . it's garish."

"My goodness, he certainly has definite opinions, doesn't he," the saleswoman said with a laugh. Cynthia found both the laugh and the tone of the woman's voice forced and annoying. "I happen to think it's very flattering."

"What color do you suggest, Barry? Remember, your mother's . . . a big woman, honey. What's right for someone else may not be right for me."

"Green," he said promptly. "Mint green."

She looked over at the woman and smiled smugly. "A light green is a lovely shade for spring, wouldn't you agree?"

The woman's hair was done up in a bun, held in place with a pencil that wiggled back and forth as she looked first at Cynthia and then at her son. "Let me check," she said briskly. "That's a size—"

"Twenty-four," Cynthia said. The number came out clear and precise, as if she wanted everyone in the store to hear. She smiled excitedly, absolutely thrilled with herself, with the progress she had made. I haven't worn a twenty-four in ten years, maybe more. And so what if it's a 'stout-shop' size and it's cut a little fuller than most. It stills shows how the diet is working, how it's paying off. I can see the results and I bet everyone else will, too.

But paying off or not, she knew she still had at least another fifty pounds to lose. The difference between weighing two hundred—if indeed she had lost that much—and two-fifty, was somehow negligible. She saw the change in dress size, but her body was still wide in all the wrong places, her breath still short when she moved too quickly. Her thighs still rubbed together and the flesh still hung from her arms, loose and flabby.

"I must tell you, dear, that a pale pastel color is definitely a mistake for a woman with a large frame," the saleslady told her as soon as she returned. Under her arm she carried two dresses. "I'm not suggesting you wear black to an afternoon affair, but perhaps a navy blue might be more suitable. I certainly didn't mean to offend your son, you understand."

"Navy blue is awfully severe."

"I wouldn't say that. Tell me, would you have any objections to wearing a coat-dress? They've been reduced from ninety-five dollars to forty-nine ninety-nine. That's quite a saving, wouldn't you agree."

"Yes, but a coat-dress is a little hot—"

"Not really," the woman said. "And certainly I wouldn't worry about being warm in March." She hung up the dresses so that Cynthia could view them more easily. "After all, the weather's been brisk, chilly."

"That's true," though she was yet to be fully convinced.

The coat-dress was a navy blue peau de soie. The dress itself was a mid-calf-length sheath, decorated with a starched eggshell organza ruff at the throat. I won't have to wear any jewelry, she thought, which is fine with me since I don't own any good jewelry, to begin with. The coat was collarless, an A-line long-sleeved jacket with additional organza trimming at each wrist.

The saleswoman stepped to the side and held the coat open for her inspection. "You'll notice it has a nice cool rayon-acetate lining. Frankly, I don't think you'll have any problems about being warm. Of course, that's just my opinion. I certainly don't want you to buy anything that'll make you unhappy."

"What do you think, Barry?" She turned her head over

her shoulder and motioned him to join her at the fitting area. "Well, do you like it? It's made beautifully."

"It's so dark, mother," he said. "But it's pretty."

"It's charming, very dignified if you know what I mean. And the neckline is so adventuresome. It's . . . it's intriguing," the woman attending Cynthia announced. "Why don't you try it on for your son. It's so hard to tell how a garment looks when it's on a hanger."

It's a smart dress, she thought, no doubt about it. And the price is right. I didn't want to spend anything higher, especially after what Barry's outfit cost.

She followed the woman behind the curtains.

"Just call if you need any help." The saleswoman parted another set of curtains and ushered Cynthia into a narrow dressing room.

"It's hard to tell without heels," she said five minutes later, emerging from behind the two sets of curtains.

The woman smiled and nodded her head approvingly. "It fits beautifully, beautifully."

"It looks nice, mom."

"You think so, really?"

He looked at her critically, finally coming out with a simple and affirmative, "Yes."

"It doesn't pull on you anywhere," the woman said, adjusting the jacket. "And the coat hangs perfectly."

"It feels a little big on me, tell you the truth."

"You wouldn't want a twenty-two. You'd be too uncomfortable. It would bind you. And besides, to be quite honest we don't have this particular ensemble in a smaller size. They've been going like hotcakes, if you know what I mean."

Cynthia turned this way and that before the floor-length mirror. It does make me look thinner than usual. And the ruff is darling. The busier the neckline the better. That way no one's going to look so hard at the rest of me. "How much did you say it was again?"

"Less than fifty dollars. How could you possibly go wrong with a price like that?"

"Do we have time to find a pair of matching shoes?"

"Certainly. Tonight we're open to nine," the woman said, beaming a smile at Cynthia and then at Barry.

"You're positive you like it now, Barry? I mean, after all, it's your party, dear. I don't want to get home and then have you say that you hate it."

"I do like it," he said. The Brooks Brothers box was still clutched to his chest. "I wouldn't lie, mom. I like lighter colors, but that looks good on you."

"I thought you liked black."

"Well I do, for me I mean," he said. He blushed in confusion and turned away.

"You made a wise choice, take it from me," said the woman. "The two of you. Believe me, you won't be sorry. The dress is a steal, a fabulous buy." She edged closer, more intimate now that the sale was just about consummated. "And between you and me, it's very very slimming."

Cynthia said, "I'll take it."

The woman smiled. "I knew you would. Cash or charge?"

"Charge."

"Stunning dress, Cynthia, simply stunning. It's so flattering on you. You lost some weight, I can see. And your son—you must be very proud of Barry. His voice was like a bell, so clear he was just adorable."

"Cynthia, that's some boy you got. And what a gorgeous dress. The collar is just heaven, dear, heaven."

"You must have lost fifty pounds, Cynthia. My God, you look marvelous, marvelous. Congratulations, darling. Your son is some handsome young man. He looks like he has parents who live on Fifth Avenue. His outfit is out of this world."

"Everything is fabulous, Cynthia. Such an adorable little place. And the chapel, so nice and simple. A real jewel-box. Your dress is exquisite, by the way. And Barry —I wouldn't have recognized him, he's gotten so tall. What a beautiful young man. Hello Natalie, darling. You remember your Cousin Eva, don't you, from Scarsdale?"

"Manny, that's some smart kid you raised. Boy, you could hear a pin drop when he got up to speak. Hello, Cynthia. Is that Cynthia? My God, you look fantastic. So how about a kiss for your Cousin Frank, you slim dickens you. Hey Manny, you could drop a couple of pounds too, feller, it wouldn't kill you. Cynthia, talk to him—"

The friends and relatives and well-wishing neighbors passed along the receiving line, shaking hands, exchanging hugs and kisses, slipping thin white envelopes between Barry's fingers. Cynthia felt droplets of perspiration trickling down her sides. She cursed the rayon-acetate lining of the coat, but didn't dare remove it, lest sweat stains be made visible, lest her bare arms be made to look like two thick and meaty drumsticks. So she smiled bravely, gathering the compliments like roses strewn at her feet, tributes she stored up to use when her mood would not be nearly as optimistic or exuberant.

The guests headed from the doors of the chapel to the dining room where they could enjoy the luncheon the caterers had prepared. Cynthia finally took her seat after Barry had made a blessing over the challah before cutting it with a large knife. She let her eyes move slowly around the crowded room. Everything was going as planned, precisely the way she had hoped. Not a sour puss in the place, she thought. If only my father had lived to see this day, he would have been so proud of both of us. She looked up at the dais. Barry occupied the middle seat, flanked on either side by a dozen of his friends and several cousins. His sister sat alongside him, bent over her fruit cup, seemingly oblivious to the laughter and tumult all around her.

Suddenly someone's warm breath brushed against the side of her face. "Don't turn around," Henrietta whispered. "I just wanted you to know how gorgeous you look. And I'm so proud of you, Cynthia, I can't begin to tell you. How many pounds is it now?"

"Forty-seven."

"Unbelievable, the change, it's . . . it's breathtaking. Go, enjoy your fruit cup. It's on the list." Henrietta laughed softly, her voice lost amid the tinkle of glasses, the steady drone of animated conversation.

Manny nudged her with his elbow. He leaned over and planted a kiss on her cheek. "You've made me one helluva proud husband, missus. I just wanted you to know that. People have come up to me, like they can't believe it's really you. I'll tell you one thing, honey, you have my word—first thing tomorrow I'm gonna try that diet out. And that's a promise."

"Go, tell your son how proud you are of him, too. It's nice for him to hear."

"Let him alone. He's with his friends. He's doing fine," Manny said, waving his hand. He lifted his spoon, removed a grapefruit section from his fruit cup and started eating.

After the dishes had been cleared and lemon sherbet was brought to the table, the accordionist began playing "Moon River." "I'll sit this one out," she told Manny when he asked her to dance.

"Can I borrow your husband?" Henrietta said when Manny remained in his seat.

"With pleasure," Cynthia replied. She looked up at the dais, hoping Barry would ask his sister to dance. But for the moment he seemed lost, dazed by the party being given in his honor. Lounging back in his chair, his thumbs hooked in the front pockets of his vest, he struck her as supremely self-confident and totally pleased with himself, not at all the picture of a boy poised on the precarious edge of adolescence and young manhood. Pretty soon he'll be shaving and going out on dates and Manny and I'll sit home and worry about growing old gracefully.

It wasn't an intriguing proposition.

I have to get out, get myself a job, she told herself. Now that I lost some weight, maybe people will stop giving me the runaround, stop making up excuses. And it has to end already, this constant worrying about money, where the next dime is coming from.

Henny and Manny danced cheek-to-cheek. She watched them glide across the floor, the skirt of Henny's pale pink dress brushing against Manny's legs. Boy, he doesn't do anything halfway, does he, she thought, frowning as she kept her eyes on them. What are you getting jealous about, idiot. She's your best friend for God sakes.

Lena seemed to be reading her mind. "That's some good friend you've got," she said from her place across the table. She motioned to the dance floor. "Friends like that don't grow on trees. She'd do anything for you."

"Yes, I know. She's one in a million." And a size twelve, to boot. With two discreet fingers she loosened the ruffled organza collar of her dress and tried to relax. Thank God I didn't have much of an appetite. I would've lost a week's progress eating everything they put down in front of me. There was enough food to choke a horse.

After "Moon River" the accordionist played "Love is a Many-Splendored Thing" and "Three Coins in the Fountain." More of the guests stepped onto the dance floor, now black with scuff marks and the movement of many pairs of feet. When Manny returned to his seat he was breathless. Beads of perspiration stood out on his forehead.

"She's a fantastic dancer," he said. He reached for the bottle of Dewars that stood in the middle of the table.

She watched as he poured himself another drink. "You didn't do so bad yourself, Forman."

"May I have the pleasure of this dance?"

"You most certainly can," she said to her son. She got to her feet with an abruptness that seemed to startle Manny. He put down his glass and looked at her, curious and almost amused. Then they were gone, moving into the crush of overheated bodies. As soon as Barry put his hand on her waist, all signs of her irritation vanished. "You should have heard the compliments I got about you. Everyone can't get over how beautiful you look."

"You know what, ma?"

"What?"

"You look pretty beautiful yourself."

"You made me very proud, that's all I wanted to say, Barry. You don't know how good that feels, to hear people say such nice things about my son." She held him tightly, closed her eyes and let him lead her in a box-step. All around her came the strains of laughter, liquor, and good humor pouring like water. Wet paper napkins littered the parquet floor. She crushed a chicken bone beneath the sole of her navy blue pump. Someone had overturned a dish of sherbet. The red-jacketed waiters moved between the grapelike cluster of tables, removing dirty plates, empty bottles, overflowing ashtrays.

It was worth it, she thought. Every penny.

"Ma," Barry asked as the music came to a sad and tremulous end, "you're still going to keep on the diet, aren't you? I mean, now that the bar mitzvah's over."

"And what do you think, Mr. Park Avenue?"

"Ma, really . . . are you?"

"For you, I'd do anything, climb the highest mountain, you name it." She laughed and kissed him on top of his head, saying, "I don't want to get lipstick on your collar. But do me a special favor, sweetheart, and dance with your sister. She loves you very much, Barry, more than you can imagine."

"Sure." He walked back to the dais, stopping to shake hands with one of the guests.

Diet diet diet . . . that's all I hear. What's worse, it's only going to be twice as difficult from now on in. At least when I started I had a good reason to lose weight. I had this party to look forward to. Now it's going to be over in another hour, just like he said. Then what? A good question—but what do they say? *Where there's a will there's a way.* Let's hope it works. God knows, something has to.

April 1963

THE BAR MITZVAH was a three-week-old memory, a flutter-ing kitetail's length of boyish thank-you notes and cordial phone calls. The days lengthened, a stretching shim-mering windowshade of light creeping across the sky for longer and longer periods of time. The sunlight playing across the Margold kitchen only served to bring out de-tails of everyday existence Cynthia found disconcerting, difficult, and unpleasant to live with. The cardinals printed on the wallpaper no longer flew. They suffered torn bills, mangled crests, their plumage faded and cracked, peeling where the glued panels pulled free of the wall's mooring. Surrounding the fluorescent fixture in the ceiling the white enamel paint hinted at discoloration, the sins of grease. The linoleum covering the floor laid bare its thin worn patches. Only the refrigerator humming merrily along testified to some small modicum of success, or prosperity. It was filled to the brim, the shelves an aluminum mine, a Tupperware party, all rolled into one.

These signs of troubled times would not have been as dif-ficult to tolerate had she been more pleased and satisfied with herself. But as her progress lessened, as her steady weight loss slowly diminished, the "genteel" shabbiness of her surroundings came to plague her nearly as much as the pounds which refused to disappear and vanish into the warm spring air.

"Could you live like this, Vivian? The truth."

"Wait a minute. I have food in my mouth." Vivian Hollander chewed quickly, trying to swallow the piece of pound cake she was eating.

Cynthia, who'd taken to smoking more obsessively, lit

130

yet another cigarette and leaned back in her chair. She watched her neighbor swallowing and felt the itch to join her, to reach across the table, slice herself a piece of cake, and give in to her compulsions. Her fingers tingled. She might as well have been a Geiger counter, clicking frantically now that she was sitting within sight of something sweet and appetizing. But she held back and inhaled deeply, as if the smoke itself were edible, tasty, as if it would fill her stomach rather than her lungs. Vivian, on the other hand, had no problems when it came to eating. They'd been neighbors for years, and for years Cynthia had tried one diet after another while Vivian ate her way steadily toward a round and waddling two hundred pounds. It was here that she stopped, while Cynthia's weight had risen close to two hundred sixty. Now she was down to one hundred eighty-four pounds, stuck there for the last two weeks. She hadn't cheated. She hadn't gone on any food binges, hadn't thrown caution and the diet to the wind. She continued to eat the three meals a day she was allowed, to snack on vegetables rather than sweets. Nothing seemed to be happening, except growing irritation and annoyance with herself.

"How can you just sit there and eat like that?" she blurted out.

Vivian shot a startled glance at her. "What?" she asked, finishing her heavily sweetened coffee.

"Haven't you ever wanted to lose weight, Viv?" she went on, trying to sound calmer, less belligerent. "I didn't mean to snap at you, but it's next to impossible for me to sit here and watch you eat without wanting to join in. The cake is Manny's, by the way, in case you're wondering."

"I wasn't."

"But," and she stopped and looked down at her hands. I can see my wrist bones, but what good does it do. "I don't know. Watching you eat like that makes me feel like a voyeur or something."

"Hah, that'll be the day. You're the most normal woman I know."

"Not quite," she said. "But Viv, why don't you try this diet with me. Maybe we can help each other."

"A confirmed chubby like me? You've gotta be kidding."

"No, I'm not. I'm a hundred percent serious. Why

131

won't you try it out, even for just a week? We're not so different. Right now you can't be more than fifteen pounds heavier than me. I mean, you've seen how much weight I lost."

"Sixty pounds—"

"Sixty-eight."

Vivian shivered. "It sounds creepy, like you cut off a leg or something. Cynthia honey, I know how fond you are of me, but it's just not my kind of thing. I have a glandular imbalance, always have, ever since I was a kid. I mean, I was a tubby when I was ten years old, so nothing's going to change things."

"You have a glandular imbalance like I had fat genes," Cynthia replied, making no effort to mask her sarcasm. She leaned forward and put both her hands on the table. I need a manicure too, on top of everything else. Then she smiled, cleared her throat, and said, "I gave myself the same nonsense excuses for years, Viv. I told myself it was bad blood—fat blood I mean. I had myself convinced it was just a case of huge mammoth bones and nothing else. But that's all a bunch of garbage, can't you see that?"

"But I like myself the way I am," Vivian protested.

"But you have such a pretty face—"

"Cynthia Margold, you're not going to start in with me, are you. We know each other too long. So I'll never wear a size seven dress. So who gives a damn."

"And you're not ashamed of yourself?"

"Ashamed?" exclaimed Vivian, her pale blue eyes expressing instant indignation. "Cynthia, you're being insulting. I didn't come here to be belittled."

"I'm sorry, I didn't mean it that way." She reached out and patted her friend's hand. She has no wrist bones at all; her arm's just smooth and round as a salami.

"Listen, if I could lose weight easily, of course I'd do it," Vivian said in a more subdued tone of voice. "But it's an impossibility."

"Aha!" she said, seizing on Vivian's words. "Now we're getting to it, the crux of the matter." She got hurriedly to her feet.

"Where're you going?"

"I have to have my milk," she said. "That's part of the diet. It helps curbs the appetite."

"Milk?" and Vivian shuddered violently. The flowers

on her housedress seemed to curl and uncurl in response. "It gives me the chills, just the thought of it."

Cynthia ignored her histrionics. She'd felt the same way, having avoided milk ever since she was a kid. I hate the taste, the smell, the way it looks, she used to tell herself. But rules were rules and if the diet was ever going to work, she had vowed to follow it to the letter. "Now let's go back a minute," she said after she poured herself a glass of milk. "You just announced it was an impossibility for you to diet. Why?"

"Why? I don't know. It just . . . I have a slow metabolism, that's the reason. Ask my doctor if you don't believe me."

"Okay." She moved to the wall phone and lifted the receiver. "What's his number?"

"Cynthia! Come on, don't be so literal. And stop putting me on the defensive. It's not nice. It's unfair of you. Okay, so it's not slow. But it's sluggish. After all, it's my body. I mean, I'm the one who knows about these things."

"Viv, I used to tell myself the same ridiculous stories. But they're all old wives' tales, can't you see that?" She paused. "No, I guess you can't. But tell me this," and she went on, feeling herself revving up like a motor, firing up with each successive word. It was a different kind of food and she went along with her instincts, not about to stop until she had convinced her downstairs neighbor that what she was saying was unquestionably the truth. "Have you ever gotten up in the middle of the night, so hungry you were short of breath, so hungry you felt if you didn't put something in your stomach, you'd just die, right then and there?"

Vivian nodded her head. She picked up her knife and cut off another slice of pound cake. For the moment, Cynthia didn't stop her.

Instead, she went on with, "So have I. And did you ever sneak into the bathroom to find some food, a box of cookies maybe, that you were keeping there, hiding for a rainy day?"

"Hey, you've been talking to Bob," she said, referring to her husband. "He has a helluva nerve discussing that with you. That's a confidence between husband and wife."

"That's just the point," Cynthia told her. "I didn't speak to Bob about your eating habits and he didn't speak to me. Viv, I used to do the very same thing. I kept a box of Fig Newtons on the window sill, for God sakes."

"You did?" Her expression softened. Interest grew in her eyes. She put down her fork and slowly swiveled her body around on the seat. Cynthia listened to the dovetail joints creaking in anguish.

If it breaks it breaks, she thought, knowing there was no way to stop herself now that she was halfway there, halfway home. And safe. "I sure did," she said, vigorously nodding her head just in case Vivian still didn't believe her. "Do you know what else I did, because I didn't want Manny or the kids to know how I was eating on the sly? I used to hide little food parcels, care packages is what they were, under the furniture, in the dressers. Under my panties, the bras with the extra strip of elastic—"

"Yeah, I have to sew an extra piece on mine, too," Vivian said, sighing as though there were nothing else she could do about it. "But I stopped hiding things under my slips. I had this bag of chocolates. You know the kind, from Fox's on the avenue, with liquid centers. I put my hand down too hard one morning and ugh . . . disgust, can you imagine kirsch and fruit syrups all over my underthings. It was horrendous." She made a face and once again shivered violently. But this time her voice wasn't filled with cake, sweets, uncontrollable hungers.

"Of course I can imagine," Cynthia said, laughing. "Because it's happened to me. Or how about this one. Did you ever stop at Normandie's . . . you know, the bakery on Utica Avenue—"

"Of course I know. I'm one of their best customers."

"You and me both. But did you ever stop in there to buy your kids a box of French cookies, or maybe some black-and-whites. You know the kind I mean. Half vanilla, half chocolate. But instead of bringing them home, you ate the entire box as you walked down the street."

"Bob *has* been talking to you. Why, it happened just last week. I bought a pound of macaroons—you know how good their baked goods are, everything's so luscious." Here she stopped abruptly and looked down at her plate. She licked the tip of one finger and dabbed at the cake crumbs. "Cynthia, what are you trying to do to me?"

Vivian's voice reached out at her, touching a responsive chord. It was her voice, the same plaintive maudlin tone she'd used with herself for years. It was the same voice that said, "Leave me alone. I'm happy being fat. I'm happy just the way I am." But the voice which had spoken to her for so long was a barefaced liar. Having come to realize that in the last month or so, she was now doubly determined to make her neighbor realize it as well.

"I'm not trying to do anything to you, Viv. But you see, we're not so different. We play the same childish games with ourselves. We say we can't lose weight because something's the matter with our bodies, our body chemistry or heredity."

"Yep, I've used that line, too," Viv said disconsolately.

"Sure, and so have I." She finished what was left of the milk and wiped her mouth with a napkin. The glass was now opaque and for a moment, no one spoke. When Vivian looked up at her, Cynthia saw a round sad balloon of a face, open and guileless and slowly deflating. "You see, what I've been trying to tell you is that this diet from Kings County is the answer. They run a clinic there, but I've always been afraid to go. Maybe, if we talk things out—you know, the way we're doing now, it'll make everything so much easier."

"You want me to try it, don't you?"

Cynthia nodded her head. "I need someone's help, Viv. And I'm asking you. I'm discovering that it's just about impossible to do it on my own, alone I mean. Henny—you remember, my friend the manicurist—is a size twelve already, and it's all a result of this diet. She can't help me anymore. But you can. And what's even more important, I can help you."

"All right," Vivian said. She drew a long breath. "You're too persuasive for your own good, Cynthia. You should go on the stage or something. But I won't fight with you. Let's just get it over with already, before I change my mind. Bring me a paper and pencil and I'll copy it down. Sixty pounds you said?"

"Sixty-eight," Cynthia repeated. Her chair nearly toppled as she scraped it back violently. Then she was on her feet, hurrying to the fridge where she'd taped the diet weeks before. She couldn't remember the last time she'd moved so quickly. And, even more than that, somehow she didn't even feel breathless. It was like getting a second wind—or maybe a second chance.

"I hope you don't mind," Vivian said a week later when she arrived at Cynthia's. Behind her stood a blonde-haired woman dressed in a shapeless floral tent, the kind of sack Cynthia kept in the back of her closet in case her will power snapped. "But when I told my friend Doris—Doris Bauer, this is the friend I was telling you about, Cynthia Margold, who lost sixty-eight pounds would you believe. Cynthia, Doris. Doris, Cynthia. Well anyway—"

"Come on in, the two of you," Cynthia interrupted with a laugh. "Don't stand in the hall." She held the door open even wider and stepped to the side to let them pass.

"Anyway, I was telling Doris about how we got to talking and wouldn't you know, she asked me if she could come along the next time we got together. I made a copy of the diet for her, and Cynthia, wait'll you hear this." Vivian put her hands on her hips and waited for total silence. "I lost *three* pounds this week with no trouble at all. And I'm not even hungry, isn't that unbelievable! I hold my nose when I drink my milk, but still. Can you imagine, *me,* not hungry?"

"Does it really work?" Doris whispered.

"You're damn tootin' it works," Cynthia said. Already, she warmed up to the task ahead, the job of making a convert out of Doris, convincing her that thin was in. "Come into the living room. I made a pot of coffee. Black. Let's call that rule number one."

A week later, Doris Bauer—down four pounds to one hundred seventy-two—brought Nan Albert and Nan's cousin, Rita Press.

"The more the merrier," Cynthia told them. "A cross-section of opinions. It can only help." There was still room to sit; the living room wasn't crowded yet. The children were in school; Lena had gone out to do some shopping. Manny was at work. No one need feel self-conscious about talking.

"I don't know how you do it," Rita Press said. Like the others, she was overweight, dressed in a shirtwaist far too tight for her. As she sat on the couch and leaned heavily against the cushions, Cynthia saw how the material pulled at her hips, the front buttons parting to reveal the woman's thin white slip. "I've tried everything and believe me, when I say everything I mean everything." She set down her cup of coffee on the end table alongside the couch. "Could I trouble you for a cookie, Cynthia.

Tell you the truth, I'm so hungry I feel a little light-headed."

"That's not a bad idea," seconded Nan Albert.

"It's not a *bad* idea. It's a *horrible* idea," Cynthia told them. Instead of cookies she brought out a tray of raw vegetables. When the women made a face, collectively frowning at the sight of carrot sticks, radishes, celery stalks and strips of green pepper, she smiled to herself and put the overloaded plate down on the coffee table. "Joke all you want, but it's good for you. Just let me ask you one thing. Why did you decide to come with Doris this morning?"

"Why?" they repeated in unison, looking at each other as though the question were out of line, unfair of her to have even asked.

"I don't know," Rita said. "I mean, Doris said she was on this new diet, that she'd lost some weight and that it was easy as pie."

And Nan went on with, "She told us how you and your friend Vivian and her sat around and discussed how difficult it was to lose weight and that it was sort of like—"

"Group therapy," Vivian piped up.

The term seemed to frighten the newcomers.

"I'm not crazy," Nan said. Momentarily flustered, she looked away. She fidgeted on the couch and tried to cross her legs. But it was an impossibility. Finally, she gave up in disgust and obvious embarrassment.

"No one said you were," Cynthia assured her. "But we're all in the same boat, don't you see? We're all women who have never been able to control our appetites. The older we get, the fatter we get. Am I wrong?"

One after another the women shook their heads.

"Fat—it's such an ugly word." Rita screwed up her mouth. Her expression was pained, chastising, despite the soft and appealing shade of her lipstick. "I'm just a few pounds plump, that's all," she said. Nervously, her fingers moved to her throat. She played with the string of amber beads around her neck.

"Plump, my eye," laughed her cousin. "You're as fat as I am, so stop kidding yourself." She looked across the room to where Cynthia was sitting. "We've been friends since we were kids. We've been through everything together, from A to Z. You name it, we've done it as a

137

pair, like regular sisters instead of just being first cousins. The two of us used to drown our sorrows in milk shakes when we were in high school together. Everyone had boy friends except Rita and Nan. You've heard of the Bobbsey Twins. Well, we were known as the Tubby Twins."

"No one's called us that in years, so why bring it up now," Rita said. And to the others, "She forgets the good times. I wasn't such a miserable teenager, believe me. I had steady boy friends, same as everyone else."

"Steady fat boys, you mean. But I'm only trying to make a point, dear, if you'd just let me finish," Nan said. "What I was saying was that if anything went wrong—if we failed an exam or had a fight with our parents—out came the goodies, quick as a wink. Food was a substitute for . . . for something. Something we didn't have, maybe, since we're all being so frank."

Rita clucked her tongue. "She's exaggerating, believe me. Am I a person you'd call fat? Chubby, yes. Not fat."

"Isn't it time we all stopped being afraid of a word?" Cynthia quickly replied. The two of them must get on each other's nerves after awhile, she thought, watching the way Nan and Rita exchanged angry sullen glances. Before either of them said another word, she hurried to add, "For the time being, let's just say we're all weak-willed, okay. But that's not the point I'm trying to make. The point is the diet, the fact that it works simply because you're never hungry, because you eat the right kind of foods. And by the way, I didn't write it. It's from Kings County, so don't go thinking I'm talking out of my hat. I'm only talking from experience, that's all."

"No more cookies?" Rita whispered to her cousin, loud enough for Cynthia to hear.

"Carrot sticks are marvelous. Try one. Or a celery stalk. Go on, they won't bite, and they won't put weight on you, either."

"Meanwhile, with all this talking going on, I didn't get a chance to tell you about *my* progress," Vivian Hollander said. "Ten pounds in two weeks, how do you like them apples, girls."

"That's marvelous, Viv," Cynthia said. "That's three pounds better than I did." She leaned forward in her chair, her eyes moving from one woman to the next. "I was at a stalemate two weeks ago," she confided.

"What stalemate?" Viv said. "Sixty-some-odd pounds

and you call that a stalemate? I call that a triumph, plain and simple."

"But I need to lose at least another fifty. And I was just staying put. My weight wasn't going anywhere," she replied. "Doris, Nan, Rita, you too Viv . . . the whole point is that we're not alone, understand? My problems aren't unique. We share the same outlook on life and we've experienced the same kind of difficulties. For instance, just the other day I was telling Viv how my daughter came home eating an ice-cream cone. Do you know what I thought when I saw her?"

"You wanted to flush it down the toilet, I bet," Rita said.

"Wrong," Cynthia said with a grin. "I wanted to ask her to share it with me. It looked so delicious. Gorgeous cherry-vanilla ice cream and a sugar cone that was so crisp and . . . you see? I've lost sixty, excuse me, *seventy-five* pounds—"

"Unbelievable," someone muttered.

"No, not at all. First of all, it didn't happen overnight. Second of all, if you want something badly enough you can do it, that's what I've been trying to tell you," she went on. "I've lost a lot of weight by anyone's calculations. But I still have dreams about food, about gorging myself on all the things I haven't eaten in months. So I'm really no different than any of you. And I'm not that much thinner, either."

"Last night I called Cynthia on the phone," Viv told them, "because I was all dressed—I mean, I had my coat on, that's how dressed I was—to go out to the York Diner, over on Empire Boulevard. That's just a few blocks from here. It's open all night and . . . well, have you ever had an urge, just this incredible desire to have a stack of pancakes with butter melting all over them and maple syrup." She shivered at the thought. "Oh God, I wanted them so badly I didn't know how to control myself."

"So she called me," Cynthia said, smiling. "She said, 'Cynthia, it's just not worth it. I'm giving up.' And you know what I told her? I said, 'Viv, you march yourself into the kitchen right this minute and open up a can of asparagus or have some sauerkraut. Or have a pear or an apple, an orange even. But don't you dare give up, not without a fight.' "

"And I did what she said," Viv told them. "I peeled

myself a navel orange. But instead of just sitting at the table and eating it, I stood in front of this full-length mirror we have in the hall. I looked at myself while I was eating. And when I was finished, I wasn't hungry. I was proud of myself, on top of everything else. I'd curbed my appetite and I hadn't gone off the diet."

"Pancakes," sighed Nan. "I love wheatcakes. And how about waffles? Are waffles allowed, Cynthia?"

Cynthia shook her head. "Afraid not. But Nan, there are so many other things you can eat, things that can even satisfy your hunger for sweets. Just look at the diet, at the sample menus they give you. You're not limited to one or two things. The choices are fantastic. Why, just this morning I made myself a beautiful breakfast, totally within the guidelines they give you. I melted a slice of American cheese on a piece of toast. It was luscious."

"That sounds good," they agreed.

"It was. It was delicious. With some fresh-squeezed juice and a cup of black coffee I walked away from the table not only full, but wonderfully pleased with myself. That's another point, to like yourself more, because the more you like yourself, the better you feel about yourself, the easier it is to stick to the diet. Ladies, the beginning of this year I weighed over two hundred fifty pounds. That's two-five-o. And now I'm down to about one hundred seventy-five."

"And you call that fat?" Doris said. "I still don't understand why you're killing yourself."

"But it is fat. It's all useless fat, totally unnecessary, totally worthless. And dangerous, besides," Cynthia insisted. "I'll tell you something else. I used to be terribly short-winded. I'd get dizzy spells, and I'd feel weak, and sometimes my legs would even swell up. Sure, carrying all that extra useless weight around put a terrible strain on my heart. That's why I said it was dangerous. But the more I lose, the better I feel. And the better I look."

Rita nudged her cousin, saying, "She's got something there. I get short of breath just walking around the apartment from one room to the next."

"And sometimes I even get tired just from eating."

"Me, too."

"Not even thirty-five and getting into the tub's already become a major operation."

140

"I thought I was the only one . . ."

"Me, too."

The voices buzzed around her. Cynthia sat back in her chair and smiled to herself. They were responding and opening up to her and to each other. It wasn't so much the fact of seeing a group of overweight women all assembled in one room like a beef trust. Rather, it was the sense that she was no longer alone, that her problems had a degree of universality. For years she'd gone around thinking no one knew or understood her suffering, the way she agonized over her eating habits. She'd told herself she was one in a million, uniquely and hopelessly afflicted. But it wasn't so. There were hundreds and thousands and no doubt tens of thousands of other people just like her, all walking around thinking precisely what she had thought: I'm fat and there's nothing I can do about it. But now, listening and then voicing their own opinions, she saw that all of the women shared a common experience, a bond that drew them close together. And when, by the end of April, there were over a dozen women sitting in her living room, her own weight loss increased proportionately. She was no longer afraid she'd quit, toss in the towel, and bounce back to where she had been months before. She was determined to go down to a size twelve if it was the last thing she did.

The question was no longer "Can I do it?" but "When will I get there?" Every day brought her closer to her goal. The idea of giving up had become as foreign to her as eating a slice of banana cream pie.

May–July 1963

"WE CAN'T AFFORD AN AIR CONDITIONER," Manny said. "As much as I'd like one, it's out of the question, Cynthia. And besides, who are all these women coming here, anyway? Yesterday when I came home early there must have been over twenty women sitting around, each one fatter than the other."

"They're friends," she said. "And friends of friends."

"What do you do, play cards, mah-jongg?"

"Not quite." She was at the sink, getting dinner ready. "We talk about our problems, about our eating habits."

"They're all dieting?" he said with a familiar and incredulous rising inflection.

"That's right. Why, is it so hard to believe?" she said. "And what about you? You promised to lose some weight and you've done nothing about it."

"And you promised to get a job and you've done nothing about that, either," he reminded her.

She didn't know what to say. Caught up with the meetings being held in her apartment, two each week and a third just about an inevitability, she'd had no time to think of looking for a job. It was her job to help herself and help others at the same time. She wasn't about to give it up when she was still thirty pounds away from her goal, nor when there were people who needed guidance, needed talking to, women—and soon men, if she had her way—who needed support and encouragement in their own efforts to reduce. The diet wasn't her idea. She hadn't formulated it. But maybe the system, the way she implemented the reducing plan, was uniquely her own. So many of the women had already said that without her,

142

they'd never have been motivated to watch their weight or stick to the diet. How could she throw that all up for a dreary nine-to-five job, a job that wouldn't be half as challenging or half as rewarding. She couldn't, that was just the point.

"Well?" he said.

"Well what?"

"Well, what about a job, Cynthia?" he persisted. "As much as I love your mother—"

"Just lower your voice, Manny," she hissed. "She can hear you."

"The TV's on. She can't hear a thing," he whispered. "Well?" When she didn't answer, he turned away and opened the refrigerator.

"I wish you wouldn't bring those things home," she said, as he pulled out a box of chocolate graham crackers. "Between you and Natalie it's getting—"

He cut her short. "Mind your business. No one's asking you." He removed two of the cookies and popped one of them into his mouth. The crackling crunching sound made her tremble. Even after all this time, all the effort she had put into sticking to the diet, she still felt a barely controllable urge to turn around and join him.

Instead, she said, "You promised. You made a solemn promise when Barry was bar mitzvahed. You said you'd go on the diet with me, that we'd work on it together."

"Next week. When you go out and get yourself a job, I'll start cutting back on my intake."

"Can I help?" Lena asked, entering the kitchen.

"You can set the table for me, mom, if you don't mind."

"You're not expecting anyone over tonight, are you?" Manny asked.

"As much as I'd like to, I'm not," she replied. "We only meet during the day, so you needn't worry about your privacy."

"Good, because that's one thing I'll put my foot down about. I won't allow my home life to be disrupted by these crackpot ideas of yours—meetings for fat women. Unbelievable, the things you come up with. If you made a couple of bucks off it, it would be something else. And it seems to me that you've been sloughing off on your jewelry business, on top of all this other nonsense."

"A lot of women can only come on Saturdays. What am I supposed to do, tell them no dice?" she shot back.

"That's not a bad idea," Manny said. "And what are you raising your voice about? I only asked a simple question."

"No one's raising their voice," she said. "I just don't like your attitude. And as far as ending the meetings, it won't happen, so you can just forget it. People come first in my book, remember that."

"All I remember is that Cynthia told me she was going to go out and get herself a job." He devoured another chocolate-covered graham.

"He's impossible," she said under her breath as he left the kitchen.

"He feels neglected, sweetheart. It's understandable."

"Ma, do me a favor and open a window. I'm burning up." She fanned herself and wiped her face before saying, "Neglected? That's a lot of hot air, pardon the expression. He comes home, he showers, he has his dinner, and then he spends the rest of the evening in the living room, doing his bookkeeping or working on his key chains. Neglected, the only one who's neglected around here is yours truly."

"Cynthia, the man works like a dog—"

"And so do I, in case you're interested. I'm trying to get through to people, mother, people who are very unhappy, who have gigantic problems. Why must everything come down to money? That's all I hear from him—money, money, and more money. It's enough to turn your stomach the way that man has an obsession with the dollar bill." The refrigerator door swung open and she jerked her head around. "Natalie, not before supper!" she said sharply. "I'm making a big dinner. You'll ruin your appetite."

"I just wanted a cookie."

"And I said no. Period! You had more than enough garbage to eat today. Pizza and a charlotte russe and a malted. It's enough."

"I can eat whatever I want to eat and you can't stop me; it's a free country!" Natalie blurted. She slammed the refrigerator shut.

"Don't get fresh with me," Cynthia replied. Natalie had already left the room. "It's Manny's fault," she told her mother. "Some example he sets. She's gotten so heavy all of her clothes don't even fit anymore." She stopped long enough to turn on the broiler. "I have no patience, mom.

144

I can't be a watchdog, twenty-four hours a day. And in the future, I forbid you to buy her candies and sodas the way you've been doing. It's the worst thing for her, believe me."

"But she's only a child, Cynthia." When the last dish was in place, Lena pulled out a chair and sat down at the table. Absently, she folded and refolded a paper napkin. "It's not as if you're dealing with a grown-up, for goodness sakes."

"Fat children end up becoming fat adults. She doesn't have to go through what I did."

"What did you go through, may I ask? All of a sudden life was such a terrible thing?"

"I didn't say that. You get so defensive—"

"Don't give me this defensive business. All I know is what a mother knows. And what a mother knows is that you were plenty happy as a child. You never had a bad word to say about anyone. And people felt the same about you, believe me."

"Mother, I am only trying to make her life a little easier." She lowered her voice and stepped closer to the table. "Do you know what the other children on the block call her? Do you? Fat Nat, that's what. How do you think she feels about that—being ostracized by her peer group?"

"Fancy words. She'll get over it."

"Sure, she'll get over it, if you'd cooperate with me instead of letting her run all over you."

"She doesn't run all over me, for your information. If the child wants a cookie, what's the big deal? Let her have it and be done with it, instead of making such an issue. That's my philosophy."

"Well it's not mine, and since I'm her mother, I'd appreciate it greatly if you wouldn't indulge her. I'm not asking for the moon—"

"No, only the stars," Lena said with a laugh.

The sound was a marble rattling inside her chest. Cynthia turned slowly around. Her mother's single explosive laugh grated on her. It was hollow, an empty tin can without warmth or substance. Lena looked down at her lap, seemingly lost in thought. The paper napkin she'd been folding and unfolding lay shredded on her plate. Beyond her the cardinals were frozen, unmoving. They looked stark and paralyzed in the thin fluorescent glare.

145

Tail feathers drooped, split, and cracked even as she stared.

"What is that supposed to mean?" she asked.

"Nothing." Lena lifted her head and smiled crookedly, her face exploding in a network of tiny unmapped lines. "I shouldn't have opened my mouth."

"No you shouldn't have." Her bitter mood made her feel momentarily defeated. It's so unlike me, she thought. But at least there's a meeting here tomorrow. At least I'll be around people who I can talk to, people who understand what I go through every day. Instead of, instead of this.

Whatever "this" was, it no longer seemed to amount to very much at all.

"Excuse me a sec," she called out. "Someone must be late."

The meeting had been in full swing for nearly an hour, but there were always a few breathless stragglers. Some were tented, expectant women. Others stood by the door, awning-striped, red-cheeked, exclaiming how furious they were with themselves. They apologized profusely, saying, "I had to take a bus all the way from Canarsie." Or declare, "There was a tie-up on the subway. I'm coming all the way from Avenue M." But when Cynthia opened the door this balmy July afternoon, she found herself staring into the narrowed and blatantly irritated eyes of the woman who lived directly below her in apartment 5-C.

"Oh, hello Mrs. Kipness," she said, surprised. "Anything the matter?" There was no sense asking her neighbor in. The occupant of 5-C was clearly not paying a social call. Her very posture was colored stiff and inflexible. But then again, they were not friends, had said little to each other over the years. When the children were small, Mrs. Kipness had made it a habit to bang up with a broomstick, demanding they put a halt to their play.

"Mrs. Margold, are you aware that there's a herd of buffalo in your apartment? I just can't take it anymore. Three times a week it's a regular stampede. How do you expect a person to live like that? My dishes are rattling around. Any minute the ceiling's going to come down on

146

my head. The plaster's already falling. What is going on up here, may I ask?"

Mrs. Kipness crossed her arms over her stingy bosom and tapped her foot. The toe of her backless slipper hit against the marble saddle of the door. Behind her, Cynthia heard the mingled voices of over three dozen women, each determined to get in her two cents to add to the vat of experience boiling up in the living room.

Did anyone ever tell you how much you resemble Margaret Hamilton? she wanted to say. You walk around like you just got off your broomstick, Mrs. K. "I'm . . . uh . . . I'm holding a meeting, Mrs. Kipness. I mean, it's only two in the afternoon. It's not as if it's late at night."

"I'm well aware of the time, Mrs. Margold," her neighbor replied. "But I can't take much more of this. I hate to be unpleasant, but isn't it a fire hazard having so many people in one tiny room?"

"I beg your pardon, but my living room is not tiny."

"Believe me, you forget I have the same apartment as you do. It's tiny by any stretch of the imagination. I don't care to have words with you, Mrs. Margold. But just how much longer is this going to go on? It seems to get worse every week."

"I will try my best to keep it down, Mrs. Kipness. Thank you for stopping by." She silently closed the door and locked it. When she returned to the living room, the voices were louder than ever.

She's right, too, that's what gets me, she thought. Nearly forty women were assembled in the living room. She'd borrowed bridge chairs and there still wasn't enough space. The ancient couch sagged dangerously under the triple threat of three stout women. Another perched like an overfed canary on the arm of a wilting club chair. Ashtrays overflowed with lipstick-stained butts.

With Doris and Vivian's help, it took nearly an hour to straighten up the apartment after the women had left.

I'm glad they're all having a good time, losing weight in the process, but there has to be a better way.

She wasted no time getting it off her chest.

"Can I have your attention, ladies, just for a moment. I want to discuss something, something I think is going to be important to all of us." The windows were wide open, but the air recalled a hothouse, scented with nearly three-dozen different floral aromas. There were enough perfumes, toilet waters, and colognes to stock a small-sized store. She fanned herself with a flapping hand, conscious of the growing firmness, the way the flesh on her arm didn't sag, loose and untoned. The women slowly quieted down and gave her the floor.

"It's pretty hot in here, isn't it?" she began, amidst a rustle of other fanning hands, nodding heads and eager attentive faces. "And it's getting pretty cramped too, wouldn't you agree?"

"You can say that again," someone muttered.

"But who cares. We're losing weight," someone else spoke up.

"Losing weight?" she exclaimed, her voice rising in a burst of undeniable pride. "We're not only losing weight, we're dropping pounds left and right. In fact, the combined total weight loss for our group has already reached the five hundred-pound mark."

A whistle or two merged with scattered applause.

"I'm so damn proud of all of you," she went on, "that I just can't even begin to express myself. But some of you may have heard the doorbell ring just a moment ago. It was my downstairs neighbor. She's on the verge of a nervous breakdown. And to tell you the truth, I can't blame her. So this is what I propose. Let's take a breather, just a week's break, no more. Not from the diet, of course. But in the meantime, I'll go out looking for a storefront to rent so we can have a regular place to hold our meetings. Are there any objections? Anyone have anything to say about it?"

"If you need help looking," Rita Press called out, "I have access to a car."

"And I think there's a small store for rent around the corner from where I live. I'll speak to the super of the building and see what he wants for it," said another member.

"But Cynthia, you're not thinking of paying another month's rent, are you?" Vivian said.

"That's just it. I wish I could. But I know I can't," she said. "So here's what I think we should do. When I find a place, I'll figure out how much it's going to run—rent plus gas and electric, the cost of renting folding chairs, whatever. I'll divide up the expenses by the number of members we have and we'll just divvy it up that way. Maybe it'll come to fifty cents a meeting. But it can't be much more than that, and probably it'll be even cheaper."

"Fifty cents is nothing," Nan Albert called out. "You know what doctors are charging these days? Fifteen bucks just for hello-goodbye, and that's not even counting prescriptions for diet pills and junk like that."

"Besides, your time is valuable, Cynthia," announced a woman who traveled all the way from Borough Park, ninety minutes plus two buses and a subway. "And girls, it really is unfair. Even if we try to be neat, we're dealing with over thirty-five people. This room just can't accommodate that many. And don't forget," and she began to laugh, "we're all big-boned women. We take up a lot of room, any way you slice it."

"I really didn't want it to come to this," Cynthia said after the laughter subsided, laughter which doubly delighted her for it was healthy and good-natured. "But I don't think there's any way we can get around it."

"It'll be a much better system," Doris Bauer told them. "We won't have to worry about lowering our voices and we'll have much more privacy. I think it's an excellent idea, Cynthia. Besides, every time you hold a meeting there are at least six or seven new women who show up."

"I'm bringing my sister-in-law the next time," admitted someone sitting behind Doris.

"And I swore on a stack of bibles I wouldn't forget to bring along one of the women from my charity organization."

"I told someone the exact same thing. What a coincidence."

"Me, too."

"I'm bringing my daughter, how do you like that," said another.

"I want some of you to start bringing your husbands," Cynthia told them. "That's right, I'm serious. Once we're settled into our new quarters, I'll try to schedule a meeting for one evening during the week. There are plenty of men who could use some common-sense pointers—"

"Plenty of men who could stand to lose some weight, period," Vivian added.

"That's for sure," Cynthia said.

There were murmurs of agreement.

"You all have my number," she concluded. "We can set up a telephone chain if it's necessary. But as soon as I find a place, and I don't think it should take more than a week, two at the most if I start looking bright and early tomorrow morning, we'll get word to you about all the particulars. How does that sound?"

When they started to applaud, she couldn't believe her ears. She felt it wasn't called for, that it was unnecessary, maybe even gratuitous. But even as she said, "Come on. What are you clapping for? I just chair the meetings, for God sakes," the women were not about to stop. Her eyes moved from one beaming face to another. They were close-knit, held together by a bond that hardened and grew more secure with each successive meeting. They were no longer alone. The chubbies, the tubbies, and the tubs of lard, the blimps and elephants, the hippos, the fatsos, the pleasantly plump and the not so pleasantly plump, those with "pretty faces, it's such a shame," the mothers and wives and aunts and bachelor girls who had all let themselves go, who had lived too many years under the delusion of big bones, large frames, lethargic metabolisms and screwed-up endocrine glands, were united in a common front and a common purpose. Yet the applause was a show of recognition and indebtedness Cynthia felt was undeserved. "I'm doing it for me, too, you know," she tried to tell them. "I'm down to an eighteen. I'm getting there. We're all going to get there, all of us. Together we can do it and have a good time, on top of everything else." And still they applauded.

I started something, she thought. Something that makes me feel good inside.

"This is only the beginning," she heard a voice call out.

"Of what?" she yelled back.

But her words were lost and the applause went on, rising and falling in waves of appreciation, gratitude. And thanks.

September 1963

"ANOTHER OF YOUR MEETINGS TONIGHT, I suppose?" No effort was made to conceal the rancor in his voice.

"I only schedule one evening meeting a week, Manny," Cynthia told him. She stood before her vanity table and clipped on a pair of earrings. There was no time to primp. If she didn't hurry, she'd be late. "Why don't you come down with me?"

"Ten pounds is plenty," he said. He'd been casually following the diet for several weeks. "Besides, it's woman-talk. I've got work to do; I can't waste my time."

"For your information, last week six men showed up. And this week there should be a few more. Everyone's starting to bring their husbands, or brothers—even their sons. We don't sit around and talk about things that are important only to women, honey. It concerns anyone who has a weight problem, male *or* female."

"No thanks." He slapped the newspaper against his thigh. She looked down and read, DAKOTA MOTHER OF FIVE. Then he turned completely away and headed for the door.

"Your pants are big on you," she called out. "You'll be tightening your belt another notch before the week is out." When he didn't answer, she turned back to the mirror, complimenting herself for having avoided an unpleasant and totally unnecessary scene. *If he doesn't want to come, that's his business. I'm not going to fight with him. He doesn't know what he's missing, that's all.* She put on lipstick and combed and brushed her hair. Now that she'd lost so much weight, she didn't feel the need to dress up her face or decorate her neckline. *I'm like a new* person, another person, she thought. Or maybe I'm just freeing the person who was hidden under all that fat; who knows? But if she wasn't sure about that, she was absolutely certain about the way she looked. She turned from one side to the other, taking infinite delight in the new Peck & Peck dress she had chosen to wear for the meeting. It was styled simply, a brief overblouse attached to a waist-shaped skirt of fine loopy wool. "Reaching new heights in city-bred elegance," read the ad in the *Times* which first caught her eye. The alternating red and brown stripes were horizontal, a pattern she had consciously avoided when she was heavy. Those stripes made a person of her former size appear even fatter than they really were. Now that she was down to a size sixteen, many of her fears, the taboos she had made for herself, rapidly disappeared. She had lost over eighty pounds. The next thirty or so were going to be more difficult to lose. For the last month and a half she'd lost not more than two pounds a week. But she wasn't worried about it. She'd already learned, not only from her own experience but also as a result of studying the statistics of the women who assembled to hear her talks, that after the initial —and major—weight loss, the rate of progress invariably leveled off. The diet still worked, but it was not a plan that called for drastic changes which might damage a person's health. That finding had been confirmed when she was advised to secure medical releases from all of the women—and now men—who attended her pep talks. Family doctors who had been shown copies of the diet agreed that there was nothing ill-conceived or potentially hazardous in the Kings County reduction plan. If she wasn't losing the five and six pounds a week she'd almost come to anticipate and expect, she was perfectly secure in the knowledge that before the year was out she would be down to her goal weight of one hundred thirty-five. No, the problem wasn't can Cynthia lose weight, but when the magic day would arrive.

Now, there were other people to worry about. She folded and stuffed some tissues into her handbag and made sure she had cigarettes, a pack of matches, and enough money in her purse. Keys too, don't forget. Then she turned off the lights and slipped out of the bedroom.

"Have a good time, mom." Barry called from his room.

152

The door was ajar. She poked her head in and saw him working at his desk. "You really look nice," he said.

She came into the room, kissed him on top of his head and ruffled his sandy-brown hair, a shade darker than it had been the year before. "I'll see you later. What are you studying?"

"French vocabulary."

"Say something for me."

"C'est dommage."

"What does it mean?" She looked over his shoulder to the page of printed text. Boy, have times changed. They gave us Latin and who the hell remembers a thing. And what use is Latin to me now? French or Spanish, that would have made more sense.

"It's a pity," he said.

"What is?"

"C'est dommage. It means 'it's a pity.' It's an idiom."

"I'll have to remember that. Work hard." She kissed him again and left the bedroom. "Are you ready to go, Natalie? Put on a sweater for me, honey. It's gotten chilly out."

Her daughter was curled up on the couch watching television. Manny worked at the bridge table. He was putting key chains through the holes of thin white plastic squares, each die-cut square faced with a metal initial he had glued on in his shop.

"Do I have to?" Natalie said, sighing loudly and unhappily.

"Do you have to what? Put on a sweater? I'd appreciate it."

"No, I mean do I have to go?"

"Natalie, we've discussed this all week. And you promised me. You're not the only youngster who's going to be there. I mean, last week there were six or seven girls, your age or a little bit older."

"What do you do? Everyone says how . . . how fat they are?" She rubbed her eyes with the back of her hands and made no move to get off the couch.

"You'll come with me and you'll see." She checked her watch. "Natalie, come on. I'm going to be late. I have a lot to do tonight."

Manny said nothing. His back was to her. He faced the television, his fingers moving repetitiously and automatically. He didn't have to look down to see what he was doing. It was like touch-typing, she decided. For a moment she stood and stared, watching his fingers move with swift and practiced expertise, exhibiting a kind of dextrous precision his overweight body never seemed to match.

"Natalie, I'm losing patience," she said. "Rapidly."

"Ohhh," grumbled her daughter. "You always force me—"

"No one's forcing you. Get dressed!"

Fifteen minutes later she unlocked the door of the storefront she had rented on Rutland Road, not far from her apartment. One of the women had contributed curtains for the window facing the street. Inside, she switched on the overhead light and let her eyes move around the long narrow room. The landlord, after pressure and finagling, consented to give the place a paint job when she signed the lease. The room was clean and simple, furnished with rows of folding chairs and an old Board of Education desk she'd bought at a secondhand shop on Canal Street. A metal garment rack at one side of the room was loaded with wire hangers so the members would have a place for their coats.

"Well, what do you think? Proud of your mom?" she asked Natalie. She took off her coat, hung it up, and moved to the back of the room.

"It's . . . okay," Natalie said with little conviction. "Plain."

What does that mean, and what is she so afraid of? Cynthia thought. She'll be with her own. No one's going to call her Fat Nat. She put her handbag down on top of the desk and turned around. Natalie slumped down in a seat near the door. She was almost eleven, but already she was what Cynthia secretly referred to as "wide in all the wrong places." It's baby fat, but it's more than that. She eats incessantly. I have to talk to Lena again, that's all there is to it. Sure, she knows her grandmother can't say no to her, that's why.

Her mother had gone out for the evening to see some old friends.

That's another story altogether. All of a sudden Manny has a new best friend, a *confidante*. What's the use of talking, wasting my energy. A thin person just can't begin to understand what it's like to be heavy. They have

154

no conception of what's involved. The problems, everything . . .

The door opened and a shy round face slipped into the light. "Come on in," she called out from the other end of the room.

"I don't know if I have the right place," the woman said. She looked down and consulted a slip of paper she held in her hand. But when she stepped inside and slowly closed the door behind her, Cynthia didn't have to look twice to realize the woman had come to the right address, a place where she might soon feel a sense of belonging and need. Clothed in a baggy coat with oversized cloth-covered buttons, the figure—engraved on the light —now began to move with a lumbering hesitancy, an uncertainty of gait that mirrored the uncertainty reflected in her face. "Are you the woman who talks about dieting?" she asked. She raised her eyes for a moment.

Cynthia caught an instant's glimmer of something shaped like hope. She'd seen the look before, now that she'd been dealing with overweight people, ever since Vivian had brought Doris and Doris had brought Rita and Nan. "That's me," she said. "It's really quite painless. And I think you'll have a good time, even while you're discovering how instructive our talks can be. Why don't you just hang up your coat and make yourself comfortable? Everyone should be along in a few minutes."

"Thank you," the woman said. She slipped out of her coat with an awkwardness of motion Cynthia immediately recognized. It was a familiar set of fumbling gestures, the same ones she herself had often duplicated.

Nothing comes easy when you're heavy, she thought. Even the simplest thing, like taking off a coat or tying a shoelace, can turn into a difficult proposition. Again she looked at the woman. She saw herself. The transformation was as simple as that. Although she had never felt particularly self-conscious about being overweight, professing and exhibiting a jolly good humor even when her obesity had gotten her down, she still saw her own image in the face and figure of the newcomer. But there's no reason why she can't lose weight, and why she can't be happy in the process. God, every week it's the same thing.

Within ten minutes the converted store buzzed with conversation, the creak of chairs, the rattle of metal coat hangers. Cynthia didn't have to count to see that there were at least a dozen new faces, bringing the attendance to nearly sixty. More men were present than ever before. When she saw a questioning youthful face—chubby-cheeked as she had been when she was a girl—she glanced at Natalie as if to say, "See, I told you so."

She realized her daughter wasn't buying it, not convinced she belonged in a room rapidly filling up with "fatsos." She's biting her nails again, Cynthia thought. Then she turned her eyes away and attended to the business at hand. She opened the top drawer of her desk and removed the roll, a chart which recorded attendance as well as weekly weight loss.

"I'm sorry I'm late," Vivian Hollander said, hurrying to the front of the room.

"No rush, take your time." Her neighbor had become a much needed assistant. By now it was virtually impossible to handle all the paperwork by herself. She insisted on giving Vivian a share of the profits. Cynthia found profits difficult to accept as fact. They amounted to no more than ten or twenty dollars a week, making up for the money she lost now that she had given up— "Temporarily, Manny, just for a month or two, I swear" —selling costume jewelry. She charged fifty cents per head per meeting. When, at the end of August, Cynthia found she had cleared nearly sixty dollars, she was surprised and confused.

It never entered her mind that speaking before a group of overweight men and women might result in monetary gain. She hadn't asked Viv up to her apartment with the idea of selling her persuasive talents, nor ultimately marketing her encouraging and helpful remarks. It had come to that, whether she liked it or not, whether she wanted to accept her burgeoning "business" as a reality or just a fluke, a passing phase. Whatever it was, burgeoning was an apt description of what had taken place since April. Word-of-mouth had spread the news of what she was doing to nearly every community in Brooklyn, parts of Queens, the Bronx as well. What had started in the spring as a nucleus of six or so overweight women had grown to embrace almost one hundred fifty people attending one of three weekly meetings. Weight loss might level off after an initial period of substantial gain. Now there was no sign that the attendance at her meetings was even approaching a plateau. The store was getting too crowded.

A few days earlier she was forced to go out and rent an additional two dozen folding chairs to accommodate the swelling ranks, "believers," as she liked to think of them.

"Good evening and welcome if you haven't been here before. My name is Cynthia Margold and sitting to my left is my dear friend and assistant, Vivian Hollander. I hope all of you who have been working with us had a good week. And I hope the figures you've brought with you, for everyone was supposed to weigh themselves at home, show that we all like ourselves a lot. But before we begin, I'd like to introduce all of you to a very special person who's with us tonight, my daughter Natalie. Natalie honey, why don't you stand up so everyone can see your pretty face."

She extended her hand and pointed in Natalie's direction. For a moment there was silence. Then a chair scraped against the hardwood floor and Natalie got slowly to her feet. Why doesn't she smile; she's so cute when she looks happy, Cynthia thought.

"Say hello to everyone, sweetheart."

"Hello." Abruptly she sank down in her chair, half hidden by the people clustered around her.

"Adorable little girl," someone said.

"Thank you, I think so myself," Cynthia said with a grin. "But Natalie's here tonight for the same reasons all of you are attending. The only difference I can think of, is that on top of everything else, she used to have a mother who weighed over two hundred fifty pounds." She gestured at herself. Still smiling, letting her eyes move from one interested and sometimes curious, sometimes skeptical face to another, she continued with, "That was me. I called myself the Blimp of Crown Heights, Miss Roly-Poly USA. Believe me, I was very happy being fat. That's *fat*, ladies and gentlemen, spelled F-A-T. It used to be the dirtiest word in my vocabulary, worse than anything else imaginable. But no more. It's no sin to be fat. But it sure is a blessing to be thin, let me tell you."

"Amen, you can say that again," whispered someone in the front row.

"It sure is, Kate," she said, lines of laughter erupting on her face. "It's the best thing in the world. Now I guess some of you newcomers are anxious to know what goes on when we hold these meetings. We talk, plain and simple. We exchange experiences. We discuss our eating habits and the difficulties we may or may not have encountered trying to diet. Not only during the past week, but all through our lives. I think it's a pretty safe bet to say that all of us have, at one time or another, tried to lose weight. And judging by our appearances—or some of them at least—we never made it. Do you know why? Because no one was there to give us the incentive, the motivation. The push with a capital P. We thought we were alone, am I right?" No one said a word. No one refuted her. "Each of us considered ourselves a solitary fat person, suffering in private. Or if we didn't suffer, we invariably thought up complicated excuses for ourselves. Rationalizations to explain away the fat, to explain why we couldn't watch our weight or control our appetite. Big bones and bad heredity were two of my own personal favorites. But anyway, that's why we're here tonight. Because we're *not* alone and we don't *have* to be alone. Not anymore, that is. Our problems aren't unique or special or very different from hundreds of other people who have put on more weight than they like to admit, or even accept as fact. But before we start getting down to basics, Viv'll call the roll and we'll see what progress we're making.

"Oh, one other thing for those of you who are here for the first time. Announcing how much you weigh isn't designed to humiliate or embarrass you. Remember, I weighed over two hundred fifty pounds the beginning of this year and I'm still not down to my goal yet. But the point is, the thing I want to emphasize, is that it didn't embarrass me one iota. It just made me short-winded, prone to dizzy spells, more than occasionally short-tempered and generally annoyed with myself. But I wasn't embarrassed, believe me. Embarrassed? With a face like mine?" She squeezed her cheeks and there was a ripple of laughter. "I was absolutely positive fat people had more fun than anyone else. After all, they never had to worry about what they ate, for starters." She shook her head. "I really deceived myself, for over twenty years, in fact. But as I said, you'll see for yourselves in the next few minutes."

Vivian got to her feet. Cynthia sat back and craned her neck, trying to catch a glimpse of Natalie. Her face was all but lost behind the broad front of a woman who had been coming to the meetings ever since the store opened its doors. For the moment she stopped worrying about her.

"Albert, Nan."

"Nan, by the way, has been with us since, I believe, sometime in April," Cynthia announced.

Nan got up from her chair. "I just wanted to say that when I first came to Cynthia's apartment this past April, I weighed, catch this, one hundred ninety-two pounds. If any of you want to come home with me, I'll show you a collection of hats that'll knock your eyes out. I knew every milliner in the city. You know why? When you weigh close to two hundred pounds, you don't want people to look at your body, your nonexistent figure. But your face is something else entirely. I had the most dressed-up face in the neighborhood, but today, tonight, I'm down to . . . one forty-nine."

"Down three pounds, exactly, from last week," Viv called out, a weight chart spread out before her.

A smile burst across Nan's face. "It's easy," she said proudly. "I'm almost never hungry anymore. And I feel a hundred, maybe a *thousand*, percent better than I did last spring. Believe me, I'm not exaggerating. If anything, I'm understating the case. And you know what else? My husband hasn't been so attentive—romantic, tell you the truth—since we first got married. Is that not a bonus or isn't it?"

"Anderson, Katherine."

"Don't forget to add Natalie's name," Cynthia whispered. "Right after me, okay."

The calling of the roll continued.

"Margold, Cynthia," Viv called out.

She got up without a moment's hesitation. It was important to project a good image, to set an example, to lead the way, so to speak. "I swear to God I didn't cheat once," she said. "But when I weighed myself tonight the scale read one sixty-three."

"One-six-three . . . and a half," Viv said. "Down two pounds, even."

"I'm getting there. Slow but sure."

"Margold, Natalie."

Cynthia looked across the room to where her daughter sat. Several heads turned with her, following the direction of her gaze. Natalie didn't move. She didn't say a word.

"Natalie?" Cynthia said. And to the others, when Natalie still remained in her seat, the top of her reddish-brown head wavering back and forth as if the girl were trembling, "She's a little shy. Come on, honey." Natalie didn't answer. Cynthia started down the aisle between the two sections of folding chairs. "I hope to start a meeting just for teenagers, boys and girls together," she said. "But we need your encouragement and cooperation. There's no reason why a youngster has to feel left out because he's overweight, no reason at all."

"You can't force me to tell," Natalie said. She pushed her chair back, swayed as if she were about to fall and elbowed her way out of the row. She was at the door when Cynthia looked back and asked Vivian Hollander to chair the meeting until she returned. The window glass threatened to shatter. The door slammed shut behind her and Natalie's small running feet echoed faintly along the sidewalk. Cynthia followed right behind her, shutting the door carefully so that no one could hear what she had to say to her daughter.

She found Natalie leaning against a car parked along the curb. Her neck was hunched down into her shoulders. The color was washed from her clothes by an overhanging street lamp. Her skin looked bleached, milky-white, translucent in the harsh incandescent glare. A chill autumn wind whipped at Natalie's feet, throwing up crumpled cigarette packs, empty gum wrappers, fallen russet leaves.

"What's the matter, honey? There's nothing to cry about, for goodness sakes."

"I don't want to go in there," Natalie said. Her words were cut short by a choking sob. Tears glittered in the corners of her eyes.

Cynthia couldn't understand what was happening. As far as she was concerned, Natalie was overreacting.

"You can't make me tell how fat I am; you can't force me," Natalie said. She opened her mouth and tugged at the air, gasping, trying to catch her breath. Her face was explosive, a brilliant shade of fire-engine red.

"No one's forcing you, I promise," Cynthia said. She moved closer to put her arm over the girl's shoulders.

Natalie jerked back, skittish as a colt, a shuddering frightened fawn. "All those . . . those people," she said.

160

"I'm not like that and you can't make me do those things."

"What things?"

"You know; you know," Natalie said. "Daddy doesn't and I won't either and you can't make me anymore, you can't."

"Natalie, what are you getting so excited about? What did I try to make you do, for God sakes. Get up and say how much you weigh? What's the big deal. *I* did it. Why, do you think people'll laugh?"

"I'm not a fatso like they are. I want to go home. I don't want to go on any diets. Never, never, never!"

She's hysterical; it's insane. "Okay, but just come back inside with me and take your seat. You won't have to say anything, I promise. But I can't walk you back home now, Natalie. You saw how many people there were. You don't want me to just walk out on them and disappoint them, do you? Some traveled a long way to be here tonight. It's just not fair."

"You're not fair, that's who," Natalie said. She skipped back a step and pulled at her sweater. The cardigan was too tight on her. One of the buttonholes suddenly gave, splitting apart like a piece of torn skin.

"Why are you so stubborn, Natalie? All I'm asking is for you to wait another hour and we'll go home together. Please. I'll—" No, I won't. I won't bribe her with food, the way Lena bribed me. I won't say, *I'll buy you an ice-cream soda.* I won't let her go through what I did, all the garbage—

"You'll what?" Natalie looked up, blotchy-cheeked, her eyes hard as rock candy, cold as Italian ices.

"You'll come back inside and act your age and act like a young lady with manners . . . breeding, that's what you'll do." She reached for her daughter's hand, thinking, If I have to drag her in I'll do it, if only for my own peace of mind. I'm not going to let her get away with murder. She's spoiled rotten and through no fault of my own, either.

But Natalie was not about to be led or dragged or pulled anywhere she didn't want to go. She threw herself back and broke free of Cynthia's hold. "I'll go home myself."

"You'll do no such thing. I don't want you out on the

streets this time of night. You'll listen to me for a change, if you know what's good for you."

"No I won't," Natalie snapped at her. No longer was she acting like a child, a puppy worrying a shoe. "I'll listen to daddy. He doesn't force me to do things the way you do." She turned around and ran silently down Rutland Road. There was no sound of leather treading and scraping against cement, no scuffing heels. All Cynthia heard was her daughter's panting breath. Natalie raced away, creating the extent and borders of her animosity by the very distance now separating her from her mother.

"Natalie, you come back here!" she yelled. "It's dangerous. I forbid you!"

Fisted hands pumped and pummeled the air. A wide apple-shaped bottom jerked left and right, swayed by the movement of the child's running feet.

"Natalie!" she screamed. The syllables cracked, tore apart. The inside of her throat felt like broken glass. She almost expected to see more glass, jagged-edged splinters, sharp-edged glinting shards, covering the sidewalk at her feet. Instead, she saw her own shrunken and attenuated shadow—nothing else. She looked down the block. Natalie slipped, slid and melted into darkness. There was no sign of her flight, not even a faint echo of running feet. She was gone. Cynthia turned back to the door set between the curtained windows.

All of a sudden I'm the bad one, the monster mother. Because I try to help my kid, make life a little easier for her. I'm a big fool, that's what I am. And I blame Manny as much as Natalie. Where else does she get her ideas, if not from him. *I'll listen to daddy. He doesn't force me* . . . she wants to grow up miserable, Fat Nat, I'm just going to stay out of it from now on in. I'm not going to fight with her or force her to do anything. Eleven years old and she's picked up all her brother's old habits. Fresh isn't even the word for it.

She turned the doorknob and stepped back inside.

"Everything okay?" asked Doris Bauer, seated near the door.

"She's at an age . . . what can I say?"

November 1963

LENA CLAPPED HER HANDS TOGETHER, keeping time to the rhythm of grief. Her body rocked back and forth, her shoulders thin as a knife edge, held tight and straining in an attitude of profound and unutterable sorrow. "Such a young man, such a beautiful handsome young man with a gorgeous wife, gorgeous children. Babies, two beautiful babies. What's going to happen? What's this country coming to they shoot the best, the best and the sweetest. Such a face, such a beautiful sweet face."

"Right-wingers. Birchites. Fascists," said Manny. He sat at the bridge table. His hands were motionless. His bookkeeping lay spread before him on the folding table. But he had eyes only for the television.

She came off the plane in a pillbox hat and a blood-stained dress. Lena started to weep. She shredded and twisted a tissue between her fingers. Cynthia stood in the foyer. Her arms were crossed, her eyes unblinking.

"But why, daddy? He was everyone's friend, wasn't he?"

"I don't know why, Natalie. It's a crazy country. It's filled with crazy people—"

"Lunatics, lunatics and murderers," Lena moaned. "His mother, his poor mother. What she's going through now."

"I don't believe it's happening," Cynthia whispered. "I just saw him on television yesterday. Stunning, such a beautiful intelligent young man. He had everything, the whole world—"

"Is Johnson okay, dad? Is he going to be a good President?"

"I don't know, Barry. We'll just have to wait and see and hope for the best."

You'd think people would have the sense to call, Cynthia thought. But no, the phone doesn't ring all night. She glanced at her watch. Who the hell wants to talk about losing weight on a night like this.

"You're not going to your meeting, are you?" Manny asked.

"I have to," she said.

"What do you mean, have to?"

"Where're you running?" said Lena.

"I can't start calling sixty-some-odd people, tell them it's canceled. When they get there I'll tell them in person. I assure you, I have no intention of conducting a meeting after what's happened today."

"So why bother to show?" Manny said. "Believe me, no one's going to be there."

"They'll be there," she said. "And there's such a thing as common courtesy, Manny, in case you've forgotten. I have a responsibility to a lot of people. I don't intend to let them down."

"Boy oh boy," he said, "you take the cake, Margold."

"Say whatever you want. I'll be back in a half-hour. Some people paid in advance. I want to give them back their money."

In the front hall she slipped into her coat with an ease that no longer amazed her.

"You disgust me, Cynthia!" Manny called out.

Go to hell. Just drop dead and leave me alone, you fat slob. The words spoke loudly in her throat. Her lips remained shut, pursed tightly together. She let herself out of the apartment, pressed the button for the elevator, and waited as patiently as she could. The burst of cannon fire reverberated up and down the dimly illuminated hallway. There was a sense of finality, something long since determined, that made her want to cry all over again.

There's such a thing as responsibility to people other than yourself, she thought. He doesn't know about things like that. Only about Forman Margold is he the world's greatest expert.

The streets were dark with a cloak of mourning. Even the arc lights seemed subdued, their orange glow somehow faltering, tremulous, and uneasy. She walked quickly, vaguely afraid of what one television commentator had called "the national madness, a growing cancer." But no one emerged from the tragic shadows. When she reached

Rutland Road she turned left, walked another block and reached for her keys. No one stood out front or huddled by the doorway, waiting to be let in. She unlocked the door and turned on the lights inside the store.

I should've listened to him, she thought. Just this once, anyway. People'll know better. They won't bother to come out on a night like this. I still can't believe it's all happened. Like when my father died . . . it hasn't sunk in yet. I just saw him, yesterday on the news. What was the word they all used to describe him? Charisma, a charismatic world leader.

"Hello?"

"I'm here," she called out.

The door opened wider. "I didn't think you'd show."

"I wanted to be here in case anyone came down. The meeting's canceled for this evening."

"I figured as much, but I wasn't sure. I'll see you next week then. I'm still in a state of shock."

"I know, I feel the same way. Good-night."

"Good-night, Cynthia."

The door closed behind her. Cynthia didn't have to consult her records. She remembered the woman had already lost twenty-seven pounds. Less a name, she was a place and statistic: East New York, minus twenty-seven. And what am I? Crown Heights, minus one hundred three. Minus half a husband, minus three-quarters of a daughter . . . minus ninety percent common sense. Plus three hundred percent giant ego.

The doorknob turned.

"Hi, there won't be a meeting tonight. I just came down in case anyone showed." She couldn't even see who it was, felt suddenly afraid, vulnerable, isolated, and totally alone.

"I live around the block. I wasn't sure—"

She relaxed, breathed more regularly, decided it was time to lock up and not take any more chances. "We'll see you next week," she said. "If you run into any problems, you know who to call. You have my number, don't you?"

The shadowy figure seemed to nod and slip back, as insubstantial as a mirage. The door closed with a whisper of metal, a soft dying click.

So your husband knew what he was talking about. Oh, but you were so eager to belittle him, weren't you,

Cynthia? So damn eager to think he was talking out of his hat, out of the side of his mouth. What, you think you're the most important person in the world, is that the game you're playing with yourself? All of a sudden, Saviour Cynthia. You big fool. You'll ruin everything at the rate you're going. The world goes on, day after day. And if you weren't around to help people lose weight, someone else would be here—right at this desk probably —to take your place. Where did you get this ego from, this overbearing vanity? Where did you come off to think worrying about weight was more important than worrying about an assassination? Talk about a growing cancer . . .

She didn't wait any longer. The voice ringing in her head was her own voice, not Manny's or Lena's or Natalie's or anyone else's. She got up from her desk and slipped back into her coat. It was a new wool topcoat, berry-colored tweed, paid for out of her steadily mounting profits. She need never feel embarrassed about looking poor or shabby.

"So?" she said aloud, the one word leaving a thousand things untouched. You learned your lesson . . . good, didn't you, Cynthia? Hopefully, hopefully. Or are you just going to forget all about it tomorrow morning, like nothing happened, like you didn't make a fool of yourself . . . in your own eyes, no one else's. Inflated egos have a way of suddenly bursting. All you need is one little pinprick and bang, you'll be put in your place so fast you won't know if you're coming or going. A word to the wise, right? Isn't that what you'd say to someone else, even a total stranger? Sure you would, bigmouth. Because if you don't watch yourself, this thing is going to get completely out of hand. Totally. Remember, don't end up becoming your own worst enemy. It's not worth it. It never is.

"So you see," Cynthia went on, "you can have that eclair or that piece of danish, that slice of banana cream pie. No one's going to stand over you and point a finger. No one except yourself, that is. It's much easier to eat . . . and eat . . . and keep on eating. You don't have to worry about things like self-control, strength of mind, will power, all those wonderful terms we have to describe the way we do battle with ourselves. But the point I'm trying to make is that there's no such thing as *one* eclair or *one* honey bun or *one* slice of custard pie for a person with a weight problem. One becomes two and then three and then half a dozen.

"I guess I've told you about some of my experiences during this past year. I've been traveling all around the city, all the boroughs, not just here in Brooklyn. I even have a group in Westchester and another out on the Island. But it's the same thing wherever I go. Invariably someone gets up and asks, 'Can't I have just *one?*' One can mean a slice of pizza or an ice-cream soda or a candy bar. Everyone has his favorite junk food. I used to love Fig Newtons, but that's another story altogether. The point is, you know what I tell them? 'You came to listen to me because you never learned to stop after *one*. If you had, you wouldn't be heavy. You wouldn't have problems with your health. You wouldn't have problems finding clothes to wear, clothes that fit. You wouldn't be dealing with unhappy husbands or wives, your kids even.' So the answer isn't, 'Yes, you can have one, whatever it is.' The answer is right in the diet. The answer is that by following the diet, the rules that are set down, you'll discover other and healthier ways to satisfy your appetite.

"Let's not fool ourselves, either. You're sitting here in Leonard Frankel's living room because you're heavy, but heavy for a reason." She began to pin down each face, making the kind of one-to-one personal contact she felt her listeners needed. "It's not a freak of nature. None of you were born that way, no matter how plump you were as babies. It's not faulty glands, bad genes, anything a doctor could lay his finger on by performing some fancy blood tests or what have you. Compulsive eating is a mental problem, an emotional problem. No matter what any of you might say to the contrary, you all eat out of an emotional hunger. Don't forget, that goes for me, too. I've probably said it ten times already, but lest you forget, I was *never* thin. Before I started the diet I weighed over two hundred fifty pounds, so I'm not talking from the viewpoint of someone who was always a size twelve. But see, eating like that—compulsively, indiscriminately—is a substitute. And when you start discovering the reasons why you eat, when you start feeling a greater sense of self-esteem, the old eating patterns start to disintegrate. They don't bind you like ropes the way they used to do. My mother used to say to me, 'What's the use of talking? You never listen anyway.' I just hope that kind of sentiment doesn't apply to any of you. It's time to start listening to yourselves for a change, to the self you've hidden under a mountain of fat, excess blubber, lard, for want of a better way of putting it. There's nothing nice about being overweight, so I'm not going to try to make it any easier by saying you're all just pleasantly plump. You're not, or you weren't, depending on the progress you've made in the last few months.

"They say a year is worth a lifetime. You know what I say? For every fifteen or twenty pounds you lose, you give yourself an extra year. Not only of existence. But of happiness, health, an extra year of feeling good about yourself." She stopped and wet her lips with the tip of her tongue. "Jeanette, how's that coffee coming? My throat feels like Death Valley." She stepped back and made a move to take her seat. "I guess that's about all I have to say tonight. Thank you."

There was no applause. She'd already told them, twice if not three times in fact, that she wasn't there to entertain, to put on a floor show. The fifteen compulsive eaters still seemed to be mulling over what she had told them. Jeanette Frankel, Leonard's wife, got up from her chair and headed for the kitchen.

"Beautiful, you were just fantastic. The way you shook them up tonight," Leonard said, "was just not to be believed."

"They need a shaking up. When you're fat you get lazy, complacent. You start accepting your weight as an end in itself, a dead end."

"Always lecturing," he said with a laugh.

"Well, I'm a compulsive talker these days, Leonard, what can I say."

"I know what I can say," he replied. "In three months I've dropped over forty pounds—"

"And you look so much the better for it, so much happier. That's the diet for you."

He shook his head. "Nope, that's you, Cynthia. You could print these diets up and mail them all over the country and it wouldn't change a thing. It's more than the diet. When you get up to speak, people listen. My friends listen. You've seen the progress they've all made. Even Jeanette, who seems to be having the hardest time of them all, has lost over twenty pounds."

"But I like to talk," she said. He stepped closer and she reached out and gave him a good-natured poke in the ribs. "If I didn't talk, I'd probably start eating again. So it's a two-way street. I help you, and you help me." She caught him staring, trying to capture her eyes. She couldn't pin down the emotion that flashed through her. Vaguely uneasy, she turned away and began to collect her notes, the papers and information she had brought with her.

"Coffee's on," Jeanette called out.

"You really made sense tonight, Cynthia. Thank you," Leonard's next-door neighbor said as she headed for the kitchen.

"You gave me a good scare," another of Frankel's friends told her. "I did cheat this week. Just a little, but I did."

She'd consented to appear before a group of his friends three months before. Leonard had heard about the classes she was conducting on Rutland Road. By now, more than a year after their inception, five classes a week were being held. She handled three of them by herself. Vivian Hollander and Doris Bauer, with her from just about the very beginning, chaired the other two sessions. In all, over two hundred fifty people were taking cabs, subways, buses, a bicycle, and innumerable private cars, to attend the meetings. Not only was she speaking before a totally willing captive audience on Rutland Road, but she had begun to make appearances throughout the city. So when Leonard had asked her to speak before a group of his friends, she hadn't thought twice about accepting. The storefront couldn't handle very many more people. And she'd discovered that many overweight individuals suffered from a complexity of social hang-ups. Some were so shy, so encased behind a wall of obesity, they rarely ventured from their homes. Others lived too far away to travel to Brooklyn. Still others, like Leonard, as well as the two groups she lectured to in Westchester and Long Island, gave no consideration to the expense of sending taxis to pick her up on Montgomery Street and take her back home again.

"Money's no object," he had told her when he called her at home for the first time. "Of course we'll take care of all your traveling expenses. It's the least we can do."

"I wasn't worried about that."

"But we'll take care of them, anyway. The thing is, so many of my friends, I guess myself included, really need to be prodded, Mrs. Margold. If you'd just come out here and speak, I think I can guarantee you'll make us Manhattan Beach chubbies a much happier group of people, a much more weight-conscious group, I should say."

She liked meeting people. She enjoyed the easy banter, the friendly conversation. She thrived on standing before a group of overweight men and women and speaking from her heart, her "guts" as she called it. No one need be alone was the motto, a kind of watchword. There's someone hidden inside of you who's dying to come out and meet the world, head-on. Thin.

The response was overwhelming.

Not "in a million years" would she have expected so many people from so many different backgrounds and communities to respond to the message she delivered. The help she gave to others made up for some of the things she had already lost. Her marriage was going by the wayside, whether she liked it or not, whether she wanted to believe it was really taking place. Quickly, almost with an effortlessness that frightened her more each day, she and Manny drifted farther and farther apart. Forty-five pounds lighter than he had been a year before, Manny now referred to her as his "absentee wife." He wasn't joking, or even being snide. Had Lena not been there to oversee the meals, to attend to all the little details that went into running a house, Cynthia knew she'd never have been able to give her lectures, to get people to talk openly and freely with her and with each other, to begin traveling throughout the city. Somehow, before she could even pull it back, rein it in, the feeling had grown that there was no way to stop what she had inadvertently started. She liked what she was doing. It wasn't her mission in life to preach the gospel of good eating habits. At least, that's what she still kept telling herself. The loan was paid in full, interest and all. The money she'd made in the last year was still very little, considering the time she gave to her work. But she wasn't doing it for any monetary rewards. What she did was accept the challenge, and accept it with an alacrity and assurance she never stopped to question. There was just too much to be done, too many people to get through to, people she wanted—and perhaps even needed—to win over to her way of thinking.

"You look adorable tonight, Cynthia. I love the dress. It's so . . . flattering," Jeanette said. "I wish I could wear something like that. Unfortunately—"

"Unfortunately nothing," Cynthia quickly replied. "You'll reach your goal, same as I did. It didn't happen overnight, Jeanette. I sweated plenty, believe me. Excuse me a sec." She stepped past Jeanette and poured herself a cup of coffee. There's a limit to how much you can talk before you get blue in the face, she thought. I don't want to think about fat anymore tonight, or else I'll start sounding like a tape recorder. Press a button and Cynthia gives her spiel. A long day, that's all. It's been a long hard, busy day, but a good day. Productive. Now, all I want is to get home, take a nice hot bath, see my kids. Manny . . . if he'd just stop being so difficult about everything. Why can't he just accept me, the new me, and be glad that I'm having a good time, that I feel useful, more than just a fat housewife?

"I never showed you my den," Leonard said.

171

"I hope that's not an invitation to do anything indiscreet, Mr. Frankel," she kidded him. She turned around and leaned back against the kitchen counter. The cup was balanced in the palm of her hand. When she looked up, Frankel was staring at her intently as he had a few minutes before.

"Indiscretion is nine parts bravado and one part valor. And it also happens to be part of my nature," he said with a laugh.

"I'll have to remember that."

"Please do." He guided her out of the kitchen, through the living room and down a narrow carpeted hall that led to the master bedroom on one side and the second bedroom, now a study, on the other.

"Is this where you do all your heavy thinking?" she asked after he had led her inside.

"No, I do most of that on the subway, believe it or not." He motioned her to a seat.

She obliged him, secretly delighted that she could cross her legs with no trouble at all as she sat back in a tufted leather wing chair. Manhattan Beach was considered an upper-middle-class community and Leonard's study seemed to reflect that, decorated to the nth degree. There were hunting prints on the wall, leather Chesterfield sofa to match the chair, campaign desk and row after row of perfectly arranged books, Literary Guild and Book-of-the-Month Club selections. There was a pipe rack on the leather-inlaid desk, the skin of some kind of wild animal, a deer or an antelope she decided, on top of the wall-to-wall tweed carpeting.

"Are you sure you're not Ernest Hemingway in disguise?"

"I'm much thinner than he was," Leonard said. "Besides, he never manufactured children's pajamas."

"But he lived well," ignoring the faint yet unmistakable tone of self-pity she heard in his voice.

"We try." He shrugged his shoulders and sat down at his desk. "Tell me something, Cynthia."

"As long as it's not too personal," she said. She tried to laugh. When it didn't work, she lifted the cup to her lips.

"Well, maybe it is. But I'm curious. Why don't we ever see your husband at the meetings? Manny, that's his name, isn't it?"

She nodded her head, trying to come up with what she

felt would be the right kind of answer. It failed to materialize, to pop full-blown into her head. So she grabbed at the first thing that came to mind. "He's busy with his own work. I mean, well . . . Manny's not my biggest fan these days, tell you the truth."

"I figured as much," Frankel replied. He picked a pipe from the rack and held it in front of his eyes, as if considering filling it with tobacco. She watched him, acutely aware that he still looked at her, even if he was pretending to be concentrating on something else entirely.

Charismatic, like Kennedy, the thought struck her. Maybe that's why, as soon as I met him, I knew I'd keep coming back. Magnetic, too, that's another word. So intense, boy he must keep Jeanette on her toes twenty-four hours a day.

A big man by anyone's standards, six-one or -two at the very least, Frankel's weight loss hadn't affected the look he seemed to want to project. As far as Cynthia was concerned, the more weight he lost, the bigger he became. Three months before he'd been a tall fat man with a handsome chiseled face and a head of jet-black hair. He'd worn custom-made suits, snappy odd jackets, natty trousers all tailored to make him look slimmer than his two hundred sixty pounds. But he still looked fat, no matter how hard he tried to hide behind an expensive wardrobe. This evening he didn't seem to be trying hard at all and yet he came off so much more self-confident, so much more handsome and impressive than when she'd first met him, that Cynthia wanted to let him know how pleased she was about the progress he had made. Something held her back.

"He doesn't really like the way I've been traipsing around the city this past year," she said. She looked down at her lap and with one hand pulled the hem of her dress over her knees.

"Has he asked you to give it all up?"

"More than once," she admitted.

Leonard drummed his fingers against the top of the desk. "Sad, that he doesn't appreciate how much good you're doing. It sort of makes me want to stop and think it over."

"Think what over?"

"There was something I wanted to discuss with you." His face seemed to visibly brighten. Except for the difference in hair color, she decided he looked very much like Jeff Chandler.

"Didn't Jeff Chandler die the same year as Hemingway?" she asked.

"What made you think of that? As a matter of fact, I believe they died about the same time. I can look it up in the almanac if you want."

"No, it's not important—just a thought." She finished her coffee and set down the empty cup and saucer on a small antique tripod table near the chair. Like the other furnishings in the room, it looked elegant and expensive without appearing fussy. "What was it you wanted to discuss?"

"Now's not the time. What say we meet for lunch one of these days?"

You can't get more evasive than that, she thought.

"Oh, there you are. I was wondering."

Cynthia found herself smiling, her facial muscles tightening in immediate and automatic response. She looked across the room. Jeanette stood by the open door. She wore a floor-length muumuu that did nothing to flatter her figure.

"I was just telling Cynthia how grateful we all are, how appreciative," Leonard said.

"Well, God knows, if I could do it, so can both of you," she said.

"Oh, Leonard's almost there already. He's within sight of his goal. He won't have any problems. Besides, my husband has a very intriguing streak of vanity. It comes out when you least expect it," she said. She hung back by the door, crossing the carpeted threshold with the tip of one flat slipper-like shoe.

"What vanity?" Frankel said, trying to sound gruff. "She's jealous of me, Cynthia, that's what it is."

Cynthia smiled once again. She got to her feet without needing to hold onto the side of the chair for support. Her body felt light, one hundred thirty-seven pounds of new-found grace. Her eyes were still on Jeanette, who looked like the incarnation of some long-dead Hawaiian princess. The woman had very brown hair and very brown eyes. Cynthia was also sure she was angry.

"I really must get going," she said. She extended her hand in Leonard's direction.

He was out of his chair and on his feet in no time at

all. Warmly, she shook hands with him. "We'll see you next week, I hope," he said, leading her to the door.

Jeanette clung to the doorway, not saying a word.

"I'll try my best," she said, loud enough for Jeanette to hear. "But I can't guarantee anything. If for some reason I can't make it, I'll send one of my assistants."

"I'd like to meet some of your friends," Jeanette said.

"They're lovely women," she said. "Very compassionate." Then Leonard led her back down the hall, Jeanette taking up the rear.

"I already called a cab for you, dear," Jeanette said when they reached the living room.

"How considerate and thoughtful of you," she replied, laying on the charm so thickly she felt that any second it would peel off like a layer of old pancake makeup.

"Keep in touch," Leonard said.

A horn honked out on the street. Leonard helped her into her coat. Before she left, Cynthia made sure to lean over and kiss Jeanette on the cheek. "You'll see," she said, "you'll be able to wear a dress like mine in no time at all."

The illuminated dial of the Baby Ben glowed a groggy and dispirited three A.M. Awakened from a deep and dreamless sleep, Cynthia turned over onto her side and stared, bleary-eyed, fuzzy around the edges. The broad rounded planes of Manny's back hovered before her. He was sitting on the edge of the bed, trying unsuccessfully to remove his socks.

When she'd returned from Manhattan Beach, Lena was still up, watching the Late Show. "He went out, don't ask me where," she said. Behind her Bette Davis was just about to discover she was going to die. "He got tired of waiting so he just put on his coat and left."

"The kids?"

"Asleep. And while we're at it, don't you think it's time Barry had his own room? I mean, he's reached an age, Cynthia. It's unhealthy that he should be sleeping in the same room with his sister."

"With what money, mother? You want us to move to a bigger apartment, tell me how and I'll do it. I just got finished paying off the bank loan, for God sakes."

Miss Davis was taking it on the chin, the picture a

blue-violet glow in the otherwise darkened living room. "I see that you're in no mood to discuss it," Lena had said.

"I'd like to know where my husband went, for starters. And you should turn on a light. It's bad for your eyes, watching like that in the dark."

Wherever Manny had gone, he'd had too much to drink. An alcoholic vapor seemed to hover around him, misting in the air, clinging to his sweaty body.

"Where were you, may I ask?" she whispered. She blinked and narrowed her eyes, squinting through the glare of the lamp near the bed.

"Wha'cha say?"

"I hope you didn't take the car. You could've gotten yourself killed. How much did you put away, a whole bottle?"

Instead of answering, he got slowly to his feet, swaying from side to side as if he were at sea. He hit the edge of the door with one shoulder, bounced back like a punch-drunk fighter and clawed at the knob until he found it. She remained in bed, watching his sodden performance with humorless eyes.

I got home as soon as I could. What does he want from my life?

The toilet flushed. The rumble made her think of the elephant house at Prospect Park. She turned toward the night table and reached out to find her cigarettes. Abruptly, she changed her mind and sank back against the pillows. Then the bathroom door opened and closed. Manny sounded like he was still staggering, hitting the walls the way he'd banged into the door. Back in the bedroom wearing only his pajama bottoms, a roll of excess fat larger than a tire around his waist, he wobbled toward the bed, shuddered, and collapsed on top of the covers.

"Just do me a favor and turn out the light."

He didn't answer, a faint snore—half a wheeze, half a warble—escaped his lips.

How disgusting can you get. Talk about lack of self-control.

She sat up in bed and reached across him. One elbow trailed against his bare, flabby chest. Even as her fingers made contact with the switch on the lamp, she was aware of something else. It was another odor, less cloying than his alcoholic whiskey breath. A perfume, faintly floral, almost like candy violets. She turned off the light. "Where were you?" she asked.

"Go to sleep, g'night," he mumbled.

She pressed her hand down against his stomach. "You're all sticky," she said. She wanted to scream, to shove him out of bed without waiting for any possible explanation he might want to offer. "Couldn't you have at least showered, you pig!" she hissed, afraid of waking up the children. "Where's your decency and who was it? Who was it, Manny? She wears cheap perfume, that's for sure."

"Sleep, gotta work t'morrow." He turned over, pressing his stomach into the sagging mattress.

I'm going to argue with him when he can't even hear me, the cheater?

She slid back until she was hugging her side of the bed. Her eyes remained open, glued wide and unblinking. She stared at the ceiling and ignored the lousy paint job, the flaking plaster, the random and occasional designs left by passing cars, their headlights reflected up toward her sixth-floor windows.

So it's reached the point where . . . it can't get much worse, can it? A father with two children. A grown man with responsibilities, how dare he? Who does he think he's dealing with, some fly-by-night? He's dealing with his wife, the mother of his two kids, that's who. Not some two-bit floozy who carries on when he's not around, when he's not looking, checking up. Oh, this is just the beginning, Forman, just the start. You want to play your little games, you go right ahead. But two can play just as good as one. I'll show that pig. I'll show him plenty, more than he ever bargained on. He wants to make garbage out of his wife, treat me like a piece of dirt, like I'm a real washrag or something, he's got another guess coming, that's for sure. Another guess coming, the phony.

She closed her eyes. It was a long time before she fell asleep.

January 1965

SHE WONDERED if diamonds on cuff links were vulgar. Maybe it was just an occupational hazard, though the very idea of thinking Leonard Frankel was someone who personified the garment center did not strike her as a very pleasant thought at all. He was more than just a sharkskin-suited sharpie, a "rag merchant" able to speak knowledgeably of piece goods and yards of cotton velvet, cheap help, and troubles with the union. Besides, even if there were diamond chips set in his gold cuff buttons, he wasn't wearing an iridescent sharkskin suit, or even a flashy mohair blend. So she pulled her eyes away from the expensive glitter at his wrists and waited for him to light her cigarette. He produced a textured gold lighter. The flame blew hotly. She inhaled and drew away until she impregnated the chair with the outline of her back.

He was nursing a drink at a small table in the rear of the restaurant, when Cynthia had arrived a few minutes before. "Mr. Frankel?" she had said, even as she saw Leonard toying with a highball glass at the opposite end of the room.

"Oh yes, right this way," replied the maître d'.

He was on his feet even before she approached the table. "Thank you," she muttered. The maître d' pulled out her chair, waited for her to take a seat, and then edged it gently back toward the table. "Well, good afternoon, Mr. Frankel," she said.

And he said, raising his glass as if to toast her, "Good afternoon, Mrs. Margold."

And the waiter said, a glimpse of red sleeve flashing

one of her cigarettes—"I'm trying to cut down but it doesn't seem to work as well as your diet"—and suddenly winked at her. "I have a business proposition for you, Cynthia."

"I know nothing about Dr. Dentons."

"Now would I have dragged you all the way into Manhattan just to involve you in sleepwear?"

"That's a very leading question."

"I'm a very leading kind of guy."

"So I'm discovering."

He looked down at his plate. "Seriously, this has absolutely nothing to do with children's wear, I promise. It has to do with you."

"Me?" She batted her eyelashes, trying to maintain the light tone and joking mood which seemed to make her feel more comfortable in his presence.

"Yes, you," he said.

"Leonard, you're so serious. It makes me feel . . . I don't know, nervous maybe."

"That's good. I like to keep people on their toes. What's with Manny?"

"That's a jump, isn't it, from business propositions to Forman Margold. Why do you ask?"

"You'd never have called me unless something happened. I think I know you by now. Somewhat, at least."

So she told him, simply, directly. Straightforwardly. Cat-and-mouse no longer seemed half as amusing as it had a short while before. He listened with an intentness, a genuine interest that was far more compassionate than merely curious. She didn't know why she was telling all this to someone she knew only indirectly, vaguely, only in terms of Frankel's efforts to lose weight. He'd nearly reached that goal, but he still seemed to want more from her. Whatever it was, and she already had a score of fantasies floating around in her head, he was yet to reveal himself. But for now, for the moment, Cynthia had all the patience in the world.

"Unpleasant," he said when she was finished.

"Very. So now you know why I called. Does that make me a winner or a loser?"

"You, a loser?" He waved his hand at her, chuckled deeply as if at a private joke. "You'll never be a loser, believe me. It's just not in the cards. You'll get whatever you want . . . if you really want it, that is."

alongside of her, "Will the lady be having anything to drink, a cocktail before ordering?"

"Cynthia?"

She shook her head. "Not allowed." She looked up at the waiter. "I'll have a large glass of tomato juice with a splash of Worcestershire and Tabasco."

"A Bloody Mary—"

"Without the vodka, thank you." She unfolded her napkin and spread it across her lap. "So," she replied, "here we are," removing her eyes from his ornate cuff links. "It's a lovely room, isn't it?" She swiveled her head around for an instant, taking in the expanse of restaurant.

"Food's not fantastic, but it's nice and quiet."

"Intimate," she said. "I've never eaten in a hotel restaurant before. Someone once told me you never get a good meal out of an institutional kitchen."

"Well, it's convenient," he admitted. "It's not far from my plant. And I certainly didn't want to meet for lunch at just any old coffee shop."

"I used to love coffee shops, luncheonettes." She stopped and smiled, took a pull on her cigarette, and put it down again. "Should I start sighing for the Cynthia who was?"

Leonard shook his head. "No, if I were you I'd smile for the Cynthia who is. You look wonderful. But then again, every time I've ever seen you, you've—"

"Tomato juice for the lady," interrupted the waiter. He set down the tall frosted glass in front of her and stepped back.

Cynthia removed the wedge of lemon bent over the rim of the glass. She cupped her hand over it and squeezed the juice out until a single pip floated on top of one of the ice cubes. Then she set the shrunken wedge down on her saucer and raised the glass to her lips. "To your health, Mr. Frankel."

"To yours, Mrs. Margold."

"So," she said again. She wiped her lips with the napkin. "Tell me everything, Leonard, right from the very beginning."

"The very beginning?"

"Yes," she said and grinned.

He seemed to visibly relax. "And you're sure now you

want to know *everything*, too?" grinning back at her from across the yard of immaculate white linen.

"Well, almost everything. After all, this is the first time I've ever accepted a luncheon invitation from a married gentleman. It marks a new—"

"—stage in the growth of Cynthia Margold."

"Thank you. That's a very nice way of putting it. I would've said something else, but I'll buy that." Rarely had she ever felt so nervous, so self-conscious of her every motion, her every gesture. It was almost as if she were at an audition, a tryout, though for what role she was yet to figure out. She had called Leonard the week before, right after New Year's. He had said all the right things, about having wanted to call, having been tied up with business, et cetera et cetera. I'm not going to wait for anybody, she had thought. If I sit around all day and wait for the phone to ring, it's never going to happen. As a result, a lunch date was set up for the following week.

"How's Jeanette?" she asked. "I'm sorry I haven't been able to get out to Manhattan Beach—"

"You haven't wanted to, that's why."

"And do you blame me?" she said. "Don't answer that. Everyone has me on the run these days, that's all. Did Doris do a good job last week?"

"Excellent. She's not half as persuasive as you are, but she speaks straight from the shoulder, so I guess people find it pretty easy to respond to her. Jeanette's lost another ten pounds, by the way. I don't know what happened, but about a week after we last saw you, she really started attacking this thing like a house afire. Won't stray from the rules one iota."

"That's how it should be. You can't diet halfway. It never works. Well I'm glad to hear she's making good progress. I always knew she would. She just needed a very definite incentive."

"You'll never guess what that's turned out to be," he said, laughing wryly, caustically.

"Don't tell me," she replied. Then she leaned forward and made no bones about the intensity of her stare. It was direct, the old one-to-one she'd long since mastered. "So what's the story, Leonard? I mean, after all—" She never finished the sentence. Whatever she'd wanted to say refused to reveal itself. There's such a thing as tact or diplomacy, she realized.

180

The waiter came back to take their order.

She told Leonard what she wanted, recalling it was the thing to do, proper etiquette, though it struck her as more than just a shade this side of antiquated and Victorian. He, in turn, spoke directly to the waiter who stood alongside the table with a pencil poised in one hand, a pad in the other. "The lady will have a filet, medium-rare, and a spinach and mushroom salad."

"What kind of dressing would she like on that? We have oil and vinegar, Russian . . ."

"No dressing," Cynthia said

"No dressing," Leonard repeated.

"Potatoes?"

She shook her head. Leonard, now aware of how she was trying not to laugh, went through the identical pantomime, shaking his head as he looked up at the waiter.

"And you, sir?" the man asked, too preoccupied to realize what was going on.

"The same."

"No dressing on the salad?"

"He's not allowed," she said. "Malaria." She clucked her tongue, reached across the table and patted Leonard's hand.

"Potato then?" asked the waiter, as unmoved as a mannequin. His expression was set and serious, so completely earnest, that Cynthia wanted to pinch him just to get a more human response.

"Out of the question," she said. "Yellow fever. It's terrible what happens when one takes a cruise to the tropics."

"No potato, thank you," Leonard said, trying to get rid of the waiter as quickly as possible. And when the red-jacketed man had left, he looked across at her. "You're terrible. You gave that poor guy heart failure."

"You're exaggerating. I was just pulling his leg, for goodness sakes. And meanwhile, you haven't told me."

"What?"

"Everything."

"I'm here, am I not?"

"*I* called."

"Well, it's the busy season."

"They told me that about bar mitzvahs. But children's pajamas?"

"Two points," he said. He finished his drink, asked for

181

"I just want to be happy, that's all," she said. "That must sound second-grade, a kid talking. But it's true. I can't put it any other way. He's a good man, Leonard, don't get me wrong. He works hard and he's a good father. Natalie dotes on him. My mother worships the ground he walks on. But . . . I don't know, I feel so confused, like I'm at loose ends. It's all so strange."

"You get a lot of pleasure from your kids, don't you?"

"Intermittently," she said with a grin. "I'm surprised you and Jeanette haven't had any children." Too late she realized she'd made a faux pas. Leonard's face darkened.

"Jeanette can't have any children," he said.

"I'm sorry. I didn't mean to pry."

"No, don't be silly. It's all right. I mean, it's no sin, nothing to be ashamed of. Just one of those things, I guess. We've thought of adopting, but . . . you know, just never got around to it."

"Medium-rare for the lady," the waiter said. "Please watch your fingers. The plate is still very hot." He set the filet down in front of Cynthia, the salad right alongside. Then he served Leonard, asked if there was anything else they might want—another of the same for Frankel, just some club soda for Cynthia—and departed as silently as he had come.

"Delicious," she said after she had taken her first bite.

"I told you the food wasn't all that bad."

"And this meal is all within the guidelines of the diet. See how easy it is to maintain your weight."

He smiled, nodded his head, and picked up his knife and fork.

Over coffee—black of course, no tempting French pastries hugging her cup and saucer—she watched him light another cigarette and turn his chair slightly to the side. He crossed his legs, slouched back and made himself more comfortable. Then he asked, "Have you ever thought of expanding your base of operations, your business I mean?"

"What business?"

"What you're doing now," he said, surprised.

"I'm not running a business, Leonard. I just go around and talk to people. And get them to talk to each other. That's not a business. That's just—"

"A crusade?"

"Billy Graham I'm not, thank you. I'm just having a good time working with people, that's all."

"So as far as you're concerned, it has nothing to do with business."

"It most certainly does not."

"May I ask a personal question? You don't have to answer me if you don't want to. But how much money did you clear this past year . . . not Manny's work. I mean yours."

"Why do you ask?"

"Just curious. Maybe I shouldn't have said anything. It's really none of my business."

"No, it's okay," she said. "Less than a thousand dollars."

"Above and beyond your overhead?"

"Yes."

"Interesting. And you only charge fifty cents a meeting." He put out his cigarette and finished his coffee.

"Actually, I wanted to lower that fee. But when I discussed it with some of my friends, they all thought I was crazy. They said I was selling myself too cheap. Fact is, I never thought I was doing any kind of *selling* whatsoever. Who wants to make money off of someone's aggravations."

"That's a very Brooklyn word, 'aggravations.' But it says a lot. And the answer to that is psychiatrists, for one. Doctors, dentists, for another."

"That's different."

"Absolutely not. You can go right down the line, Cynthia. You're performing a service, a valuable one at that, just the way a dentist does when he fills a cavity or cleans your teeth. People get paid for their time, so I don't know why you've gotten it into your head that you're any different. But to get off this for a minute. I wanted to ask you something else. I have a friend, a business associate, who lives up in Purchase, not far from White Plains. I've told him all about you, about your work I mean. And he's seen the fantastic progress I've made. Well, when I mentioned to him I was going to see you for lunch, he asked me to extend an invitation."

"Invitation?"

"That's right. You see, if you thought I had a weight problem, Gerald's is even worse. He's *fat*, Cynthia, very very fat. And like lots of overweight people, most of his close friends are all in the same boat. Well, he thought that it might just be an excellent idea for you to come up to his estate in Purchase for the weekend and talk to him and his friends. Sort of give a crash course in weight reduction. He has a beautiful home, an indoor swimming pool . . . I think you should seriously consider it. And Gerald Evans is a very successful businessman, I might add."

"Married?"

"Divorced."

"And?"

"And he's very heavy and he's reached a point where he'd like to lose weight . . . painlessly, of course."

"Of course. So where do you fit in?" she asked. "Yes, please," as the waiter bent over to fill up her cup.

"More coffee, sir?"

"No thank you." And to Cynthia, "Evans is a friend of mine, that's all. I'll sort of act as a go-between."

"Otherwise known as a chaperon."

"All right, you might say that."

"And how does Jeanette feel about all this, your going away for the weekend with a married woman?" She decided it was definitely the wrong time to laugh. Then why do I feel like giggling? Nervousness, that's what it is. He makes me feel so damn jittery and I can't even put my finger on it, either.

"I haven't mentioned it to her yet, tell you the truth."

"Well when you do, you get back to me, Leonard, and we'll discuss it further. How's that?"

"Sure, whatever you say. I just wanted to get your reaction."

"My initial reaction is hesitant, to be quite honest."

"You're playing games with me, Cynthia."

For a moment she said nothing. The room came into sudden focus. All through lunch she'd been aware of Leonard Frankel, no one and nothing else. Now she heard knives scraping against plates, the tinkle of glasses, snatches of conversation, heavily padded footfalls, the kitchen doors swinging back and forth on humming well-oiled hinges. The flocked wallpaper directly behind him appeared in sharp relief, framing his face. Leonard's black hair looked glossy, each single hair claiming a share of reflected light. It was the color of India ink. Again, she saw the diamonds on his cuff links. Again, she wondered if they were vulgar, ostentatious, or merely just a random and inexplicable lapse in taste. Maybe Jeanette bought them for him and he couldn't say no. Maybe. She decided to ask.

"As a matter of fact," he said, "they were a gift. But not from Jeanette."

"Aha," she said, with a grin.

"No, it's not what you're thinking, much as I'd like it to be. Actually, my partner and his wife gave them to me for my thirty-fifth birthday. Three years ago. I think they're a little flashy, myself. But once a month or so I wear them to the plant just to show him I'm still appreciative. He's funny about things like that."

"So are a lot of people."

Leonard glanced at his watch, then waved his hand at a passing waiter. He scribbled in the air and a moment later a check was laid discreetly alongside his place. "Think about what we discussed," he said when they were outside on the street.

The previous evening's snowfall had melted, leaving a two-inch accumulation of gray slush. Everywhere she looked it was wet and sloppy. She stepped through it as carefully as she could. "I will," she said. "And thank you for a lovely lunch."

"Thank *you*."

She decided not to stand there and watch him as he started across Fifth Avenue, heading in the direction of Broadway and the loft where he had his business. Instead, she turned on her heel, pulled up the collar of her coat and hurried toward the subway. He puts Jeff Chandler to shame, she thought. Then she tried to forget how handsome and demanding he was. After all, there was Manny. And Jeanette. Maybe we can arrange a match, get the two of them together. She decided she'd hate herself if she laughed. But as she walked down Fifth, threading her way through the soot-colored puddles, she thought it just couldn't be helped. All of a sudden so many things were so very very funny.

And sad.

On Monday afternoon Cynthia came up with a solution. She was certain Manny would never object to her going away for a weekend, provided her friend Henny came along. And who knows, maybe Henny and this Gerald Evans'll hit it off. You never can tell, and won't it be something if it happens. She's been single so long she's given up hope. But there's no reason. She's sweet, she has a good figure. Everyone adores her. It'll be so much better for her than going to Roseland or the Lorelei. Sure, she goes to a dance hall and she has her pick of garbage. She's too old for the single bars and too young to be around cheaters, all those phonies who probably give her a line when all they want is to get her into bed and forget all about it the following morning. Besides, even if Leonard's friend is heavy, he can lose weight just like everyone else. That should be the biggest problem at this point.

She had no meeting to conduct that afternoon and spent an hour shopping on Utica Avenue, catching up on odds and ends. She did her banking, brought in clothes to the dry cleaner and the Chinese laundry, picked up some oaktag Barry had asked her to buy, and decided that instead of going home, she'd stop off and speak to her friend. Monday was Henny's day off. She lived right nearby, just around the corner from her, on Crown Street, several houses down from the Carroll movie. The streets were dry again and she didn't have to walk slowly for fear she'd slip on the ice.

Now I don't have all that extra padding, cushioning for a fall, she thought. But that's just the way I want it. Two sheets of oaktag were rolled up under her arm. She had a small bag of groceries in her other hand. After crossing Utica Avenue, she stopped for a moment to read about the coming attractions at the movie theater. *Send Me No Flowers* was arriving in less than a week. She decided she could do without Doris Day, even if Rock Hudson and Tony Randall would be keeping her company. A revival of "Splendor, Savagery and Spectacle You'll Remember for a Life-Time!" was currently completing its run. She'd seen *Quo Vadis* over ten years before and decided to save her money. "The abandoned pleasures of the world's wickedest city" couldn't compare with the pleasurable abandon of going on a food binge. "The evil priestess, prey to every unspeakable passion," was yet to indulge in the hedonistic delight of consuming a pound of peanut clusters while immersed in a hot sudsy tub. So she slipped past "The Arena of Death, ablaze with human torches," and kept on walking, only to stop with a suddenness, an abruptness that wiped the smile off her lips and brought to mind a screeching line of cars pulling into a dingy subway station. There was the pale blue Ford station wagon with the commercial plates, the back loaded up with cartons, "items," he called them. And there was Manny coming down the steps, taking them two at a time. In a pair of baggy wool trousers, a nylon jacket zipped up to his neck, the bottom edge of a pull-over visible below the hem of the windbreaker, he looked just as he had when he'd left for work that morning. Now, he walked quickly, purposefully, even jauntily, cock-ily, she thought. She remained where she was. She made no attempt to hail him, to call out in a delighted voice, to hurry to catch up to him. Manny got into the station wagon and a moment later pulled away from the curb.

She turned away, caught sight of a phone booth on the opposite corner, and crossed the street. A minute or two later, after she'd gotten through to Information, she had memorized the number. Fumbling for a dime, she dialed. Through the cracked, smudged pane of glass she could see the poured concrete steps with their rounded edges, leading right to the door of the four-family house where Henny rented an apartment.

"Dreamtime Togs, good afternoon."

The voice, thin and brittle as gold leaf, grated on her ears. She kept her eyes on the empty parking spot in front of Henny's building. The words "Spectacle You'll Remember for a Life-Time" flashed on and off in her head. "Good afternoon, this is Mrs. Margold. Could I please speak to Leonard Frankel?"

"One moment please, I'll connect you." As if from a distance far greater than the length of an office, she heard, "Mr. F., it's for you. A Mrs. Margle."

Someone picked up another extension. "Hello?"

"Leonard? It's me, Cynthia. How have you been?"

"Cynthia, what a pleasant surprise. Where are you call-ing from, the city?"

"No, I'm at home," she said. "In Brooklyn, I mean." Then, without waiting, she rushed into, "Leonard, I just wanted to know if you were still serious about that week-end thing we discussed."

"At Evans' place?"

"Yes, I've thought about it and I . . . I think that a

crash course would be a terrific challenge for me." I'll remember it for a lifetime. "Is your friend still interested?"

"Absolutely," Frankel said.

She hoped he was smiling, grinning up a storm, making a spectacle of himself. Any second the tears would start trickling splendidly and savagely and then there'd be no stopping the waves of self-pity, that sinking depressive feeling she hadn't suffered from in months. Don't, she thought. Control yourself. It's not your fault, no way is it your fault. "Will you set it up then?" she asked. "Any weekend is fine with me. My schedule's completely . . . open."

"Manny gave you the go-ahead, I take it."

"Manny thinks . . . it's a splendid idea, just adores it," savagely, with abandon. She tried not to sound bitter but she was failing miserably. "He thinks . . . yes, there won't be any problems at my end."

"I'll give Gerald a ring then, see when he's free. Probably in two weeks, I'd imagine. But I'll get back to you as soon as I hear."

"Wonderful. If I'm not home, just leave a message. Someone's usually there."

"Great. Well, I'll be in touch. I'm delighted you called. I think the weekend will be very good for you."

"I hope so. Have a good day. And," pausing for just an instant, "send my best to Jeanette."

"Will do."

When she stepped out of the phone booth, a car had pulled into the vacant parking space across the street. It wasn't pale blue. It wasn't a Ford or even a station wagon. It didn't have commercial plates, "bread and butter items" stacked up behind the front seat. It wasn't "loaded to the gills" as Manny would often say. It was just a nondescript car on an otherwise nondescript Brooklyn street, parked in front of a four-family house whose red brick facade resembled a hundred others in the neighborhood.

Upstairs, a slimmed-down manicurist who's scared to death of ending up an old maid is changing the sheets and making the bed. My best friend, can you beat that? Just another good-time girl, just another taker like all the rest. You give and you give and what do you get in return, just a lot of fancy words, that's all, one lie after another.

How could you? How could you do this to me? The both of you.

She set the bag of groceries and the oaktag at her feet. Robert Taylor and Deborah Kerr crowded their way across the marquee, splendidly savage and abandoned. She looked away, pulled out a Kleenex from her coat pocket, and wiped her eyes. They weren't even wet. The tears had merely been imagined, like a dream or a wish.

February 1965

―――――――――――――――

"So NOW I'm going to start thinking about myself for a change, because you know what gets me, what really hurts? He denied it, right down the line. He said, sure he was at Henny's apartment. But not because he's been having an affair with her. Oh no, that wasn't the reason he stopped by. It was for something else entirely."

"Such as what?" Frankel asked, both hands on the wheel.

Eyes like Kit Carson, he's so completely responsible it's unreal. At which point she replied, "Such as what did she suggest he buy me for our anniversary, that's what."

"Well, maybe he was telling the truth. Maybe you should give him the benefit of the doubt, instead of just jumping the gun, Cynthia."

"Leonard, come on," she said, visibly annoyed, piqued. "He sounded like Ricky Ricardo on *I Love Lucy*, for God sakes. Talk about phony stories. An anniversary present, my eye. Our anniversary isn't even until next month, the end of March. And believe me, he's never made a stink about it before. An issue, I mean."

"So you banished him to the living room."

"What's this 'banished' business? I didn't banish him anywhere. I just told him I didn't want to sleep with him for awhile, in the same room that is."

"That's all?"

"Yes."

"And he just took it?" Frankel asked. "Just like that? No fight, nothing?"

"No fight, nothing," she repeated. "I'm sorry I brought

191

it up. There's no reason I should subject you to my problems. It's unfair."

He reached across the seat and pressed his hand down against her knee. "You're playing games again," he said. Frankel looked at her for a moment—a mere instant that still had to count for something, she decided—before turning his eyes back to the road.

They were driving along the Hutchinson River Parkway, heading toward Purchase and a spring that still hid its face, as shy and uncertain of itself as she was. The air coming through the open window was green, alive with promises, the first tentative stirrings of growth. Crocuses, like the kids would bring home from school, bulbs planted in wax-coated milk containers, so proud of themselves. Manny has a green thumb, too. When we first met he always brought flowers. All kinds—tulips, roses of course, carnations, candytufts I think the little ones were called. Always with something in his hands. Sweets to the sweet or flowers for the flower of my heart, my life. I believed him. I loved him, too. I guess I still do, mixed in with all the . . . the other nonsense. Not hate though. No, not hate. But anger, because I'd be a real fool, a total ignoramus, if I said it wasn't true, that I wasn't angry, furious even. But you just don't stop loving, even in the midst of anger like that. You just go on. And on, and on.

C'est dommage, the pity is I want more now, more than I ever realized. "Besides," she said, "I called Henny right after I spoke to him. I asked her what kind of gift she'd suggested Manny buy me," hating playing Sherlock Holmes, but what choice did I have? I'm not naive.

"And?"

"And she didn't know what I was talking about, that's what. In the dark isn't even the word for it."

"So you're convinced?"

"Beyond a reasonable doubt," she said, trying to forget that one of Manny's favorite programs was "Perry Mason."

It's like a whirlwind, a fantasy, she decided. I feel like a little girl lost in a doll house. God, and to think I live in four rooms. This floor alone has twice that number. She wanted to bounce up and down on the bed, start to do a tap dance across the Oriental carpet. But the atmosphere of money, lots of money at that, subdued her, keeping her emotions in check. She unpacked her overnight bag and freshened up in a bathroom that was marble-floored, mirrored on all four sides.

I could use some new clothes, some sporty outfits, she thought. She did a pirouette, examining her reflection from every angle. No trace of a tummy . . . it's still hard to believe, even after all these months.

"Cynthia, are you ready?" Leonard called out.

"One sec," she said. She hurried out of the bathroom and moved swiftly toward the bedroom door. When she opened it he was standing there with his legs crossed, one elbow against the jamb, his palm against the side of his head. His eyes swept up and down her body. She felt naked, completely undressed in the space of a mere split second.

"You look pretty pleased with yourself," he said, grinning.

"I am," she said. "But there's a lot of work to do. One look at your friend and I realized I'm going to have my hands full this weekend. You were being kind when you said he was heavy."

"Shh, not so loud," he whispered.

And she whispered back, "You said he was wealthy. But he's not. He's rich. This house is incredible. It's like out of a movie. How many rooms again?"

"I'm not sure. Over twenty."

"Unbelievable." Then she was walking right alongside of him, down the hall with its dark polished wainscoting, down a flight of carpeted stairs to the first floor of the old Tudor house.

Evans, an urbane cross between Monty Woolley and Jackie Gleason, waited downstairs in the living room. The personification of a Westchester County country gentleman, he wore a tweed sports jacket with leather patches on the elbows, whipcord trousers, and soft ankle-high leather boots. A paisley scarf was tied loosely around his neck like a halfhearted ascot, while his fly-fronted shirt was the softest and most subtle shade of eggshell Cynthia had ever seen. His dress did not hide the fact that Evans was grossly overweight. No amount of custom tailoring could hide his huge pot belly and flabby barrel chest, not to mention a behind that stuck out like a seat cushion, an oversized jellyroll. Yet his face wasn't nearly as full and round as the rest of him. The fat seemed to have stopped just short of his double chin and nonexistent neck.

"Mrs. Margold," he said, extending his hand in a greeting whose warmth immediately made her feel more comfortable and at ease. "I've been looking forward to meeting you for quite some time. Leonard," and he nodded in Frankel's direction, "has been telling me how successfully your weight-reduction plan has worked for him. And judging by his appearance, I'm inclined to agree. You'll have some coffee with me, won't you? My friends should be arriving within the hour."

"I'd love some coffee," she said, thinking, He's got to be kidding, faking or something. No one talks like that except in Hollywood. He even has a phony accent, like he thinks he talks the king's English when he was probably born on Kings Highway, right near me in Brooklyn. The more she thought about it, the less surprised she became. Even as she and Leonard followed their host into the dining room, where a silver coffee service was set on the long mahogany table, it gradually dawned on her that many overweight people she had known in the past had also played games with themselves. Many, in fact, had assumed strange roles, all designed—at least in their estimation—to detract from their obesity. One thing was certain; Evans wasn't just overweight. He was obese, probably close to three hundred pounds. No wonder he fancies himself a fat James Mason. What else does he have going for him but a lot of money and no one to spend it on.

She was still sorry Henny could not have come along. Something, a sixth sense of human understanding perhaps, told her they would have hit it off very well together, despite their considerably different social and economic situations. But now it was too late for that, too late for good deeds, matchmaking, favors for friends.

After an exhausting afternoon of nonstop talking, she finally relinquished the floor to Leonard so she could catch her breath. She sensed that Gerald Evans' carefully groomed and manicured façade had cracked around the edges. His cultivated veneer seemed in danger of peeling off, falling by the wayside. Underneath, she detected a man who hid his uncertainties and self-doubts beneath all the trappings and paraphernalia of the high life, the

194

good life. But if the truth were known, she would not have minded a taste of it herself.

At dinner the cook served all the wrong things, but she kept her mouth shut, not about to spoil what had otherwise been a nearly perfect afternoon. Evans and his friends had finally begun to talk about their eating habits, sad and sometimes amusing stories about their particular "misadventures" with food. She felt the groundwork had been laid and she didn't want to spoil any of the good work she—and Leonard, too—had accomplished.

"Tomorrow I shall begin," Evans promised, raising a Venetian wineglass filled with a fine old claret. Cynthia didn't know if it was either fine or old, but Frankel had whispered how his friend kept one of the best-stocked wine cellars in Westchester County. "But now, let's all enjoy ourselves. Don't you agree, Cynthia?"

Ignoring the curious eyes of the other guests, sorry too that she hadn't brought along a dressier outfit, something more suitable for a formal dinner party, she said, "I think people should have a good time, Gerald. But sticking to the diet and still having fun aren't necessarily in opposition to each other; they don't have to clash, I mean. You can have one with the other. It's just a matter of self-control."

His guests said nothing.

"Your friend never lets up, does she, Leonard?" Evans said, trying to smile.

"She's not supposed to, Gerald. She has to set some sort of example. If she didn't, what would be the point of this entire weekend," Frankel replied.

"Well, I don't think we should talk about losing weight for the rest of the evening," one of the guests (whose rubies Cynthia couldn't help but covet) announced, toasting Evans with an upraised glass. "We've heard so much this afternoon, I'd just like time for it to all sink in."

She smiled and lowered her eyes. She picked at her food, not nearly as hungry as she had first thought. Two years ago I would have eaten everything in sight. How strange. Now it just doesn't do it to me. Maybe it was a mistake coming. They're not here to lose weight. It's more of a social function. Who knows, maybe they're all laughing at me, thinking it's just one of Evans' crazy little jokes, a new way to spend a weekend in the country.

She wanted to get up and excuse herself, but that would have been rude and she didn't want to embarrass either Leonard or herself. After all, she was still a guest in Evans' home, even if he had taken her aside earlier that evening to press a check into her unwilling hands. "You've done more good than you can imagine, Mrs. Margold," he had said. "This is just a small token, just to cover your expenses."

"What expenses? I had no expenses, Mr. Evans. Leonard drove me up. Please, I didn't accept your invitation because I was going to get paid for it."

"Then consider it mad money. Buy yourself a present; you deserve it." He turned away, leaving her with the neatly folded bank check still held loosely, uncertainly, in her hands. Later, alone in her room before getting ready for dinner, she unfolded the check she had stuffed between her papers. PAY TO THE ORDER OF CYNTHIA MARGOLD. $150.00. All that Leonard had said at lunch, several weeks before, came back to her. *You're performing a service . . . people get paid for their time.* But still, $150 is going overboard. Fifty, before I left, that I could see. But not three times that amount. I'm just talking from the heart, telling them things that I really feel, that I really believe in. Why should I get paid just to be honest?

"Because," Leonard said hours later as the two of them sat alone in the living room after Evans and the other guests had retired for the night, "you're doing more than just being honest, Cynthia. That's what I tried to tell you when we had lunch together. I'm not saying to suddenly start charging everyone five bucks a meeting. You'd price yourself right out of the market. People couldn't afford that much. But what's going to happen when more people hear about your work? What's going to happen when there are twenty people calling you from New Jersey, say—desperate for someone like you to talk to them? You're going to drop everything and run to Newark, or wherever they are? Of course not. You won't be able to, it's as simple as that. There's a limit to how much one person can do. I mean, even by coming up here this weekend, you had to get one of your friends to cover for you. But if you start hiring people, ex-members who've reached their goal weight, for example, you can establish the nucleus of a staff—"

"A staff for what?"

"Cynthia, the country is hungry for something like this, don't you see? It's ready for you. It's wide open. Up to now you've restricted yourself to Brooklyn, with a foray into Westchester and Long Island. But imagine what it would be like if there were classes held all over the country. There are fat people in Cleveland too, you know. And in Chicago, L.A., Miami."

"And how does this all get going, this . . . this scheme of yours?" she said. "With what money, for starters?"

"You know why you're cynical? Because you're scared, you're afraid. But what the fuck are you so afraid of, that's what I want to know? Not twenty-four hours ago, less even, you were telling me how you're on the verge of a divorce. Can Manny afford to pay you alimony, to pay two rents at once? Can he? The truth, Cynthia."

"No." She got up from the couch and remembered a film she had seen years ago when she was Tilden High School's favorite fat girl. Alone in the balcony of the Loew's theater on Pitkin Avenue, she had sat with a jumbo-sized box of buttered popcorn, letting the tears stream down her cheeks. Fredric March had just returned home. The moment Myrna Loy saw him standing by the doorway, Cynthia had felt total empathy, total understanding. When Myrna Loy trembled, she trembled. When Myrna Loy cried out and ran to her long-absent husband, she too had wanted to cry out, to jump up from her seat into the arms of someone she loved more than anyone else in the world. It was *The Best Years of Our Lives,* the worst years of mine, she had thought. There was no stopping her. Never before had she felt love coming off the screen with so much fervor, so much intensity it left her weak with a sense of her own emptiness. She had decided, then and there, never to compromise, to fall in love with someone to whom she would feel that selfsame devotion, that heartrending teary-eyed loyalty. Then Manny had come along two years later. There had never been a time for tears after that. We ate our way through our courtship, our honeymoon, our first thirteen anniversaries.

"This room, this entire house in fact, is a perfect movie set," she said, her back to him. "Why don't you be Paul Henreid and light my cigarette? I can stand by the fireplace watching the flames crackle and someone can be playing the violin in the background."

"And then what?"

She heard him getting to his feet, felt the heat of the fire, the glowing coals, the flickering flames that were like snapping bluish tongues saying things she didn't want to hear. His hands were on her waist, urging her slowly around. Isn't it what I wanted, from the very first? she asked herself, even as his lips pressed down against her mouth. No longer a schoolgirl, she didn't melt in his arms. She wasn't carried away, transported to some silver-screen realm of filmed caresses and Technicolor ecstasy. She knew exactly where she was and what she was doing.

"Come," he said. He took her hand. Her fingers felt lost in his, his grip strong and yet gentle, too. "It's time for bed."

She laughed to hide her fears. "Are you going to tuck me in, tell me a story before turning out the light?"

"I'm going to tuck both of us in. And I'm going to leave the light on. I want to be able to look at you. I'm the last person in the world who's afraid of the dark."

"What are you thinking about, Leonard?"

"You."

"No you're not. You're just saying that."

"To be nice?"

"Maybe."

"No, I'm too honest for that."

"How can anyone be too honest?"

"It's easy. Come, snuggle up to me. That's it. Feel okay?"

"Very."

"That's the way it should be."

"Tell me."

"About honesty?"

"Yes."

"It's not an overrated virtue, contrary to popular opinion."

"You're making fun—"

"I am not. How could I ever make fun of you, Mrs. Margold?"

"That sounds very nice, comforting."

"Then I'm glad."

"I know you feel good."

"But are you glad?"

"I don't know," she said. "You're the first—"

"No," he said. "The second."

Late the following afternoon, Cynthia sat in the living room with Leonard and Gerald Evans. The other guests had departed after she had given them a last frantic and determined pep talk. She had no way of knowing if the crash course had been a success, but judging from her host's ebullient mood, he was more than pleased with her performance.

"There's something I've been meaning to discuss with you, Cynthia," Evans said as he sat across from her. "Have you ever given thought to incorporating, making this a going operation?"

"Making what?" she said, though by now she knew what he was referring to, thanks to Leonard's little impromptu lecture the night before.

"Your classes. I happen to think it would be a very sound business venture. Wouldn't you be inclined to agree with me, Leonard?"

"Cynthia has no desire to exploit the overweight."

She shot a puzzled glance at him. His expression remained stony, unchanged. That's a switch, she thought. Last night he couldn't get me to go public quick enough. This afternoon he's down on the very same idea. I wonder what got him to change his mind.

"Well, I wouldn't call it exploitation," Evans said with a laugh that made his stomach shake and jiggle. "Would you, Cynthia?"

"What?" she asked, smiling as if it were the thing to do.

"Do you think it would be capitalizing on the fact that there are thousands of overweight men and women in this country, all eager to be just as slim and trim as you two are?"

"I don't get what you're driving at, Gerald."

"What I'm driving at, my dear, is that you should seriously consider incorporating, establishing this as a growing business. Certainly there's no reason to think your good works should stop in Brooklyn. Why limit yourself that way? Why deprive others of your skills, your know-how? Imagine if there were weight-reduction classes held throughout the country. You could become a very wealthy woman, independently wealthy I might add, in no time at all. And it's an original idea, that's the main point. It hasn't been done before. The public is ripe for this kind of operation."

"Cynthia does this for her own personal self-satisfaction, Gerald. Her husband makes a very fine living, as a matter of fact. She certainly isn't wanting for very many things at all."

"I didn't mean to imply that Mr. Margold—"

"We're quite comfortable, Gerald," she interrupted. "My husband does very well for himself." Then she made a point of looking at her watch. "Leonard, I promised Forman I'd be back before five. We're going to get caught in all the Sunday traffic unless we get going."

"You're right. I forgot," he said. He got quickly to his feet.

Cynthia, not even sure why she'd played the scene the way she had, the way Leonard obviously wanted it to be enacted, joined him in saying goodbye to Gerald Evans.

"Think about it anyway, Cynthia," he told her as she waited for Leonard to bring the car around to the front of the house. "I have a considerable amount of capital at my disposal. I'd be more than eager to invest in your future."

"Thank you very much, Gerald. That's very kind of you. But I don't think it's in the cards. Not for now, anyway."

"Well, if you change your mind, you know how to get in touch with me."

"And if you have any trouble sticking to the diet, you have my number. Please feel free to use it."

"Let's hope I won't need to." He laughed heartily, too heartily for her to believe he was serious about losing weight, following the suggestions she had given him and his friends.

It's all a game, she thought. And maybe this entire weekend was just a setup, just to lead into our last conversation. Just a business proposition. I hate that word and why the hell did Leonard act the way he did, that's what I'd like to know.

"Simply because I didn't bring you up here to become Gerald Evans' business partner, that's why," he explained once they were alone in the car, heading back toward the city.

"But *you'd* like to be my partner, wouldn't you?"

"You're damn right I would," he admitted. "But I care about you, Cynthia. He cares about what you can do for him. There's a difference. I had a feeling he'd pull this kind of shit with you. I wasn't wrong, either."

"Well, the man has money to burn, so what do you expect," though it still amazes me how they're all so anxious to get in on the ground floor. Maybe they have something there. Maybe I should start thinking about making a lot of money, instead of worrying about taking advantage of people. Even if I charged a dollar a meeting everyone would still be able to afford it. And maybe Leonard has a point when he says there are people in Cleveland, Chicago, all the big cities in fact—and the smaller ones too, probably—who'd jump at the chance of getting the kind of help I've been able to give people in Brooklyn. If there were ex-members lecturing all over the country, running . . . what do they call it? Franchises, that's the term. What if successful ex-members ran classes in every big city, giving the same pep talks and good sound advice I give in Brooklyn? But who ever heard of a nationwide chain of schools for the overweight? It's ridiculous. The whole idea just doesn't seem plausible.

"I'm going to get in touch with my attorney, find out what you'd have to do to incorporate," Leonard told her. "I have some money put aside I can invest. Not as much as Evans, but there's no reason we have to start big. We can take everything step by step, one thing at a time."

"We?" she said. "I haven't agreed to anything yet, Leonard, just remember that. Everyone's giving me the bum's rush and I don't like it. I didn't start this thing just to become a millionaire."

"But it would be nice, wouldn't it?" Then he began to grin. His voice seemed too loud, booming out at her. His smile was frozen in place, recalling the gaping jaws of a shark. "And then you wouldn't have to worry about dirtying your hands with alimony suits or buying your clothes only when they're on sale. And wouldn't it be nice to know there was a bank account with enough money for your kids' college education, enough money for your mother to have her own place again. Well, wouldn't it, Cynthia?"

There was no sense kidding herself. "Yes," she said. "It would be very nice to have all those things, that kind of security, Leonard. But you have to sacrifice something to get it, isn't that the way life works? You always have to give up something—"

"What do you have that you're so afraid of losing?"

Self-respect, she thought. Or maybe just peace of mind.

May–July 1965

BUSIER THAN EVER BEFORE, Cynthia moved through the days and weeks of spring without looking back. She didn't want to retrace her footsteps, returning to a time when images and memories were sharp and unpleasant, filled with bitter words, snide and stinging asides. Instead, she looked into the future, which, at least in Leonard Frankel's estimation, was hers for the asking. *Wide open* seemed the word of the hour. He always repeated it to her, trying to drum into her head that there was more going for her than the daily classes held at the storefront on Rutland Road. Yet she was still reluctant, afraid to make what she saw as the big plunge, to transform herself from the ardent energetic amateur into the profit-conscious and diligent professional.

Despite the fact that they now saw each other once and sometimes twice a week, she still managed to keep a cool front whenever he started in on her. His harangues had reached a predictable point. She knew his arguments and beseeching by heart, just as she knew his body and the ways of his lovemaking. She realized he was there for her, but she was still not ready to accept his other more businesslike demands. For the moment she was content, anxious to avoid unpleasant scenes, anxious to maintain the precarious balance of harmony she and Manny had settled into. He now slept in the living room, having relinquished his bed to Lena, his marriage rights—unknowingly—to Leonard Frankel. She knew that Barry and Natalie were aware of the growing rift between their parents, though they said little if anything about it to either of them. "I can't break up my home, not yet anyway," she told Leonard. She never asked him if he was considering divorcing Jeanette, or even pressing for a separation. If anything, she avoided all talk of his wife, though she knew that the first (and perhaps the only, she often wondered) Mrs. Frankel had slimmed down to an amazingly attractive size ten, a metamorphosis as complete and unequivocal as her own considerable weight loss.

If you don't think about any of it, it won't bother you, she told herself that spring. Yet change was in the air, whether she wanted to accept it or not. She knew she couldn't continue playing games with herself. By the end of May her defenses had weakened, her arguments grew more feeble, less spirited, less determined. There really was no reason to fear incorporation. And rumor had begun to spread, to get back to her, that Manny and Henny were still seeing each other as she had suspected months before. She made no attempt to stop them, nor break it up. After all, she was having an affair with Leonard, so it would have been hypocritical to impose a double standard of morality on her husband, declaring his adulterous conduct unacceptable when she was behaving precisely the same way with someone else.

In late May she was approached by a man who introduced himself as Richard Jameson. The Tuesday evening meeting had ended. The members were filing out, animated and excited as they talked among themselves. Cynthia was putting her papers away when a young man who clearly had no difficulty maintaining his weight stepped in front of her desk and handed her a card by way of introduction.

"Channel 7? Oh, now I remember," she said. "I've seen you on the news."

"We'd like to see you on the news, too, Mrs. Margold," he said with a grin she found as infectious as his collegiate good looks and confident bearing.

"I beg your pardon?"

"Perhaps you've seen the Sunday evening show I do for the local network, 'Faces & Places.'"

"The name's familiar. I don't watch much television to tell you the truth. I just don't have the time." She looked over his shoulder. "Goodnight, Viv, Doris. See you Thursday."

"Goodnight, Cynthia. You were wonderful. You had them in the palm of your hand."

"You really did," Jameson agreed. "Mind if I take a seat?"

"Oh please, I'm sorry." She swept the papers off the chair alongside her desk and motioned him to sit down. Then, when she, too, had taken a seat, Jameson told her how he happened to come to her meeting.

"We've been hearing rumors about your work, Mrs. Margold. Very good reports, I might add. I think there's a story here, a half-hour TV special. You see, 'Faces & Places' is aired for a New York audience. We concern ourselves with people who live in and around the city, who make the metropolitan area their home, individuals who are doing vital and important things with their lives. Your work with the overweight has begun to attract a considerable amount of attention and I'd like to get your permission to be the subject of one of the shows I produce and narrate."

"You can't be serious," she said. She glanced at the card he had handed her. There was nothing frivolous about it. It was right there in black and white. RICHARD JAMESON, ABC-TV.

"Oh, I'm completely serious. We'd like to get our camera crew in here and film one of your meetings, film you at home too, if that's okay with you. There must be hundreds of people in New York who could use the kind of help you've been giving here in Brooklyn. What better way to acquaint them with your methods than by showing you in . . . in operation, so to speak. As I see it now, there'll be some brief introductory remarks and then we'll turn the cameras over to you, show you in action. Then, toward the end of the program, I could interview you here or at the studio, whichever you prefer, though I like to keep 'Faces & Places' as much out on the streets as possible, if you know what I mean."

"I know what you mean," she said with a nervous laugh, "but I don't believe what you mean. Say this again. You want me to be the subject of a TV show, is that it? A half-hour TV show devoted to Cynthia Margold?"

He nodded his head, flashed a grin of even white teeth, and reached into the inside pocket of his blue blazer. He pulled out a bulging white envelope, removed its contents, and spread them flat on the desk before her. "This is just a standard contract, more of a release than anything else," he said. "Because 'Faces & Places' is just an adjunct of our local news coverage, I'm afraid we have a rather tight budget, limited funding from the network. But it's standard procedure to pay our subjects minimum Equity rates. The scale is somewhere between three and four hundred dollars."

She looked down at the contract and then at Jameson. He was still giving her an All-American grin and she recalled having seen him on the news less than a week before. "You're better looking in person," she said. "You're their drama critic too, aren't you?"

"Only on occasion. They're grooming me for the job, you might say," he replied. He found a gold fountain pen in the opposite inside pocket, uncapped it and laid it out before her. "But 'Faces & Places' is my real baby. It's a show that I think is really in touch with the people, with . . . well . . . faces and places I guess is as good a way as any to describe it, which are important to New Yorkers. As a representative of the network, Mrs. Margold, I can assure you that we're all inclined to agree that what you've been doing here in Crown Heights and East New York is *very* important. And we want our viewers to know about it."

"How did you hear about me, actually?"

"As a matter of fact, the credit should go to my secretary. A couple of weeks ago she received a phone call from one of your ex-members, a businessman who lives out in . . . Manhattan Beach I believe. He spoke so highly of you and felt your work was of such importance, that she relayed the information to me. I sent one of my assistants out here last week—a young man with a weight problem, by the way. Well, all I can say is, he came back praising you to the skies."

"You'd like me to sign? Now?" she asked, still incredulous, though not about Leonard's involvement in the entire affair.

"If you don't mind. As I said, it's a standard contract. We just like to get the paperwork out of the way, you understand. There's no small print, nothing to worry about. It just gives us permission to film and use your name, that's all. You won't have to worry about script approval because you can tell us exactly what you don't want us to shoot. The contract's been made out in triplicate. Again, that's just standard procedure."

"You can shoot anything you want," she said. "I mean,

206

I don't have anything to hide. I'd just like to get my apartment in order—"

"We won't be doing any of the actual footage for several weeks. And if it'll make you feel any better, I'll arrange for one of our studio set decorators to come to your home, liven it up a little, if you like," he said, smiling diplomatically.

It needs a lot more than just some livening up, she thought. But she appreciated his tact. Without another word, she reached for the fountain pen, recalling the day she had gone for a bank loan, right after her father's death. I'm the one with the magic wand these days, Flynn. Isn't that a switch.

"Aren't you going to read it first?" he asked. "Look it over at least?"

"What for? If you can't trust ABC, who *can* you trust." He still monitored a plastic video grin as she waved the pen in the air and then wrote her name with a flourish. Her hand had never been more steady, her signature more legible. Her mind had never been more set, than at that moment. It's what you'd call a turning point, she told herself. If ever someone's been given a sign, this has to be it. You might just say the gods have spoken. So who am I to disagree?

The camera crew arrived after the Fourth of July weekend. Jameson said, "Let's get one of your meetings down on film before anything else. After all, it's the focal point of the show, the major interest. The thing I most want to emphasize."

A dozen men and women clustered around Cynthia's desk and demanded to be heard.

"What is going on around here, that's what I want to know?"

"Cynthia, who are these people, all these wires, and those lights overhead?"

"Is that a television camera? I don't want to be seen on television. I don't want people to look at me and see how—you know. I've only lost eight pounds. I still have more than fifty to go."

"What are you all so worried about?" Cynthia said.

"They're going to put us on display? Who gave them permission?"

"I did," she said weakly.

"You did? Cynthia, how could you? I'm going home. This is ridiculous. We come here because there's privacy, our kind of people. We don't have to feel ashamed, feel like . . . like freaks in a sideshow. Isn't that what you always tell us?"

"Yes."

"Well, what kind of privacy do you call that . . . that evil eye over there?" and the woman, as heavy as Cynthia had been that January over two years before, turned her head around and jabbed a pointing finger in the direction of the television camera. "I for one will not be subjected to . . . to scrutiny."

Others joined in. Loud, increasingly irate, directing their annoyance at her and no one else. She pulled Jameson aside, asked for a few minutes to be alone with her members, realizing she should have said something earlier, prepared them in advance. "Have the boys take a smoke outside," she said. "I'll get them to cooperate, don't worry. But just understand, Dick. People who are heavy have more problems than just their weight. They're all very shy, self-conscious."

"It's understandable," he said. He turned to his crew. "Guys, drop everything for a few minutes. I want to talk to you outside."

Cynthia made her way back to the front of the room. She waited for the door to close before trying to quiet everyone down. "I'll explain everything," she said, "if you'd just give me the courtesy of listening instead of . . . yakking away like a bunch of chickens who've lost their heads." She sat down at her desk and folded her hands, waiting for the fifty men and women to give her their attention. When there was silence—however sullen—she got to her feet, moved around, and leaned against the front of the desk.

"It's hard to believe how selfish all of you have become," she said, pinning down as many blustery faces as she could. Her eyes were narrowed, piercing. She stared at one member after another, refusing to accept defeat, to give up without a fight. "It's really incredible, you know that. I thought you cared about people, above and beyond just thinking of yourselves."

"What does that have to do with anything?" a woman

208

in the back yelled out. She was immediately seconded by those around her.

"I'll tell you exactly what it has to do with," she replied. "That camera over there belongs to Channel 7. They own that and the wires you've been tripping over and the lights strung up along the ceiling. They also schedule a program each Sunday evening called 'Faces & Places.' It's about New Yorkers, for New Yorkers. They want to do a show about me, about us, and that's why they're here this evening."

The door swung open. She half-expected to see Jameson stick his head inside, waiting to get the go-ahead signal. Instead, she smiled to herself as Leonard Frankel closed the door softly behind him. With a barely noticeable wink he caught her eye, then silently took a seat.

"But all that really has nothing to do with you, right? Wrong!" she said. "Tell me something, Adele." She pointed to one of the women who had been loudest a few minutes before. "How did you find out about these meetings?"

"Me?" she said, as though she were on trial, having been accused of some terrible and heinous crime.

"Yes, you, Adele."

"I . . . I heard about them from a friend of a friend."

"And you, Charlie O'Hara, who once told us he'd sooner die than give up Hostess cupcakes—"

"Twinkies," came the beefy voice from the rear.

There was general laughter and she smiled, sensing the mood had begun to change, however slightly. "Okay, Twinkies . . . I was a Fig Newton freak myself. But seriously now. How did you hear about our get-togethers?"

"The brother-in-law of a cousin of mine told me about them."

"Thank you. It was all through word-of-mouth, that's what I'm trying to bring out. I don't advertise. I don't put notices in the papers. You all found your way to Rutland Road through the good word of friends and relatives and neighbors. Well, what about the hundreds of overweight men and women all over the city who haven't been as lucky as you? Well, what about them? How are they going to get any help, may I ask? That's why I said you were selfish. The goddamn TV camera isn't even going to show your faces, for your information. Just your

209

backs. I made that clear to them before they even arrived this evening. And now you have the gall . . . it's downright audacity how do you like that, to sit there and complain? You want to know something? I've never patted myself on the back, not once. But I will tonight. I may regret what I'm going to say, but I'm going to say it anyway.

"You should kiss the ground I walk on, that there's someone who's not pumping your system full of diet pills or charging you an arm and a leg for phony advice and quack cures. This store isn't a shrine. It's not holy. We don't sell miracles here. We all do it by hard work, just remember that. So how dare you sit there and tell me you want your privacy? I want those hundreds, those thousands if that's the case, of overweight people in this town to know that they're not alone, that they can be helped, that there's a way to lose weight. Painlessly and easily. And most important, safely. There isn't a doctor you've spoken to who hasn't said anything but the most favorable things about this diet. It was written by doctors, nutritionists—" She stopped, cleared her throat. No one stirred. No one said a word.

"So I can't believe for one minute that any of you, *all* of you as a matter of fact, are sorry you ever decided to come here and try to lose weight. Are you going to deny that same right to someone else, just because they haven't been lucky to find out about what happens here on Rutland Road? Well, are you? Because if you are, I'll send these men from Channel 7 back to the studio and we can just continue where we left off. So it's up to you now. I bust my backside for all of you and when I ask a favor, a little cooperation—"

Leonard started to clap. Even then, she had no way of knowing if his approval was self-serving. But as the applause came back to her she stopped, just long enough to catch her breath. She felt angry, hurt as well. Someone joined him and then someone else.

"A show of hands," she said. "All those who want the camera crew to stay please raise your hands." The chairs creaked, seams strained, fabric pulled as hands were raised aloft. "All those opposed?" She waited, smiling to herself. "I think the ayes have it." She hadn't expected almost unanimous approval. But that was exactly what they had given her. Leonard got up, opened the door and stepped outside.

"Thank you," she said. "We'll go on with the roll, if that's okay with you. And just remember, the camera won't be able to see any faces. That's a promise."

The meeting continued, and ten minutes later the camera crew was hard at work. Under the heat of the arc lights mounted on the ceiling, she felt droplets of perspiration trickling down her back, her sides. The storefront was yet to be air-conditioned and with the door closed to keep out the curious, the air became close and oppressive. Somehow, the mugginess wasn't nearly as stifling as it might have been. Somehow, it just didn't seem to matter. She'd made her point. It wasn't a victory nor a personal triumph. She meant every word she had said. Now, the only thing that worried her was how she would be able to accommodate the scores of people who would undoubtedly show up at Rutland Road, eager and desperate and clamoring for a chance to try out her methods. The only solution was one Leonard had already given her.

If the public response was going to be anything like she imagined, as Jameson and Frankel had predicted, she had no other choice but to go ahead and start opening up other branches.

And that means incorporating. And that means making Leonard a partner. It means I'm in this over my head. Sink or swim, Cynthia, win or lose. That's the name of the game because it's all up to you now. I don't have to be a nobody from Brooklyn. I've got my work, maybe my whole life cut out for me. But it's not going to be easy, that's for sure.

BOOK TWO:

The New Body

September 1965

"WHY DON'T WE GO AWAY, just for a weekend? Up to the mountains somewhere, or even Atlantic City? If you want to know the truth, Leonard, I miss the Holiday Inn. It used to feel like home."

"I just don't have the time, love, and neither do you. There's too much to do."

Several things stood out in her mind during the Indian summer of their incorporation. She missed weekday afternoons, no lunch but a room with a double bed at the Holiday Inn on lower Broadway. Now, there was neither time for lovemaking nor time for even a modicum of privacy, intimacy together. She never called him anything but Leonard, Frankel only on occasion. But it was never Lenny or Len or anything soft and diminutive. Only Leonard, one of two partners who owned Dreamtime Togs, and now one of two partners who had established what was legally and officially and henceforth to be known as the C & L Corporation. Cynthia was President, Leonard her moneyed VP. He provided the capital and she provided the know-how. They had decided to work it out that way but as things became more complicated, she missed the simplicity of her former status. She wasn't Cynthia Margold who spoke on Rutland Road. Now she was in charge of two branches, with a third already in the works.

She was billed as "A One-Woman Crusade" on the "Faces & Places" episode which had been aired to a city languishing through a late-August heat wave. But the uncomfortably hot muggy weather didn't seem to prevent people from turning on their sets, watching the documentary footage, watching Cynthia in action. At home she had stared in disbelief, finding it hard to accept the fact that there she was, right there in black and white, saying, "Fat is just a state of mind." Saying, "It's time you discovered who's hidden underneath all that excess poundage." Saying, "I never would have been able to do it without the love and cooperation I got from my family."

"Boy, you really put one over on them," Manny said with a laugh that was more derisive than amused.

Natalie giggled in tempo and said, "It doesn't even sound like mother."

She talks like I'm not in the room, like I'm dead already, Cynthia thought to herself. She gripped the arms of the club chair and kept her eyes glued to the flickering images passing across the screen. Manny and Natalie sat side by side on the couch. Lena had dragged in a chair from the kitchen, while Barry was curled up at Cynthia's feet.

"You're fantastic, mom. Boy, do you come off sounding smart," he said. "I just can't believe it's you, that you're really on TV. I told all my friends about it, when to watch, everything."

She reached down and tousled his hair. My most loyal fan, she thought. At least he hasn't forgotten who his best friend is, the one who'd do just about anything to keep him happy.

When there was a break for commercials, Manny got to his feet, yawned, and stretched his arms above his head. "I'm gonna take a walk," he announced. "You want to go to the park with your pop, Nat?"

Lena turned her head back, even before Natalie literally jumped to her feet. "What, you're not going to stay to see the rest? How often does your mother get to be on TV, Natalie?"

"Let her go, mom," Cynthia hissed. It was a hiss because she remembered for weeks afterwards how the words had started to explode inside of her, only to be repressed, held back between clenched teeth. The anger and hurt feelings had no way of escaping. She kept them back, along with the harsh biting words she'd stopped herself from saying.

"You look stunning," Lena said. The words rushed out,

216

as though she were trying to erase the sound of the door, slamming shut behind her son-in-law, her granddaughter. "Who did your hair? It looks wonderful. I never thought Leon's did such good work."

"I didn't go to Leon," she said while her other self, her filmed counterpart, told Richard Jameson that, "Anybody can lose weight if they really want to, if they really start being honest with themselves." "I went to a new shop, over on Empire Boulevard." She wasn't about to have her hair done at the same place where Henny worked. She wasn't about to subject herself to playing at cold shoulders, at turning the other cheek. They can do whatever they goddamn please, just as long as they keep it out of my home. It was *my* home, not ours. The difference wasn't nearly as subtle as even Cynthia would have liked to think.

But then there were other things to worry about.

The phone began to ring, even before the credits rolled across the screen, even before there was a station break, time for the network to identify itself. They called from as far away as Stamford, Connecticut, as near as down the block and around the corner. "Where do I sign up?" "When can I start?" "What do I have to do?" The following evening she arrived at Rutland Road not to confront hordes, not a desperate clamorous stampede, but at least fifty men and women, ready, willing and eager to enroll, right then and there.

Now, as Indian summer lingered with the color of wheat toast, the streets once again alive and littered after the Labor Day weekend, she sat at her desk and tried not to think about anything which might draw up images of family strife or marital discord. It was a new desk in a new office. A real office, not just a space in the back of a narrow, hastily painted storefront. With Vivian Hollander's help, she had tabulated the addresses of all the people who had called or written or who had arrived to find there wasn't even standing room at Rutland Road. The largest percentage of those interested in joining her classes lived in the Flatbush section of Brooklyn, an Italian-Irish-Jewish middle-class neighborhood cut down the middle by the busy thoroughfare of Flatbush Avenue. It was here that they rented a large spacious room with an adjoining office. A real-estate agency had leased the space before them, the second floor of a three-story building located near the corner of Flatbush Avenue and Glenwood Road, not far from Brooklyn College.

Now, they were already up to their ears in work. Within a week, Cynthia and Doris Bauer—now a fully salaried assistant—had signed up over two hundred men and women. The four classes currently being scheduled each week —two in the evening and two during the day—were nearly full. A fifth class for teenagers was in the works, as was a third branch to be opened in Queens, probably Forest Hills if they could find a suitable location. Meanwhile, the storefront on Rutland Road continued to turn away both the idly curious and the genuinely interested, directing them to Flatbush Avenue. Motivated by the seventy-five dollars the C & L Corporation was paying her each week, Vivian had taken over the bulk of the work in Crown Heights. Already she begged Cynthia for a helper, swamped with the job of running the classes almost entirely by herself.

Cynthia lectured three nights a week, two evenings on Flatbush Avenue and one evening to her "regulars" on Rutland Road. The phrase, "there just aren't enough hours in the day," constantly passed through her thoughts. There was always something to do and attend to. When she wasn't working in her office or speaking before a group of eager-eyed men and women, she traveled throughout the city, giving the kind of free advice and encouragement she had given the year before. Everywhere she went she was asked, "When will you open up in our neighborhood, Mrs. Margold?" "I know of fifty people right here in Jackson Heights who'll sign up tomorrow." "Mrs. Margold, there are chubbies in Yonkers too, don't forget." "Jersey City's on the map, too, you know. We need help out here, desperately."

"Soon," she kept repeating. "You're not forgotten, believe me. It just takes time. Just try to be patient. I'll come out here in two weeks to speak to you again, I promise."

At Leonard's insistence, she had been forced to raise her prices. They were now charging $1.50 per meeting, but this increase in cost didn't make anyone turn away. Membership climbed. Again, as she had experienced when she had first rented the storefront in her neighborhood, there was no sign of a leveling off, no indication that a plateau would soon be reached. Enrollment mounted as steadily as the young corporation's profits.

"It's like a dream, isn't it, Cynthia? A fantasy come true," Doris Bauer said on one September evening, an evening after a day which had been even more hectic than most. That morning, Cynthia had spoken to a packed crowd in Jericho, Long Island. Sixty women jostled each other for space in someone's furnished basement. Then, in the afternoon, she had conducted one of her regular classes on Flatbush Avenue. Now, she still had her hands full with paperwork. Doris continued, "Hard to believe that from a handful of fat women it would have grown so . . . so rapidly. It makes me dizzy, all the excitement."

"It makes me tired," she replied. "It seems like I haven't had a minute to myself."

"Well, even though you're going to tell me there isn't enough money, you could use a regular secretary, someone to handle all the busywork. And now with all this bookkeeping . . . it's too much for a two-girl office."

She had to smile then, amused at her friend's choice of words. "A two-girl office," she repeated. "Yep, that's us, all right. But just keep one thing in mind, Doris. We used to weigh enough for four."

"It's the one thing in the world I don't think I'll ever forget," Doris replied. She sighed loudly, rapped her knuckles against the nearest wooden surface, and finished applying her lipstick. When she was done she dropped the lipstick in her purse and snapped it shut. "I still have to cook dinner tonight. God," and she shook her head, "where does all the time go? Seems like I just walked in here ten minutes ago."

"Get home safe," Cynthia said.

"You too. G'night." The door closed behind her.

She remained at her desk, her eyes blurring as she confronted the long list of names which lay before her. You're having a good time, so what are you complaining about now? she thought. And you're clearing over a hundred dollars a week, on top of everything else. Before you know it you'll have money in the bank, money to do with as you please, money to use to . . . to move out if need be. If that's what you want.

I love you, Cynthia. I love the way you look, the way

you talk. I love the way you feel when I'm deep inside you, part of you. We can do so much together, so much for each other. You weren't meant for Brooklyn; the world is a hell of a lot bigger than a four-room apartment. You can have anything, baby, anything you want.

"Sonuvabitch," she whispered. What lines he gave me, what absolutely ridiculous cliches. But I fell for them. Oh boy, and how. And now you're having dinner in Manhattan Beach with the love of your life—ha, while I'm busting my brains out, trying to get this whole thing organized, on the right kind of footing. Why aren't you here tonight? Why aren't you sitting alongside of me, helping me tally all these numbers, total up all the moneys? Why, because you're quick to put your hand in your pocket when it comes to laying out cash, but when it comes to laying your feelings on the line it's another story altogether. If you only knew why I did this, Leonard. It was as much for you as it was for me, Mr. Frankel. You pressured me into it, with all your stories. Sure, Doris was right. I did think it would be like some kind of dream, a fairy tale. Once upon a time in the kingdom of Crown Heights there lived a merry roly-poly fat girl, Cynthia the Blimp. The charming Chubby Margold. She was loved near and far . . .

She reached for the phone, crossed out the number she'd unconsciously scribbled across a piece of scrap paper, and dialed as automatically as she signed her name. "Hi. Yes, busy busy, all day without a letup. Good, I'm glad, mom. Is my kid there? Barry," of course. "Could you put him on?" She heard Lena call the boy's name. A moment later a breathy adolescent voice, still cracking in the upper and lower registers, was heard at the other end. "How'd you like to come down here this evening and have Chinese with me? Lobster cantonese, you name it. Anything you want, it'll be my pleasure." She listened for a moment and then interrupted to say, "Well, can't you put it off for a couple of hours, honey? I'll tell you what, grandma'll give you money for a taxi so you won't have to wait for the bus. How's that? Then when we're done, you can go right back home and finish your studying. Well . . . tell her to wrap it in aluminum foil. It'll keep. I'll talk to her. You know how to get here, don't you?"

An hour later she sat across from her most loyal fan,

220

her staunchest ally. "Now just because I reopened that charge account at Brooks Brothers doesn't mean you can go haywire, Barry," she said. "A couple of sweaters, maybe some shirts and a new pair of pants, okay. But you don't need a suit . . . not this year, anyway. Next year, when you've grown some more, you can have your pick, I promise you. And has your mother ever broken a promise? Come on, have I?"

"No," he said. He put down the menu and folded his hands in his lap. "I'll have the lobster cantonese . . . no, the lobster soong. With wonton soup and pork fried rice. What'll you have, mom?"

"Jumbo shrimp with Chinese vegetables, number seven."

"Is it allowed?"

"Of course it is. I can show you where it's right on the diet, right there in black and white," she said. "I've come this far, Barry, so it's time you stopped worrying. Your mother's never going to be fat again, I can assure you. And that's not just a promise; that's the God's honest truth." She opened her bag and fished out a pack of cigarettes. "So tell me about school, your friends. Do you have a steady girl friend yet?"

"No."

"We hardly ever get time to talk these days."

"That's because you're always so busy."

"Are you sorry about it?"

"Not me," he said, picking at the fried noodles she tried to ignore. "I think what you're doing is the greatest. But you know what, mom? I don't like sleeping in the same room with Nat. I've been wanting to talk to you about that. She . . . she's always nosying around, going into my stuff, my drawers I mean. And I'm going to be sixteen soon. She cramps my style, ma. I mean, I'm not a little kid anymore. D'you understand?" He leaned forward, looked at her intently, and then suddenly lowered his eyes. "I know about, you know, the facts of life, ma. I want my own room. Isn't it time already?"

"Soon," she promised. "Here's the waiter. Go, have some soup. You must be starving."

"Are you and dad going to get a divorce?"

"Who told you that?"

"No one. I'm just asking, that's all."

"Have your soup. Besides, your father doesn't make enough money to support two households."

"Who'd be in the other household?"

"Barry," and she stopped, trying to think of the right thing to say, "let's talk about this later, okay. Now's not the time." I don't want to lose my appetite. Then, trying to make it up to him, she said, "But when I get home tonight I'll suggest to your father that he share the bedroom with you, and your sister can move in with me, sleep in my room I mean. Grandma can have the living room again."

"He snores," Barry said. "And he always gets up in the middle of the night to eat. He makes so much noise—"

"We're not moving so quick. I can't afford it, Barry. Not yet, anyway. So please, just try to be patient, honey. You'll have your own room, I promise."

"That's what you said six months ago."

"The soup looks lovely. Mind if I have a taste?"

"You're not allowed," he said, his lower lip trembling. "And I want my own room. It's not fair."

"You want a lot of things, Barry. But you can't always have your way. I'm well aware of the problem, so do me a favor and stop reminding me about it. I said it'll be attended to and it will. Everything just takes time, just remember that. The world wasn't built—"

"—in a day. Yeah, I know all about it. Besides, it was Rome that wasn't built, not the world." He made a face and looked down at his plate. Steam rose in a small fragrant cloud. Bubbles of fat broke apart at the rim of the bowl. The bok choy floated across the surface, wrinkled and green. "This soup stinks. It smells like dirty dishes, toes even."

"Barry! People are eating," she whispered. She glared at him even as he continued to frown. "Where are your manners, for God sakes."

"Well it's true. It's not my fault. What kind of place is this, anyway?" He turned his head from side to side, taking everything in with a single hooded glance. "I thought you were going to take me somewhere nice, otherwise I wouldn't have bothered to come. It looks like a restaurant for poor people. And there's crud on my silverware, besides."

222

It took all of her self-control to keep her mouth shut. She pulled her hands down under the table as if to sit on them. If not, she knew she wouldn't be able to stop herself from slapping his face. Which he deserves, she thought, and which I just can't bring myself to do.

January 1966

AGAIN, it was Chinese food. Only now, it was served up on small Wedgwood plates to a select group of guests, close friends of the Frankels all assembled in their Manhattan Beach home to see the old year out and usher in the new. Cynthia sat in an armchair with a high rounded back and button upholstery. Her legs were crossed demurely, a spartan array of Oriental tidbits and hors d'oeuvres balanced on one knee.

"Sweetheart, it's all within the limits of the diet. I checked everything out beforehand. And I told you not to have dinner," Jeanette said. "Such a pity Forman couldn't make it. I hope he'll be feeling better by tomorrow."

"Just one of those things," she replied with an official Flatbush Avenue smile. "You know how stomach viruses are. They just come on out of the clear blue, without any warning at all."

Jeanette clucked her tongue, nodding her head as if to reinforce her apparent concern over Manny's health and welfare. "And Leonard's always telling me how hard he works. What a pity he's not here to share in the festivities."

"Yes, everything is so very festive," she said, choking on the word though that was not all what she intended. "Your home looks lovely. And I adore the new couch. Silk, isn't it?"

"Of course. My decorator helped me pick the fabric at Scalamandre, in New York. You've heard of them, surely."

"Indeed I have," she said, gritting her teeth. "They have some reputation."

"The best."

She had no idea what Jeanette was talking about, whether Scala whatever she'd called it was a person or a department store, both or neither. Ignoring the woman's inquisitive brown eyes, she daintily removed a spare rib from her plate and took a small tentative bite.

"Excuse me, dear," and Jeanette turned around and moved gracefully across the room.

Cynthia followed her with her eyes. You wouldn't know it was the same woman, she thought. I'll have to get her to come down and lecture, share the burden with me. And when did she get that rock on her finger? It must be five carats, if it's a day. And the dress, the way she has her hair done in all those intricate little ringlets. Everything, her makeup, the way she carries herself, the way the house is furnished. I wonder if she was so thin when she and Leonard got married.

"How's everything going?" he asked.

Speak of the devil, she thought, saying, "Fine. And don't you look zippy this evening, very man-about-town, if I do say so myself."

"We try," Leonard said.

Not hard enough, remembering him saying that once before. Don't tell me Leonard Frankel is running out of lines? Heaven forbid! She kept her eyes on him, smiled to herself, and continued to stare. A moment later Leonard looked away, brushing at an invisible ash along the front of his white dinner jacket. Cynthia had unhappily discovered she was the only woman in attendance who hadn't thought to wear a floor-length gown, never realizing the Frankels would be giving such a formal party. She once again began to feel sorry for herself. I need some new clothes. Desperately, she thought. But I don't want to use the money yet. There are more important things, like getting the hell out of the apartment, for starters.

"I'm sorry Manny wasn't feeling well."

"He was feeling fine, I assure you," she said. "He'd made other . . . plans, that's all."

"That's too bad."

"Why? It's not too bad at all. We would have ended up having a fight or he would have had too much to drink, anyway. Besides, how would it look for slim Cynthia to be seen with her fat slob of a hubby—"

"Hey, come on," he said. "Cool it, Cynthia. It's a party, New Year's Eve, you forget. Leave the poor guy out of it."

"The poor guy and I have been married for close to seventeen years, the poor guy."

"I don't want to talk about your marital problems. Tonight is just the wrong time."

"Whatever you say, Leonard." She put down her plate, wiped her fingers with a linen napkin spread across her lap and then got to her feet. "So why don't we talk about us, for a change. And I don't mean the business, either."

"Excuse me, Jeanette wants me for something." Abruptly, he turned away.

"Leonard," she called out, only to be tapped on the shoulder by a man who introduced himself as Frankel's partner in Dreamtime Togs.

"I've been meaning to meet you for quite some time, Mrs. Margold," he said.

"Thank you, but can you excuse me for a moment?" Without waiting for a reply she hurried across the thick pile carpet and out of the living room. She moved down the hall which led to the study. The door was open, but the book-lined room was empty. Behind her came the swish of rustling fabric. She turned her head over her shoulder to again confront Jeanette's tall poised figure.

"Surely you're not looking for a good book, dear," Jeanette said. She wore very red lipstick. When she smiled, her mouth looked smeared with blood.

The perfect color for her, she decided, all things considered. "No, I was just—"

"Well, I suppose now is as good a time as any."

"For what?" she said, even as Jeanette took hold of her arm and steered her through the doorway and into Leonard's study. She closed the door behind them and Cynthia had the feeling that she was trapped, that she had no more excuses on the tip of her tongue, no alternatives left open but to turn around and deal with whatever was about to happen. "Is anything the matter, Jeanette? You look very perturbed about something. Have I said anything that I shouldn't have?"

"My dear, you couldn't say a wrong thing if you tried. After all, aren't you the one-woman crusade, the one who everyone runs to when they've reached the end of should say—has already told me. That ring must have cost you a small fortune. But I suppose nothing is too good for the first Mrs. Frankel—the *only* Mrs. Frankel."

"Come on, Cynthia, what do you expect?" He held the pipe in both hands now, but the bowl was empty. It didn't warm his fingers the way it might have looked at first glance. "Did I ever make any promises I didn't keep? Did I ever tell you I was going to get a divorce? Well, did I? Answer that."

"If I didn't care about you as much as I did, as much as I *do,* rather, I'd . . . no, I wouldn't even spit in your eye. You're probably not worth it."

"Lot of good it would do, anyway," he said, half a laugh getting caught in his throat. "Why don't you stop playing games with yourself and face facts, for a change."

"And what facts are those, Leonard?"

"Simply that you're married and I'm married and it would be the worst thing to start changing the status quo."

"Why?"

"Because it would."

"Because it would, he says. Because sometimes, if you really want to know the truth, I get the feeling you used me royally. How do you like that, Mr. Frankel?"

"Used you?" he said, raising his voice. "D'you know how much money I've shelled out for the corporation so far? Close to four thousand dollars, that's how much."

"Her new ring probably cost you twice that."

"Four thousand dollars," he repeated. "You asked for a typewriter, I bought you one. You needed chairs, a desk, new lighting fixtures, I didn't say a word. You wanted stationery, we got you stationery. We put your two friends on salary . . . not even under the table, mind you. What more do you want from me, Cynthia?"

"Obviously, the one thing I really wanted from you you're not willing to give. So that's all there is to it," she replied. "Funny, that I didn't even see this coming. Oh, I knew it was probably inevitable, but still . . . that's the way the cookie crumbles, right? Sure, right."

"Stop feeling sorry for yourself."

"Sorry? Me sorry? Not me, Mr. Frankel. But do you know what else is funny, now that I think of it? When I first found out about Manny—what was going on when I wasn't looking—I vowed to start worrying about Cyn-

230

their rope? I mean, if it weren't for you I'd never be able to fit into this gown in a million years. No, I thank *you* for letting me see the light, sweetheart. For helping to save my marriage."

"Well, that's . . . that's very nice of you to say, Jeanette," she stammered. "I couldn't be more pleased," you snide, catty bitch.

"But what gets me, what really surprises me, Cynthia, is that you must have taken me for a complete idiot."

"Pardon?" She blinked rapidly. But her false eyelashes weren't about to fall off, nor were they too heavy, difficult to wear. The light wasn't harsh or glaring, either. If anything, it was soft as amber, flattering too. "I don't think I quite understand."

"You don't?" Jeanette threw her head back, the motion exaggerated, theatrical. Her neck seemed to twist, to snake back and forth. The long slender veins standing out on either side were like taut vibrating bowstrings. Then she began to laugh.

"I think I'll go and have some champagne," Cynthia said, slurring the words with the speed of her delivery.

"When I'm finished, when I've said all that I have to, you can have all the champagne in the world, *Mrs.* Margold."

"Jeanette, this is ridiculous," she said loudly, hoping against hope that someone would hear her, would enter the study and interrupt them before anything else was said.

It didn't happen.

"Ridiculous?" Jeanette exclaimed with another laugh, as cool and bitter as the first had been. "You're the ridiculous one, Cynthia, chasing after Leonard all these months. Did you think I was so naive I wouldn't realize what was going on behind my back?"

"This isn't 'As the World Turns,' Jeanette. You're making a soap opera out of a . . . a business relationship, for God sakes."

"You do have snappy answers when you need them, don't you. But then again, I always thought you had a big mouth. A little coarse, perhaps, a little common—"

"If you'll excuse me, I don't have to stand here and be insulted." She made a move toward the door, but Jeanette blocked her way.

"The affair of the century is over, Cynthia," she said.

227

"Some neighborhoods just don't go together, I'm sorry to report. They don't mix well, if you know what I mean. Besides, he never loved you, anyway. Leonard only knows how to love himself, if you haven't guessed by now." Her face was set as if in plaster. If Cynthia slapped her, she was certain Jeanette's features would shatter like a china plate, like a Coney Island plaster-of-Paris Kewpie doll. "Nevertheless, I think it's . . . wonderful that you and Leonard are business partners. But that's as far as it's going to go, I assure you."

"The affair of the century?" she said, seizing on the first thing that came to mind. "You have a lurid imagination, Jeanette."

"Not at all," she replied. "Leonard and I have already had it out, as a matter of fact. So if you don't believe me, you can speak to him about it." She waved her hand before Cynthia's face, the five-carat marquise-cut diamond winking at her, malicious and insistent, demanding to be noticed. "Sort of an I'll-make-it-all-up-to-you kind of present, if you know what I mean. I've always admired Winston's—"

"Winston who?"

"Harry Winston, the Fifth Avenue jeweler," Jeanette said. "Bulgari's settings are just a little too much for me. And of course, Leonard was also interested in the investment value, needless to say."

"I don't know who Bulgari is or Harry Winston either, but I'm very pleased for you, Jeanette. Wear the ring in good health and when you try to sell it, I hope they give you a decent price. And now, if you don't mind—"

"I don't mind anything you do, Cynthia, so long as you stay away from my husband. It would be most unfortunate if Forman found out what's been happening behind his back all these months. Most men don't take to being . . . cuckolded."

The word didn't ring a bell, though she couldn't help but get the gist of it. "Forman keeps someone just like you on the side, Jeanette. We have an understanding, an arrangement you might say. Because of the children, of course." She paused and stared into Jeanette's eyes. "But then again, that's something you'll never have to worry about. Isn't that so?" you poor barren s.o.b.

She hadn't expected Jeanette to answer and she didn't. The color rose in her powdered cheeks with a speed and intensity Cynthia marveled at. Unkind though the remark had been, she hadn't been able to stop herself. Her eyes fixed on the large stone in its platinum setting. Jeanette stepped back as if she'd been stung, groping with one manicured hand for the doorknob. Before she could get a grip on both it and herself, Leonard opened the door and stepped inside the study.

"You have a houseful of guests, Jeanette, in case you've forgotten," he said.

"Of course. Excuse me." Several ringlets fell along the back of her neck as she turned away. Cynthia looked down at the floor, pretending to study the shape and subtle gradations of color that marked the antelope skin. Or was it the hide of a deer? She'd never thought to ask. When the door finally closed, Leonard spoke.

"What were the two of you talking about?"

"Don't be naive." His point-blank question came as no surprise. "Why did you go and tell her about us?"

"Why?" he said.

"Yes, why?"

"She knew anyway, that's why," recovering his tongue. "She's not stupid."

"But you told her, that's the point."

"Okay, so I told her. But we haven't slept together in weeks, anyway."

"*Months*, anyway."

Leonard moved past her. He stopped in front of his desk, looked down at its polished brass fittings, and then reached for a pipe. Jabbed between his teeth like a baby's pacifier, it made his voice sound gravelly, as if he had pebbles in his mouth. "Okay, months. What's the difference."

"What's the difference, he says! It's a considerable difference, that's what. Here I've been about as patient and understanding as a person can get and you really don't give a damn, do you?"

"It's not a question of that, Cynthia."

"Then what is it a question of?"

"I don't think it's in our best interest anymore, becau of our other, our business relationship."

"I see. Now that we're partners on paper, we do have to be partners between the sheets, is that it?"

"Sometimes you have a way of turning a phrase—"

"So your lovely slim wife—your blushing bri

thia for a change. I guess I forgot all about it. But seeing as this is New Year's Eve and a time for making resolutions . . . well, my first resolution of the new year will be to start thinking about Cynthia again. Seeing as no one else does."

"That's a joke," he said. "Every time you get up in front of a class you have fifty people thinking about you, just about at your beck and call. They never forget who's doing the talking, not for one minute."

"Good, that's just the way I want it," she said, feeling not only angry, but defiant as well. "Because Cynthia's nobody's fool. Because Cynthia's finally gotten wise to herself. I got the right idea, Leonard. I'll make everyone know who I am, what do you think of that?"

"If that's what you want, I wish you the best of luck."

"That's just what I want. The nobody from Brooklyn who fell for some garment center sharpie—"

"Cynthia, come off it. Give me a break."

"—some garment center sharpie," she repeated. "Well, this nobody is going to be Miss New Body. That's right, isn't that goddamn clever of me." She pretended to laugh, scornful, sarcastic. "From a nobody to a new body. We'll have to remember that, Leonard. Maybe someday it'll come in handy, like a corporate motto or something." There wasn't anything left to say, except, "Goodnight," and have a good life.

She didn't wait for him to see her to the door.

She was up earlier than Natalie, earlier than Barry and Manny who slept in the other bedroom across the hall. "I already made a pot of coffee," Lena said when she walked into the kitchen. "I couldn't sleep anymore. My arthritis was bothering me."

"I feel a little stiff myself," she said. "Did you take anything for it?"

"Just some aspirin. It must be the change in weather. It feels very damp out," Lena said. "Can I make you breakfast, a scrambled egg?"

"I guess I have to," for three full meals a day was the very cornerstone of the Kings County plan. And even though she'd reached her goal weight, the only insurance against slipping back into the old patterns was to continue following the diet, until death do us part.

She sat down at the table, got up just as quickly, and gave her mother a kiss on the cheek. Lena looked up in surprise. "What's that all about?"

"It's the New Year and your daughter wants you to know how much she loves you, that's all."

"Well thank you, dear. Your mother loves you just as much, believe me," Lena said. "You'll always be my baby, that's all I can say."

"You've been really good to me, mom. Helping out around the house, doing most of the shopping, the cleaning up. What I said on TV was true. I couldn't have done it without you."

"And if it wasn't for you and Manny, I hate to think what would have happened," Lena replied. She cracked an egg over a bowl, and beat it rapidly with a stainless steel fork.

"When did he get in last night, anyway?"

"I don't know. I was sound asleep," Lena said quickly. "You want me to put a little milk in the egg?"

"Just a drop." She poured herself a cup of coffee, took a sip and then lit a cigarette.

"You smoke too much, like a regular chimney."

"An occupational hazard," she said. Suitably fortified, she didn't hesitate or think twice about lifting the telephone receiver off the hook and dialing. When I say something, I mean it, she thought. The phone rang once, twice, three more times in even-paced succession. Finally a voice still drowsy with sleep got on at the other end. "Good morning," she said. "Happy New Year."

"Good morning and happy New Year to you, too," Leonard said. "What time is it, anyway?"

She glanced at the clock which sat on top of the refrigerator. "Twenty after nine."

"Cynthia, let me go back to sleep. I'll call you later."

"Just let me tell you what I have to first. Just let me get it off my chest."

"I thought we discussed all of that last night, before you made your dramatic exit."

"It wasn't dramatic. No one was even standing by the door to say goodbye to me," she assured him. "But this has nothing to do with that, I promise. Just listen for a minute, because when I was coming back here last night, sitting in the cab, it all came to me. Like a flash." She stopped for a moment, took another sip of coffee, and hurried into, "We've been playing at this like amateurs, even the name—the C & L Corporation—sounds like some kind of gang front or something. It's phony. It doesn't have a ring to it, if you know what I mean. Leonard, if you're investing all this money, let's at least make sure it pays off, instead of just gambling and taking chances. Let's do it the right way, like getting ourselves an advertising agency, for example. Flatbush Avenue's fine, so is Rutland Road, Forest Hills even. But weren't you the one who told me about franchises? Leonard, we could make thousands, selling my idea, our idea, I mean, to ex-overweights all over the country."

"So what else is new."

"Leonard, I'm serious. So it'll cost you another couple of hundred bucks—"

"Another couple of thousand, you mean."

"But Leonard, it's a long-term investment. Why should we be small fry when . . . Do you really want to manufacture children's pajamas for the rest of your life, the truth?"

"You're really out to conquer the world, aren't you?"

"Your egg's gonna get cold," Lena said.

"Maybe," she said. "Because if I don't, someone else will. Leonard, why don't we change our name, for starters? Remember what I said last night, about going from a nobody to a new body? Well, listen to this. The New Body School of Weight Reduction. Doesn't that sound high-class?"

"It's too long. It'll get caught on people's tongues."

"Then just drop it to the New Body School or something like that. That's why I'm telling you we need an advertising agency. That's part of their job, to come up with clever little names and gimmicks like that. Don't you know anyone in the business, someone we could get a deal with so it won't cost all that much just to get started?"

"Cynthia, it's going to taste like rubber in another minute."

"Just a second, mother, this is business. We're talking about money, my future, for God sakes."

"Go fight with children," Lena mumbled.

"I do know someone," Leonard said. "We grew up together, as a matter of fact. I spoke to him a couple of months ago and, if I remember correctly, he was telling me that his son is some hotshot copywriter on Madison Avenue. In fact, unless I'm imagining it, he told me his kid handles a diet soft-drink account."

"Perfect," Cynthia said. "Find out where he works and I won't even bother you about it. I'll do all the calling, whatever legwork's necessary."

"And I'll shell out all the money, right?"

"We're partners, Leonard," she said. "What you put in you're going to get back in spades."

She thought she heard him laugh. "Boy, when you get on a kick, there's no stopping you, is there?"

"What else do I have going for me, Leonard? I got it from both ends last night, you forget."

"Okay okay, I'll take care of it. But if they're going to charge us an arm and a leg, Cynthia, you can just get it out of your mind, because somewhere along the line I have to put my foot down."

"What can it possibly cost just to talk to them?"

"They'll bill you for creative time."

"Leonard, just call and find out how I can get in touch with . . . what's his name, anyway, your friend's son?"

"Something Eisenstern, I don't remember."

"Well, I want to meet this Something Eisenstern. And Leonard, the sooner the better."

February 1966

"NOT THE NEW BODY SCHOOL. That's boring, Cynthia. And it sounds too much like the New School, anyway, Besides, it has no . . . no zip, no *joie*, no ring to it. No, you want something short and sassy, something sweet to the ear, that'll sing on the tongue. But highly original, unique. Lemme think, lemme just think for a sec."

She wasn't sure if he was putting on a show of razzle-dazzle, playing at being a twenty-five-year-old boy wonder. But as she sat in a molded plastic chair alongside his cluttered desk, Cynthia had to smile. Eisenstern—"D. Wayne Eisenstern to my birth certificate," he had said, "D. W. to people who know I'm bananas"—seemed to possess unlimited sources of energy, creative drive. He reminded her of a character in a silent movie, not his physical appearance so much as the swift, jerky quality of his hyper, frenetic movements. His office was a study in disarray, disorder, and eccentricity. But there was also a calculated air to the tottering piles of paper, the deflated balloons tied to the grid of the ventilator, the overgrown hanging plants fronting the windows, and the vaguely obscene posters tacked on the wall, which all seemed to say he was trying very hard to live up to his image.

Whatever that might be, she thought. Though he looks like one of the devil's helpmates with little pointed ears and that heart-shaped face. Adorable on the outside and smart as a whip inside, which is just fine with me.

"No, they don't call me an *enfant terrible* for nothing," he said, as if he were talking to himself. "No, that's not

235

what we want. This has to be dynamite or else forget it. Wait, give me time—"

"No one's rushing you," she said.

He looked up at her. "Have a Smartie." He tossed her a small cardboard cylinder.

She caught it in both hands. "What are they?"

"Chocolate mints like oversized M & M's. From London. Very rare, very classy."

"I can't," she said, and set the box of candies down on top of his desk.

"Suit yourself. Now let's see. The New Body School, the New Body School. What was it you told me you thought up before?"

"From a nobody to a new body."

"Not bad, not bad. I love your red hair. It's a fabulous color like brand-new copper pennies. But how does this grab you? Not new body but NuBody, with a capital N and a capital B, like so." He scribbled across a piece of paper and held it up for her inspection.

NuBodies!

"I love it already," he said.

"Why the *ies?*"

"Because if you just say NuBody, you have to use another word, otherwise people'll think, 'NuBody what?' But if you call your outfit NuBodies, it's all there under one umbrella, a nice neat little package. And then you can use your line for a corporate slogan or whatever. 'From a nobody to a NuBody.' Or better yet, if you dare and I don't see why not since no one else has come up with your idea so far, 'From a *fat* nobody to a NuBody.' Though it might be offensive to some . . . but in any event, you've identified your product, the item you're selling, so at least there's no confusion in the mind of the consumer."

"NuBodies?" she said, trying to judge how it would sound in someone else's mouth. It rolled off her tongue, but she still wasn't absolutely sure if it was right.

"It's faab-ulous, faaab-ulous," he sang. "You wouldn't want it to sound like someone was speaking with a

236

mouthful of mashed potatoes now, would you? Of course not. Now maybe we'll use a Janus-like logo—"

"A Janice what?"

"Ja*nus*, the god with two faces. Only the logo, you know . . . Esso has its tiger and Shell has its scallop shell. A logo . . . how do you explain a logo? It's something that will immediately be associated with your company. Do you ever go to see Otto Preminger's films?"

"Sometimes, when they're in the neighborhood."

"I won't ask you which neighborhood since I got out of mine as soon as possible. But anyway, he makes fantastic use of logos. He hires Saul Bass, I think that's the guy's name, to design these images for him that are immediately associated with the film."

"Oh, I see. Like they used . . . what was it, pieces of a body almost, for *Anatomy of a Murder*."

"Right, right," he said with a grin. "Or that upraised arm with a gun for *Exodus*. That's a logo. Now what I was saying before was that we could use a figure that's fat on one side and thin on the other. That's what I meant when I said Janus . . . that's J-A-N-*U-S*."

"And how much is all this going to cost?" she asked, even as he began to scribble across a fresh sheet of paper.

"Money money money," he said. "Ugly little word. Did you notice how tacky the outer office was? You know why, because this is a cheapo agency. They don't think big. They don't know how to project the right kind of image. They don't even know what the word image means. Don't make that mistake with NuBodies. The name is so fabulous, I can't begin to tell you. Image is everything, the heart, the crux, the capstone of it all. But that's the reason why Endicott, Tucker & Groves is worth piss; if you know what I mean."

"So why are you working here, if they're second-rate?"

"Why?" he repeated. "Cynthia, you don't mind if I call you Cynthia, do you? Do you know the origin of the name? You don't? Fantastically interesting story, to digress for a moment. It's Greek, actually. Cynthus . . . I believe it was originally spelled with a K, but no matter, is a mountain on Delos, one of the Greek islands. It's considered the birthplace of Diana, otherwise known as Artemis, the goddess of the moon, the huntress—" He drew his arm back as if to shoot an arrow.

"Which means I'm a genuine lunatic, no doubt," she said, laughing.

"Don't ever denigrate yourself, even in jest. It's bad for the image." He tapped the point of his pencil against the desk until it broke. Then he shoved it under a bunch of papers and said, "I have a fantastic idea."

"You've already come up with several. I think I'm starting to love the name, NuBodies. It does have a nice ring to it. But one other question. Why that kind of spelling? Why not N-E-W?"

"Because it's much too obvious. You have to be subtle in this business, Cynthia. Cynthia-Artemis-Diana, love that name."

She grinned and said, "You're crazy, do you know that."

"Of course I am. One has to be crazy to be a love goddess; to work at Endicott, Tucker & Groovy. But pardon my asparagus on the firm's good name." He leaned toward her. "If you think *I'm* crazy, you should meet my parents. Genuine certifiables, the both of them."

"If it wasn't for your father, I'd never have found out about you."

"Sweet man, daddy. Misguided, of course. You didn't happen to tell anyone else you had an appointment with me today, did you?"

"Just my partner."

"Yes, Leonard Frankel. I suppose I'll have to cater to his ego too, but no matter. Because I have a splendid idea. Do you have the time? I've stopped wearing a watch. It makes me feel very paranoid."

"A quarter to twelve."

"Lovely." He got abruptly to his feet, centered the buckle of his alligator belt over his fly and reached for his blazer, hanging over the chair. "Why don't I take you for a nice two-hour lunch? Omelettes at Madame Romaine's, over on Sixty-first, if that sounds amusing. And I'll tell you how we can work the entire ad campaign out for next to nothing. Have you ever heard of the word freelance?"

"I think so."

"Terrific." He dropped his voice an octave, though not the speed of his speech pattern, saying, "It means I'll work for you . . . NuBodies, I mean; and Endicott, Tucker & Groans won't be any the wiser. I'll just bill you directly

238

and it'll cost you a fraction of what it would if you went directly to my bosses."

"But I told Mr. Tucker. Or Leonard . . . Mr. Frankel, did."

"Shit," he said. "That kills that idea. Well, we'll think of something. But in the meantime, Cynthia-Artemis-Diana, let's get out of here before I go positively buggers. Does your diet allow you to eat omelettes, by the way?"

"Plain ones," she said.

"Wonderful. We shall have a regular funfest," and with that he took her under the arm and guided her to the door.

March 1966

D. W.'s FUNFEST turned out to be an ad campaign that would have blitzed all of NuBodies' competition, had there been any. Within three weeks of their initial meeting, space ads appeared in the *Post* and the *Times*. The response was immediate, though in D. W.'s eyes it was fully justified, "Only to be expected when you're dealing with a class-A genius like myself, sweetheart." Classes were now held six days a week, plus double sessions for teenagers on Monday evenings and Saturday afternoons. Cynthia had located ideal office space on Austin Road in Forest Hills, Queens. The branch would be ready to open its doors to the general public by the beginning of April, earlier than she or Leonard had anticipated. For the moment, D. W. had said nix to the Janus logo. Instead, he presented her with a highly stylized letterhead, the word NuBodies presented in a tall, elongated, sans-serif typeface. It was, as he insisted and as she readily agreed, the essence and embodiment of a firm which stood for slimness and weight-reduction. Good to his word once again, he managed to work out a deal with Endicott, Tucker & Groves. NuBodies would be charged far less than the agency's usual commission.

"I merely told Mr. Grovel that it was simply a matter of good business. Encourage a young up-and-coming company now, when they have limited moneys for advertising, and they'll never forget the agency when they hit it big. And you're going to hit it big, my dear, no doubt about that, no question in my mind whatsoever. Have another carrot stick. They're very good for your eyes. Combats night blindness and assorted infirmities . . . you name it, the works."

Cynthia put down her glass of milk and helped herself. She sat in the living room of Eisenstern's apartment, her third visit in as many weeks. Familiarity was breeding anything but contempt. The railroad flat on East Eighty-ninth Street continued to both delight and intrigue her. It was, as D. W. had described it, "shockingly now, convincingly decadent." Personally ascribing to a different set of adjectives, she referred to the three-room apartment as "unbelievably busy, but fascinating all the same." She was still as fascinated—since that was the word she felt fit the best—as she had been the first time she had walked up the five flights of stairs to reach the top floor of the Yorkville tenement.

Gladys, a Siamese cat with a permanent back injury, the result of "an unforeseen collision with the bottom of the air shaft," now rubbed against her stockinged legs, demanding to be lifted onto the couch. "She's lazy," D. W. said. He munched on a pretzel as he sat opposite her, his legs crossed in what he had said was known as a double lotus position, one squeezed almost painfully and impossibly on top of the other. She privately marveled at his ability to twist his body into strange and outlandish positions. "Do you happen to know of a good taxidermist, Cynthia?" he asked as she worked her way down to the bottom of the carrot stick.

"No, I haven't been in the market for one for several years," she replied. Already, she had begun to pick up on his sense of humor, macabre by any other name or standard of good taste.

"Pity. I'm thinking of having Gladys stuffed."

"Stuffed? You can't be serious."

Of course he wasn't, or so she hoped. Still, he continued, "Oh, indeed I am. There's not enough fur there for a rug, so why not have her stuffed. She'll become an *objet d'art,* just like Roy Rogers's horse, Trigger. Besides, then Gladys won't be such a terrible bother, a real pain in the ass if you want to know the truth. I mean, who the fuck wants to cater to a crippled Siamese when you're still young and beautiful and . . . and the whole world beckons. Oh, I tell you, life's not easy, kiddo. But then again, I wasn't put on this planet to suffer. That I can assure you."

"I don't see you doing any great amount of suffering,"

she said. "You're certainly not living like you're down to your last ten cents. Drinking Berninis—"

"*Bellinis*, please," he corrected. He lifted the oversized wineglass and took a sip of the drink which bore that name, a mixture of inexpensive champagne and Bartlett pears, run through a blender "for anywhere from thirty seconds to a minute and a half depending on how thirsty you are."

"Berninis, Bellinis . . . what's the difference. You have it too good, that's your problem. Your parents must have spoiled you rotten, that's all I can say."

"My parents? Ugh, I don't want to lose my appetite." He recrossed his legs and reached for a cigarette. "Someday," he sighed, "everything will just be peachy keen. We shall be rich as Midas, you and I. Won't that be delicious, Cynthia? All that money, oh what a joy not to have to worry about paying bills, not to think of taking buses instead of cabs. I wasn't meant for poverty, I assure you. It's not in my genes."

"I don't trust genes of any kind," she said. "And while we're on the subject, yours look like they're about to run away from you."

He glanced at his tattered dungarees. Patched and repatched with all sorts of fabric and scraps of suede and leather, the cut-offs still seemed to be hanging by a thread. "Well, the least you could do is buy me a new pair. You haven't bought me a present in weeks, not since you picked out that garish and I mean garish tie at Bonwit's."

She winced, but let it pass. "You'll just have to teach me about all the finer things, that's all there is to it."

"Sarcasm will get you nowhere," he replied. "But keep your eyes and ears open. You're learning, believe me. And you're getting there too, slow but sure. Your hair doesn't look like Dynel, for starters. Sure, you pay a little more, you go—at my advice, don't forget—to Elizabeth Arden instead of Marty's of Montgomery Street, and you get results . . . noticeable ones, at that."

"Sure, when you pay through the nose, you're supposed to get results. Thirty-five dollars for a wash and set. It was outrageous, that's what it was. I don't even pay that much for a pair of shoes."

"You will, rest assured. Everything changes. After all, you're Cynthia Margold, President of NuBodies. You're going to be a very wealthy woman, very rich I should say."

"You're convinced, aren't you?"

He nodded his head. "Absolutely. Why, aren't you?"

"I'm not so sure."

"Well stop doubting yourself, for God sakes. Remember what I told you about self-denigration? Well, just keep that in mind, kiddo. Because as far as I'm concerned, there isn't a kernel of doubt in my mind that you're going to make it, that you're going to be very rich and very famous and very soon, on top of everything else. I mean, look what you've got going for you, Cynthia. No competition, not yet anyway, for starters. A one-of-a-kind product, for another. People are fatter than ever, in case you haven't noticed."

"Oh I have," she said. "I'm trying to reach them, all of them."

"And you will, you will. Just be patient. Everything takes time, though in your case I'd venture to say less than most. My dear, don't you see? This is just the very beginning. You've barely scratched the surface. You haven't even hit the heartland yet."

"And when I do?"

"There's no telling what kind of gifts you'll buy me, no telling what miracles will take place, too." He got to his feet, asked if she wanted a refill and disappeared into the kitchen.

"What do you think, Gladys? Think I'll be rich and famous?"

When the cat didn't answer, she leaned forward and lifted her onto the couch, trying to forget about all the mole-gray hairs which would soon cover her skirt. He gets crazier every time I see him, she thought, one eye on a poster of Greta Garbo, suspended by a thread of wire which was fitted to an eye hook screwed into the wall. Beneath the one-time movie queen—"I beg your pardon," she had told him, "but I happened to have been only a child, an infant, when she was in her heyday"—hung a pair of ceramic lips, full and pouting. Bee-stung in the great tradition of Clara Bow. To the left of the vampish disembodied mouth was a small engraving. He insisted it was an original Beardsley. She wouldn't have been able to tell the difference between a copy and the real thing, any-

243

way. Next to her, Gladys seemed to have settled in for the evening, burying herself down into the cushions.

"Are you hungry? You want some more nibblies?" he asked when he returned.

"Not yet. I'll let you know."

"Do you mind?" He didn't wait for an answer, but pulled his polo shirt over his head with a single fluid motion. "The only problem with this apartment other than the intermittent hot water, the five flights of stairs which give me such excellently muscled legs, and the general air of decay, is that it gets no ventilation whatsoever. I never stop sweating."

"Make yourself comfortable. It's your house." She glanced at his bare chest, firm and thinly haired all the way down to the waistband of his cut-offs.

"Now," once again settling back in the chrome and leather Bauhaus chair, "where were we?"

"We were talking about how famous I was going to be."

"Well you are, so you'd better get used to it." He closed his eyes and rocked back and forth, his hand a baton which beat rhythmically at the air. "Barbra, Barbra," he whispered as Streisand sang "How Much of the Dream Comes True." "She's going to be on TV again, end of this month. 'Color Me Barbra,' it's supposed to be fantastic. Don't you adore her? She's like you, you know."

"Like me? Why, just because we're both nice Jewish girls from Brooklyn?"

"First of all, don't start thinking of yourself as nice, because you're not. Second of all," and he paused to keep time, inadvertently flexing his chest muscles even as his hand cut across the air.

"Second of all what?" She stared at him from across the marble-topped coffee table, surprised she had never realized how handsome he was. He certainly has a streak of exhibitionism, that's for sure. But I can understand why. And it certainly doesn't offend me. If anything, it's a pleasure to be with someone who's proud of his body, his physique.

"It's obvious, Cynthia, can't you see. God, sometimes you play at being so humble it's not to be believed. She's going to be the biggest star that ever came down the pike, and you're going to be just as much a Cinderella in your own right. She was the ugly duckling of Erasmus High—"

"I went to Tilden, right next door."

"—and look how far she's gotten already. Everyone laughed when she got up to sing and now she's the one who has the last yuk. And look at you. Self-styled Blimp of the Western World now about as sexy and smashing looking as anyone would want, yes, I mean it so don't start making humble-pie faces at me. This is D. W. you're talking to, not your partner."

"That's unfair."

"It's the truth though, isn't it? But as I was saying, you've got it made, kiddo. You think two branches—"

"Three."

"Okay, three branches in Greater New York is the be-all and end-all? It's nothing—it's peanuts, kid stuff. Picture a chain of branches in every state in the union."

"I already have."

"I should hope so," he said. He edged forward, making his point even more apparent and physically immediate. "And what about TV appearances and maybe a national magazine devoted to helping people lose weight? And another thing, pretty soon you're going to have to hire someone to come up with some new recipes. The ones from Kings County are getting a little tired."

"I know; one of my members was talking about that the other day. In the last six months she's tried every recipe in the book and she's getting a little bored. So am I, to tell you the truth."

"See? So you have to start thinking of new things, Cynthia, ways of improving NuBodies, making it the best possible company of its kind. Even though you're lucky enough not to have competition now, just wait another couple of months and you'll be seeing a dozen Johnny-come-latelies all trying to get into the act. You'll have to go out on the lecture circuit, too, that's another thing. I mean, the possibilities are endless, limitless. All you need is someone with a little imagination and a flair for p.r. and you're all set."

"Aren't you that person?"

"Of course I am. You're going to help make me a very rich young man, have no fear. Let's be honest with each other, Cyn. I'm bullish about NuBodies, gung ho, because I believe you can make a killing and I want to be part of it, right there when it happens. The whole concept is so exciting it makes me dizzy."

245

"So do all your fantasies."

"But they're not fantasies, don't you see. It's going to happen. It's just as inevitable as the two of us ending up in bed together."

"Excuse me?"

"You heard me," he said. He was out of the double lotus and on his feet before she could figure out what was about to happen next. Instead of moving toward her, he turned away and headed for the stereo. He flipped over the record, lowered the volume, and stepped across the bare hardwood floor. Then, gripping one arm of the couch, he leaned forward and kissed her. It was full, direct and lingering. One minute he'd been filling her head with all sorts of delightful dreams and the next his tongue was tickling her lips and palate. One hand snaked around to the back of her neck and pushed her closer to him. His other hand let go of the couch and slid down across the front of her blouse. She tried to pull back, but his grip was tighter and closer than she had realized.

I didn't want this to happen, she thought. I didn't even think of it. Yet she responded, despite herself, despite her second thoughts and inhibitions.

"Close your eyes and relax," he whispered. He licked her ear and slid his lips down along her neck, saying, "Trust me, just trust me and everything will be cool."

Cynthia leaned back and went limp.

Unfortunately, so did D. W. Try as she might, she was unable to rectify either the situation or his infuriated sense of embarrassment, humiliation, as if his body had betrayed him. "It's okay," she said when nothing else came to mind, the two of them lying side by side in his darkened bedroom. "It happens, what can you do. It's all right. I certainly don't think the less of you because of it." She pulled the sheet up to her neck, feeling modest and sad, unhappy she had given in to her desires. It had been so long since someone had held her, since Leonard had lingered lovingly over her body, that she'd almost forgotten what physical pleasure was all about. And, though she refrained from telling him, D. W. had shown her that he had all the right moves at his disposal. All except one. But it hadn't hurt when he'd pressed down upon her. His weight had felt comforting, not oppressive. He was trim, agile. His body was warm, hard, and aroused. And then . . . then nothing.

"Sorry," was all he said. He slipped out of bed and hunted up a cigarette.

Her eyes, accustomed to the darkness, watched him as he moved across the bedroom. She wanted to say, "Let's try it again." Instead, she propped her head up against the pillows and closed her eyes. Suddenly she felt ravenous for something to eat. The bedsprings creaked lightly as he slid back between the sheets.

"Want a smoke?"

"No thanks." I'd love a cookie but I don't dare.

"Well, can't say that I didn't try."

Why *did* you try? Why did I *let* you try? "Am I complaining? Am I? You're very good, believe me."

"Up to a point, *the* point." The sigh that escaped his lips made her understand the full meaning of self-pity. She too had often sighed just as woundedly, lost in her own maze of unhappiness, content to feel sorry for herself because that had always seemed the easiest way out. Then she had learned that it was about as hateful and self-destructive an emotion as any. She wanted to tell this to him, especially since he preached so long, hard, and vigorously about the dangers of self-denigration. She wanted to reassure him, as best she could. The words failed to materialize, as if they were drying up, evaporating inside of her. She lay there in the darkness, her skin still warm, moist with a fine sheen of perspiration and thwarted ardor, passion that really hadn't had a chance to explode.

"Well," he started to say.

"Come on, enough. Just forget it. It was my fault. I should have stopped you. I mean, we like each other for different reasons, better ones maybe. We'll be good friends, and for a good long time to come. So let's not even worry ourselves about it. It's over and done with."

"Not quite," he said. "But thanks. I'm touched."

"Are you going to be bitter for the rest of the evening? Because if you are, I'll go home and we can just . . . are you crying?"

"Don't flatter yourself," he snapped. "The cat's purring. You imagine things to suit you. That's your problem."

"Hey, Eisenstern," and she turned her head to the side and kissed him on the cheek. "I like you. Isn't that enough? So it didn't work. So what? The world goes on, just like you said. We've got other things to worry about, you and me. You're going to help make me rich and famous, remember?"

"Who can forget?" Then he laughed. Tension released itself, floating up to the ceiling with the thin quick puffs of smoke. Gladys purred more loudly and jumped up on the bed. "See? What did I tell you? She's a goddamn lazy feline, that's all there is to it. She can get up if she wants to. She's just like dear mother. The two of them love to be catered to."

And you don't? she thought.

"Would you like to be the first to use the lavatory facilities?" he said with calculated flipness. "I don't want to be accused of using up all the hot water."

"No, go ahead. I'm in no great rush."

"Sure now?"

"Positive."

He got out of bed again, gave her what was left of the cigarette, and kissed her on the mouth. It made her think of Barry, a sexless caress, mother and son rather than man and woman, lover and mistress. "You prefer men, don't you?" she heard herself say.

"Ask me no questions and I'll tell you no lies." He pretended to laugh, botched it, and wiped the smile off his face. "Do you want to know if I'm gay or straight, is that it?" He stood over her, his face another plaster cast, easily breakable. Jeanette and Manny and Natalie, maybe Leonard as well. All the faces she had seen hard and frightened, angry, hurt, now came together in a single mask. Brittle, molded by the darkness, fragile as a delicate china figurine.

"Yes," she said in a whisper.

" 'Yes and his heart was going like mad and yes I said yes I will Yes.' Thank you Molly Bloom courtesy of Jimmy Joyce and of course I am," he said. "But you've known that all along, haven't you? So why bother asking."

"I wasn't sure."

"I don't know if I should take that as a compliment or not. But now you can be sure, okay?"

"Okay."

Then he was gone. White, his bare buttocks made her think of marble statues and made her see in her mind's eye young Greek gods cool and aloof in the Metropolitan Museum. Now that's social significance, she thought, and laughed. He was beautiful now, rather than handsome.

248

It's just as well. Who was it who said you can't mix business with pleasure? Frankel, obviously.

Trouble was, there seemed to be too much business and not nearly enough pleasure.

Two weeks later, D. W. was arranging his vaguely obscene posters, deflated balloons, *New Yorker* cartoons, and hanging plants in the office at Flatbush Avenue. Cynthia, during one of Madison Avenue's famous two-hour lunches, had convinced Mr. Tucker who had, in turn, convinced Endicott and Groves, that it would be mutually profitable if she "leased" D. W.'s services.

"Lent, you mean," Mr. Tucker had said. "He'd still be salaried out of our office, needless to say."

"Certainly. But it'll just be on a consultant basis, that's really all that it amounts to," she had replied, later asking herself where she'd ever figured out the right vocabulary, where she'd picked up the nomenclature of the ad game. But the words had come to her, just as they had come to her in the past, whenever she'd felt squeezed, pinched, in a bind. "Besides, how long is six months, when you get right down to it? He'll be back before you even realize he was gone. And Mr. Tucker, we're willing to sign a contract with your agency, if you find that desirable. I mean, Nu-Bodies owes a tremendous amount to Endicott, Tucker & Groves. Don't think we're about to forget what you've done for us."

"You're really certain about this, Mrs. Margold, aren't you?" he asked, already on his second Rob Roy.

"Absolutely," she said, nursing a ginger ale with a twist of lime. "Our gross is up forty percent from last month alone. With D. W., Mr. Eisenstern I mean, as advertising and promotional director—consultant I should say, I don't doubt our gross will be double that in no time at all."

"Have you broached this with Eisenstern?"

She nearly choked on her drink. The bubbles went up her nose. She coughed and turned her head away. Broached it? she thought. It's his idea. He came up with the scheme and now I'm only doing his dirty work for him. "Naturally, I wouldn't think of going over your head, Mr. Tucker," she finally managed to say. "I certainly wouldn't want you to think I was being underhanded, unethical, or anything like that. But I did make it a point to ask Mr. Eisenstern if such an arrangement would interest him. He seemed to indicate that it would."

249

"Well, speaking for myself, I don't see why it can't be done. But I'll have to toss the idea around with my partners."

Run it up the flagpole or whatever it is you people do on Madison Avenue, so long as the answer is yes.

It cost NuBodies more than she—and certainly Leonard Frankel—had bargained for. But then again, talent didn't come cheap and she was absolutely positive D. W. would prove to be worth his weight in gold. When it came to matters of business, he was, "Impeccably potent, my dear. So have no fear, Eisenstern's here. And he intends to stick around for quite some time."

That was just the way she wanted it.

September 1966

THAT SPRING AND SUMMER she traveled from Maine to Miami. It was alliterative, as D. W. took poetic delight in reminding her, but it wasn't planned that way. Early in April, Eisenstern had sent out press releases to just about every TV and radio station up and down the East Coast. Would they be interested in interviewing his client? Would they find it suitable programming to schedule a talk with a woman whose whole life was devoted to helping people become slim; dedicated to an ideal that was thin, trim, even athletic? Cynthia trusted him as she had trusted few people in the past. "As long as it doesn't cost us a helluva lot, I'm in there with you," Leonard had said. His response was typical, exactly what she had come to expect from him. Squeezing out the value of a penny like a drop of blood, like the last lukewarm trickle from a bottle of soda pop, seemed to be the cornerstone of his business ethic. He watched over corporate expenditures like a guardian at the tomb of a long-dead Egyptian pharaoh. As long as she kept within his budget, she could do just about anything she chose, anything she pleased. So D. W. had worked up a press release—snappy copy, flashy headline—mailed bulk rate to save the few dollars Leonard constantly sought to conserve. In Portland, Maine, she was met at the airport by a small contingent of overweight downeasters. A bouquet of long-stemmed American beauty roses was thrust into her hands. Her mouth dropped open in amazement. How had they found out about her? Wasn't Maine provincial, rural, isolated? It may have been, but D. W. had done his homework, having gone up to scout the area a week before she ventured off the plane. A poster reading WE NEED NUBODIES was waved before her startled eyes. MAINERS FOR THIN LIVING read another, alternating black and red Magic Marker letters scrawled on the familiar sheet of oaktag. And where are they now? she thought. And is he going to serve me with divorce papers and pretend to be the wounded breadwinner, the suffering daddy? At least he'll get free manicures for the rest of his life. *Isn't that the truth?*

"When are you going to open a branch up here, Mrs. Margold?"

"As soon as I find a woman who's lost a hundred pounds through the NuBodies method," she said. There was no need for a prompter, no need for someone to write her speeches, to put the promised words into her mouth. She was in her element now—neither air nor fire nor water. Just earth and earthy and earthbound. The salt of the earth, Manny would have called the women whose husbands worked in the textile mills of Biddeford and Saco, the lobster men plying their trade along the waters of Casco Bay and the North Atlantic. She was as far from Brooklyn as she had ever been, geographically as well as culturally. Weight seemed to be a common denominator, bringing people together where they had never been together before.

She spoke on a local radio station. The program's format encouraged telephone calls from interested listeners on a three-hour nonstop talkathon, a marathon of both heated accusations and equally heated approval, fervent approbation (so said the moderator in a complimentary aside). Someone told her she was persecuting fat people. Another begged Cynthia to visit her home because she was ashamed to be seen out on the street, because she couldn't even fit behind the wheel of the family car. "What little is left of my family, Mrs. Marg'ld, and I wouldn't say it if'n it weren't so."

They wanted help. Who was she to deny them? "It's not a miracle cure. I'm not a saint," she said in the glass-enclosed, acoustically secure room which faced the sound engineer with his headphones and controls. She didn't worry about the electronics nor the mechanics and theory of broadcasting.

"What was that I just heard?" the woman with the Yankee twang asked with a start of surprise.

252

"I just slapped the host of Cumberland County's favorite all-night talk show," she replied. "He was getting very fresh with a married woman. One with two children, mind you."

Lots of laughs, that one. Lots of pats on the back. "You're too much, a real killer," he said, getting in a feel when she wasn't looking. Earthy, down to earth, back to the people. She loved it, happy as a clam in high tide. She ate up all the attention, the exposure, the chance to speak her mind.

"You're not alone. We have a system that works. It doesn't happen overnight. It takes months of hard work and diligence, but it hasn't failed yet. And it's medically approved. The one thing NuBodies isn't is a quack cure."

From Portland she flew a nervous-making ten-seater plane all the way north. Radio spots were plentiful the farther she traveled from the mainstream. But this too was the heartland Eisenstern had spoken of. She wanted to make herself known wherever they would listen, whether in Deer Isle or Presque Isle, Caribou or Millinocket. Forty-eight hours later she was flying down to Portsmouth, New Hampshire. There, in a live broadcast taped at a local seafood restaurant which overlooked the quaint and scenic harbor, she explained why fish was one of the best foods to eat when you followed the NuBodies plan. The Junior Chamber of Commerce got into the act. The following afternoon she spoke at a hastily assembled luncheon at that same pierside restaurant. Several local businessmen—haberdashers and clothiers mostly—were instantly ready to put up money to underwrite a local Portsmouth branch. "Get me someone, a man or a woman, it doesn't matter, who's dropped a hundred pounds by using my methods and we'll sell you a franchise without blinking an eye." No franchises had yet been sold. Nor had prices been established. Cynthia was certain that if NuBodies was going to make itself known up and down the coast and clear across the country, it was going to happen as a result of honesty and integrity. No one was going to get up before a group of overweight men and women who hadn't first suffered as they did, who hadn't known what it was like to wake up in the middle of the night and devour an entire box of cookies, a cold lamb chop, a loaf of day-old bread, a pint of ice cream still hard as a rock and straight from the freezer.

When she got back to New York she told Leonard

about her experiences. "Right here in New York, the only people who lecture are former members. I want that to be a rule of thumb we use for the rest of the country."

"The rest of the country?" he said with a rising inflection that first made her think of Manny, before putting doubt in her mind where there had never been doubt before.

She rose to the occasion. D. W. was feeding her the non-caloric fantasies of fame, the daydreams and delusions of wealth, both financial and emotional independence. "You're damn right, the rest of the country. I was wined and dined wherever I went. People begged me to open my NuBodies branches. You think New York's the fat capital of the world, but you've got another guess coming. No way, Leonard. There are chubbies all the way up in Aroostook County."

"Where the hell is Aroostook County?"

"Don't you ever eat Maine potatoes? No, of course not, you're not allowed and neither am I. But I didn't tell that to the people in Caribou and Presque Isle. I merely said that if they want to lose weight, we have the answer they've been looking for. I mean, how can you tell a potato farmer he can't eat his own product. They would've stoned me."

The following week she went down to Richmond for her first television appearance since "Faces & Places." It was junior league Johnny Carson, third-rate Merv Griffin, but the people were warm, friendly, responsive. She loved the naked eye of the television camera. She loved the publicity, the banter, the questions thrown in her lap and tossed back with smooth talk and good-humored alacrity. If she knew about anything, it was NuBodies. It was part of her now, an extension of her very being. She wondered what she would be like without the company, if she would be the same Cynthia who still trudged up and down Utica Avenue, though now without her costume jewelry case. How did I live so long without it? she wondered. How was I content to vegetate, getting fatter and fatter? No need to keep asking herself, because other people did. There were new twists to old stories: women whose husbands had fled from ravenous mountains of gluttonous fat; teenage girls who drowned their sorrows by stuffing their faces, as Rita Press and her cousin Nan Albert had done, be-

254

neath gooey ice-cream sundaes, malteds, banana splits. "I don't know when to stop, how to control myself," they said. She promised to leave a hundred copies of the diet with the TV station. And again, to the first person who successfully shed an even hundred pounds, the promise of being able to open a franchise in the Richmond area.

In August they were forced to sit down and establish the necessary guidelines. A man in Wilmington had successfully completed the NuBodies course, to the tune of a whopping one hundred twenty-three-pound loss. What amazed Cynthia more than anything else was the fact that he had done it entirely on his own, without the benefit of classes and without emotional and psychological reinforcement from others afflicted just as he had been. He was in New York with medical statements, as well as before and after pictures, to back him up—and the promise of a loan from the First City Bank of Wilmington, Delaware.

"Fifteen thousand," Leonard said, snapping his fingers. "Plus thirty-five percent of the annual net profit."

"He's crazy," she said, nudging D. W. in the side. They sat around her desk at Flatbush Avenue. The man from Wilmington waited for an answer. He could be reached at the Biltmore as soon as they came up with a figure. "You'll price yourself right out of business, and then we'll really be up shit's creek without a paddle."

"Spare me the folk sayings," Leonard said. "And you're wrong, on top of everything else." He yawned and cracked his knuckles as he rocked back and forth on two rickety wooden chair legs. "Other franchises go for just as much."

"We're not selling soft ice cream or fried chicken or hamburgers, in case you've forgotten. This man took me up on an offer I made and I'll be damned if he's going to go back to Wilmington and tell people New York's filled with a bunch of sharpies, phonies of the first order."

"Maybe fifteen thou sounds like *mucho dinero* to you now, kiddo," said D. W. "But mark my words, a year from now you'll be sorry you decided to sell yourself so cheap."

"Well, why can't the figure fluctuate, according to the marketplace? You know what I'm saying, like cabbies and medallions. The price for one is always changing, going up, isn't that so?"

255

"Not a bad idea," Leonard said. "What kind of money were you thinking of for this Wilmington character?"

"This character lost over a hundred pounds. We should all have members who are so much a character as he is."

"Okay, okay, you take everything so personally," he snapped. "Name a figure, Cynthia, and stop beating around the bush."

"Five thousand and ten percent," she said without a pause or moment of hesitation.

"Now that is what I would call genuinely bananas," D. W. said. He picked up his coffee, raised it to his lips, made a face and put it down on the desk. Then, from behind an ear he removed the stub of a pencil and began to doodle across the reinforced cardboard container. "You want us all to end up in the poorhouse?"

"Some poorhouse," she said. "This one here," and she motioned to Eisenstern, "is taking home close to two hundred bucks—*after* taxes, mind you. That's more than I'm making and I'm the one who's busting my backside—"

"And I'm not?" he barked. "Just get off your high horse, lady. Endicott, Tucker & Groves sign their name to my checks, not Cynthia Margold."

"I'm sorry, sorry, I didn't mean it that way. Except that I've been traveling around like a regular gypsy and I want to get through to people, to help them help themselves."

"Admirable sentiments," he said and stuck out his tongue at her.

"Why don't we compromise?" Leonard suggested. He sighed and checked his watch. She wondered if he was late for a date. She was curious to know if there was someone new in the picture, someone who'd sweet-talked her way into his pants and then his wallet. Or vice versa. "For the fiscal year 1966, let's establish a price of ten thousand, plus twenty-five percent of the net annual profit. Next year we can rework the figures, if it's warranted. If it's not . . ."

"Then we're in big trouble," D. W. said, "because if all we've got going for ourselves is Wilmington and Brooklyn, it's time to do some serious thinking about where this outfit is heading."

"Don't tell me you're getting cold feet all of a sudden?" she said, surprised.

"Not at all, kiddo," he told her. "My contract's up the end of September. You've got six weeks to sell your act."

She had no way of knowing until he told her a month later—point-blank and to her face—that his words were merely designed to shake her up a little, to keep her on her toes. He'd bargained on frightening her because he felt certain she depended on him. Nor was he wrong. The idea of a NuBodies without a D. Wayne Eisenstern was quickly becoming anathema. She went out on the circuit again, wangling her way onto TV talk shows and radio interviews that sent her winging as far south as Miami Beach and Atlanta. Before Labor Day had arrived the papers for the Wilmington branch were almost signed. The initial down payment for the franchise was deposited in the bank. Not only was Wilmington on the NuBodies map, but Portland, Maine and Yonkers, New York, as well. Negotiations had also begun for the sale of the Forest Hills branch to a former member. The Friday after Labor Day, after she had personally chaired the evening class, Nu-Bodies ended its first year with a small catered party at its headquarters on Flatbush Avenue, near the corner of Glenwood Road.

The Frankels were there; Vivian Hollander with her assistant, a current member close to goal weight that the corporation had finally decided to provide her with; Doris Bauer, who looked after things on Flatbush Avenue when Cynthia wasn't around to personally supervise the operation of the branch; Mrs. Donner, the woman who was currently in the process of negotiating the purchase of the Forest Hills chapter on Austin Road; Lena and Barry; Cynthia's part-time secretary; and of course, NuBodies' creative flame—burning progressively hotter—D. Wayne Eisenstern, otherwise known affectionately as D. W.

"Rules may be rules," Leonard announced, "and diets may be diets. But there's nothing like a good bottle of champagne to see the old year out and usher in the new. So I propose a toast, ladies and gentlemen. To NuBodies—"

Glasses were raised high. Cynthia gave her mother a hug, glanced over her shoulder, and smiled at Barry, engaged in a heated discussion with D. W.

"—may she become everything we want her to become, the best service organization of its kind . . . anywhere in the country!"

"In the world!" a tipsy Vivian Hollander called out.

"Amen," Lena said, the glass to her lips.

Cynthia added, "I'll second that."

"Hear, hear," yelled D. W.

And Leonard said, "Cheers," and downed his drink neat, one arm over Jeanette's shoulders as if he were somehow afraid she'd stray out of his sphere of influence.

The champagne was cool and tart against Cynthia's tongue. She let it trickle down her throat, savoring its piquancy, the sharp acidity of fermentation. It was a taste she had gone out of her way to avoid, having denied herself all alcoholic beverages since she had promised to stick to the diet. That seemed like ages ago in another place far removed from the present, physically as well as psychologically. She took a sip of her champagne as Leonard refilled everyone's glass.

"I don't know what's keeping them," she said to Lena.

"Do you want me to make you up a plate of cold cuts?"

"No, not yet," she said. "It's the least he can do, to show his face. And he was supposed to bring Natalie. It's just unfair, mother. I don't know how he can be so inconsiderate, insensitive too. He knows how much this means to me."

"I'll see if Barry wants a sandwich," Lena said.

She turned away and Cynthia leaned against the side of her desk. She looked around, wondering when the bubble would burst. Weren't things going too smoothly, too quickly, moving so fast she felt dizzy with her accomplishments? In little more than a year she had put away several thousand dollars in her savings account, not to mention the weekly salary she earned, nor the rising payroll and the mounting business expenses. The corporation wasn't pinched for funds. Leonard watched over like a hawk the cash reserve of nearly ten thousand in the bank. That's okay too, she thought. He's more responsible than I am. Let him attend to the bookkeeping. I'll worry about the people. It's a perfect division of labor.

But at the moment she was less concerned with Nu-Bodies' future, than she was about her husband and her daughter. The apartment had been quiet for a long time in an unspoken truce like a lull before a storm, but the storm hadn't broken and she was perfectly content to maintain the status quo.

Natalie was nearly fourteen and an eighth grader at Winthrop Junior High, a five-minute walk from home. She had entered puberty with all the disadvantages Cynthia had tried so hard to help her overcome. If she was swathed in baby fat two years before, she was now more firmly entrenched in what Cynthia considered a self-destructive shell, a wall of fat. Natalie was more than overweight and Cynthia blamed Manny for catering to the girl's compulsive eating habits. She looks up to him like he's the sun, moon, and stars put together. If he curbed his appetite a little more, the way he did last year, so would she. She certainly doesn't make any attempt to cut down, or model herself after me.

Recently she had noticed the bruises, perhaps permanent black-and-blue marks, along the insides of Natalie's thighs. She was sitting cross-legged on the couch, watching television. The folds of her terrycloth robe had parted, just long enough for Cynthia to observe the same kind of friction marks—"fat tattoos," she once had called them—that she too had suffered, up and until she'd begun to watch her weight. To see those kind of lurid bruises on a youngster, a girl who was barely a teenager, had made her want to shake Natalie into an awareness of what she was doing to herself. Even Lena, who for years had catered to her granddaughter's propensity for all the wrong kinds of food, had commented about the problem just the week before. "Maybe you're right," she said. "It's not healthy for a young girl to be so heavy. Even you weren't that chubby when you were her age."

"Talk to her, mom. Do something. Something," she begged, more of a plea than a suggestion. "I can't get through to her. No matter how hard I try she just turns the other cheek, turns away. She doesn't want to listen to me and Manny isn't making any effort to help. So maybe you can reach her, mom. Try, that's all I'm asking. Just try. Maybe she'll open up to you."

Lena had tried. She'd even given Cynthia a "progress report" a few days later. The answer was no, prognosis negative. "She got fresh with me, honest to God. She told me to mind my own business, it's her house."

"I should wash her mouth out, what kind of thing is that to say to a grandmother."

"She's sensitive about it. It's okay. I know she loves me."

Why hadn't Lena said, "I know she loves you, *too?*" It was no wonder that she was beginning to believe, deep inside her where gut emotions never lied and never made up stories, that somehow Natalie had done more than turn against her. I can't remember the last time she even gave me a hug and a kiss, or said a kind word. What did I do to her that she's so angry? Maybe that's why they're not here tonight, because she, not Manny, was the one who refused to come.

By the time the party broke up, less than an hour later, she had downed three glasses of champagne in quick succession. She'd filled a paper plate with more food than the diet prescribed for the evening meal. The slices of cold roast beef and breast of turkey were perfectly acceptable. But she had far more than she knew she should have, far more than she had allowed herself to eat in recent memory.

Sure, she thought, out of aggravation that's why, just like the old days—that's a laugh. What's so different about the new days, anyway? I'm still stuck living along a demilitarized zone. Sure, that's what they call it. An armed camp. There's a lull in the fighting, a truce no one talks about. No one's dropping bombs but no one's sitting around a conference table either, trying to work up solutions for a lasting peace.

"Come, let's go home . . . to World War Two and a half," she told Lena. The joke seemed to go over her mother's head. "I just want to get Barry first. Why don't you go downstairs and see if you can hail a cab. There should be plenty around at this hour. And don't worry about the neighborhood. Flatbush Avenue is one of the safest streets in the city."

Barry was still involved in what seemed to be the same animated conversation with D. W. which had begun an hour before. She was pleased that they got along. Maybe he'll pick up D. W.'s drive, ambition, the way he pushes himself. He's gotten too damn lazy for his own good, nearly failing French last term. He used to be such a studier, a real bookworm. I don't know what's happened to him all of a sudden.

"I was just telling Barry about how I got into advertising," Eisenstern said when she approached them.

Impulsively, she hugged Barry to her side. No attempt was made to wiggle free. He merely stood there, his eyes on the glass of champagne he held in both of his hands. The bubbles had escaped, vanishing into the smoke-filled air. The champagne was flat; the party was over. It was time to go home.

"Tell him how he should buckle down more," she said. "Tell him what kind of marks you brought home when you were in high school."

"Mother," Barry said.

"My son gets embarrassed very easily. He's a very refined young man. High-class," she said with a laugh, knowing how Barry hated to be teased. "Sure, why not, Brooks Brothers suits, fancy loafers—"

"Weejuns," Barry said.

"Mr. Preppy," D. W. said. "Well," and he grinned and drained his glass, "we'll be seeing you. Take care of yourself, Bar. And watch out for your ole lady. She's a tough cookie, hard as nails, Mrs. Margold is."

"What did he mean by that?" Barry asked when D. W. had turned away.

"I have no idea. But your grandmother's waiting for us downstairs. And you had too much champagne for your own good."

"Only two glasses."

"And you're already wobbly. I'll have to carry you home yet."

"I like it though," he said as he helped her on with her coat. "It makes me . . . I don't know, forget a lot of things."

"And what do you have to forget about at sixteen-and-a-half, may I ask?"

"Oh, you'd be surprised, Cynthia," he said mysteriously.

She was less surprised about his vague and enigmatic comment, one which should have puzzled her under any other set of circumstances, than she was about the way he tossed off her name as if it were common practice. It's the alcohol, she thought. I had no business letting him drink. But he's not a baby, either. I guess sooner or later he's gotta learn, same as I did. Trouble is, I wish it was later. He's growing up too quick and I don't have a chance to enjoy him the way I'd like to.

"Manny, you up? What happened? I thought you and Natalie were coming to the party?" she called out as soon as she fitted the key in the lock, turned the cylinder, then the doorknob, and stepped inside. The lights were on, but she didn't hear the TV going in the living room. She slipped out of her coat and walked into the foyer. "Man-

261

ny?" She turned around. "They must have gone to the corner for a soda or something."

"I'll boil water. You want Sanka or tea?"

"Tea."

"Barry, you want anything?" Lena asked. "A nice hot drink?"

"No thanks. I'm going to sleep. I have a headache."

"Drinks like it's going out of style," said Cynthia, even as she moved from the kitchen to the hall and then into her bedroom. With one hand she reached back, grabbed hold of her dress zipper and began to pull it slowly down. She kicked off her shoes, wiggled her toes, and turned on the light near the bed. Two dresser drawers, belonging to Manny's highboy, were slightly ajar. She stepped out of her dress and moved to the closet, reaching out to push the drawers back into place. It was a gesture so automatic, compulsive in its own right, that she would not have thought twice about it had the drawers not been empty.

She tossed the dress onto the bed and pulled the drawer all the way open. Sligh Furniture, she read. Holland, Michigan. The label was burned or permanently inked into the inner side of the drawer. Other than that, there was nothing. She shoved it closed and tried another. It, too, was empty, showing where the joints were separating, drawing apart from each other either through age or overuse or both.

"Mother!" she grabbed a robe and hurried out of the bedroom, stockinged feet rustling, whispering loudly in her ears. A thousand feather fans, egret plumes, and muscular Nubians at her disposal, D. W. once had said. Once. When? she thought. When did this happen? Tonight of course. I can't even think straight.

In the hall, standing in front of Barry's door, she listened to the whine of the teakettle, a high-pitched whistle that felt as if it were cutting right through her. In one ear and out the other, she said to herself, tying the robe tightly around her. Then she knocked on the door. "Are you decent?"

There was a scurry of sheets. A moment later Barry said weakly, "All right, come on in."

She let herself into the room and looked down at him. He lay in bed, his hands draped carefully over the covers, his face inexplicably red. "Sorry," she said, wondering how he'd gotten so overheated in such a short period of time.

The champagne, probably. "I just wanted to check something." Natalie still kept her clothes in the smaller of the two bedrooms in the apartment, although she slept in the other room with Cynthia. She had her own dresser and Cynthia reached for the top drawer, amazed at the way her fingers seemed to tremble of their own accord. It pulled out easily, lightly, gliding on its track with no weight behind it. The drawer was empty.

"Your tea's ready," Lena said. She appeared in the doorway, having changed into a drab faded housedress and backless slippers instead of high heels.

"What is going on in here?" Barry demanded. "Can't I have a little privacy, for God sakes?"

She ignored him. "What's going on here is right. Absolutely. A hundred percent." She searched her mother's face. The lines of age and worry, told her nothing she already hadn't guessed, hadn't figured out for herself. "Where are they, mother? What's happened to all their clothes?"

"Whose clothes?" Barry said, his eyes sparkling, opening wide in surprise, interest. He sat up in bed, pulled the quilt around his waist and leaned forward, trying to peer into the opened dresser drawer.

She slammed it shut. "Your sister's clothes, your father's too. They took everything."

"What? Fat Nat took all her clothes? What for? Did she run away, is that it?"

"No, not *she,*" Cynthia said, still staring at her mother. "*They.* She wouldn't go anywhere without him. Well mother? Mother?" She felt like screaming, throwing herself against Lena, and crying and beating her fists in frustration and rage that rose up so quickly inside of her that she wondered if her hair was standing on end. Her fingers curled and uncurled like the petals of a flower caught by time-lapse photography. "Well, where is my husband, my daughter, mother!"

"Let's talk in the kitchen. Let the boy get some sleep," Lena said in a soft voice, the words as fluttery as Cynthia's stomach. She stepped inside the room with a tentative slippered foot, bent down, and kissed Barry on the forehead. "Sleep tight, sweetheart. Sweet dreams. Go to sleep now."

She used the same words thirty years ago. The same words I used when the kids were little. But everything

263

does change; that's just the point. It doesn't stay the same, even if you want it to.

"Who wants to sleep?" Barry said, making a sound that was and wasn't a laugh. "This is too exciting. You mean they just abandoned us, just like that? Didn't he tell you he was leaving, mom?"

"He told me nothing," she said. "Nothing."

"Rien," Barry snickered.

"Just wipe that smug expression off your face before I really tear my hair out," she yelled. "I want my daughter, your sister. That's all I give a damn about. How dare he take her like this? Who does he think he is, walking out without a word, no goodbye, no explanation, nothing. He's like a kidnapper."

"Well, if you know Nat the way I do," Barry said, "she went with him because she's always been daddy's good little girl. Besides, the two of you don't get along, anyway."

"Cynthia," Lena said. "It's not for him to hear. He's too young. Come outside and we'll talk about it. Let him get some sleep."

"Not for him to hear?" she repeated. "What, I should tell him his father's on vacation, went to the Fontainebleau, Grossinger's with his daughter, is that it? He should drop dead on the street—"

"Cynthia! He's the boy's father! Please," Lena cried, "I beg of you."

"—that's what he should do. I can't help it, Barry. He's just a goddamn s.o.—"

"Cynthia!"

Everything was red: the walls that should have been a soft cocoa brown; the carpet, a russet tweed when it was new; the dust ruffle on the box spring that was dark-brown corduroy. But everything was fire-engine red now.

"Go to sleep. We'll talk about it in the morning. You're not a child anymore, not after tonight. You're learning about the facts of life," she said to him. "Firsthand, that s.o.b. I'll kill him. He took my kid, mother, he took my baby. Where did he take her?"

"Mom please, come on, don't cry. I can't stand that. Don't, please." Barry threw the covers back and hurried towards her, his arms over her shoulders, his breath puppy warm, boyish against the hollow of her neck.

"How do you like them apples," she said, one hand wiping back a tear. She tried to laugh, but gave up in despair. "My own kid doesn't give a damn if I live or die, doesn't love her own mother like I've been a witch, a monster all her life."

"Of course she loves you, Cynthia," Lena said.

"Love, another joke, another bellyache, that's what it is. But he's not going to get away with this so fast, I assure you. I'll speak to a lawyer, that's what I'll do. We have an attorney working for us and I'll speak to him. What kind of home can he provide her with when—" She stopped short, stopped herself from saying it. There were certain things not so much sacred as profane, things she didn't want Barry to know about. "Your father deserted us, Barry, he deserted us and that's all there is to it."

"You deserted him a long time ago, Cynthia," Lena said. The voice leaped out at her from the doorway. Yet at the same time it was subdued, as gentle as a caress. "And if he hadn't left, you would've, sooner or later. So why make an issue when you saw it coming for as long as you did? It's what you wanted, isn't that so?"

"Not with Natalie," she replied. "Not even to discuss it with me first, talk it over? She's my child, mother. She's my own flesh and blood. She came out of *me,* don't you see that?"

"Mom, let's not talk about it now, okay?"

"Sure, you're right, right again," she said, trying to sound less hysterical. She took a deep breath as if she were coming up for air. "Go to sleep. Your mother'll be fine. I'm just overwrought. It caught me off guard, maybe. Shh, go to sleep." She kissed him again and tucked him in the way she had done when he was still her littlest and her sweetest, her baby boy, her first-born, Barry who was going to grow up to be whatever he wanted, whatever his heart desired.

"You're gonna be okay, aren't you?" he whispered.

"Sure," she said, winking as if they had a secret no one else could ever share. "Your mother's a fighter, just remember that. She doesn't give up so easy. Tomorrow everything'll look better in the light of day. Now go to sleep and don't worry about a thing. I mean, don't we all have each other? So what's the difference, right? Right?"

Wrong, she thought. W-R-O-N-G. Wrong.

265

Business was business, R-I-G-H-T. If that's the way it is, that's the way it is. Besides, a lot of these kids are paying for the classes out of their own pockets, using allowance money, or the money they make from part-time jobs. I have an obligation to other people's children. Isn't that another joke to add to the long list of many.

So she was getting dressed, ready to leave the house, and catch a cab for Flatbush Avenue where she would conduct a class for teenagers that Saturday afternoon. She put on a slacks set, a bulky knit sweater so she wouldn't have to worry about wearing a light fall jacket. Then she tied a scarf around the handle of her shoulder bag. It was pure silk, signed Hermès. D. W. had given it to her "as a small token of esteem, my dear, on this your first anniversary as an official new body." I never would have spent so much money on myself, that's for sure, she thought.

She was glad she had a class, especially one that would only be attended by teenagers, youngsters all in need of an answer to their weight problems. Like a den mother, that's what I am. Aunt Cynthia. At least somebody needs me.

The telephone rang. "I'll get it!" she yelled out. She hurried into the kitchen as it rang a second time. Lena was sitting at the table, reading the obituary column in the morning paper. ("What's so morbid about it, may I ask? How else am I supposed to know if someone's died? Believe me, when you get to be my age, you'll understand.") She looked up and Cynthia put a finger to her lips, certain it would be Manny.

It wasn't.

"Hello, mother? This is Natalie."

Natalie who? "Hello, Natalie," she said, trying to be calm, even-tempered, cool of voice and heart and spirit. It didn't work. She felt her stomach fluttering, turning somersaults just as it had done the night before. "Where are you, Natalie honey? My God I've been frantic. I didn't sleep all night. Not a note, nothing. Are you with your father, at least?"

"Yes," the girl said. "I just wanted you to know that I was okay."

"Well where are you, for God sakes?"

"We're staying with . . . just a minute."

Gobbledegook, garble, and more garble as someone pulled the phone away from her. She heard muted voices, too. Apparently, Natalie was now waiting for instructions, cupping the receiver with the palm of her hand. Lena mouthed, "Is it?"

She read her mother's lips, nodded her head.

Then Natalie got back on. "With friends, friends of daddy's," she said.

"And when are you coming back home, Natalie?"

"I'm not."

Two words, simple as can be, she thought. They cut into her like sharp, well-honed knives. "What d'you mean, you're not?" her voice rose, not so much tormented as aggrieved.

"I'm gonna stay here with daddy. I want to live with him, that's why I took all my clothes. Here, I'll put him on."

"What'd she say, what'd she say?" Lena whispered. She got to her feet and stood near the phone, her arms crossed in a kind of sign language of resignation, imminent defeat.

"Cynthia?"

"Yes, Manny, I'm here," she said. Where else should I be? This is the only home I know, you forget. All of them, out of heart, out of sight, out of mind.

"It wasn't my idea, believe me. The kid wouldn't listen. She wants to live with me, if that's okay with you."

"It is not okay with me. I want my child back, you, you—" Calm down, down, it won't work any other way. Lena said it, you get more flies with honey than with vinegar. Go slow, easy now. Just take your time, compose yourself. "Where are you? What are you exposing her to, Forman?"

"I'm not exposing her to anything but a father's love."

"Oh what bullshit, what paltry bullshit, you phony!" she yelled. "I want my child back, do you hear me, Forman. There are laws. You have no right to just, just steal away in the middle of the night."

"It wasn't the middle of the night," he said. "And I want a separation."

"A what?"

"You heard me. A separation. And Natalie is old enough to make up her own mind. I didn't twist her arm or force her to do anything she didn't want to, Cynthia. She wants to live with me. And that's that."

"That is not that, Forman," she said. She pressed one

hand over her heart, as if to stifle the frenzy of irregular thumping beats. A muscle or a nerve, both perhaps, pulsed and danced along the inside of one trousered thigh. "I'm protected by laws, for your information. A mother's children can not be taken away from her so easily. I'll go to court first. I'll sue for divorce on the grounds of adul— desertion. No judge in his right mind would allow a youngster, a child at such an impressionable age, to live in some tawdry love-nest if you want to know the truth. You're around the corner, aren't you? You're at Henny's?"

"Shh, Barry'll hear," Lena whispered.

"I'm not at Henny's," he said. "And don't give me your highfalutin crap about 'tawdry love-nests'. The only thing that's tawdry was our marriage. Well, now you're married to NuBodies, Mrs. Margold, I hope it warms your bed at night."

"I want Natalie back. Now. Today. I'll come and get her myself, if it's necessary."

"Why, so you can aggravate the kid about her weight, try to turn her into a junior version of you? Well, it doesn't work that way anymore, Cynthia."

"You're poisoning her against me, you bastard!" she screamed.

"In any event divorce on grounds of desertion is invalid in this state unless the husband's been gone for more than two years. Less than twenty-four hours is a considerable difference in time, wouldn't you agree?"

"You'll hear from my attorney."

"NuBodies' attorney, you mean. Do they wipe your ass for you too, now that they own you?"

"Drop dead and go to hell. If I see you on the street, Forman, I'll tear your eyes out!" What am I saying? What's going on? I can't even hear myself think. I want my daughter, that's all I give a damn about. "Just . . . just please, bring Natalie home and do whatever you want. I'll give you a divorce, anything, but I want my child."

"But she wants to stay with me. I can't force her to do what she doesn't want to. She's almost fourteen—"

"And she's still a baby. She's a baby, Forman. She won't be able to go to school like other children—"

"She'll go to school. The term starts Monday and she'll be there, just like everyone else. I'll be in touch, Cynthia. Give my love to my kid, Lena too." He hung up with a loud, resonating click.

"What'd he say?" Lena asked, tugging at her sleeve.

"Click. He wishes you a long life. Good-bye mom, I'm gonna be late."

"Cynthia," she called after her.

"Click," she said again. "Click, click, click."

December 1966

SHE HEARD THAT *click* all through the fall—"Not the winter," D. W. reminded her—of her discontent. Manny called every Friday evening. Ostensibly, it was to speak to his son, to ask after Lena, to let her know Natalie was doing fine and that she was happy and healthy. But when everyone had gotten on and off the phone that hung along one tired kitchen wall, it would be her turn, either to hang up or exchange a few meager words with her husband. The corporation's legal counsel had advised against pressing for a court battle over custody rights. Although Natalie was clearly a minor, Forman still made a good enough living to support the child. And if the girl wanted to live with her father, nine judges out of ten would go along with the youngster's wishes.

"Even if they're living with his . . . you know. His mistress?"

"You don't know that for certain, Mrs. Margold, do you?"

"No," she admitted. "In fact, I don't even think they are living around the corner. Not now, anyway. I would have heard something from the neighbors. Or somebody."

All through September she refused to talk to him. She returned his checks, unopened. Yet as the weeks dragged on her resolve faltered and the first few tattered comments were exchanged. Brief, ragged and heartless though she felt them to be, it was still better than nothing. But if her marital life was floundering, undergoing its death throes, the other side of her that was business with a capital B, was skyrocketing. Endicott ("End-the-cut just won't do," said D. W. "It's not zippy enough. It's too obvious.

Just give me time. I'll come up with something clever, rest assured."), Sucker ("Again my dear, let's not be obviously shabby and call the man by what he hasn't been able to perform in years.") & Grave (". . . isn't even the word for it when I hit him for a raise, gave me this look like he was on his last.") had renewed D. W.'s contract with NuBodies for another six months. Their commission went up accordingly, but even Leonard was inclined to agree that the higher cost of advertising was, in the long run, ultimately worth the expense.

"Adrift on a sea of fat," lamented D. W. the day the call came through that he didn't have to pack his wilted plants and head back across the East River. "Flesh peddlers, that's all they are, selling my soul, my creative spirit, the very fair flower of my youth, to the highest bidder." He sighed and buried his head in his hands. "A mother who's a dragon, a father who's a shark, and me, a nice bar mitzvah boy at their mercy, at the beck and call of ex-chubbies. My God, and I thought I was going to be a star, Cynthia, a star!"

"You love it," she laughed.

He raised his head, brushed aside imaginary tears. "Of course I do," he said. "If I didn't, I wouldn't be here. So let's go over your schedule for next week. We've already booked you on Delta's seven-thirty flight to Memphis—"

"Memphis?"

"Yep, as in Tennessee. The Jack Paar of the *Volunteer State* would you believe that's what they call themselves, is hot for your bod. Wants you to tell those Southern belles why it's bad news to stuff their faces with grits and corn pone."

While in Tennessee she did a stint in Nashville to get the most out of her mileage ticket, which entitled her to a free stop on the way back to New York. The week after her sojourn below the Mason-Dixon line, she did two radio spots in Philadelphia and one in Camden. Wherever she went she met the same kind of people: vocal, eager, all anxious for her to show them how they could help themselves. Thanksgiving was occupied with a new round of negotiations, this time for the sale of a franchise to a group of women from South Orange, New Jersey. Among the five of them, they had lost over six hundred four pounds.

"I say we up our figure to twelve-fifty," Leonard said. "Remember, we're dealing with five people, not just one, like Lewars in Wilmington. If they've gotten this far, they're not about to give up so easily. Another five hundred a head isn't going to kill anyone or break the bank."

"But Leonard—" she said.

"But Leonard just remember what you told me about the fluctuations of the marketplace. Well, this is it, Cynthia. So you might as well sit back, relax, and enjoy yourself. Twelve thousand five hundred. Same percentage figures as last time."

"Twelve-fifty," she said, knowing it wasn't wise to argue. Besides, he usually got his way, so what would be the point. And so it was that by the time the holiday weekend was over, she had secured another colored pushpin to the map of the United States which hung in the office. Now there were seven red pins clustered around the upper right-hand corner of the country. NuBodies Land, she decided to call it. And this is just the start.

Every Friday evening, punctual and reliable as Naval Observatory Time, the phone rang and the knife cut just a little deeper.

"Talk to him, talk to him for heaven sakes," Lena hissed as she held the telephone receiver in one hand, a white molded plastic club to beat her into insensitivity and submission.

She sounded weary saying, "Hello, Forman. How's my Natalie? Is she happy? Is she feeling good? How's her schoolwork coming along? Yes, yes everything is fine. We're all . . . hunky-dory, peachy keen. Yes he's dating. He's going out tonight in fact, to Greenwich Village. I don't know. That's where all the kids hang out these days."

In December, after several weeks of belaboring the point, after seemingly endless days of hearing Lena berate her for her stubbornness, she agreed to meet with him, "To see if we can iron out our difficulties, Cynthia, now that we've given each other a breathing spell. I mean, after all, we're two intelligent people who loved each other, remember?"

"Who can forget," she said. She made sure to laugh, nervous though it may have sounded.

The location where they would hold their "reunion"

was at his suggestion, not hers. "Coney Island," he said when she asked him where he wanted to meet. "Remember what it was like, eighteen years ago? We had our first date there, remember?"

Again, "Who can forget," only now she refrained from laughing. Somehow, there was nothing humorous about being reminded of the roots and origins of their marriage. It would be, she decided after she hung up, like laughing at myself. And I'm not brave enough to do that, not yet. But I will be. I'll learn. Because if I don't, then I'll really be in big trouble. She picked up the phone again and called D. W. to tell him, "Momentous news, straight from the horse's mouth. No, I'm not the horse in question, Eisenstern. Well I don't care if you're in the middle of . . . whatever. Just listen for a second, will you . . ."

A pale skinny sun hung like a Necco wafer in the sky. The Coney Island boardwalk was deserted, save for small huddling groups of old men and women, sitting on benches and folding chairs, heads turned up to face the thin and fitful winter light. They had blankets wrapped around them as if they were on shipboard, voyaging to warmer climes. She saw her father reflected in a dozen different wrinkled faces and she wanted to cry for the loss. But she didn't. Tears get you nowhere, she decided. I'm as slim-trim as he ever dreamed. Of course, it seems to have cost more than I bargained on. Like maybe a husband and a daughter.

"I thought it was you," he said, "but I wasn't sure."

"You mean to say you've forgotten how good ole Cynthia looks? It's only been two months, Forman." Give or take an eternity.

"The dark glasses, that's why. They're new, aren't they?" He shook the spare loose change in his trouser pocket. His hand jiggled up and down as though he had a frog in his pants.

"Yes," she said. She wanted to laugh, if only to break the barrier that had somehow been thrown up around them. It was like an unscalable electrified fence, alive with hot sparks of tension, nervousness. "Shall we walk?" she suggested.

"Thanks for agreeing to come," he said.

"Don't thank me, thank Lena. She was the one who did all the convincing. You'd think she was trying to get me married off, the way she was so determined we get together. But she liked you from the very beginning, the very start. Remember?"

"So did your father, if memory serves me."

"Yes, sure. So did my father." She jabbed her ungloved hands down into the pockets of her coat. I lived with this man all those years and now it seems like I'm walking with a stranger. When did all this start to happen, these changes, this inability to go back? We were so happy for so long, I just don't understand what went wrong. Did he stop growing with me or did I? What did he want from me that I didn't give him?

It was a New York December with an offshore breeze and no premonition of snow in the sky. The air brushed cold and dry against her cheeks with no hint of brine or moisture. The sun rose up higher in the washed-out blue sky, but there was no warmth to speak of. She wondered why the old people craned their necks, as if they were intent upon catching a glimpse of heaven, some kind of radiant shore she knew nothing about.

"Remember?" he said, and before she could pull back he slipped his hand through hers. They walked like a weak chain, not even forged, merely linked for the moment. "Remember how we took the subway, the elevated actually? How the two of us stopped at every counter Nathan's had to offer, sampling the entire menu? Remember when we went on the roller coaster? They called it the Cyclone, didn't they? Or was it the Hurricane? I'm not sure, but you almost lost your lunch, you got so sick."

"I thought you were the one who got sick," she said. "And didn't I have to drag you home? You looked green. I remember. You were positively green. I took you back to your parents' and your mother nearly had a fit. She took one look at you and clapped her hands together like you'd just had a brush with death."

"Come on, it wasn't that bad. A little dizzy, nauseous maybe, but I wasn't all that sick, not that I can remember."

"It was a different kind of place then, after the war. A different element."

"Yeah, it's gotten kind of honky-tonk, hasn't it? But I always liked the boardwalk in the winter. Makes me think of Atlantic City. Remember the time we drove down with the kids, maybe five-six years ago? We stayed at . . . what was the name of that hotel where they served kippers for breakfast and there was a cage of monkeys in the pool house?"

"The Morton," she said. "And Barry got lost on the boardwalk and Mr. Peanut found him, remember that?"

"Remember?" he laughed. "Who can forget. You were going nuts, tearing your hair out and getting so hysterical when we couldn't find him."

"Well he was a little boy then, Manny. Of course I was worried. But remember how you got up one morning, six o'clock I think it was, to go bike riding with him?"

"It nearly collapsed under me, but I managed," Manny said. "We biked all the way down to the end of the boardwalk, or just about, before coming back." Suddenly he squeezed her hand, stopped short by the railing which overlooked the empty beach and the steel-gray ocean, and turned to face her.

She slipped her hand free and looked down at her feet. Thirty-dollar shoes from I. Miller, she thought. So things *do* change, even when you don't want them to. "We had lots of good times, the four of us together," she said. Her voice was low and ached for a past that had escaped. Over his shoulder, the gray water peaked and foamed, revealing an undercoat of green surviving like the memory of warm and drowsy summer days.

"We still can," he said.

She felt maudlin and uncomfortable. "How?"

"By going back to what you were, by being a mother and a wife again."

"Instead of?"

"Instead of someone who's wrapped their entire life in a phobia—"

"Is that what NuBodies is to you, just an obsession, a phobia of mine? Is it, Manny, is it?"

He said nothing. The answer was revealed in the short curt nod of his head. She noticed twin streaks of gray where there had never been gray before. He's not even forty yet, but didn't he once tell me his father turned gray overnight, something like that?

"I made nearly as much money this year as you did," she felt urged to announce. "I'm not saying that just to throw it up in your face, believe me. But the point I'm making is that my little business means a lot to me. It makes me feel like someone, a useful person, I guess."

"And being Mrs. Margold isn't useful?"

"I didn't say that, Manny. There you go putting words in my mouth. But . . . but it's not as if this just started last week, or the day before yesterday. I started holding those meetings. Almost four years ago. It didn't happen overnight. You had ample time to adjust to the changes, to make some kind of concession, compromise."

"You ignored your family in the process, that's all I'm trying to say."

"And I disagree."

"Well, there you have it. You want your cake and you want to eat it, too."

"And what's so difficult about that? I'm ten times more attractive, more of a woman, I mean, than I was when I was heavy. One would think you'd appreciate that. But no. Instead you gave me a hard time every step of the way. And now, on top of everything else, I'm getting blamed for being a lousy wife, a worse mother."

"Because you have no distance. You can't just step back and see yourself, the way you act, Cynthia. But I can. I have a ringside seat."

"The way I acted wasn't much different than the way you acted. I don't know if you're interested in hearing it, Manny, but don't think I've gotten over the fact of you and Henny. It's not the affair. It's the fact that you picked my best friend. Out of all the people in the world to choose from, you went and picked someone who was as close to me as a sister."

"And you never fooled around?" he snapped. "You think I'm such a big dummy I didn't see what was happening between you and your partner, the pajama king."

"It only happened after I found out about you and Henny. And it's over, has been for more than a year, longer even. And it was nothing to begin with. I got fooled. Okay? Are you satisfied? Your wife got taken for a ride, plain talk." Far off there were screeching gulls, riding the air currents over the oil spills and floating garbage.

"Well?" he said.

"Well what? What do you want me to say, Manny?"

"Look," and he pulled his hands out of his trouser pockets. The tips of his fingers were calloused, the mounds of his palms rough, weathered. His blunt cropped nails were thick, cracked, worn. They were the hands of a worker, hands that struggled day after day to bring home a decent living, "a good living" he always called it. "Are these the hands of a lazy man, are they?"

"No. No one ever said you were lazy, Manny. Never. You work like a dog. I know that. You always have."

"These hands have been at it for a long time, Cynthia. Nothing comes easy, right? Isn't that what I always used to say? But Cynthia, these hands are good for another thirty years. Look, we don't have to stay in the old neighborhood if you don't want to. I . . . I went looking at houses last week, out on the Island."

"Houses?" She cocked her head to one side, her expression at once incredulous and disturbed. "What kind of houses and with what money, may I ask?"

"Nothing fancy. In a development. They only want ten percent down and the rest I can get financing through my bank. But at least I won't be paying rent to some crummy landlord. Like I'm my own boss now with my business, I'll be my own landlord, too. And there'd be room for Lena, a separate bedroom plus bath. We can try to make things better, Cynthia. I'm willing to compromise, to make concessions. Isn't that what you said you wanted from me?"

"A house, our own house," she said. The laughter escaped, lilting and nervous.

"All I'm asking is for you give up this—"

"Phobia."

"No," he said. "NuBodies. What do you need the headaches for, the aggravations? My business is picking up. I still make enough for all of us. So you won't have as much money as you do now. But there's more to life than just that, Cynthia."

"I can't," she said. The words tore at her. Her insides felt as if they were being flung back and forth by winds of hurricane velocity. The seagulls were now circling overhead, screeching loudly. "It's part of me now, Manny. I've watched it grow just like a child."

"But your other one, your real child means shit, is that it?"

"You took her away from me, Manny," she said, trying to control her rising temper. "You said she wanted to go with you. You said she didn't want to turn into a junior me. Well, you're going to have your hands full raising her, that's all I can say. Because she's a very unhappy youngster. She could use seeing a psychiatrist, if you want to get down to the nitty-gritty. Fat children, teenagers who eat compulsively, obsessively the way she does—the way she has for years, are emotionally disturbed. And you're not helping her any or setting any kind of example for her to follow."

"I won't tell you the things she said to me."

"No, please. I don't want to hear. Don't hurt me any more than you already have, Manny."

"Don't hurt *me? Me?*" and he thumped his fist against his chest with such force she was afraid he'd crack a rib. "Always the villain of the piece, the fall guy. I'm the one who's always at fault, always wrong."

"I didn't say that. No one's wrong anymore. Okay? We're both wrong. So let's not drag it out any longer."

"Fine, whatever you say, Cynthia. If that's what you want, it's your decision. We'll make the separation legal. And if you want a divorce, we'll worry about it when the time comes."

"And Natalie?"

"Stays with me, no discussion." He turned abruptly away, grabbed hold of the metal guard rail, and stared out over the water. The gesture was so dramatic, so unlike him, that for a moment she nearly forgot who she was with.

That was the only real surprise of the afternoon. The rest had been expected, as if she had known what he would say even before he spoke. You can't go back, she thought, telling herself—convincing herself, too—even as the words drummed into her head. "It just doesn't work anymore, Manny. But at least we tried. Right?" she turned her mouth up. A "brave little grin," one she hadn't worn in months, flashed across her lips like an echo of the past.

"I really tried," he said, turning back to her. "I did the best I could, the best I knew how. Obviously, it wasn't good enough."

"When can I come and see my daughter, Forman?"

"Soon," he said. "I'll let you know. And if you don't come to her, I'll make sure she comes to you."

"Just as long as I can see her and spend some time with her. It doesn't matter where."

"You'll see her," he said. "Sooner or later."

June 1967

SIX MONTHS LATER, she wrapped the last dish and wedged it carefully inside the reinforced cardboard drum. "I can't think of anything else, can you?"

Lena stood with her in the kitchen. She swiveled her head around, completing a half-circle. "Nope," she said. "Looks like we've got everything. Whoever moves in is going to get themselves a beautiful apartment, no matter what you say."

"Beautiful for two people. A young couple, yes. But it's still hard to believe, isn't it?"

"It's an accumulation of years, that's why."

"I hope he gets good use out of the furniture. At least my kid will have a decent bed to sleep on again."

"You did the right thing," Lena told her, "giving all that stuff to Manny. Do you have any idea what it costs to furnish an apartment these days? A small fortune, that's what."

"Which is precisely why I was so insistent upon subletting a furnished apartment, mom. I just didn't want to look at all my old furniture. I just wanted it out, know what I mean? And this way, everything'll be fresh, new. Mr. Caulfield hardly lived there, from what he tells me; less than a year at most. And you saw the kind of taste he had. He may just agree to sell everything when the time comes, but the important thing is that it's big and the location is perfect. Three bedrooms right on Riverside Drive—"

"And with a river view, don't forget."

"Who can forget," she said, laughing. "And as soon as we move into our new offices downtown, it'll just be a short hop to work. It couldn't be more convenient. The idea of living in Manhattan gives me the chills. I'm so excited."

"I'm all done, mom," Barry said as he came into the kitchen. He turned his head around in a survey that took in all the empty spaces, the round light patches on the walls where pots once hung. Finally, he looked back at her. "I'll miss the cardinals on the wallpaper."

"Who can see them, they're so faded."

"I'll miss them anyway, and the noises from the back alley and Mrs. Kipness banging up with her broomstick."

She couldn't tell if he was being sarcastic.

"When are they coming?" he asked.

She checked her watch. "Any minute. You sure you took everything you wanted now? I don't want you moaning about how you forgot something, when it'll be too late."

"No, everything I wanted is packed and ready to go," he said. He stuck his hands into the back pockets of his tight-fitting Levis and rocked back and forth on the balls of his feet. "Unreal," he said. "So we're finally making the big time, eh mom. Fun City, doo-wah diddy." He whistled between his teeth and she found herself smiling again, shaking, too.

"Well, you wanted your own room and I told you you'd get it, sooner or later." Sooner or later—the sonuvabitch, it's been two months since I saw her. Her skin was all broken out. My heart went out, and when I tried to give her a twenty-dollar bill to buy herself something, anything she wanted, she just pulled her hand away like it was stung, like I was a snake trying to poison her or something. Oh God, when does it get better?

"Better late than never," he said. "And at least I can finish up at a new school with decent people. Wingate's the pits, lemme tell you."

"A beautiful school," she said to Lena. "I don't know what the kid wants. They went out of their way to be nice to him, believe me. I had talks with guidance counselors, the assistant principal. They were ready to do anything—"

"Except to pass me," he said.

"Well whose fault is that, Mr. Smart Guy? When you don't study, when you pass fresh remarks to teachers and when you fail two Regents—not one, mind you, but chemistry *and* French—of course you don't get promoted."

"It's another year the army won't grab him," Lena said. "And he's young anyway, so it's no great tragedy. It'll give him more time to find himself."

"The boy's seventeen and he's still a junior in high school."

"Mother, it's enough already. I don't want to hear about it, okay? Get off my back for a change." His mood, almost wistful a moment earlier, had altered dramatically. Mounting anger painted broad harsh strokes across his face.

It was the wrong time for arguments or heated discussions of any kind. "Okay, okay I'm sorry," she said quickly. "It's over and done with, no use talking about it now, anyway. Maybe you're right. A new school, new friends, a new start." She looked at her watch again. "What's keeping them?"

The cue was perfectly timed, synchronized. At that instant the doorbell rang loud and shrill. She felt herself stiffening, snapping to attention. She took a deep breath and stepped out of the kitchen. The wall-to-wall carpeting had been pulled up a few days before and carted off in Manny's station wagon. The floors had never been finished and now they gave up their age, their pre-Depression vintage in a hundred splatters of paint, ancient scuff marks, loose lengths of hardwood, and rusty nails.

"Right on time," she said, smiling broadly as she let the movers into the apartment.

"Beautiful day to move," one of the men said with an equally broad grin. "Not too hot, not half as humid as it was last week. If the traffic isn't bad, you'll be in good shape, Mrs. Margold."

She had the money all ready. "Try to be careful," she said. "I'd hate to have anything break." She slipped each of the three men a ten-dollar bill.

"Will do," the foreman of the job replied, thanking her for the tip with a brief nod of his head. "Well, let's get going, guys."

The acquisitions of married life, that part of her past she wished to save in order to carry into the future, were packed away in over seventy-five cartons, drums, and portable clothing racks. Barry was drinking milk from the waxed container when she came back into the kitchen.

"No sense standing around," she said. "They'll get everything, and we'll only get under their feet. When you pay through the nose, you get service; that's one thing I've learned in the last couple of years."

"The car downstairs?" he asked, a white moustache still foamy and wet across his top lip.

"Yep, everything's set." She'd never learned how to drive, but Vivian Hollander had a license and rented the car in her name.

The moving men wore identical gray uniforms, crisp and clean. They loaded six or seven cartons onto a hand truck and rolled it out of the apartment. The wheels thumped and thudded over the wooden threshold. She heard the elevator door squeaking loudly in the hallway.

"I'm ready when you are," Barry said.

"Mom, you have everything?"

Lena nodded.

"I'll meet the two of you downstairs. I just want to . . . give all the closets a last check. I'll be right down."

"No rush," said Lena. She and Barry threaded their way through the pile of boxes. When they were out of sight, Cynthia turned away and walked down the narrow hall which led to her bedroom. She poked her head inside Barry's room. Satisfied he had made sure to pack everything he wanted, she continued down the narrow hallway. She ran her fingers, the palm of one hand, over the pebbly kraftex walls. The landlord's painters had always complained how difficult they were to cover. She looked more closely, noticed a patch of beige paint the size of a dime, surrounded by the more recent antique white. When the walls were beige the kids were how old? Barry was ten, eleven maybe. It used to be a squeeze walking down this hall. Sometimes if I didn't aim perfectly straight, I'd hit against the sides, that's how wide I was. Now there's all this room to spare.

She stepped over a second wooden saddle, rubbed smooth and satiny from countless coats of floor wax, the friction of many feet. Nothing, just the old double bed Manny said he'd pick up. The rest are gone—highboy, lowboy, mirrors and vanity table, carpeting, shades, curtains, nightstand and lamp—all carted off to the apartment he now shared with Natalie on Clarkson Avenue. She moved across the room and peered out the window. The two-family houses on East Ninety-first Street, East

New York Avenue, the offices of Dr. Bolen the orthodontist—thank God both of them have straight teeth,
good bites—and Crazy Moshe's candy store where Barry
once came home insisting he'd seen a mouse running circles in the ice-cream bin, were all made painfully visible.
She saw everything she had taken for granted year after
year. There was the grocery store where the owner rub-
ber-stamped his checks "Sol the Refugee." Next door, Old
Man Grushka still helped the women of the neighborhood
pick out patterns for custom-tailored skirts, walking suits,
and winter coats. His hems were flawless. He shortened
sleeves of every cut—dolman, raglan, three-quarter. He
even, she recalled, had a special book of patterns designed to soothe the vanity of women with large frames,
big bones.

The downstairs buzzer rasped loudly from the front
hall. Barry was probably leaning against it—impatient,
anxious to get started.

"One minute," she said aloud before she realized she
was alone, except for the movers working through the
piled cartons in the living room and foyer. She turned
away. She'd seen enough.

It'll be a new view and a new life, she thought. You
wanted this for so long, so what are you afraid of? Change
is good; it keeps you on your toes. In September you'll
be moving into your new office downtown and everything'll be fresh and clean.

It was time to go and there was no point standing
around, getting wet-eyed and nostalgic for a past she had
knocked into the ground long before. The bedroom closet
was empty. She shut the door and stepped back into the
hall. She turned on the light in the linen closet and peered
inside, her eyes roaming from one shelf to another. Sad
and bare, until something caught the light, a paper reflection of coated glossy stock. She reached up, and, with
two fingers, snagged a bag of Sugar Babies, teardrop-
shaped caramel candies.

It's been here for years, she realized. When I was eating in secret, hiding things, I must have stuffed it behind
a pile of towels and then forgotten all about it.

Suddenly, everything snapped and crumbled. The tears
welled up and trickled down her cheeks, leaving wide
damp furrows in her face powder. She slammed the door
shut and shoved the bag of candies into her leather purse.

Then, still crying, she ran from the apartment as if fleeing a ghost, a specter of the way it used to be, the life she once had led. Again, there was no turning back, no way to retrace her steps and start all over; she'd made up her mind long before. Now, there was only one goal in sight—to make it.

And make it big.

October 1967

SEVENTEEN PUSHPINS ON THE MAP of the United States; Portland, Richmond, and Cleveland, the three points of a triangle, defining the borders of NuBodies Land. In her new office at Worth and West Broadway, Cynthia had no view but plenty of room. That was okay too, because at home every morning when she got out of bed she could throw the curtains back to reveal the Hudson and the Jersey shore at the other side. Occasionally she'd see an ocean liner, tugs like baby whales flanking the sides of the mother cruise ship, making its way slowly to a berth farther downriver, farther downtown. She had more closet space than she knew what to do with. These days Lena's presence was never an imposition, but almost a necessity, since she had little time to deal with the mundane realities of running a household. Lena always attended to the shopping, the laundry, the hiring—and sometimes firing—of a woman to come in once a week to clean. Cynthia had repeatedly offered to hire someone on a more frequent basis so that her mother wouldn't have her hands full taking care of the apartment. Lena had refused, saying that if she didn't have something to do with her time, she'd go crazy.

Another year and she won't have the energy, the strength, Cynthia thought as she affixed her name to a contract which gave a group in New Rochelle the right to establish a branch of NuBodies and to use the corporate name, the corporate slogan, corporate literature, and the mimeographed corporate recipe book.

There had been other changes, too, in the past few months. After three weeks of wheeling and dealing, at least seven or eight business lunches plus a cocktail party at her new apartment; Endicott, Tucker & Groves had finally given their consent to an exclusive three-year contract, lending D. W.'s services to NuBodies. Before the negotiations, she offered to hire D. W. outright, to put him on the NuBodies payroll, rather than continue the arrangement he had with the advertising agency. For reasons she was yet to figure out, he had turned her down, telling her he preferred being lent, rather than owned.

It really didn't matter who signed his weekly salary check—now up to $290—so long as he continued serving NuBodies with the same degree of excellence and creativity which had marked his first year with the firm. His schemes were even more imaginative. She would have been a fool to think the seventeen pushpins had little to do with the fact that right across the hall he was ensconced in his own carpeted office, replete with a new IBM typewriter and a full-time secretary.

Leonard grumbled about every new change, every addition to the list of expenditures. At the same time, he was capable of compromising, willing in the long run to do what was best for the corporation. He was playing with the idea of selling out his interest in Dreamtime Togs, now that NuBodies was well on its way to success. For the fiscal year 1966, NuBodies had shown a net profit of over $25,000, above and beyond the money put out for the upkeep of the office, for salaries and sundry business expenses. Now, as 1967 drew to a close, the last figures she had seen indicated that NuBodies would clear close to $50,000. And since her salary was now up to $20,000 a year, not including traveling expenses, she was more than just pleased with the progress she was making.

Her *phobia* had begun to blossom into a highly successful institution. It was the rare week indeed when she wasn't getting on a plane at LaGuardia or Kennedy, still traveling tourist class but traveling, nevertheless. Certain trips she put out of her mind as quickly as possible. There was the fiasco in Pittsburgh, when she'd been pitted against a local physician whose lucrative six-figure practice catered to the wealthy overweight of Squirrel Hill. He had all sorts of fancy figures at his disposal, complicated rhetoric which tore holes in all her arguments. Pittsburgh was still without a NuBodies branch and she didn't doubt it was all a result of her poor showing on the local television station. Afterwards, she'd made a point to do her home-work, to arrive not only with countless facts and figures, but signed statements from dieticians, nutritionists, and medical specialists. D. W. saw to it that she was always met at the airport by a loyal contingent of NuBodies fans, mostly women—though occasionally men—who had heard about her "fat crusade," and were eager for her to soothe their consciences by describing the ease with which they could lose weight . . . if they followed the diet, of course.

NuBodies was well on its way to achieving the kind of success she had often dreamed about. She had come to think of the firm as a lover, since there was no one else around who was equally as capable of drawing her out of herself. Although the first rushes of fame and notoriety had come and gone, she had no doubts that it would eventually happen all over again, but on a bigger scale. It was no longer the greatest of treats to sit in a TV studio under hot lights and banter with a local talk-show host. But at the same time, she still hadn't been asked to appear on Johnny Carson and she still preferred—infinite-ly, at that—gabbing in Cincinnati or Rochester to dusting furniture in Brooklyn.

Still, all she had to keep her warm at night was an electric blanket. And if she missed the presence of some-one who had blood pulsing in his veins rather than corpo-rate figures and budgetary proposals, she also missed the uncomplicated existence that had been the cornerstone of her married life.

You'd think that as Barry got older, he'd quiet down and give me more pleasure. But no, it gets worse, one trial after another. The more money I make, the more ways he figures how to spend it. If it isn't a new winter coat which he has three of already, it's another sweater or a pair of shoes. When did he become such a clothes-horse, a fashion plate? He has more to wear in his closet than I do and he still wants. Plus an allowance, plus now he wants to go to Europe this summer. Europe? I haven't even been to Canada or California and my kid wants to go to Paris, London, Rome—you name it.

She had an appointment that afternoon with the prin-cipal of the high school where Barry had started his junior year for the second time, the month before. She knew it wasn't going to be a mere social call, an informal chat. The principal, Mr. Wickers, had intimated that unless she

288

met with him, her son would surely face the threat of expulsion for, "Activities I'd sooner discuss in person, Mrs. Margold, than over the telephone."

Whatever those activities happened to be, she realized they weren't going to land him on the dean's list or the honor roll. If I was home every night, maybe it would be different, she thought. But Lena can't discipline him. She's too old to be his bodyguard and he wouldn't listen, anyway. And when I'm out of town he takes advantage and comes in at all hours. Eighteen in February and all of a sudden the Village is his second home. Where does he go; what does he do when he's down there? What's the great draw, the attraction, with all those hippies taking drugs and panhandling on the streets—that's what I'd like to know.

She'd tried to discuss the situation calmly with him but Barry, in turn, had given her his usual snappy comebacks, fresh remarks that infuriated her more than anything else. She quickly exhausted her patience and when Lena had said, "If Manny was around, he wouldn't let his son get away with murder the way you do," she wanted to claw the walls in absolute and total frustration. The truth of it was, Lena spoke from the heart. Sure, if Manny was at home to discipline him he wouldn't carry on, but he isn't at home.

She headed uptown after the lunch-hour crowds had thinned out. Broadway was congested, but no longer jammed. Riverside High School was located five blocks south of her apartment, but it might as well have been in another city, another era. Spray-paint graffiti defaced the front doors of the gaunt red brick structure. When she stepped inside she noticed how years before the school had maintained separate entrances, blocks of red sandstone proclaiming BOYS on one side and GIRLS on the other. Now there was a single set of doors, covered with protective wire screens.

This place looks like a bomb hit it, she thought.

She stopped at the information desk in the hall. A uniformed policeman advised against finding the principal's office on her own. She decided she didn't want to know why he was being so protective and followed him down a wide, paint-scarred corridor, then up a flight of enclosed metal stairs which led to the second floor of the building. They went down another bleak hallway. As the

289

bell rang to announce the end of a period, she found herself in Mr. Wickers' outer office.

"I'm Mrs. Margold, Barry Margold's mother," she said to the blue-haired secretary. "I have an appointment with Mr. Wickers."

Ten minutes later, after leafing through a dog-eared copy of *Scholastic Teacher* while a pregnant student sat across from her filing her nails with an emery board, she was asked to step inside the principal's office. The bare, cold room was dominated by an oak desk.

"Mrs. Margold," he said, rising halfway from a wooden swivel chair.

"Mr. Wickers," she replied.

He was a thin man with sparse, thinning hair; thin, narrow lips and long, thin fingers which now gripped the edges of a manila folder, no doubt Barry's permanent record card. She took a seat even though he hadn't offered one, immediately taking a dislike to what she felt was an air of dry and officious pedantry—if that's the word I want—his ideas on education as outmoded and behind the times as his shapeless pinstripe suit and skinny black tie.

"I would not have asked to see you, Mrs. Margold, had the problem with your son not been as serious as it is," he announced.

"And how serious is that, Mr. Wickers?" she said directly. She'd come to expect—to like, as well—the forthright quality which marked her business contacts. People invariably spoke their mind. She didn't know why that kind of practice couldn't be applied to Mr. Wickers.

"Quite," he said. "Your son's a bright young man. His records indicate that he's of above-average intelligence, which makes his performance here at Riverside all the more difficult to fathom."

"I never thought Barry was that complicated a boy," she said, sitting demurely with her bag and hands arranged neatly on her lap, the hem of her modest wool dress well below her stockinged knees.

"Well," and he paused as if searching out the right word, "complicated is not exactly what I had in mind. To be quite frank with you, Mrs. Margold, and I wouldn't have asked you here this afternoon unless I fully intended to speak freely and with an open mind, Barry has been a considerable disciplinary problem since he entered last month. I've had complaints from nearly all of his teachers, particularly Mrs. Jacoby, his homeroom teacher. He's repeatedly used abusive language and two days ago one of the teachers on hall duty discovered him smoking . . . marijuana in the boys' bathroom."

"Mara what?" she said.

"Marijuana. Grass. Pot I think is another word that's used. It's becoming more and more of a problem in our school system. Surely you must remember reefers from when you were in high school."

At least he thinks I'm halfway educated, she thought. "No," she said. "The word doesn't ring a bell. Sorry. But marijuana's what they're all smoking these days, isn't it? It's like a drug, a narcotic."

"Close to it, I'd venture to say," Wickers replied. "And it's definitely illegal. But that's just part of the problem. Barry has been a disruptive influence in most of his classes and I'm hard-pressed to figure out what's troubling the boy. His records seem to indicate a slow but steady deterioration in academic performance ever since about the ninth grade."

Now it's marijuana. Like he doesn't carry on enough, he has to fool around with drugs. But what does Wickers expect me to do about it now, when the boy's almost eighteen and refuses to listen, to take any direction, advice. "I try my best, Mr. Wickers. I don't know if you know, but the work I'm involved in requires a considerable amount of traveling. My mother, Barry's grandmother that is, lives at home with us—"

"And the boy's father?"

"The boy's father and I are legally separated."

"I see, I see," he said, his voice thin and narrow and barely audible. He opened the folder and proceeded to examine the rows of figures, grade marks and handwritten evaluations. " 'Refuses constructive criticism,' " he recited. " 'Constantly argumentative, disrupts classroom environment.' " He waved his hand. "And so on and so forth."

A balloon popped inside her head. It could have been a blood vessel, too. Or someone hanging up a phone with a loud and never-to-be-forgotten click. It was a gingersnap, a cookie crumbling. It was a ball bouncing. A minor explosion, something else to always be remembered. "For eighteen years my son's life has been a little more than *so on and so forth,* Mr. Wickers," she said, her voice as harsh and grating as she could muster. "And judging from the deteriorating physical plant you supervise, Riverside is certainly far removed from what one would call an ideal educational environment. I'm quite sure Barry isn't getting the kind of attention and creative help a fine school would be able to provide. So I don't think he'll be disrupting any of your classes in the future."

"I beg your pardon?" he said. His eyes blinked rapidly and he closed the record with a quick little jerk of his wrist. "I don't quite follow you, Mrs. Margold."

"There's nothing to follow," she said, already getting to her feet. "I don't think Barry can receive adequate preparation for college here at Riverside. I think he'll respond much better to a private school atmosphere, one that's culturally enriched," as Riverside certainly is not. No one's going to talk about my kid like he's a so on and so forth, just a number and nothing else. I'll pull him out so fast they won't know if they're coming or going. I'll enroll him somewhere else, that's all. That's the answer. The nerve . . . who does he think he's dealing with anyway, some kind of welfare case? No wonder he's not doing his best, when the school's so depressing. It's a fire hazard, too, I'm sure. And what's the point of working like a dog if my kid ends up getting an inferior education. He'll go to private school. And that's all there is to it.

There was, as she discovered a few days later, a little more to it than that.

"That's the situation, Leonard. That's how it stands. I have to pull the boy out and get him settled in a private school."

"So what are you waiting for? Do it," he said. His arms were crossed over his chest. He leaned against the back of her office door, and Cynthia rolled her chair away from her desk, feeling cramped, stifled.

"I fully intend to," she said. "In fact, I've been calling schools all morning. Rhodes and York don't have any room whatsoever until the second term starts in January. But Lenox Hill has room for him. The only problem, it's going to cost."

"Well, that's a private school, Cynthia. You knew that all along. How much?"

"Over two and under three. Closer to three thousand,

more than likely," the way my kid spends money like it's going out of style, like it grows on trees or something.

"So?"

"So I need a raise to cover my expenses, to pay for the tuition." She held her breath, searching his face for an early warning, some kind of reaction to her words. She saw none. Hard, impassive, he remained with his arms crossed, his shoulder blades flush against the back of the wooden door. His crossed legs revealed three diamonds' worth of woolen argyle sock, the top of one sand-colored chukka boot, and then the impressive length of his firm muscular legs. His eyes narrowed for an instant.

"A raise?"

She nodded her head. "I just have to cover myself," she said again.

"You just gave yourself a raise, this past June. When you moved."

"Well . . . I had to. I have a very big rent. And now the boy has to go to private school. You should have been there with me, Leonard. The place is a disgrace. It's ready to fall down."

"And it's obviously not good enough for your kid."

His words were edged with sarcasm, something else that went beyond cynicism, too. She chose to ignore his quickly changing mood, saying, "Absolutely not. So I'm going to give myself a three thousand dollar raise."

"Why not five? Why not fifteen even?"

"I'm not asking for the moon," she started to say.

He interrupted. "You're not *asking*, period. You're telling."

"It's a necessity," she said. "I just wanted you to know . . . beforehand, that's all."

"And shall I up my salary accordingly?"

"If that's what you want," thinking, Why does he make me feel so guilty about money? It's not like it's coming out of his own pocket, for God sakes. "What's the big deal, Leonard, anyway? You've recovered every penny you poured into the company. What am I working so hard for unless I can see a little pleasure out of it, a little return. The boy has to get his diploma, one way or another."

"I can't stop you, so what's the point of the discussion? You control fifty-one percent and I'm left with the other forty-nine." His face was now as sour as a lemon drop. His mouth puckered and he said, "So when you decide to give yourself a raise, I just have to learn to sit back and keep my mouth shut."

"But you don't approve."

"Cynthia, do you want me to pat you on the back and say you're a very good girl because you're asking for money that could be better spent elsewhere? Do you have any idea what kind of rent we're paying for these offices? We didn't rent the IBM typewriters you insisted upon having, either. We bought them, outright. Each goddamn ribbon runs us something like four or five bucks—"

She cut him short, saying, "I am far from extravagant." Then she pretended to shuffle papers from one side of her desk to another. "You don't see me going hog-wild, spending money left and right," buying five-carat diamonds, either. "I still travel in coach, for your information. And I work very hard, too hard. What I need more than a raise is a vacation."

"On company money?"

"Yes, why not?" she said, raising her face so that the entire length of her neck felt as if it were uncoiling, arching upright like a cobra about to strike. "I'm Nu-Bodies and NuBodies is me, one and the same. What's good for Cynthia is good for the company."

He laughed: wry, dry, short, and to the point. "You have a lot to learn, Mrs. Margold, a helluva lot. More than you can imagine. And not only about business, either." And with these cryptic words ringing coldly in her ears, he turned on one crepe-soled heel and stepped out of her office. The door closed behind him, another click to add to many.

"I don't believe him," she said aloud. And to herself, What kind of games is he starting to play with me now? The answer eluded her. She picked up the phone and asked her secretary to connect her with the headmaster of the Lenox Hill Day School. "Tell him it's Mrs. Margold calling, Barry Margold's mother." The President of Nu-Bodies too, in case anyone's interested.

January 1968

OUTSIDE THE APARTMENT on Riverside Drive, the river and sky drifted together in a wintry embrace, black as onyx. Inside, Lena called out from the kitchen. "Everything's on the table, so come to supper." There was a pause before, "Barry, dinner's ready. It's gonna get cold."

"One minute," the voice faint and tinny as it echoed down the hallway.

Cynthia stood by the dining table, all eyes on the meal her mother had prepared. "It smells delicious," she said.

"Fresh filet of sole, beautiful baby peas, and fresh broccoli, not the frozen. So sit, sit. I'll be right there."

"Barry!" Cynthia called out as she took her place at the head of the table. "Supper's on, honey."

From the kitchen, Lena said, "So what happened with that group out in Hempstead? They sign yet, or what?"

"Day after tomorrow," she replied. "They were trying to give us a little bit of grief, too. Wanted to make their own rules, can you imagine. The whole point of a franchise is to keep the classes as uniform as possible. Not only in New York, but throughout the country. If one branch starts to do things their way, the word NuBodies'll end up meaning nothing. So obviously we had to put our foot down."

"Hempstead's beautiful," Lena said. "Cousin Fran used to live there, had a gorgeous home, before she moved down to Miami. You should look her up next month, let her show you around when you're down there."

Barry nodded his head by way of greeting and took his seat. "Looks good," he said. He unfolded his napkin and spread it out on his lap.

"Do me a favor, sweetheart, and comb your hair. It's all over your eyes," Lena said.

"I just did," he said.

"Mom, come on. This isn't a restaurant," Cynthia said loudly.

Lena finally sat down, but not before she'd brought out a container of milk for Cynthia and Barry. "I can't eat milk and meat," she would say. "It's not a question of religion. It just turns my stomach, that's all. But go ahead, drink all you want. I know it's good for you." Tonight, however, she didn't say anything about it.

For the moment there was silence. She watched Lena and Barry digging into their entree.

"So how's Dwight?" she asked, spooning out a grapefruit section that had been sweetened with liquid saccharin.

"Eh," he said.

"What's *eh* supposed to mean?"

"It's a school. They're all the same."

"That's all, just a school? You know what that school's costing me? Thirty-two hundred dollars a year, that's what. It's more expensive than Lenox was."

"That's because I have to go this summer," he said, making a face.

"Well, whose fault is that? You forfeited going to Europe because of your marks. If you don't take summer courses they won't promote you in September. Do you want to be a high school junior for three years running?"

"Cynthia, let's enjoy our dinner," Lena said.

She sighed and finished the grapefruit. He didn't *flunk* out of Lenox, she thought, he was *kicked* out. There's a big difference. Pulled the same kind of shenanigans he did at Riverside and they weren't about to put up with it, not for two minutes. I warned him. I begged him to buckle down and start behaving himself. Sure Dwight accepted him. For the two-thousand-dollar contribution I forked over they would have kissed my you-know-what and where's all this money coming from, that's what I'd like to know. Twenty-three thousand sounds like a lot before taxes. Afterwards it's a crying shame what the government takes out. And Manny always used to say rent was never supposed to be more than a fourth of your income, one week's salary, tops. What I'm paying to sublet Caulfield's co-op is closer to two weeks salary. And then there's food and clothes and expenses and telephone bills. It doesn't end.

"Have you made any nice friends?" she asked as she motioned her mother to remain in her seat. She got up and stacked the dishes, carried them into the tiny kitchen, and brought back the broiled fish.

"A couple."

"Just a couple? Any nice girls?"

"Most of them are skuzzy," he said, his eyes on his plate. His long straight brown hair—the color darkening with age—fell over his brow. "Pass a lemon wedge, please."

"Pardon?" she said. "What's that supposed to mean?"

"They're all . . . I don't know. Lemme eat, mom. I'm gonna be late as it is."

"For what?" she asked.

"Have some lemon on the fish, Cynthia, it's very good for you," Lena said.

"I have a date," he said, "an appointment I mean, at eight."

"With who?"

"With whom?" he corrected, giving her what she felt was a sly grin. "A friend, a buddy of mine from Riverside."

"A buddy of yours from Riverside," she repeated. "And what about your homework, your studying? You know, Barry, Dwight is considered much harder than Lenox Hill. You haven't been there two weeks and already you're starting to pull the same kind of nonsense you did at Len—"

"I'm not pulling any nonsense and just get off my back, mother. I'm going out. I don't have any studying to do for tomorrow, and I made this appointment a couple of weeks ago."

"And what're you going to do? Where're you going?"

"Cynthia, honey, eat your fish before it gets cold. You were just telling me how hungry you were."

"I will, mom, in a minute," but this has gone far enough. "Well? Barry, your mother is talking to you. The least you could do is look at me."

He lifted his face and stared her straight in the eye. She didn't see anger, or even hostility. Just a look that was cool and composed, making her realize her words were futile.

"Well? Where are you going tonight, may I ask?"

"To a movie, okay? We're going to see a movie over on the East Side. Satisfied?"

Eighteen next month and he talks to me like I'm beneath him, like I'm dirt or something. The whole thing is just getting out of hand; it's getting to be too much for me. I have no more patience left . . . Miami next month, what a blessing in disguise. I need a good rest. I need to unwind and start thinking about myself for a change. Just to lie by the pool like a lady and be waited on hand and foot.

Barry wiped his mouth and pushed his chair back. She noticed that his eyes were red-rimmed, bloodshot. His movements brought to mind a puppet, jerky as a marionette. She recalled what the principal of Riverside had said to her. "I want to talk to you a minute, Barry."

"I gotta go," he said. He stepped around and kissed Lena on the cheek. "Great dinner, gran'ma. See you all later."

Don't tell me he's on something! But what's he so nervous about, darting around like he can't get out of here quick enough? She started to rise from her seat, about to follow him to the door. Instead, Lena caught her eye, said without words, without moving her lips, "Let him go. It's not worth the aggravation."

"So long," he called out. The chain lock rattled and then the door swung open and shut. Running footsteps drifted under the door sill. She heard the elevator lurching up along its shaft, cables straining and Barry standing there in the hall with one finger glued to the Up button.

"What am I supposed to do with him?" she said. "Doesn't even kiss me goodbye. Like all I'm good for is money; like I'm his worst enemy instead of his best friend."

"It's a phase he's going through," Lena said.

"That's what you said a couple of years ago, if I remember correctly. So it's about time he got over it, if you ask me. He's been getting away with bloody murder for too long already. Enough is enough. And he never brings any of his friends to the house anymore. I don't know, mom. There was a time when he didn't invite them over because he was ashamed of me, I was so fat. Now he can't use that as an excuse. So what is it? Who are all these kids he's hanging around with, that's what I'd like to know?"

"It's a different world," Lena said, on her feet again, piling the dishes atop each other.

"Everything was delicious," she said. "But that's no excuse, mom. I'm trying my best, am I not? He goes to private schools. He has beautiful clothes. I give him a nice allowance every week, instead of making him get himself a part-time job like he used to do when he worked in Manny's shop a couple of hours on a Saturday morning . . . which didn't kill him either, by the way. But what more does the boy want from me?"

"Go figure out children," Lena said, "the younger generation's beyond me." She shrugged her shoulders and collected all the utensils that were left on the table.

"It's beyond me too, if you want to know the truth. I need this vacation more than anyone can imagine, more than you can dream."

"Soon," said Lena in the voice she had used when Cynthia was sixteen and seventeen and eighteen and crying herself to sleep at night because she still hadn't been asked out on a date. "February'll be here before you know it."

"Let's hope I live that long."

Lena gave her a startled look and the two of them turned silently into the kitchen.

February 1968

HAIR BLEACHED PALOMINO by the sun, the pool boys in their faded ragged-edged jeans circulated between the rows of chaises. Upraised muscular arms carried trays of orange juice. In her reclining chair, Cynthia lay stretched out, facing the sun. Already, she had lost her winter-white skin, replacing it with a coating of red that was hot to the touch, but one that promised to darken into a more attractive—and less painful—tan before the week was out. After three days she felt refreshed, rejuvenated. She was still operating on a New York rhythm, but that excess of hurrying energy now seemed to be the least of her problems.

That morning she had placed a call to New York, first to Lena to find out how everything was at home (meaning, was Barry behaving himself), and then to her office to see if anything needed attention. On Riverside Drive things were, in Lena's words, "copesetic." On Worth and West Broadway, D. W. had gotten on at the other end to berate her for going off without him, for leaving him alone with "a pack of fanatical ex-fatties."

Do you know that I miss you, Margold, I really do. It's no fun coming in every morning and having my coffee all by my lonesome. Just take care you don't get a bad burn. I want to be able to give you a hug without hearing you yell 'Ouch!', understand. She had laughed, saying, *Believe it or not, I miss you too, Eisenstern. This place is filled with so many Social Security types, I feel like I'm a social director at an old age home. Well, you were the one who picked Miami. If it was up to me, I would've bundled you off to Cozumel and gotten you stoned, so don't start com-*

300

plaining now, kiddo. Oh, I'm not complaining, she assured him. I'm just . . . maybe I'm not used to sitting still and being waited on, left and right. It's good for you, he said, and don't go worrying about the office, Margold. Everything's under control. Have a good time, baby, and if anything untoward comes up, you'll be the first to hear.

She wondered what he meant by *untoward.*

"Orange juice?"

"Yes, thank you." She raised her hand like a visor, shielding her eyes as she accepted the plastic cup the pool boy handed her.

"Watch the sun," he said before moving off. "It can get pretty gruesome. You don't want to take too much all at once."

"So I've discovered," and she grinned, sizing him up in one fell swoop. Too young, she decided. But that doesn't mean I can't look. Oh God, Margold, what's to become of you, all alone in a beautiful two-room suite and no one to share it with. Maybe I should've gone to the Club Med, or something more daring, exotic. A place with a younger crowd. It's not as if I'm ancient; I'm not even forty yet. Yet.

"Mind if I join you, Cynthia?"

She swiveled her head around and her mouth dropped open in surprise. "Well I'll be . . . what a small world. Here, there's plenty of room." She lowered her bare suntan-lotioned legs over the side of the reclining chair, winced when they touched the burning hot concrete, and then slipped into her rubber zoris. The go-aheads had cost her $1.79 at the hotel notion shop. A day later she saw them heaped in a pile, selling for 59¢ at the Woolworth's on Lincoln Road.

Gerald Evans sat down on the edge of the chair. "Don't you look fit and healthy," he said, his eyes invisible behind dark-tinted sunglasses. "And rested, too."

"Well, we try," she told him. "But what brings you down to Miami? I must say right off that you've obviously been following the diet, somewhere along the line. You look wonderful, Gerald, just terrific."

"Forty-seven pounds . . . plus a neck," he said and laughed. "I could stand to lose another forty, but we won't go into it." He smiled and crossed his arms over his chest, as if he were self-conscious of his belly, a loose tire of fat visible right above the top of his baggy swimsuit.

"Just great," nodding her head to emphasize her approval. "And how is everything up in Purchase?"

"Couldn't be better," he said. "I'm down here just for a few days, just to get out of the city for awhile, get a little color. And you?"

"The same. Just to unwind, though I must admit I'm getting a little bored, sitting around without having to worry about business."

"And how is it . . . your business, I mean? I understand you've incorporated."

"September marked our second year," she said proudly.

"Wonderful. Lots of luck. How's it doing?"

"Very well, thank you. Better than I expected, in fact."

From the pool came squeals of laughter, someone splashing, a mother crying, "Shawn, stay out of the deep end, I'm warning you!"

"Small world," she repeated. Funny, but I don't have anything else to say to him. But he looks good though. A smooth operator too, I bet. A real charmer.

"Yes," he said. "You never know who you'll bump into when you're on vacation. Can I get you a drink?" and he motioned to the bar at the far end of the pool.

"I'll take a raincheck, if you don't mind. I never drink this early . . . and I hardly drink at all these days, actually."

"It shows," he said, his eyes moving behind his sunglasses.

Involuntarily, she pulled in her stomach, wondering if it was a mistake to have worn a two-piece. "Thank you." Again she thought, What else is there to say?

"What say we have dinner this evening? I understand you're . . . how shall I put it and still be discreet? No longer responsible for what you do on your own time."

"My my, but word does get around, doesn't it?" She pretended to laugh, botching the attempt. "I wouldn't have thought anyone was interested. But your sources are correct. My husband and I have been separated for a little over a year now."

"Drinks in my suite first and then dinner? How does that sound?"

"Sounds fine, Gerald. I didn't bring anything terribly dressy, though."

"Doesn't matter. Do you like stone crabs?"

"Never had them."

"You like seafood, don't you? And I know it's a staple
302

of the diet, because that's all I've been trying to eat for months."

She nodded her head.

"Then you'll love stone crabs. I know a great little place up. Nothing pretentious but the service can't be beat and the wine list couldn't be better. What say I see you around seven-thirty—eight?"

"Lovely. What's your room number?"

"Oh I'm not staying here," he said. "I'm at the Doral. Down along Collins. Just get into a cab. They'll know how to get you there." He got to his feet and she remained where she was, once again aware of the way he took her all in, gobbling her up with his eyes. "Have a good day. And watch the sun, Cynthia. We don't want the president of NuBodies burnt to a crisp."

Then he was gone, no longer a waddling fat man but someone with a lot of money who was merely over-weight. She followed him with her eyes for a moment. Strange, she thought. What was he doing here if .he's staying at the Doral? It's not because the pool is better, that's for sure.

"Can I get you a fresh towel, Mrs. Margold?" asked the pool boy. He was the same tanned and solidly built young man she had already given a healthy tip. D. W. again: *Let them know who they're dealing with, kiddo. Service always costs, but when you pay a little more, you always get treated like a star.*

"Don't mind if I do," she said. "And could you tell me something, Ronnie . . . your name is Ronnie, isn't it?"

He nodded his head.

"What's the difference between this hotel and the Doral?"

"The difference?" he repeated. "The Doral's quieter. It's not as much a family hotel. And it's not so . . . you know."

"New Yorkish?"

"Yes, that's what I mean. Sure."

Jewish you mean, she thought. So what was he doing here, anyway? He's the snob of Westchester County. Strange, very strange.

There was nothing strange about Gerald Evans' hos-pitality. A bottle of champagne was chilling, cloth-covered in a bucket of ice, when she arrived at his suite at eight o'clock that evening. He wore a striped seersucker sports jacket with matching blue linen trousers, white patent leather loafers, and three triangles of white silk jutting out over the top of his breast pocket. She decided it was a very natty outfit. The vertical stripes of the jacket made him look thinner than he really was.

"Champagne?"

"Love some," she said. "But just a tad," and that was D. W. speaking, too, so many things remembered, filtered through her consciousness and recycled to be used again. She took a seat and when the cork popped, couldn't help muttering, "Cheers." Then he joined her on the couch, sitting a little too close for comfort. Well, what the hell, she thought. You only live once, right?

He raised his glass. "To your health."

"And to yours, Gerald." The champagne was nutty and wonderfully dry. In fact, it was far and away the best champagne she had ever tasted. She read the label: Dom Pérignon, 1953. "Is that supposed to be a good year?" she asked, not afraid to show her ignorance. D. W. was well on his way to becoming her fashion adviser-cum-coordinator, but wine tasting was still one of the self-improvement courses he had yet to offer.

"A very great year," he said.

"I'm very glad."

He leaned back against the couch and turned his head to the side. "So, you must tell me all about NuBodies. I'm very curious to know how it's doing. After all, I knew you when—"

"I was afraid to go professional," she said, completing the sentence. She put down her glass, wiped her lips with a cocktail napkin, and accepted a cigarette. "But everything's been going very well, Gerald. We have over twenty franchises now and we're negotiating for at least another half-dozen. And there's talk of publishing a NuBodies' cookbook, among other things. I've been doing a lot of traveling—you know, promotional work. So far, well . . . it's growing. I wouldn't say exactly by leaps and bounds, but it's growing. It's doing better than I ever expected, actually."

"Wonderful," he said, blowing a smoke ring into the air. "But the moment I met you, I just had a feeling you had . . . how shall I put it? The right touch. You knew

304

how to deal with people, how to handle them. Instinctively, I suppose. And that's an incredibly important asset when you're in business for yourself, especially these days, when everything's so dog-eat-dog. And Frankel's still your partner, isn't he?"

"Yes." She had a feeling Evans wouldn't mind being in Leonard's shoes, recalling, too, the offer he had made her. But that's over and done with, she thought, water under the bridge. Leonard didn't trust him and I trusted Leonard, so there's no sense crying over spilt milk. Besides, I really have no great complaints. At least Leonard's a hundred percent behind NuBodies.

"Some more champagne before we go out?"

"Just a drop. It's marvelous, but I really don't like to drink all that much, Gerald."

"I sympathize with you completely," he said, though when they were seated at the restaurant an hour later, he nevertheless insisted upon ordering a bottle of white wine for dinner.

She was not so naïve as to believe he was trying to get her drunk. But the champagne, and now the wine, made her feel mellow, her tongue loose and unhinged. She visibly relaxed, putting aside everything that was bothering her. Here she was, sitting at a quiet banquette in a dark and atmospheric candlelit restaurant, the guest of a man who had always struck her as the very personification of a gentleman. Self-assured too, knowledgeable. Not suave, for that was far too obvious. No, Gerald Evans had all the right moves down pat, as if nothing he ever did or ever attempted could possibly end in failure. But she was curious to know how he had found her at the pool, refusing to believe in small-world statistics or the improbability of coincidence. Certain there was something more to it than that, she tried to turn the conversation around toward that particular direction.

She wasn't successful.

He dodged her questions with an ease that at first intrigued her, later amazed her even as she tasted a rough sour edge of irritation coloring her remarks. But the stone crabs were as superb as he had promised. And the Pouilly-Fuissé he and the wine steward had selected was just as dry and nutty, vaguely aromatic, as the champagne had been.

"I think a little dessert is in order, don't you? Just to

305

clear the palate. They have a wonderful cantaloupe *granité*. It's usually served between courses, as a relief. But it's light enough to be ideal for someone who follows the NuBodies plan . . . to the letter."

She had no idea what a *granité* was and opted for the fresh strawberries. "Without cream or sugar. And espresso would be lovely, thank you." *He's doing a snow job on me the likes of which I've never seen, and the question is, why?* But before she could ask him, point-blank, there was the ritual of dessert and postprandials. The captain flamed her lemon peel before adding it to the espresso. Gerald ordered a brandy. Then he lit a cigarette, wiped his mouth fastidiously with his napkin, and swiveled around so that he was better able to see her as they sat side by side on the banquette.

"Now," he said, "we can relax. That's another thing I love about this place. They never try to hurry you along. It's wonderfully Old World the way everyone is so calm, easygoing. We can sit at a table and spend three hours over dinner and no one could care less. Not like so many restaurants—fine restaurants too, I might add—in New York."

She smiled, thinking, *If I had a walkie-talkie I'd sneak into the ladies' room and call D. W. What do I do now? He's on to something and I still haven't got the foggiest—*

"I've been meaning to discuss a business proposition with you, Cynthia."

Aha! Here he goes, she thought, suppressing a triumphant grin. *Now it's finally coming out.* "I had a feeling everything was leading up to that," she admitted.

"Now please," and he laughed, too jocose and too hearty to be convincing, "don't think I asked you out this evening merely to toss around some business ideas."

"May I ask you one question then?"

"Certainly."

"How did you happen to know I was staying at the Americana?"

"Oh that," whereupon he smiled, serene and beatific, as if her question didn't faze him in the least. "Just a mere coincidence, nothing more. I happened to have bumped into Frankel's partner—his *other* partner, that is—last week, when I was downtown. It just came up in conversation, that's all. He mentioned that Leonard had told him you were going to be down here on vacation

306

and so after I checked into my hotel, I called your New York office. I thought it would be a lovely idea if the two of us got together after all this time. Surely you don't think that was underhanded, do you?"

"No, of course not," she hurried to say. "I'm not offended in the least, Gerald. Just curious, that's all."

When he smiled at her once again, she saw Porky Pig for a flickering instant. The candle lent a golden cast to his skin, as if his face were being modeled by the flame. As she recalled from her visit to Purchase, his was not a round face, the face of a fat man. It was surprisingly oval—more so now that she could see his neck—even a little bit angular, though right below his shirt collar everything widened and swelled, taking on rounded lines, heaving curves. "So," and he tapped his fingers against the edge of the table. Lifting his cup with two fingers, he took a sip of espresso, set it down again on its gold-rimmed saucer, puffed at a cigarette and said, "I think you'll find my offer rather intriguing, Cynthia. Attractive, too."

"Go on, I'm all ears. And I don't mean that sarcastically, either."

"Who thought that? After all, it's only a proposition. The choice is still in your hands, certainly not mine. But this is what I have in mind. From what you've told me, I gather you've had your hands full—"

"To put it mildly."

"Not only have you been traveling up and down the East Coast—"

"My goodness, you're well-informed. But yes, that's true. And now the Midwest, as well."

"And the Midwest," he repeated. "But you've also had to deal with financial matters, matters of pure business, shall we say. I understand Leonard still owns half of Dreamtime, so it must be difficult working with a partner who can only give you a portion of his time."

"We manage," she said. The unsugared espresso, strong and syrupy, masked the taste of the berries the moment she took a sip.

"Would it not be more advantageous for you if you didn't have to concern yourself with problems of franchise contracts and office supplies and petty nonsense like that? Wouldn't it be more in line with your natural talents to be on the road more, speaking before groups of overweight men and women, officiating at the opening of branches, appearing on radio and television? By the way, I caught you on 'Faces & Places' and you were too beautiful for words. But that way you wouldn't have to be bothered with the business end of NuBodies. You could devote all your energies—and I realize how considerable they happen to be—to helping others . . . help themselves."

Where did he get my lines from? she wondered. "And how do you propose this all come about, Gerald?"

"Now we're getting to the crux of the matter," he said, beaming a smile at her. He leaned closer. She saw his nostrils flaring for an instant. "I propose to buy out your interest in NuBodies and hire you as a permanent kind of . . . goodwill ambassador, you might say. You'd be responsible for making public appearances and lecture tours and the like. In return, the corporation will pay you handsomely for your services."

"Are you serious?" she said, making no attempt to conceal either her surprise or her growing interest.

"Absolutely. I'm prepared to assume your interest in NuBodies and pay you thirty thousand a year in return."

She didn't bat an eyelash. And she didn't hesitate when she said, "Thirty thousand is peanuts. I make nearly that much now, so what's the big advantage?" Aren't you becoming hard as nails, the way you can just sit here and bandy about figures the likes of which Manny never made in two years, if not three.

"You won't work half as hard. You won't be killing yourself, for one," he said. "I know how involved you are in getting this diet to the people. But right now, as things stand today—correct me if I'm wrong—you can't give them a hundred percent of your time because of business responsibilities."

"So you're saying I hand over my fifty-one percent interest in NuBodies in return for a yearly salary of thirty thousand. For how long?"

"For the life of the corporation," he said with a grin she had already begun to distrust. "Or better yet, we can work out a sliding-scale contract, an arrangement whereby your yearly salary will go up at the same rate the company's profits increase. But either way I think it's something you should seriously consider . . . if only for your own peace of mind."

"It's an attractive offer," she said. "Though thirty thousand is out of line, especially since you're not considering any cash settlement right now, right on the line I mean. It would have to be higher than that for me to even begin to consider what you're suggesting."

He waved his hand, erasing one set of figures, erasing the *three* in particular. "That should be the least of our worries. But . . . but think about it, Cynthia. I'm certainly not pressuring you for an immediate yes or no answer."

"Oh, I realize that, Gerald. I *will* think about it." She made a move to rise. "Excuse me a moment."

He got to his feet.

No headaches, she thought, looking for the ladies' room —though without a walkie-talkie. Maybe I should do it. Then I wouldn't have to fight Leonard every step of the way. I'd let the two of them deal with finances while I went around doing my thing, giving my talks, meeting with people, helping them.

He invited her for a nightcap at his suite, but she respectfully declined the invitation. The last thing she wanted to do was end up in bed with someone who just might soon become her boss. And from the way he was looking at her, she wasn't flattering herself thinking that was what he had in mind. "Breakfast then, tomorrow morning at your hotel?" he asked as the cab pulled up in front of the Americana.

"Elevenish," she told him. "I'll be by the pool. And thank you for a lovely evening, Gerald. I had a wonderful time." She kissed him, quick and fleeting, and let herself out of the taxi.

But instead of going straight to bed after she had undressed, she picked up the phone and asked the switchboard operator to get her an open line to New York. It took five minutes for her to get through. When she did, the voice at the other end was drenched in sleep, a low-pitched basso drone that bore little resemblance to D. W.'s usual tone of voice. "Who . . . what time is it?"

"It's Cynthia and it's not even one. I'm sorry. I thought you'd be wide awake."

"I'm not. Wait a minute." The telephone receiver fell from his fingers and she jerked her ear back just in time. She made herself comfortable. When D. W. got back on, she asked, "Are you up now?"

"Barely, but go on."

"Here's the thing." Then she launched right into it, telling him what had transpired since she had met Gerald Evans—or he had met her, as the case happened to have been—earlier in the day. She outlined the business proposition he had made to her and concluded by saying, "So what do you think I should do? I'm calling you because I consider you my friend, because I think you're behind me every step of the way. Do you think Leonard has anything to do with this? The truth."

"No," he said without a pause, a moment of thoughtful hesitation. "I would've heard something, gotten wind of it, one way or another. No, I don't think he's cooked up anything with this Evans character. I don't think he's that clever—between you and me."

"Don't underestimate him," she said. "But what should I do? It's an attractive offer, any way you slice it."

"D'you want to be a figurehead, Cynthia? You want to sit on your ass and have a cushy job for the rest of your life, go ahead and do it. But I wouldn't, if I were you."

"Why?"

"Because you built this thing up from the very beginning, that's why. You want to give it away to the highest bidder, the only bidder, in fact? Do you think for one minute, kiddo, that you're going to be happy traipsing around the country, a puppet for the bosses in New York? That's not the Cynthia *I* know. That's someone who's lazy, who hates responsibility."

She took it all in, swallowed it, sifted it through. "D. W., let me ask you this then. What do you think the future's going to be like for NuBodies? I know it's a tough question, but answer as best you can. Is it going to become a million-dollar outfit or have we already reached the top?"

"The top? My God, you've got to be out of your ever-lovin' head, the top," he exclaimed, his voice loud and persuasive. "Kiddo, we haven't even scratched the surface. We haven't hit the big time by any stretch of the imagination. Come on, Cynthia, it's only been two years, for Chris' sakes. And from raking in a grand total of a hundred bucks a week, you're now making over . . . you tell me, I don't know."

She said, "Over twenty thousand a year."

"Okay, not bad for two years, is it? Nothing I've seen,

no figures, no reactions from people, have indicated that NuBodies is about to hit a slump. How can it, when people are fatter than ever. You should've seen the statistics HEW just came out with. Obesity is a national disease, sweetheart. So what is it, you're getting scared all of a sudden? What are you so afraid of that you're about to sell your baby on an auction block? Christ, I knew I should've gone down there with you. Leave you on your own and there's no telling what you'll do."

"You make it sound like I'm totally irresponsible, a real ignoramus or something."

"Those are your words, my dear, not mine. But to be as concise and simple as possible, you asked for my opinion. If he offered you seventy grand a year, it would still be the same." There was a pause. She waited, able to hear a match flaring, D. W. inhaling, sucking in his breath. "Cynthia-Artemis-Diana, fire of my loins, love of my life, don't give it all up now. Don't. When I say you're going to be worth a million bucks, I'm not talking out of my hat. I mean it. Besides, I'm being selfish. Right now I need you as much as you need me. We're a terrific team. If you sell out, there's no telling what'll become of me and Gladys. I'll have a nervous breakdown and she'll fall down the air shaft again. I'll be sent back to the salt mines, sweetest ex-fat girl in all the western hemisphere. So listen to your D. W. Trust me."

The words were strained beneath the glib patter, the verbal fireworks. She heard the message loud and clear. "Well, you've said it then. But I'm going to sleep on it, anyway."

"Cynthia. Don't."

"Whatever I do, whatever decision I reach, you'll be the first to know. Call me tomorrow from the office. I'll be here at the hotel. And I'm sorry I woke you up, love. It was a very heavy evening, that's all. I'm still an old-fashioned girl, what can I say. The man announces thirty thou and I go bug-eyed; I start seeing dollar signs. I don't know what I'm so afraid of, if you want to know the truth."

"I don't know either. You've got a beautiful thing going, kiddo. Don't fuck it up now, just because some jerk's dangling a carrot under your nose. I mean, holy shit, Cynthia, if you want to start jumping hoops for some con

man, go right ahead. But if I were you, you know what
I'd tell him?"

"No. What?"

" 'Kiss my ass, mister,' plain and simple."

"He'd do it, too," she said. Then she began to laugh.
She didn't have to fake it. Hopefully, D. W. wasn't faking,
either.

"So the answer is thanks but no thanks."

"I think you're making a mistake."

"I don't agree, I'm sorry."

"I'll go as high as forty-five thousand with a guaranteed
ten percent raise within eighteen months."

"Such figures you reel off, Mr. Evans. My God, you'll
have my head spinning in another minute," she said, playing the coquette. "S'more coffee?" She lifted the insu-
lated coffeepot the waitress had left on the table. When
it's fifty cents a cup, you're damn tootin' refills should be
free.

"No thank you."

"Could I interest you in another slice of toast then?"

He shook his head. "I think you're making a rash decision, Cynthia. I think you're making a big mistake."

"Perhaps," she conceded, "but if you're so eager to buy
me out *now*, when NuBodies has barely gotten on its feet,
I tend to suspect that it's heading toward a period of very
healthy and very substantial growth, financial and otherwise. I want to be part of it when it happens, Gerald.
Come on, it's my baby, has been from the very beginning.
You don't separate a mother from her child, do you?"

"Only if something's basically the matter with the child."

"Well it's not retarded and it's not stillborn and I'm
quite confident that the mother's neither of those things,
either. But why speak in metaphor and play games with
each other?" Thank you, Eisenstern. From your mouth
to God's ears, as Lena would say, the lines you've given
me since we've met. I could kiss you. "The truth is, I
like what I'm doing, Gerald. It's exciting. It's challenging
work. I don't want to give it up and be . . . a puppet, a
Betty Crocker. A figurehead."

"Someday you just might turn into one."

"Someday I'll worry about it when it happens. Right

312

now I don't consider it very much of a problem at all. Why do you?"

He didn't answer.

She bit off a piece of whole-wheat toast. It went crunch. Not click.

October 1968

A WEEK BEFORE LABOR DAY and two weeks after the Dwight School's summer session had ended, Cynthia received a thin white envelope in the mail. Enclosed was her check for the fall semester's tuition, along with a terse note from the headmaster. "It grieves me deeply to have to inform you that I will not be able to admit your son Barry to the term commencing this September. It is my firm belief that he requires a different kind of classroom approach than the one we have tried to give him here at Dwight. The staff and I hope you will be able to place him in a school more in line with his needs. Sincerely yours."

"Why?"

"How the hell am I supposed to know why?"

"Barry, there's a reason why they've expelled you—"

"He didn't say anything about expelled. What are you getting so excited about? The school's not for me, that's all there is to it. Besides, that bunch of phony snobs used to bum me out all the time."

"And what do you think is going to happen now?"

He threw his hands up in the air, shrugged his shoulders, shifted his weight from one loafered foot to the other. It was, she saw clearly, a show of boredom and disinterest. He really doesn't care what happens to his future or anything, she realized. "Something," he said at last. The two stood in the narrow kitchen. Always a battleground, she thought. Nothing sweet and tender ever happens in kitchens. Only horror shows. If I didn't eat myself to death in a kitchen, something else just as bad would happen.

314

"Send him to a shrink," advised D. W., as succinct as the headmaster's note.

"Psychological counseling isn't something you'd call a sin, you know," Leonard concurred.

"Maybe a doctor'll knock some sense into his head before the army tries to grab him, God forbid," said Lena.

The doctor in question was Simon Hirsch, a Freudian-oriented psychiatrist who had his office around the corner from Bloomingdale's. As soon as the holiday weekend was over, Barry had his first appointment with the doctor. These continued, twice a week, all through September and on into October. In the meanwhile, she tried to enroll him in one private school after another. But she had no luck on that score. No luck with my husband, my children . . . only my business, she thought, having exhausted nearly every private day school within commuting distance.

She called Dr. Hirsch early in October. "I can't cope," she said. "I don't know what's bothering him, why he keeps getting kicked out of one school after another. Doctor, I'm at my wit's end. Just let me talk to you, ten minutes even."

"I can't discuss the boy's problems, Mrs. Margold," he informed her, "without running the risk of destroying professional confidentiality."

"I'm not asking you to show me the notes you've made or his file or anything like that. Can't you just tell me how I can . . . I don't know, relate to him better? And maybe suggest a school that can deal with him." It has to be more than the fact that I made the mistake of spoiling him, catering to him like he was a prima donna or something. There has to be an answer somewhere.

"Certainly, I can help you with that," he said. "I'll explain the situation to Barry, so he won't start jumping to the wrong conclusions. He has an appointment to see me this coming Thursday afternoon at four. Why don't you drop by the office at close to five. I'll see you then."

"I'm very grateful, doctor," she said, refraining from mentioning that since she was sending him a two hundred dollar check every month, the least he could do was sit down and give her ten minutes of his time.

October was also the month she had finally gotten her way with Leonard, having worked on him all through the summer. "What I spend in cabs is obscene," she said.

"Outrageous, too. The corporation can afford to provide me with a car and driver, Leonard. I'm not asking for a Caddy. Just a decent enough car to get me around. It's not such a huge expense, when you get right down to it. And God, it's all tax-deductible, anyway. It'll end up costing us less than what I take off in cab fares, believe me."

"Where will it end, Cynthia?"

"Have I asked you to advance me the down payment money for Caulfield's co-op? Have I? Well, have I?" And when he didn't answer, she said, "It's coming out of my own pocket, nearly everything I've managed to save up in the last three years, for your information. So stop giving me poor-mouth." D. W. had provided her with the term. She now used it even more freely than he did. "Besides, do you know how many franchises we've sold, altogether?"

"The figure eludes me."

Keep at it. Snappy remarks will get you nowhere, I assure you, she had thought, saying, "Thirty-four. At an average of fifteen thousand per, that comes to something like half a million dollars."

"For one, that's over a three-year period. For another, we never cleared a quarter of that gross in terms of out-and-out profits. Our expenditures are skyrocketing, in case you haven't seen the latest figures."

She waved a manila folder under his nose. "This is a market research forecast I had D. W. prepare. You know what the analysts are saying, what they predict, according to our current rate of growth? Next year we just might hit the $750,000 mark, that's what."

"Again, you fail to see the point . . ."

"And what point is that?" pray tell.

"Those figures cover the last three years with a projection for 1969, not just next year alone. Last year we sold seventeen franchises. That brought gross revenues to about two hundred fifty thousand. Then we deducted thirty thou a year for you and thirty thou a year for me and too damn much to Endicott and his bloodsucking partners. That left about one-sixty. Then we had to pay out Doris and Vivian and Vivian's assistant and Doris' assistant and your secretary and D. W.'s secretary, plus the girl who works the switchboard out front. Plus rent. Plus office supplies. We still own the operation on Flatbush Avenue and Rutland Road and we have to pay for everything *they* need. If we put away sixty thousand it was a lot."

"I want a driver. You didn't even mention the share of revenues we get from the branches. Next year we'll net double sixty thousand."

"For a woman who spent almost all of her life in a four-room apartment, you've certainly come a long way. Now you want chauffeurs. You're unbelievable, Cynthia, just unbelievable."

But she was still president. And she was still able to get what she wanted. For the time being, anyway.

"Where to?" Phil asked when she left the office late that Thursday afternoon. Even the Wall Street canyons, monolithic and cold with scurrying white shirt fronts crowding the small strips of pavement, seemed to reflect the change of seasons. The steel and glass façades caught a burnished reddish light from a slowly dipping sun.

"Sixtieth between Park and Lex," she said. "Hasn't it been a gorgeous day? Fall's my favorite time of year. It's when New York's the most alive. Did you have a good day, Phil? Do anything exciting?"

Her driver glanced back and smiled, even as he shifted into first and slid away from the curb. "Yeah, I got the tires changed, oil too. Real exciting." He laughed, truthful in his admission that when he wasn't driving her back and forth from work or wherever she happened to need to go, he didn't have a hell of a lot to do with all the time on his hands.

She caught his unkempt black and bushy brows. They hooded his eyes as he peered back at her through the rearview mirror. "Anything the matter?" she asked.

"Nope."

He let her off in front of Hirsch's office, the entire first floor of a three-story brownstone. The two sycamore trees which flanked the entrance had already begun to change color. Their leaves were a pale and brittle orange-gold, muted and soothing, perfectly in keeping with the work she imagined went on behind the heavy and ornately paneled front door. Hirsch shared the office space with another psychiatrist, a Jungian named Seymour Asher and author of two best-selling works which had attracted a large and considerable cult following, *The Universal Ego* and *The Ego that Swallowed the Universe*. Hirsch specialized in the psychological problems of adolescents.

317

Asher, on the other hand, was a favorite of New York theatricals and Broadway types, as Barry had informed her the week before. He had arrived home with two autographed copies of Asher's books. "I met him in the hall," he said, with the characteristic mysteriousness that had now become almost ingrained, ingrown too. She'd tried making sense out of them and gave up in disgust.

She checked her watch. She was early. It wasn't even twenty to five. She stopped at the door, turned around, and looked back at the curb, thinking she'd have a cup of coffee with Phil, but he'd already pulled away, no doubt circling the block in search of a parking spot. So she pressed her finger against the buzzer and let herself into the office.

"They should be done in a few minutes," the receptionist told her. "Why don't you take a seat and make yourself comfortable."

She did, curling up with the current issue of *Time* Magazine. There were no articles or features stories even remotely connected with weight loss. She read reviews of *The Great White Hope* and Marlene Dietrich's limited engagement at the Mark Hellinger, making a mental note to have her secretary call and get tickets. She decided to surprise D. W., take him out to one or the other or maybe even both since no eligible bachelors were banging down her door and it was the rare Saturday night indeed when she went out "on the town." Then she closed the magazine and left it on her lap, suddenly fantasizing how it would feel if someday her picture would be on the cover. If not Woman of the Year, then Woman of the Week would do nicely. Inside there'd be a three- or four-page spread, outlining her humble origins—That's what D. W. called them and it wasn't a put-on, either—how she built up NuBodies until it became an American institution, unique and one-of-a-kind. The one-woman crusade, her flaming red hair a national trademark," registered" just as they had recently registered the name NuBodies to protect themselves against competitors. There were two of the latter now, the Thin Set and the Slim Way. *Leave it to me, there's nothing to worry about. They're fly-by-night operations, D. W. had assured her. But I understand they're copying our methods . . . stealing them. Well you can't patent or copyright the way you run your classes, ma bête. But there's nothing to hassle*

318

your head about. They're two-bit outfits. And did you ever really have your heart set on making it big in Staten Island? referring to the Slim Way's headquarters, the location of its one and only branch. The truth?

"Do me a favor and go take it in the ear!"

A door slammed shut and she jerked her head up, following the direction of the sound. The buckles of the forty-two-dollar Gucci loafers he'd insisted upon having —"If D. W. can wear them, then why can't I? All the kids at school have them now, anyway"—were a loud, high-stepping rattle. Barry, his hair down to his shoulders —Prince Valiant in blue jeans, a crewneck sweater and a Brooks Brothers blazer—suddenly occupied not only all of her thoughts, but her entire field of vision as well. He stood in front of her, one inch under six feet, his hands buried down into the front pockets of his faded Levi's.

"What was that all about?" she whispered, at least grateful that the office was empty with no other patients waiting to see either Dr. Hirsch or Asher.

"If I told you, you'd say that I deserved a good slap in the teeth, so what's the point. I can't bear that man," he said.

Totally at a loss for words, she got to her feet and reached out a hand she wanted to rest on his shoulder. The consoling gesture was roughly rebuffed. He pushed himself back and the horse-bit buckles adorning his Italian calfskin loafers made another grating sound. "Just do me a favor and wait here for me. Phil'll drive us home. I'm just going to speak to the doctor for five–ten minutes, that's all."

"About what?" he said. His eyes narrowed. But at the same time, he reached out and picked a stray thread from her camel-hair coat. She couldn't tell if the gesture smacked of concern or condescension, as if he were suddenly embarrassed about her appearance, the way she looked and even handled herself in public.

"Nothing that you don't want me to know about. Satisfied?"

"The doctor can see you now, Mrs. Margold," the receptionist announced.

"Thank you." To Barry it was, "Sit still for a minute and wait for me. I want to talk to you."

"I wanted to buy something at Bloomingdale's. What d'you want from my life, anyway."

319

"You don't have a bit of kindness left, feeling for me, do you?"

"You have a real martyr syndrome, a complex . . . just like Natalie." His expression changed abruptly, a grimace she'd come to anticipate, to realize he favored and relied upon, far too often as far as she was concerned. His lips curled down so that the lower half of his face took on the lines of a puppet, woodenly carved from each corner of his mouth and down to his chin.

"I'll be right back," she said and headed for the door that had just slammed shut.

"Mrs. Margold?"

"Good evening, doctor."

Hirsch with his bland, untroubled face, was a universal father figure if ever there was one. He got up from his chair and motioned her to take a seat alongside of his desk.

"I hope he didn't get fresh with you," she said, already searching for the cigarette that would be a pacifier, once she got it lit and wedged between her lips.

"It's okay. I work with teenagers every day. It's not all that unusual. The boy's only directing the anger he feels for himself out at me. We call it transference. Actually, it's far from abnormal and ultimately it's a healthy process. So don't worry yourself unnecessarily. He's getting all the help he needs, I promise you."

"He *does* need help, doesn't he?"

The psychiatrist nodded his head.

So there it is, in black and white, she thought. So I wasn't wrong. So I didn't send him to a psychiatrist, one of the top men in the city, just on a lark, just because everyone told me it was the thing to do. *He does need help*.

Hirsch closed a folder she had seen spread across his desk, filed it away in a side drawer and then looked up at her. Having never been in a psychiatrist's office before —mental illness as much a taboo as cancer or TB—she turned her head around for a moment, surprised when she didn't see a couch. He must sit in this same chair. Sure, it's still warm. Lot of comfort that is, my kid who used to be such a gorgeous baby is growing up to be some holy terror and I don't have the answer, *any* answer for that matter. And I'm losing patience too, by leaps and bounds, on top of everything else. Which is worse and I know it is, but I can't seem to do anything about it. *Cope*, that's the word. Again and again: *I just can't cope.* Like some over-weights can't bend down to tie a shoe, I can't cope with a son, and I bend over backwards for him, too, and that isn't even a joke. If it was funny at least I could laugh. But it isn't. It's tragic. And it's a disgrace.

"What can I do, Dr. Hirsch? You tell me, because I just don't know anymore."

"I think we have to get Barry enrolled in a special school, Mrs. Margold. I think that's the only viable answer we have at this point in his life."

"What do you mean, a special school?" her eyes became instant slits, suspicious, and almost hostile. She didn't like it when people criticized her son, even if it was deserved. I'd steal for them if I had to, she used to say. Now it wasn't *them*, because Natalie was living in Brooklyn with her father, her Sweet Sixteen party the end of the month and she still hadn't received an invitation in the mail. *It's coming, don't worry,* Lena said. *She loves you, as God is my witness, would I lie to you?* "Special," she asked, "like in *sick?*" A frog jumped in her stomach. She decided it was the perfect time to feed it an eclair.

"The boy's not sick, Mrs. Margold. You mustn't jump to erroneous conclusions like that. He's having problems right now, that's all. Emotional difficulties, let me say. But he's not *sick*, not by any stretch of the imagination."

She still wasn't sure if he was saying that just to make her feel good.

"You see, the difficulty stems—at least in part—from the fact that now that you and Mr. Margold are sepa-rated, Barry has no male figure, a father figure I should say, to model himself after."

"Am I to blame then?" She wasn't snapping at him, but she knew she was coming close. "Is it my fault my husband and I . . . you know, discovered we were incom-patible?"

"No, of course not," he replied. "I'm just stating the situation as I see it, Mrs. Margold. It's open to a hundred different interpretations, depending upon your school of thought or which psychiatrist you consult. But what I do think is necessary, an important first step in the right di-rection, is for Barry to return to school, complete his studies, and get his diploma."

"Aren't there any schools . . . geared to boys like him?"

Hirsch nodded his head. "Indeed there are. I've been considering one in particular, the Lincolnwood School up in Monterey, Massachusetts. It's a little town about ten or so miles outside of Great Barrington. The school is run by a trained psychologist. It's experimental, but only in the sense that it was established just for youngsters like Barry. It's apparent that he can't adjust to a normal classroom routine, a regimented academic environment. Well, at Lincolnwood they believe in giving their students a certain degree of independence, freedom which sometimes works to make the child more emotionally secure, stable in his own right."

"In other words, a military school would be a mistake?"

"Were you considering that?"

"Yes, yes I was."

"My God, it would be absolutely the worst kind of error in judgment," Hirsch said, his laugh as cool and brittle as the leaves which fell from the trees outside his office window. "Absolutely a mistake. It's not a question of mere discipline, you see. It goes beyond that."

"Well how can we get him up there?" she asked. "To Massachusetts, I mean," the question all but answered, the problem all but solved. If Hirsch recommended Lincolnwood, it was good enough for her. First things first, she thought. Let him get his diploma and then we'll worry about what happens next, when the time comes.

"The school is expensive, Mrs.—"

"That's no problem, no barrier," she said. "The problem is Barry, Dr. Hirsch. Something has to be done. He gets worse every day, not better. And like I told you, it's not even a question of patience anymore. I just don't know how to even begin to handle him.

"Lincolnwood might be the answer," the psychiatrist said with a nod of his head, a thrust of his chin. "Let me do this then. I'll get in touch with the headmaster this week and see if he can find room for Barry. Chances are he won't be able to start until January or February—"

"Which means he's going to lose another six months," she said, frowning. "What if the army wants him? What if he gets a notice to go down for a physical? What then?"

"No problem. That's what I'm here for. All I have to do is write a letter and there'll be no difficulties, I assure you."

"Wouldn't that hurt him . . . later on? I mean, don't

they keep that kind of information on file all the time, for the rest of your life?"

"Not necessarily. But let's cross that bridge when we come to it. Right now Lincolnwood is our best bet. I'll devote my energies to getting Barry accepted."

"And in the meantime?"

"In the meantime I suggest he continue seeing me as he has since September."

"I see," she said, sensing the interview was drawing to a close. She started to get up from her seat. "But what's the matter with him, doctor? What's wrong with him?"

Dr. Hirsch smiled, Buddha-patient, cryptic, and reticent, all at the same time. "Whatever Barry's problems are, they're not insurmountable, Mrs. Margold. Try to be patient with the boy. Adolescence is a most difficult period in one's life. He's just having a little harder time of it than most."

"So you're not going to tell me," she said, trying to smile.

"No." He reflected her smile, mirror-perfect, got to his feet and extended his hand. "As I already mentioned when we discussed this earlier on the phone, patient confidentiality is sacrosanct. I wouldn't dare do anything to jeopardize the professional relationship I've been trying to build up with your son. If I did, all the progress he's been making—and believe me, there *has* been progress, Mrs. Margold—would be endangered. I wouldn't run the risk of taking that kind of chance."

She sighed and nodded her head. "You're the doctor," she said, her cigarette bent and lifeless, a crumpled butt in his glass ashtray. "I'm just a mother." When she stepped outside, Barry was nowhere to be seen.

"My son . . . ?" she started to say to the receptionist.

"He left," the woman said. "Ten minutes ago."

No end, she thought. No end in sight.

"Aren't you going to come?"

"No way," Barry said. "When I spoke to her on the phone last week she said it was just gonna be a bunch of her girl friends from school. It'll be boring as . . . you know. No, I think I'll stick around and stay in the city. Catch a flick or something."

"Did you buy her a birthday present, at least?" she asked.

"Sure I did. What do you think, I'm a cheapskate or something?"

"What did you get her?"

"I sent it already. In the mail."

"What?" she persisted, curious, glad that at least her two children were getting along, even if they saw each other infrequently, at best.

"God, are you nosy, mother. I sent her money. Okay? Satisfied?"

"Money?" she said, taken aback. "What kind of birthday present is that? It's so . . . so impersonal." And it came out of my own pocket, on top of everything else. "Couldn't you have bought her a nice little piece of jewelry or something?"

"She told me she needed money so that's what I sent her."

"What does a sixteen-year-old kid need money for, that's what I'd like to know."

"Don't ask me," he said. "That's what she said she wanted, or needed, I should say, and that's what I sent her. Maybe she needs an abortion, who knows."

"Very funny, bigmouth."

"See you guys later."

He was out the door in a flash. She'd stopped asking him where he spent his time, his ultimate destination. She had a feeling he lied about it anyway, not telling her where he was really going or what he really did. A call to the city's department of health had brought her a thin twelve-page brochure, not unlike the stapled pamphlet put out by Kings County Hospital. Only this one wasn't entitled "You Too Can Be Thin." It read, "Drug Tips For Parents." And underneath that, in smaller but no less bold type, "How To Detect Drug Abuse Before It's Too Late." Inside were a list of symptoms corresponding with particular drugs, from marijuana to LSD, from amphetamines to downs, cocaine to heroin. She wasn't about to go into his room and ransack his dresser drawers, searching for some kind of proof. Certain things were sacred (along with professional confidentiality), and when it came to a person's privacy, it didn't matter if the person happened to also be her son. She wouldn't expect Barry to go through her drawers. Likewise, she had no intention of

324

performing that kind of illicit act when he was not around, when the coast was clear. D. W. had told her that if all he took was marijuana, she shouldn't hassle her head about it. If he was into pills and heavier stuff, she wouldn't need a booklet to detect the symptoms. *You'll see them, and you won't need Merck's Manual, either.* What she did see were quick outbursts of temper, nervous irritation and then the opposite spectrum of emotions: sluggishness, lassitude, boredom, everything brought down to a common denominator which went something to the effect, "Just leave me alone and stop getting on my back, mother."

If Barry's mental health was now in doubt, at least she was thankful that Lena's was not. Her mother had gone —at her repeated insistence—for a complete physical checkup, only to report that the doctor had given her a clean bill of health. In fact, other than her arthritis, for which he said they could do little if anything, Lena had returned home to report, "They told me I had the constitution of a woman fifteen years younger than me. When I told them how old I really was, the doctors, and the nurses, too, just couldn't believe it. They thought I was pulling their leg."

Knock wood for one and pray to God something gets through to her kid, for another.

But he was gone now.

"Mother, are you dressed yet? Phil's waiting for us downstairs. We don't want to be late," she called out as she stepped from her room, one hand securing a gold macaroni earring D. W. had helped her pick out at Tiffany's.

"One second. Just let me run a comb through my hair."

Ten minutes later they took the West Side Highway down to the Battery Tunnel. Once they crossed over into Brooklyn, Phil got them onto the Belt Parkway and from there it was a fast thirty minutes to Sheepshead Bay and Lundy's, the seafood restaurant where Manny was holding his daughter's Sweet Sixteen party. Leonard and Jeanette lived near Lundy's but she had no intention of paying them a visit. It was enough she saw Frankel nearly every day when he showed up at the office—to check up on me, no doubt. She didn't want to be reminded of his newfound marital bliss, nor made to ogle Jeanette's five-carat diamond.

Over and done with, she thought, just like everything else. But that's all right, too, because you always go on to the bigger and better, that's my philosophy. Because if you sit around and stew in your own juices, you never get anywhere and you never accomplish anything.

"I'm gonna have myself some clams across the street, a dozen cherrystones, at Tappans's," Phil said when they got there. "I'll be out in a half-hour, tops."

"No rush, but littlenecks are sweeter. That's my opinion, anyway," she said while Phil got out of the car and opened up the door for Lena. He helped her out as well and she said, "Take your time. We should be here for a good two hours, maybe a little more than that."

"Have a good time."

"Thank you, Philly," Lena said. "Whenever you drive I feel in safe hands."

"That's what I'm here for."

"Isn't he a terrific guy?" she said to her mother. "Always a gentleman." She took Lena under the arm and headed for the main entrance to the restaurant.

"One in a million. How do I look?"

"Like a dream."

After checking their coats, she asked the captain where the Margold party was being held. He directed her to a side room in the rear of the restaurant. It was a great barn of a place, with high arched ceilings and countless white-clothed tables. Everywhere she looked, mouths were moving. Lundy's was known not only for the freshness of its fish, but also for its buttermilk biscuits, "prepared right on the premises by our very own bakers." She knew that was one item she would go out of her way to avoid.

She had offered to split the bill with Manny, but he told her it wasn't necessary. *You paid for Barry's bar mitzvah, so this is the least I can do. Besides, it's not running me all that much. She's only having a dozen or so friends, the most.*

Lena said, "I haven't been here in years. But from what I remember, you can always count on getting a good piece of fish."

"I've heard that, too." Then she saw her from across the room. Natalie wore a pink dress (the wrong color, it only makes her look heavier it's such a pastel shade) very lacy and frilly, with a full skirt, matching shoes, and a corsage of carnations and gumdrops on her wrist. Her skin's clearing up, thank God, she thought. But she put on more weight than when I last saw her. She's like a balloon and half her friends are just as heavy. Why do they let themselves go like that? I don't think I'll ever understand it. Even when I get up in front of a group of people and talk my heart out, one part of me's just always in the dark.

"You didn't tell me your mother was the same Margold from NuBodies," she heard one of Natalie's friends exclaim in a high-pitched, excited voice.

"Lena, Cynthia," and Manny kissed his mother-in-law on the cheek.

"Hello, Manny. You're looking well," Cynthia said. Henny, she noticed, was conspicuously absent. But it would've taken more gall than he could have mustered.

"So are you." He turned his head around. "Natalie, look who's here."

She moved toward them, a small tub with short-cropped, reddish-brown hair, her eyes fixed on her grandmother. "Is this a Natalie," Lena said with a grin, "is this a gorgeous sweet sixteen or isn't it." They kissed. Lena looked more birdlike—frail and flightless—than ever, dwarfed by her grandchild.

"You think you can spare a little kiss for your mother?" Cynthia said, working so hard to smile, trying with everything she had to feel relaxed—and wanted.

"Sure, why not," Natalie said. Cavalier, as if she were doing her mother the greatest of favors, her lips touched Cynthia's cheek for an instant. It was as fleeting as one of Barry's departures.

"You look lovely," she said.

"Doesn't she though," agreed Lena. She reached into her black leather bag and pulled out a small square box wrapped in brightly-colored gift paper. "Happy birthday, sweetface. Wear it in good health."

"Thank you, gran'ma." She kissed Lena again. "I'm not supposed to open it now, if that's okay with you. At the end of the party they," indicating her friends, "make a kind of funny hat with all the ribbons and wrapping paper and stuff. And daddy's going to take pictures."

"No rush," Lena said.

"And this is from me to you, sweetheart," said Cynthia,

extracting a similarly gift-wrapped package from her handbag.

"Thank you." She turned away without a kiss, a hug, or a squeeze of the hand. Both gifts were deposited on top of a pile, heaped high on an adjacent table.

"Mrs. Margold, I go to your classes, on Flatbush Avenue," one of the girls rushed up to tell her.

"You do?" and Cynthia smiled. "I hope you like them."

"Oh I do, I do," the girl replied. "I already lost fifteen pounds. The people are so nice and the woman who talks to us, Mrs. Bauer—she lets us call her Doris, she's the greatest. She's so understanding and you should hear the things she says about you. I never thought I'd get to meet you but now I have and I want to thank you, for what you're doing I mean."

She smiled, pleased and yet embarrassed. It was Natalie's party, her show and no one else's. She didn't want to do anything her daughter might misconstrue or interpret in a bad light. No sooner had one of the girl's friends stopped to speak to Cynthia, when another teenager stood before her, announcing in a loud and animated voice that she, too, attended the NuBodies class for teenagers. "On Rutland Road, with Mrs. Hollander, Viv."

A third girl said, "I'm afraid to go."

She couldn't help herself. "Why? There's absolutely nothing to be afraid of, dear. A lot of teenage girls have problems with their weight. It's not a sin."

"I know, but still—"

"It's time for everyone to sit down and have lunch," Natalie announced, there was nothing cordial in her tone of voice.

Cynthia looked up, half expecting to see her daughter stamp her foot with the same kind of angry, petulant impatience which had marked her childhood. Instead, Cynthia confronted a pair of red apple cheeks and a stout, pear-shaped body which literally trembled like a piece of fruit being pulled off a branch.

She heard herself say, even as a hand reached out to automatically pat Natalie's friend on the shoulder, "We'll talk about it later." In an entirely different voice, one she used when she stood in front of a group, she said, "But now it's time we all sat down and enjoyed our lunch ... and Natalie's birthday party."

Don't tell me she's mad at me, she thought, taking a

328

seat next to Lena. She unfolded her napkin, looked around, and smiled at Natalie's friends. Sweet girls, she thought. Nothing cheap or loose about any of them, all from nice families no doubt. Thank God for that. It's enough I get the other extreme from her brother.

Two waiters first dispensed New England clam chowder. Cynthia waved her hand. "Not for me, thank you." She didn't expect nor did she want any of the others to follow suit. But that was what happened. No sooner had she asked the waiter to leave her plate bare, when at least half of Natalie's friends chose the same course of action.

Manny glared at her from across the length of the long narrow table.

Is it my fault? she thought.

Lena nudged her in the side. "The soup is fabulous. A cup wouldn't kill you. It warms the insides." Then she said loudly, addressing the table, "Isn't the clam chowder luscious? Personally, I've always liked New England style better than Manhattan. It's so much creamier, richer."

Several of the girls picked at dry sea rounds, salt-free crackers stacked in the basket with the biscuits. Cynthia listened to the scrape of spoons against china. Don't tell me I'm going to feel this uncomfortable for the next two hours, because if I am, I had no business coming. I should've stayed home and minded my business instead of acting like a mother.

She allowed herself to partake of the steamers, though she avoided dipping them in the monkey dish of melted butter the waiter left alongside her plate. For awhile, ten minutes or so, there was very little talking. When the fried shrimp came out, it struck her that nearly a dozen pairs of eyes were turned her way, as if all of Natalie's girl friends were waiting to see if she would eat the main course. Fried foods were a no-no, prohibited and stipulated as such on the diet. But she was afraid to decline, afraid she'd start another chain reaction which would only have disastrous consequences.

"Vivian says that when you see fried food you should say, 'Thanks, but I value my health,'" one girl whispered all too loudly to the youngster sitting next to her. "Isn't that the funniest thing you ever—"

A foot shot out under the table. Cynthia gave a little jerk, a little cry, a little start of pain and surprise. And when she looked to the side, there was Natalie, her face redder than ever. Swollen and inflamed, more of a balloon now than an apple. The girl mouthed, "I hate you." She didn't need a course in lip reading to understand.

"Everyone eat hearty!" she called out, too gay and frantic but there was no other choice. Something had to be done to change the atmosphere, so tense and electric with hostility she wanted to crawl into a corner and be forgotten.

It was too late.

Natalie scraped her chair back and got to her feet. Her eyes were like puddles, wet and muddy-brown. "I'm not staying if she stays, daddy. She's ruining my party. It's for me and my friends, not for her; she's skinny as a skeleton and I don't want her here, daddy!"

"Natalie honey, please," Lena said in pacification. "That's your mother you're talking about."

"I don't care if everyone hears because it's true. Henny'll be my mother. She loves me more. More!"

Crawl under the table. Hide your eyes. Two hysterical children and you're the one who's always caught in the middle. From both ends you get it, so be smart, get out of here but go, get out before she tries to overturn the table, before you start to cry. What good would it do, what possible good in all the world if she hates you? She hates you. *HENNY'LL BE MY MOTHER*. "Manny'll drive you home, mom," she said to Lena, already making a move to push her chair back and get to her feet.

The full meaning of "stunned silence" came to her, loud and crashing without anyone saying a word. Just those dozen uneasy pairs of eyes, embarrassed, all looking down at generous portions of fried shrimp, French fried potatoes turning cold and soggy on lukewarm china plates.

"I'm sorry if I did anything to hurt or upset you, Natalie," she said. She stood there, straining to remain calm, trying not to tremble with a terror she felt only a mother could possibly understand. "I would give you my life, that's how much I love you." Then she turned away, her steps faltering but moving her forward, out of the side room and the long narrow table of hushed whispers, furtive glances.

"It's a party, everyone!" Manny said loudly, the words ringing in her ears as she made her way to the checkroom to get her coat. "Eat up, there's plenty, there's more to come!"

She was already outside, looking in vain for Phil who no doubt was still finishing off his dozen clams on the half-shell, when a hand caught her on the shoulder. She forced herself to turn around.

"I'm sorry," he said. "The kid's hysterical. She's super-sensitive, what can I do."

"What can you do?" she said with a voice that cracked like a broken plate. "She hates my guts, the very ground I walk on, that's what you can do. 'Henny'll be my mother.' And who told her that, who put that . . . that lie, that garbage in her ears!"

"I didn't tell her anything of the kind. She's hyper-sensitive about her weight. It's not my fault."

"Then is it mine then? Am I to blame for everything that happens, even when I'm not around? You turned her against me. But why, what purpose could it have solved, that's what I'd like to know." The air smelled like a fish store. The wind which blew at the hem of her coat was briny, wet. She shivered and pulled up her collar.

"Turned her against you?" he repeated, the voice of innocence and reason protesting, or so she felt, far more than necessary. "I never did anything of the kind, Cynthia."

"I get it from my other one, too," she said. "Now it's both of them, like I'm the worst mother in the world, like I went out of my way to get my kids to hate me."

"She doesn't hate you."

"Then what do you call that . . . that performance she just gave? Love? That's a laugh. That's a load of bullshit, pardon me, if ever there was one. What in God's name have I done to that child to make her despise me so? You didn't see how she looked at me when I walked in, or maybe you did. Sure you did. The invitation came to Lena, in case you don't know. To Mrs. Lena Winick, care of Margold. Doesn't even ask her own mother to come to her Sweet Sixteen."

"If you weren't invited, you should have stayed away, if that's the case."

"If I slapped you in the face for that, it wouldn't do any good. So what's the point. You created a little mon-ster, Forman. You turned that child into a walking, talk-ing—" She stopped, clutched at her bag, opened it, found a tissue, changed her mind, snapped it shut. Her eyes were dry. Just like the last time, she thought, saying, "What's the use of talking. I'll talk till I'm blue in the face and it won't do any good, so maybe I should keep quiet for a change."

Behind her came, "I'll be right with you, Mrs. Margold."

"Who's that?" he asked.

"My driver." She wasn't *Cynthia* any longer, now that someone was with her. Phil observed the proper amenities, even in the midst of something she decided was the closest she had ever felt to a complete and total breakdown.

"So the lady has a chauffeur," Manny said, both hands buried inside baggy trouser pockets, lots of change jingling as he stood there, stood his ground too, she decided.

"Is that so terrible?"

"I didn't say a word," he replied. "But you're right. What's the use of talking because you've got one helluva nerve blaming me for Natalie's behavior. What about your other one, now that we're on the subject?"

"What other one?"

"There's only one, Cynthia. My son. The one with the pageboy haircut and pants that look like they've been painted on skintight, that's what."

She narrowed her eyes, hysteria replaced by a mixed bag of anger and disbelief. "What are you talking about? What tight pants?"

"You heard me," he said while behind her the car pulled up, and Phil jumped out to open the side door.

"Five minutes," she said, waving him off. "What was that supposed to mean, Forman?"

"Just what it sounds like," he said. "You can stand there and accuse me of turning Natalie against you, well then I can stand here and be just as . . . as self-righteous and accuse you of turning Barry into a sissy, that's what."

"A sissy!" she yelled. "What's gotten into you? You're sick, you're a sick man, Forman. Don't you ever say such a thing to me again, do you hear? Do you hear? I'd kill for him, you . . . you . . . my son is not a sissy. He never was a sissy and he'll never be a sissy. What kind of sick things are you trying to make up? The way you distort reality, Forman—"

"Hah," he said, "some distortion. You're blind to it,

332

that's all. You won't be happy until you've destroyed everyone."

Once before, the evening she had discovered he had left with Natalie like a thief in the night, her world had come tumbling down, red as a fresh coat of crimson paint. Now the red enveloped her like hot licking flames. Unable to think straight, to see things clearly, unable to stop herself, she raised her arm and brought her hand down across his face. Once. Twice. It was a thunderclap in her ears. A scream strangled and clawed at the back of her throat.

"Don't you ever come around and bother me again," she said. "I don't want to know you're alive, that you exist."

"If I wasn't a gentleman I'd take you in hand, Cynthia, knock some sense into your head."

"That'll be the day, you and your crummy two-bit operation—the real businessman, Mr. Ferris the big wheel. You're lucky you're not starving to death." That was all she had left to throw in his face. His business was his whole life. She wondered if it meant more to him than NuBodies meant to her. She couldn't be sure, one way or another.

"You'll be getting the papers in the mail," he said, his cheek still blotchy with the tattoo of her palm and five fingers.

"What papers are you talking about now?"

"From my lawyer," he said. "Henny and I are getting married as soon as the divorce comes through. I'm going down to Haiti or out to Reno or wherever the hell people go when they want a quick divorce, because that's exactly what I have in mind."

"You . . . you yokel, you greenhorn." She was sneering, her face contorted and still she didn't care. "They'll take you for everything you have, every last penny . . . which wasn't much to begin with, anyway. Go, get a divorce. I'll give a party when it comes through. I'll bake a cake for you because it'll be my lucky day, you phony. Talks about his son like he's filth, like he's someone who walked in off the street, a nobody."

She got into the car, slammed the door behind her and clutched at her hands. The tips of her fingers tingled. They were still warm, still going through the motion of slapping him across the face, even as she held them down, in check against her lap.

"Where to?"

"Cross over the bridge into Manhattan Beach," she said. She looked out the window, half expecting Manny to rap his knuckles against the glass. He loves pulling scenes, she thought. But he'd already turned away, a wide figure in loose trousers, the seat of his pants shiny too. His shoulders seemed to pull in on each other like a puckered seam, short-circuited.

Phil pulled out of the parking lot.

She found a tissue, blew her nose. There were no tears. I've cried too long and for nothing, no good whatsoever. "On second thought," she said, "don't bother, Phil."

"What?" He glanced back, his face a Kodachrome in the saltwater light.

"Just take me home."

November 1968

THE GOLD CHARM BRACELET with the single charm—"16" on one side, "From Mom with Love" on the other—was returned in its original box, unopened. As Cynthia finally discovered, Lena had signed for it when it came in the mail. She hadn't told her about it for nearly a week, breaking the news only after NuBodies had signed on a group in Washington, D.C. It was the first franchise to be bought by blacks. Cynthia considered it a breakthrough. If she could do her bit to encourage the growing black middle class, she felt she had accomplished something that went above and beyond helping people lose weight. So she was in a good mood, in excellent and even high spirits, when she returned home that evening.

Then Lena brought out the box.

She took one look, recognized the florid girlish handwriting, i's dotted with little circular balloons, and said, "Just put it away in a drawer for me, mom. The store won't take it back because I had it engraved."

"Such a shame," Lena said, "a real pity."

She made the effort of laugher, the smile of someone the world considered a good sport. "That's life. Right?"

"Some answer. This time I blame Manny, how d'you like that?"

"Don't blame anyone. It's not worth it. I'll give it back to her one of these days." Don't ask me when. "Maybe when she's old enough to understand." Don't ask me what, because I still don't know how I went wrong; what I did to her that was so terrible.

She worked on a speech she was scheduled to give the following week. A hall had been rented in Detroit. Posters had been put up. Ads were appearing daily in the *Detroit Free Press*. It would be her first trip to Michigan and since the state was still virgin territory, wide open to the Nu-Bodies "idea," she was anxious to make a good showing and an equally good impression. She turned in early. It was useless to wait up for Barry, and the Late Show was a movie she had already seen twice before. It didn't have the greatest of memories associated with it, either. Myrna Loy and Fredric March. *The Best Years of Our Lives.*

"How'd it go?"

"Without a hitch," she said. "Like clockwork, smooth as silk. I had close to three hundred people eating out of the palm of my hand."

"And a new branch?" D. W. asked.

"Well, none of our lecturers want to move to Detroit, so I made the same offer I have in the past. First person to lose a hundred pounds by our methods gets the opportunity to open a franchise. I think this time we'll even help with the financing. The city's that big and I think it's important we get a foothold. Early."

Christmas was less than a month away now and even Orsini's was caught up in the holiday mood. Great rustic wheat and pine cone wreaths hung in the entranceway when she stepped in off the street to meet D. W. "I made reservations for a smashing lunch," he had told her.

"Just ask for Eisenstern?"

"Nope. Ask for Eliot."

She didn't know what *that* was all about. But the previous evening, when she'd gotten in on a Northwest jet, she came home to find a stack of messages. He'd been trying to reach her most of the evening. As mysterious as Barry, she decided when she finally got through to him. "What's the problem, love?"

"No problem. Just a lot of news. Meet me for lunch tomorrow and I'll tell you everything. You're not coming in in the morning, are you?"

"No, I'm going to sleep late. I feel exhausted. It was hectic, to put it mildly. And that talk show interview you arranged—it was like going through a meat-grinder. God, they wanted blood. It was worse than Joe Pyne was, last year. Worse than Pittsburgh, even."

"Worse than Pittsburgh? Really?"

"Really," she said. "I mean, I never thought Detroit was particularly worried about its weight. But . . . I'll tell you when I see you."

"Right this way please," said the black-tied maître d' when she told him she was expected at Mr. Eliot's table.

I dressed perfectly, she thought, her eyes moving from one table to another. My God, what an elegant place. I'm surprised he hasn't taken me here for lunch before. It's right up his alley . . . high-class. She wore a simple light wool dress with a narrow chain belt and alligator pumps. A single strand of pearls—"real" as opposed to "cultured" —hung softly around her neck, earrings to match. The dress was cuffed and long-sleeved, basic black. It also made her look very slim, which was an added bonus, a "benny" as D. W. would have called it.

"There you are," he said, which wasn't all that predictable since he was the last person she knew who relied upon cliches, pat stock phrases. He got up from his seat and waited until the maître d' had helped her to a chair. "I've ordered a liter of their house white, if that's okay with you. It's palatable . . . actually, not too bad at all."

"Fine."

"You look delicious, good enough to eat. I see that some of me's been rubbing off."

"Just a little," she said and raised her glass. "You look as adorable and put-together as always. New suit?"

"Pierre Cardin, Bonwit's. Like it?"

"Very. And it fits you beautifully."

"Thank you."

"Okay," she said with a grin, "now that we've dispensed with that, what's this *Eliot* business all about and why were you so funny last night on the phone?"

"I wasn't funny."

"Mysterious then. You reminded me of my kid, everything hush-hush, top-secret."

"How is he, by the way?"

"Don't ask."

"Did you hear from that school yet?"

"Lincolnwood? Not yet. But the psychiatrist says there's nothing to worry about so I'm keeping my fingers crossed. But what about you?"

"First a toast."

She raised her glass a second time.

"To my new career."

337

She drank without asking another question, though something was intent upon doing a swan dive from the back of her throat all the way down to her stomach, and it wasn't the wine.

"I adore you, you know that, Margold. You're a dynamite lady and I want you to be the first to know," and he checked his watch, "that less than two hours ago I handed in my resignation to End-it-All, Pucker & Grubby."

"If I did a double take you'd only accuse me of being unnecessarily dramatic. Say this again. You did what?"

"Resigned," and he made a face that made her think instantly of Danny Kaye in either *The Court Jester* or *Merry Andrew*.

"Endicott, Tucker & Groves and D. Wayne Eisenstern are no more?" She shook her head in dismay. But there were no cobwebs to clear out. Everything was perfectly obvious, though far from understandable.

"Very good," he said. "You're catching on faster than a speeding bullet—"

"That's because you've got me well-trained."

"It's taken forever and at great cost to my mental health and well-being—"

"But it's been worth the effort, hasn't it?"

"Absolutely, my darling. Are you hungry yet? Because if you are, we can order."

"No, not yet. Let's just sit a while longer. You did what now? Resigned? But why? They were paying you good money I don't understand."

"I wanted to be a free agent."

"But what about, what about the contract we have for you? Your services, I mean. It doesn't expire until . . . what is it, sometime next year, March I think. What about that?"

"What about it? The firm has the contract, my dear. I'm not chattel you know. This isn't the Middle Ages, *le moyen age* as it were. I'm not a serf. Since I've severed my relationship with the agency, that in effect absolves any contractual obligations of which I've been a part. Don't forget, Cynthia my sweetest angel-puss in all the world, that I was never under contract with Endicott. Only NuBodies was. There's a difference."

"I don't understand. I don't get it. Why? You still haven't told me your reasons. What was this, just a whim, a spur-of-the-moment decision?"

"Would you like to order now, sir?" the waiter asked, discreet as possible as he stood alongside the narrow table, his hands behind his back.

"Cynthia?"

"Not yet. A few more minutes. And where does this . . . this decision you've reached, leave *me,* that's what I'd like to know."

"Do I detect a note of panic, hysteria in your voice?" he said.

"You're damn right you do. I don't have to sit here and feed your ego when you know how I feel about you."

"Look at it this way, sweetheart." He leaned forward, both elbows flat on the table. His wineglass was upraised, suspended like a pale amber globe between his hands. "I was tired of having my brains picked, tired of working for someone else. I want to be my own boss for a change. My decision has nothing to do with NuBodies, I assure you. I mean, I didn't quit Endicott because of NuBodies, if that's what you're worried about."

"Frankly, that *is* what I'm worried about," she told him. "I don't want to lose you, D. W. Not now, not-when things are starting to take off again the way they did when you first came to us."

"When you first came to me, you mean," he made a point of correcting. "Well let's order first, because they have a very slow kitchen. Then we can talk about it." He picked up the menu. "The veal piccata is to faint over, it's that good. And very NuBodies, if you know what I mean."

She was in no mood to sit there and pick and choose. "Fine." She took another sip of wine, decided it was going to be a very scary lunch. A waiter was right there to refill her glass, even before she put it down on the table again.

"Ready sir?" the captain asked.

"Yes, I think so," D. W. said, still eyeing the elaborate menu. "My daughter will have the veal piccata and a green salad, no dressing. I'll try your mozzarella in carrozza."

"And for the main course?;"

"Scampi." He handed the captain the menu. "Oh, and another liter of white, when you get the chance." Then he turned back to her, saying, "Where were we?"

"What is the mozzarella in whatever?"

"It's fabulous. They deep-fry mozzarella cheese with anchovies. It's extraordinary."

"Don't tell me any more or I'll get heartburn. If not that, paupitations," she said, straining at cheerfulness, an excess of good humor. "Now tell me about Eliot."

"I'm coming to that. First things first."

"Such as?" Behind her she caught a flurry of motion, the buzz of a sudden dozen different whispers. She turned her head to the side before looking back at D. W. with wide eyes. "Did you see what I just saw?" she whispered along with half the restaurant. "Isn't that Jackie Kennedy? My God she looks fabulous. I don't care what they say about her big feet, bones like hers don't grow on tress. They're plain remarkable."

"It's Jackie O., all right," so blasé he couldn't tell whether or not he was faking it. "I told you Orsini's was divine. Always has been, even though they don't allow two single gentlemen to sit downstairs."

"Why not?"

"The room's too dark, the fools," he said. "But stop gaping and let the poor woman have her privacy. The limelight can get to be so tedious after awhile."

"I should be half as poor."

"That's the one word which no longer applies to you, Cynthia. So let's not get into your favorite poor-mouth routine. Just let me get back to our discussion. Basically, what I want is all pretty simple and straightforward," he said, hurrying along now as though he were short on time. She was forced to lean forward, to concentrate on every word and syllable. "I'd like NuBodies to underwrite the cost of establishing my own advertising agency."

"Either my ears are clogged this afternoon or you're not speaking clearly."

"I said, I'd like NuBodies to underwrite the cost of a new advertising agency, D. Wayne Eliot & Friends."

"That's the name of the agency?"

"Yes. Clever, isn't it?"

"Who are the friends?"

"I haven't found them yet."

They both laughed, though it didn't make things any easier for her. "You've gone off the deep end or I have," she said, "because one of us is crazy. Do you have any idea what Leonard will say when I tell him this? He'll laugh in my face, that's what. I didn't even go to him . . .

340

the corporation I mean, when I bought the co-op. It came out of my own pocket, my savings, because I didn't want to get into any arguments, discussions with him. How much is this . . . extravaganza going to cost?"

"Initially? Not more than fifteen thousand."

"Insanity," which was just one of the many things he'd taught her to say.

"Ten then, though I'd be pinched," he said before she could even catch her breath. "I also have two thousand of my own saved up. So what it comes down to is eight grand to get me on my feet."

D. W.'s mozzarella in carrozza and her salad arrived sooner than expected. She took one look at his plate, felt her mouth water, and closed her eyes. A nervous shiver went through her like an eel. I don't dare, not even a taste, it's so rich, she thought. And he's got me wrapped around his little finger, just like Barry, on top of everything else. And he knows it, too; that's what kills me. I've always been a sucker for a fast talker. You'd think I would've learned by now.

"And what would be the advantage to NuBodies, if we set you up in business?" she asked, still trying to keep her eyes away from his plate.

"That's the beauty of it. One sec." He stopped long enough to take a bite. Melted cheese clung to the tines of his fork. He wiped the excess off his lips and smiled contentedly. "All right, let me go over it with you, step by step. The last thing I want is for you to think I'm trying to put something over on you, because I'm not. So just listen for a minute and if you have any questions, save them to the end."

She picked up a fork and approached her undressed salad, still wary-eyed, still finding his proposal nearly impossible to swallow.

"Now first of all, why the fifteen . . . okay, the eight grand. Very simple," he began. "I need the money to rent office space, for legal fees for incorporation, to have a letterhead and logo designed; I mean, I can't do everything, especially if I'll still be up to my ass in work for you people. Then a credit line has to be set up with suppliers. You know—type houses, layout artists, the media. That kind of thing. And there has to be money for salaries. Not only for me, but for the people I'll have to hire, an art director and such. Okay? Got that?"

341

"Okay. You just spent eight thousand dollars. Now what?"

"Do you know how agencies make their money?"

"All I know is, Endicott always gets a big fat check the end of every month."

"Because the agency bills you a percentage of the price of the media, for starters. In other words, if it costs you say a thousand bucks to run a full-page ad in the *Detroit Free Press,* he billed you fifteen percent of that. Plus the production costs."

"Which are?" surprised at herself for not having asked him—or Leonard, for that matter—about any of this before. She was getting an education (however belated) and the idea pleased her.

"Close to eighteen percent. It sounds like a lot and it is. But it's standard, up and down Madison Avenue. What it does is cover the moneys he laid out to have the ad set up, designed and what have you, the type set, the mechanicals made, et cetera et cetera. So that's how he makes his money. Now what I propose is instead of billing NuBodies the standard fifteen percent media commission, I'll only bill you ten percent. In effect, that means a hefty five percent kickback to you and Leonard for all NuBodies advertising."

"That sounds lovely," she said, "but there has to be a catch."

"That's just it. There isn't. You're wondering how I can afford to do it, right?"

"Agreed."

"Very simple. What I lose on NuBodies I'll make up on my other clients. In other words, when our NuBodies campaign really takes off, I'll have all the clients I want begging for my services. I mean, look at David Ogilvy for example. He's got a castle out of his agency. Lester Wunderman's a millionaire in his own right, all through advertising. The possibilities are endless. And the beautiful part is you save money and I make money. One hand greases the other." There was nothing left of his appetizer but a small pool of orange liquid. "Olive oil, nothing to worry about," he muttered when she looked across the table. "So what do you think? Like the idea?"

"The idea sounds feasible, but not because we'd be billed less. I mean, Leonard'll love that. I'm more concerned with you, to be quite honest. Is this what you really

342

want? Do you want all the headaches of being a boss? Wouldn't it be easier for you to work for us as our creative director say, instead of giving yourself all these new responsibilities?"

"I'll always be NuBodies' creative director," he said, "simply because I'll continue being the brains behind your promotion and ad campaigns. But this is what I think I want, Cynthia. If it doesn't work then it doesn't work and we go on from there. But right now I think it's a fantastic opportunity for both of us."

"Now explain why the Eliot and not the Eisenstern?" All around her affluent New York reeled through the social process. She was part of it, a new body with a rich string of pearls and no more costume jewelry. Right across from her sat a young man, handsome by anyone's standards. He looked at her with what she interpreted as a hopeful smile, intent—if not dependent—on her every word. Tantalizing aromas hovered in the air. She wanted to turn her head around and stare, studying one table after another. I'm Cynthia from Brooklyn even though I'm Mrs. Margold of NuBodies. You can't separate the two, even with a new name.

"Why I've begun the legal process of changing my name?"

"You've started it already?" surprised at the speed he reached decisions. At least he's not talking out of the side of his mouth.

"Absolutely. Time waits for no man and all that bullshit. Because Eisenstern's too ethnic. On Madison Avenue, the whiter you are, the better. And what's more, I have a doozy of a name picked out for you, a real winner. How does Cynthia *Morgan* grab you, kiddo?"

She didn't answer him. The waiter arrived with their main courses. "The plates are very hot," he cautioned. D. W. attacked his scampi with gusto. Her veal looked as perfect as he had promised, but she waited for it to cool a moment before taking her first bite.

"Well?" he said, clearing his mouth with a swallow of wine. "I'll handle all the paperwork. You wouldn't have to bother with a thing. I mean, kiddo, after all . . . you're not Manny Margold's wife anymore. He's getting a divorce, right? That's what you told me. And you're on your way to becoming a celebrity, on top of everything else. Who the hell wants to be announced on coast-to-coast TV as

Cynthia Margold, a formerly fat Jewish housewife from Brooklyn? It's dreary. And why bother keeping Manny's name, when all that's gonna be left of your marriage is some stinkin' little piece of paper."

"Streisand didn't change her name."

"She would've, had she been born Barbara Joan Schmuckler and I went to school with a girl who had that name, so don't tell me I'm exaggerating or making it up, either."

"Well Margold's a far cry from Schmuckler," she said, laughing. "And why Morgan, of all the names to choose from?"

"It doesn't have to be Morgan, if that doesn't grab you. I wrote out a whole list the other night. Yes I did, on a piece of paper, no shit. There was . . . let's see. March and Maremont and Margo. Moran. But I like Morgan the best. Think about it, that's all. But what do you think about the agency?"

"The veal is luscious. How're your shrimp?"

"Beautiful. Well?" He was as impatient as Manny used to be when he came home from work and wanted his supper on the table.

"Well I'll have to sweet-talk Leonard, for starters. I can see your point and eight thousand isn't that much money, not if we're going to save five percent a year on advertising costs. Besides, it's only a loan, anyway. But you know how he is. I mean, just because I have controlling interest in the corporation doesn't mean I can do everything and anything I want. He's been talking about going public, instituting a board of directors to help make decisions. I need that like a hole in the head, right?"

"All I know is," he said as the waiter poured more wine into both of their glasses and he urged Cynthia to have another drink, "that when you want something bad enough, you always end up getting it. One way or another."

She was already feeling a little high. But that's okay, too, she thought. It's time I learned how to relax, unwind, enjoy myself and have a good time. And he can be so much fun, such a sweetheart, when he wants to. "Do you really want us to be D. Wayne Eliot and Cynthia Morgan?"

"Would I try to pull the wool over your eyes, you who dragged me out of the morass of my miseries, out of the

344

salt mines of tedium." He mopped up some of the garlic sauce with a crust of bread. "How can you even contemplate such a thing?"

"Everything is delicious, the best veal I ever had. Soft as butter," she said quickly. "How are your shrimp?"

He put down his fork and fixed her with two bright dark eyes. "That's the second time you asked."

"Sue me for caring," she said and took more wine. He wanted something from her and it was obvious by now that he wasn't going to stop or let go or do anything even remotely akin to easing back, until he got his way.

"Well?" he asked. "Yes or no? I have to know, that's all there is to it."

"I can't say no to you, can I?"

"Of course not. I remind you too much of Barry, Mrs. Morgan." When he grinned he resembled one of those cloven-hoofed satyrs she'd seen dancing around fancy picture books, the kind people put on top of coffee tables and then forgot about. But then again, she'd decided he looked like one of the devil's helpers the first time she met him. Maybe that's all part of the appeal, she told herself. 'Ladies and gentlemen, it gives me the greatest of pleasure to introduce the founder and president of NuBodies, a person who's helped change the eating habits of a nation, a one-woman crusade, the very lovely and vivacious . . . Cynthia Morgan.' But she didn't hear the sound of applause, live or canned.

Once again he asked, "So the answer is yes then? You'll loan me the money?"

"What do you think," she replied. "And finish your food. Children are starving and you're leaving over half your lunch, Mr. Eliot."

"Whatever you say, Mrs. Morgan."

She realized it was going to take time to get used to.

February 1969

Dear Mom,

Don't ask, that's all I can say. I raised a wild Indian, a spoiled brat who thinks the world owes him a living, from start to finish. I'm sick of blaming myself but who else is there to blame. Whatever went wrong, it's on my shoulders now; I only HOPE they knock some sense into his head and get through to him, that's all I can pray for. It was a gorgeous drive, all the way up the Taconic State Parkway to Hillsdale and then on past Great Barrington (G. B. they call it around here) into Monterey. Lincolnwood's a dream, that's the only way I can describe it. The school has every facility imaginable and the quality of the kids is out of this world, just fantastic. From the finest homes, the best families. You'd think he'd be pleased. No way, no how. Sulked all the way up, again he started carrying on about how he wanted to go to Europe this summer, not summer school which he'll need if he's ever going to graduate. The headmaster took us around and it's everything Hirsch said it was. And more, besides. I told him if he didn't have to go to summer school, providing he did good work in the next couple of months, I'd get him a job in D. W.'s agency. He looked at me like I was out of my mind or something. Nothing pleases that child, mother. He only wants blood, just like the other one.

Anyway, after Phil and I finally helped him unpack and get situated, we went back to G. B. I had a gorgeous luncheon with the Women's Club there and now I'm spending the night at the Great Barrington Inn which is very snooty and high-class; you'd love it, like out of a pic-

346

ture book of American history, that's how charming and well-maintained and immaculate it is. Tomorrow Philly's driving me on to Pittsfield where I do two different radio spots. Then, later in the day we have to trek down to Springfield where it'll be more of the same. But from what I've seen, lots of people around here could use a good talking to, weightwise I mean, and no pun intended. So I should be back a day or two after you get this letter. I'm going down to dinner now with this lovely man I met from the Chamber of Commerce, a real gentleman and refined from head to toe.

After Springfield we do a quick stop in Hartford and then I should be home in time for dinner Thursday evening if the traffic isn't bad. So the trip up to Lincolnwood/ Monterey paid for itself. They sure know how to get mileage out of me, their money's worth. Well, that's what running a business is all about, I guess. Now if I only got as much pleasure from my kids as I got from you and NuBodies, I think I'd be the happiest woman in the world. Miss you and don't forget to double-lock the door at night. Even though we've got a doorman, I still worry about you.

Your daughter loves you like you wouldn't believe!

Cynthia

September 1969

A THOUSAND DIFFERENT BODIES and a thousand pairs of eyes: blue, brown, black, hazel, gray, green, colors in between. All these bodies and eyes staring back at her as she stood behind the podium at the Stamford Civic Center. "Four years," she repeated. "Fifty-two NuBodies branches in fourteen different states, from Maine to Illinois, from Georgia to Massachusetts. And now Connecticut. Of course I'm proud. But wouldn't you be? Four years ago I sat around my living room with half a dozen of my closest . . . and heaviest friends. We were fat. We were *very* fat. But we wanted to do something, something to help ourselves. We did. And you can too, because if you haven't found the answer yet, I'll tell it to you, right here and now. The answer is NuBodies. The answer is that we all work to help each other. No one goes it alone, the hard way. It's a group effort and because of that, the number of people who can't lose weight by going to our classes is negligible compared to the number who can. But all my talking, bragging, too, I guess because I am very proud and I think I have a right to be—at least a little right, anyway," and she paused to grin, to catch her second wind. "But all my talking means next to nothing until you attend one of our meetings. Until you see our system in action. There's nothing miraculous about it. It's not a wonder cure. It's rooted in safe, down-to-earth common-sense methods, doctor-approved. Weight loss is slow but steady so that your body, your system, has a chance to adjust to the change of eating habits. But as one week piles on top of another, so do the disappearing pounds. Would you like to see what I used to look like before I started the

NuBodies diet?" She had the slide controls in her hand. Behind her a screen was set up, taut and white, ready to throw the projection back at the audience. The cues had been worked out in advance. Now the lights dimmed in the civic center and she pressed her thumb down against the button. There were all the oohs and ahs, a regular chorus of astonishment she'd hoped to hear, a faint rustle of applause as well. She clicked the button down again and the after picture, Cynthia Morgan weighing in at a little under one hundred forty pounds, vied for attention with the before. The last was a snapshot Manny had taken at the height of her compulsive eating. She weighed over two hundred fifty pounds and not even the shapeless pup tent dress could hide her fifty-six-inch hips, her exaggerated Rubenesque proportions.

"Something, isn't it?" she said with a laugh. "The difference between the two is one hundred and twenty pounds," exaggerating slightly but that was okay, too, because the photographs said more than any figures she could reel off to the audience. "Here are some others, members who have lost even more weight than I have. Here's a woman from Detroit, Michigan, one of our best lecturers up there." The slides went click and click again. This time she was too engrossed in what she was doing to make the usual auditory connection. "—from Portland, Maine. And here's a gentleman from Wilmington, Delaware. A woman from Brooklyn, New York. Here's a before and after shot of a couple from Cleveland, Ohio. Between the two of them they dropped two hundred and ten pounds. Remarkable? Absolutely. Miraculous? Not at all. We teach you how to eat properly, for starters. When you join our classes, you discover that dieting and being hungry aren't necessarily one and the same. On our diet you're *never* hungry and that's not a promise, that's a fact. So I've come a long way in four years, thanks to hundreds of men and women just like you, overweight individuals who worked together to achieve a solution to a problem which had plagued them throughout their adult lives, and most of their teenage years, and even, in some cases, back when they were children. But now we have a branch, right here in Stamford, right in the heart of downtown. There's no reason any of you can't come and pay us a visit, attend one of our classes, and see if you like what we're doing. There's no reason in the world why being overweight should be embarrassing, not when it's so easy to lose all the excess poundage you've put on over the years. And that can mean ten years or two, it doesn't matter to us. What matters are people, people just like you and me, people who have reached the end of their rope, who want some help. We can give you that help.

"Ellen Reinhart, a native of Stamford, born and raised right here in this city, will be running the classes downtown. She lost ninety-seven pounds through the NuBodies way. She's ready and eager to tell all of you how she did it, how you can do it, too. So give her a try. There's no cost for a trial class. And if any of you sitting here this afternoon think NuBodies might be too much for your pocketbook or your wallet, let me alleviate your fears by stating that our weekly class costs less than a movie. Only we don't serve hot buttered popcorn. Just a lot of good honest talk and friendly advice. And help, the old-fashioned kind, where people care about other people. So isn't it time you cared, too? Do come. I don't think you'll regret it."

The "thank you" was drowned out in applause, alternately polite and animated. Believers and skeptics filled the rows of seats. But looking out at her audience, she felt confident she had helped get the Stamford branch off to a rousing start. Ellen had told her that within one week of opening her doors, three out of the six weekly classes were already filled. Cynthia hoped her appearance at the civic center would change those figures to six out of six. But now she listened to the applause, hands clapping over and over again. The sound made her tingle, little hot sparks and electric charges of pleasure. She didn't think she'd strained or overstated her point. D. W. had said that excitement was contagious, interest infectious. She hoped she'd infected all of them, put a bug in their ear, gotten them started. There were women out there who could barely squeeze into the ample-sized seats. There were men who suffered dizzy spells merely by bending over to put on a pair of socks. There were even teenagers in the audience, alone or with parents, who ate as compulsively and mindlessly as their elders. But NuBodies was for everyone, young and old alike. She had her job to do, the work set out for her. Now, she basked in the reward, the applause and the smiling faces.

She stepped down from the podium and the new owner

350

of the Stamford franchise, Ellen Reinhart, took her hand, bent over and kissed her on the cheek. "You're a miracle worker," she said. "They loved it, every minute."

"Honesty's the best policy," Cynthia said. "I didn't want anyone to think we're trying to put something over on them, especially when we're not."

"You'll be at the dinner tonight, won't you?"

"Of course. I wouldn't miss it for the world." How could she, when it was being given in her honor. "I'm just going to go back to the hotel and take a nap. I'll see you later." Phil waited by one of the exits, looking slightly rumpled and slightly bemused. As she stepped off the stage, a group of women hurried up to her.

"Can I have your autograph, Mrs. Morgan?"

"I think what you're doing is just fantastic, the way you get through to everyone. So eloquent."

"I already enrolled. Tomorrow I go to my first class and boy, can I ever use it." Nervous laughter, a hand without wrist bones, definition, squeezing her fingers. "I just hope it works as good as you say it does."

"Follow the rules and it'll work like a charm," she said. "You shouldn't have any doubts. If it worked for me, it can work for you. And you're thinner than I was, believe me."

Scraps of paper were thrust in her direction, copies of the program that had been distributed at the door. The women pressed in all around her. She thanked the higher-ups for keeping the air-conditioning going, accepted a ballpoint pen and wrote her name in loose broad letters, slashing her signature across the sheet of paper. She didn't understand what the appeal was, why they had to have her autograph. She wasn't a movie star, a congresswoman, a Broadway favorite.

"Can you write, 'For Louise'?"

"With the greatest of pleasure." She didn't have to turn the smile on and off. It stayed in place with no effort at all. Her hand was as steady as it had ever been. Phil waited patiently beyond the rounded shoulders and double chins. His arms were crossed over his open-necked sport shirt. She was amazed that there were so many, a dozen autographs and yet another dozen women, men too now, clustered around her like worker bees around their queen. Don't get a swelled head, whatever you do, she told herself. All you represent is a chance, a second chance to make things work. Sure there are happy fatties in this country. But they're in the minority, no matter what anyone says. The vast majority of overweight people have emotional difficulties they can't even begin to deal with. Even psychiatrists have a hard time getting through to them. But at NuBodies we know how to talk their language. We've all been in the same place, the same situation. We've all gone through the same self-destructive . . . syndrome, is it? Something like that. But look how I'm still convincing myself, lecturing too. Amazing . . .

"For Frank MacKinnon, if you don't mind, Mrs. Morgan."

"Mind? Why should I mind? Have you signed up yet, Frank?"

"Tomorrow," he said. *Portly* was an understatement. He made Manny look like Slim Jim, skinny by comparison.

She took his felt-tip pen and wrote it out the way he'd asked. At last she could move forward. She slipped out through a side door the way she once had slipped inside Dubrow's Cafeteria. From one extreme to the other, she thought. Phil opened the car door for her, and she sighed as she sat back and closed her eyes.

"The hotel?"

"Please. I want a hot bath and a comfortable bed."

"I don't think you've ever been more . . . convincing," he said as he drove out of the parking lot. "Honest, that's the word that comes to mind. You spoke from the heart. Who wrote the speech?"

"Who do you think? Yours truly. But it was a good showing, wouldn't you say? I mean, we never had a thousand people before. I was a little shaky when I got up on stage with everyone staring at me, like they were holding their breaths or something. But once I got going, started talking, I could've kept it up for days."

"They would've listened, too."

At least somebody does, she thought. But no, stop thinking so negatively. Things've been going beautifully. You have no complaints so don't start in on yourself.

It was true. She had no reason to feel sorry for herself. If her bed was empty, her bankbook was full. Leonard had finally sold out his share of Dreamtime Togs, so he was able to assume more of the responsibilities that went

352

along with running the company. She had more time to travel, to promote the corporation. Even Barry had been cooperating. Two weeks before, Phil had driven him up to Lincolnwood for the start of his last term. Applications were already completed and in the mail, sent to ten different colleges recommended by the school. Even the headmaster had written her personally to remark about the boy's progress, how he was finally applying himself and calming down. The apartment on Riverside Drive was empty for the first time since she'd moved in. She'd sent Lena down to Miami for a month to bask in the sun. She felt her mother justly deserved the vacation. It would have been nice if D. W. had come to Stamford with her, but he'd begged off at the last minute. His agency kept him constantly on the go and he was busier than he'd ever been before. Besides dealing with a growing client list, impressive in its own right, he was working out the details for a national NuBodies magazine, one that would be devoted to weight reduction. It was going to be geared to the same growing market which had already been responsible for putting corporate earnings over the million dollar mark.

A million dollars, she thought. My God—I used to take home thirty or forty at the end of a week and I thought that was a bundle. Not that I have a million in my back pocket, but now that we've gone public my stock should be skyrocketing if all the predictions the brokers and analysts made pan out.

The initial offering, thirty percent of hers and Leonard's holdings, had been snatched up the day it was placed on the market. Now that NuBodies was a publicly held corporation with three-quarters of a million shares outstanding, a board of directors had been established and a financial counselor–investment analyst had been hired on a permanent basis. There were so many new details, things she still had to learn about the business the way D. W. had taught her the rudiments of advertising, that she hardly had time for herself. Some days she felt it was just too much for her. Those were the days she felt most strongly the way her life had changed. There was no going back. "To the bigger and better," she muttered. Phil glanced back at her with a pair of questioning, half-amused eyes. She smiled and nodded her head.

353

"Why don't you spend the night, rest up?" Ellen Reinhart suggested. She was a slim, horsy-faced woman with a tightly coiled bun of straw-colored hair and short, pale lashes that seemed out of keeping with her darkly intense brown eyes. When she spoke her hands touched at her hips, her wrists, her elbows, as though she were still uncertain if this was really her body or someone else's.

"There won't be much traffic," Cynthia said. "And you know how it is. It's always nicer to sleep in your own bed."

So they drove down the middle lane of the Connecticut Turnpike, the FM radio tuned to WPAT. The music was the "easy-listening" variety. She let the familiar Broadway melodies slide in and out of her thoughts. So much to do, so many things to accomplish, and we've barely touched the Midwest, and we haven't even ventured into California. Not to mention Texas or the Deep South, or places like Seattle, Denver. Wide open . . . our competitors can eat their hearts out, as Eliot always puts it. *Kiddo, they're the scrabby end. The pits, take it from me. They've sewn up Staten Island and Astoria. Big deal. If Staten Island and Astoria aren't smart enough to know that they're being had, taken by a bunch of second-rate Johnny-come-latelies, that's their problem. Not yours.*

"That was fast," she said when he got off the West Side Highway. "I must've dozed off."

"What time you want me to pick you up tomorrow?"

"Make it ten . . . no, on second thought, ten-thirty. I deserve a break. It's been a rough day. Hectic. Sit, Phil. I have hands, too, you know." She let herself out when he pulled up in front of the building.

"I'll wait until you're inside," he said. Two weeks before a woman had been raped less than a block away. He wasn't about to ignore his responsibilities until the doorman had let her in and the elevator door had closed safely behind her.

But the doors were open, unlocked, and the uniformed attendant was nowhere in sight. They have a helluva nerve, after what we pay for maintenance, upkeep alone. And then they want big tips for Christmas. Unreal. Only after she had pressed seven and the door slid noisily along its metal track, did she hear the night-duty man call out her name. "Mrs. Morgan," which was refreshing because it was usually "Margold" or "Morgold" or any combination in between. The man's voice had an anxious questioning ring to it. The door slammed shut with a clang. The car lurched upwards.

Damn right, 'Mrs. Morgan,' she told herself. When it comes to service, doing their jobs, they're never around when you need them. She got off at seven, dug her key out of her bag and fitted it into the Duo cylinder. Recently installed, it promised to remain pick-free, burglarproof. But the moment she turned the knob to let herself in, she realized something was wrong. The chain lock was in place, which was impossible since it could only be secured from the inside and nobody was supposed to be at home.

She pressed her index finger against the doorbell. The buzzer rasped into the darkened living room. A tombstone slab of moonlight, rectangular and self-contained, revealed a rubber tree plant with broad, drooping, ghostly pale leaves and the hard edge of a glass and chrome cocktail table, sharp and cutting as a newly opened wound.

"Anyone home?" she called out. "Mom?" But Lena was in Miami. At least she was supposed to be in Miami. "Barry?" But he was at Lincolnwood, behaving himself. Being a good child, as she herself had put it when she'd last spoken to him, a few days earlier on the phone.

A light went on in the hall beyond the living room. Nothing to be afraid of, she thought, remembering the night after Kennedy had been killed, when she stood alone in the storefront on Rutland Road. She remembered the door opening and the feeling of vulnerability, insecurity, and she felt it all over again and tried not to tremble. Less than a moment later the trembling stopped as she caught his moving shadow, a silhouette of invisible moving fingers, sliding up and down his chest. What's he doing here and what's he buttoning his shirt for? The apartment's warm as toast and I'm his mother. Then the silhouette stepped into the elongated square of moonlight. Ruffled feathers of shaggy brown hair, a familiar face—not from her side, but his father's—familiar petulant lips. The last work shirt button closed to cover his bare chest; faintly fuzzed down the middle, it made her realize that either she was getting old or he was. Barefooted, too, and in tight blue jeans he came to the door and undid the chain lock. He stepped to the side and she reached for the hall light. She flicked the switch and his face sprang up before her in high relief.

"What are you doing home?" she said.

Beyond him another silhouette sat and waited on the tufted velvet couch, highball glass with acid-etched initials —C. M.—clamped like a permanent extension of his hands and fingers. D. W. raised the glass to his lips, took a long thoughtful swallow, and set it down on the coffee table. It was one-fifteen.

"Good evening," said the president of D. Wayne Eliot & Friends to the president of NuBodies, Inc. "How'd it go in Stamford? I thought you were spending the night. That's what you said."

"I'm not following," she said. She stopped long enough to hang up her coat in the front hall closet. Barry hadn't moved an inch. A cursory search of his face revealed a basic flaw, a dab of anxiety here, a smudge of fear there, like grease paint he'd forgotten to wipe off. The actor of the family, faltering in his favorite role. It wasn't right. The whole thing was somehow warped and jarring, out of phase, out of gear. "What are you doing home; you're supposed to be at school?" she said again, steeling herself through her uncertainty.

His hands disappeared into his back pockets. It made her wonder if he was afraid to show her his fingers. "I," he said and glanced over his shoulder at D. W. She didn't need a cue card to catch the look of helplessness which flicked on and off across his reddened features. D. W. picked it up off the floor where the word—the single *I*— had fallen, broken and shattered so that Barry couldn't speak.

"The kid called me, said he needed someone to talk to," he told her. He remained where he was, stuck to the seat cushion.

"Talk to? He has a mother to talk to, a staff psychologist, a roommate." So what does he need you for? "And the boy is supposed to be up in Massachusetts, at school. That's where he should be, anyway."

"There's no such thing as *should*," said D. W.

"Don't give me any of that, not tonight, not at . . . this late hour." And to Barry, "Kindly explain what's going on."

"I hitched down," he said, still hitching four fingers of each hand inside his back pockets. The stationary posture, a pose of almost languid affectation, seemed to contradict his look of fear and uncertainty.

"You hitched down?" she repeated. "You idiot kid you,

what kind of new game are you playing? What about graduation? They'll throw you out on your backside, moron. What about that? Well? Say something instead of standing there like the world owes you a living because goddamn it, it does not, Barry Margold. It doesn't owe you anything!"

"Stop yelling at me," he said. "I don't like it when you raise your voice."

She looked at D. W. For an instant it was for condolence, moral support. Then she realized that even though little had been said, somehow he was in on it, whatever *it* might happen to be. The idea was slowly forming. It was the last thing she wanted to deal with but now she had to because that was what being a mother was all about. That was what everyone talked about when they spoke of adult responsibilities, parental guidance, the Golden Rule.

"All right," she said. "I won't yell. Just explain yourself. Now."

"I told you. I hitched down. The school was getting to be a drag. They were getting on my nerves. I wanted to be here, in New York I mean, for a couple of days."

"I'm delighted. I'm absolutely posititutely . . . positively delighted. Well, for your information you had no right to sneak out of school. You didn't tell them you were leaving, did you?"

"No." He looked down at his feet, at his bare clipped toenails.

An immaculate child, always was. The thought flashed across her mind's eye like a neon sign. "So you called D. W. to hold your hand and tell you you were a good boy, is that it?"

Something she had said made him flinch. "Do you have a cigarette?" he said, still avoiding her eyes, the questions she still hadn't gotten around to asking.

"Since when are you smoking? Something new, or does that go along with marijuana?" She raised her head, pulled at the air with her nostrils. The smell had a familiarity to it. D. W. had smoked grass in her presence, when she'd last been at his apartment, the time before that as well. Like French cigarettes. She wasn't about to stand there and wait for an engraved invitation. She moved past him, leaving him immobilized with his stunned, frightened look. The look was one she hadn't seen since he was a child,

357

since the time he had thrown a pailful of Brighton Beach sand out the window when she and Manny had gone to visit her parents. She'd returned home two hours later to find him hiding, huddled under the covers of her bed and saying, "I did a terrible thing, mommy." But then fear had been replaced by cockiness, smug self-satisfaction. She left the two of them, D. W., whom she blamed for catering to his whims, and Barry, whom she blamed for going out of his way to make a mess of his young life; and moved through the living room. She stepped into the hall and then proceeded down it, the thick pile of the wall-to-wall carpeting muffling her footfalls. There was a light burning in his room at the end of the hallway. The door was ajar. She stepped inside, wanted to clamp a hand first to her lips and then his, and stepped back, jerky as a windup toy.

Eyes assailed, vision violated. The bed unmade, the sheets greased and sweaty, damp and wrinkled. Nose assaulted, smell corrupted. The air thick with the bittersweet French tobacco smell of marijuana and something else, something that bothered her much more. Cloying, fetid, it made her think of dirty toes, sweat socks unlaundered and forgotten in some moldy closet. It was a locker room smell, but chemical and repellent. She couldn't identify its source, but she knew it meant nothing good or wholesome for her or her son.

She came back into the living room. She had been accused of hysteria, of taking a morbid delight in making scenes. Now, she wanted to avoid that kind of bitter confrontation at all costs. It was too late, both the time of day and the time of his life as well as hers. "Barry, will you kindly go to your room and stay there. I want to talk to Eliot in private. I'll speak to you later."

Had he refused, standing a ground that was shaky and crumbling at best, she knew she wouldn't have hesitated to reach out and strike him, to hit him across the face because he had forced her hand. He had forced that ultimate of confrontations, the one with herself, the fact of her own failures. But he left without so much as a word of protest, without a whimper.

Will he huddle under the covers? she wondered. Will he cry and try to hug me and say, "I did a terrible thing, mommy. I made a terrible mistake." But this couldn't have been the first time . . . or could it?

She listened. The bedroom door closed with a hiss like

an outrush of breath, sending the foul rancid odor into the living room as if on a stream of air anxious to reveal all kinds of sordid family secrets. She was afraid to breathe. "How could you? You couldn't wait, you . . . you pig, you pervert you!" Her voice was pitched low. Her teeth were clenched though she struggled not to appear unnecessarily dramatic. It was all coming out and she couldn't help herself. She stood by him, leaning over the glass and chrome table. D. W. raised his boyish face. He avoided her stare—persistent, increasingly enraged.

He said, "How could I what?"

"What was that shit I smelled in there?"

"A popper," he said, tea-party coy, nonchalant, untouched by her own burgeoning terror that somewhere along the way she had made the most basic of errors.

"A what?"

"A popper," he repeated. "Amyl nitrite. It gives you . . . a rush. What are you getting so overwrought about? You weren't supposed to be home, anyway. And it's not as if this was his first time, you know. It's been going on for years."

"What years? He's nineteen years old—"

"Twenty soon enough."

"I'll kill you for this," she said. In her head there was another voice, a mocking echo repeating like a broken record, *Barry is a sissy Barry is a sissy Barry is*—"He's just a baby, you piece of filth . . . he doesn't even know what he's doing with his life and you could just, just . . . I can't even say it it turns my stomach so."

"Say it," he replied. "The kid's a fag. It could be a lot worse. He could be into S&M—you know, leather games. Or transvestism."

"You want to goad me on, don't you? Why, what did I ever do but the nicest things for you. Eight thousand dollar loans at the snap of your fingers, whatever you asked for you got. Like you were my kid brother, my son even—"

"Look, I didn't seduce the kid, if that's what you're thinking."

"No, he seduced *you*, is that it?" she said, on the verge of exploding and then having to deal with neighbors overhearing her; Barry in his room at the end of the hall, the door probably an inch ajar so he, too, could listen in and get an advance preview of what she would say when she got back to him, once she was finished with D. W.

"As a matter of fact, that's about it, in a nutshell. The kid called me up, sounded like he was on the edge of an anxiety attack or a nervous breakdown or something. He asked me where you were, and I told him you were in Stamford for the day and wouldn't be back till tomorrow. He said, 'Please come on over. I just gotta talk to someone.'"

"So you ran. You couldn't get here fast enough. You couldn't wait to get your hands on him."

"Let's not go overboard about this, Cynthia. I didn't *run*, for starters. I took a cab." When that joke didn't work, he went on, "And I came over here because he's your kid and since I love you . . . like an older sister, I felt I had a responsibility to placate the boy, calm him down."

Some calming down, she thought. "You know what? A week ago, yesterday even, this morning in fact, I would've believed you. I would've fallen for your bullshit; hook, line, and sinker. But now it doesn't work that way anymore. You're not weaseling out of this one so fast, Mr. Eliot. Oh no, not by a long shot." She grabbed the first cigarette in sight. She wanted to slap him, throttle him, shake what had happened out of his system so that she could stomp on it and say it didn't exist, it wasn't so, it hadn't happened. Her son wasn't a homosexual. Wasn't and never would be.

D. W. got to his feet, gold lighter in hand. She jerked back as though he were trying to burn her with the butane flame. "Aren't we reacting a little hysterically, Mrs. Margold?"

"Morgan," she said. "Thanks to you. The way you've connived right and left. Unbelievable. And idiot that I am, I trusted you. I trusted you and look where it's gotten me . . . in a sewer, a real sewer that's where."

"I'll speak to you in the morning. I can find my way out by myself, thank you."

She stepped in front of him, made a move to grab for his arm. He avoided her and inched back. "You're not leaving so fast, Eisenstern, not with all the dirt you've left behind. I'm tired of cleaning up after you. Because this time I'm not finished, because when I get through with you and your dirty tricks, D. Wayne Eliot & Friends

360

is going to be a joke, the laughingstock of Madison Avenue."

"And how do you propose to do that, may I ask?" glacier cold, so supremely confident she couldn't bear to look at him.

"You're finished with NuBodies, for openers. Endicott would bend over backwards to get us back again. Now they won't have to bend. I'll give them the account on a silver platter."

"Try something like that, Cynthia, and there won't be a NuBodies to do an ad campaign for. Because kiddo, you're the last person in the world who's as pure as driven snow, just remember that. Poor Cynthia, more sinned against than sinning. Poor Mrs. Margold, has a fat daughter who hates her guts, a husband who married her best friend and a son who's gay as a goose. Oh yes, and a partner who got in her good graces by first getting into her panties and then pumping her like a real stud with nice hard stallion thrusts. But as soon as he got what he really wanted, and not just a little pussy either, as soon as he got the vice presidency of the corporation, he went back to wifey so fast it must've made you dizzy."

"You really are despicable, the lowest of the low," she said. She stared into his eyes and saw daggerlike taunts. His forehead was creased with the effort of concentrated venom, acid remarks. "What do you run, a scandal sheet or something? Who told you about Leonard and me? It's past history, anyway, long since past history."

"Oh, Jeanette has a very big mouth, my darling," he said. One hand reached up to scratch the pointed tip of a half-seen ear. His hair was as shaggy as Barry's, but much more wiry and not nearly as long. "And she loves fancy lunches, just like you. She loves to wear that five-carat boulder of hers. Between you and me the stone has a major flaw, probably a crack. But that's neither here nor there. What is here is that I'm not to blame for what happened this evening. And I don't intend to be your scapegoat just because you raised a son who turned out queer."

"He is not," she said. She felt herself deflating inside, energy rushing out like air, conviction escaping like a balloon with a puncture . . . a major flaw.

"So send him to a new shrink if you're so convinced. But don't hang it all on me, kiddo. Because if it wasn't for D. W., NuBodies wouldn't mean shit today. How do

361

you like that? Because without me," and he tapped one finger against the top of his head, "without these smarts, you'd still be a nobody and NuBodies would be nowhere."

"Don't flatter yourself," was all she could come up with. It was emotional blackmail. Or maybe just blackmail, plain and simple. "There are plenty of bright young men in advertising who could have done as good if not a better job than you."

"Perhaps," he admitted, "but the fact is, none of them did, so you really don't know that for sure. But your competitors would love to learn all the secrets of your success, my darling. I understand these days you conveniently forget to acknowledge whose diet it is you're really using. And wouldn't they love to know how Natalie is a basket case when it comes to losing weight. And all about Forman Margold and Barry Margold and anything else that might come to mind. So don't stand there and give me your high-and-mighty righteous indignation. Because it doesn't hold water, sweetheart. It's leaking out all over the place. You're standing in a puddle of bullshit . . . doll."

They stood there, the two of them facing each other. What is there left to say? she thought. I loved him like I loved my two kids. I gave him whatever I could because maybe he used to give me more than they did, just plain pleasure and respect. And now he can threaten me with blackmail, like the words were right there all the time, right on the tip of his tongue.

"And don't forget," he said, not waiting for a response, "that you're sitting on something like a quarter of a million shares of NuBodies stock. If the company goes, baby, you go too, because the stock won't be worth the paper it's printed on."

"And you're so convinced that you can topple us, just like that, just by shooting your mouth off, is that it?"

"Maybe. In big business, anything and everything is possible. So if I were you, I wouldn't push me, Cynthia. Not if the reason is something that boils down to a single sexual encounter. I haven't been having an affair with the kid. I'm not a chicken-queen, in case you've been wondering."

"I don't know what that means and I don't want to learn. So do me a favor and go home," she said. She stubbed out her cigarette and felt the need for something else, but not a drink. If it's an eclair, a doughnut, a candy bar, then the world can say Cynthia Margold Morgan whatever the hell her name is, is as predictable as April showers. Right? Right? Sure, absolutely, positutely. "You won, okay? Satisfied? You're a winner, a big man, D. W. You've got all the cards and you called the shots and I'm just shit, just plain garbage, a piece of nothing you managed to manipulate any which way you pleased. But if I find out you and Barry do something like this again, a second time, I'll find my own cards. I'm not threatening, either. I'm just promising. I'm not everyone's big fool, in case you're interested."

"I never thought you were a fool, Cynthia," he said, already buttoning his jean jacket. His tone was conciliatory, but as far as she was concerned, it no longer mattered. "Sometimes you're just misguided, that's all. Believe me, it isn't the worst thing in the world to be gay. It complicates your life a good deal. But there's a helluva lot out there that's ten times more impossible to deal with. Or live with, for that matter."

"What? Next you'll be telling me I should thank my lucky stars he's not a junkie."

"Maybe."

He let himself out the way he had come in. She didn't bother to put the chain lock back in place, but went directly to Barry's room. He was sitting up in bed, still dressed and propped up against the pillows. He puffed at another cigarette.

"The smell in here is repulsive," she said. She opened one of the two windows near his bed and let the night seep into the room. He also had a view of the river. But she had no patience or desire or interest in cityscapes, the play of moonlight on water, the rare few twinkles of neon and incandescent light flickering back across the water from the distant shore.

"Did he leave?"

"What do you think, I invited him to stay?" She sat down at the foot of his bed, turned her head to the side and picked up something she saw on top of his dresser. It was golden-yellow in color, a small ampule covered with loosely woven meshlike fabric and knotted at each end with white thread. "What is this? Something new? Is this the . . . what did he call it?"

"A popper," Barry said with a voice that had no expression, conveying neither sorrow nor remorse, neither smug defiance nor anxiety. All of his former terror seemed to have evaporated, as the smell did now that the window was open and fanning the curtains and sending crisp eddies of air into the bedroom.

"More garbage, stuff to kill yourself with," she said, and threw it down where she had found it. She looked back at him. "So what am I going to do with you, Barry? You tell me, because I just don't have the answer anymore. It's not even a question of being at my wit's end. I just don't know how to deal with you, how to get through."

He said, "I'll go back to Lincolnwood."

"You're damn right you'll go back, first thing tomorrow morning. I'll have to call the headmaster and make up some kind of story. But I'm sick and tired of lying for you and I won't. This is the last time. Just to get you graduated and into college. That's my primary concern."

"And your secondary concern?" he asked with a laugh that sounded like a hiccup.

"I don't want to discuss it." If his father was here he'd know how to handle him, but I . . . I can't even think straight anymore. Such a beautiful day and I have to come home to this, this—"You want to ruin your life, destroy yourself, that's your business."

"Some terrific answer that is." He snorted, contemptuous of what she had thought was a shred of tolerance.

"What do you want me to tell you, Barry? That I'm happy about what you've been doing, that I'm tickled pink about what went on here, right in this room as a matter of fact, tonight. Well I'm not and I can't give you my approval, so don't expect me to and don't ask for it, cause it isn't there." And I don't think it ever will be. "All I know is, D. W. is not the happiest, most well-adjusted man in the world. And if that's the person you've decided to take on as a model, you picked the wrong one, from A to Z."

"Did you tell him that?"

"What I told him is no concern of yours. I'm talking to you now, my son, not someone I deal with in my business." She reached out, her fingers grasping at his arm, swooping up to tangle themselves in his thick leonine head of hair. "You're such a beautiful boy—and smart. You can be so good if you want to so why do this to yourself, sweetheart? Why ruin your life before it's even gotten started?"

"Tears aren't going to change anything, so don't cry," he said. "I do what I want to do, what makes me happy."

"And I don't, is that it?" Did Manny say this to me, too? Or did I say these very same words to Manny? I can't remember. I can't even form a sentence I'm so . . . so. What? Overwrought? Disappointed? Both. Both and more, my God, what has he gotten himself into, what kind of hole he can't climb out of again and is it my fault, did I see it coming, did I wish it on him or plan it this way? I did not. I did not and no one but no one can convince me otherwise. It's not my fault, goddamn it, it's not!

"I didn't say that," Barry said, puffing away like a choo-choo train from his favorite childhood picture book. *The Little Choo-Choo* that something. *The Lonely Caboose* . . . she couldn't remember. It was too long ago, when she read to him as he ate, saying too, 'Open your mouth and close your eyes and Mommy's gonna give you a big surprise.' What's the use? she thought. It's all past history, like so much else.

"Does the headmaster know about this?"

"Of course not. What do you think, I tell everyone my life story?"

"You don't have to get sharp with me or snappy, Barry. I merely asked a civil question and it wouldn't kill you to give me a civil answer. Did Hirsch know?" at least. Or did all my money go down the drain, out the window like the smell of that shitgarbagejunk he was taking?

"Sure he did." He yawned and put out his cigarette. His motions—the slow cavernous opening of his mouth, the suggestion of boredom in his listless fingers—struck her as deliberately exaggerated. "He said he couldn't do anything for me unless I wanted to . . . you know. End it."

"And you said?"

"I'd think about it."

"And that's almost a year ago."

"I'm still thinking."

Feeling weary and old she got to her feet. You can talk till you're blue in the face. It goes in one ear and out the other. Like his sister. The two of them. Lena said it: two rebels. A team, a real pair. I raised wonderful normal children, right? Wrong. "Phil'll be here in the morning. Ten-thirty, so set your alarm. Make sure you're ready to leave when he gets here. I'll take a cab to work."

"Isn't that white of you. Isn't that oh-so-self-sacrificing. My martyred mother." The words were filled with blood.

Mine this time, she thought, not his. Without answering, she shut the door behind her as tightly as she could.

January 1970–December 1971

"THINGS HAPPEN," she wrote Barry after Lincolnwood's headmaster had personally telephoned to tell her the boy would definitely be graduating in June, "which make us wonder if we're the ones who really control our lives, or maybe it's someone else. Forgive my grammar, but what I'm trying to say, my sweetest boy, is that nothing is irrevocable, insurmountable. (So my high school education wasn't all that bad, after all!) You must have heard the phrase, 'Where there's a will, there's a way,' a hundred times already. But it's true. You *CAN* change, as long as you apply yourself, as long as that's what you want. What I want from you is a happy young man. That's all that interests me. I can't tell you how to run your life or what to do and how to behave when I'm not around to watch over you. And I realize you've reached the age where you wouldn't want me prying, either. But the fact is, I still don't know why this thing had to happen or why you've taken it into your head not to write or call—to refuse phone calls, too—ever since what happened this past September. At first I was so angry with you I was fit to be tied. But you know, son, time is a great healer, just like medicine. The more distance you give yourself, the easier it becomes to be objective, understanding. I want you to do what's best for YOU. But please Barry, don't jump into things half-cocked, without thinking about the consequences of your actions. Come graduation I have a beautiful present all picked out for you and if you agree to go on to college in the fall—providing you're accepted which we'll know for sure May fifteenth and for which I pray day and night, I promise I'll send you to Europe for the summer, the way you've been after me to do for God knows how long. So just stay well and don't do anything to make people think the less of you. You know what I'm talking about, so a word to the wise. I love you with all my heart and soul. Your mother."

Your only mother, she thought.

In the end she forgave D. W. too, if only because it was easier that way, if only because the first issue of *NuBodies* Magazine was such an unequivocal out-and-out success. "Morgan's Monthly or It's NuBodies Business," he called it, sending her three dozen long-stemmed roses and a laminated plaque of the cover of the first issue, on the day of publication. "Don't ask me to get down on my hands and knees," read the note he enclosed with the flowers. "I'm too prideful a guy for that. But isn't it time to forgive and forget? I regret what I did. I'm genuinely sorry. And I miss those rare moments we shared together. I haven't stopped caring about you, you know that."

What she did know was that he hadn't stopped working for NuBodies. And why not, when Leonard just about forced me to allow him on the board, with all sorts of lucrative stock options, the works. He's got just as much a vested interest in the company as I do, so sure, he wants to make up. But what's the point of carrying around a grudge. It only drains you of energy. And basically I don't think, deep down inside where it counts, that's he's really such a bad person. He just has a big mouth, a streak of thoughtlessness. But don't we all? God knows I'm not a saint, either.

So things were glossed over as if with lacquer, nail polish, spray paint. The new outer surface was smooth and shiny and hard, but just as vulnerable and liable to crack as it had been before when everything, from making money to losing weight, was a constant uphill struggle. But she had to work with him just about every day. You couldn't get things done in an atmosphere of an armed camp. He took her to lunch, Lutèce this time, dropped a cool hundred-dollar bill and got on her good side by getting her a little tipsy.

"Life's too short, kiddo," he said while outside the intimate dining room January peaked like NuBodies stock. "There's only one Cynthia-Artemis-Diana. I'll be indebted to you for the rest of my days."

In front of everyone in the restaurant he got down on

his hands and knees alongside her chair and told her how F. Scott Fitzgerald had done the same for Isadora Duncan. She couldn't help but laugh, tousle his hair, call him "my centurion" because that was what he said Isadora had called Scott. What made it even nicer was that no one interfered, looked askance, or cast disparaging glances in their direction. If anything, a bit of romantic horseplay, tomfoolery, was all too welcome now that the post-Christmas doldrums had settled over New York like a stifling inversion layer.

Two days before Barry's graduation, NuBodies common stock split. Much to her surprise, she discovered she was sitting on over half a million shares. On paper, that amounted to a net worth of upwards of six million dollars.

She bought Barry a Corvette, specially painted B. R. G. —British racing green—because that's what he said he wanted. It was waiting for him when he came back after spending two months in Europe. He left New York with a lot of pocket money, "spare change" he called it, a few days later. Intent on driving all the way out to Denver, where he was due at the university to register for fall semester of his freshman year, Barry kissed her good-bye, revved up the engine, and disappeared down Riverside Drive, leaving rubber. She wondered if she hadn't made a mistake getting him such a high-powered automobile. But Phil had gone with her to the dealership, saying, "You might as well get your money's worth, if you're paying this much already. Another few horsepower ain't gonna kill anyone." The school's alumni association was five thousand dollars richer, but in this instance she felt the money had been well-spent. As long as he got in and he doesn't have to have any hassles with his draft board, that's all that interests me. And he's never looked better or sounded more sensible and respectful in all his life. So who knows, people *do* change, even when you least expect it.

After his departure, after the collect call from Denver —"I made it, safe and sound, no sweat"—she threw herself into her work with the recurring image of standing on a diving board and peering down into a swimming pool. But the pool wasn't filled with water. Instead, endless papers, lists of figures, lecture notes, airline tickets, hotel room keys, copies of *NuBodies* Magazine, cassettes upon which she had begun to dictate her recollections for the "autobiography" about to be ghostwritten, before-and-after photos, and all manner of memorabilia, rose up to the rim of the pool. She saw herself jumping headfirst into her labor of love as she called it. The papers and tickets and tapes and keys and photographs slid back, undulating like waves of gelatin dessert. What else do I have to do with my time? she thought. Besides, like Manny used to say, work keeps your mind off the war . . . with yourself.

"It was just a little business, just a crazy idea of mine," she told the men and women in business and local government who had all paid fifty dollars a plate to see her awarded the honor of becoming Brooklyn's Woman of the Year. "I was wallowing in fat and self-pity. I knew there had to be an answer, a better way. But I never realized, not until I had those dozen women sitting there in my living room, that I wasn't alone, that the world was filled with fatties just like me." What she didn't tell them was that she was wearing a girdle for the first time in years, that she was now dangerously close to one hundred fifty pounds—fifteen pounds more than she would have liked, that the television commercial she had insisted on doing for NuBodies brand cream soda had been a near disaster.

"Take two . . . take seven . . . take thirteen," one of the production assistants kept calling out. No matter how she sat, legs crossed and uncrossed, arms over her stomach, or hands on her thighs; no matter how she dressed or what she wore, jacketed and bloused, skirted or in flaring pants; the director insisted that the moment she moved her arm to hold up the bottle of soda that bore her svelte gowned photo, she looked fat. "The camera doesn't lie, Mrs. Morgan. You're selling thin and if you don't come off that way, people are going to laugh their heads off." She asked for a lunch break, bought a new girdle and a roll of adhesive tape, called Lena and got her down to the studio. When she emerged from the dressing room they had assigned her for the day, she could barely breathe. They printed the sixteenth take and she didn't eat anything for two days, though that in itself went against everything the diet—the NuBodies way, the NuBodies idea—stood for.

But by the time she was signing autographs at Double-day's for copies of the *NuBodies Cookbook*, she had man-aged to get back down to an even one hundred forty pounds. The book, with the same slick Avedon photo used on the soda bottle, Cynthia in a long slit gown looking more like a size seven than a twelve, went through five separate printings, stayed on the *Times* best seller list for thirteen weeks and eventually was sold to paperback—as *Publishers Weekly* dutifully reported—"for a healthy $125,000. The author is now on a nationwide TV and radio promotional tour."

The last, with first-class accommodations and a hectic three-week cross-country itinerary, landed her on the Johnny Carson Show for the first time. She was invited back. "I'll take you up on that," she told him during one of the commercial breaks, right after Patrick Casey had broken up both her and the audience with one of his hysterical comedy routines. "Do, I'm serious. And when are you opening up out here?" Next to her, Casey whis-pered something marvelously obscene into her ear. She was barely able to get the words out, to say, "Beginning of next year, if all goes well." She almost wondered if that was a problem, because things *were* going well, all *too* well, in fact.

When another Labor Day weekend came and went and NuBodies got around to celebrating its sixth anniversary, Leonard returned from a business trip to the West Coast with the news that he had wrapped up a million dollar deal. The result of the week of meetings and negotiations would be the simultaneous (or just about) opening of Nu-Bodies franchises in Los Angeles, San Francisco, San Diego, Sacramento, Santa Barbara, and Long Beach.

"And guess who's going to be there to get them off on the right foot?"

She held up a bottle of their first successful venture into the food services industry, yet another of D. W.'s many brainstorms. One manicured finger tapped at the glossy label with its expensive four-color print job: *After all, let's let the public know you've got gorgeous red hair, kiddo.*

"You guessed it," he said. He kissed her full on the mouth. Jeanette wasn't standing nearby to watch the way their tongues got tangled together, a *True Romance* "mo-ment of breathless abandon." Trouble was, she felt neither breathless nor abandoned. When she kissed him, she tasted nickels and dimes. His tongue was a bank deposit slip, his lips fat and fleshy dollar bills. And when he released her and she looked into his eyes, she saw a cash register ringing up NO SALE.

"Happy?" he asked.

"Totally," she said, wondering how long it would take to get the taste of small change out of her mouth.

January 1972

"I JUST SENT YOU A CHECK." The receiver was cupped to one ear. On top of her desk sat a shrimp earring, a miniature paperweight holding down nothing more substantial than the weight of her recollections. She waved her other and free hand at the woman who sat alongside of her, steno pad in readiness. "Well whose fault is that, Barry? I can't help it if Omaha's boring. You should thank your lucky stars they at least took you in as a sophomore, instead of making you repeat your freshman year. Of course it's not as pretty as Denver. I know you miss the skiing. But am I to blame for that? Look, what more do you want from me, this phone call is costing a small fortune." A beat. She examined her nails. His whine went through her like a police siren. "You have your own apartment so what else do you want? Yes, I'll send another check. Of course I don't want you to starve; what kind of talk is that? Finals are in two weeks, aren't they? I expect a good report. You pass this semester and we'll talk about Bermuda for Easter, fair enough? No, I will not commit myself this early, Barry. It is not a question of money so don't you dare call me a cheapskate. For your information, it ran me close to five thousand bucks last year in Denver. That's right, five grand, with all your carryings on and having the car fixed after you nearly broke your neck." Not to mention the same amount to the alumni association which I don't even want to think about or I'll get nauseous, sick to my stomach the way I throw out money. And does he appreciate it? Does he ever say thank you? Forget it, those kind of miracles can't be had for love or money, for all the tea in China. "Look, I have to get off now. I have work to do; the woman is here. Who? Lynne Cohen, who's working on the autobiography with me." He said something. She frowned, bit at her lower lip like she was trying to remove a fleck of wet tobacco. But no cigarette was burning in the small-footed Steuben bowl D. W. had given her, the fourth Christmas gift out of twelve. *Who in their right mind would want to get just one gift? It's criminal. Face it, you're loved, Morgan. You're adored by a young man on his way to the top.* "I said I will mail it and I'll mail it. Have I ever lied to you before, or broken a promise? Then keep your mouth shut for a change. You heard me. You're getting out of hand." Click. She looked at the free-lance writer whose legs were crossed at the edge of her desk, dark stockings, a sensible shoe. "Would you believe the little bastard hung up on me?"

The ghost writer shrugged her shoulders. "I was never a mother," she said.

"You're not missing a helluva lot, let me clue you in." She put down the receiver, replaced her earring, and got up to pour herself another cup of coffee. "Need a refill?"

"No thanks, Cynthia. It makes me . . . you know, gassy."

"Some people are like that," she said, as if dividing the world between those who were addicted to caffeine and those who weren't. "Me, I couldn't live without it. I must be up to eight cups a day by now. It's like adrenalin." Gift number six or seven, she wasn't all that sure, was an oversized, cobalt blue china mug from Ginori on Fifth Avenue. The coffee was the color of bittersweet chocolate. But it had no sweetness or texture to it until she added some liquid saccharin. She returned to the desk, while behind her, through the narrow crack she had made in the double-thick Thermopane window, the traffic snarled and coughed, groaning along Broadway as it headed toward Wall Street and the Brooklyn Bridge. "Now where were we?" making herself comfortable again.

Lynne consulted her notes. "You were just getting into the hassle you went through finding a place to hold the meetings."

"Oh yes, now I remember." She blew across the top of the mug and felt the steam condense on her upper lip. "Hassle isn't even the word for it. I was up against a lot of shyster landlords, phonies from beginning to end, for openers. Sure there were people willing to rent me a place, but the prices they were asking for lousy little roach-infested holes were just not to be believed. I finally cornered this one man, a recent refugee from Hungary or some place like that, and got him to act like a gentleman. He gave me a paint job, though it was like pulling teeth."

"How much was the rent?"

"Is it important?"

"Might be," and she shrugged her shoulders again, the gesture so repetitive Cynthia wondered if it was a nervous tic or if the woman had permanent accordion creases, pleats on her back and the sides of her neck.

"Let me think for a sec. So much has happened since, it's hard to remember."

She was saved by the opening of the door. "Can you give me five minutes of your time?" Leonard asked. He looked over at Lynne Cohen. "Hi. Aren't you looking like the dapper career girl this morning."

"Career woman," she corrected.

Good for her, Cynthia thought, saying, "I was just telling Lynne about how I rented the storefront on Rutland Road." She glanced at his tall tweed presence and then back to her co-worker. "It's still in operation, needless to say. And it brings in a very handsome income every year, even though we no longer own the branch outright. I sold it to my friend Vivian Hollander for peanuts," adding quickly, "but don't put that in. It's no one's business what she paid. She was a good friend—still is, though I don't see her as often as I'd like—who deserved a break, a little financial security, that's all."

Leonard stepped across the room and put down a thick sheaf of papers on top of her cluttered blotter. "The contract from Random," he said. "Lynne's already signed it. But we need your signature as officer, president of the corporation. In triplicate."

She asked if he had read all the small print.

He stuck his hands into his trouser pockets and signaled his amusement with a sudden flash of recently capped teeth. "There isn't any small print, Cynthia. It's a standard contract. And we're dealing with a reputable house so don't hassle yourself reading it over, word for word." He leaned forward and pointed with one buffed fingernail to where it read on page three, "This Agreement shall be interpreted according to the Law of the State of

New York. IN WITNESS WHEREOF, the parties have duly executed this Agreement the day and year first above written. AUTHOR," and a black line of several inches in length across which she was supposed to affix her signature.

"That's where I sign, yes, I realize that," she said, momentarily put off, annoyed he took her for such an idiot, a goose—a term D. W. had taught her to prefer. She flipped back to page one of the first copy, reading down the left-hand margin. THE GRANT, ADVANCE, ROYALTIES, SUBSIDIARY RIGHTS. "Who owns movie rights?"

"We own ninety percent of them. Come on, hon. I don't have all day. It's not like Hollywood's banging our door down. Besides, there's a messenger waiting outside to take it over to them as soon as you sign."

"What's the big rush? They can wait an hour." She flipped to page two. STATEMENT & PAYMENTS. MANUSCRIPT. FAILURE TO DELIVER. She looked over at Lynne Cohen. "You'll have it ready on time, won't you?"

"If you keep finding time for me between now and when you leave for California, I don't think there'll be any difficulty at all. Besides, I still have all those cassettes you've been dictating. So there's more than enough material to work with."

"True." She continued reading down the margin. EDITING RIGHTS, that's not my problem. COPYRIGHT. "What does this mean, Leonard? 'Publisher is hereby authorized upon first publication of the Work, to secure copyright to it in the name of,'" and here it was typed in, " 'NuBodies Inc.' I don't understand."

"Well who's going to get the royalties, along with Lynne's percentage?" he said in a voice she interpreted as one which strained at patience, as though he were addressing a child and not his superior.

"We are, of course."

"Exactly. Well, that's why the copyright is in NuBodies' name. It's for tax purposes, pure and simple. It's a NuBodies project, isn't it? So how can it be copyrighted under your own name. It wouldn't make sense."

"Where do I sign?"

He showed her for the second time. The pen skipped and she tried again, saying, "This is always the worst part of being in business, all this damn paperwork. It's endless.

376

I'd sooner speak straight from the shoulder to a group of people. That's when I feel in my element, accomplishing something valid, worthwhile." Three times she wrote out her name in characteristic broad, confident letters. No sooner was the last N set down when Leonard gathered together the three copies of the contract, bent low at the waist like a courtier, and excused himself.

The door closed softly behind him, as if he feared disturbing them any longer. "Now," she said again, "where were we?"

"Rutland Road," Lynne said, brushing black bangs out of her eyes.

"The neighborhood's changed completely. Poor Viv, still stuck in Brooklyn, too. But when I spoke to her a couple of weeks ago, more like a month ago actually, she said she was starting to look for a new apartment, probably on Ocean Avenue if she finds something she likes. Her husband left her. Some men just don't know when they have a good thing going. You're not married, are you?"

"Not this year," Lynne said and wrote a line of stenographic symbols across the page.

"Be smart. Stay single. Less aggravations in the long run. But anyway, Rutland Road was where things really got moving, in a big way you understand. Professionally speaking, of course.

"Of course."

Late that afternoon she devoted one hour to looking for new office space. Even Leonard, the sometime Scrooge of weight reduction, had agreed with her that it was time they got out of the financial district. They were pinched for space, not money. And since they had the funds and now the growing prestige to go along with their mounting capital, he suggested they try a midtown location which would be more convenient and accessible "for all concerned." The last was a catch phrase, the kind of cliché he often used. She failed to really understand who the "all concerned" might be. Though she was certainly part of the collective, they'd said nothing to her about moving, even though it was her idea, from the beginning. Leonard only latched onto it when he discovered he couldn't put his secretary in an outer office since no such space existed on the floor they currently rented. So she checked out several Fifth Avenue addresses. She didn't see anything either prestigious or large enough for the company's needs. Maybe a new building, one that's in the process of being built. There was that amazingly futuristic one going up on Fifty-seventh, where Avon would have its corporate headquarters. Maybe that would be perfect for them. She made a mental note to check it out as soon as she found the time. She hailed a cab and went less than a dollar on the meter to the Running Footman, on East Sixty-first. A couple of five o'clock stragglers overflowed the stools at the bar. She didn't bother to check her black mink polo coat—Cynthia's Christmas present to Cynthia. *Why didn't you tell me that's what you wanted, Leonard said. I didn't think you cared. You know I'll always care, you big dummy. How many Cynthias do I love in this world? Only one.* The sign above the checkroom read, WE ARE NOT RESPONSIBLE FOR THE LOSS etc. Besides, she was still chilly, having been out on the street with the temperature dropping steadily all afternoon until now, at dusk, it was nearly twenty degrees.

D. W. sat at a table on the lower of the two first-floor levels. It was a long narrow space; much like a sunken living room, one gained access to it by going down three little steps. The heels of her shoes were broad, chunky as current fashion dictated. She held onto the polished brass handrail and stepped down carefully. He chewed on a plastic straw, a perfect Rob Roy sitting in front of him, the absence of ice and the clarity of the drink telling her without words that he'd been waiting quite some time. She slid onto the banquette and sat across from him.

"Penny for your thoughts," she said because that was the first thing that came to mind. It was the wrong hour for being clever and self-consciously witty.

"I usually command a helluva lot more than that an hour." He got halfway off his seat, bent over the table, nearly upset his drink, and kissed her on the cheek. "You look so flushed and ruddy and healthy, it's depressing." Then he laughed, signaled the waiter with a flourish of one gold-ringed hand. "What're you drinking?"

"Just a glass of white wine."

"A glass of chablis for my niece," he said.

No one laughed or even smiled. She chalked it up to the late hour.

"Hear from your kid?"

"This morning. Hates Omaha with a passion."

"Who can blame him. It's the armpit of the nation. And how's business?"

"You know as much about that as I do. I'm looking forward to finishing up the book and going out to the Coast. It'll be a nice change for me, a chance to really put my time to good use."

"What is it, another two three weeks?"

"Something like that." She thanked the waiter with a nod of her head. After opening her coat a little wider— "to get some air"—she took a sip of the chilled wine and put it down on top of the cocktail napkin that bore the imprint and logo of the Running Footman. "You look preoccupied."

"I'm trying to figure out how to stage a coup."

"Where?"

"I haven't decided yet." He tried to laugh. "But I guess I am. I'm up to my ass in work." He slipped one hand into his jacket pocket and pulled out a silver key ring through which one metal key with the name Segal hung like a lavaliere. "Aren't you going to congratulate me? Or say, 'Use it in good health.' Isn't that what people from Brooklyn say when someone buys a co-op?"

"I'm not from Brooklyn anymore." Then it registered. "You didn't?" and she opened her eyes wide with pleasure as if she were looking out at an audience, hungry, desperate even, for the curative of truth.

"I sure did. I'm in the big time, kiddo. No more games. I'm a regular homeowner." He blew the last word at her, making two great gaping O's with his lips.

She reached across the table and caught his wrist. Then she let go, only to squeeze his small unlined hand with its even rounded fingernails and gold Tiffany bands on one pinkie. "I can't wait to see it. Is it the one you've been negotiating for on Park?"

He nodded his head. "Hot stuff, eh? Park Avenue here I come. I'll take you over there in a cab if you're really hot to take a look at it."

"Sure I am," she said, something telling her it was a good idea to humor him, perk up his flagging spirits. Though why he seemed depressed she was yet to figure out. "And it's on my way home, anyway, so why not."

"Finish up. We've missed the sunset but I think you'll

still be able to get a good idea what a spectacular view I command."

He told her in the cab going uptown, "I haven't had a woman in to clean yet, and it's not even painted."

"Everything comes in time. The world wasn't built in a day."

"Rome," he corrected.

She looked at him, her eyes focusing slowly, knowing her expression was curious and surprised, bewildered too. "Half the time you and my kid sound exactly alike."

"That's nice," he said.

It wasn't what she had expected to hear. But as for the apartment, a duplex on Park and Seventy-ninth, was as spectacular as he had insisted. "It makes my little hovel look shabby by comparison," she said as he flicked on overhead lights with a sudden gaiety that bordered on abandon. With the same kind of feigned drunken exuberance, he took her on a grand tour, escorting her from one room to another. "What's your maintenance going to run you?"

"Let's not talk about it. I'm just thankful I'm making money and socking away as much as I can. Do you have any idea how much it's going to cost me to get this place decorated the way I want? I had two guys in this morning, just for estimates. Frightening, the cost of furniture. Sinful, as my mother would say."

"Have they seen it yet?"

"Who?"

"Your parents," surprised he hadn't followed her train of thought.

Clinging to his preoccupation like an actor concentrating on verisimilitude, he scowled, his black eyebrows coming together to form a single crooked dipping line across his forehead. "What, are you kidding? I haven't spoken to *la belle mère et le gros père* in six months. I'm on their current shit-list. *C'est la guerre.* But what do you think?" He stopped in the middle of the living room with its high beamed ceiling and massive picture windows.

"I think it's an extraordinarily beautiful apartment," she said. "Very . . . dramatic," totally honest, not thinking what she would say or choosing her words beforehand. "And I just hope you're going to be very very happy here, that's all I can say."

"You'll always be the archetypal Jewish mother."

"Is that good or bad?"

"It's whatever you want to make of it, love. But I'm glad you approve. I'd hate to think I spent half the Eliot fortune on a lemon.".

"A lemon is the last thing it is. It's . . . it's breathtaking, actually."

"Let's not exaggerate," he said, grinning. He completed the tour, spinning lewd stories about how he would do "dirties" in the sunken marble bathtub. He also told of the kind of lavish dinner parties he would hold thanks to the kitchen with its up-to-date appliances and more than adequate counter and cabinet space. He told her how he intended to decorate the living room with its view of Park Avenue and its glimpse of Central Park. "If you stick your head out far enough," he joked, "you might even be lucky enough to see an old man exposing himself at the entrance to Dog Hill, up the block." Gathering his self-assurance— so she interpreted this forced kind of patter, merriment, this borscht belt song and dance—he said, "And the bedroom is going to be mylar for days, that or mirrors, a mirrored ceiling for sure. I haven't decided exactly what else yet. But the rest of the house will be terribly top drawer, lots of good English furniture if I can afford it, the whole substantial tasteful number. After all, I *am* the president of one corporation, an officer of another. So I have to put up some kind of front against the heathens. But I want the bedroom to be sensual, get my point? Hedonistic. Maybe even bordering on the cheap."

"No, cheap is the wrong word."

"True," he agreed. "Risqué then. Womblike. Or maybe like some kind of ultramodern brothel, furnished in Danish Bordello . . . as opposed to French Provincial. But we'll see. Anyway, it's going to be fabulous, that I can guarantee. It's just too bad it won't be done up in time for Leonard's birthday party."

"I thought Jeanette is taking care of that."

"Oh she is, but wouldn't it be lovely to have it here on Park instead of everyone trooping out to Manhattan Beach. Who the hell wants to travel to Brooklyn, anyway, even if Phil is doing the driving. I still don't know why they haven't rented here in town, even a studio, a *pied-à-terre*. It's such a boring trip back and forth, day after day."

"He drives."

"Still, it's a drear." He stopped and tapped his finger

against the glass. "Windows have to be cleaned, too," he said out of the corner of his mouth. Then his lips widened as though trying to form the right shape for something he was yet to tell her. "What are you getting him for his forty-fifth? Decided yet?" He turned completely around and faced her with a swiftness that nearly upset her balance.

She shook her head.

"I know how you feel—"

How can you? You can't even begin to—

"—What can you get a man who has just about everything?"

"A new set of cuff links, for starters."

"Pardon?" he said.

She brushed it aside like a piece of lint, a fly landing on her shoulder, unwelcome. "Nothing. Just a private joke."

"I bought him a painting."

Was he too proud of himself or was his chest just swelling because the air was tight, close with all the windows drawn against the night? She couldn't tell, had no way of knowing for sure. His lips widened once again and she wondered what he would tell her next. "A painting? How . . . extravagant of you."

"Well, it's merely a matter of good business, my dear." The last grated on her ears as never before. "And it's all tax-deductible, so what's the difference. Another thousand isn't gonna kill me or break the bank, one way or another."

"That much?" She was visibly amazed. Two hundred dollars for a gift, yes, that she could understand. But a thousand seemed above and beyond the call of duty. Yet Leonard had been responsible for getting D. W. appointed to the board, with profit-sharing benefits—his favorite kind of *bennies*—and stock options and the like. No wonder he wanted to express his gratitude. Or was it merely that? Something told her she was missing the boat, but she couldn't put her finger on it.

"I really should be getting back. Lena must be starting to worry."

"So have you thought of anything?" And then, when she didn't answer right away, he said, "Just let me shut some of these lights."

382

"No," she repeated. "I haven't given it all that mucl thought, frankly."

"Well there's always stock."

"NuBodies stock, you mean."

"What else is there? That's the best kind. And it won't cost you anything because you've been sitting on it since the company went public. I mean, course it'll cost you, but only on paper. You won't miss the actual bread, that's what I'm saying. And you might as well keep the shares in the family. Right or wrong?"

He's far from family, she thought. "Stock is . . . so impersonal," reminded of the gift Barry had given his sister for her sixteenth birthday. Money, "cold cash on the line" he had called it.

"My darling, there's nothing impersonal about giving him something he'll value for the rest of his life, remember that. Chances are, knowing Leonard, he'll sell the painting I bought when the market value goes up. But that's okay, too. I'm not giving it to him to kiss his ass, needless to say."

"Needless to say." She turned toward the door, hoping he'd get the message and start turning off the lights he'd mentioned a moment before. But apparently, he wasn't ready yet.

"Think about it, Cynthia," he said. When she glanced back his face was wan in the thin incandescent light, his manner halting, casual in all the wrong ways.

"I will," she said, if only to appease him, to end the conversation. "How much would you think would show him . . . how much I cared, D. W.?" She grew uneasy at the way he now looked at her: straight and hard, his attitude no longer half as circumspect as it had been earlier.

"I really haven't even given it all that much consideration," he replied. "I suppose one percent would be more than plenty, wouldn't you say."

She began to laugh just as he turned out the overhead light. The sound came back at her like an echo, like the tinkle of crystal pendants on a chandelier, the kind D. W. would probably end up buying for his new apartment. Even in the darkness, he was transparent.

"What's so funny?" he said.

You are, she thought. But she said instead, "Life." That was all. "Just life."

Between finishing up work with Lynne Cohen and getting Lena situated in a new apartment, Cynthia had her hands full. She spent three days in Miami Beach with her mother, helping her unpack. A furnished apartment on Collins Avenue with an ocean view had been rented for the winter. Lena looked forward to the change. She had several cousins living near Lincoln Road and South Beach and as she'd admitted, "I hate New York winters like poison." Cynthia, though she never breathed a word about it to her mother, relished the opportunity to enjoy a little privacy. If anything, she'd encouraged Lena and, needless to say, provided all the money that was required for the move. Then, when she got back, she had Leonard's birthday party to deal with. But the problem had been solved, even before she left for Miami. At Cartier she found a salesman with taste she decided was "impeccable." He helped her choose a pair of lapis cuff links, two oblong bars of the blue- and gold-flecked stone set atop simple gold fittings. She decided the five-hundred-odd dollars was well spent. One percent . . . unbelievable the way everyone takes me for an idiot, a *goose*. But instead of letting the entire episode—distasteful, shabby, even a little bit slimy too, when you got right down to it—pass unnoticed, never to be mentioned or alluded to again, she wrapped the Cartier jewelry box in a single share of NuBodies stock, currently valued at thirteen dollars and change. If Leonard was disappointed, the expression on his face didn't betray him for an instant. "Now I can finally hock those old diamond ones you and I hated so much," he said. "And I love the wrapping paper; it's my favorite kind," kissing her on the cheek while Jeanette smiled—an iceberg in a matching ice-blue gown—less than three watchful feet away. She began to wonder if D. W. had cooked up the scheme all by himself, without letting Leonard know about it beforehand. Maybe he thought it was the perfect way to get in his good graces. But he and Frankel got along without any difficulty at all. As far as she knew, there was no friction there whatsoever.

So she still couldn't figure it out, and there was no one to take aside and ask, point-blank. Had she given Leonard one percent of her holdings, each of them would have had equal control of the corporation. Thirty percent in the hands of dozens upon dozens of stockholders, thirty-five percent in her control and the same in his. Now, she was still sitting on thirty-six percent. Even with the board of directors, she maintained controlling interest in NuBodies. She didn't intend to give it away so quickly, so easily, to be taken for "an ignoramus of the first order." This time, it wasn't even a question of forgiveness. D. W. was greedy and that was all there was to it. In the space of a little less than six years, he'd come a long way. From junior copywriter to president of D. Wayne Eliot & Friends and member of the board of NuBodies Inc. As far as she was concerned, he'd gone far enough. She promised herself that she would exercise considerable more judgment in the future. Even though she still liked D. W., even though he knew how to cater to her ego, how to flatter her, how to make her laugh and forget that her life wasn't nearly as bright and carefree as the press releases and articles in *NuBodies* Magazine had it appear, the trust and personal commitment she had staked in his future was eroding by leaps and bounds.

I may not know how the corporation functions inside and out, she thought, but I'll be damned if I'm going to just sit back and let someone take everything over lock, stock, and barrel. I've worked too hard and I'm nobody's fool. Not now and not tomorrow and not the day after that, either.

Two days before she was scheduled to leave on what Leonard had called the most important p.r. trip of her career, guest of honor and major participant in the opening of the first California franchises, NuBodies dropped from thirteen and three-eighths to four and a quarter. "There's nothing to get upset about," Frankel said. "Some bastard might have set off a rumor we were having problems, for all I know."

"Who?" she asked. "And why?"

"How the hell am I supposed to know, Cynthia? Maybe one of our competitors, someone like that. But I've been on the phone with a guy from the SEC all morning. People have been dumping shares like we're about to announce we're filing for bankruptcy or something. But I intend to get to the bottom of it, I promise."

He was good to his word. She was packing, ready to fly out the following morning, when he called to tell her to have a good trip. "And get there safe. We closed at ten and a half. Go figure the stock market, because I can't."

His wasn't the last call she received that evening, however.

She was selecting her jewelry and cosmetics for the trip when the downstairs intercom buzzed sharp and shrill. "Yes? Mrs. Morgan here," immediately sorry she hadn't pretended that no one was home. But he'd seen her come in, so it really didn't matter.

The static was like chalk on a blackboard. "This is Rudy, Mrs. Morgan," the doorman called up, having finally learned to get her new name straight. "There's a gentleman down here wants to see you.",

"Who?"

"A Mr.—" and then in a voice that was farther away, "What's your name again?"

"Margold," she made out.

Rudy got back on, louder than before. "A Mr. Margold to see you, Mrs. Morgan. Shall I send him up?"

"Please." I don't believe it.

"What?" he yelled. "I'm sorry. We have to get this thing fixed. It's hard to hear you."

"I said yes, send him up. Yes," she yelled. The intercom went dead and she stepped away from the grill. The pocket-sized speaker was set into the wall near the front door. She stayed where she was, rubbing at her elbows. The skin was rough and chapped and she wondered why. All winter she'd been wearing long-sleeved dresses and what the hell does he want from me now, of all the times to pick, he has to come tonight. Outside, halfway down the hall, the elevator gurgled like an upset stomach. It seemed to throw up its charge like something it couldn't swallow. The doorbell rang a moment later. Her fingers flew at her hair, smoothed the long trailing panel of her quilted housecoat, brushed away invisible crumbs at the corners of her lips. "One minute," she said. Idiot, ignoramus, stop shaking. She undid both sets of locks, turned the knob, and opened the door.

"Hello," he said, both hands in his pockets, face red with cold. "I hope I haven't come at an . . . inopportune time."

"No." I'm only entertaining all my lovers, en masse.

"I would've called but the line was busy and then I had to look for a parking spot."

"You could've put the car in a lot," she said, motioning Forman to enter.

386

"They charge an arm and a leg," he said, his eyes widening as he stepped into the foyer and looked around. "Pretty high-class," he muttered. "Lena around?"

"She's down south for the winter. Miami Beach. Her arthritis was acting up again. Would you like a drink?"

"Sure," he said. "The usual."

"I'm sorry. I forget." *Why am I lying, playing games?* Once again he looked surprised. Mechanically, without emotion, he said, "Scotch-and-water, one cube. Just a splash."

"Make yourself comfortable." She pointed to the living room. "Take off your coat," *the same nylon shell he's had for years. It probably isn't even warm enough.*

"Great view you got," he said, tugging the zipper down so that the jacket opened to reveal a faded but still gaily patterned overshirt. The curtains weren't drawn. Outside, the river was shot with winking color. Breaking it up like a prism, it sent the shifting reflections swimming across the gentle, troughlike waves. "You bought it, didn't you?"

"What?" she asked.

"The apartment."

"A couple of years already." She handed him his drink. "I'd join you but I have to fly tomorrow," *as if that has anything to do with it. I just want my wits about me, period.*

"Really?" He raised the glass. *"Salud."* After a swallow, he said, "Where're you heading?"

"Out to California."

"How nice."

"I hope so. We're opening our first branches out there and, you know, I'm going to be a guest speaker, that kind of thing. Forman, take a seat, please, no reason to stand there like—" *you know, a total stranger.*

He sat back on the tufted velvet sofa, put the drink down on top of the coffee table. "You look terrific. Still keeping your weight down, I see."

"I try. You lost plenty yourself. What happened, get the bug?"

"Went to NuBodies a couple of months ago, would you believe," he said, grinning.

She was pleased and let him know it. "Told you it works." She sat down in a chair to the right of the couch, folding her hands in her lap. "And how is Natalie?"

387

"Well," he said. "How come you haven't been out to see her? Holidays, I mean."

"I haven't been invited," she said. "And Henny?"

"Working hard," he hurried to say, "same as me. Same as usual, it's always tough making a living, you know that."

"Yes, nothing ever came easy for you, Forman."

He let it pass, showing none of his old spirit. She decided it was just as well. "It's harder these days." He took another sip of his drink and smacked his lips. "And I guess I might as well put all my cards on the table, Cynthia, because that's why I decided to see you tonight. It's about Nat."

"What about her?" Doesn't call, doesn't write, doesn't let me know if she's alive or dead. Nineteen years old and she's managed to pick up all her brother's bad habits, even though they haven't lived together in years.

"You know she just started the second semester of her sophomore year. She's out in Madison, on partial scholarship."

"Madison?"

It finally rang a bell, just before he said, "Wisconsin, the University of Wisconsin. Barry wrote from Nebraska, told me he passed. They're in the same exact grade. Funny, the way things work out, isn't it?"

"If you knew the half of it you wouldn't laugh," she said. "But it's water under the bridge, like they always say. I ruined him, spoiled him rotten. I guess I must be learning something, right? I mean, if I can admit it."

"You tried, Cynthia."

"Lot of good it did me," she said and frowned, annoyed at herself for having made that kind of admission. It's not his business anyway, she thought. He didn't contribute, help out. I had my hands full for years so why should I complain to him about it. He wasn't interested before, so why should he be now. "What about Natalie?" picking up the conversation where it had somehow dropped, a few minutes before.

He said, "I need your help. That's why I'm here."

His hair's gotten thinner, grayer. Tired too, everything about him, like he's aging from the inside, too quick. And whose fault is that? Am I supposed to take another blame, is that the way it works? "What kind of help, Forman?"

"I can't afford to send her anymore, Cynthia," he said, drawing out his breath with a sigh and a wheeze. "The business has been . . . well, it's been falling off in the last year. I don't know what it is but I can't seem to make a day's pay the way I used to. That's why Henny went back to work at the beauty parlor. But still, it's not enough for what they're asking for tuition, room and board." Hunched over, he looked as if he were getting more uncomfortable with each passing second, each word he managed to utter, to get out into the open before it choked up inside him.

"Let her go to Brooklyn College," she said, her lips drawing shut like a purse-string. She got abruptly to her feet and went to mix herself a drink. "That way it won't cost you a penny," she added, the words trailing over her shoulder. "Just for books, school supplies, that's all. She's a big girl now. She has to be made to understand." After all, hasn't she always worshipped you? Hasn't she always been daddy's good little girl?

"Sure she can go to Brooklyn College, City College, too, for that matter," he said as she kept her back to him and poured herself a fingerful of scotch. "But how can you do that to a kid? All her friends are there. The school's been good to her, Cynthia. It's much better, scholastically I mean, than Brooklyn. Has a better reputation, always did. And she's made dean's list three semesters in a row. It's lucky they're even giving her a partial scholarship."

She turned around, drink in both hands, cupping the highball glass as if it were a brandy snifter. "Why lucky? With marks like that I should think they'd bend over backwards to keep her."

"It's because of the admissions application, where it had to list your name, occupation. She had to tell them things she didn't want to, when they called her in to the dean's office, the scholarship committee."

"What kind of things?"

"About . . . you know, about how the two of you haven't—" He couldn't finish the sentence.

"Well whose fault is that, goddamnit!" she said, raising her voice. All the accumulated bitterness rushed out into the open. "I'm so tired of being used, Manny, so sick and tired. I'm weary, that's what it is. Everyone takes me for a horse's ass and I've had enough, more than my share. The child doesn't speak to her mother for three

389

years and all of a sudden she expects me to foot the bills for her college education. It's ludicrous. It's a real joke."

"She doesn't know I'm here, Cynthia. I didn't tell her."

"Why not? You tell her just about everything else," she snapped. She took a quick swallow of her drink. It burned, all the way down. "I'm sorry. I didn't mean that." She could hear herself speaking, but the words seemed to come from someone else's lips. Yet she had no trouble believing in what she heard, a belief that was shared by a sense of loss, desire both emotional and physical. It can't be, she thought. Never again the way it was. If he took her right then and there, on the floor, on the couch, in the bedroom, up against a wall, nothing would change but the rhythm of her breathing. Knowing this, her mood softened. She couldn't blame him any longer.

"All the Margolds have too much pride," he said. "It's our Achilles' heel. No one wants to give an inch. You, me, Barry, Natalie, all four of us. But someone has to sometime, Cynthia."

It isn't four anymore, she thought. Hasn't been for a good long time. His words, so tempered, so well thought out, made her shudder all the same. How could she say no? In spite of everything that had happened, Natalie was still her daughter, flesh of her flesh. She'll grow out of it, she had told herself so many times during the last five years, ever since she'd found Natalie's hastily emptied dresser drawers. She'll wake up, like in the middle of the night, sit up in bed, snap out of it. 'What have I done to my mother?' And now her mother's being put on the spot all over again.

"You knew I'd say yes before you came, didn't you?" she asked, taking another quick pull at her drink. She wore one ring, but not her wedding band. It clicked against the glass.

Manny looked down at his lap, his legs bowed, as if he were contemplating the hollow space he had made within himself. "That isn't so," he said. "I only hoped to reason with you, that's all." He raised his eyes. She noticed how pale they were, dry and with an unguarded focus. "I just wanted to tell you the way things stood."

"I want to see her," she said, "that's the only stipulation. I have no intention of being an anonymous benefactor, if you get my drift. You forget that she's still my daughter same as Barry is still your son."

390

"He writes me, just about every week."

"What?" She had heard him, all too clearly. But she wanted him to repeat the words, perhaps to drum them into her head, make them stick like two surfaces glued firmly together, make her see what a fool she'd been.

"He writes, at least," Manny said again.

"Consider yourself among the fortunate. If I get a post card it's—what's the use of talking. When he wants money, he knows who to call. And what does he say, my darling son? About himself, I mean?" Has he told his father? No, he wouldn't be that stupid, exposing himself, leaving himself so wide open to . . . recrimination, is it? Is that the word I'm looking for or something simpler, like disgust? Or less crucifying and easier to deal with, like disappointment?

"Lots of things, different things," Manny said evasively. "Is he seeing, you know, a psychiatrist out there?"

"Why, did he say he was?"

"No, I just asked, that's all."

"A good man from the medical center there. One of the best in the state. Once a week," as if it'll help, God only knows.

"That's good." He sighed once more, got to his feet and straightened up. His hands smoothed out his trouser legs so that they broke right above the top of each shoe. She noticed how the back of his cuffs were frayed. The empty glass with its melting, smooth shaving of ice, sat in a ring of moisture, condensation which floated on top of the glass table. "So when do you want to see her?"

"Don't you think it's time, Manny?" she said hurriedly. "Don't you agree? I don't want the kid to threaten to drop out, but I'm not an ogre and it's time she made her peace with me." And me with her. He knows that, so why say it, why slay a dead horse when maybe, maybe just maybe, things'll turn out the way you've always wanted. Even if she didn't sit up in bed in the middle of the night and feel it hit her like a blow on the top of her head, God forbid, maybe she's old enough to understand what's happened, how we were so alike she couldn't even begin to grasp, to deal with it.

This confusion made her want to tremble. But the shaking was internal. She wasn't about to demonstrate to Manny that she was not in complete control of herself and her emotions.

"How long you plan to stay out in California?" he asked.

"Less than a month. Two or three weeks, tops."

"Can you stop in Madison on the way back?"

"I can arrange it. There's a branch in Milwaukee and what's that, an hour or so away?"

"Something like that, ninety miles or so. Maybe less."

Everything vague and she didn't know what Milwaukee had to do with it. But it was too late to erase the sentence and say something else.

"Should I tell the kid to expect to hear from you? I'll leave you her number at the dorm."

She nodded her head. "I want you to tell her that *and* about the tuition. But Manny, tell her we're splitting it. Fifty-fifty, even-steven. All right?"

"I appreciate that," and his eyes were soft now, docile and almost fawning.

She looked away in embarrassed silence, amazed and not pleased that she had managed to gain the upper hand, to dominate a man she once described as "one who never let me get away with murder, blue murder like so many other husbands I know." She still wanted to be liked, to be considered a good person. She wanted Natalie to fill those long-emptied dresser drawers and maybe, she reasoned, this was as good a start as any.

The p.r. man D. W. had hired, particularly with her California trip foremost in mind, had already earned his pay and done his homework. When she got off the 747 at Los Angeles International Airport, there was an advance guard of photographers and newspapermen there to meet her. The flashbulbs burned white-hot while above her the California sky was the color of Sea Island blue ink.

She fielded their questions with ease. She wasn't a politician out looking for votes; she didn't have to say one thing while she really meant another. Ten minutes later, pinwheels still dancing before her eyes, a friendly arm steered her gently away, disentangling her from the sweaty crush of journalists. "Welcome to California, Mrs. Morgan. I'm Burt Heflin. Mr. Eliot contacted me several weeks ago, if you recall."

"You staged a great reception, Burt," she said.

"Nothing was staged, Mrs. Morgan. I just informed the

papers you were arriving in town. Wait till you see the crowd that's waiting for you in the terminal." He opened a metal door, and they stepped inside one of the buildings, Heflin explaining that the portable ramp which usually hooked up to the airliner had been put out of commission by a faulty electrical connection. "That's why you were delayed deboarding. Which was fine with us since it got all the photographers out of the terminal and right out in front to meet you." He guided her onto a moving sidewalk. He said it was both a pleasure and honor to finally meet her, "A woman of your caliber."

She felt the ground move beneath her feet and said, "I look all right?" suddenly aware of all the tanned, healthy faces which surrounded her, the casual glossy air of the people who lived three thousand miles from Riverside Drive and Rutland Road.

"Perfect. Don't sweat it," Heflin assured her. He was a ruddy-faced man with a firm, brotherly grip and a white linen suit.

"Who else do you handle?"

"Only the biggest names. Now watch your step, they're right on the other side of the gate there."

Were they screaming? She couldn't believe her ears. Okay, so she was Cynthia Morgan, so her face belonged to the public, seen daily by millions of shoppers driving their carts down the aisles of supermarkets from here to Boston, from Dallas to Detroit. Thousands of bottles of NuBodies brand diet soda, each dressed out in a square four-color label bearing her svelte, gowned figure, were sold every day of the year. Thousands of copies of *Nu-Bodies* Magazine were read daily. Thousands of men, women, and teenagers attended NuBodies classes in eighty-seven different locations in twenty-two different states. And within a few days, those figures would change to ninety-three branches in twenty-three states. Then there were the several million who had seen her on Johnny Carson, not to mention talk shows in just about every major city in the country. The mayors of fifteen different cities had given her gold keys. The governors of Minnesota, Louisiana, and Maine had all proclaimed NuBodies Day at various times during the past few years. There were countless other scrolls and plaques and proclamations hanging in her office. So she wasn't what one would call a stranger, a nonentity. And when she heard the screaming and saw the waving posters, she smiled to herself, involuntarily straightened her shoulders back, sucked in her stomach and stepped forward to become part of the excitement and the tumult.

They were screaming, "Cynthia! We love you!"

Let the papers call them fanatical fat people. They're not, because they need me and they recognize that nothing is final, that no book is ever closed. They all have a second chance. And a third if they need it. And a fourth, too, if they don't make it right off the bat.

"You're beautiful," she said. "This is the happiest day of my life. I love you—all of you. I love California."

"Keep smiling," Heflin whispered into one ear, half hidden under a lacquered curl of red hair. He failed to realize that she wasn't faking it, putting it on to please her well-wishers. "Walk forward and don't mind the flashbulbs. It's all good p.r., baby, and that's what counts."

She did as she was told, confident she was dealing with a professional, someone who knew his business the way she felt she knew hers. There were seemingly endless hands to shake and shoulders to squeeze, even a baby or two to kiss. She got ink on her fingers from leaky fountain pens as she autographed copies of the *NuBodies Cookbook*, well-thumbed issues of the national magazine, scraps of wrinkled paper and even a warm capped bottle of Nu-Bodies black cherry soda.

"When are you opening up in San Bernardino?" someone yelled.

"And don't forget us in the Valley, Cynthia."

"Pomona's on the map, too."

"And so is Riverside."

"—Anaheim."

"We need you in Pasadena!" shrieked a woman who wore a hat with an oversized button which read: NU-BODIES, WHERE THIN IS IN.

"Just make sure to come and see me this afternoon," she yelled back, thinking it was just yesterday she got off a plane in Maine and heard very much the same kind of thing. "Three o'clock at the Hollywood Bowl," and in a whisper to Heflin, "That's where it's being held, isn't it?"

"The Hollywood Bowl, there's no admission charge," Heflin said, loud enough to be heard. He took her arm again, waited for her to acknowledge the thanks of three nuns who had already signed up at the Long Beach branch, and then urged her forward.

Dazed, though jet-lag was the last thing she felt, she turned her head back and said again, "I want to see all of you there this afternoon. Don't forget." Then she was holding onto him as people swarmed around her. The baggage area loomed ahead.

"Can you see your bags?" he asked, one hand on her elbow, the other waving in the air for a redcap.

"Right over there, with the Gucci stripe. And the small one, the Vuitton case." *It's all right to be label-conscious, kiddo. But just don't be so obvious about it that people'll think you're vulgar, that's all.*

A plum-colored Mercedes was parked outside the baggage claim area. Heflin held the door open for her and she slid onto the front seat, the leather interior sunbaked and warm against her thin clinging dress. He got in at the other side. She caught him frowning when he discovered an ink stain on the sleeve of his suit jacket. "It'll come out in the wash," she said, "like everything else." Then he turned the key in the ignition. As soon as the engine responded, the p.r. man hit the air-conditioning switch and slid into the stream of outgoing traffic.

"So how does it feel to be a celebrity, Mrs. Morgan?" He turned his head to the side and flashed what she saw as a professional smile, all good humor and camaraderie sitting comfortably and effortlessly on the surface of his tanned face.

"Nervous-making," she admitted, forgetting the exact figure he was getting each week, somewhere in the vicinity of two or three hundred dollars. She hoped he would do something other than just feed her ego.

Heflin got them onto the San Diego Freeway with no trouble at all. "You'll even have time for a short nap," he said as they headed toward Beverly Hills. The car tore through the flat pastel-shaded landscape at close to seventy miles an hour. She sat back and tried to relax. But there was too much to do, too much to think about, especially her appearance at the Hollywood Bowl.

"How many people you think will be there?" she asked.

"Where?"

"This afternoon."

"Ten or eleven thousand maybe, maybe fifteen if we're

lucky. And don't forget you'll be appearing on the Carson show, end of the week."

"Who can forget," she said. "That's the one thing I'm looking forward to most of all. Will you be picking me up or have they hired a car like the last time?"

"I'll be around whenever you need me. But there's a car and driver waiting at the hotel, so you won't have any trouble getting around. I'll take you over to the Bowl personally this afternoon, if you like."

"Yes, I'd appreciate that. I've only been out here once, and I don't think I'd know the Hollywood Bowl from," and she stopped to think, "Candlestick Park."

"That's in San Francisco."

"See, what'd I tell you. I'm still a New Yorker, hopelessly so."

"Oh, I wouldn't say that. You might even decide to settle out here one of these days. You never can tell."

"I'll worry about it when the time comes," she said with a laugh. Straight ahead of her the smog was an orange stain on the horizon. Relax, she told herself. You're going to have a ball, a marvelous time. It's going to be fun . . . I hope.

But it was fun, more fun in fact than she'd had in a long time. Her appearance at the Hollywood Bowl touched off a deafening roar and when she mounted the stage to address the crowd, she received a standing ovation even before she began her half-hour talk. She hadn't expected so warm a welcome and the last traces of nervousness, an anxiety akin to stage fright, slipped away, immediately replaced by a sense of confidence that did not desert her for the next thirty minutes. She spoke from the heart and from her experience. "It only works if you want to make it work," she cautioned them. "I don't sell miracles. You won't wake up two days after you enroll and find yourself skinny. It takes weeks, sometimes months. But it's worth it. I promise you, it's the one decision you'll make that you'll never live to regret." They believed her, perhaps because she had no difficulty believing it herself. It had worked for her and all those months of effort came back to her. Even as she spoke she heard voices other than her own. Lena complaining her face was getting pinched up like a peanut. Manny saying she was going to drive him out of his "everlovin'" mind. Barry telling her how fabulous she looked and Natalie, her face darkening, purpling like a bruise in the downfall of light, saying outside the storefront, "You can't force me; you can't make me. Daddy doesn't—"

"So wake up and start believing in yourself," she told them. "Do something constructive for a change. Get yourself down to one of our new branches out here and sign up. And don't wait until tomorrow because tomorrow is always a week and then a month and then a year away. You finally have the opportunity to change the course of your lives, because if you think being fat, heavy, overweight, whatever you want to call it, hasn't colored your entire existence, you've got another guess coming. So give yourself the gift of a second chance . . . because no one else can do it for you. Thank you."

Screams, yelling, shouts, and whistles, and wild applause —wave after wave of adoration came back to her. Her body tingled in response, her eyes and ears alive to every sight and sound. She shivered and gripped the sides of the wooden podium, moving her eyes back and forth across the tiers of seats. People scrambled to their feet and clapped like mad. She glanced over her shoulder to where the lecturers of the new California branches sat, assembled in a thin, well-dressed line across the stage of the bandshell. They, too, hurried to join the crowd. Beaming smiles spelled money, but affection, too, she hoped. Because they have to feel something, even more than just compassion. Because they've been where I have, they've been fat and they've changed their lives just like all these people can do. She took the mike again and said, "We're all in this together, one big family. I love all of you." She couldn't think of anything else. Nor did she know if she was heard. But it didn't seem to matter, either. They were still going crazy, some thirteen thousand overweight and formerly-overweight men and women crying out for an encore as if she had just given an award-winning performance.

There were more flashbulbs and more reporters. Then the handshakes from the lecturers, the franchise owners sitting with dollar signs in their eyes in the front row, as though they were all protecting their investment. I'll get through to them at tomorrow's reception, she thought. They're always like that in the beginning. Until they see that they have to earn their money, that they're performing a public service and they better not forget it, either, or else they'll make fools out of themselves, out of me, too.

She had all the money she could possibly want, but it wasn't going to solve every problem. Now, under an immaculate blue Southern California sky, she wanted the love and respect she felt should go along with her hard-earned material success—even if there was no such word as *should*. But like everything else, it too had to be earned. It'll just take time, so stop worrying about it. Be smart for a change.

It was easier said than done. After all, wasn't asking for happiness asking for just about everything.

She had a pink stucco bungalow, a suite consisting of two small but "charmingly appointed" rooms at the Bel Air Hotel, right off Stone Canyon Drive. Birds she had never seen before, with alternating black and white stripes on their wings and tail, flew like noisy little dive bombers from one rim of the canyon to the other. There were hummingbirds, too, and if she looked out one window she saw unbroken greenery dotted with lush scarlet flowers. Scrub pine, more in keeping with the climate, traced dark green paths along the hillside. She would have liked to follow one, to end up in some cool and mysterious place, as secluded as a page in a book of fairy tales. But there was never enough time, nor enough hours in the day. From the window she saw other things. At the top of the canyon wall, a pink marble villa looked down at the cluster of buildings which made up the hotel. If she looked out from the opposite direction, the jutting shelves of half-seen private homes captured her eye and her imagination. She wondered which movie stars lived where and if she'd ever be invited into their homes to become part of the *Photoplay* fun and games, their madcap theatrical diversions. The last was a phrase she was absolutely certain D. W. would have used, though his tone would have left a little to be desired, condescending more than anything else. Well, he's not here and I intend to have a good time, despite myself. She fully expected people—and that meant the Hollywood set, if such a "set" indeed existed—to accept her on her own right, on her own merits. She didn't consider these minor or inconsiderable and so it pleased her to discover that her suite had been invaded by

398

a massive floral tribute. When she returned from the Hollywood Bowl she found a horseshoe-shaped arrangement of red, yellow, and white flowers. It stood in the center of the living room, and would have been equally at home in a funeral parlor. She supposed that was part of the joke and when she read the attached card, she started to laugh. There was no doubt in her mind that he was pulling her leg. But she loved him for it, wondered when he'd gotten married, and reached for the phone. She dialed his service, asking them to forward a message. "This is Mrs. Morgan, a friend of Mr. Casey's. Will you tell Pat I wouldn't miss it for the world. No, he'll understand. Yes. Thank you."

What to wear, what to wear?

Patrick Casey lived in Beverly Hills, ten minutes from the hotel and five minutes off Coldwater Canyon. The note had read: "Bernice and I are giving a party this evening and guess who's the guest of honor? Don't forget I lost thirty-five ugly lbs. when I lived in Fun City, thanks to NuBodies. We expect you around nine. Do not fail to keep this assignation. Thinly, P. C." She was delighted he had thought of her, doubly delighted that he thought enough to give a party in her honor. Flattered and excited about meeting the "natives" firsthand, she tried on three outfits before she settled on the one she felt did her figure the most justice. Black satin man-tailored pants, a black glitter sweater of rayon and Lurex, and a touch of gold at her ears and wrists and she decided she was neither over- nor under-dressed. He hadn't mentioned whether it was going to be formal, dressy. But knowing California—at least on the surface—she had a feeling the guests would all arrive in casual attire. The climate didn't lend itself to ties and high necklines and she certainly didn't want to come off looking like a transposed New Yorker, an unsophisticated East Coast greenhorn.

She had heard of Casey long before they'd met on the Johnny Carson Show. Originally, he'd attracted attention as a result of his Tony-winning efforts on Broadway. She remembered seeing him in the revival of *By Jupiter* ("It's dated and it doesn't have a shred of social significance, if you ask me," Manny had complained), as well as one of Ben Bagley's nostalgic "tune-filled" revues. He received a Tony as best supporting actor in a musical for *Jupiter*, a nomination in the same category for his work in the revue. Then, so he'd told her when they talked after the show, he'd gone out to the Coast, "to seek my fame and fortune." Nowadays he was known for his daily appearances on "The Trivia Game," a daytime quiz show cashing in on the growing nationwide nostalgia craze. Evenings, he often made guest appearances on various musical comedy shows. A minor TV personality at best, so D. W. had made a point of telling her when she returned from her first trip to California, Patrick Casey was still Hollywood. And if that was not a plus in its own right, she also genuinely liked him as a person, even when he wasn't "on," performing his routines with or without the benefit of a live audience.

She left the hotel at nine-fifteen, not wanting to appear too eager or pushy. Her driver, a Chicano who said little, but whose driving made Phil look like an amateur, knew the way as if he'd been there several times before. Coldwater Canyon was dark with eucalyptus trees. When she turned her head back she saw the lights of the city, strung like a rhinestone necklace across the throat of the sky. She wondered if L.A. deserved more than that. Somehow, diamonds would never have worked amidst the stone-green canyons, the serpentine twisting roads. One such snaking avenue led from Coldwater to Hyacinth Way, where Casey lived, "among the homes of the stars," she recalled him saying. "The great and near-great, the forgotten, the lamented, and the still remembered. That's Hollywood, baby. But you're gonna love it as much as you love the Big Apple, mark my words."

A fawn-colored pug, more apricot than beige, announced her arrival the moment the driver let her off in front of the comedian's unpretentious ranch house. "Bernice," his familiar nasal voice called out in the darkness. "Control your emotions, my beauty."

She was still laughing when the door opened wide and Pat stepped out to welcome her. "I thought you'd broken your vows and gotten married," she said.

"Me, the confirmed bachelor boy of Yorba Linda and Tinseltown? You must be joshing and how *are* you, you thin gorgeous devil. Meet Bernice, my companion for the next twelve or thirteen years we hope; if her adenoids don't kill her, I will." He took her in his arms, kissed her on one cheek and then the other, grabbed for her nearest hand and moved back. "Fabulous, you look like you just stepped off the set of *Hush . . . Hush, Sweet Charlotte*. Now come inside and meet a hundred of my closest and dearest friends."

Immediately upon entering she saw two faces she recognized, the host of "The Trivia Game," and the star of the popular weekly series "City Hospital." She couldn't get over the fact that she was finally at a party with "honest to God" celebrities. Pat literally dragged her down three steps into the sunken living room.

"This," he announced, presenting her like a trophy, "is the Cynthia Morgan. The president of NuBodies and one of my all-time favorite people." She was nervous, aware that she was on display, some kind of strange door prize, a white elephant or a rare bird—she couldn't make up her mind which was more applicable. But she hid her anxieties as best she could under a smile she hoped would look not only genuine, but ingratiating as well.

They're people, same as me. They just entertain for a living, that's all. I teach people how to lose weight and they teach them how to laugh. Something like that . . . Jesus, calm down. He likes you. You'll be home free in another minute if you just give yourself half a chance and act natural.

But it was one thing to think that and quite another to put it into operation. Only after Pat had gotten her a drink did she start to relax. He took her around, never relinquishing his hold. "This is Jackie Treager, a fantastic paintress though I like her graphics better than her oils. And this is my manager and shill, not to mention the heir apparent to the Casey millions, my indecent friend, Gene Burr."

"That's quite an introduction," she laughed.

"That's quite a client I've got," Burr replied. He was a silver-haired man with a turquoise Indian bracelet and an amazing collection of bulldog jowls. "I caught you on Carson last time you were out here. We must get together and talk about your career before you go back to New York. You're a natural for television, Cynthia, in case no one's told you."

"Really?" Her eyes lit up at the very thought. "I did a half-hour documentary, but that was years ago. But thank you anyway. I'm terribly flattered," she said, letting herself be dragged off again.

"Justin, this is the one and only NuBodies lady—you've seen her on soda bottles I'm sure. But in all seriousness, this gorgeous specimen of femininity is totally responsible for making me what I am today . . . slim, trim and devil-may-care." He clicked his heels. "Justin Rodell, Cynthia Morgan."

"How do you do," the young man said, extending a well-manicured hand. "With an introduction like that, you don't need a press agent."

"From what I gather, introductions are Pat's specialty."

"Absolutely," he agreed. He wore blue jeans, broken-backed moccasins and a shirt she decided was custom-made. The initials J. R. were sewn over his heart as if to stanch a wound.

"He's adorable," she told Pat when they were out of hearing distance.

"He thinks so, too," Casey said. "One of Gene's protégés. He's going to write The Great American Novel . . . or so he's been telling everyone, ever since he got out here. When I read it, I'll believe it." Then, in a louder voice, "Paul, you haven't met my heart-throb and guiding light. Paul Antonio, Cynthia Morgan."

"A pleasure," he said, squeezing her fingers rather than shaking her hand. She decided it was a very suave Continental kind of gesture. "Pat's told me all about you."

"Good things I hope," she said, unable to stop staring into Antonio's eyes. They were pitch-black. No other word and no other color could describe them.

"Oh, the very finest things, I promise," he said. When he grinned right after, his teeth were as perfectly white as his eyes were black.

"Paul's an actor," Casey told her. One arm swooped around her shoulders, gathered her closer. She wondered if he was suddenly being overly protective or merely demonstrative now that he'd had a couple of drinks under his belt. "But he can't sing or dance, so how the hell is he going to win his way into the hearts of Mr. and Mrs. John Q. Public. That's his problem. I mean, God knows, America is the last place for a true-blue Stanislavskyan. I told him to get his ass into musical comedy while he still has his looks. At least that way he'll be able to make a living. But he's not about to listen. He tells me it's not *pure* enough, whatever the hell that means."

"I don't think he'll lose his looks for quite some time,"
402

she heard herself say. Immediately afterward she clamped her lips shut, momentarily distressed. She blamed it on the alcohol, though she had hardly touched her drink.

"Well thank you, Mrs. Morgan."

"Cynthia."

"Excuse me," Pat said, releasing his hold. "I hear Bernice barking . . . as per the usual. Someone's at the door, some stagestruck kid looking for love . . . I hope."

She was left alone, both hands on her highball glass, both eyes still on Paul Antonio. She didn't know what to say. He was Italian, unless Antonio was a stage name, which it might well be since his skin tended toward the fair rather than the olive and she was pretty sure Shakespeare had once written a character of that name into one of his plays. And he was slightly taller than she was, though not nearly as tall as Frankel, and as perfectly featured as a piece of Greek art. She estimated he was somewhere between twenty-six and thirty. Closer to twenty-six, she thought. A moment later she said, "Well," because that didn't mean anything and at least it didn't make her look foolish, either. Then she brought the glass up to her lips and took a sip of her drink.

"Pat's told me all about your work. Should I be thankful or sorry I've never had a need to turn to NuBodies?"

She thought it a gratuitous question. "Thankful, believe me," she replied. "And what do you do, Paul?" Even though Pat had called him an actor, she still wanted to hear him talk about himself. If only to get to know him better. If only because she was quickly discovering that his voice was just as hypnotizing as his eyes.

"Act," he confirmed. He found a pack of cigarettes in the front pocket of his snug-fitting cowboy shirt. When he offered her one, she shook her head.

"It must be very . . . exciting." *What the hell am I supposed to say when I'm acting like a schoolgirl; I can't even keep my eyes off him he's so—*

"Not always. It's hard getting work, specially out here when everyone's so oriented to TV. Live theater's a dying medium. And as for serious drama, forget it. People aren't interested. They want to go to a show and be entertained mindlessly. No one wants to sit through a play that'll make them feel."

"What?"

"Uncomfortable," he said and winked at her, as if he

were letting her in on some kind of trade secret. "Emotions is what I'm really saying."

"Yes, I gathered that." She smiled and moved a bracelet around on her wrist so the clasp didn't show. "But you want to act in that kind of play, am I right?"

"Sure," he said, one hand running through thick raven-black hair, the other flicking cigarette ash into the nearest empty beer can.

"My goodness, what is going on here, a regular tête-à-tête?" Casey said, his sandals flapping. Back across the room after welcoming the latest arrivals, he struck a pose she'd seen him use on television countless times before. Even if his material seemed to be getting a little tired, the latest *Variety* poll had listed him number seven in its survey of the popularity of more than fifty other comics, male as well as female.

"Pat, you'll embarrass me." There was a trace of something in his voice she couldn't pin down or define. Alarm maybe, she thought. But what for? What's he getting so nervous about all of a sudden that he's straining like he's giving a bad performance.

"It's good for the skin color, darlin'. You look a trifle peaked." He turned to Paul Antonio and widened his eyes like Eddie Cantor. "She has a fabulous and I mean *fabulous* suite at the Bel Air Hotel. I mean, when this kid comes out here she doesn't play games. So you'd think she'd at least take advantage of the sun, the pool, our gorgeous California weather . . . not to mention our inimitable life style. No way."

"I just got in this morning," she protested, knowing it was a mistake to take him seriously.

"That's no excuse. But I expect to see you out there tomorrow, bright and early, taking in those rays by the handful." He glanced over his shoulder and then back at her. "By the way, I want you to meet Loretta Wyckoff, New York's answer to Sue Mengers." Before she had a chance to turn around, he added in a whisper, "She can be very helpful."

With what? There was no time to go into it.

She didn't know who Sue Mengers was and, too embarrassed to ask, she turned to one side and shook the woman's outstretched hand. Immediately she noticed the mole on her left cheek. Something her mother's mother had said when she was a little girl, suddenly came back to her. *In Russia they know about these things. A mole like that, on the left cheek especially, means no good. It means she's going to have an unhappy life. Now you, Cynthia, knock wood, don't have a mark on your body.* Then she blew between her fingers to ward off the evil eye. If those weren't the exact words, they came pretty close. After all, it was more than thirty years ago.

Bangle bracelets sounded a fanfare. "Don't tell me how much I could use NuBodies," announced the stout peroxide blonde. The words were accompanied by a muffled and horsy laugh. "I'm on an ice-milk diet and it suits me fine."

"I didn't say a word," Cynthia replied. She forced herself to smile and tried to project, to be charming the way she knew she could. But she didn't want to discuss Russian superstitions or offer to recommend a good plastic surgeon. She didn't like New York's answer to Sue Pinkus or whatever her name was. At the first opportunity she managed to turn away. *Help like that I can do without,* she thought to herself. *Years ago I had to deal with another Loretta too, if I remember. A job interviewer. They're both far from being prizes, that's for sure.* When she looked up from her drink, Paul Antonio still stood nearby, posed like a piece of statuary.

He leaned over so far she thought he would lose his balance and fall into her arms. Not that she would've minded, but still . . . there was such a thing as propriety, one of many rules of thumb Lena had laid down, drumming into her ever since she was old enough to understand. Nevertheless, she remained motionless as one hand reached for a red curl and lifted it up off her ear. He leaned still closer and told her she used too much hairspray.

She was disappointed. "Occupational hazard," she said, not even knowing what she was talking about.

"What occupation and what hazard?" he whispered, warm breath fanning against her ear, the side of her neck.

"It's a good question." She tried not to shiver. The disappointment was gone so quickly she scarcely remembered it at all. "But give me time and I'll come up with a suitable answer, I swear." *Why swear; why not promise? For God sakes, act your age, Cynthia!*

"I have all the time in the world."

Either I'm imagining all this or it's really taking place.

405

What is he saying and, better yet, what is he doing to me and what am I doing to myself, that I can't even think straight? So she laughed. It seemed to cover a multitude of sins she was trying her best not to think about.

He edged back, flexing his muscles. She wondered if he was doing it on purpose, forcing her eye to first notice and then admire his physique. Paul then looked beyond her, to some point and some person or persons on the opposite side of the crowded living room. "Barbie and Ken," he said, nearly spitting out the words. For the first time since they'd been talking, his face turned ugly, contemptuous.

Everything went sour. She finished her drink, but held onto the glass. "Barbie and Ken what?"

"Barbie and Ken, those two sexless dolls. That's California in a nutshell, a state filled with handsome plastic people. Androids. Mannequins. Don't move out here, whatever you do. It ends up destroying people, killing them. You get caught up in looking pretty and tanned and relaxing the way everyone else is relaxing and living high off the hog which usually means way above your means. Pretty soon that's all you're doing, just lying about wasting your time. Your life too, I guess."

"Aren't we bitter at twenty-six?" She glanced over her shoulder. No one seemed even vaguely inhuman, puppet-like. They were all getting too drunk and too sloppy to be stiff-limbed, smoking marijuana also because it was a smell she knew she'd never be able to forget.

"Closer to twenty-nine, but yes we are. Do you want another drink?" He took her glass even before she had a chance to make up her mind.

"Gin and tonic."

Left alone, she thought it would be a perfect time to either involve herself in another conversation and thus beat a hasty retreat, or else stand there and watch like someone in an audience for a show that's selling SRO. At the top of the steps, leaning dangerously against a wrought-iron railing that seemed destined to come loose as it marked off the sunken living room from the foyer and adjoining den, Gene Burr waved one hand about in violent and opinionated self-assurance. She was certain of this just by the expression on his face. The multitude of deep-set lines made her think of a clay bust upon which someone had jabbed unfriendly, unkind fingers, far too deep. There were three crooked lines across his forehead, one on each side of his mouth and, amazingly enough, several making tracks and valleys down his cheeks. He was talking to that Wyckoff woman. Back-lighted, her dark roots were now clearly visible and just as clearly in abundance. Cynthia heard her snorting, "Oh Gene, Gene come on now, you know it's not my fault. He's not good enough and that's all there is to it. I can't waste my time being a mother *and* an agent."

She moved closer, intrigued by what was going on.

A door slammed farther down the hall. Justin Rodell . . . yes, that was his name, she remembered, stepped out of what she supposed was the bathroom, the top two buttons of his shirt undone. "You want a drink, Burr?" he asked, ignoring Loretta Wyckoff completely, as though she were invisible.

"Why not," the manager said. "How're ya doin', Loretta?"

"Deliciously."

No love lost between those two, she thought. Well I don't blame the kid. She looks like a bitch on wheels.

"I couldn't find lime. I hope lemon'll do," Paul said, tapping her on the shoulder.

She turned around, feeling guilty at having been caught spying. But no, I was just eavesdropping. There's a difference. "Thank you. But what you said before sounded very depressing, self-defeating almost."

"Well let's forget it then. Having a good time?"

"Trying to."

"What say we grab a drink at your hotel? To tell you the truth, I'd just like to sit down someplace quiet and talk to someone who isn't always *on*, putting on a show."

"So early?" the *yes*, the affirmation, as yet unspoken.

"It's after ten."

"Give me ten minutes to say good-bye and bow out gracefully, okay?" thinking, It's done, simple as pie.

"Fine. I'll wait for you outside. Do you need a lift? I have my car."

"Well, if you're driving—could you do me a favor and call the hotel? Ask them to page Mrs. Morgan's driver. He said he'd be in the bar or the lobby. Tell him not to bother to pick me up."

"What time you want him there tomorrow?"

"My, you think of everything," and she made a show of

407

laughing. "Ten-thirty—eleven. That should be early enough. I have a big reception to do in the afternoon, but most of the morning I'm free.

"It's all taken care of," he said and turned away.

The way everyone works out here like they're all taking speed pills or something, but why not. After all, it's a kind of vacation for me, isn't it? I mean, why shouldn't I have a good time, accept a date from an eligible bachelor. So stop asking yourself questions and start enjoying yourself.

"I was serious about lunch," Gene Burr said, appearing before her in the spot Antonio had just vacated.

"Then lunch it is." She was happy now. Two drinks and she was dangling over the edge, doubly pleased with herself because the best looking man at the party had paid her the ultimate of compliments, having asked her to join him in another five minutes.

"How's tomorrow sound? I know a place that's so *you* it's to die over."

Everyone has a line. "I have a reception to attend at the Century Plaza. But if you can make it early, like not much later than twelve, I'd love to have lunch with you."

"I'll pick you up at ten to."

"Lovely. I'm looking forward to it."

"There'll be lots to talk about," he said. He patted her arm and turned away.

All of a sudden I'm a hot property. Who would've thunk it—good ole Cynthia Margold of Brooklyn having drinks with the stars. And half of me is taking it seriously, too—that's the real joke. Wait'll Lena hears.

She put down her glass, tasted lemon on her tongue, and went to make her goodbyes.

There was some difficulty with the management.

"I don't make the rules, the manager does. And when he says a gentleman must have a coat and tie, it's his word against mine."

"In 1972? In California? You must be kidding. I'm Mrs. Morgan, of NuBodies." She bent over the bar, one hand pinning Paul down to the stool he was about to relinquish. She lowered her voice, thinking that whatever was going to be said was just between her and the bartender. "I am paying over a hundred and fifty dollars a day for my suite and if I want to entertain a guest, I am not going to be embarrassed in public by ridiculous antiquated rules. Put us in a dark corner and if the manager gives you any grief, blame it on me because I really don't care. You're charging me through the nose, an arm and a leg as it is."

"Okay, Mrs. Morgan," the bartender said. He dropped his eyes with a pained, cringing look. "I'll send a waiter over in a minute." His very manner—suddenly obsequious, subservient—seemed to imply an impulse to lose himself, to disappear under the bar and not be seen again. Or at least for the rest of the evening.

"Thank you." *You have to open up a mouth, kiddo, D. W. said. Otherwise people'll try to step all over you. It's the law of the jungle. It's only natural.* And to Paul, "Unbelievable, the way people around here try to intimidate you; it's a disgrace. Come, we'll sit over there." She motioned to the proverbial dark corner. "I was ready to take *his* tie off in another second, he got me so angry."

"It's always been considered a stuffy hotel," he said. "But it's not worth getting upset about."

"Who said anything about upset? Do I look upset? Not me. He just has a helluva nerve and he didn't use his head, that's all. In my book, the customer is always right, no matter what." He followed her across the room, pulled out a chair and waited until she had sat down before joining her. "So," she said and took him up on the offer of a cigarette.

The waiter came as promptly as the bartender had promised. "I'll have a brandy, Benedictine on the rocks. Paul?"

"The same," he said with a nod of his head. He placed the ashtray between them.

"So," she said again. Here we are. Now what?

He looked at her, searching her face. For what, she was yet to figure out, to understand. It went beyond the moment, the possible outcome of the evening. *Come-hither* seemed pale in comparison. "Is it really true you used to weigh two hundred fifty pounds, or is that just something a publicity man cooked up for the public?"

"Publicity man? For the public?"

"You really did weigh that much?" he said, surprise flashing in his eyes.

"More than that," she said. "I don't know who told you it's a gag because it isn't. I was a hippo, plain talk."

409

"And now you're a gazelle."

"Not quite."

"Oh, you're doing pretty okay, Cynthia, rest assured." When their drinks arrived he raised his glass and toasted her, saying, "Why should a woman want to be thin unless she is thin? The ideal of female beauty that all great men, from Julius Caesar to myself, have held, is much more like a barrel than a clothespole. Thank you, Mr. Dooley."

"Mr. who?" she said, the thick amber liquid warm and syrupy as it slid down her throat.

"Mr. Dooley. Don't ask me who he is or was because I honestly don't know. But when Pat told me he was giving you a party, I made sure to do my homework, thanks to *Bartlett's Quotations*. Here's another one that grabbed me." He made a point of clearing his throat, apropos a dramatic reading. "That which is everybody's business is NuBodies' business."

"That's fabulous." She stared openly now, a talent scout at an audition.

"Wait, one more, just for the road." And he launched into a florid rendition of, "Choose a firm cloud before it fall, and in it catch, ere she change, the Cynthia of this minute."

She clapped her hands like a little girl. "You're making it up, aren't you?"

"Would I do something nasty like that to you, Cynthia NuBody? Alexander Pope wrote it, but don't ask me what it means because I'm yet to figure it out."

"The Cynthia of the minute," she repeated. Her face brightened. "It means the moon, the fleeting moon."

"Really? I never knew."

"It does, honestly. A very crazy young man told me that. Years ago . . . well, not that long ago, but long enough."

"Is he still crazy?"

"Worse than ever. But did you really look up all those sayings, quotations, just for me?"

"You're fishing for a compliment," he said. He bent forward from the waist, leaning toward her with such sudden urgency it looked like he was about to scramble over the table to reach her side. Both hands captured her wrists and held them steady. "You are a very amazing woman, do you know that? A very beautiful woman, too. Not pretty. No, that would make your features

410

flabby, ordinary. You're too strong-minded, independent to be just good-looking, attractive. What I mean is, your face has strength in it; it's the character that gives it the beauty." He let go of her. "There, now I've blown the whole thing out the window and made a perfect ass of myself."

"You have not," she said. "Don't think that, not for a minute. Just . . . thank you, Paul. That's very kind. I'm very," and she stopped long enough to smile, to moisten her lips with the tip of her tongue. "Well, here we go again because the only thing I can think of saying is that I'm very flattered."

"There's nothing the matter with that. Or this." His lips parted and the tip of his slim pink tongue waved into view. Then he leaned back in his chair and began to laugh, both hands wrapped around his chest like a tourniquet.

She giggled. "If I wasn't well on my way to being honest-to-God fresh, I mean drunk . . . see? I blew it, same as you."

"But I'm not fresh. Just . . . arousing."

"Enticing's a better word but you know it too, don't you."

He nodded his head and continued to grin. "It's one of my many gifts," he said. "And now you know how true it is, which is even more important."

"I don't know yet."

"You will," he said, about as confident and self-assured and salacious a person as she had ever come across. "But you know what else? Ever since I moved out here I've wanted to see the inside of one of the Bel Air bungalows. I hear they're really something." He got up from his seat and made a great display of adjusting and centering his oversized metal belt buckle. Without waiting for her to reply, he said, "So how about giving me the grand tour, Mrs. Morgan?"

"Cynthia."

He waited outside while she paid the bill, making sure to tip the bartender for being so cooperative.

He lay nestled against her, one spoon fitting perfectly into another, a thin trickle of saliva wetting the freckled curve of her shoulder. Cynthia's eyes were open but she didn't move. Through the slats of the blinds the morning came back to her in narrow rectangular ingots, shapes not unlike the bars of lapis she had bought for Leonard Frankel's birthday. A shifting patchwork of green leaves continued to form and re-form. No shafts of golden sunlight, no dusty sunmotes, spilled into the bedroom like she had read in so many novels of romance and heartbreak. The day looked gray and brooding, and she knew that when Pat Casey got out of his "bed of pain," as he once had called it, he would not be pleased to note that all his predictions about the glorious California weather had come to nothing, unanswered and unfulfilled. Puppy warm as he snuggled against her, the bony caps of two knees fitting into the backs of her legs, one arm thrown haphazardly around her waist like an anchor, Paul Antonio continued to sleep. She wondered if he was dreaming, what form his fantasies were taking. Was I drunk or what? she asked herself. No, not that drunk. I knew what I was doing, what was going on. I wanted it to happen, probably more than he did. It had been so long—*ages*, in fact— since she had felt anything remotely akin to fulfillment, sexual pleasure, physical gratification, that now a touch of sadness intruded upon her thoughts. It was as if all the barren years had been wasted, as if she had given up part of herself to claim another part, the bitch goddess. *That's success, baby, D. W. said. You can't have your cake and eat it, too. Manny told me the same thing. Is it that all men are alike, ultimately? she asked. Nope, it's just that he's probably not stupid, that's all. You busted your ass getting where you are, so of course certain things got left behind, put in abeyance. But only temporarily, remember that. She said, I'll try.*

He lay nestled against her, permanently fixed, attached. *No one ever did those things to me before. And he said, There's always a first time, specially if you want to catch the Cynthia of the minute.* Or am I just acting like a complete and total ass, forgetting the fact that I'm forty-two years old . . . an older woman. Are people gonna look at me now and cluck their tongues and say, Look what's happened to our Cynthia, Chubby Margold. Look how she can't control her urges like a regular you-know-what so don't say it; it's an ugly word and I'm hopelessly middle-class. All of Lena and Jack's values just can't be dislodged. And will they say, Look how she has to go and take herself a young lover. Shameful, shocking . . . but who said

412

anything about take? Or lover? It just happened like all things just happen. No plans have been made; God knows it's only a . . . one-night stand, or is it?

She didn't know, and she didn't want to think about it any longer.

What had been good, what had made her feel passionate, alive again, animalistic, she clung to as she once clung to scraps of half-remembered dreams of slimness, small bones, no appetite. Waking up on hundreds of mornings-after, she recalled how she would refuse to pull the covers back, still seeing in her dream's eye a vision of Cynthia that was lithe, trim, graceful. A size seven. Then reality intruded, again and again. "Breakfast's on the table, sweetheart," Lena would shout from the kitchen. "Poppa left for work already and you'll be late for school, darling." Or later Manny shaking the same fantasies out of her system, the sad recollection of days now lost forever, saying, "How about a hot breakfast for your hard-working hubby?" Or later still, she was the one who did the shaking. "Barry, time to get up. Natalie honey, I made a gorgeous breakfast, eggs and everything." Everything. Now she lay with the single sheet drawn up tight and modest around her neck, unwilling to move, to give up the pleasure of remembering.

Behind her, a yawn like the hesitant growl of a bear cub. A teddy bear, she thought, but hard as a rock. Every muscle works, the whole thing so perfectly constructed, put together, it made her shiver just to look at him. But sweet Jesus what's the matter with feeling lust, for a change. His lips chewed at the back of her neck, slid down to momentarily savage her bare shoulder.

"G'mornin', moon lady," he whispered, his tongue stabbing down to flick in and out of her ear.

Trembling, she wiggled back, turned over onto her other side. She kissed the half-drawn shutters of his eyes, windows leading back into herself, to places she'd nearly forgotten she'd ever visited. Not since Manny and I were first married, she decided. Not since Leonard and I claimed the Holiday Inn for our very own, and she watched him as he yawned and opened his eyes wide. Thin straight lips slid back to reveal two rows of perfectly aligned white teeth. He smiled, kissed her on the tip of her nose.

"How're ya doin'?" he said. "You're doin' another number on yourself," he said, "I can tell."

"How can you tell?" She moved one hand back and forth across his chest, memorizing him all over again.

"I read you loud and clear," and grinned again. Then, with an Indian war cry, some kind of boyish whoop last heard when it was common practice for her to stick her head out the bedroom window and throw Barry nickels and dimes wrapped in paper napkins for the Good Humor man and all the kids on the block were screaming and playing tag or stickball or ringalevio or whatever it was they used to play, he threw himself down on top of her. And picked up where he'd left off the night before.

"I'm gonna be late," she said later, trying to make herself heard as she stood under the shower. The needle spray stung and prickled. She leaned against the side of the tiled stall and let the hot water come down with full force.

"When's he picking you up?" Paul asked. Stationed on the other side of the sliding glass door, she could see his silhouette moving in front of the sink and medicine cabinet.

"Aren't you glad I had a razor?"

"It helps."

"What time is it now?"

"Eleven-thirty."

"Christ, I knew it was late." She turned the single control knob from hot to cold, gave a little cry of pleasure, and then turned the faucet off completely. "Can you hand me the towel, love." How easy it is, natural, she marveled. He pushed back the glass panel and passed the towel across the wet threshold, eyes averted as if to respect her modesty.

"Want me to dry your back? I'm a regular whiz."

"No thanks. I'm managing." Have for years.

"Should I order a pot of coffee?"

"If you like."

After she'd made up her face and put on a dress, she found him lounging on the couch in the living room of the stucco bungalow. He nodded his head, admiringly she hoped. "Very classy. You're doin' okay for yourself, Mrs. M."

"God knows it's taken just about forever," she said, smiling. "So what are your plans for the day, Mr. Antonio?"

"Well," he drawled, "I thought I'd rustle me up some
414

breakfast and then head back to my grungy little hole and catch a little more shut-eye."

"Tired?"

"Kind of."

"Don't you have work to do?" She was genuinely surprised.

"Wish I did. Last week I went to my last class."

"Why your last?"

"Ran out of bread, simple as that. No *dinero,* no *dramática.* But seriously, drama coaches out here—everywhere, I guess—don't take Master Charge. And they don't give credit or believe in deferred payments, either."

"I wouldn't think so," she said. "But how do you pay the rent?" Maybe I shouldn't have asked but it's too late now.

"Oh, I scrounge up a little here and a little there. We manage. Paul survives . . . not in the style of a prince, the style he'd like to be accustomed to, but he manages."

"Well, let me at least pay you something for the gas," she said without thinking twice.

"What gas?"

"Last night, when you drove me back here."

"Come on, Cynthia, don't be silly. It was nothing."

"That's what you think." In the bedroom, she found her Gucci shoulder bag with its identifying double G's and red and green stripe, where she'd left it on top of the dresser. Inside there was a matching wallet. She removed a wrinkled dollar and a crisp twenty, covered the larger bill with the smaller, and returned to the living room.

"Thanks," he said, pocketing both bills without a second glance. "What are your plans for the evening?"

"I'll be busy until tenish. Why, want to take me on a tour of the town?"

"I thought we'd have dinner."

"Marvelous. How does Chasen's grab you?" picking the first restaurant that came to mind, a popular—and expensive—meeting place for movie and television executives.

"I hate to put on a tie if I can help it," he said. He got to his feet. "Why don't you meet me at Cyrano's. It's very informal, intimate."

"How do I get there?"

"Tell your driver to get on Sunset. It's right off Sunset

Plaza Drive." He stepped closer; both hands reached out to press against her shoulders.

"Lovely." She bit down on her lower lip. Aren't you ashamed of yourself? No, no I'm not. Absolutely.

He licked her lips with what she'd already discovered was an amazingly prehensile tongue, then fitted his mouth into place, lips against lips. She clung to him, a moment of suspended animation that made her think of a cartoon character who, after having raced off a cliff, continues to walk through the thinnest of air. When he finally let go, she heard the ringing of the house phone, and she felt dazed.

"See you at ten," he said. The door closed with a click. She picked up the phone.

"I'm ready when you are, doll," Gene Burr said, overly familiar.

"I'll be right out. I'm just putting on my makeup." She wondered if he'd bump into Paul. But even if he does, she thought, it's none of his business, anyway.

There was no doubt she enjoyed being catered to. Burr's yellow XKE zipped through downtown traffic and when they reached an area below the Strip, a section of town where antique shops vied for business one right after another, he found a parking spot right on San Vincente and led her across the street to a narrow and cobblestoned alley. Above the two rusty iron gates, thrown back in a position of permanent welcome, she read the flowery hand-printed script. The Green Café.

"I told you it's so you it's to faint over," Burr said.

He was on intimate terms with the manager, made a great show of knowing several of the waiters and the woman tending bar and, no doubt as a direct result, got them a table she decided was choice. From where she sat everyone coming in could see her. Likewise, she could see just about everyone dining in the outdoor garden, an eclectic space built around two trees and dozens of flowering shrubs.

"Now *this* is California," he said, ordering them a liter of white wine. "So," and he put his hands on the table as if that were more than enough to let her know he was going to be honest, forthright, no managerial bullshit whatsoever. "When are you moving out?"

416

"I just got here," she said.

"That's why I'm asking. I can tell it's in your blood . . . now don't tell me I'm wrong. Wait and see. You're so California, Cynthia, it's just not to be believed."

"I always thought I was so Brooklyn it was just not to be believed."

"Where?"

Her silence let it go at that.

For lunch they had cold salmon and a fresh green salad. "Don't tell me you've ever tasted a salad like this before, because if you say yes I'll know you're pulling my leg. Everything tastes better out here, fresher."

"The salad is delicious," she said. "How long have you made L.A. your home?"

"When Pat moved out, I moved out. I used to have a two-bedroom down by the U.N. Great apartment and the rent was nothing, a steal. One of those canopied rent-controlled jobs. But now that I'm here, I don't know how I stayed in New York for as long as I did."

Then he launched into what first struck her as a snow job and then, gradually and by degrees, increments of persuasion made her wonder if he really did have a point. "Pots of money," he repeated at intervals, telling her that if she thought she'd already made her fortune, all she had to do was turn to television to realize her judgments were premature, that she was selling herself short, "before you've even hit your prime." He visualized a daily half-hour show in a morning time slot, say between nine and ten-thirty. "Not just weight control. Of course, that'll be the biggest draw. But you can really go much farther than that, Cynthia. You'll have guests talking about every kind of topic imaginable, so long as it's of interest to women. If Barbara Walters can do it, there's no reason in the world, no sane reason I can think of, why you can't. And better, besides."

"Who's going to put me on television?" she said. "I don't even have . . . what is it called in this business? A track record?"

"There's where you're wrong. Again. You have one of the all-time great track records because you're already established. You're a known product. The networks'll know what they're buying, beforehand. You sell magazines. You sell soda pop. You sell thin to millions of people. Do you know that if some smart Seventh Avenue

417

designer, some shrewd merchandiser, came out with a line called," and he waved his hand to pluck an answer from the air, "The NuBody Collection or whatever, the public would go apeshit. Don't make a face because this is my business. That's why I'm a successful manager, one of the best out here, if you don't mind my saying so. You know, Pat isn't my only client. Who do you think won the Tony last year for best supporting actress in a musical?"

"I forget."

"Well, she's mine . . . I mean, I'm her manager. And what about the Bette Davis of the West End? London, I mean. You know who I'm referring to, don't you? Well, she's been with me ten years now and they're selling out over there, now that she's got the starring role in the new Williams play. So you see, doll, I'm not talking out of the side of my mouth or off the top of my head. And when I tell you, when I make a statement to the effect that you could make a fortune, pots of money, with your own TV series, I'm not bullshitting or feeding your ego because what for? What good would it do me?"

"How much does a personal manager get?" she asked, edging back in her chair so the waiter could pour her coffee.

"Twelve-and-a-half percent," he said promptly. "And that's standard and it's peanuts, besides. When you're raking in ten, fifteen, twenty thousand a week and believe me it's a very definite possibility, a percentage like that means crap. Get the picture?"

"The big picture," she laughed. She drew a square in the air with one polished fingernail, the four sides forming an invisible frame around her face.

"You're not kidding, the big picture," he said. "So think about it, Cynthia."

"I'm thinking about it now," she admitted, "and it sounds very lovely, very exciting. Of course I'd love to be on television, five days a week. I love talking and I love meeting people and I love the attention, you know that. Or if you don't, now you do. But how would you go about setting it all up?"

"Now we're talking," he said. He hunched over, both elbows flat against the edge of the table, oblivious to everything else. "The first thing I do is convince—negotiate's a better way of putting it, because no one but no one likes to be strong-armed—one of the studios to underwrite the cost of a pilot. That's for starters. That's gonna run anywheres from a hundred to maybe even a hundred and fifty thou. When we've cleared that hurdle, we can start worrying about the next step."

"Which would be?"

"Selling the pilot to one of the networks. But knowing you the way I think I do, doll, you're a natural. I can't put it any other way. You were made for television, Cynthia, so it's high time you got wise and took advantage of your talents instead of sitting on them, nipping them in the bud. And on top of everything else, NuBodies is bound to make a fortune if you're on the tube five days a week."

"That part I can see," she said. Behind her, along the margin of her thoughts, she heard someone say, "Now the weather that you find on the other side of a low pressure area is even more intriguing." She glanced back, as intrigued as the weather pattern. Two men, meteorologists she supposed, were bent over in heated conversation, mapping something out on a shredded paper napkin. It seemed so out of place with the general tenor of the restaurant—everyone else working very hard at laughing too loudly or else appearing fashionably bored and unconcerned, that she couldn't help but smile. They obviously love their work, which is something I have more respect for than just about anything else, she thought.

"Well?" Burr said.

Close up, in the strong natural light, the wrinkles on his face were even deeper than she'd first imagined. "Do it."

"You're serious now?"

"Of course I'm serious. If you think it's possible, then do it. Start the negotiations."

"I'll have my secretary mail out a contract first thing this afternoon."

"What contract?"

"Standard manager-client form, that's all. It's merely to protect you and to protect me. When everything's aboveboard, on paper that is, no one gets hurt."

"Fine."

"More coffee," the waiter asked. "How are you doing, Mr. Burr?"

"Couldn't be better, Tony. Cynthia, more coffee?"

"No thanks, I'm fine," she said. There was so much

going on inside her head she didn't need the extra caffeine to buoy her up or give her energy. A TV show and an autobiography coming out and don't forget we've got people working on a new line of frozen foods, everything prepared beforehand, just heat and eat. And Paul. Or am I jumping the gun I don't even know what I want half the time. She refused to dwell on it. "What did you say I was in?" she asked.

"When?" He looked confused.

"Before. Something about selling myself short."

"Before you've even hit your prime."

"That's it," she said.

"Move over, Jean Brodie," Burr said.

"I never saw the film."

"That's all right. You'll be watching yourself on TV soon enough."

"You're really sure of that, aren't you?"

"What do we have to lose? It doesn't cost anything to sit down and talk to people, does it?"

"No."

"Then stop worrying."

"I'm not worrying," she said.

"You're going to be one of the biggest names in daytime TV. Mark my words."

It came back to her. "I've used the line before," she said, "but I still think it stands up."

"And what line is that, doll?" friendlier than ever.

She smiled to herself. The *doll* went along with the flashy XKE and today's god-awful gold bracelet he wore on one hairy wrist. It went along with giving snappy lines, being a theatrical manager, making wonderful promises, and having one's secretary send out contracts at the drop of a hat. I learn something new every day, she thought. But at the same time, she chose to end the lunch by saying something old, something she'd learned long ago. "From your mouth to God's ears."

He laughed and she was pleased to note his teeth weren't capped. "I'll have to remember that, write it down."

"Do," doll.

The reception at the Century Plaza went off without a hitch. She warned the new franchise owners, their lecturers as well, to follow the rules and regulations laid down by the home office, to give people their money's worth in every way imaginable. "Morale is the most important thing you have going for you," she said. "If you show that you're losing heart, your members'll have no use for you, no matter how workable the diet happens to be. And since we're all here this afternoon because we believe in the NuBodies way, I don't think I can stress this point enough. NuBodies works. It's safe; it's sound; it's medically approved. Your job will be to help our overweight members conquer their particular fears, food fetishes, stumbling blocks, whatever. Encourage them to talk freely and at every opportunity. Remember, this isn't a lark, ladies and gentlemen. And we're not running a factory, either. You're dealing with people, very sensitive people at that. I don't want you ever to forget it, and I don't want to ever receive a letter when I'm back in New York, stating that so-and-so hasn't been helpful, constructive. Think of yourselves as teachers. And act accordingly."

The applause was tempered, if only because her closing remarks had been spoken with an edge of severity. She didn't mean to lecture, but it was important—vital for the well-being of the corporation—to establish guidelines from the start. There'd been incidents in the past, incidents she didn't want to see repeated if she could help it. NuBodies was providing a valuable service to the public and this was the crux of what she had tried to tell her audience, to drum into their heads and hearts.

It didn't take very long, not much more than ten or fifteen minutes, to get from the reception at the hotel to Cyrano's. All along Sunset Boulevard neon lights flashed like beacons, marking the way into topless bars, massage parlors, storefronts serving up XXX-rated films. She glanced at her watch, hoping it was fast. "Do you have the correct time, Luis?"

The driver glanced back, meeting her eyes. "Eleven o'clock, Mrs. Morgan."

"Shit," she said under her breath. I knew I should have left earlier but it was next to impossible. They all came to see me so how could I have bowed out without looking bored or rude. Well, he's probably sitting at the bar, anyway. Tight, and I don't blame him either.

Luis waited for her outside the restaurant as she passed from the narrow outdoor terrace into the first of two dark and spacious rooms. It was sizable but intimate, probably the result of candlelight, dense shadows, and private booths. The bar was a long line of swivel stools and slouched-over figures in the second room. She walked quickly down the length of the bar until she reached the service area. "Has a Mr. Antonio been in?" she asked the bartender.

"Paul's come and gone."

"Did he leave a message or anything?"

"Nope, can't say that he did."

Goddamnit, couldn't wait a half-hour for me. I said tenish, not ten o'clock right on the dot.

"Drop me off at the hotel, will you, Luis," she said as soon as she got outside again.

Stop getting overwrought. It's for the best, right? No, it isn't right, absolutely not. I wanted to see him. I don't care if he's starving or ten years younger than me, more even. I just wanted to see him and have dinner and talk and relax and look at him. And know that he was looking at me.

The bungalow's pink stucco façade was ruby red in the dim light. She let herself in, locked the door behind her, and felt hunger rearing up like a dragon awakening from years of hibernation, inactivity. Unlike St. George, there was no way to slay it. I could always order in a sandwich, a nice bacon, lettuce, and tomato. She flicked on the overhead light—too bright. She switched to a lamp alongside the couch. Then, after kicking off her shoes, she listened to her stockings whispering the way into the bedroom.

"What took you so long, moon lady?" Propped up against the pillows, the sheet tucked neatly around his trim and athletic waist, Paul Antonio looked at her and winked. He snapped shut a copy of this month's issue of *NuBodies*. "Don't tell me that wounded look means you thought I'd just given you the ole shafteroo, the old heave-ho."

"No," she said. "There won't be any more disappointments. I've had more than my share. And like they say, enough is enough. Right?"

"Absolutely. So trust me."

"I am," she said. "That's just what I intend to do."

"What?"
"Trust you," she said.
"Now you're talkin', Mrs. M."
I hope so.

February 1972

"OF COURSE I WANT TO MEET HER. She's your daughter, isn't she? And you're not going to start telling me you're embarrassed to be seen with a handsome stud like yours truly."

"You always put things so . . . tastefully," she said. She put down her comb and brush. "Then come with me, if that's what you want. Of course I'm not embarrassed. What do I have to be embarrassed about, anyway? I'm not doing anything I shouldn't."

"That's what I like to hear, Morgan," Paul said.

She left the room key at the front desk, and Paul held the door open for her. Outside, State Street was still trying to forget about last week's blizzard. Perfect timing, she thought, bracing herself for the cold. She'd brought along her fur coat, knowing beforehand that she was stopping in Madison before returning to New York. Paul's wardrobe conspicuously lacked winter wear. The problem was solved easily enough. After they checked into the Badger Inn, off State Street, she helped him select a forest-green loden coat at Redwood & Ross, right next door to the motel. And woolen socks. And a Pendleton shirt. "And a pair of gloves, don't forget."

Well what's the difference? It's either now or later because people must be freezing their tootsies off in New York.

"Thanks," he said. "But I can get away with my boots so don't hassle your head about galoshes. My feet are plenty warm, specially in bed at night."

She didn't want to stop and question herself for the umpteenth time. He was with her. She wanted him to be with her and he accepted the invitation and as far as she was concerned, that was that. *Why don't you come back with me to New York? I have a huge apartment. There's plenty of room, so there's no problem about getting on each other's nerves. You can have Barry's old room if you like and . . . well . . . we'll see if we can't get you enrolled in the Actors Studio or wherever you think is best. Uta Hagen, he said. But there's no sense sitting around L.A. and wasting your life, your talents I mean. At least this way, you'll be able to accomplish something, start going to auditions—Go-sees, he corrected.—Okay, go-sees. But you'll be doing something constructive with your time, Paul. Well, it's your decision. I don't mean to pressure you or force anybody. You want to come, I've extended the invitation. Now it's up to you.*

Cars were still buried in the knee-high snowdrifts. Students, heads hunched down and thus barely seen, trudged through the snow, books pressed up against the fronts of ski parks or loden coats similar to Paul's. The air was crisp as a fresh apple, rare and sharp as cider. Cynthia's breath swirled before her like pipesmoke, a thick little vaporous cloud that hung in front of her face as he took her arm and guided her down State Street. They sloshed past Brown's New & Used Books, the Kollege Klub, Ye Olde Pancake House, and Rennebohm's Pharmacy, heading in the direction of the Student Union.

"Why the fuck does your daughter want to bury herself up here? I'm freezing my tits off," he said.

"Don't ask me. I guess the farther away from Brooklyn she got, the better. And I told you to put on a muffler but you wouldn't listen, know-it-all. You're as bad as my kid."

"One thing, Cyn honey. No comparisons with Bar, okay? He's a boy and I is your *muy macho hombre*. Get the picture?"

She said, "I'm sorry," wondering why he was getting so sensitive all of a sudden. All I said was he should've put on a scarf so he wouldn't be cold.

When she'd spoken to Natalie the night before, her daughter had told her she'd be waiting at the Rathskeller in the Student Union, the Rat as it was popularly known. "I'll be sitting in the back, mother, near the windows which face Mendota."

"Face who?"

"Mendota, Lake Mendota," impatient as ever. "You can't miss it. Two o'clock okay for you?"

"Why so late, honey?"

"I have classes all morning and I just can't cut. Don't you have people to see up here? Daddy said you had some business in Madison."

"Your father made a mistake," she said. "The only business I have in Madison is with you. That's the only reason I'm here. To see you, Natalie."

"Two o'clock. I just can't make it any earlier. See you tomorrow."

They cut through the library, the marble floor a continuous slippery puddle of melted snow. Having never been on a college campus before, she couldn't help but marvel at everything she saw. The study rooms were crowded. Everywhere she turned students moved with a purposefulness that recalled New York pedestrians at the height of rush hour. None of them seemed to have a weight problem.

Outside the library, they crossed Langdon Street and hurried through the doors which led into the Student Union. She shivered and rubbed her hands together. I really must look like a mother, a tourist with this fur coat on but I didn't have anything else half as warm and it must be ten degrees out, maybe colder. "It goes through you like a knife," she said, her eyes searching out directions, a sign which would lead her directly to Natalie like a well-marked trail.

"You're telling me. Hot coffee, that's what I could use, in a big way."

"Me too."

An obliging student pointed out the way. She turned to the left, descended a single flight of wide marble stairs, and found herself at the entrance to the Rathskeller. It was a huge vault of a place, with a high groined ceiling, massive unfinished beams, and a three-sided wall of over-sized mullioned windows. Each was decorated with stained-glass shields through which the afternoon sunlight filtered, mottling the plank flooring with luminous hazy patches of red, green, and blue.

"You take it black, don't you?" Paul said.

"Yes. She said she'd be by the windows."

"You go look for her and I'll get us some coffee. Want a doughnut or something?"

She shook her head, stepped into the Rathskeller and
426

narrowed her eyes. Paul disappeared into the cafeteria at the right and she moved across the room, aware of the way her black mink coat was being carefully scrutinized. She heard something like, "endangered species," and wanted to say the skins were ranch-bred, but didn't.

Natalie sat beneath one of the stained-glass windows, her face buried in a thick, unwieldy-looking textbook. My daughter, the honor-roll student, she thought. It surprised her, because Natalie hadn't expressed much interest in schoolwork when she lived at home. When we *had* a home, she thought. She reached out, touched the girl on the shoulder. Natalie's head jerked up. Her dark and penetrating eyes took her in in a single well-defined glance. She pushed the wooden chair back and got to her feet.

"Long time no see," Natalie said as a hand swept back straight, reddish-brown hair, glossy and growing down to the small of her back.

"Too long," Cynthia said, unable to get her voice above a whisper, hushed and nearly reverent. "Just let me look at you, because I've dreamed of this moment for so long already and let me enjoy it. You look wonderful. You look so . . . so beautiful, happy, Natalie. I'm so very pleased, delighted for you." She stepped forward and pressed Natalie against her. The girl found her shoulders, squeezed them for just a moment, as if an embrace of any longer duration would be some kind of unspoken commitment, one she was unwilling to make. At least for now. When she let go, Cynthia stepped back again.

"So thin, I wouldn't have known it was the same Nat—"

"Fat Nat, remember?" smiling crookedly.

"Never. Natalie, Thin Natalie," she told her. "And your hair . . . everything in fact. You look fabulous. Fabulous."

An intruding voice said, "It tastes like the L.A. *Times* but still . . . well hello. You're Natalie, of course. I should've guessed, just by looking at your hair. Like mother like daughter. Great looking kid you've got there, Cyn."

"Paul Antonio, Natalie Margold," she said, trying to gloss over Paul's attitude, which she didn't appreciate.

"Not Morgan?" he asked.

"No," Natalie replied. "I've always liked things the way they were. Nice to meet you." Her eyes were suddenly restless, alert.

"Paul's a friend of mine from California," she explained, aware of the way they were both staring at each other, taking in the measure of each other's worth. She took a sip of the coffee Paul had given her. "It isn't bad, not *too* bitter."

"Witch's brew, they call it," Natalie said, looking down at her pile of books. "Puts hair on your chest, even if you don't want it to grow there."

"I'm gonna sneak around, give the place the once-over," Paul said, as though sensing her growing embarrassment, a feeling of discomfort she was reluctant, even unable, to put into words.

"There's a terrific art exhibit on the second floor," Natalie volunteered. "Six architectural canvases by John Day, one of Albers' pupils."

"Never heard of them," he said, his dark-green loden coat thrown open to reveal the partially unbuttoned front of his woolen shirt, a V-shaped wedge of tanned and muscular chest. "But I'll give it a look, anyway. Nice meeting you, Natalie." And to Cynthia, "Have a happy reunion, Mrs. M."

"A friend," she said, trying not to look distressed and thinking, Sure it would've been easier if he didn't come with me but it's too late now and how could I have done that to him, or to myself even. I can't live like it's a secret, like he's not my—

"A good friend, I gather," Natalie said, a smile Cynthia interpreted as sly, teasing its way across her lips.

She let it pass. One hand slipped into the side pocket of her coat. She pulled out the small box with its faded wrapping, its ribbon bow wilted and beyond repair, past caring too she imagined. "It's been sitting in my drawer for more than three years already," she explained as she handed the package to her daughter. "But I still wanted you to have it even . . . even if you think it's silly or I'm being sentimental which I guess I am, but I love you, Natalie. I've never stopped loving you. Or thinking about you, worrying what you were doing. Day after day."

"From my Sweet Sixteen?" turning the box over and over in both of her hands. "Jesus, wasn't that a trip, like ages ago."

"Like yesterday," she said.

"Thank you, mother. Like they say, it's the thought that counts, right?"

428

"Yes," she said.

"What is it, anyway? Can't be half as useful as splitting the bills with daddy, which I appreciate, even if I haven't gotten down on my hands and knees to kiss the ground you walk on. But I am grateful, mother."

"It's a charm bracelet, gold," she said.

"A charm bracelet! That's too funny. God, do people still wear things like that?"

"Some people do," she said.

"Do you want me to open it now? I mean, right this very minute?"

"Not if you don't want to, Natalie," she said.

"I'll save it for later then. The girls at the dorm'll pee in their pants. A charm bracelet, what a goof. Shades of Wingate High School, mascara, and lots of turquoise eye shadow. And shaving your legs, too. Oh, that's right. You weren't around to share in all those teenage trials and tribulations I went through. It's just as well, anyway. From what I gather, you had your hands full with my adorable big brother."

"I'd rather not talk about it," she said.

"That's cool."

Maybe there's a plane out early this evening, instead of tomorrow night, she thought. There was nothing else to say, except to show an interest in Natalie's studies. "What are you majoring in?" she asked.

"Sociology."

"How unusual. What does it entail, exactly?"

"A sociologist is a person who studies the reasons why mothers desert their children, for example."

"Marvelous, then you'll be able to apply all your own firsthand information," she said. She got to her feet, maintaining her balance and poise and even a brave little grin, on top of everything else. "Where did you say that art exhibit was being held?"

"On the second floor."

"I think I'd like to give it a look-see before I go. Will you be able to have dinner with me tonight?"

"I'd love to have dinner with the two of you of course, but I'm afraid I can't. I have to book it for a big exam tomorrow. So please tell your friend it was nice meeting him."

"Well, good luck," she said. She shivered, even though

the Rat was quite well-heated. "Drop me a line now and then. Tell me how you're doing. Your studies, I mean."

"I will."

"Good."

SANDWICHED BETWEEN EVERYTHING ELSE, meaning the company and Paul and lectures and Paul and guest appearances and D. W.'s ego and Leonard's cryptic remarks which, in their increasing frequency, seemed to go nowhere yet hint at things she was afraid to hear, Cynthia once again had to contend with Barry. He was still Margold, not Morgan, and he was still, "a giant pain, the likes of which you can't even begin to imagine that's how impossible he's become." Only this time, less than two weeks after returning from California, Wisconsin, and all points west, "He got himself into *more* hot water than you can possibly believe," she told her mother. They sat opposite each other, facing overstuffed deli sandwiches and a bucket of sour pickles and green garlic tomatoes, at the original and still popular Wolfie's on Collins Avenue. "Hot water to the tune of—and I don't mean to alarm you—a broken leg and a fractured rib."

Lena's tongue clucked like a Teletype.

"That's right, an accident, *another one,* in that sports car that idiot me had to go, had to run to buy him. And his friend got hurt, too. A concussion and a multiple fracture in his right arm. Getting himself into trouble isn't enough for him. He has to go and involve someone else."

"The two of them?" and her tongue went at it all over again.

"If it wasn't so familiar, so old hat, I think I'd be even more upset. But it just gets worse and worse, or whatever the word is for a brat who's not only spoiled—and it's my fault, I agree—but fresh. Such language, the likes of which you've never heard before, I don't even know where he picked it up except in the gutter. So if it's not too much trouble for you, mom, a hardship I mean, I'd appreciate it if you'd stay on here through the summer." Knowing that one set of facts had absolutely nothing to do with the other, she nevertheless had already decided that this was the perfect time to broach the subject. Lena, Cynthia, and Paul, all in the same Manhattan apartment, was a situation she didn't have to try on for size to know that it wouldn't fit, that it would prove intolerable and something to avoid at all costs.

"Whatever you think is best," said Lena. "But where is he, my grandson? He's here in Miami, so why didn't he call?"

"He never had the opportunity. And there you have it. And don't ask me what he was doing driving from Omaha to Florida, because at this point that's the least of my worries." Because at this point, her major worry was the payment that was still to be made to Detective Lieutenant Ryan Kaplan.

Well my mother, bless her soul, was Irish and my father came from Poland. So I got the best of both worlds. But what I wanted to talk to you about, Mrs. Morgan, concerns a little matter I tactfully neglected to include in my report. And what is that? she asked. Coke, he said, as the two of them sat at a table in the hospital cafeteria. Coke? Cocaine and several ounces of hashish. You see, my wife lost twenty or so pounds at NuBodies, right here in Miami. It's helped our marriage a helluva lot. So I certainly didn't want the papers to get wind of the fact that your son was involved in a drug charge, seeing as you've been on TV, Johnny Carson and all. In fact, Mrs. Morgan, the boy was under the influence of drugs when the accident occurred. I really think a contribution to the Policemen's Benevolent Association is in order, she said. Cash, if you don't mind, he said right after. They frown on checks . . . it involves too much paperwork, you understand. How much would you suggest? she asked. Kaplan cracked his knuckles and looked inside his coffee cup as if he were reading the grounds. Then he looked up at her and raised his hand, displaying five stubby fingers. That should do the trick, he said. Nicely.

After she left Wolfie's she went over to American Express to get a cash advance since she had no way of cashing a check that size in Miami.

Barry informed her—in passing—that he had no intention of returning to Omaha to complete his studies. "I want my own apartment," he repeated later that afternoon, as Cynthia blotted her neck dry with a damp tissue.

"You know when you'll get your own apartment, Barry? As your grandmother would say, when hair'll grow on the palm of my hand, that's when."

"You're always giving me these folksy sayings. I want to live my own life, my way," he said, one leg plaster-white, raised high in traction.

"As long as I pay the bills, you mean," she told him. "How old are you now, Barry?"

"You didn't even give me a decent birthday present," he said. "Twenty-two."

"At twenty-two your father was already busting his backside trying to make a living. It's time you got wise to yourself, cause I'm not gonna be around forever, always there to clean up the mess you make with your life. And need I tell you how much it cost me to keep this latest escapade of yours out of the papers."

"How much? That detective was a real prick. You know what he had the nerve to call me?"

"I don't care what he called you, because you probably deserved it. And do me a favor and watch your mouth, mister. I'm still your mother and don't you ever forget it. I don't have to stand here and listen to language like that. I never talked dirty and neither did your father."

"No, you were too busy trying to prove to the world what a saviour you were."

"Keep talking, cause I'm not paying to have the car repaired, I'll tell you that."

"It was nearly totaled, anyway."

"Just be thankful you weren't nearly totaled," she replied. "And to get back to what I was saying, it cost me five hundred dollars—five big ones as you'd put it—to pay off Kaplan, that's what. Not to mention paying the orthopedist and all the other bills."

"You're covered. I have Blue Cross."

"And what about your friend?"

"David?"

"That's right, David Fisher who, as it turns out, has a mother on disability and no father in sight. Who's going to pay his bills, may I ask?"

"Can't he get welfare?"

"You are the most—" She couldn't say it, so instead she told him, "Your mother is picking up his bills too, in case you're interested."

"Thank you."

"What? I must be hearing things."

"You're not. I said thank you."

"Well it's about time, because if that isn't the surprise of the century, I don't know what is."

Pat Casey was in town, doing a benefit for CARIH, the non-sectarian non-denominational asthma research foundation. Burr was with him, all their traveling expenses having been paid for by the Mike Douglas Show. Pat was going to tape a show in Philadelphia after his charity stint, and Gene had decided to stay on in New York for a few days. "So it'll be a perfect time for us to talk about what's been happening, doll."

"Why don't you come over for drinks then?" she suggested.

"Who's going to be there?"

"Just Paul and me. Very cozy."

"Yes, I heard about that," he said. She was sure she heard a chuckle getting snagged somewhere between his words. "How's it working out, by the way?"

"Not bad. Better than expected, actually." There was no sense lying about it, keeping it a big secret, hush-hush and all that sort of adolescent nonsense. But she hadn't even given herself the time to sit down and think about the change which had come into her life, a change best described as an intense, sporadically moody, dark-haired young man of twenty-nine who bore a strong resemblance to "either the bust of Menander at the Boston Fine Arts Museum, or else a statue entitled the 'Dying Gaul' I saw at the Capitoline Museum, last time I was in Rome." But whoever Paul resembled, D. W. had been effusive in his praise, saying too, "I don't know what the guy's head is like, Cynthia. But you picked yourself a winner, looks-wise, I mean."

There was no question about his physical appeal. If anything, she felt it strengthening, day after day. But it was his mental state that worried her, that gave her cause for doubt, unhappy self-examination. Paul had been accepted by the Actors Studio, but when she returned from the office every day, she found him lying on the living room sofa, a joint between his lips, a drink near at hand, and the television tuned to the afternoon movie. She'd gotten over harping about his smoking, making it clear she didn't approve but wasn't going to be a square about it. "I just don't want to try it and that's that." But even more than the inordinate—so she thought—amount of grass he was smoking, his lackadaisical and lethargic attitude was doubly difficult to deal with.

"Why don't you start going to auditions, making the rounds?" she suggested. "You might be able to get in a showcase or something like that. Isn't that what it's called?"

"Sure," he said.

When she pressed him for a more definite commitment, he bounded off the couch and grabbed her. "Let me get out of my things at least," she said, her concern turning to desire in the amount of time it used to take her to consume a Fig Newton. And if that was not romantic it didn't matter, because she had already learned to make the definition between love and lust.

"Fuck the clothes. I'm in charge now." A line like so many others she'd heard in her life, it nevertheless worked like a charm.

Paul had all the right moves at his disposal. The unsettled feeling that traveled with her from the apartment to the office and back again seemed to evaporate like mist and haze burning off under a high-noon sun. She gave in to his physical demands, her own as well, and stopped questioning him. Yet an hour later she was always back at the beginning, trying to figure out a way to make him happy.

She wondered how Brando had gotten started, who had given him his first break, thinking nothing of making comparisons, drawing parallels between the two of them. Because now, she was certain that's what Paul needed, one small break and he'd be well on his way to the big time, getting the acclaim she instinctively felt he deserved. But she'd never seen him perform, not until a day or two before Burr arrived from the Coast. Paul invited her down to the studio to watch him do a ten-minute scene, an exercise for one of his classes. He played Stanley Kowalski to a simpering and forgettable Blanche du Bois. Afterwards, Cynthia—who had never depended upon the kind-

435

ness of strangers—was more convinced than ever that he had all the ingredients to become not just a fine actor, but a great actor. He hadn't played the scene as a derivative of Brando, which certainly would have been the easiest way to go about handling it. No, his interpretation of the gutsy and primitive Stanley had been wholly his own, with a touch of bitter and sardonic humor—"The humor of an intelligent man who (a) has already been pegged as a beast, and (b) who's never figured out how to go about using his smarts," Paul explained later—that left her shaking her head in wonder. He wasn't Brando. He was Paul Antonio—"That *is* my real name, moon lady. I wouldn't shit ya"—and he could act, finally managing to give her the proof she realized she'd needed all along. Now, it was her turn to do something about it.

The chance came up when Gene Burr joined them for drinks at her apartment.

"So how come you haven't returned my contract, doll?" he said as he sat in the living room, legs crossed and a slight, affluent paunch visible beneath his cashmere turtleneck. Paul bit his nails and paddled one finger back and forth across the top of his glass. Cynthia didn't have to remind him that Burr was in a position to be of considerable help to his fledgling career.

"I didn't? I thought I had already. I'll check with my secretary tomorrow. But what's the difference, Gene. Nothing's been signed, right?"

"True," he said. "But I might as well tell you that the deal's about to be closed."

"Are you serious?"

"You're damn right I'm serious," he said, grinning and showing his uncapped teeth. "What do you think, I've been sitting on my ass all these weeks. I've got Warners interested in underwriting the cost of the pilot. For a hefty percentage of course, but still. Somebody has to come up with the bread and they seem to be the ones who are most turned on by the project."

"I can't believe it," she kept repeating, even as she got up to freshen their drinks. "Paul, isn't that fantastic news."

"The best," he said. He slouched back in his chair, his legs stretched out in front of him. The darkened soles of his bare feet stuck up in the air like two slabs of charred wood or overcooked meat.

"And what's with you these days, Paul?" Burr asked.

"I'm working my balls off."

Cynthia missed a step, recovered her balance, and continued to the bar. "I saw him do a scene, a couple of days ago," she called out.

"And?"

"And he has more talent in his little finger than half the big names out in Hollywood, that's what."

"I thought he was strictly into Broadway, *pure* and serious drama," Burr said, talking as if Paul weren't even in the room, away and out of earshot.

"Who said he isn't? I was just speaking figuratively, that's all." She returned with their drinks, set them down on their respective coasters, and took a seat across from Burr. "I wanted to speak to you about an idea I've been playing around with."

"Such as?"

"Such as investing in a Broadway play." She glanced over at Paul, satisfied her words had had the desired effect. Strings pulled taut, he sat up straight in his chair and leaned forward. Shoulders hunched together, he kept one eye on her and the other on Gene Burr.

"Did I ever tell you Cynthia's got one of the best backs in the business," he said.

"Come again?"

"Ever read Nabokov?"

"*Lolita.*"

"*Ada*'s even better."

"I didn't know you were so literary," Burr said.

Cynthia agreed.

"Lots of things I don't talk about," Paul said with a touch of self-importance. "But ole Vladimir has a thing about a woman's back, specially the hollow curve right at the base of the spine. Anyway, Cynthia here—"

"I'm sure Gene has other things to worry about," she said. It was none of Burr's business. Besides, what kind of thing was this to talk about, when she wanted to feel Gene out on the business of producing and backing a play. So she spoke up before he had a chance to continue. "As I was saying, wouldn't it be a good investment for Nu-Bodies, taxwise or what have you, to underwrite the cost of mounting a play? A *good* play, mind you. Not a piece of crap the critics would write off in three sentences."

"Starring Paul Antonio, of course."

"Hey, come on now, Burr. Let the lady, finish," Paul said.

"Why not? Why shouldn't he get the break, instead of someone else. I've seen him work. Audiences would eat him up. He's got great . . . animal magnetism, that's how they'd react to him. And not only does he have the ability to project, but he's now, for the seventies I mean. So why not cash in on it," she said.

"Because it costs as much to mount a play as it does to tape a pilot. Maybe more. And you haven't dug into your own pocket for that little project, doll. Look it, you're not dealing with ten thousand bucks, Cynthia. More like ten times that, a hundred and fifty thousand, probably."

"Well the corporation can afford it. D. W. can't even think of enough ways to diversify our interests fast enough. And even if the play doesn't make it, we can always write it off as a tax loss, so what's the difference?"

"There's a big difference," he said, the wrinkles on his face deepening like the banks of a river made visible after a month-long drought. In the soft light his skin looked pitted, cratered with shadows, and his silver-gray hair was a network of metallic threads.

She didn't like his attitude and she wasn't about to pretend otherwise. "I don't know what you're objecting to, to begin with."

"Who said anything about object?" He turned to Paul. "Did I say I objected? Did I even imply you didn't have talent? Okay, I haven't seen your work, but there's no reason in the world for me not to believe Cynthia. Right?"

"Then let's do it," she said.

"Do what?"

"Gene, stop playing dumb and worrying about saving my money. You know what I mean. Isn't there a decent property around suited for Paul's talents?"

"You really want to gobble the world up whole, don't you?"

"Now what the fuck is that supposed to mean, Burr?" A muscle twitched on his jaw. Paul put down the drink he'd been cupping in his hands like a pacifier. "What the fuck is she busting her ass for if she can't enjoy her money? And why shouldn't she try something other than weight reduction, for a change. Cynthia Morgan and Nu-

Bodies Inc. Presents is a perfect way to start. So don't give us your holier-than-thou bullshit."

"Look what I started," he said. He smiled, this time without showing teeth, and slapped his hands against his suede-covered thighs.

"Wait a minute, Paul. Don't get so excited," she said. Measuring his temper with a quick and guarded glance, she decided it wasn't going to go anywhere, more for show, a dramatic reading, than anything else. "Gene only has my best interests at heart. Am I right, Gene?"

"You're damn right I do," Burr said. "You want a TV series and you want to back a play, produce it too, for all I know. Okay, I'll work on it, doll. That's the best I can do, and that's what a manager's for. I'll shop around, see what kind of script I can come up with. But this isn't kid stuff, just remember that. You're in the big leagues now, and I don't want to see you get hurt—burned, I should say, that's all."

"How the fuck is she gonna get hurt backing a play?"

"My friend, if you get half as worked-up and animated on the stage as you do in person, you probably have all the talent Cynthia here says you do."

"You're damn right I have talent."

"Well, you don't have to prove it to me. It's not my money," Burr replied. He glanced at his watch. "Gotta run, gang."

"Why so fast?" she asked, thinking that they might have all had dinner together.

"Heavy date," he said, "with a prospective client. But Cyn honey, you won't forget about mailing out the contract, signing it too, will you?"

"It was an oversight." She got to her feet. "So when do you think you can have something to show us—me I mean." She didn't want him to think Paul was calling the shots, or at least some of them, telling her what and what not to do. He hadn't even said a word about her being a Broadway angel, as she remembered it was called. No, it was her idea, from the very start. And why not? He's right. What am I killing myself for unless I can enjoy my money. I certainly haven't gotten tons of pleasure out of it, that's for sure. It's just sitting there. Why should I start worrying about my old age when I'm not even old?

"Rodell has a script he worked on with Loretta Wyckoff for over a year. I'll see what I can do."

"Is she involved in it anymore?"

"No way," Burr said, shaking his head.

"I didn't think so," she said.

Even as she locked the door behind him, Paul was out of his chair. He clapped his hands, did a little dance she couldn't even begin to describe or duplicate, and grabbed for her as if she, and she alone, had the means to solve his life for him. She decided it was going to be a very expensive solution.

RODELL'S PLAY, *Four for Dinner,* was much too experimental and avant-garde, "artsy-craftsy" she termed it, for her more conventional dramatic tastes. But despite her lack of enthusiasm—"He writes good strong dialogue but the play just doesn't seem to go anywhere, Paul. Nothing's resolved at the end"—Paul called it "the best American play since *Virginia Woolf,* bar none." Even more important, he felt that the role of Robbie was so perfect for him, "It gives me goose bumps. It's like Rodell's been inside my head and under my skin. It's like he's pulled my guts out, hung them up to dry and turned them into words. It's not that I *am* Robbie. God knows I'm not nearly as fucked-up . . . I hope. But I know where Robbie's at, understand?"

"I thought Robbie was a whiner, if you want to know the truth."

"Yes, my pet, but what a brilliantly literate whiner. He intellectualizes all his emotions, so that his responses are all mental, rather than visceral. Just the opposite of a character like Stanley Kowalski, by the way. You see, Robbie refuses to feel because he's afraid of feeling, of committing himself to anything he can't understand and therefore dissect in psychological terms. Now if that isn't the dilemma of twentieth century man, I don't know what is."

Burr sent three other scripts and though she liked one of them—James Outman's *Tony the Blest*—much more than *Four for Dinner,* Paul wouldn't hear of it. "Dreary stuff," he said. "It's just not for today. And for your information, I know theater a little better than you do and

Rodell's play's a winner. It's gonna take everyone by storm."

"In that case, let's hope we don't get hit by lightning, burnt to a crisp," not even trying to be either funny or clever. She was merely nervous and there was no way to hide it, especially now that she had to confront Leonard with her plans.

"But you're the president of the corporation. You hold the controlling interest, don't you?"

"Sure I do, Paul. But still, it's not going to be fun if he categorically refuses, or the board doesn't go along with me. I can use my veto power, but still—"

"He won't, so stop worrying. Let him read the play if he has any doubts. Let the entire board read it, for that matter. I'm telling you, Cynthia. This isn't a turkey. We're not dealing with a bomb. It's going to be a hit, a smash hit the likes of which Broadway hasn't seen in years."

There was a Russian folk saying that went along with that, but she refrained from using it. Too much of a good thing, overkill, trampled originality right into the dust.

"So that's the story, Leonard. I wanted to lay my cards on the table, so to speak, instead of beating around the bush. But to repeat, I think no matter how the play is received, it can only be advantageous for both our corporate image and our tax structure. We haven't lost a penny in years. Isn't it about time we took a decent write-off like everyone else does?"

"It never ceases to amaze me how little you know about business, Cynthia," he said. "But tell me this. When are we moving, relocating to Madison Avenue?"

"This summer," she said, looking down at the papers strewn like dead autumn leaves, from one corner of her desk to another. Behind him the closed door stood just as resolute, just as firm and implacable.

"And how much is it costing us?"

"Leonard, stop treating me like a child or something. You were never a father and the role doesn't suit you," she said. She couldn't help getting in a dig at Jeanette. Not that it mattered, because the whole thing seemed a losing battle. Try as she might, she couldn't recover her quickly dwindling confidence.

"Why is it that whenever we discuss a matter that's

purely business, you invariably go down to the level of personal involvement?"

"Because we would never be in this room together if there hadn't been personal involvement, that's why."

"Don't yell at me. I'm not Barry."

"Then don't insult me and act like a goddamn cold fish. You conveniently forget that we used to be . . . that's right, no sense kidding ourselves. Lovers. This was a lovers' business, wasn't it, Leonard? And we used to have such good times, too. So many laughs, so many moments of tenderness and compassion. And all those plans we had, dreams we shared together."

"You're breaking my heart." Immobile, the thorn-proof country gentleman in a tweed takeoff of a hacking jacket, Frankel leaned back against the door and pressed down on his unseen hands. "So please don't start that again, whatever you do."

"There's nothing to start. You killed it, ages ago."

"And stop feeling sorry for yourself, Cynthia. It doesn't become you. It doesn't ring true, either. In fact, it smacks of self-pity, since we're being so honest with each other."

A show of anger or grievous outrage would only intensify his obstinacy. The sun slanted through the venetian blinds. She found a sucking candy in the top drawer of her desk, removed the cellophane wrapping, and popped it into her mouth. The taste of sour green apples and summers in the country she had never spent, neither as a girl nor as a woman, bit at her tongue. "The move to Madison Avenue has nothing to do with it," she said at last.

"It has everything to do with it. It's costing us somewhere in the neighborhood of two hundred thousand dollars. Have you already forgotten the big stink you made about the need to have a fancy outer office, not to mention a brand-new office for yourself. Have you called that decorator, by the way?"

"Not yet. He's still out of town," doing something for Jackie O., whose marriage contract—according to D. W. —had more clauses in it than Eleanor of Aquitaine's.

"Well I guarantee you that when he comes by to give you an estimate, or sends over one of his high-society flunkies, which is much more likely, it's going to run five figures, that's what. But I said, if that's what you want, you go ahead and do it, as long as it'll make you happy."

"Happy!" she exclaimed, nearly choking on the hard

candy. "What do you know about happy, anyway? All you know is to worry about Leonard, can't even enjoy your own success, take pleasure in it, that's what. I want the money for the play. I'm the president of NuBodies and I still have controlling interest—"

"No, I'm afraid not." He tilted forward, his hands slipping down into the pockets of his twill trousers so that she caught the subdued gleam of blue stone, lapis lazuli.

"What?"

"You heard me the first time, Cynthia. You don't have controlling interest in the corporation, not anymore you don't. Not since January."

Was he hoarse or was he whispering? She couldn't tell. "What are you talking about? Of course I do. Do you want me to produce each and every share and count them up right in front of you? Is that the only way to satisfy you, Leonard?"

"It wouldn't do any good," he said. "Jeanette and I bought up forty-five thousand shares when we dropped from thirteen to four and a quarter. That gives me thirty-seven, not thirty-four, percent of our total holdings. And since you're still sitting on thirty-six percent, or five hundred forty thousand shares to be exact, you no longer retain even nominal control of NuBodies. It's as simple as that."

"I don't believe you," she said. "You always did have the gift of gab, a real bullshit artist of the first magnitude." She dug a tissue out of a box in another desk drawer, removed the sour apple candy from her mouth, wrapped it in the kleenex and dropped the sticky package into the wastebasket near her feet.

"That's really of no interest to me, Cynthia. I couldn't care less what opinion you have of me. I haven't cared for quite a long time, to tell you the truth. But I can have an audit done for you at the drop of a hat, if you still don't believe me."

"You're bluffing."

He shook his head. "You wish. But what I want you to know is that it's good for our image for you to stay right where you are, Founder and President in capital letters. Only, in the future, Cynthia, decisions will be made either by me or by the board. If you recall, we changed our charter, bylaws I mean, so that the president could override any decision made by the board of directors. I didn't approve at the time, even though I felt I had all the votes I needed. But now I'm quite delighted. Because if you take this little matter up before the board and even if they go along with you which I'm absolutely positive they will not since it's just another example of fiscal irresponsibility to feed your all-consuming ego, I will veto their decision. Is that clear?"

"But *I'm* president. *Me,* not you."

"In name only. And that's just because I'm a nice guy, a gentleman."

"A gentleman! A gentleman he says. You are unbelievable, Frankel. I don't know if I should take you seriously or what."

"Take me seriously, Cynthia. It's all very clear-cut."

"What's clear-cut is that you pulled the wool over the eyes of the SEC, that's what's clear-cut," she said. She held onto the arms of her chair, stabilizing herself, afraid she'd either go spinning off or toppling backward in a kind of enraged epileptic seizure. She bit down on her lower lip, tasting lipstick and a residue of artificial green-apple flavoring. She tried to control the involuntary trembling which spread out in concentric waves from her mouth to her shoulders, to her arms, and down to the tips of her fingers. It didn't work.

"That's something you'll never prove," he said. "And besides, an in-house battle would do more damage than I know you care to inflict on the company. After all, you *are* in control of over half a million shares of common stock. That's not something to sneeze at or take lightly. Or jeopardize."

I'll jeopardize his skull in another minute, she thought. "I want to ask you something, Leonard," she said, for it was becoming apparent that now was as good a time as any to air dirty laundry, even if it looked like an impossibility in terms of reaching a compromise, an amiable solution. "Did you send Gerald Evans down to Miami to try to convince me to sell out? I'm just curious, that's all. You might as well be honest, love, because if you did, you know as well as I do that it didn't work."

"I don't see what that has to do with anything," he said.

"I'm not sure I do either. But answer me, Leonard. Yes or no."

"Yes," he said.

"Thank you for answering my question. It's the nicest

thing you've done for me in years. And tell me one other thing, Leonard. Was it your idea or D. W.'s to try to get me to hand over one percent of my stock as a birthday present, right before I left for California?"

"I don't know what you're talking about. And what's the difference, anyway. You didn't and that ended that."

"Oh, so you *did* know about it, beforehand I mean."

"Rumor spreads very rapidly around here, in case you haven't gathered by now. Would you like me to give you the details of your current love affair? It's common knowledge, in case you think you've been keeping it a big secret, because you haven't. Even my secretary talks about it."

"I'm glad for her," she said.

"Look, the point is, you're no longer in a position to destroy NuBodies with your harebrained schemes, and that's all that counts, as far as I'm concerned. The rest is not worth discussing. It's over and done with."

"If I wasn't a lady, I'd get up and slap you for that; but it's not worth my energy, Frankel. You know what slime is? Mud? You're what lives underneath that kind of filth, not even on top, not even on the surface. As soon as Burr swings that deal with Warners, I'm going to be on the Coast so fast you won't know if Cynthia's coming or going. And I'll stay out there, too, so I won't have to see your smirking garment center face, you weasel you, you sonuvabitch." Everything was voiced in a hiss, low-pitched, carefully modulated, perfectly enunciated.

"And you call yourself a lady? That has to be too funny." He rocked back and forth on the balls of his feet, his leather shoes squeaking, never moving away from the door. "But since everything's out in the open, cards on the table and all that bullshit, I might as well make corporate policy clear on that particular issue too, while we're at it. Burr can take his deal with Warners and shove it up his ass, for all I care. I have a better deal lined up for a syndicated series that'll cost less than sixty thousand for a pilot and for which we won't have to be beholden to anybody, meaning Warners and the percentage Burr's about to hand over to them on a silver platter."

All she could do was look at him, open her mouth, and laugh. His face seemed to swell, then darken. His lips were pulled back just enough for her to see how he was gritting his teeth. "Don't tell me you're getting angry, Leonard? You, of all people? And don't give me orders.

446

If I want to do a series for Warners, I'll be damned if I'll let you tell me how I can and cannot run my life."

"You once said something that made me want to wring your neck," he said quietly. "'I am NuBodies and Nu-Bodies is me.' Remember? It haunted me for a long time, right up until I had those forty-five thousand shares in my pocket. But Cynthia, you were right."

"Pardon?"

"Yes, you were. You are NuBodies. But since I control NuBodies, I control you. You're no longer a free agent, kiddo. The corporation owns your rags-to-riches story, lady, the rights to your life. Get the picture?"

"No."

"Then I'll try to make myself even clearer. This September your autobiography—if I dare call it that—is coming out, to coincide with our seventh anniversary."

"So?"

"The copyright is held by NuBodies Inc. Not by Cynthia Margold Morgan. Now have I made myself perfectly clear? You can't use your inimitable God-given talents without my permission. You are, in effect, responsible to me, from now on in. You don't even own your past anymore. You wanted to be NuBodies and now you are. Absolutely, beyond a shadow of a doubt. But just remember, you may be NuBodies, but I control the corporation. Have I finally made myself understood, Mrs. Morgan?"

"You're out of your mind, Leonard. A corporation can't own a person's life."

"The *rights* to a person's life, my dear, not the life itself. But if you don't like it, you can always leave the corporation and get back all those wonderful years in Brooklyn that you've been trying to forget for so long. But by then, Warners wouldn't want to touch you with a ten-foot pole."

All she could say was that she'd get herself a lawyer.

In response, Leonard was the one who now began to laugh. "You see, Cynthia, things catch up to you. Money in particular. While you were busy playing superstar, hiring chauffeurs and buying co-ops and sports cars and paying off admissions officers, left and right, hobnobbing with second-rate celebrities, I was sitting in my cubbyhole across the hall, working my tail off."

"And I didn't? I didn't work, day in and day out? I never stopped working, for your information. I . . . I broke up a family for this business, that's how important it was to me."

"That was probably your first and biggest mistake. But no matter, it's too late now. After all, you're the Grace Kelly of weight reduction, Princess Pound-Loss. Do you think, do you really believe people attend NuBodies classes because some fat nobody from Brooklyn went down from a size forty-six to a size twelve. And if you don't watch yourself that figure's about to change, I might add. But the answer is that they could care less, Cynthia. They come to us because we give them what they want, what they need, a way of losing weight you didn't even think up, since we've decided to be so candid with each other for a change. I never told you about the market studies we did, when we first came out with our line of diet sodas. You wanted your photo plastered across every fucking bottle and we went along with you, didn't we? But you know what? Our market researchers told us that consumers were going to buy the brand name NuBodies. Anything else was extraneous. Your fancy Avedon photo that makes you look like a horse's ass, some kind of over-the-hill Jewish vamp, didn't mean shit."

"Why did you end up hating me? For what reasons? What did I ever do to you, Leonard, to make you feel such venom, such loathing?"

"I don't hate you, Cynthia. I just think it's time someone took the wind out of your sails, that's all."

Screaming would solve nothing.

Crying would spell defeat as if each tear were a lettered tile from a Scrabble set, or else YOU LOSE in florid sugar script, the icing on the cake.

Slapping him across the face, tearing with bare hands at his thorn-proof smug exterior, that façade of self-satisfaction, would be more in keeping with the cover of some lurid piece of pulp fiction—"She killed for the company" in five thousand words or less. Or else, "Underneath his tweed jacket, her partner was an s.o.b., was—"

"The lowest of the low, Leonard," she said, unable to raise her voice, barely able to catch her breath. "So you wanted to deflate my sails, isn't that something? Well you know what? No one deflates these sails, mister. I have taken it for years. From D. W., from my son, even from your wife, who probably has been behind this for all I know, goading you on every step of the way. And now from you. But I will tell you one thing, Frankel. I'm here to stay. If I go down, NuBodies goes down with me, whatever you might think to the contrary, whatever your all-knowing market analysts might tell you. For thirty-some-odd years I survived. No, not in the style of . . . how did you put it? Oh yes, the Grace Kelly of weight loss, something like that. But I managed. There was food on the table. No one went hungry. There were clothes on my back and the bills got paid. Weak I am not. I come from a long line of survivors and nothing you can say or do will ever change that.

"And if you want to go on believing that NuBodies would be what it is today without me, you can do whatever the fuck you please. Because *I* know different. Those keys hanging on the wall to all those cities, those proclamations from governors, that plaque for Woman of the Year . . . that's bullshit, you're right. That's just good p.r. and a lot of fancy footwork, being in the right place at the right time. But in the bottom of that closet there," and she pointed with one trembling hand, "there's a box filled with something like forty thousand letters. Three boxes actually. Two are back in my apartment. The ones I've already answered, personally, over the years. People flocked to NuBodies because I was their inspiration. I gave them something to believe in. Neither you, nor your wife, nor D. W., nor anyone else for that matter, can take that away from me. And if I want to produce a play, do something that goes beyond helping people lose weight, I intend to do it. So keep your eyes open and tell your stockbroker to be on the watch because I'll be putting up some of my hard-earned shares, selling them to the highest bidder. It'll be the chance of a lifetime for you and Jeanette, a not-to-be-missed golden opportunity. Because I don't break promises. Because I don't go out of my way to destroy a person, inside and out the way you do. Now please get out of my office Leonard, because the very sight of you turns my stomach, I feel that ill."

"Just remember, Cynthia. And that was a very dignified and impressive little speech, by the way. But just remember, the deal with Warners is off. So if I were you, I'd get on the phone and call your new friend Burr and tell him to stop whatever he's been doing. The corporation won't allow it."

She reached down to take off her shoe and hurl it across

449

the room. But then she changed her mind, straightened up, and swung the chair around. Her eyes were trained on the wall, focused on a single oversized gold key that opened up all the doors of gratitude and appreciation in Portland, Maine.

"Where to?" Phil said.

"Brooklyn. Flatbush Avenue and Glenwood Road. Any route you take's fine with me."

A year before, she'd loaned Doris Bauer fifteen thousand dollars to purchase the Flatbush Avenue branch, outright. One-third of that loan, something Leonard had known nothing about, had already been paid off. It was Doris' security against the future. And the only security I have is a lot of money and a life that belongs to a registered trademark. Now if that isn't the joke of this or any other year, I don't know what is.

Phil was going on and on and Cynthia, sensing that he was trying to get her out of her bad mood, said, "I just don't feel like talking." So he clammed up and they silently drove a well-remembered route down the FDR Drive and across the Brooklyn Bridge, down Flatbush Avenue past Grand Army Plaza and Prospect Park. The heartland, D. W. used to call it when he was young and pushy, but never innocent. And Leonard would hold my hand and beg me to incorporate, telling me how I was needed, how there were people out there in the heartland, yes the great wide-open heartland, who needed me, who needed help and how I was the only one who could get through to them and now, now ... what?

She laced her fingers together, held back from reaching for a cigarette.

There was a class in session when she mounted the stairs to reach the meeting-hall which looked out on Flatbush Avenue. She keeps everything so neat and clean, presentable, Cynthia thought, running the tips of her fingers over the freshly painted walls. She stopped in front of the door with its crisp shiny gold-leaf letters, NU-BODIES INC. And underneath, "A thinner way is a better way." The original "Fat Nobody" campaign was a thing of the past, gone, over and done with like so much

450

else in her life. She fitted the palm of her hand to the cold rounded cheek of the metal doorknob, turned it, and let herself into the room.

The sad set expression she'd been unable to control or fight off all morning and afternoon easily slipped away. She replaced it with a smile and silently took a seat in the back of the crowded hall. Business was better than ever. There were barely half a dozen vacant chairs. At the other side of the classroom, not yet aware of her presence, Doris Bauer stood at the lectern. Behind her a hand-painted oaktag poster charted the total weight loss of the Flatbush Avenue branch, from the day it had first opened its doors nearly seven years before.

It's like a dream, isn't it, Cynthia. A fantasy come true.

Sure it was. But whoever thought it would turn out to be so complicated, a dream that paid for all the better things in life but left you sitting home alone with nightmares. So there's Paul now. So I'd be a bigger fool, the goose of all time, the horse's ass that phony said I was, to think that'll go on till death do us part. So you always end up back where you first started. Square one. Only this time it's with a real education, the kind you never get from books, the kind you never wanted to learn about to begin with. That and a hundred pounds gone out the window like all the things I used to think I wanted, the things I needed to make me happy. And when Barry said thank you I thought *that* was the surprise of the century. I was selling myself short, jumping the gun and even that would be too good for him, that crumb, that lowlife, that despicable—

"Of course it's not easy, Barbara. But anything that's important in life never is. You've got to remember that and make the distinction between what's good for the Barbara of yesterday and what's good for the Barbara of today and tomorrow. And you can't lose hope, whatever you do. We're all in this together, remember that . . ."

The words drifted back to her, honest and effortless, all so familiar. Safe, she thought, holding her smile in place. She had a good teacher. Not me, but experience, the best helpmate of all. There was a rustle of fabric, the creaking of a chair. The woman sitting in front of her glanced back for a curious and disbelieving second. Like someone pantomiming surprise, her eyes opened wide, her mouth following suit an instant later.

451

"You're Cynthia Morgan, my God, aren't you?"

"Yes, but let's listen to Doris. She's giving you very good sound advice."

The woman, her striped tent of a dress so familiar that Cynthia wanted to laugh until she cried, tapped her neighbor on the shoulder and whispered into her ear. A few minutes later a faint buzz could be heard above the level of Doris Bauer's voice.

"Anything the matter?" Doris said. She stood on tiptoe and peered across the room. "Well I'll be!" a smile like a flower bursting fullblown on her lipsticked mouth. "I'm going to stop for the time being because there's someone with us this afternoon who knows more about what I've been trying to tell you, than just about anyone else in the world. Because if it wasn't for her, there'd never be a NuBodies and I'd probably still be weighing in at close to two hundred pounds. Come on, Cynthia, don't be shy. You know you love to talk."

All heads were turned her way.

"You're embarrassing me, Doris."

"Come on now. You can't let us down, disappoint us."

She got to her feet.

Applause—spontaneous, warm, animated and delighted —greeted her ears. It was the best medicine in the world for what ailed her. "Hey," she said, "I haven't even said a word yet."

"Who cares, you look fabulous," a woman on the aisle said loudly, hands going like cymbals, over and over again.

She walked down the aisle and kissed Doris on the cheek. "What brings you to Brooklyn?" her friend whispered.

"Memories." She took her place in front of the old wooden lectern, one she remembered buying down on Canal Street. Back then when my life was a helluva lot simpler, nothing to complicate it, nothing to get in the way of what I thought I wanted. Had I known . . . no, I guess I wouldn't have done it any other way or changed it one iota. You can't see into the future so why get yourself depressed with hindsight.

"Boy, am I glad to be here today," she said, taking a deep breath. "It feels like home, like I'm home free, it really does." She was in her element now. No matter what, she knew she was wanted, needed too. Nothing and no one could change that, could destroy the sense of ac-

452

complishment. "Nine years ago . . . wow, is it that long already? I guess it is, because it was sometime in January or February of 1963 that I went on a diet that was going to end up changing my entire life. Yours too, I hope." All these faces before her were somehow her face. Leonard can't take this away from me. No one can. "I didn't write the diet; I want you to know that. Maybe some of you think I did, but that's not really the case. But what I did do was figure out a way to make it work, better I mean, a kind of takeoff on group therapy, you might say. I figured that if you put a bunch of overweight people together and got them going, got them talking and exchanging experiences, pretty soon they'd all come to the realization that being heavy wasn't something that was unique, something that just applied to them and no one else. No, they'd discover that lots of other people were all in the same boat . . ." The words spun their way back and forth across the room, touching on everyone she saw. She didn't need a script, notes, a speech written by someone else, prepared in advance. "Tell it the way it is, the way it happened," D. W. had once advised her, "and you'll never go wrong."

". . . Fig Newtons? My God, I used to eat whole boxes while I was hiding in the bathroom. Well, who wanted anyone to see?" she said with a laugh that burst the last bubble of tension, freeing her completely. "It wasn't the prettiest sight in the world, let's face it. And I can see by the way you're all nodding your heads that you've been in the same kind of situation, just like me. But wait, how about leftovers? Now that's a subject that used to be near and dear to my heart. I never told you the story how my son didn't eat his dinner one night. I made a gorgeous meal but he wouldn't touch a thing and you know you can't fight with children, especially if they're thin. But at three o'clock in the morning, I slipped into the kitchen, looking for all the world like this amazingly chubby ghost in a pink nightgown under which you could have easily slept two, if not three. Oh yes, I was two hundred fifty-two pounds . . . wait, closer to two-sixty. But I was also a thing of grace. Oh I was, you shouldn't laugh cause it's true. But I can still taste that cold breaded veal cutlet, that's how luscious it was. Now, when I go to bed at night, I'm out like a light and I don't get up till the following morning. How do you like that for progress?"

And even as she spoke, as she claimed the attention of every single smiling upturned face, she thought, I'm not through yet, Leonard Frankel. I'm not finished, washed-up. Not by a long shot.

September 1972

CYNTHIA THE SURVIVOR—alias the one-woman crusade, alias the subject of *With a Face Like Yours, the Cynthia Morgan Story*—continued to do just that. She went about her business as if nothing had happened, save for a rather traumatic and unpleasant phone conversation she had with Gene Burr. That had been a few days after Leonard had lashed into her. If she hadn't told him she was going to sell some of her holdings to underwrite the cost of mounting Rodell's play, she didn't even want to think what the result would have been. Not that it troubled her that Burr would be furious. She hadn't signed his contract, having decided to wait to feel out Leonard on the subject. Now, it was just as well. But since Justin Rodell was one of the manager's clients, she made up for the debacle of the TV series and his broken promises to Warners by throwing herself into the Broadway project, giving it her total financial and emotional commitment. The result was that a few days after Labor Day, *Four for Dinner* went into rehearsal.

The summer, she decided, was a perfect time to clear the air, tie up loose ends, recoup her energies, so to speak. First on the list was Lena, still ensconced in an air-conditioned apartment in Miami Beach. "I'm getting too old to lie, mom, to fib and make up stories," she told her mother over the phone. She proceeded to explain the situation—that was her word for it, no one else's. Paul was there to stay, at least for the time being. Lena was having a good time in Miami so unless she had any serious objections, could she stay on through the winter. Then, come Christmas, she'd see what was what. "You're not a little girl anymore, Cynthia," her mother replied. "You like him, this . . . gentleman friend of yours?" "Yes, very much. And it's been very good for me, mother. Can you understand that?"

"Sure I understand. A woman is nothing without a man around. Your father, may he rest in peace, has been gone ten years this November. A lot of water under the bridge, a long time, right? Sure it's been a long time, sweetheart, but for me it's like yesterday, understand?" "Yes," she said. "Then you go ahead and have a good time, for a change. It makes me want to cry the way you work, the way you break your back and for what? What's the point unless you can enjoy your success a little. And don't think, not for one minute, your mother is sore or angry or anything like that. It's a beautiful place you gave me down here. My arthritis is a thousand percent better, knock wood. And Cynthia, daughters like you don't grow on trees, I want you to know that. I could tell you stories about some of the people I've met that'd make your hair stand on end, the way children treat parents it's an absolute disgrace."

Barry called once a week from San Francisco, where he had gone in search of "God knows what," as Cynthia had already put it. "I'm doing fine, mother, just fine. The apartment's shaping up and I don't even limp so don't hassle your head about a thing. And once I'm all settled and know my way around, I promise to go out and look for a job."

It should only happen, she thought, saying, "Just don't go wild or crazy all over again. Did you find yourself a new psychiatrist yet? And what about your friend, David Fisher? Did he go back to school?"

"Yeah, I got a letter from him the other day. He's doing fine and . . . oh, that's right, I didn't want to forget. He sends his regards to you, thanks and all that. And no, I don't need a psychiatrist so don't harp about it. I just want a little peace for a change."

"That happens to be one of the funniest things you've ever said to me in years, Barry, years."

"Well I'm not laughing, mother. It's my life and I don't see what's the big joke."

"You just said it," she told him. "In a nutshell." And every other week she sent a check, knowing there had to be a better way but unable to figure out what it was.

As for Natalie, "my sociology major," Cynthia received a card from Boston—two actually, several weeks apart. Together they read, "I'm up here at B.U. for summer school so I can graduate early. And I just wanted you to know that your daughter is alive and well and appreciates the help you've been giving her/me. Don't ever think I hate you, mother, because it isn't so and hate is an ugly word, besides. Let's just say we had a 'personality clash' and leave it at that. Got a card from Barry. What's he doing in San Francisco? He sounded spaced-out and maybe I'm not being cool about it, but it worried me a little. Daddy said if I ever write you to say he sends his best and hopes that you are well and happy. If, by any chance, I get down to N.Y. this summer, I promise to call. Thinking of you, Nat."

D. W. bought a two-bedroom house at Fire Island Pines and invited her out for a long weekend. She respectfully declined.

At Brentano's, between the chess sets and the Modern Library editions, space was cleared and a table and chair set up for the autographing party NuBodies had organized—and was paying for—to herald the publication of Cynthia's autobiography, *With a Face Like Yours*. She'd wanted to have it called *A One-Woman Crusade*, as opposed to the title which, as she remembered after seeing the artist's proof of the jacket, she herself had thought up years before. But D. W. and Random House had voiced their objections, saying that (a) it was too self-congratulatory and, (b) would infringe upon the rights of ABC's documentary of the same name. It appeared that the network was interested in doing a follow-up story, running clips of the original "Faces & Places" episode to tie in with the autobiography and Cynthia's work over the last seven years. But when that project—much talked about over lunch at several of New York's finest French restaurants—fell through, she devoted he last two weeks in August to working on the pilot for the syndicated half-hour series Leonard was banking on selling to independent stations throughout the country, i.e., stations who were still unaffiliated with either NBC, CBS, or ABC. She had to go on a crash diet—"On TV, everyone looks ten pounds heavier than they really are. So it's no stigma, nothing

457

personal against you, Mrs. Morgan"—and the work was grueling. Her attorney, Jerry Brennen, had agreed with what Leonard had told her.

There were no snags with the autobiography. Advance orders were so heavy that it went into two additional printings prior to publication day. And just to "sweeten things up," D. W. had made sure to bus in two chapters' worth of members, so that the TV camera crews he had also arranged to be on hand would be able to "film a spectacle worthy of the accolade *cinéma vérité*." Within half an hour, she'd signed her name to nearly a hundred copies of the book. "Eyewitness News" had sent down Betty Oliver to cover the event. Cynthia had already learned the value of publicity—especially when it was free. The sight of a microphone being thrust under her nose was something she didn't have to be coaxed into putting to use.

OLIVER: How does it feel being a best-selling author, Mrs. Morgan?

CYNTHIA: (*returning a pen and an autographed copy of the book*) Unbelievable, Betty. It's like a dream come true. I never thought so many people would be interested in reading my life story. But it's very gratifying, it really is.

OLIVER: I understand there's talk in Hollywood about a movie version.

CYNTHIA: (*smiling radiantly*) Oh, I'm sure that's just something some bright-eyed p.r. man thought up. I mean, who could play *me*? (*laughs loudly*) I'm an original, right? I'm kidding, I'm kidding. But I did want to say that it's a very exciting day and I hope my book will be an inspiration to thousands of men and women all over the country. Right now I'm involved in another project though. (*accepts another book to be autographed*)

OLIVER: What's that exactly, Mrs. Morgan?

CYNTHIA: (*looking up with another smile*) A play, Betty. I've decided to try my hand at producing a play. It's a brilliant work entitled *Four for Dinner*. New Yorkers will be able to make up their own minds about it when it opens on Broadway.

OLIVER: And when will that be?

CYNTHIA: (*returning the book*) Enjoy it. (*to Oliver*)

Right now it's in rehearsal. But it should be opening in Boston sometime in October, with a New York opening at the Broadacre a few weeks later. We've got a brilliant cast lined up, with a young actor, Paul Antonio, playing the lead. He's going to take Broadway by storm, he's that exciting a performer. (*reaching for the mike as Oliver starts to step back*) And I just finished the pilot for a new TV series and the first Canadian branches of NuBodies will be opening their doors in Toronto and Montreal, later this month.

OLIVER: Sounds like you have a very busy schedule.

CYNTHIA: (*smiling radiantly once again*) The busiest, but I love it that way.

OLIVER: Well thank you, Mrs. Morgan, and good luck.

CYNTHIA: Thank you, Betty. It was a pleasure talking with you.

OLIVER: (*turning away*) This is Betty Oliver at Brentano's Bookstore on Fifth Avenue, reporting for Channel 7, "Eyewitness News." Now back to Roger.

Four for Dinner
a new play
starring
Paul Antonio

BELOW THE MARQUEE with its optimistic, twinkling lights, the crowds gathered early. The ticket-holders, in anything from black tie to blue jeans, were for the most part affiliated with NuBodies in one way or another. Advance sales had been nil and the house was papered. Cynthia arrived with Gene Burr in a rented limousine, but wasn't about to fool herself. She knew D. W. had arranged for the distribution of free tickets to franchises in the New York area. The *Boston Globe* had summed it all up in the closing paragraph of its review: "*Four for Dinner* is a theatrical meal I found both unappetizing and barely palatable. Mr. Antonio, who gets ample opportunity to display his bare chest and barely bearable talents, is joined by an undistinguished cast that appears to have been blocked by a director more in tune with the needs of radio drama than live theater. All in all, an inauspicious and disappointing debut for all parties concerned."

Two directors later the cast still seemed to be stumbling around the stage like the blind leading the blind. Justin had worked on one rewrite after another and now, on opening night at the Broadacre, Cynthia imagined he was still slugging away at the typewriter, still trying to play doctor to his first dramatic effort.

"Look, doll, plenty of shows bomb in Boston and end up becoming smash hits on Broadway. Just because some jackass in Bean Town didn't like it, doesn't mean Barnes and Watts, Kerr too, won't flip out when they see the play. And I thought the last dress rehearsal went very well, a hundred percent improved. So stop getting yourself all worked up, depressed. You don't want your maribou to get all damp and sticky, do you?" His laugh was hearty, boisterous, encouraging. But it wasn't infectious. Nevertheless, she flashed a smile that was known in the trade—meaning *With a Face Like Yours*—as Cynthia's "brave little grin."

When the limousine door opened, flashbulbs started going off left and right, courtesy of the two photographers sent down by *NuBodies* Magazine. She put on her best party air, posed for pictures with Burr and even with Clive Barnes, whom she bumped into on his way to his seat. Rodell arrived in a taxi a few minutes later, bags under his eyes and a nervous tic at the corner of his mouth like a signpost betraying his unspoken fears, anxieties that were impossible to put to rest.

"There he is," Burr said, taking Justin in hand. "Come on, you two. You look like death warmed over, Justie. You've written a brilliant play so cheer up, for God sakes. We all know we've got a winner on our hands, so let's cut all this morbid shit. It doesn't make good copy, anyway. Listen, every play that's got something going for it, that's worth its salt, goes through its share of troubles. It's only natural. So smile Justin, and you too, Cynthia. They're taking our picture. Everyone say cheese."

"Everyone say turkey," she muttered, the yellow maribou on her dress hanging down like a limp handshake, too tired to perk up and wave about as she stood below the glittering marquee.

Once inside, it wasn't much better.

Papered though the house was with loyal NuBodies fans, *Four for Dinner* and its Brandoesque star were unable to hold the audience's attention. When the curtain came down after the first act, people started making for the exits as if they'd seen flames shooting out of the empty orchestra pit. She wanted to get up and tell them it was all a mistake, that she was sorry she'd dragged them into Manhattan with the promise of an exciting evening, only to subject them to a play that should have closed in

Boston. But she was committed to Paul, if not to Justin Rodell, and that commitment had—according to her last calculations—already run her something in the neighborhood of one hundred thirty-seven thousand dollars.

Well, Uncle Sam'll just have to bear with me this year, that's all there is to it, she thought. But Christ, I'm embarrassed more than anything else. And poor Paul—

She stayed in her seat, rather than mingle with the smokers stationed by the theater doors. "I don't want to hear what they're saying," she told Burr. Justin, who had been sitting on her right, didn't return when the house lights dimmed and the second act got under way before a considerably thinned out and frosty audience. And when the final curtain went down at the end of the third and last act, she was already hurrying across the street to Sardi's. The second floor of the restaurant had been rented for an opening night party, replete with open bar, champagne, caviar, the works. Now, she would have preferred crawling into bed and closing her eyes, only to wake up the following morning without any memory of the fiasco, just a bad dream and nothing else.

"You were wonderful," she told Paul when he arrived twenty or so minutes later.

"Stop bullshitting, Cynthia. You weren't even out there when we made our curtain call. Only one by the way."

"I . . . I was just too nervous," she stammered.

"It shows." He turned away, picked at the caviar, and headed toward the bar.

"Now we wait," Burr said.

The management had brought in a color TV and the cast and crew hung around it as if it were an object of worship. Burr went off to telephone the *Times* to find out when Barnes' review would be out. The director, the third in what she felt had been an undistinguished and inept triumvirate, switched to Channel 11. Ten minutes later she slipped between the stage manager and the costume designer as the drama critic looked out at the TV audience, the watchful, nervous faces.

"If the play's the thing," he said, "then the new offering which opened tonight at the Broadacre theater is the strongest element in an otherwise uneven production—"

"Shit," she whispered. Behind her, someone dropped a glass, spilling a drink. She decided it was the most dramatic moment of the evening.

"—but in what is shaping up to be a far from memorable Broadway season, *Four for Dinner* has its definite moments. If you like your theater seasoned with liberal doses of black comedy, existential ennui, and semi-nudity, you might just find Mr. Rodell's mordantly witty play your cup of tea."

"Mixed," someone said loudly. "It's not all that bad."

Not bad my foot, she thought, and what does *mordant* mean, anyway? Besides, no one listens to Channel 11. It's Barnes that counts. If Barnes likes it, people'll stand on line to get tickets. I should have had the notices put up backstage, right after they took their bows, and that would've been the end of that. Would've spared everyone this . . . this wake.

"Another twenty minutes," Burr said, returning from the pay phone near the bar. "I heard Eleven gave us mixed notices."

"Mixed to tepid," she said, finishing her drink and going off in search of another.

At eleven-twenty, after hearing Channel 2's out-and-out pan, the drama critic for "Eyewitness News" faced the expectant and unhappy gathering. She edged closer, grabbing at Gene's elbow. "You know who that is?" she whispered.

"Not really."

"That's Jameson," she explained. "Richard Jameson who produced the documentary I was in, years ago. I didn't know he was reviewing for them."

"He just replaced Derek somebody or other, a month or so ago. It was in the trades. But let's listen, doll."

"—the latest turn in her career opened this evening at the Broadacre theater. *Four for Dinner*, billed 'a new play' though in my estimation it's all pretty much old hat, has as its major draw the appearance of former X-rated superstar, Paul Antonio. Known to West Coast audiences for his audacious blue movie performances, Mr. Antonio is ill-equipped to handle the complexities of live theater. It's unfortunate, because Rodell's play might have fared better had it been entirely recast and mounted in a smaller and more intimate Off-Broadway setting. But as it stands now, it's bloated and logy. It's too bad that Mrs. Morgan, known throughout the country for helping thousands of people lose weight, just wasn't able to trim this one down and work the same kind of magic—"

Someone reached out, stabbed at the controls, and the picture went blank.

"Sorry kids," she said, not even sure if her voice had carried. She looked around. Paul was nowhere in sight. She found Burr at the pay phone. He put down the receiver, turned to her, and shook his head.

"That bad?"

"Worse."

"Barnes hated it?"

"Barnes hated it," he said.

"Well that ends that, right?"

"Sorry, doll."

"Don't be. Can't say we didn't try. We did the best we could," under the circumstances. If she let go now, her face would sag, would melt, would go dripping off into tearful self-pity. So she held herself tightly and said, "What did he mean about Paul, that's what I want to know?"

"Who?"

"Jameson. What did he mean, X-rated superstar? What blue movies? Paul never told me he was in—"

"He never told me, either. I wish he had, too," Burr said. He looked down at the polished tips of his patent leather dress pumps. His black tie was crooked. "How's your drink?"

"Finished."

When she got back to Riverside Drive, less than an hour later, she knew she was too late. One glance and she saw all the telltale signs, the familiar half-open and emptied dresser drawers, the gaping jewelry box—velvet-lined like the case she had lugged up and down Utica Avenue, from one beauty parlor to another—which once had held the gold watch, the cuff links, the signet ring, the thin chic eighteen-carat chain he had to have because everyone who was everyone was wearing them, all the things in fact she had given Paul since returning from Los Angeles. Even the piece of Vuitton luggage she'd bought him when he'd left for Boston was now an empty oblong space on the top shelf of her closet.

She sat down on the edge of the bed, removed one shoe and then the other. One of the bedroom windows was open, but she didn't get up to admire the view. Something flapped like a lame wing. She turned her head to the side, one hand flying up to brush back damp tendrils of hair, off her brow and away from her eyes. There was a scrap of paper pinned to the pillow, rustling like a feather in the drafty room. She flicked on the light near the bed, pressed the piece of ragged-edged, freshly torn newsprint onto the polished surface of the rosewood nightstand and read, "Exclusive N.Y. Showing. Double Feature. ARDIS AMARE (Miss Mouth) & PAUL ANTONIO (Mr. Macho) in *Bucking Gigolo* and *Tongue in Cheek*. Plus assorted short subjects. 'Amare and Antonio deserve the title King and Queen of Hard-Core!'—Walker, *Love Rag Mag*."

Muy macho hombre, she thought. Me *mucho* ignoramus, period. Well, you win some, you lose some. Right?

She prepared a grilled cheese sandwich. "It's always better to eat a little something when you're feeling under the weather," Lena said in her head. When she got into bed and pressed her face against the pillow, she caught his smell, a mixture of sweat and after-shave. She wanted to cry, but refused to allow herself to be anywhere near as extravagant with her emotions. No, she thought, it's not even that, either. Because what possible good would it do, anyway? He's not coming back. I couldn't make him materialize even if I wanted to, so what's the point of tears. He took what he needed from me and maybe I did the same thing, too. Except I didn't take everything. I needed something more and now it's too late. He'll never be able to give it to me if I stand on my head. Laugh. Go ahead. Laugh.

The following morning Cynthia made plans to move out to the Coast.

BOOK THREE:

Somebody (Justin Rodell's Story)

December 1973

IT'S OVER A YEAR ALREADY since my play fell on its face. But like Burr says, "What are you worried about, Justie? You've got talent up the nose. And you're the last person in the world who's going to be a one-shot author. If you want something bad enough, if you want to be somebody that is, then go out and do it instead of sitting around on your face, mewling and puking and bemoaning your fate." That's easy enough for him to say, because ever since Mama Burr died a year or two ago, he's been sitting on something like half a million bucks. But far be it from me to talk about someone else's money. I'm sure his father, buried these last fifteen years, didn't rip off poor unschooled darkies and immigrant Jews just to make his fortune. No, I'm absolutely positive he made his money the same way good ole Cynthia Morgan did, with the sweat of the brow and a clever profitable gimmick. Can't say that I'm angry with her, though. I mean, fair's fair. When you get right down to it, she did pour a fortune into *Four for Dinner* (I should have retitled it *Gastric Upset* or just plain *Indigestion* with an exclamation point at the end). At least the critics didn't rip me to shreds or put most of the blame in my lap and on these poor rounded creative shoulders of mine, so I guess that's worth something, even if it is a pittance and doesn't pay my American Express bill.

What I'm getting at is that I'm out here in Los Angeles County thanks to Frank Wakeman, the executive producer of "City Hospital," now in its third lucrative season. I told Burr to get on his tail since they're supposed to be such good friends and get him to buy a script of mine. Otherwise I'll have to commit suicide or apply for welfare, in that order. "None of your smartass remarks, Rodell. Just spare me the histrionics, for a change," said my manager, friend, rich uncle who hasn't loaned me a goddamn penny since I've been his client, amanuensis, you name it. But I sent Frank a partial, a real weirdo scenario about this young couple who contract ergot poisoning (it's like LSD), and I'll be, the guy—who happens to be a gentleman from the old school—bought it! So that's why I gave up my studio in Fun City and took a cheap little place below the Strip.

So with forty-five hundred bucks in my pocket and one teleplay credit under my belt, I was ready to conquer the world . . . or Hollywood. And when Gene told me Cynthia had moved out here, that she'd been asking about me, I didn't know if I should clap my hands or turn around in the opposite direction and just keep walking. But as I said, I don't dislike the lady, even if she is a little loud and pushy, among other things. Then Gene announced he was giving her a party and don't ask me why, because he gives parties for everyone, his maid even, just like Patrick Casey. It's all a calculated way of getting people over to drink with him, as far as I'm concerned. Anyway, he asked me if I wanted to come and I said, "Sure I want to come. Why not? For old times sake, right?" That's how I got to see her again.

Won't this be a treat, I thought after I'd parked my rented car in Burr's driveway, way up at the top of a street—now catch this for urban planning—called Whipstick Way. Very ritzy address though, right above the Bel Air Hotel. But Burr always has had a knack for spending money. Anyway, there I was parked between a white Mercedes and Burr's yellow Jag, my cream-colored Pinto looking like a Schwinn racer, not even a ten-speed.

"I don't believe it I wouldn't have recognized him with his new beard; he looks fabulous!"

That's Cynthia, one run-on sentence and this head of bright copper hair that puts Medusa to shame. I closed the door behind me, did my soft shy little-boy routine —just got off the farm and ain't them there city slickers somethin' else, with a hangdog expression and a shuffle or two thrown in for good measure. The next thing I knew

470

she was sweeping me up in her arms like Mother Courage herself.

"You smell delicious," she said, lots of wet sloppy demonstrative kisses on my cheeks and forehead.

"And you look as dramatic and successful as ever," I replied. She still held my hands but that didn't stop me from stepping back and giving her a quick review with both of my beady eyes. "You've still got the biggest knockers in the business, Morgan."

"And you're still as fresh as ever and don't embarrass me, I don't even know all these people."

"That's all right, neither do I. Where's Burr? Drunk already?"

"Not yet—and he asked me to tell you to behave yourself, whatever that's supposed to mean."

"How's your drink coming?" I asked, because I didn't have a ready comeback just sitting there at the tip of my tongue.

"Fine. There's plenty of wine," obviously remembering that that's all I drank. "But it's so good to see you again, Justin. You look wonderful."

"So do you," I said. "California obviously agrees with you."

"We try."

I gave her a little squeeze and went off to pay my respects to Burr. He likes to show his clients off to people who come to the house. Since it was only late afternoon, one of those hell-I-can-get-away-without-giving-brunch-so-long-as-there's-plenty-to-drink affairs, most of the guests were outside on the deck near the pool. Burr's house commands a fantastic view of the canyon and because the Bel Air Hotel owns most of the land, they haven't allowed any developers to build or wreak havoc with the "untamed countryside," as he once called it. Tamed or untamed, it's all pretty spectacular, with a pink Monopoly set San Simeon sitting way at the top of the opposite ridge.

"How ya doin', doll," he said when I came up to him. It's an affectation, this "doll" business. Male, female, black, white, Christian, Jew. It doesn't matter to him. The world, at least for Gene Burr, is composed of those people who are dolls and those who are dogs. All his clients are the former until they leave him. Whereupon

471

they're automatically shoved into the denigration category.

"Your doll's doin' okay," I said, hoping I wasn't smirking enough to piss him off. But it's hard to tell, now that I've grown myself a beard. But anyway, we argue too much. He likes to play all-knowing avuncular Gene and it's a bore.

"Let me introduce you," he started to say.

"In a minute," not feeling as social as I knew I should —for my career, I mean. "I just want to get something to drink."

Most of the guests looked like minor TV executives he was in the process of ass-kissing and sucking up to so his acting clients would be able to get work. I wasn't particularly impressed or interested in middle management or why it was so difficult casting "Wide World of Entertainment." So I poured myself a glass of humble California white and started rapping away with a very together young lady, Jackie Treager. Burr already owns a couple of her canvases (and keeps promising me one too, when I hit it big, would you believe), Pat Casey too. For all I know, Cynthia bought a dozen when she moved out. I wouldn't put it past her, especially since it always struck me she had a thing for conspicuous consumption.

"I heard about your 'City Hospital' script," Jackie said, very Israeli sabra-looking even though she's actually Scotch-Irish.

"It's a script," I said, playing it down. "And I heard you're going to be hanging your work in that new restaurant . . . what's it called again?"

"Pierpont Plaza."

"Sort of a Green Café revisited."

"Something like that."

Then, since there wasn't much else to say, I slugged down my wine and went off in search of a refill.

Back in the living room with its museum collection of Biedermeier furniture. I saw Cynthia and Pat Casey with heads bent over and shoulders shaking, either from the strain of laughing too hard or plotting too gleefully. But whatever it was, she caught my eye and right away motioned me over to join them. "There's the young man I've been looking for," she said. "Has Gene told you about the plans for the musical yet?"

"No, should he have?"

"Now Justin's the perfect choice to write the book," she told Pat. Then to me, "Pat's going to direct a musical version of my life. Isn't that going to be fabulous?"

"Seriously, Pat?"

"Well, you know Cynthia. Her enthusiasm is infectious. It's an idea we're playing around with, that's all."

I don't think I've ever seen him half as serious as he was at that moment. But whether or not it had anything to do with the musical, I was yet to figure out. In any event, Cynthia said, "What d'you mean? It's more than just an *idea*. We have someone to write the music and lyrics, Kaaren Blyer to play me—"

"Gene's client, who won the Tony a year or two ago, right?" I asked.

She nodded her head, one hand rising up to sweep back all that wavy red hair. "She'll be fabulous, fantastic. A voice that Merman wishes she still had, let me tell you."

Gene was obviously feeding her good lines. But I must say I was intrigued. "When did all this come about? Last I heard you were still on the best seller list."

"Well what do you think I do, just sit around and vegetate out here? No way, no how."

Pat managed to make himself scarce and Cynthia and I were the only ones left in the living room. She plunked herself down on one of the sofas and I followed suit. She's a real mother figure and I guess I was in the market for a little maternal ego-boosting. Besides, it's a lot of work trying to be charming on a nonstop basis. And since Cynthia and I had once "enjoyed" a working relationship, I knew I didn't have to put on any airs or give her any lines. I could just be me. So I asked her to tell me what she was talking about, meaning the musical comedy.

She launched into a real animated blow-by-blow, telling me how Kaaren, and Billy Whiz-bang or some music-writing ace like that, and Pat to direct, and me to write the book, would all make pots of money—which came out of Burr's mouth, not hers—putting together a musical comedy-cum-extravaganza for Broadway. "Based on?"

"*With a Face Like Yours*, my autobiography," she said.

Your auto-whitewash, I thought, though the smug reviews hadn't seemed to have affected sales any.

473

She dug into her zippy Hermès bag and pulled out a cigarette. I had my handy-dandy, all-purpose disposable lighter ready and waiting. "Don't think I'm being chauvinistic," I said. The remark seemed to go over her head. She got her cigarette lit, inhaled, crossed her legs and swiveled to the side to get a better view of my handsome rakish Austro-Hungarian features.

"Think you can do it?" she asked, showing a lot of thigh.

I forced my eyes away from that remarkably unveined, unlined expanse of womanflesh. "You're serious now?"

"Sure I'm serious. Look, I don't know if you were embarrassed, or reluctant, or what have you, to see me this afternoon. You're not mad at me or anything, are you, doll?"

There was Gene, popping up all over again. "Of course not," much protestation and chest-thumping. "Why should I be mad at you?"

"Well, you know, because of the play and all." She let out a deep, world-weary sigh. "You'd think life would be easy but it isn't. With all the luck I've had with my business," whereupon she pulled the hem of her skirt down over her knees, "it's been the exact opposite with everything else. I bet you never opened a fresh mouth to your mother, did you?"

"She was too busy protesting against the bomb," I said.

Cynthia cocked her plucked eyebrows and said, "I didn't catch that."

And I said, "She was a professional left-wing Congregationalist pacifist demonstrator. That's why half the time I wonder if I'm turning into a reactionary sonuvabitch. Sort of a rebellion in reverse, you might say."

"Either I'm stupid or you're speaking too fast, cause I don't follow. But I know about rebels, believe me. I have two kids who wrote the book. But let's not go into it because I want to know how you feel about doing the musical."

"How do I feel?" I repeated. "I would love to do it; no shit, Cynthia. I mean, Christ, I've always been a sucker for Broadway types. And you know you can't get much more Broadway, much flashier than Burr. So it wasn't such an accident I picked him to be my manager. But what do you want me to do, prepare a treatment?"

"Only don't make it so experimental as—"

"*Indigestion!*"

That too slipped off into the universal ether.

"You know what I'm saying," she tried to explain. "This is gonna be . . . more commercial. Lots of singing and dancing."

"Does Gene know about the project?"

"Sure he does."

"I'll talk to him then. When would you want something?"

"As soon as possible. Because the quicker we get this thing—show—on the road, the better. Right?"

"Right."

"Excuse me."

"Sure." She left me sitting alone in that museum of a room, with all the highly polished surfaces and the extra added attraction of Gene's rose medallion collection. Actually, he inherited it from his mother, but we won't go into it. Not now, anyway. I sat back and must have smiled to myself or something because the next thing I knew these wonderful long languid hands were sliding down the front of my ready-to-be-scrapped workshirt with the hole in the pocket. I looked down and saw there was paint under the short, workmanlike fingernails, so, I knew who was going to get the benefit of my next line. "Are we ever going to end up in bed or is that just a persistent dream I keep having?" I asked.

"I thought you only went for weak-willed women, stay-at-homes who bake bread and make babies," Jackie Treager said. She swooped down and her hair fell over my face and I was looking at the blood rushing to her head and her tits flopping by my chin as she hovered over me.

"Someone's been handing you the wrong cue cards," I said. I reached out to grab her but she snapped back to attention.

She straightened up and came around to the other side of the couch. I patted the cushion next to me and Jackie slipped down with a wonderful graceful ease she sometimes shows in her work, especially if she's using pen and ink. Everyone says her oils aren't half as good, but she's getting better. "Bored?"

"Not at all, just a little tired," she said.

"How'd you like a ride in my luxurious Pinto coupé?" I asked, making sure to pronounce the *accent aigu*.

She wasn't amused. "Let me take a raincheck, Justin. It's the wrong time—"

"—of the month. Yeah, I know all about it." Story of my life, I thought.

It was nearly seven when the door closed for the last (next to last, since I hadn't made my dramatic exit, not yet anyway) time. I sat in the living room, nice and mellow after having downed four fast glasses of white, hoping I was still in a decent enough condition to drive home without killing myself. "Is she serious about the musical?" I asked when Burr finally stopped playing Harriet Craig and plopped his ass down on the armchair across from where I sat.

"Did she discuss it with you?"

"Sure did."

"Want to do it?"

"Shouldn't I?"

"Didn't ask you that, doll. I asked if you wanted to do it, that's all."

"You're drunk," I said.

"Now don't give me an argument, and what makes you say that, anyway. I had two drinks, tops. And one joint and I'm feeling fine. Up for dinner tonight? Early, cause I have a date after ten."

"Can't, but thanks anyway. I have an appointment with a very high-class hooker."

"My ass you do," he said. "You've never paid for it in your life. That's your problem. You're spoiled rotten."

"Me and Cynthia's two kids."

"Now who told you about that?"

"My my, aren't we being protective of Lady NuBody."

"Not true. I just think too many people shoot their mouths off. Unnecessarily, that's all. Who told you what?"

I was surprised at his show of curiosity. "Just something I heard, that's all," I said evasively, avoiding the issue. "But tell me about the musical. What do you think I should do?"

"What do you want to do?"

"Come on, Gene. You're the manager. You tell me."

"I think you can do anything you set your mind on doing, that's what I think," he said. "And if you want my God's honest opinion, her life story really would make a damn good musical, especially after seeing the crap that's been around the last couple of seasons."

"Who's going to back it?"

"Write it first," he said. "Then worry about the backers."

"And what would my percentage be?"

"No more than two percent of box-office, probably a little less since you'd be using someone else's material, the autobiography I should say."

"No shit," I said, pleased. Very pleased, actually. "Two percent of a weekly gross of say one hundred thirty-five thousand dollars is roughly what? Twenty-seven hundred a week," and I smiled.

"Your face is filled with money, Rodell. You're a greedy little sonuvabitch, aren't you?"

"Is that supposed to be news or something? Come on, who else is supporting me, Burr? Somebody has to worry about Justin and it might as well be yours truly."

"What about your parents?"

"What about them? Their entire fortune consists of six or seven municipal bonds, okay? Next question."

"No question. Write a treatment. I have a library filled with plays, musical comedies, you name it. Take your pick. Just a treatment, Justie. You don't have to write the goddamn book, you know. And how long would it take you? Tell the truth. Shit, the way you work, you'll have it done tomorrow night, more than likely."

"Not quite," I said. I got to my feet. My trousers didn't need straightening out since they were unpressed painter's pants. "I'll speak to you tomorrow. But you want me to go ahead and give it a try?"

"Fuck, yes," he said, which meant, "Absolutely."

"Who's tonight's lucky starlet?" I said at the door, about to let myself out.

"Spare me the snide remarks, Justin. I'm twenty years older than you. When you get to be my age—"

"I'll find out it just takes a little longer to get it up," and keep it that way, "that's all."

"Smartass!" he yelled, but he smiled, too.

"Somebody has to keep the world on its toes."

"And you're that somebody, right?"

"Absolutely, ole buddy. Beyond a shadow of a doubt." Then I stepped out into the California night, chlorophyll, smog, and a cream-colored Pinto leading me back to a Smith-Corona portable and a brand-new ream of erasable bond. Broadway, I thought. Well, why the fuck not?

February–April 1974

I GAVE MYSELF A MONTH, from right after Christmas until I was tickling the toes of February. I said to myself, Don't rush, Justin. You've got plenty of time. If not all the time in the world, then still enough to do a good job. Figuring she'd be far more impressed with a working book—or a treatment that came as close to a finished product as humanly possible—I didn't prepare any ten-page outline. Oh no, once I got started the whole thing sort of came alive by leaps and bounds. For four weeks I was at that Smith-Corona portable, from rough draft to first draft to second draft to final draft. I was pretty impressed with myself and all those drafts, all things considered. I mean, it's one thing to write a straight play, a *drahma,* but it's something else altogether to figure out how to write a book for a musical comedy. It started off with a great rousing montage scene, film and live actors, with the kind of set Boris Aronson wins Tonys for—plenty of chrome railings and levels, all wonderfully stark yet at the same time totally sophisticated; with turnstiles fat people didn't fit through and pay phones they get stuck in and lots of good shit like that.

You know, when I get into something, especially a project of this kind of magnitude, I just can't approach my work half-assed, half-cocked, half-heartedly. Oh no, it's got to be the whole effort or no effort at all. So I worked my ass off. That's all there was to it. And when, early in February with maybe a thousand bucks left in my checking account, I arrived at Burr's Bel Air "retreat," I wasn't feeling like a smartass in the least. A little smug, a little self-satisfied and self-congratulatory, yes. But not snide. I mean, I had nothing to be snide about. I'd done my homework, as it's called. I'd worked hard, very hard, and I had a feeling he was going to love what I gave him to read.

"Done?" which sort of said it all.

I nodded my head. I wanted the script to speak for itself, no exaggeration intended. And I figured he'd take a week or so to read it over. So imagine my surprise—if that isn't the cliche of all time, I don't know what is, except that I *was* surprised, so there—when he said, "If you've got an hour to spare I can read it this morning and let you know what I think. Instead of keeping you guessing . . . since I know you'll murder me if I do."

Rodell wanted to dance around he felt so pleased. "You are my ace in the hole, Burr," I said. "So if you'll lead me to your porn collection, I'll busy myself until you've finished the kid's latest magnum opus," He had a stack of *Playboy* magazines maybe a foot and a half high, which wasn't my idea of real honest-to-God hard-core. Well, beggars can't be choosers.

It must have been an hour later when he came out on the deck where I was catching a few rays and wondering why they always but always airbrush out the pink. I'd put the treatment, tentatively entitled *Pounds, a new non-fattening musical* in an impressive black spring binder and now he slapped it down on one of the deck tables, pulled up a lounge chair and said, "You blow my mind, Rodell."

"Is that good or bad?"

"Bad? Christ, I don't think you could write bad if you tried. Do you have any idea what you've done? You've put the whole goddamn history of musical comedy inside of a hundred typewritten pages."

"That's what I was trying to do," I said. I started to explain how I thought the show should encompass the musical idiom of each period, since it started with Cynthia as a kid back in the thirties and then went right up to the present. He waved all my elaborate explanations aside.

"That's not what I'm talking about," he said. "What I'm talking about is the fact that you've written a show that she's going to flip over. It's fantastic, just amazing, a delight to read."

I nearly split my lip I was smiling so hard. "You really think so?" the thought of two percent of box-office dancing around in my head like those proverbial sugar plums.

"She has to be crazy if she doesn't," Burr replied. "I mean, Christ, Rodell, you've written the part of the century. And if this won't be the supreme ego-trip for her, nothing will. Besides, when Kaaren sees this, she'll go bananas. My God, she's in just about every scene."

"I couldn't get around it, even with the subplot."

"It could be a little funnier."

"We'll get Doc Simon in to inject a little—"

"We don't need anyone. You can do it yourself. After all, it's just a first draft. Right?"

"Of course right. Sure. Just a first draft," I said. "I wasn't even sure if it was ready yet." (Boy, sometimes I just amaze myself, no shit.)

"Now he plays humble pie," Burr said to the overhead clouds, splattered thick as thieves across the sky.

"But you like it, you really think it's good?"

"I really think it's good. And I think she's going to adore it."

"So now what?"

"We wait till she reads it, and then we'll see where we stand," he told me.

And that is where all the fucking aggravation and trouble started.

Okay, so she was out of town for two weeks. That couldn't be helped. It was understandable. I tried my hand at writing a couple of short stories but they've never been my forte and my agent back in New York thumbed his nose and said, in effect, "Try again. Thanks but no thanks." Okay, that's understandable, too. You can't be an ace at everything. But the money was running out faster than a speeding bullet and Wakeman had all the scripts he needed for the rest of the season, so "City Hospital" was out of the question. No transfusions, no new blood required.

"Write another play, try a novel. But stop being so goddamn impatient," Burr said.

"Easy enough for you to say," I told him. He's sitting on five hundred thou so of course he doesn't have to worry about paying rent, phone bills, gas and electric, laundry, credit card charges, etc., etc. But I started work on another play, anyway, if only to keep my sanity, maintain my equilibrium. Day after day he called and kept firing me up, telling me it was going to be a smash-

481

hit musical, that I had nothing to worry about, that patience was a virtue, and all that kind of soothing bullshit managers hand out like pablum to their unhappy clients.

Oh yes, I was getting unhappy, that's for sure. Very unhappy. February goes by like a shot in the dark, like all I have to do with my time is sit by the phone and wait for someone to come to terms with their ego. No word from Cynthia. Lady NuBody's back from her whirlwind promo tour to Canada and the Food Fair at the New York Coliseum. Ten different varieties of "Thinner Dinners" (a registered trademark of NuBodies Inc., New York, New York) are now building miniature igloos in the frozen food cases of American supermarkets. Last time I looked, shares of common stock were going for something like twenty-seven bucks, while the rest of us poor suckers can't even afford to pay our taxes. So of course I'm getting pissed-off, royally and rapidly. I know for sure, for positive, she's sitting around her Malibu Beach Colony villa, gazing at her boring collection of signed testimonials and Ispanky porcelains, waiting for the decorators to finish up the work so she can move into her new—"The company paid for it," Burr confided just the other day—marble-floored mansion at the top of a hill in Trousdale Estates. So why the fuck can't she sit out by the pool or the beach or wherever she wants and read my script?

A good question.

I said as much to Burr, when the roar of leonine March was already going through its transformations, an ovine bleat of "Help!" if ever there was one. "Well what do you want me to do, doll?" he said when I called him.

"What do you want me to do?" I repeated, incredulous, as I tried to temper my voice, if not my words. "I want you to get her to read it. Is she ever going to read the script, Gene, or have I just been given the royal shaft? I mean, come on, fair's fair. I busted my chops for four weeks and the least the lady can do is come up with a yes or no answer, instead of sitting around and jerking herself off while I'm about to starve to death."

"You're not starving," he said, his telephone voice more grating than I'd ever heard it before.

"I owe the government something like six hundred bucks in back taxes, come April fifteenth. I don't even have that much to my name, so don't give me your . . .

that's right, whatever, about starving. I have no more money, Gene. What am I supposed to do, stand on the corner of Hollywood and Vine and beg?"

"Well, write something."

I hung up, thinking of classic paranoid conspiracies, plots, and a lot of neurotic garbage—offal of the mind—that didn't help my mental well-being in any way whatsoever. So I had no choice. I got into my creamy-dreamy Pinto two-door and headed out, taking the scenic route over Laurel Canyon. At Ventura, the original "Boulevard of Broken Dreams," I turned left towards Encino and Suburbia U.S.A. O Los Angeles you stupid fucker, you murdered Scott Fitzgerald and even if I'm not half as good, not in his league by any stretch of the imagination—mine or anyone else's for that matter—you're killing me. O Los Angeles, goddamn stucco graveyards and pastel ash heaps, dreams picked clean as the bones of last year's news ... well, at least I got it out of my system, which is more than you can say about most people. But the thing is, look what it's all come down to. I gave up my snug and comfy Manhattan studio to travel around in a rented car I can ill afford, knocking on the door of Sleaze Ltd., otherwise known as Sensuo Press Inc. I hadn't dealt with them in about three years, when I gave up six months of my time, energy, and self-esteem to do a series of forty-five-thousand–word porno epics. I knocked off four a month, five hundred bucks a shot. It was money, coin of the realm. It paid the bills. It didn't do much for my creative juices except to keep them going. But it did improve my typing speed and my standing with my landlord. And believe it or not, one of the first "books" I ever did for them was picked up for the movies. Entitled *Tongue in Cheek*, it was turned into a seventy-five-minute expletive deleted. I never got a penny in royalties and I never got a chance to see the skin flick, but at least it did wonders for my reputation at Sensuo Press. So I'd given them a call right after hanging up on Burr, hoping they'd have some work for me.

They did.

I spent an hour in their grimy offices, shuffling and scraping, the conversation turning alternately from "Don't worry about plot. Just give me a lot of action, but no four-letter words because of the Supreme Court business, get the picture" to "So how do you like the Coast and what's the story with that play of yours." In turn, I was alternately serious, smutty, humble, and charming. And when I finally made my goodbyes, I had a ten-day deadline in my back pocket and the promise of seven hundred badly-needed dollars, in addition. I stopped at a taco stand for lunch before returning home. The theme of the book was female dominance, something I knew nothing about. It meant lots of leather, black rubber, whips, and chains. I dragged out a dusty copy of Krafft-Ebbing, fortified myself with two Ritalins and a fresh pot of coffee, and went to work. After all, somebody had to support Rodell.

I don't think I've experienced a worse April than the one of seventy-four. And I don't mean because of Watergate, the inflation, or the shortage of gasoline, either. I mean that it was in April, my checking account momentarily revitalized but my ego languishing in the dustheap of broken promises, that Cynthia Morgan came out of the oceanfront closet of her retirement to pronounce judgment.

"She's coming over for drinks, so if you want to find out about the script, get your ass out here by seven," Burr said.

"Well, what did she say?"

"She didn't say anything."

"Is that good or bad?"

"How am I supposed to know, Justie. I can't read her mind. When we're all sitting around the coffee table, you can ask her. Not before."

I didn't like the way that sounded, but figured it was useless getting myself worked up into a pessimistic sweat. But when I arrived at Whipstick Way my stomach was playing the same kind of lashing games and goddamn if my hand didn't shake when I went to pour myself a glass of wine.

"Well, what a surprise," she said after her driver—a hard-boiled Mafioso reject, if ever there was one—let her out in front of the house and Burr led her inside his Biedermeier mausoleum. "I haven't seen you in weeks, Justin. I thought you were going to come out to the house, get in a swim or something."

I smiled, thinking, but not saying, I wasn't invited.

She settled in with a drink, and I'm sitting there on

real-live pins and needles, waiting for her to wade through the debris of her last promotional tour and the "gratifying" success of Thinner Dinners, selling out across the land like tickets to a Broadway show I was yet to write —or thought I'd already written.

"Justin's naturally been . . . anxious about the treatment," Burr said maybe forty-five minutes later, interrupting Lady NuBody's monologue and nonstop ego-trip.

"I meant to bring that up," she said.

"Well?" I said.

"Well, what can I say?" she said.

"Whether you liked it or not would help," considerably.

"Justin!" Burr said.

"It just didn't do it to me, Justin," she said.

"I see. Why not?"

"Does it matter?" she said.

"You're damn right it matters—"

"Justin!" Burr said, louder.

"Stop yelling at me, Gene. I sweated bullets over the treatment and the least she . . . Cynthia I mean, can do is tell me why she's dismissing a month of hard work with three little words."

"Well, I didn't know you felt that way about it," she said.

"Well how do you expect me to feel about it? I've been waiting for you to give me an answer, an opinion, anything, for close to three months now."

"It hasn't been that long," she said, looking over at Gene.

He kept his mouth shut, which was about as diplomatic and unhelpful as you can get.

"Most of February, all of March, and it's now three weeks into April," I said like *Poor Richard's Almanac*.

"Well you can't expect me to just drop everything, Justin—"

"You did when we were dealing with *Four for Dinner*."

"This is different," she said, "and I wish you wouldn't look at me like that. As far as I'm concerned, I came off very . . . snotty, unappealing, if you want to know the truth. Your conception of me, I mean. Very sarcastic, nasty. I didn't know you thought that little of me, frankly."

"I do now."

485

"Justin, just grow up for a change and apologize and stop acting like a spoiled brat," Burr said.

Then Cynthia said to Burr, not to me, "I've been in touch with Morton Avery. You know, the one who wrote that wonderful little book, *The Wishing Tree.* He seems very interested in the project."

That's when I decided (a) to leave and, (b) to get back at her like no one's ever gotten back at anyone before.

TIME: the following afternoon, a rare and smogless April lunch hour.

PLACE: the newest in-spot, the Pierpont Plaza, below the Strip in the heart of the decorating district, five minutes by Pinto from my studio apartment.

IN MEDIAS RES: which means we can skip over all the preliminaries such as "How are you?" "I'm not well," "What are you eating?" "My heart out," in order to get down to the real crux of the issue, the nitty-gritty as it were and as it is.

"You know," said Burr as he raised the carafe with an inexplicably trembling hand, poured himself more wine, and watched me wave my palm to ward off a refill, "the world doesn't revolve around Justin Rodell. I just want you to know that, for starters, doll."

"Do me a favor and cool it with the doll. The last thing in the world I am, especially at this moment, is a doll."

"Oh, we're so angry, so embittered, such an angry young man, today. We didn't get our way, things didn't work out the way we wanted, so we're out to kill. It doesn't cut with me, Justin. I just want you to be aware of that."

"I could care less."

He looked at me, shook his head, and glanced down at the menu. I wasn't particularly hungry—And do you blame me, or am I doing an ego-trip worthy of Ms. Morgan?—so I ordered a shrimp cocktail and let it go at that. Then, when the waitress departed, he cleared his throat dramatically, self-consciously, rubbed an invisible whatnot from the corner of his mouth and looked at me with a pair of small and reddened eyes. "What am I going to do with you, Justie?" he said, sighing.

"Nothing," I said, trying to see everything as a totality,

486

a symphony divided into neat and recognizable movements. We'd passed through the introduction and now things were revving up, quicker than I'd first thought. I didn't feel like being slow and tempered, somewhere between hither and yon, largo and larghetto. It just wasn't where my head was at; it just wasn't the right kind of sound, either.

"Look," he said. "It goes a helluva lot beyond the fact that she didn't like it."

"Meaning?"

"Meaning NuBodies, and not Cynthia, owns the rights to her autobiography. Listen, I invested a couple of grand entertaining her last year, trying to get her to sign with me. We had a series all lined up—this is before your play—and her partner, Leonard Frankel stepped in and said nothing doing. So what happened was, he invested something like eighty thousand in his own project and needless to say, it fell flat on its face. No one but no one wanted to pick it up, it was that much of a bomb."

"But you told me she was serious about the musical."

"She was . . . is, I mean. Except she told me, after you made your dreary adolescent exit last night, that Frankel announced his opposition."

"But she can open up her mouth and talk about that nothing writer, Morton Avery."

"She's a talker, what can you do," Burr said.

"But you knew she didn't own the rights to her life when this whole thing started, back in December. Am I right?" I stopped long enough for the waitress to put down our lunch, filet of sole amandine in front of Burr, the shrimp cocktail in front of me. I still wasn't hungry.

"Well," and he hemmed and hawed and said after another throat-clearing while, "I thought we might be able to get around him, Frankel I'm referring to now. I took her seriously, doll. Believe me. Would I have put you through all this shit if I hadn't taken her on her word?"

"That's not the point," I said. "You're a manager, a professional. You're supposed to figure out these things in advance. I worked my ass off for four weeks and you know what it gets me . . . it doesn't even get me on the subway, that's what."

"You learned how to write a musical comedy. Is that so bad?"

"It doesn't pay the bills, Burr."

"I'm sorry that's the way you feel about it. I did the best I could."

"It wasn't good enough," I said.

"Hey, come on now, Justie. This is Gene you're talking to. Get off your high horse for a minute and face the facts, buster. You're still an unknown out here. Do you expect everything to happen overnight? It takes a lot of hard work, effort. So you wrote something on spec, and she didn't buy it. So big deal. There's more going for you than Cynthia Morgan, for God sakes."

"I'm not through with her yet, not by a long shot," I said. "And these shrimp taste like they've been dipped in iodine."

"I'll send them back."

"Don't bother. But Lady NuBody hasn't heard the last of me, I assure you."

"Don't threaten me, Justie, because, just like you, I could care less," Burr said, his mouth filled with sole and his creased and furrowed face no longer holding the promise of success, big money, the good life.

"You knew all along that she didn't own the rights to *With a Face Like Yours.* But that obviously didn't bother you one iota. No, it was all right for me to go and kill myself—"

"You didn't kill yourself."

"You know what, Gene? You can shove your contract and your twelve and a half percent right up your ass. And if you don't like it, take me to court and sue."

He put down his fork with a great stainless flourish. "Now what the fuck is that supposed to mean?"

"Just what it sounded like. A good manager would never have put me through all this shit. And you said it a minute ago, not me. I've been sitting around, thanks to all your bullshit promises and kind words, waiting for something that wasn't going to happen even *before* I started writing the treatment. You said so yourself. Well you know what? You know what I intend to do?" And I stopped myself—smart cookie—just in the nick of time. It was none of his business. The less people who knew about it, the better off I'd be. "Enjoy your lunch," I said, pushing my chair back.

"Come on, Justin. Don't tell me you're going to make another one of your spoiled-brat dramatic exits."

"You know what, Burr? All my smartass remarks and

flashmouth comments are just a means to an end. Since we're being so honest this afternoon, I'll let you in on a well-kept little secret. My big mouth and snappy comebacks are just my way of trying to hide a very insecure ego, creative and otherwise. Contrary to popular belief, I am not the most well-adjusted, most confident guy in the world and you've done your best to whittle away a little more of my self-esteem."

"Are we finished, Justin? Are we done with the verbal pyrotechnics, and are you finally ready to grow up and face facts?"

"No," I said. "And I'm not finished with Cynthia Morgan, either. Because when I get done with her, she'll know precisely what it costs, the price you pay when you shit on someone's head and just . . . just dismiss them with three words like they're a lackey, like the world's a stageset for her benefit and no one else's. Oh no, I'm not through with her—"

"You're talking like a two-year-old."

"Thank God I don't write like one." I got to my feet, shoved my chair back in place against the edge of the wrought-iron table. "Have a good life, Burr. You're a terrific manager. You'll go far with all your second-rate talents."

"Rodell," he called out.

Rodell was already figuring out the cheapest way to get back to New York. Rodell was already plotting. This time it would be a book, not a play. A real killer of a book starring guess who.

You guessed it.

May 1974

THE ENGINE OF HATE AND VENGEANCE is a powerful motor, an equally powerful incentive. It constantly refuels itself. It got me where I wanted to go, though we won't talk about the cross-country ride on the Greyhound bus. Certain things are best forgotten, but it was the cheapest way to get back to New York, to see if the proposal I'd airmailed special delivery to Lloyd Tudor & Sons had found a receptive audience. Lloyd Tudor & Sons: a publisher known for its sexplicit novels, raunchy exposés, and muckraking tracts all designed to cash in on the public's quest for vicarious thrills, whether thinly veiled as fiction in the manner of a *roman à clef,* or else purporting to be "the real thing," no holds barred, straight from the horse's mouth.

From what I'd heard, they had money to burn, heaps of ready cash to invest in any property they felt they might be able to make a buck on. It was this kind of property I'd suggested in my five-page proposal—quite a comedown from the hundred-odd pages I'd written for Ms. NuBody, alias the Beast of the Ball. But this time I didn't intend to get burned—not if I could help it, that is.

My ex-fiancée, a Barnard graduate who'd broken our engagement at next to the last minute to run off (and eventually return unaccompanied) with the lead singer of a quickly forgotten rock group, wasn't averse to letting me use her Yorkville railroad flat as a base of operations. "Just a week, tops," I said. I didn't have enough for a hotel room. Since she was going to be out of town at a feminist convention in D.C., she really didn't mind having me around to take care of her cat. Barnabas, as she had christened her neurasthenic feline, slept curled up in a lump on top of her pillow, that and little else. As long as I cleaned out the kitty litter box every other day and left some wet and dry food on the counter near the kitchen sink, we got along fine.

In twenty-four hours I recovered my equilibrium and started to feel, if not my old self, then at least in rhythm with New York. And a few hours after those initial twenty-four, during which time I didn't want to think of anything but a hot shower and a warm bed, I arrived at the swank offices of the Messieurs Tudor. I'd mailed the précis to Hal Otis, their senior editor. His secretary led me down a narrow, carpeted hallway, bureaucratic doors ajar on either side, her pillow-soft bottom outlined and wiggling provocative invitations beneath a skirt made out of old and faded blue jeans. The women in L.A. were wearing the same. Nothing changes, I thought, except the level of my checking account.

"Mr. Rodell," and Otis got to his feet and extended a warm, slightly moist hand. He had a salt-and-pepper beard, trimmed very much like mine. I had a feeling we were going to get along just fine.

"Mr. Otis," I said, shook hands and took a seat alongside his very Danish modern desk. The secretary murmured an unintelligible something and closed the door softly behind her.

"How was your trip in?" he asked.

"They say leave the driving to us. Don't believe it for a minute."

"The bus?"

"Unfortunately. My play was not a smash hit, if you remember."

"Four for Dinner?"

"Yes," pleased that I had escaped literary obscurity, the label of nonentity.

"Interesting reviews though, if I recall."

"That didn't stop Mrs. Morgan from closing it the night it opened."

"Oh," he said and smiled and rocked on his sway-back chair, "so that's how you know her."

"Among other ways. So what did you think of my proposal, Mr. Otis?" I figured there was no sense pussyfooting

491

around. If he didn't want to do it, I could still hand-deliver the outline to my agent and get her to handle it. I'd avoided that up to now simply because she's not the swiftest person in the world and, for all intents and purposes, time was really running out.

"I'm interested," he said. "I would've sent it back if I didn't like it. Who's your agent?"

I told him.

"She's good, well thought of."

"Takes forever," I said.

"Well she's not getting any younger. Did you tell her about this or what?"

"Not yet. I figured if there was going to be a contract, I'd let her handle it, even though I've done all the legwork. She's been good to me, giving me her time and all."

"True, no sense being bad-mouthed," Otis said. "So you want to do an exposé based on," and he stopped just long enough to examine the first page of the proposal, spread out before him like a map of the New World, " 'the life and hard times of Cynthia Morgan.' "

"Yes," I said. "I think it's very marketable. It has built-in audience appeal, because of the tens of thousands of readers who have come in contact with NuBodies in one way or another."

"But you're not going to really get into the actual operation of the firm, are you?"

"To be quite honest with you, Mr. Otis, when I was writing a treatment of a musical comedy for her, Cynthia Morgan I mean, I went to several NuBodies meetings in Los Angeles. You know, to sort of get the feel of things, local color and all that. So I can say in all truth that I buy their methods, I really do. I don't think they're putting anything over on the public. I think their system works, probably better than most. We're dealing with its president and founder now, not the company itself. And from what I've been able to gather in just a week's time, there are a lot of interesting skeletons in her closet."

"Such as?"

I enumerated. He nodded his head and smiled.

"Separating the person from the myth, I take it."

"Precisely," I said. "At this point, the only person I've tried to find, and just can't seem to get a bead on, is Paul Antonio."

He consulted the outline again. "The young Italian lover?"

"Yes," I said. "But other than the fact that he's playing Judge Crater, I don't foresee any other great problems, difficulties getting people to talk."

"You'll have to work closely with our legal department, of course."

"Of course."

"You intend to make tape recordings?"

"Cassettes, yes. As long as I'm quoting exactly, I don't see how she can touch us."

"She can, but the idea's too intriguing to just forget about. What kind of advance were you thinking of, Justin. It is Justin, isn't it?"

"Yes." I figured that was the turning point. So I told him I appreciated his candor and forthrightness and all that, and said that I'd just about exhausted my resources, and that if I was going to make it the best possible book of its kind, it would cost me a considerable amount in air fares and travel expenses. "And you know what they say. Money talks and nobody walks."

"You really think that'll be necessary?"

"It might. No sense taking chances."

"You have a point there," Otis said. "I was thinking in terms of seventy-five hundred, if that's agreeable." He swung back and forth in the chair, trying to fix the price with an equally steady and unwavering expression, his eyes unblinking, his mouth set.

I smiled and looked down at my lap, saying, "That's very generous of you, Hal. But I really think ten thousand is more in line—"

"Out of the question," he said promptly, a bit sharply, too.

"That's too bad," I said. "Just the other day my manager out on the Coast was telling me how *NuBodies* Magazine already has a circulation of a million plus. And at least as many people, if not more, have gone to NuBodies classes. You've heard about the phenomenal success they're having with their new frozen food line, Thinner Dinners, haven't you?"

"Claiborne devoted his entire column to it, yesterday in the *Times*."

"I see you do your homework, too," I said, and laughed.

"On occasion."

He wasn't making any move to usher me out and so I added, "And just before I left Los Angeles, I was reading in *Variety* that she's been signed to co-host the Carson show, she and Pat Casey, a friend of hers out there, when he goes on vacation next month. That'll be close to two weeks of nightly exposure. If people don't know who she is by now, they will after she gets done playing the Perle Mesta of late-night television."

"That I didn't hear," he said.

"It was in *Variety*. Front page."

"Ten thousand," he said with a question mark, two fingertips stroking the underside of his chin. In that split second he brought back to mind one of my high school English teachers, the first person to ever encourage me to think about writing in terms of a career. I figured it was a good sign, prophetic or something like that.

"I know Avon wouldn't think twice about it, wouldn't hesitate. But I'd rather see the book in hardcover first. That way we're assured of a big paperback sale."

"In publishing, no one is assured of anything, unless you're dealing with a Robbins or a Michener. But okay, I see what you're driving at. It's not the kind of book you can research at the Forty-second Street Library."

"No, it isn't."

"Five thousand at signing and five thousand after I see a finished manuscript."

"First draft," I said. "The five thousand is going to go awfully quickly."

"You'd make a good literary agent," he said, nodding his head.

"I'm a better writer."

"Let's hope so."

I started to get to my feet.

"Oh, one other thing. When do you think you'll have something to show me?"

"January or February, barring any unforeseen difficulties."

"Sounds fine." He got up from his chair and once again extended his hand. "If you run into any problems, just give me a ring. That's what I'm here for. I'll have the contract sent out to your agent by the end of the week."

"That'd be great," I said. "I think we've got ourselves a winner on our hands."

"If her closets are filled with as many skeletons as you say they are, I don't see why not."

I couldn't have agreed with him more.

"I'VE NEVER BEEN INTERVIEWED by an author·before," Henrietta Margold told me as she sat in the living room of her three-room apartment in the Crown Heights section of Brooklyn. "My husband should be coming home any minute now. He knew Cynthia better than I did. You know why, of course."

"Of course," I said. "But you did tell him that I called, didn't you?"

"Oh sure. Manny and I are very open with each other. Can I get you another cup of coffee, Mr. Rodell? I made a big pot. There's plenty."

"No, I'm fine, thank you. The tape recorder doesn't bother you, does it?"

"Should it?" she asked and something seemed to burn behind her suddenly narrowed eyes.

"I don't see why," I said. "It's just a machine." Then I smiled and tried to imagine myself as her nephew, rather than a total stranger. I was still new at the game, so new in fact that this was the first interview I'd arranged since signing the contract for the exposé I'd already decided to call *The Fat Lady*. So if Mrs. Margold was a little nervous, sitting on the edge of her chair, I was just as anxious in my own right. I wanted to get her to come out with all the "good stuff" I was positive was lurking just below the surface of her affability and charm. She was a heavyset woman with frosted hair and short pudgy fingers looking strangely exotic with their complement of long, blood-red nails. She'd already told me that she worked as a manicurist at a beauty parlor in the neighborhood, the same shop where Cynthia—more than ten years before—had sold costume jewelry on a part-time basis.

"You used to be great friends with Mrs. Morgan, am I right?" I asked, trying to ignore the fact that while it was 1974, the Margold living room seemed stuck somewhere back in the Eisenhower years. The furniture was old, shabby, tired as the persistent wrinkle caught across the bridge of her prominently shaped nose. It gave her face a shopworn look, blunting my feelings till they were dulled with sadness.

"Like sisters," she said. "Isn't that disgusting the way she went and changed her name? Like she was ashamed of being Jewish or something." She glanced at the cassette player and then leaned back in the faded armchair. Lace doilies, antimacassars, were placed strategically on both arms, as well as the back of the chair. She was still wearing her operator's uniform, a shiny white synthetic zipped up the front to the collar. A rectangular enamel pin—white letters on a black field—declared MISS HENNY in small block letters. "There wasn't anything I wouldn't have done for her. I mean, I was this close," and she held up two fingers pressed tightly together. "I don't know who you've spoken to already, but I was the one who was responsible for getting her to lose weight, finding out about the diet she ended up using for NuBodies, I mean. She's managed to keep her weight down. I haven't. That's life, right?"

"Right."

"Sure, I mean, I've got more things to worry about than keeping my figure. Manny doesn't complain so I'm not gonna kill myself, break my back starving the way I used to when I was single. But that's another story altogether. If you want to know the truth, if Cynthia hadn't involved herself with this business of hers—and I'm not knocking it, mind you—I'd still be thin and I'd probably still be single, too. But she gave up a beautiful home, a family, for a career. Some women are like that."

"Yes, I imagine so. But tell me, Mrs. Margold. You went to high school with Cynthia, didn't you? What was she like then?"

"The same, basically," she said, offering me a chocolate from a box of paper-skirted miniatures. When I shook my head, she took one and settled back again. "But a pusher, know what I'm saying? I'm not begrudging her

her success, though if you'd see how the daughter turned out you wouldn't think she was such an angel. Barry I don't know too much about. Manny's not a talker when it comes to his children. And it's none of my business, on top of everything else. Believe me, to this day I wish Cynthia only the best. I don't have anything against her and I'm certainly not the guilty party, either. But now that I think about it, she wasn't much different even when she was fat. And she was fat, Mr. Rodell. When I say fat, I mean a real truckhorse, that's how heavy she was. I'm skin and bones now, in comparison to the Cynthia of ten years ago."

"What about in high school?" I asked again. "She went to Tilden, right?"

Mrs. Margold nodded her head. "The two of us. We were just starting to be friends then. She alienated a lot of people in those years. She had a chip on her shoulder. Well, who can blame her. I did too, a little, until I quit and went to beauty school and learned how to get along with people, which you have to do in my line of work. But she wasn't what you'd call a happy girl. Terribly self-conscious about her weight and she had bad skin, terrible in fact, from eating so much sweets, besides."

"Why did you say she was pushy, a moment ago?"

"Did I really say pushy?"

"Yes. I can play the tape back if you like."

"What for? I believe you. Well, it's true, actually. I mean, it's a feeling I've always had about her. She used to jam that jewelry she sold right down people's throats. Now *that* was when she was pushy. People used to shy away. They were afraid to say no to her, like she'd take it as a personal affront or something, like she'd turn around and say to them, 'So you don't want my kid to get bar mitzvahed like everyone else, is that it.' That's why she sold the jewelry, to pay for Barry's Bar Mitzvah. But then she goes and ignores her husband, takes up with some manufacturer or other and bingo, of course Manny starts looking for a little affection elsewhere. Can you blame him? When a man comes home from a hard day's work and his wife is too busy to cater to him, to be attentive is what I'm really saying, of course he's bound to get antsy. It's the human condition, as far as I'm concerned."

"Human nature, you mean," I said, unable to stop myself.

"Yes." She looked beyond me to the door, as if she expected her husband to arrive at that instant and confirm the sentiments she'd unconsciously raised her voice to express. When he didn't, she glanced back at me again and smiled mysteriously, about to share a secret. "Has anyone told you about their marriage?"

"Not yet."

Mrs. Margold leaned forward. Another grin settled on her lips and remained for maybe all of five seconds. Then she said, "Well, put this in your pipe and smoke it. Because if anything should go in the article—" needless to say, I'd avoided any detailed explanation of what I was doing, "this is one thing people should know about. And I'm not bitter, believe me. But you'd at least think she'd loan Manny a couple of bucks now and then, especially with his business failing and his having to declare bankruptcy last year. And the troubles we went through as a result. Forget it, selfish isn't the word for Cynthia Morgan," the last spat out like another expletive deleted. "When you're a celebrity—and if you ask me she looked like a horse's ass when she was on Johnny Carson last month—you always forget your roots, your people, your own kind. That's my opinion."

By the time she finished, I knew I had the material for a chapter no reader would ever forget. Talk about marital intrigues. Talk about children hating their parents. Talk about the ubiquitous Mr. Leonard Frankel, of whom I was beginning to discover lots more than I'd even hinted at in the outline. Oh yes, the second Mrs. Margold was a veritable fount of information. She'd obviously been holding her venom back for a long time. But now that she had a willing ear—a captive audience if ever there was one—she poured out her pent-up hostilities in a great and animated rush of recollection.

She hadn't ended her story soon enough, because right then a key scraped in the lock and her husband opened the front door. "There he is," she said. "I was wondering what was keeping him." You could tell by the look that came into her eyes that here was a woman who was genuinely in love. It was no wonder her remembrances had presented Cynthia as the villain, Miss Blackguard U.S.A. Since I'd quote her directly, that was fine with me. I hadn't started this project thinking people (other than the overweight) adored Cynthia Morgan. Now, my

499

assumptions were fast becoming fact. It remained for me to convince Forman Margold that I was on his side, too.

As heavy as Henrietta was, Forman made her look trim and slim. His frayed leather belt was a case history in itself, a study in faltering will power. Nearly every hole looked as if it had been used at one time or another. Now, the belt was fastened so close to the end, the last notch, that there was hardly enough to cover the buckle. His wife was out of her chair, the model and attentive spouse she'd so adamantly declared Cynthia not to have been. She threw her arms over his shoulders, kissed him full on the lips and squeezed one blue five o'clock shadowed cheek. I also got up, aware of the way he tried to size me up in a single circumspect glance.

"Good afternoon," I said, though it was well past five. "I'm Justin Rodell. I called last week, remember?" I extended my hand and he returned the handshake.

"How do you do," he said. To his wife it was, "Excuse me, honey. I want to wash up. Have you offered Mr. Rodell a bite to eat? Maybe a beer."

"I tried but he said he's not hungry. I made him coffee. How'd it go?"

"No good," he said and excused himself with a nod of his head.

Mrs. Margold turned back to me. "Can't find work. They don't want to hire a man close to fifty. And he was his own boss all his life, besides. What are you supposed to do, go on relief or what?"

"It's a terrible situation," I said, commiserating with a cliché she seemed to overlook.

"As far as I'm concerned, she's the one who ruined his business, the one who's responsible. He's a defeated man now, tired before his time." She edged closer, a whisper that implied all the walls had eyes and ears. "It's demoralizing, when the wife ends up being worth God knows how many millions and the husband can't even afford to buy himself a decent pair of shoes. You think I like doing nails, washing heads, day in, day out? I hate it, like poison. But who has the choice? Money's money. The landlord wants his check, right on the first."

"My . . . uh . . . publisher, has provided me with a small amount of expense money, Mrs. Margold," I said, figuring she'd already laid the groundwork for me. "He's

500

a great believer in the old adage that time is money, money is time, if you know what I mean."

"You must be joking," one hand on her throat in a gesture that said she was taken aback.

"No, I'm serious. I'm prepared to offer you a check for one hundred dollars, thanks to your cooperation. Your husband's too, I hope."

"A hundred dollars?" she said.

"That's right. I have the check all written out," which I really did.

"You're a young fellow. I can't take money just because I spoke to you from the heart."

"It's not my money, Mrs. Margold. My publisher's a very wealthy man. He believes in reimbursing people for their time, as I've said."

"Manny, did you hear that?" she said when he came back into the living room. Beads of water still clung to his hairline. A fresh shirt replaced the banlon pullover he'd worn earlier.

"What?" he asked. "And what's the matter with the air-conditioning?"

"It's been on the blink, on and off, all day. But Mr. Rodell's publisher has authorized him to give us a check for a hundred dollars."

He stopped short, halfway across the living room. I was still sitting in my chair, trying to look like every mother's son. "What kind of article you writing, Mr. Rodell?"

I told him I was going to be interviewing people who knew Cynthia before she got involved with NuBodies.

"What is this, *True Confessions* type stuff?" he said.

This guy's nobody's fool, I thought. Defeated or not, he's no pushover. "Not quite," I said. "What would Mrs. Morgan have to confess about anyway?" I pretended to laugh.

"Honey, do me a favor and get me a cold drink, some juice or something." He fiddled with the air-conditioner and then turned back to me, standing with his hands in his pockets, the jingle of small change a coppery melody rising above the drone of the old and antiquated machine. "Plenty," he said at last and I had to do a fast rewind in my head to realize it wasn't a *non sequitur*.

"Plenty to confess about, you're saying."

"Exactly," he replied. "Some social significance this is,"

501

and he laughed, exposing a set of teeth badly in need of dental care. But there was no money for vanity, not much money for anything, it seemed. I think at that instant, with Forman Margold's bad teeth staring me in the eye, I came pretty close to not just hating, but despising Lady NuBody. She's sitting on a fucking fortune and her former husband, the father of her two kids, is living like a welfare case. And whose fault is it, that's what I wanted to know.

"My wife sold herself to the highest bidder, plain honest talk, Rodell," he said, finally taking a seat as his wife returned with a glass of orange juice and a plate of cookies. Again I waved aside the offer of more coffee. "You've heard of her partner, Frankel, I take it?"

"Yes."

"He knew a good thing when he saw it, that's my opinion. Took her for a real ride."

It must have been a hell of a ride if she no longer owned the rights to her own life. But I decided not to tell him what I knew, to play dumb yet interested, as innocent as all get-out. So I said, "I'm not sure I follow, Mr. Margold."

His wife sat down next to him on the couch, self-consciously playing with the skirt of her uniform. She smoothed it out like she was making a bed, folded her hands neatly, and turned her head in my direction. "What I'm saying is," he went on, "I would've gone along with her, and no offense to you, Henny—"

"Of course," she said, smiling.

"—but she never gave me half a chance. Do you know what it is to sleep with a woman who thinks you're garbage?"

"Forman!"

"I understand, Mr. Margold. My fiancée left me two days before we were supposed to get married,"—an exaggeration, but pretty much close to the truth, give or take a couple of months.

"What a shame," Mrs. Margold said.

"So you can follow what I'm driving at, then."

"Yes," I said.

"All right, that's what it boils down to. And believe you me, when you start making it, when things start happening one-two-three, no one in the world matters for one minute. She didn't let anything get between her and success. Who else have you spoken to, may I ask?"

"Just some people out in California."

"Did you see her on the Carson show?"

"Yes."

"What'd you think?"

I shrugged my shoulders, not wanting to say anything which might influence him, one way or another.

"Not talking, eh?" He grinned at me and took a sip of juice. "I thought she was pretty good, myself. My wife here can't bear the sight of her. Me, you get older, you get mellower. Not necessarily wiser, mind you. Remember that."

"I'll try," I said and searched my pockets for the pack of cigarettes I knew I'd stashed away before I left Manhattan.

"Has anyone told you about how she treated Natalie, her daughter? Our daughter. What's the difference, you know what I'm saying."

"No, not yet."

Mrs. Margold got up to find me an ashtray.

"Is your tape recorder going?" he asked.

I nodded my head.

It was more than an hour later when I turned down their invitation to stay for supper. Mrs. Margold was ready to take the check, but at the last minute her husband folded it in half and handed it back to me. "Believe me," he said, "I didn't talk to you because I need your money. As far as I'm concerned, she's pulled the wool over everyone's eyes. And this is not gonna be just any old article, is it?"

"No."

"Maybe you'll turn it into a book, right?"

Shrewd cookie, I thought. "Maybe." Margold had played it straight with me, and I was already feeling a little guilty, holding back on him.

"Well, get the truth then. This is a real American story, Rodell. This is what Horatio Alger never wrote about, believe me. If I were you, I'd concentrate on that, finding out what success and love of money . . . and power, don't forget power . . . does to a person. I don't know what my wife told you before I got here. But before Cynthia started carrying on with this NuBodies of hers, she was . . . well, I had no complaints. She was a good wife and an even better mother. Then she started to change and there was no stopping her from then on in." He led me to the door and reached for the knob. "You wrote a play a year or so ago, didn't you?"

"I beg your pardon?"

"Sure you did," he said, and he gave me another toothy grin. "I read the *Times,* cover to cover, most every day. Rodell, Rodell, I knew the name rang a bell. Wasn't that the same play she got herself—"

"Yes it was. Well, thanks for your time, Mr. Margold." I looked beyond him to the living room. "And thank you again, Mrs. Margold. You've both been very kind. I appreciate it."

"It's been our pleasure," she called out.

Forman Margold opened the door and walked me to the elevator. "Don't tell anyone I told you," he said. "But if I were in your shoes, I'd go out and get the goods on Frankel. There's more going on there than meets the eye."

"What kind of goods?" I said. The elevator door creaked open. On one of the wooden panels, someone had carved *Fat Nat Does It.*

"You're the writer," he said with a laugh. "I'm just the poor schmuck who got caught in the middle." He turned away. The sound of his backless slippers followed me all the way down to the lobby and out onto the noisy, steaming Brooklyn street.

August 1974

THE AIRPORT WAS CLOSED DOWN in Santa Fe, which meant I had to fly into Albuquerque and then rent a car. It was some seventy miles or so along I-25; as bleak, hot, and defeated a landscape as I'd ever seen before. But I had plenty of gas and a gallon's worth of extra water, just in case. Actually, I needn't have worried. It wasn't Death Valley and the rented Pinto—notice how consistent I am—didn't give me any grief. Once I got into town, I stopped at the first traffic light and asked the driver of the car right alongside of me the quickest way to Garcia Street.

There were several "turns lefts" and one or two "turn rights" and before I'd quite figured out what I was doing, I was pulling up in front of number 613. She was expecting me, though I hadn't been able to give her a definite time. If she wasn't home, I'd already decided to drive around until I found a place to get something to eat.

Henrietta Margold had saved me more time and energy than I think she realized. "I'd like to get in touch with Natalie," I had told her, a week or so after I'd been to the apartment. "Just a letter. But I'm afraid I lost the address her brother gave me in California." I was lying through my teeth, but at this point I had no choice. I couldn't worry about ethics when I was writing a rather unethical and unapologetic kind of book, nor when I had a deadline that loomed up before me, getting closer with each passing day.

"I don't have it in my directory," she said. "But wait, Manny got a letter a couple of days ago. Maybe there's a return address on the envelope. She's out in Santa Fe, I guess you know."

I hadn't, but I said I did.

"Here it is," she said a few minutes later. "Hard to read her writing. Six . . . yes, It must be. Six-one-three Garcia Street, Santa Fe, New Mexico. You need the zip?"

"Sure," I said, to be authentic.

"Eight-seven-five-o-one."

"I can't tell you how much I appreciate this," I said.

"It's nothing. After you left, you know what my husband said? That he'd give his right arm for his son to be half as aggressive—that was the word he used—and well-spoken as you."

"Thank him for me," I said.

"I will and Mr. Rodell, when you write Natalie, tell her I say hello. Her father, too."

"Certainly." I don't know why I found that so funny, but I did.

Contrary to what I'd told Hal Otis, I really hadn't gotten myself involved in Cynthia's background when I was out in California. I tried to find Paul Antonio, as I said, but no one seemed to know what had happened to him. As for Barry, Cynthia's son, I heard through the grapevine that he'd been living in San Francisco, but that he moved into Cynthia's Malibu beach house shortly before our "blowup." So I was taking things by degrees, moving steadily across the country and back toward the West Coast, or so it struck me as I got out of my car, locked up, and mounted the warped wooden steps which led to the front door of 613 Garcia Street.

At this point, I had a pretty clear picture of Cynthia's marriage, the "something" that had happened as it were. Even if it was a one-sided view, half of a stereoscopic slide and nothing else, it was more than enough to get my readers' interest going.

The daughter could help pull more of the pieces together. I'd managed to have lunch with two of Natalie's high school teachers, under the academic guise of documentation and research for an article I was preparing on the Margold clan. The consensus was that she had been a brilliant but erratic student, much like her mother in that she'd been very self-conscious about her weight. "Natalie never smiled," her English teacher confided. "She was reading Kafka when the rest of her peers were struggling through Tom Sawyer. Keen mind, but no participatory sense, understand?" Her guidance counselor, the woman who had been responsible for helping her gain admission to the University of Wisconsin, told me that Natalie was blessed with a streak of self-criticism, selectivity—whatever that was supposed to mean. When I tried to pin her down to specifics, she said, "She was not the usual type and I daresay most of that rubbed off from her mother. Mrs. Margold . . . Morgan now, as I understand . . . was, is, an achiever of the first order. Naturally, Natalie lived under that kind of competitive shadow. A cloud, you might say. She struck me as being in constant battle with herself, always demanding more from her young resources. Will that be helpful, Mr. Rodell?" I told her it would be very helpful and made sure to pick up the tab for lunch.

By this time I'd managed to get in touch with Natalie through the mails. I told her I was interested in interviewing her for a piece I was doing on NuBodies, "all of the Margolds, as well." Something about the fact that she was living in Santa Fe prompted me to add that it would involve remuneration for her if she was, in so many roundabout words, cooperative. She replied with a postcard mailed less than a week after I'd sent out my letter of inquiry. "Remuneration is what I'm most in need of and if you want to come out here, I'll let you know why. Natalie Margold."

Ms. Natalie Margold, I thought, and rang the downstairs bell to let her know I was on my way up. The door didn't have an inner lock, but she rang back all the same. Glad that she was home, I trudged up the stairs. Apartment 6 was on the third floor of the old wooden building, the kind of multiple dwelling which has seen better days, like maybe thirty years before. Cynthia was living high off the hog while everyone else who'd touched on her life seemed to be suffering from financial difficulties, dire straits of one degree or another.

"Rodell the playwright," she said. The door opened to reveal an absolute knockout of a chick—and I don't mean that derogatorily or chauvinistically, either—standing there and filling the threshold with a bod that seemed to go on for days. I mean, she was that beautiful, that exciting just to look at. To ogle, actually, since that's what I was obviously doing. So of course my stare was accompanied by a classic double take. I'd been prepared for the exact opposite, an acne-coated chubby clutching

507

a half-eaten banana in one hand and the remains of a cupcake in the other. But this was no plump, pimply wallflower standing before me. No way.

"Surprised?" she said.

"Very. I'm Justin."

"Of course you are, greedy Rodell."

I didn't know where she'd picked that up from, but it didn't delight me, certainly not the way she did. She had reddish-brown hair that hung down Cherokee fashion, just the slightest hint of a natural wave as it cascaded over her back and shoulders. Her belly was tomboy flat, her breasts small and girlish, her eyes large and rimmed with kohl. She wore a pair of repatched jeans and an old white oxford shirt rolled up to expose a bare and desirable midriff. "You are one beautiful lady," I said, unable to help myself. I must have been licking my chops or something—she was that much of a turn-on. And for reasons more psychic than substantial, I had no sense of being a total stranger, either.

"You're damn right she is," someone called out from within the apartment.

Natalie beckoned me inside. If it was ever time to be wide-eyed and openmouthed, this was it.

"I don't believe it," I said. "I just don't believe it."

"Believe it. How ya doin', buddy?" He came forward, barefooted and blue-jeaned like Cynthia's daughter. A hand shot out and he clasped me around the shoulder. "Scared the shit out of ya, didn't I?"

"What the fuck are you doing here, that's what I'd like to know." I heard Natalie locking and bolting the door behind her.

"Oh it's a long long story, ole buddy," Paul Antonio said. "But you've got plenty of time to hear it all, I gather."

"Yep, you gather right."

He let go of me, stepped back, put his hands on his hips and shook his head. "Don't you look like a real city slicker," he said. "Nat and I are on food stamps and you look like you've stepped out of Magnin's window."

"Well—"

"He's playing Edward R. Murrow so of course you've gotta look the part," Natalie said. "How about some wine?"

"Great." I was still dazed. I took the tape recorder off

508

my shoulder and set it down on a vintage Salvation Army table. They had one room with a closet kitchen. It might have been home for the two of them, but it brought to mind Hoovervilles and Quonset huts like you wouldn't believe. "Do you know that I tried to find you in L.A. and it was like you were swallowed up whole. No one knew a fucking thing. Even your old friend, the guy who bartends at Cyrano's, didn't even know if you were alive or not. What's been happening, man?"

"Have some smoke first, unwind," he said. He had a joint ready and I rolled up my shirt sleeves and settled back on their moldy but functional living room sofa. "So what do you think of the moon lady's daughter?"

"The who lady?"

"The moon lady. Cynthia. What do you think of Nat? A piece, am I right?"

"Flattery gets him everywhere," Natalie said. She came back with three glasses of Dago red, made herself comfortable next to me on the couch, and looked expectantly at Paul.

"I'm still confused," I said as he handed me the joint.

"Take it slow," she said. "It's very trippy stuff."

That's not what I was confused about. But I nodded my head, held the smoke down and then passed it over to her. After I'd cleared my lungs, they fielded questions fast and furious, even before I got a chance to catch my breath, get my bearings, or turn on my cassette player. What kind of thing was I writing? Did her mother know about it? When was the last time I'd seen her and who was giving me the money for the story? Who had I spoken to and what had they said? Wasn't I worried about a libel suit, a knock-down-drag-out legal battle?

The grass lowered my defenses. I felt relaxed and self-confident, sure of myself, sure of them as well. I figured that if Cynthia's old lover was shacking up with her kid, they obviously weren't on anything but her shit-list. So this time I didn't play at being the Sphinx, cryptic and all that nonsense. I told them how she'd shafted me with the musical comedy—mentioning in particular her (now infamous, at least in my estimation) line about Morton Avery, which I still believed said it all and summed up my case. Then I explained how Tudor & Sons had given me a contract to do a big fat nasty book, "telling it the way it was."

"The way it is," Natalie corrected. "And grimy's not the word for it, either. You don't know the half of it."

"But you will," Paul added right after.

I couldn't figure out why they were so eager to tell me what they knew. But I certainly wasn't unhappy about it. I managed to get the tape recorder going, though by this time I was already far gone, stoned out of my head.

"Told you it was dynamite dope," he said.

"Unbelievable. And I have bread for the two of you," figuring it wouldn't hurt to sweeten up the pie, right from the start. "I take it money's in short supply."

"Paul had to make another one of those—"

"Art movies. It's not important."

Natalie, who was giving me wonderful once-overs with those big black-rimmed eyes of hers, settled back with a glass of wine. "I don't know why I'm telling you all this," she said.

I said, "You haven't told me anything yet."

Paul said, "That's how stoned she is."

"It's better than being straight and uptight," she said, which in my mind sort of dated her as a post-teenybopper.

After *Four for Dinner* flopped flat on its face, Paul took off like a scared jack rabbit, a bat out of hell. He went back out to the Coast, where he lined up a couple of parts in skin flicks, quickie blue movies for equally quickie salaries. Turns out, too, that *Tongue in Cheek,* the porn novel I'd written which had been sold to the movies, starred Antonio and someone else I'd never heard of, a Ms. Mouth or something like that. Anyway, he finally did land a more "respectable" job, waiting tables at the Pierpont Plaza. Well, L.A. isn't all that big and sooner or later—sooner, as it turned out—who should come in for lunch with one of his clients, but Gene Burr. Cynthia had just rented a house in Malibu and Burr obviously was a little plastered, or mean, or maybe just plain mischievous, because he suggested Paul come over to his place when Cynthia was going to be there. Some party or other, as per the usual. Paul thought it might be a goof—the casualness of all these complex couplings really blew my mind—and so did Natalie. She'd just graduated, had gone out to the Coast on her mother's invitation—and air fare. Well, Natalie showed up at the party without Lady Nu-Body in tow (Cynthia had a headache or stomach ache, or some ache like that, and bowed out at the last minute). Natalie meets Paul, Paul meets Natalie. And Gene Burr, the old bastard, sort of smiles malignantly in the background. Nature took its course, as they say. Next thing happens is Mother Morgan is kicking Fat Nat out of her heart and home. "Called Paul a bum, a junkie, a sex freak, do you believe. After they've been boffing for months. She's weird, Rodell. I mean, she's on an everlastin' ego-trip that just doesn't end." So Nat's out on her ass and Brother Bar doesn't have bread to hand out and so they decide to do the let's-hitch-and-worry-about-it-afterwards number. "Forget the commune scene," she said, knowledgeable about things I never wanted to know about to begin with. "A lot of losers get together and ball up a storm and pretend to plant beans and corn and crap like that and it's such a joke, it's sad." So they quit that particular scene in Taos, tried several others, and ended up in Santa Fe, 613 Garcia Street—after being kicked off Apodaca Hill and then Canyon Road, when they failed to meet their rent.

Well there it was, all wrapped up, just waiting to be transcribed from the cassette onto my typewriter. Natalie took a deep breath, Paul rolled another joint, and I hunted up more wine and let all the words buzz around in my head like a hive of fat and contented honey bees, drunk on the most libelous nectar imaginable.

We finished off the half-gallon jug and I flipped the cassette over and punched the record mode. "The thing is," Paul said, "is that Cynthia's basically a joke."

"Why?"

"Come on, man, it's obvious. Aside from the ego number she's doing on herself, and aside from the fact that between you and me she's having trouble keeping her weight down, all over again, she plays games with herself. Constantly. How for example? Okay, take me. I came along and of course I knew a good thing when I saw it. I came prepared in fact, because her friend Casey let it be known she was available . . . in the market, I should say. That was his opinion, of course. But it panned out, as you already know. Thing is, here was an old lady—and I don't mean *old* old—who had a lot of bread and an empty bed. Right? Nat knows how I feel about it so don't look so scandalized."

"I'm not," I said, and I wasn't. I was just amazed how everyone had to get in their digs, how free they were to shoot their mouths off, doing half of my work for me. I almost felt sorry for Cynthia. Almost, but not quite.

"Okay, cool. She was horny. She was lonely. She wasn't getting it on with anyone or anything but her bankbook. Fine. I came along and I filled her heart—" whereupon he started laughing and gagging so hard that Natalie had to thump him on the back before he recovered and caught his breath. "Very strong shit we get out here," he finally managed to say. "But wait, wait, lemme try it again. Rodell, I ain't a bullshitter, right?"

"I hope not."

"Well I'm not. Cynthia wanted a lover, and I was there at the right time in the right place. So it worked, for a while, anyway. I mean, I wasn't disgusted getting between the sheets with her—"

"Stop being so goddamn clinical," Natalie said. Her face was suddenly red. Looking at her, I saw how she bore more of a resemblance to her mother than I'd first realized. "Who gives a shit anyway how she is in bed. I'm not interested."

"Ohh, aren't we being sensitive today," Paul said, chucking her under the chin. "Just remember, precious. Speed kills."

She pulled back and I thought to myself, So Ms. Nat's speeding along, on top of everything else. Interesting, very interesting and unexpected.

Paul glanced at me and shrugged his shoulders, as if he didn't even realize what he'd just said. "Women are all the same. Young, old, it doesn't matter. But what I'm trying to say is that I knew she could do good things for me—meaning my career. I still think I wasn't half as bad as the critics said, but that's finished, so why hassle our heads about it. Thing is, she started getting possessive, like real early on in the relationship. If I didn't come home at such and such an hour, she'd get all uptight, start playing suffering wifey. Now *that* is when it got to be a drag, lemme tell you. Then the other thing is, do you know the people she surrounds herself with, businesswise I mean?"

"I haven't met them yet."

"Oh man," he said, "they are something else altogether. First of all there's this slick little fag who's got her wrapped around his fuckin' sapphire pinkie ring. D. W., would you believe that's what they call him? Well they do, no shit. Anyway, this D. W. is one slimy bastard, lemme tell you. Takes advantage of her, like you wouldn't believe. Then there's the partner, another Jew-boy . . . sorry, Nat, but you know what I'm saying—"

"Dagos are all anti-Semitic," she said with a bare hint of a smile. "It's part of their ethnic insecurity. But go on, Paul. I'm all ears. I'm sure Rodell is, too. Aren't you Rodell?"

"Sure," I said and smiled, trying not to stare too hard at her tits, trying not to watch the way she was suddenly rubbing her arms together like a boy scout does with two sticks when he wants to build a fire.

She looked cold and the apartment was warm, hot even. Speed kills, I thought, and stopped smiling.

"Okay," Paul went on, missing the story that was probably reflected in my eyes. "This Frankel character is like the puppetmaster. Get the picture? He pulls the strings and Cynthia dances. D'you know what that fucker did to her? Fiddled with the stock market, that's what. Look how he's lookin' at me, Nat, like he don't believe me or somethin'."

"I believe you," I said. "Every word."

"He believes you," Natalie said.

She laughed now, rubbing at herself and shivering, too, as he said, "Okay, maybe that's just my opinion. But there has to be a reason why she's no longer the head honcho of the company, Justie, in case you haven't heard." He stopped and looked over at Natalie. "You okay?"

"Yeah, I'm fine. Just a little cold."

"Put on a sweater."

"No, I'm fine. I'll be all right. I'll just wash my face, that's all." She got up and disappeared into the bathroom.

"She all right?" I asked.

Paul waved his hand, minimizing whatever was wrong with her. "She'll be fine. She doesn't know her limits, that's her problem. But there's nothin' to worry about, so forget it. Anyway, like I was saying," a one-track mind if ever there was one, "this Frankel, probably working with the other one, D. W., managed to get controlling interest. Now that's something you don't read about in the papers—"

"Or *NuBodies* Magazine."

"Exactly," he said. "Believe me, I really don't give a shit about it, one way or another. But the lady's pathetic. I mean, she's sad. She's so wrapped up in Cynthia she can't see the forest for the trees, can't tell her ass from her elbow, either."

This was all news to me. Not that I'd chalked off that particular angle of investigation, her business relationships, but I figured the best place to start was close to home, meaning Morgan's family. Now, I realized I'd eventually have to go back to New York and pick up the trail all over again. "So you really have nothing against her, then?" I asked.

Behind me, I heard the toilet flushing. The bathroom door opened and a whiter-faced Natalie came back into the room. She wasn't shaking nearly as much as before. "You okay?" I said again.

"Fine."

Paul said, ignoring the exchange completely, like all he could think about was Cynthia and no one else, "She never hurt me, man. Not personally. She put up all the money for the play, right? But what really rubs me the wrong way is that she knows Nat doesn't have a fucking penny to her name. The chick's written for money, made apologies up the ass, the whole bit. And we've both looked for work too, no shit. But forget it. Santa Fe's still suffering from the Depression and the moon lady doesn't want to know Nat's alive or dead. It makes me kind of wonder if the business with the play wasn't just another ego-trip of hers, like it had nothing to do with me at all."

"What's the difference, one way or another. She gave me up years ago," Natalie spoke up. "And she fucked up my brother good. But that's not for public consumption, Rodell. I mean, it'll kill her if it ever gets into print, like she won't be able to deal with it, on any level whatsoever." She looked down into her empty glass, back in her hands since she didn't seem to have anything else she wanted to hold. For some reason, I felt embarrassed to keep staring at her. Not because I knew she was on meth or anything like that. It went way beyond drugs to something I guess is called privacy, plain and simple. I didn't know what to expect after that, but a moment later she said, "Sometimes I wish she'd drop dead and leave me alone, stop trying to love me so much, ugly as it sounds. But I don't want her murdered, know what I mean?"

No, I didn't. She wanted Cynthia to drop dead, but at the same time she needed her for money. Very confusing,

I thought. I also knew that this time I'd really gotten my hands dirty. Filthy, in fact. It was mucky business, to put it mildly, and it didn't do much for my peace of mind or self-esteem. Nevertheless, I still asked her what wasn't for public consumption.

"You mean you haven't met Brother Bar yet?" Paul said. He snickered, stuck out his little finger and waved it about. "Its a better story than Cynthia and the chauffeur."

"Him too?" I said. "The dude with the bushy eyebrows?"

"You got it," Paul said, snickering all over again.

"Have you met my brother?" Natalie asked.

"Not yet."

She looked over at Paul, saying, "He's got a lot of surprises in store for him."

"That's for sure," Paul said. "But you're gonna be our guest and stay the night, aren't you, Justie?"

"Sure." Where was I running off to? Besides, I had a feeling that if I played my cards right, I might even be able to make it with Natalie, not to mention finding out more about the black sheep of the family, her older brother Barry.

Nat and I zipped off to the nearest supermarket and I laid out thirty bucks for groceries, steak and wine, and all the trimmings. On the way back she put her hand on my thigh. I felt a dry heat, just like the Santa Fe Weather Bureau had predicted.

"Why do you want to crucify her so?" she asked as the two of us unloaded the groceries from the back seat of the car.

"Why do you want to kill yourself?"

"That's my business. And I'm not, so don't worry about it, Rodell. Just answer my question."

"Who said anything about crucify?"

"Come on. I was straight with you, so be honest with me. It wouldn't kill you, you know, to trust someone."

I grinned, glad to see the color had finally returned to her cheeks. They were ruddy now, the way they should be, instead of ashen, bedsheet-white. "I trust lots of people," I said. "But as far as my feelings for your mother, they're pretty much at a low ebb. Okay? Satisfied?"

"No. Why do you feel so strongly about her?"

I noticed the way she avoided the word *hate*. "Why?

Because your mother uses people like tissues, that's why."

"Don't we all?" Natalie said.

"I don't."

"You've given yourself a royal snow job, Justin. Besides, more than a million people in this country would kiss her feet, given half a chance."

"I'm not part of that million."

"Funny," she said. "I never was, either."

September–October 1974

BARRY REALLY DIDN'T LOOK LIKE HIS MOTHER. And there wasn't much of a facial resemblance to his father, either. But when he opened his mouth, out came the Margold pearls. "How much you willing to spend, Rodell?"

"Depends on what you have to sell."

"I shouldn't be telling you this, but my sister called me yesterday—collect, of course. She warned me about you."

"I never thought I was that dangerous a character."

He smiled slyly. "She said it was a pity you weren't half as good in bed as you were getting people to talk."

I didn't tell him that speed usually loosens the tongue. "No one twisted her arm, either way. Besides, I don't perform well in groups."

"You and Paul and Nat?" a lot of dirty books rustling around behind his eyes.

I returned the lecherous grin and puffed away at my cigarette. The chlorine from the pool came back along the breeze, sour and briny. I hadn't been invited to take a swim.

"Nat's new thing is that sex is like Lay's potato chips. You know, 'betcha can't eat just one.' " He threw his head back and laughed, derisive, exaggerated. His hair fell into place, layered like a dark-brown shingled roof. Then he cracked his knuckles. I imagined it sort of finished the set, just another way of telling me he was bored—which I knew he really wasn't. The gold bracelets he wore on one of his wrists clicked together like a pair of maracas. "Pretty convenient for you that my mother's out of town."

"Where?" I asked.

"A swing through the Deep South," he said, affecting a drawl. "Something like that. The usual p.r. bullshit." He took off his sunglasses, dark-tinted aviator specs, rubbed his eyes with a thumb and forefinger and kept staring beyond me to the pool. His eyes looked forty years old, so used and tired I don't think he could have given them away, to Good Will or anyone else, for that matter. A circular purplish patch made me wonder if someone had given him a black eye.

I sat on the deck chair and tried to stay one step ahead of him. It wasn't going to be easy. He was as much a smartass as I. Thanks to Natalie—despite her put-downs which really didn't bother me—I hadn't had any trouble getting in touch with him. Barry was staying at his mother's new house in Trousdale Estates, until he figured out what he wanted to do with the rest of his life. Those were his sentiments, not my conjectures. Now, as we sat out by the kidney-shaped pool and I sensed how he was enjoying the feeling of holding court, I felt stymied and at a loss for words. It was a new sensation.

"What exactly do you want from me, Rodell?" he asked. He turned his head back in my direction, his sunglasses in place again and his eyes invisible behind their polarized shield.

"Good question," I said and attempted to smile. My tape recorder was within reach, next to me on a terra cotta garden stool. For the moment, it wasn't consigning anything to the realm of electromagnetic permanence, much as I would have preferred. "First off, did your sister mention what I was working on?"

"A book Rhonda Grahame would be afraid to write. Or should I say *offended* to write?" referring to the popular Hollywood gossip columnist and scandalmonger.

"Something like that," I admitted.

"So, big shit," he said. "What do you think, you're on your way to writing a best seller?"

"Maybe."

"It'll probably be as successful as your play and don't turn on that machine yet, either. But what do you want me to say? For ten bucks I'm gay? For fifteen I'm gay as a goose? Besides, you probably knew that before you got here. So come on, Rodell, what is it you're looking for? People could care less about my sex habits."

"I agree with you. I had no intention of using that. I

518

was never one to judge a person by whom he went to bed with." He was right, too. There had to be more to my story than just a collection of sexual intrigues. But so far, no one had provided me with the key to unlock that particular—and perhaps forbidden—door.

"How very white of you," he said. When he grinned, I got a chance to see what must have been a good three thousand bucks worth of dental care. His uppers and lowers were a symphony, a toothpaste ad, so perfect that even the slight chip at the edge of one of his front teeth seemed planned that way. "You smoke? Grass I mean."

"On occasion."

"I can see you're a better bullshit artist than I am," he said, and once again gave me a chance to notice the attention that had been paid to his mouth when a faint grin pried his lips apart. He found what he was looking for in a silver cigarette case with a tree bark finish. The kid had all the right accouterments.

I knew when to keep my mouth shut and waved aside his offer of a joint. I stubbed out my cigarette as he lit up. The bittersweet aroma of marijuana mixed with the pervasive odor of the chlorinated water. He blew the smoke out through his nose and I wondered if it was possible to get a contact high. "Sure you don't want a poke?" he asked.

"Positive, but thanks."

"How's Natalie getting along?"

She'd taken me aside before I left to tell me she'd only dropped the speed so she could handle my visit. *You have a way of making people nervous, she said. And this business with Paul . . . believe me, it's only temporary, until I can get my shit together, that's all. Besides, I wanted to get back at her and don't start asking me for what, because it's the story of my life, all wrapped up in a neat little package. Like mother like daughter, dig it?* I understood, or I thought I understood, which is the best I can say under the circumstances. To Barry I said, "Not very well. They had to apply for food stamps." Everything else just didn't seem worth getting into.

"Sonuvabitch," he said, shaking his head. "What do you think of Paul, by the way? He's a slick motherfucker, wouldn't you agree?"

Not as slick as you, I thought, saying, "That's exactly what he said about D. W."

519

I'd hit oil. The corners of Barry's lips turned up. "Now there is one helluva smart operator," he said. "Boy, he knows how to get around my mother better than just about anyone I know. Better than me, probably." He stopped long enough to take another pull at the joint. "You know, about five years ago . . . yeah, that's right. I'm almost twenty-five and I wasn't even twenty then. Christ, I'm getting old fast." When I didn't say anything he launched right into, "Five years ago, she caught me in bed with him. Well, not exactly in bed, but she figured out what was going on, anyway. My mother's not a fool, contrary to popular belief. D'you know that he managed to talk his way out of it, no shit. And the real joke is, she thinks—to this day, mind you—that that was the first and last time we ever made it together. Now my dear, that has got to be one of the funniest things going, Rodell. Shit, we'd been having an affair for months, if not longer. Sometimes my mother's like a dizzy queen. Dense. Know what I mean?"

"Sure," I said, watching him carefully. Behind his sunglasses I was certain his eyes were getting pinker and pinker. "Who introduced him to you?"

"That's a stupid question. What are you, naive or something. Who do you think?"

"I hate to assume things, or take anything for granted; that's why I'm asking."

"You assumed a lot when you called me, isn't that so?"

"Not really, Barry. No one's forcing you to say anything."

"True."

I changed the subject as fast as I could. "Do you still see him?"

"D. W.? On occasion. He's not my type, actually. And I don't think I'm his, either. You are, but we won't go into that. Anyway, these days he's into leather; dreary scene, far as I'm concerned. But I will say that when I first met him, I thought he was King Shit. Not Mr. Right, mind you, but a real put-together kind of guy, a finished product, you might say. He made himself a small fortune, thanks to my mother . . . misguided creature that she is. It's sad too, because nowadays she doesn't seem to be on terrific terms with anybody, except maybe Pat Casey, Gene Burr, too, I guess. Have you spoken to my father?"

"He's having hard times."

"So I've heard. But as far as that goes, he fucked things up, not my mother,. He could've been on easy street now, instead of living in some dump with a manicurist . . . not even a hairburner, do you believe."

Cynthia's secretary stuck her head out from the office which overlooked the pool and deck. "You're wanted on the phone, Barry," she called out, ending abruptly a look which had come into his face, an expression of such consummate distaste that it was almost scary just to sit there and watch him.

"Excuse me a sec." He got up, flung the towel he'd had around his shoulders onto his chair and stepped gingerly over the hot mosaic of tile which surrounded the pool. He was wearing a narrow black swimming slip and nothing else. I guess it was a kind of invitation, one he'd prepared in advance and one he was probably sorry I was ignoring. As soon as he was out of sight, I flicked on the tape recorder and leaned back against the scratchy nylon slats of the deck chair. From where I sat, I could see the initials C. M. tiled along the bottom of the pool, wavy but legible. The empty glass near Barry's chair also bore the same legend, as did the towel he'd tossed aside a moment before. I wondered if Cynthia had a subconscious fear of amnesia, like one day she'd wake up from between her three-hundred-dollar Porthault sheets, not knowing who she was. Then all she'd have to do was examine her monogrammed linen and her monogrammed life.

Forgetting the mother's insecurities, I turned my attention back to the son. I really didn't want to make a big deal about the kid's homosexuality. Barry wasn't making a point of blaming his mother for his sexual proclivities, and I really wasn't into using that kind of information, anyway. Not that it was a sacred cow, or anything like that. I mean, by now I'd gotten my hands as dirty as they were ever going to get. But the fact that he was queer just didn't seem all that vital, certainly not essential for the ultimate success—I hoped, I hoped—of *The Fat Lady*. Besides, I was getting bored with everyone's fucked-up libidos. If only someone was ready to tell me that Cynthia had cheated on her income tax returns, or that Nu-Bodies was a front for a black-market baby operation, or that there were rat droppings in Thinner Dinners and

521

insect debris in NuBodies cream soda, or that Paul's suspicions about Frankel and the stock market were fact and not fiction, I'd be a hell of a lot happier. In any event, I did have a pretty strong feeling that there was more going on than just the fact that Barry had had an affair with Lady NuBody's creative director, Mr. I-Magination himself. And sure enough, when the kid came back a few minutes later, I finally saw what I'd missed, what was now as obvious as the gold bracelets clicking and jingling carols on his wrist. "What are you into?" I asked. "Smack? Snow? What?"

"What?"

I reached out, caught one of his wrists and turned his arm over to expose the tracery of bluish veins just below the surface of his tanned skin. I saw the telltale tracks left by more needles than I had the stomach to count. Barry jerked back, pulled his hand free, and crossed his arms, trying to hide the evidence of his habit.

"What the fuck business is it of yours?"

"I never got a chance to tell you how much money I was willing to part with," I replied. "How many bags a day do you use?"

"Don't give me your social work savvy, Rodell. I don't have a habit . . . besides, she sent me to Croydon, just a couple of months ago."

"Croydon?" It didn't ring any kind of bell at all.

"A nice quiet place where rich old fuckers go to dry out, and rich young fuckers go to get detoxified."

"She paid for it."

"She pays for everything. It's called a strong maternal instinct. After all, I'm the only one who ever stuck by her. Me and my grandmother. Besides, she doesn't have a husband, so at least she has me . . . on a string."

"Well, it's your life. I could care less." I caught myself and tried to gloss over my scorn with, "What I meant to say is, I'm not making any value judgments. Each to his own, that's my philosophy. But I do know that coke's going for close to a small fortune these days," assuming he wasn't into heroin.

"I only snort it now, anyway," making a face that reminded me of a little boy sulking in front of a toy store window because his mother wasn't taking him inside to buy him what he wanted.

"Who started you on it?"

"Who do you think, my mother?"

"I have no idea."

"D. W." He suddenly pushed his chair back, the gesture so blatantly phony, dramatic, that it was all I could do not to laugh or call out "Cut!" But he followed through, got to his feet, and stood over me, blotting out the sun. I raised my hand to my eyes to see him better. "I don't like you, Rodell."

"Few people do," I said, trying to stay glib and cocky and not at all serious.

"You're an evil prick, that's the kind of vibes you send out. What do you want to do to my mother, anyway, see her crucified?"

"Everyone in your family has some kind of hang-up about Christ," I said. He missed the allusion completely. But the fact that I was chuckling, trying to remain unmoved, unimpressed by what I guess he considered manly behavior, didn't please him in the least. It was obvious Barry knew that I was laughing at him and it was equally obvious that I'd made the interviewer's primary mistake: alienating his subject.

"Look, I don't need your blood money, Rodell. My ole lady picks up the tab for me, wherever I go. I don't want to fuck up a good thing. Besides, she's helping a lot of people in this country, in case you're interested."

"I never said she wasn't. I think NuBodies is a wonderful idea. A national institution. But does she pick up the tab for your habit, too? Is that part of her maternal instinct? Or is your dealer strictly cash-and-carry?" At that moment the fucking cassette got jammed and the machine automatically stopped. It clicked off. The sound was like a clap of thunder. Barry looked down at the tape recorder. Before he could say or do anything else, I had the machine strapped over my shoulder. "Three hundred bucks could buy you a nice little stash, Bar," I said, already on my feet.

"How long has that been running?"

"Not long. And I told you I wouldn't use the fact that you're a queer."

"Gay."

"Gay, whatever. I just want to find out what you know about your mother, in relation to NuBodies, that is."

"I don't know anything, Rodell. I may be fucked-up or spoiled rotten like she always says, but I'll be goddamned if I'll sell myself to the highest bidder." He started to turn away.

"Your sister did," I said. Your mother did too, remembering what Forman Margold had told me, weeks before.

Barry looked back at me, removed his sunglasses, and kept on staring. "My sister could have had anything she asked for, that's how badly my mother wanted to make up with her. You weren't there when Natalie walked out on her. But I was. My mother cried all that night."

"That's not what I heard. Nat says your mother kicked her out, soon as she found out about Paul."

"I'm not talking about that, you asshole. I'm talking about ten years ago, when Natalie ran off with my father without a word of explanation. But what's the use of talking. It's none of your business, anyway. All I can say is, my sister blew it, just like always. This last time she threw it away for some muscle number, well-hung but in no way well-heeled. Fortunately for me, I'm not nearly as stupid as she is, Rodell. You'll probably be hearing from my mother's lawyer, soon as she gets back."

"I'll worry about it when the time comes," I said. "Because it won't be happening for quite awhile, like not until the book is finished."

"That's what you think. Keep deluding yourself."

"If you open your mouth to her about the book, Barry, I won't think twice about telling her all about your long-term affair with D. W."

"She could care less."

"Perhaps, but she will care about the fact that those scars of yours, the tracks on your arm, weren't all made *before* you went to Croydon, but after."

"You're bluffing," he said. "You couldn't tell if they were old or new, anyway."

"Think whatever you want, Barry. But if you don't fuck with me, I won't fuck with you. It's as simple as that."

"You wouldn't tell her—"

"Don't test me, because I would."

Lena Winick, Cynthia's mother, lived in a one-bedroom apartment in Westwood, not far from UCLA. Fortunately, her grandson hadn't thought to alert her or to tell her to avoid me. When I called to see if I could arrange an interview, I told her I was writing an article for the *American Jewish Quarterly*. "For such a good cause, of course I'll speak to you," she said. "It'll be my pleasure." The *American Jewish Quarterly* existed only in my imagination. That didn't bother me—or Mrs. Winick—in the least. After all, I was trying to make *The Fat Lady* more than just your everyday run-of-the-mill exposé.

Mrs. Winick turned out to be the paradigmatic American Grandmother: frail, birdlike, blue-haired, and anxious to please. She had a pot of coffee and a chocolate layer cake waiting for me when I arrived at the apartment. Here at least, there was no indication of poverty rearing its ugly head. It was quickly apparent that she was well provided for, that someone was taking good care of her.

"I'm really very appreciative, Mrs. Morgan . . . Winick I mean, that you're giving me your time."

"Don't be silly," she said. "What else do I have to do. My daughter takes care of everything. It gets a little boring, understand?" She winked and fluffed up her hair, becoming wonderfully impossibly girlish even with the liver spots on her hands and the pouches of fatty tissue making permanent bags beneath each of her pale, watery brown eyes. "You'll take some coffee and cake, won't you?"

"How could I say no to such a charming hostess," I replied, thinking of the Dale Carnegie course I had never taken. I placed my tape recorder on the dining table and took a seat.

She poured me a fresh cup of coffee, said she preferred tea for herself, and finally sat down across from me. The formica table was covered with a plastic cloth. Not a speck of dirt was caught in the faux-linen pattern. "Oh an ashtray," she said when she saw me reaching for a pack of cigarettes. "I almost forgot."

It was black plastic. The name Chasen's ran around the rim, up to the spot where a pack of matches was designed to fit neatly in place. "Do you mind if I turn on the tape recorder?" I asked. "The coffee's wonderful, just the way I like it."

"I always put in a little extra for the pot," she said. "Some people like to doctor it up with salt or egg shells or nonsense like that. Me, I just make it good and strong. That's the way my husband always liked it. And sure, put it on. I don't mind. It's a pity my daughter's out of town. Her business keeps her very busy."

"Yes, I would imagine," I said. She cut me a piece of cake and I bent my lips up and continued to smile.

"So what kind of story, article I mean, are you writing, Mr. Rodell?"

"Human interest," I said, pleading further silence until I had swallowed what was in my mouth. "Marvelous cake. Did you bake it yourself?"

"No, I'm not a baker, never was," she said. "But eat, enjoy. There's plenty there and I don't touch sweets, myself. I have a little sugar; these things happen."

I nodded my head. "I was surprised to learn you had your own apartment, Mrs. Winick. I thought you were living with your daughter."

"Not for six months, a little more," she said. "She likes her privacy and I like mine. We spent enough time together over the years. It's time I gave her a break, you follow?" She laughed and covered her mouth with the palm of one hand.

"Certainly, I see your point," I said. "It's always nice to have your own home. And I must say yours is furnished very handsomely. Tasteful."

"You like it?"

"Very much."

"That's Cynthia for you," she said. "For her mother, the best isn't even good enough. She always has her hand in her pocket. There aren't many daughters around like mine, Mr. Rodell." She stopped short, tilted her head to the side. "What kind of name is that, 'Rodell'? You don't mind my asking, do you?"

"Not at all. I'm writing for the *American Jewish Quarterly*. Remember?"

"Oh that's right," she said. "What a silly question to ask. But it's an unusual name, Rodell. But anyway, what I was saying was that she's as good as gold. D'you know what a saint is? Well my Cynthia's a saint. And believe me, I'm not exaggerating. She's what every mother dreams of having from a child, that's all I can say."

The tape deck was still going and I was still smiling, eating cake, and drinking coffee. I nodded my head at what I hoped were effective and inspiring intervals. This wasn't where I wanted the interview to go. "But I can see right off that you've never had to worry about your weight, about joining NuBodies, that is."

"Knock wood," she said, though she didn't demonstrate. "I eat like a bird. Besides, I never had a glandular problem the way she does."

"Does?"

"Well you know what I'm saying. She was always a big-boned kind of girl. It's right there, right in her autobiography. Even her new doctor says so." She stopped in the middle of a breath and looked away. I felt like Columbus landing in the New World. Well it's about time, I thought. If this isn't the key I've been looking for, nothing is.

"You know," I said, trying to get her attention again, trying to make her forget what she'd said, the fact that the color had risen explosively in her powdered cheeks, "to this day my mother has a slow metabolism, an endocrine problem. Small world."

"You don't say?" her eyes owl-wide. "What does she do for it?" She sipped her tea. I noticed how steady her hand was, steadier than mine.

"Well, she's tried just about everything," I replied, trying to be as circumspect as possible. "It's a pity she can't locate a good doctor, someone who really knows what they're doing. There are a lot of fakers around these days, a lot of phonies."

"You're telling me," she said, agreeing completely. "But Dr. Mackenzie is fabulous, the best. You're from out here or what?"

"No, New York."

"Your parents, too?"

"Yes."

"Couldn't be better. He's in Manhattan, in the book. More coffee?"

"Just a drop. I can't resist, it's so good."

She got up to get the pot and I sat back in my chair and felt happier than I'd been in months. I made sure to drop the subject completely, turning the conversation back to Mrs. Winick's feelings about Cynthia and NuBodies. She gave me a glowing testimonial, painting a picture of someone who exhibited the utmost in devotion, both to business and family, making a point of adding how Cynthia had helped hundreds of thousands of people "assume normal healthy lives."

"You've been so kind and gracious, I just don't know how to thank you," I said just before I left.

"Think nothing of it," Mrs. Winick replied. And again she said, "It's been my pleasure. It's made my day."

Mine too, I thought.

I'm sure she could have handled an ingenuous kiss on the cheek—*Say good-bye to grandma, Justin.* But I figured there was such a thing as going overboard. So we just shook hands and let it go at that.

January 1975

AFTER ALL, he was giving out speed, liquid amphetamine —"diet drops" is what his patients called them. So you'd think that at the very least, Dr. Mackenzie's nurse would be a model for his clientele to emulate, to dream of becoming: a svelte youthful vision, slim of waist, dainty of trotter. Well it didn't happen that way. Miss Verna Baylor was Marion Librarian revisited, a displaced Yankee with a dog-eared copy of *Downeast* magazine and a nasal "Ayuh," hanging on the thread of her every breath. She was no help at all, though she did confide that she would have much preferred living back in Bangor than in Fun City. But that was the extent of her secrets. With ringleted hair done up like a plastic helmet and meager, barren breasts protruding like twin pencil points from her functional double-knit dress, she categorically refused to advance my literary career.

"Doctor's files are doctor's files. If a body invited the fox into the henhouse, what do you expect might happen?"

"There'd be a lot of squawking, but who's to hear," I replied, two crisp hundred-dollar bills stuck like flypaper between the fingers of my right hand. But I muffed it. She wasn't into payoffs and revelations. She threatened to call the doctor out to bring me to task, or take more drastic measures.

I knew Cynthia had seen Dr. Mackenzie, had gone to him on more than one occasion. But the particulars of her visits remained a mystery. The key was in the lock, so to speak, but the door wasn't opening. If the woman who had founded NuBodies no longer relied on the system's tried and proven methods, all of her sexual machinations and family squabbles would pall in comparison. But I couldn't substantiate the facts, especially since there were four other Mackenzies, all practicing physicians with offices in Manhattan.

After finding a tolerable and inexpensive furnished studio apartment in New York's Chelsea section, I began work on the first draft of my book. I'd dug up most of the facts surrounding Cynthia's brush with the law in Miami, the payoff she had made to keep Barry's accident out of the papers. But in my mind it was still minor, barely worth the plane fare, second-string stuff and not the big leagues by any stretch of the imagination.

From what I'd heard about D. W., I was reluctant to try to see him. He had a vested interest in NuBodies, if not in Cynthia, and it didn't seem likely that he'd be willing to cooperate with me, advancing the cause of my dreams of financial and non-fictional glory. As it turned out, I couldn't have been more wrong.

Right after New Year's and right about the time when a record snowfall gave me the needed self-discipline to stay indoors and finish writing the last pages of my first draft, I got a call which made me immediately wonder why I'd been so stupid as not to have requested an unlisted number from Ma Bell. "Justin Rodell, please," the voice said.

"Speaking." I put down my number 29 Magic Marker felt-tip and straightened up in my chair. The hairs weren't bristling along the back of my neck, but something in the moment of palpable silence which followed right after told me my day of reckoning had finally caught up to me.

"This is David Eliot . . . of NuBodies."

"Hello David Eliot of NuBodies. What can I do for you?"

"I was digging around in the bottom of my closet, rummaging through some old discarded emotions of mine. Guess what I found?"

"I haven't the slightest idea," I said.

"You don't?" His voice rose up, three contralto notes before it dropped back into a more basso register. "Well let's see now. They were all perfect fits, actually. One was

530

greed. The other was blackmail. The third was Barry. Am I getting warm, Mr. Rodell?"

"Subtropical," I said.

"I was hoping as much. But in case you're curious . . . I won't even belittle you by saying 'worried,' Barry hasn't said a word to La Belle Cynthia. Does that please you?"

"It might."

"I'm so glad," he said and I felt like smashing his face in, which was an impossibility, at least for the moment. "I think the two of us should get together for a nice friendly . . . informative chat. Don't you agree?"

"Sure."

"Drinks at my place?"

"If that's what you want," remembering what Barry Margold had said and thinking it was certainly better than meeting him at a leather bar.

"I knew you'd be amenable." He set up a time, gave me his address, and clicked off without another word.

Six hours later, Eliot's Filipino houseboy made me feel somewhat less than welcome when I arrived at the Park Avenue duplex.

"Are you drinking or smoking?" D. W. asked, emerging from a side hall like Count Dracula from a coffin.

"Drinking," figuring I needed all of my smarts and self-assurance.

"What?"

"Wine."

"Red or white?"

"Doesn't matter."

"Andres, will you open the chilled bottle of Beaujolais?" And to me, "Well, take a seat, Rodell. I'm not going to bite you, you know."

"Fantastic apartment," I said, thinking, The ill-gotten gains of trading in flesh, preying on the broken egos of fat people.

Maybe I was being too harsh. After all, nothing I'd unearthed cast any aspersions on NuBodies' methods. I was dealing with personalities, not corporate policies.

"I think so, too," he said. "It's home."

He motioned me to a seat with a wave of a gold-watched hand. I found myself disappearing into the maw of an overstuffed, oversized burgundy sofa. It was so large that my feet barely touched the floor. Talk about feeling childlike, if not childish. When the drinks arrived in frosted, equally oversized goblets, he raised one chilled glass and smiled with yet another set of perfectly fixed teeth. "To the success of your venture, your new book."

"Thank you," I knew he wanted me to choke on the words. The wine, though, rated eight on a scale of ten. I put the glass down on a trompe-l'oeil stack of books, sheet metal fashioned into the remarkable likeness of three heavy Victorian tomes, and crossed my arms.

D. W.—dark-haired, intense of eye, vaguely demonic, silk-shirted and groomed to within a peacock's inch of his life, smiled from his vantage on an opposing sofa and said, "The most remarkable fact is that Cynthia hasn't discovered you're writing this . . . work of art. Your luck's been holding out, I take it."

"It was," I said and tried to laugh.

"Yes, *was,* until now. But you needn't get all anxious and sweaty, Rodell. After all, I haven't informed on you. Yet."

"My publisher is handling all the legal odds and ends."

"I'm sure there'll be plenty of those. How far have you gotten into the book? And what's it called, may I ask?"

I told him.

"Love the title," he said. "Sort of says it all. Oh yes, it's very delicious, very nasty too. But that's okay, 'slong as it sells. I can just see the expression on her face when it comes out. She'll squeal like a little piglet, our darling Mrs. Morgan. But are you debunking NuBodies, in addition to everyone else?"

"The classes? No. I think they work."

"They do. You're a smart boy, staying out of mischief like that. But it'd be foolish alienating millions, as you've probably realized. So you're just going after your pound of flesh, nothing more, nothing less."

"Something like that." I can't say I was feeling comfortable and at ease, because I wasn't. Too late I realized I should have met him on neutral ground, not on his home turf. An animal—human or otherwise—is always more confident in its own territory. David Eliot was no exception to the ethological and behavioral rule.

"You scared little Barry though, which is a pity. He's not used to being frightened by anyone except his mother.

And then only on occasion. How did you figure out he was still shooting up?"

"Just a good guess is all."

"It made him keep his mouth shut, I'll say that. Not that I really care what he does with his life, one way or another. The world is filled with fuck-ups, of which he's just a prime example. And his mother gave him more chances than I care to enumerate. Well, it's enough I have to look out for myself twenty-four hours a day. No one else does. So I really have no time or inclination when it comes to worrying about Barry Margold."

"I look out for myself on that same kind of nonstop schedule," I said.

"How nice, a young man after my own heart. But Rodell . . . you don't mind me calling you that, do you, kiddo? After all, Justin implies a degree of familiarity that just wouldn't be *comme il faut*."

"You serve excellent wine," *spirits* if I was going to be half as affected and pompous as he pretended, "and you have a beautiful home. But where does that—"

"Lead you?" he interrupted; his words fit perfectly to the end of my sentence. "To a mutually profitable understanding, that's where, Rodell."

"Mutually profitable?" I said.

"Indeed." His eyebrows flew up to the edge of his kinky black hair. "Simply put, I propose that for ten percent—a mere agent's fee, you must agree—of your royalties, and that includes your advance of course, I'll put myself at your disposal. Not myself, per se, but the information I have available to me."

"Such as?"

He twisted his lips into a semblance of a grin, pulled at the attached lobe of one ear, took another swallow of wine, and said, "If you haven't heard of Dr. Speedgood by now, I hate to think what the rest of *The Fat Lady* is going to be like. A lot of boring erotic intrigues, no doubt."

"I've heard of Mackenzie."

"Good boy, you've done your homework. I take it though that you reached a dead end."

"You're one step ahead of me," I admitted.

"That's why I live overlooking Central Park, my dear. And that's obviously why you have to write garbage instead of *literature*. But David Wayne Eliot learned a good

533

many years ago that if you don't keep on your toes, someone's bound to come along and try to smash your fingers."

He had a letter of agreement all written out. If I signed along the dotted line, promising ten percent of my earnings from *The Fat Lady,* in addition to the inclusion of a strongly worded statement making it clear that NuBodies was an efficacious and sound system of losing weight, he would secure Mackenzie's file on Cynthia, along with her income tax returns, personal correspondence, and other tidbits of inflammatory fact.

"Not to mention," and he let the phrase hang as if suspended in the air, obviously and purposely trying to tempt me, to tantalize me into accepting his offer, "a most intriguing and informative item, one I know your book would suffer the lack of, and suffer strongly."

"Meaning what?"

"Meaning that in the last year, Cynthia has paid repeated visits to the same spa, health farm they call it, where a former First Lady used to go to dry out. Under an assumed name, needless to say. Cynthia as well as *la première femme.* Which is about all they had in common, I'm afraid."

"She has a drinking problem?" I was amazed. "Since when?"

"My dear fellow, not a drinking problem. An eating problem. A pound problem. She went to have the flab pounded off her. Now do you follow?"

"You mean to say NuBodies no longer works for its founder, that she can't even keep her weight down eating Thinner Dinners?" I knew I sounded like the teaser for a soap opera, but it just couldn't be helped.

"What a dramatic way to put it," he said, affecting a laugh. "Thinner Dinners, by the way, were a brainchild of mine, as was just about everything that's made pots of money for them. But that's what I've been saying for the last ten minutes, Rodell. Wouldn't you agree that kind of information makes excellent copy?"

"And all I have to do is sign?"

He nodded his head.

"And if I don't?"

"Very simple." He stopped, seemingly in mid-sentence. As I watched him, he refolded the cuff on a shirt sleeve, scratched behind his ear, lit a cigarette, rewound his watch. For the first time since I'd arrived, I could hear music. It seemed to come from another room, something tinkly, a harpsichord tapping out a piece by Couperin, tip-tapping a deadline. When he finally spoke, it was as if he'd needed time to compose his thoughts, dramatize his point. "If you don't sign," he said, "your book won't be half as interesting scandal-reading as it might be. And lest you forget, it'll be awfully difficult to get any work done with Cynthia's attorneys breathing down your neck, hounding you day and night which they'll do—rest assured. So I really can't see that you have much of a choice to make, when you get right down to it."

Once again I read over the letter of agreement. It looked straightforward and clear-cut. When I raised my eyes, he was standing over me, a gold pen clasped between two slim, ringed fingers. "What about Leonard?" I said, figuring that I might as well get my money's worth.

"What about him?"

"I want the info on his relation with Cynthia, business and otherwise. And what about his stock market manipulations, his wheeling and dealing? And the fact that he was able to gain control of the corporation?"

"My goodness," Eliot said, smirking, "you really have opened a can of worms, haven't you. You have to realize of course that I can't substantiate any illegal hanky-panky with the market . . . and that shouldn't imply there was any, either. But, after all, my position would be placed in jeopardy if I opened my mouth too wide, shall we say. You don't want me to suffer now, do you? But I can fill in certain gaps in your story, providing of course they don't implicate me. Personally."

"Of course. Who'd want to implicate *you*, D. W."

"Pity you're not gay," he said. "Because I could teach you so much and we could have become wonderful friends, close as sisters. Well, one can't bemoan one's fate forever. As they say, life's too short and honesty's in short supply. I hope you don't object to a fountain pen. I find ball-points decidedly inferior writing instruments. They never allow a person's character to come through. Don't you agree?"

I signed on the dotted line.

EPILOGUE:

Everybody

August 1975

"ULTIMATELY, the book is not damaging to our corporate image," Leonard Frankel told her. "If anything, now that it's number three on the *Times* Best Seller List, the publicity has only helped generate a fresh resurgence in sales and revenues. Haven't you read it yet, Cynthia? NuBodies comes out smelling like a rose."

"And I hate to tell you what I come out smelling like," she replied.

"I'm sorry. He said some pretty unflattering things about me, but you don't see me carrying on, making an issue out of it. There's nothing I can do about it, Cynthia. The corporation's not going to waste its financial resources by filing a libel suit. NuBodies hasn't been slandered in the least. On the contrary. So if I were you, I'd just ride out the storm."

"No way," she said. "If NuBodies doesn't bring suit against them, then I will, on my own if necessary."

"If that's what you want, go right ahead. No one's stopping you, Cynthia. But a word to the wise," cautioning her with an upraised finger, a pushed-back cuticle, a crescent of buffed nail, a half-moon of ivory like a single wan and tepid smile. "Don't make an ass of yourself."

Ten days later, an out-of-court settlement was urged on her by her attorney, Jerry Brennen. "Absolutely not," she told him.

"Mrs. Morgan, it would behoove you to listen to the facts. I can't institute a libel suit if there aren't any grounds—"

"What do you mean, there aren't any grounds? You've

read that piece of . . . that's right, crap, that's all there is to it, a piece of filth, garbage. So how can you say I'm not within my legal rights? Did you read the words he put into people's mouths, the unbelievable things he quoted everyone as saying? I might as well change my name again, become the Monster of Crown Heights, after the way he ripped me to shreds."

"I want to arrange a meeting with their attorney. Let's hear what they have to say first, before we jump into anything," Brennen replied.

"Why is it, Jerry, that everyone is so goddamn afraid of getting their feet wet, that's what I want to know?"

"I'm your legal advisor, Mrs. Morgan. I'm not afraid of anything or anyone, believe me. I just want to do what's best for you."

"All right," because she knew she shouldn't argue with her lawyer, not if he was ever going to be of help. "Whatever you say, Jerry. You want me to meet with them, I'll meet with them. Is that little . . . is Rodell going to be there?"

"He'd better."

"You can say that again. What I have gone through in the last three weeks, no one but no one knows. Or understands." Or gives a good goddamn. On your own again, lady, that's what it boils down to. No one wants to raise a finger, unless it's to accuse, to warn. When you need help from people you made wealthy and successful, you can't find them, no matter how hard you look. "Okay, Jerry, I'm going along with you," because I have no one else to turn to at this point. And if that isn't the God's honest truth, I don't know what is.

And meanwhile, everywhere she looked, everywhere she cast her eye, copies of *The Fat Lady* pyramided and ballooned and mushroomed into view. He was getting window space in nearly every bookstore she passed. Even Bloomingdale's had given the book its own display on Lexington Avenue. The window dresser had managed to arrange the copies of the book to spell out NUBODIES.

Rodell had appeared on the "Today Show." Then, for two weeks following his appearance in New York, he'd been out on the road, hitting nearly every major talk show in the country. All the shows I had to finagle my way on to, when I was a nobody, Cynthia thought. And he gets on at the drop of a hat. At last people aren't stopping me on the street.

She'd read the book, but nothing would make her believe he'd written fact instead of fiction. She refused to accept the possibility that she wasn't loved, that people looked down at her as if she had clawed her way to the top, not worked and sweated and nearly killed herself for an idea she had believed in. Rodell hadn't knocked Nu-Bodies. That was the only saving grace in what she considered to be over three hundred pages of filth and corruption.

But what about my members? she thought. What about the people all over the country who thought I was being straight with them. What are they going to think when they get their hands on the book and read how I . . . I ruined two children, threw away a husband like a used tissue, went to a milk farm because I needed a rest after the aggravations I went through with Barry and Natalie. What lies, what out-and-out fabrications, that I went there to have the fat pounded off me. So I was five pounds over my goal weight, so big deal, what's five pounds in ten years, anyway? It's not like I'm a kid anymore, like I'm a youngster. I'm forty-five years old so of course it's hard to keep my weight steady as a rock, my system on an even keel. And what normal person, what everyday person, could watch their weight after the nonsense the two of them pulled. Barry with that garbage he used that I thought I'd lose my mind when I found the . . . set of works, that's what it's called, in his room. Not even in a dresser drawer which I wouldn't have touched. And did I criticize him because of his other sickness? Did I forbid him to bring those people into the house, into my own home. Oh no, I was a swinging liberated mother—that's what he called me, the little bastard. A real swinger who's lucky she never thought of swinging at the end of a rope. Yes, sure, and what about the other one, my sociologist, went off with a leech is what he was from the word go and I knew it but I was a fool, a horse's ass cause he fed my ego, made me feel . . . young and desired or was it beautiful or all three? So of course I got angry. It was normal. Dr. Mackenzie gave me tranquilizers, appetite suppressants, cause how could I have shown up at a meeting saying I was having trouble keeping my weight down, keeping it steady. People would have looked at me like I was out of my mind. So is it fair that now my members, people who trusted and believed in me, should think I went out of my way to put something over on them, to ridicule them by ridiculing NuBodies? I'd cut my arm off first than make fun of them, my bread and butter.

She threw her past up before her like some swiftly unfurling parchment scroll, some kind of certificate she had been awarded in the years since she had fled a life which hadn't seemed to be going anywhere. She read the riot act on herself, as well, trying to figure out if and where she'd gone wrong.

Phil picked her up at the Sherry-Netherland where she was staying, driving her downtown to meet Brennen at the offices of Wyatt & Linden, attorneys-at-law. "New dress?" he asked. The car's air-conditioner made her feel as though she were sitting in a vacuum, the city sounds muted and distant, unlike her mood.

"Yes. Like it?"

"Looks great on you," he said.

Cost enough, too, she thought. It would have paid for a month's rent in Brooklyn, gas and electric too, probably. She smiled, the expression bitter and resentful. Ten years of change and growth was somehow reduced to a price tag, the cost of a St. Laurent new-look chemise. It was a floral print, one whose shades of bordeaux, lavender, and pink highlighted her reddish hair, picked up the color of her glossy, polished fingernails. High-heeled strapped shoes finished the simple yet fashionable outfit. The one-piece dress was top-of-the-calf length. The thin fabric moved when she moved. It was a perfect dress to dance in, to be seen in. But at the moment, sitting in the back of the car, she didn't want to be seen by anyone. Not to be recognized, nor photographed, nor stopped by someone wielding either a pad and pencil or a hand mike. I don't want to be on the news, in the news, or part of the news. I just want to be vindicated . . . yes, that's it. Maybe it's too late to stop them from publishing more copies of the book, selling them all over the country. But it's not too late for them to make a public statement, retracting their lies. And it's not too late to pay me for damages, to make Rodell pay through the nose. That glory-seeking phony, that libelous little s.o.b.

The office bespoke modesty, jurisprudence, soft-spoken words and compromise. She found it heartening, even a little bit encouraging. A portable cassette tape recorder sat like a centerpiece in the middle of Howard Linden's desk. Jerry was already there, sitting back in a leather wing chair. When she came into the room he got to his feet, extended his hand. His grip was cool and firm and she felt encouraged.

"Mrs. Morgan," he said, "this is Howard Linden, senior counselor for Lloyd Tudor & Sons and for Justin Rodell, of course."

"How do you do," she said, a curt nod of her head, no outstretched hand to seal the pact, the introduction.

"It's good of you to come down here this afternoon, Mrs. Morgan. This is my associate, Mr. Wyatt."

"Hello," she said, taking in the measure of both men with a swift, critical, and discerning eye. They were just names with LL.D.'s attached, pinstripe suits and well-modulated voices. She wanted to know nothing more about them. "May I ask where Rodell is?"

"We feel it's unnecessary for our client to be present, at this time," Linden said.

"Unnecessary?"

"Mrs. Morgan," Brennen said, his voice cautioning her to say no more, to nod her head and take a seat.

"But Mr. Rodell has provided us with some of the materials he made use of for his book," Linden continued. "I think that once you've heard them—"

"Heard them?" she interrupted.

"Yes," he said. "You see, they're all on tape, cassettes I should say. But I think that once you've listened to the evidence firsthand, I don't think either you or your counsel, Mr. Brennen here, will be inclined to pursue this matter any further."

She shot a startled, uncomprehending look in Jerry Brennen's direction. He was six-four, but now he seemed to have shrunk, his shoulders bending in on each other as if he were cardboard wilting after a heavy rain. His very size had seemed a promise of exoneration. Now, she felt something shrinking, sinking down, weighing heavily inside her.

"You'll of course allow Mrs. Morgan and me to listen to these tapes in private, won't you?" Brennen said.

"Certainly," Wyatt told them. "But you realize that we can't permit the recordings to leave our office. My secretary will show you to a conference room down the hall. You'll have all the privacy you and Mrs. Morgan require."

"I'm not following, Jerry," she said, dazed and disbelieving. How could it be possible? Were they going to get away with blue murder, because that's the word she used to describe *The Fat Lady*, just like that, no discussion, nothing?

He leaned toward her, his breath medicinal as opposed to minty. "I'll explain in due time. Trust me."

They all say the same thing, she thought. And what's worse, I fall for it. I trusted everybody, everybody and his mother. That was my problem. I was an idiot, naive isn't even the word for it and gullible's putting it too mildly. Everybody had a story and a line and I fell for them all because I believed in people and I'm not feeling like a martyr now, either. But I believed everybody was honest, decent.

Brennen took her hand, guided her to her feet, guided her to the door and led her down the corridor to the walnut-paneled conference room. Austere, poorly lit, it made her feel not only depressed, but unnerved.

The tape recorder ran on batteries. He selected a cassette from a box that held at least a dozen. There was nothing for her to do but sit there and wait. And listen. "They're not labeled," he said. "Or if they were, it's been erased though I don't know why." He gave the machine a moment to warm up, then pressed his finger down against the button marked Play.

Static. A chair scraping. Something she decided was the creak of springs, a couch or a bed. She couldn't tell for certain. Then the voice, agonizing over old wounds, petulant bruises. "Just plain jealousy. She couldn't handle it that maybe I was more desirable than she was, that she had to pay for Paul and I didn't."

"Turn it off."

"But that's to be expected of my mother—"

"What?"

"Turn it off," she said. "Try another one."

He pressed Stop and said, "Would you rather I waited outside?"

"Yes. Yes, that's the best way, Jerry. I can figure out how to work it. I'm not a dum . . . yes, please."

When he was gone, when the door closed like a whisper she needed to forget, she punched Fast Forward. The tape rushed with an angry hiss from one enclosed reel to another. She waited, ten seconds, fifteen. Then she hit Play. "—horny. She was lonely. She wasn't getting it on with anyone or anything but her bankbook. Fine. I came along and filled her heart—" and then laughter, horrifying, jeering laughter. She pressed down on Stop, removed the cassette, found another.

"—pays for everything. It's called a strong maternal instinct. After all, I'm the only one who ever stuck by her. Me and my grandmother. Besides, she doesn't have a husband," she heard Barry say with a voice that smirked, that reached out at her like a hand holding a knife to her throat, "so at least she has me, on a string." It didn't seem to matter when, a few minutes later, she heard him say, "I don't need your blood money, Rodell . . . she's helping a lot of people in this country."

She tried to listen to several others. Finally, she stopped the last tape she had selected and sat back. Everything he used, she thought, everything he wrote down was word-for-word, verbatim, right out of their mouths and onto the printed page. Natalie and Barry, Henny, Manny. Even that creep from Miami. Even Lena, though God knows how he ever got in touch with her. He didn't leave any stone unturned, did he? And on top of everything else, the IRS is on my back, as if I don't have enough to worry about. It's the accountant's fault, but it'll cost plenty to have it straightened out. And who gave him that kind of information, I'd like to know . . . as if I don't know already. More slime. So how many people does it take to fill Shea Stadium? What was that figure I quoted? Fifty thousand, fifty-five? And almost half a million members. And three times as many have been with us at one time or another. And what about *Newsweek*, what kind of terrific cover story are they going to write after what's happened? I'm a laughingstock, that's what I am. Just, just a fool, a big fool everybody's laughing at, pointing the finger. What, I'm going to sue my own kids, my own flesh and blood for saying things they're too stupid to even have thought about beforehand? Manny doesn't have a pot to pee in and whose fault is that and I'm gonna sue him, too? That's a laugh, another joke. Maybe we should just cancel the gala and forget about it. Maybe I should call it quits, while I'm ahead. If I dragged Rodell into court he'd produce these . . . these . . . whatever they are they were taken out of context, but the words are still there, the voices leaping out at me, saying things, lies.

"Yes, I'm finished," she said when Jerry Brennen knocked on the door.

"Well? What do you think?"

"I wonder if it's been worth it," she said.

"What?"

"Everything, Jerry," she said. "Everything and anything."

"I knew what they had, but I guess it was important for you to hear it for yourself. There just isn't a basis for a libel suit, for an infringement . . . a violation of privacy. Not when they have those tapes in their possession."

"So we just forget about it, is that it?" she said.

"Looks that way."

"What are my members going to think, that's what I want to know. I must look like the biggest hypocrite to come down the pike. Sure, I'll be speaking to row after row of empty seats next month, that's what it boils down to. Isn't that funny. Isn't that the most hysterical thing you ever heard." She reached into her leather tote. Underneath the address book and the wallet, the hairbrush and loose change, the tissues and cigarettes and lighter, she felt the smooth worn wrapper of the bag of sweets. Sugar Babies, they were called, teardrop-shaped caramel candies. Satisfied that they were there, that she hadn't forgotten them when she'd dumped the contents of one handbag into another, she got to her feet. "As long as I don't open them, I'll be all right. I'll be fine," she said.

"Don't open what?"

"It's like a good-luck charm, a rabbit's foot. Like an old Brooklyn superstition," she said. "Besides, I'm not a quitter, never was. If I quit the diet years ago, I wouldn't be here today. I'd be back in Brooklyn. And it wouldn't be any better than this, I'm positive. If anything, it would have been much worse."

FOR THE FIRST TIME IN SEVERAL YEARS, Halston didn't dress her. His current collection of evening gowns seemed too young, more suited to someone with a body like Natalie, though of course her daughter would never be caught dead in anything that smacked of high fashion. So she went by her instincts and allowed the head buyer at Saks to play salesman, helping her make the right selection.

When she arrived to pick up the gown, he wisely avoided any mention of what she supposed people—at least people whose lives touched upon her like the pages of a book—were calling her "current difficulties." He told her what shoes to wear, what jewelry to use to accent the gown, how to wear her hair so that it rippled like whitecaps, breezy as sea spray blowing off of her neck. "The dress is so you, there's nothing to worry about," he said. "And don't feel stiff, Mrs. Morgan. Believe me, the dress just falls and floats. Like the chemise, it moves when you move." He even had a bottle of champagne already chilled, waiting for its cork to pop, to bubble into crystal stemware he held high in one raised hand. He toasted both her and the success of the gala. She knew he hoped to make her a steady customer, but she also hoped his well-wishing expression of good luck and congratulations went beyond shrewd business sense. Yet when he said, "To the next ten years," she couldn't help but wonder if he was laughing behind her charge account, the thousand-dollar-plus price tag he snipped off with an agile flourish of one hand.

Manny once told me you never shit where you eat. If I

said that now they'd all look at me like I was vulgar, incurably common or something. But I don't think you can put it any better than that. And that's what all my members are probably thinking, right this minute, that why should I bother bucking traffic and traveling from God knows where to come to Shea Stadium and applaud a woman who turned her back on us. But I didn't. And there's no way to let them know that. There's no more time left.

Lena and Barry had arrived on the same flight from Los Angeles. They were staying with her at the Sherry-Netherland, each in separate rooms. Bob Hope's manager had called that morning to confirm any last-minute changes, details. D. W. too had called several times already, leaving messages with the desk when she wasn't in. Even Peter McGuire, the young *Newsweek* photographer, had left word that when the flashbulbs started going off, he'd be part of the shutter-clicking pack of photographers expected to cover the event. Two days before, she'd attended a run-through, a kind of undressy rehearsal out at Shea. They were paying something like twelve or fifteen thousand for a prominent Broadway director to shape the gala into an evening not only newsworthy, but theatrical. Standing on the makeshift wooden stage, carpenters and lighting technicians still at work all around her, she had looked out on the empty stadium, row after row of unclaimed seats. She couldn't hear the sounds of spontaneous pleasure, excitement, hands burning in a frenzy of recognition. She didn't want their gratitude so much as their compassion, their expression of sympathy, their belief that she was still the same Cynthia she had always been, the woman who once had told five other compulsive eaters, "If you want something badly enough you can do it. We're all in the same boat, don't you see? We're all women who have never been able to control our appetites. The older we get, the fatter we get." And now she wanted to say, "The older I get, the more confusing it becomes, the less I understand, the more I need your help." But the seats were empty and the green playing field stretched out before her like some clipped and manicured threat, the difference between the Cynthia who used to attract thousands to her breathless and invigorating pep talks, and the Cynthia who had been called the

"Fraud of Fat." Maybe I'll just get up and tell them I'm bowing out, that NuBodies works just as well without Cynthia Morgan to emulate, to follow, to copy. Maybe I should just stand up here and say that they really don't need me anymore, that I'm just a walking-talking ego with an insatiable appetite for fame, power, glory, prestige. You see, I wanted so much from my life, so many things, so much more than just living in Brooklyn and eating myself into the ground. I wanted to touch at the heart of something, but not make it bleed, not make a fool of myself in the process.

Cynthia's dress was an elusive and perhaps even indescribable shade, a peachy orange, a saffron-tinted red. Loosely pleated panels of silk chiffon floated from the waist to the floor, featherlike and wispy. A stole of the same gauzy material and mutable hue hung like twin pendants from her arms, all trimmed in maribou which rustled like leaves on a warm and breezy Indian summer night. A gently scooped V-neck, bare shoulders, and that was all there was to it—simple, classic, flattering. In front of the hotel, Phil was already waiting for her in a black Cadillac limousine. She finished getting dressed, buckled the ankle straps of her open-toed shoes, fastened the safety clasp of her necklace, and made sure her earrings were secure. The buyer who had wooed her at Saks had written down what makeup to use. Arden's Red Door Red on her nails, Revson's Crystal Red on her lips. "And whatever you do," he said, "don't stop smiling. Because when you smile, Mrs. Morgan, you've got the world right in the palm of your hand." As long as I don't have the world on a string, maybe things'll work out. Not that they have in the past, except when it came to money. Everything else sort of fell apart at the seams like the dresses I used to wear when I was two hundred fifty-two pounds, Chubby Margold, the Blimp of Crown Heights.

Ever since the book had been published, she'd followed the NuBodies regimen as closely as she had followed it ten years before. She'd told herself she was only ten pounds heavier than she should be (even though, as she tried in vain to fondly remember, there was no such word as "should"). But it was more than ten pounds, more than fifteen. Somewhere along the line, nineteen pounds of old Brooklyn memories—tents for dresses, candy bars for breakfast, peanut brittle under the mattress and entire strawberry shortcakes devoured on the street between the bakery on Utica Avenue and the front door of her building, and always the refrain "Why are my clothes getting tight again?"—had come back to haunt her. But as Lena had once said, "Where there's a will, there's a way." And Cynthia, as she had told Jerry Brennen, wasn't a quitter. Or a whiner, either.

When she was dressed, when the image which came back to her in the pier glass looked as good as it was ever going to look, she stepped into the bathroom. She pulled the scale out into the middle of the black-and-white tiled floor and mounted it with the same unhappy anticipation that brought to mind yet another flood of memories —meetings on Rutland Road; Natalie running out into the Brooklyn dark; fights with Manny; everyone saying it wasn't worth it, that she was killing herself for what, for what—like a headache no two aspirins could ever cure.

There was a time when I couldn't even see past the hot cross buns of my knees. My thighs were like sides of beef, my calves like Christmas hams. Now, all she had to do was tilt her head forward and read the figure bisected by the jiggling wavering black line of the bathroom scale. One-three-seven.

Well it's about time, she told herself, grinning and looking again just to make sure it wasn't wishful thinking. One-three-seven, clear as daylight. And it's about time I got wise to myself, too, on top of everything else. Because whatever I say tonight hasn't been written out in advance, beforehand. Because whatever comes out of my mouth is going to surprise a lot of people, including myself.

The stadium looked deserted.

In the black dark that surrounded her, she steeled herself for a disappointment she had considered and put aside, knowing it would be too difficult to handle, to deal with on any level whatsoever. It would draw upon whatever reserves of courage she possessed. She was afraid there wouldn't be anything there, or not nearly enough; afraid what might happen as a result.

Phil drove around to the main entrance and the lights were suddenly in her face, the voices rising up above the sounds of the engine, the air-conditioner, and Barry's buzzing in her ear.

They weren't going to let her pass unnoticed.

Security police and men in blue held the crowds back behind ropes of wine-colored velvet. When the door of the limousine opened and she stepped out into the arc light, the mob of fans threatened to break free of their restraints. With Lena on one arm and a black-velvet-dinner-suited Barry on the other, she emerged out of the darkness of the Cadillac to a wild cacophony of adoration. The screams, the whistles, the hoarse jubilant shouts, the cries of "We want Cynthia! We want Cynthia!" came back to her like thunder breaking overhead. She was prepared for maybe ten thousand out of a possible fifty-five. But not this, not by any stretch of the imagination. After all, she'd come so close, just a hairbreadth away from thinking of herself the way Rodell had written, thinking she was nothing more nor less than Princess Pound-Loss, the Grace Kelly of weight reduction, the Fraud of Fat.

But no.

She was Cynthia, just Cynthia Margold who'd gotten a little too carried away one afternoon, who'd let D. W. and her own inflated ego get in the way of what she'd always valued as an ample helping of good plain common sense. So she had become Morgan, La Belle Cynthia, Artemis-Diana, Lady NuBody, the Moon Lady, a martyr and a saviour and a one-woman crusade. But she was still Cynthia Winick Margold and she knew that the screams and wild cheering were calling for the woman from Brooklyn, a woman just like them, someone who'd made good out of the energy and drive of her own convictions, turning weaknesses into strengths, lack of will power into the entrenched solidity of perseverance.

"Thank you, thank you," she yelled back, framed by a spotlight, coated with white incandescence. Her voice was lost in a rush of full-blown belief equal to the faith of purpose which had brought her here on this warm and languid September evening. She wasn't a myth, a demi-god. She hadn't swindled anyone. She couldn't sing or dance or tap her feet, give an Oscar-Emmy-Tony-winning performance. She was Cynthia, just Cynthia, the lady from

Crown Heights who one day realized that if fat people got together, chances were they'd be able to change the long-established and destructive patterns of their lives.

Lena squeezed her arm. Barry leaned forward and kissed her on the cheek. "They love you, Mom," he said. "They can't get enough of you."

In that split second he was an awed little boy again. She laughed and said, "I don't believe this. I think I'm gonna faint." And then she smiled. And felt something lifting up within her, inside of her, not so much her spirits as a growing awareness that nothing had changed, that they were still on her side . . . not Rodell's, nor Leonard's, nor D. W.'s, nor anyone else's who had tried to come between them, to put distance and skepticism in the way of trust and honesty. These were her people: solid, dependable, mindful of promises made and promises yet to be kept. These were the people she had tried to woo in Portland and Memphis and Philadelphia, in Chicago and Detroit, Cleveland, Miami, Pittsburgh, Denver, Atlanta, and Houston. She had spoken from the heart in cities like Los Angeles and San Francisco and Minneapolis, in Boston, Richmond, Kansas City, New Orleans and Seattle. Smaller towns too, like Buffalo, Akron, Jersey City, and Tulsa. And Flint, Nashville, and Newport News. These were the men and women who had lived too long under the self-defeating delusion of big bones, bad glands, lousy heredity and lousier genes, screwed-up metabolisms always slower than the most ailing timepiece. And when she stepped inside the stadium, taking a route which led her to the edge of the stage, she couldn't handle all the tears she had held back for so long, too long, always fretful and fearful and just plain scared of the luxury of a good healthy cry.

"Your makeup'll run," Lena said. But when she looked over at her mother, Lena's eyes were even wider and wetter than her own. "Something . . . it's unbelievable, it's just . . . just, I can't even say it. Oh, if Jack was only here to see this, to see the good things you did with your life, the way you helped people."

They held each other for a moment, saying nothing else. Her mother's strength was part of her strength now. She understood, and when Lena let go of her there was a glow on her face to match the glow of the spotlights. They turned and looked out at the crowded stadium. Men and women had come from thirty-seven different states, from more than one hundred fifty different chapters. They had come in cars and buses and planes because it went far beyond the fact that they were losing weight and looking better for it. They were feeling better, inside and out. That was what she felt was more important than anything else. Being fat and being thin was more than just a straight line of vanity separating one point from the other. It meant that people were caring about themselves, being more productive, fulfilling whatever unique destiny they had chosen for themselves. She knew she had to tell them that they weren't merely more beautiful or more handsome, but that it was like a chain reaction that transcended pounds lost and meals carefully planned.

"There isn't an empty seat," Lena said. "And that's no exaggeration, either. Not a one, in the whole place. And you were worried—"

"Not worried. Frightened."

"Well there's nothing to be frightened about now," Lena said. "Because it gives me the chills just to look out and know all these people came to see you. And no one else. And if you blame yourself for anything tonight, anything at all—"

"I won't," she said. "No, not tonight."

"Not tomorrow, either," Lena said.

And she repeated, "No, not tomorrow, either."

She waited by the side of the stage, caught in the shadows, as yet unseen by the crowds which overflowed the bleachers. There was music, a great brassy fanfare, drum rolls, a circle of white light hitting the stage and the edge of the velvet curtain which was its backdrop. "Ladies and gentlemen, Mr. Bob Hope!"

She saw past history, past sins, past errors, past triumphs too, in the movement all around her, in the rows of folding chairs which faced the stage. Gowned and black-tied, she saw them all stiffly erect, conscious of who and where they were, laughing too when Bob Hope launched into his nonstop monologue, giving the audience their money's worth. Her eyes stopped and catalogued, hesitating before each of them: D. W., Leonard, Jeanette, Vivian Hollander, Doris Bauer, Pat Casey who was going to join Hope in another minute. Even Gene Burr was there, bending over to say something to his client, Kaaren Blyer. She would sing a medley of Broadway show-stoppers before the night was over. She saw Peter McGuire snapping pictures and she saw Phil being ushered to a seat alongside her secretary. She saw Lena and Barry finally take their seats, leaving her in the shadows, unmindful of the laughter Hope was enjoying with his slick rhythmic patter. She saw someone who looked like a very thin version of Gerald Evans. She saw Halston with an impeccably attired *haute couture* model on his arm and smiled because that was as much a surprise as the presence of her attorney, Jerry Brennen, and his wife. Or the presence of Richard Jameson, drama critic and one-time producer of television documentaries. She saw Ellen Reinhart, the owner of the Stamford franchise, and Mrs. Donner, whose first name eluded her, owner of the Forest Hills branch. Mr. Lewars of Wilmington, the man Leonard had once deprecatingly referred to as a "character," was there, and he was as trim and fit-looking as the day he'd signed the papers for the purchase of the first NuBodies chapter. She saw Lynne Cohen, who'd made a tidy sum ghostwriting her autobiography, saw, too, the publisher of *NuBodies* Magazine, flanked by his editor-in-chief on one side, his managing editor on the other. But she didn't see Natalie, or Manny. She looked in vain for Paul, Henny, Justin Rodell.

Pat Casey made them howl and stamp their feet when he did a takeoff on Hope. Kaaren Blyer brought the house down when she pulled out all the stops, singing a medley consisting of "He Touched Me," "Being Alive," and "Everything's Coming Up Roses." Then, after she had taken her bows, she stepped back in front of the mike and said, "And now, it gives me the greatest of pleasure to introduce the vice-president of NuBodies International Incorporated, Mr. Leonard Frankel." The applause which followed, polite at best, hinted at disappointment. Cynthia had the sudden brainstorm of calling upon these fifty-five thousand men and women, many of them stockholders, to vote her back into control at the next board of directors meeting. With all their proxy votes in her back pocket, she saw herself beating Leonard at his own game, proving to him that she was still alive and kicking, that there were more ways than one to skin a cat, that controlling a corporation went above and beyond the amount of money you had behind you, backing you up.

The director of the gala came up to her. Venerable and white-haired, tweed-suited and with a hat to match, he had staged nearly as many Broadway shows as there were NuBodies chapters. Now, as Frankel rambled on, he tapped her on the shoulder, wished her luck, kissed her on the cheek.

"But I know that you're all here this evening to see one person and one person only," Frankel said, "the woman who has made this all possible. She doesn't need a fancy introduction, because you all know and love her. So with delight and great respect, I give you Cynthia Morgan."

"Do your stuff," the director said.

She mounted the steps at the side of the stage and the applause rose up: loud, clamorous, deafening. Again and again it roared and broke above her head and roared again. Then they were rising up, giving her a standing ovation, tier after tier, row after row. In front of the stage the gowned and jeweled, the black-tied and formally attired, all got quickly to their feet, put down their programs and began to join in the rushing thunder of clapping hands, voices screaming out at her. But they weren't screaming that she'd failed them, lied to them, deceived them. No, the voices and stinging palms affirmed a belief that hadn't been swayed by the printed page, by the glib slick prose of someone she had never meant to offend, had only tried to be honest with, still firm in her initial judgment that the musical Rodell had written for her made her look like death warmed over, if not a complete and total s.o.b.

"Thank you," she said into the microphone. "Thank you, all of you. I'm . . . I'm overwhelmed. And honored."

They didn't stop to listen. The applause continued, filling the stadium with its ardent fire, its unabashed and unrehearsed enthusiasm. She felt the heat of the spots above her head, filling the circle of light with her Maribou-trimmed dress and her coppery-red hair and her eyes brimming, awash with tears. And when they finally let her speak, more than five minutes later, there was no need to pause, compose her thoughts, bring to mind something she had planned and memorized and thought out beforehand, way in advance. She hadn't thought what words she would use until now, as all fifty-five thousand pairs of eyes watched her, cognizant of her every move.

"You deserve nothing less than my total honesty," she said. "My total gratitude. You've stood by me, and you don't know how good that feels, how deeply that affects me. I guess you're probably thinking, too, that I'm going to say something about that book, *The . . . The Fat Lady*. Say something like it's all a bunch of nonsense, a lot of lies. But it's not all lies." She stopped, looked down at the loose folds of silk chiffon, the dress changing color—peach to pale orange to saffron to red—with each breath she took. Not a single program rustled. A distant subway train rumbled and shook into the brittle green September night. "You see, I think I got lost somewhere along the way. I think there was a moment, a point when I almost stopped believing in myself, believing in you. Here I was, traveling back and forth across the country, appearing on radio and TV, telling all of you to follow the NuBodies way, because a thinner way was a better way—"

Someone cried out, "It is!"

She laughed and nodded her head. "You're absolutely right, it is a better way. But you see, I was telling you even more than that. I was telling you to follow the rules, to go to every meeting you could, to believe in yourselves, in your own strength of purpose, character . . . and then I was cheating. Not only on you, but on myself. Boy, did I lose out as a result."

There wasn't a sound but the echo of her voice, the words throbbing in the air, welling up out of the depths of her growing conviction, filling the stadium. Wherever she looked she seemed to feel the mounting and silent surprise, hushed, mirrored on thousands of curious, intent faces. But it was too late to stop. And even more than that, she didn't want to stop.

"So please forgive me," she said, "Forgive me for being a hypocrite. This last month I've given myself a lot of time to think things over. I also lost nineteen pounds . . ." She smiled, a big brave grin. "Not by going to a health farm or a doctor who handed out diet pills left and right. But by following the diet that worked for me ten years

556

ago, when I lost not just nineteen pounds, but almost a *hundred* and nineteen pounds. Maybe I should have just walked into a meeting, here or out on the Coast, where I live. But you know what? I was ashamed, I really was. What an awful thing to admit, but it's true. I was embarrassed. I thought all of you expected something like a miracle from me and I didn't want to disappoint you. But, I guess in the long run, I did. And so now I want to use this opportunity to ask all of you to accept my apologies. You're the most important people in my life. And I say that from the bottom of my heart, with every ounce of sincerity and honesty I possess. I'm on your side, believe me. But I'm just a person, just like you. I'm not a movie star. I'm not holier than you are. I'm really not even a celebrity, when you get right down to it. What I used to be was a very fat woman who lived in Brooklyn, who one day decided there had to be a better way. That's how NuBodies got started. I used to eat because I didn't think there was anything better to do with my life, anything more important than food. And more food. But the more I ate, the unhappier I became. So I said to a group of my friends, all just as fat and compulsive when it came to food as I was, 'Let's sit down together, talk things over, find out why we're doing this to ourselves.' That's the way NuBodies began. That's why over a million people, more even, have reached their goal weight in the past ten years. So I guess tonight really is a good cause for celebration. To start the next ten years in the best possible way, the surest footing. I'm still going to be around to help you. But you know what? From now on I'm going to turn to you when *I* need help, too. It's going to be a two-way street, the way it was ten years ago. We're going to work together like we've never worked together before."

She stopped to catch her breath, not to end all the things which hurt inside her. The address wasn't over, but the audience didn't seem to realize that. The cheers and the shouts and the cries of "Yes!" and "Yes!" and "Yes!" again, pulled her toward them, reached out at her, touched at her every nerve. She trembled and the audience shivered and trembled too, having been a part of something unexpected, reassuring, honest. Then they were on their feet again, a stampede of applause, a cannonade of wild, bursting, adoring and devoted voices.

Now I know for sure, she thought. Yes. Because this is what ten years means, what it all comes down to. Nothing more, nothing less. And it's been worth it. Yes. No matter what, good times and bad, it's all been worth it. Yes.

"FASCINATING!"
The New York Times

Move over, world—here comes the year's
most glamorous, exciting heroine, in the
super-sensational novel about men and women,
love and sex, success and the advertising game!
Her name's Rosemary ...

and she's got

The Rosemary Touch

A Novel by *Lois Wyse*

Bestselling author of
LOVETALK
and
A WEEPING EYE CAN NEVER SEE

23531/$1.75

THE BIG BESTSELLERS
ARE AVON BOOKS

THE TOWERING SAGA
OF A WOMAN'S RELENTLESS RISE—
AND THE DESTINY SHE CARVED FOR HERSELF!

Frances Casey Kerns

A Cold Wild Wind

THE
SPELLBINDING
NOVEL OF DESIRE
AND OBSESSION

She spent her childhood in a tarpaper shack, the daughter
of bitter, neglectful parents. Out of her poverty she fashioned a vision of wealth and success and set out to achieve
it. Propelled into the tumultuous world crowded with
jealousy, greed, and lust, she succeeded in her goal . . .
only to realize—too late—the price of her dream.

AVON ◆ 26575 $1.75

A NOVEL OF POWER, INTENSITY AND
BURNING TRUTH

Anya

SUSAN FROMBERG SCHAEFFER

*The story of the magnificent life-odyssey of Anya Savikin
—from an idyllic European childhood, to the terror of the
death-camps, to survival and escape to America, to middle
age...*

*"ANYA is a myth, an epic, the creation of darkness and of
laughter stopped forever in the open throat. Out of blown-
away dust Susan Fromberg Schaeffer has created a world. It
is a vision, set down by a fearless, patient poet ... A writer
of remarkable power."* WASHINGTON POST

27789 $1.75

"BASIC AMMUNITION FOR THE WORKING WOMAN"

Library Journal

getting yours

LETTY COTTIN POGREBIN

HOW TO MAKE THE SYSTEM WORK FOR THE WORKING WOMAN

The most important and informative guidebook you can read on the pitfalls and possibilities of the workaday world, GETTING YOURS is absolutely indispensable for the career-minded woman who is looking for a job opportunity that suits both her skills and her spirit.

From handling on-the-job sexism to dealing with conflicts between career and family, GETTING YOURS is filled with the facts and understanding you need to get your future moving.

"COGENT ADVICE, SOLID INFORMATION... POGREBIN'S SPIRITED ADVICE SHOULD STIFFEN THE RESOLVE OF WOMEN ON THE WAY UP AS WELL AS THOSE TOTTERING AT NEST'S EDGE."
—The New York Times

GY 3-75